LUDVÍK VACULÍK
A CZECH DREAMBOOK

MODERN CZECH CLASSICS

Ludvík Vaculík
A Czech Dreambook

Translated from the Czech by Gerald Turner
Afterword by Jonathan Bolton

Karolinum Press

KAROLINUM PRESS is a publishing department of Charles University in Prague
Ovocný trh 3–5, 116 36 Prague 1, Czech Republic
www.karolinum.cz

First published in Czech as *Český snář* in 1981 by Edice Petlice, then by Sixty-Eight Publishers
of Toronto, Canada, in 1983. This English translation is based upon the fifth edition
of *Český snář*, published in 2002, by Atlantis of Brno, Czech Republic.
As the Iron Curtain was collapsing, Milan Heidenreich, a Swedish citizen of Czech origin,
contributed to the English publication of *A Czech Dreambook* with a generous donation
for its translation.

Cover and graphic design by Zdeněk Ziegler
Typeset by DTP Karolinum
Printed in the Czech Republic by Tiskárny Havlíčkův Brod, a. s.
First English edition

ISBN 978-80-246-3852-2 (hb)
ISBN 978-80-246-3889-8 (ebk)

To Jiří Kolář

Last night, I don't know why, I couldn't sleep. I got up about six times for a drink of beer or milk, thinking my restlessness to be of chemical origin. I felt excited and tense, not tired, as if I'd had a strong coffee late in the evening, although that happens to be one thing that helps me sleep better. Anyway I had had nothing of the kind, just a cup of tea at Eda Kriseová's much earlier, during the afternoon. Then we all trooped along with our Hamburger to a mime performance which I very much enjoyed, and after it we went home at a very respectable hour. Next it occurred to me that my extreme distress might have been caused by the stroboscope which Hybner uses to such brutal effect in his performance.

The thought tossed around in my head the whole night and it struck me that one's biology and neurology really do start to rebel against one – against me. I am not aware of exerting myself, yet I end up feeling exhausted. I am not afraid, yet I shiver as if I were. I speak German all day with no bother, but then at night all sorts of phrases come back to me over and over again clamouring for grammatical corrections, which only goes to show how much it exhausted me. Only three years ago I was able, at interrogations, to suppress the onset of an insidious gall-bladder attack by stubbornly cursing to myself and willing it away with all my strength, causing, to my shame, beads of cold sweat to appear on my forehead. I have felt this past year to be a turning point for my strength, my resources, my sanity and my time. And to outward gaze, even my own, nothing has changed. So there are ascertainable thresholds we have to cross one by one. It looks as if my fiftieth birthday has finally caught up with me after two years. Or something.

These are joyful days for Jiří Gruša. He has received the German edition of his *Questionnaire*, together with the Czech one from the Škvoreckýs. He is delightfully over the moon about it, as if it were his début, and I observe how all those around him wisely and generously wish him well. Ivan prophesies him not only a reputation but also money, although he refuses to predict whether it will be a quarter or half a million. We all chuckle. Jiří rubs his little hands, comically feigning belief in Ivan's prophecy, and declares: "I can quit the housing co-op, at last."

So last night I was obliged (you won't catch me going to a psychiatrist) to do some investigation in this field too: Could I possibly be eaten up with envy? And once again I come up with the following conclusion: God be praised – Jirka at last has what we sort of promised him when we coaxed him along our "wicked path" to Jürgen's publishing house, which then kept him waiting interminably. It was a bit like encouraging someone with promises of astounding views over the next hill. Then at last you get there and they are overwhelmed, and your only fear is whether they are sufficiently so.

And so I discovered yet again that I most likely lack the requisite ambition to be a writer. I appease the equally requisite sense of duty by listing all the different things I do. I feel fully employed. But at night something comes, from time to time, to torment me, and I get the agonizing urge – desire would be an inappropriate word! – to switch the light on, sit down and write – anything. It was back again last night. But I did not do it because it would have worried the family. Yes, it's perfectly all right for me to sit down and write into the night or all night, for that matter. But to begin writing in the middle of the night, or before dawn, even – that's abnormal! And I know it full well. That is why last night I made myself postpone the urge until this evening. So shall I really start keeping a diary like this? After resisting it for years!

I've received notification from the State Security, the StB, that my regular monthly "official discussion" is tomorrow. The best name for it without quotation marks would be intimidation. There is just no way of getting used to it and pretending it's of no account.

The temperature was up a bit today, as if a thaw was on the way. And I had originally planned to write a feuilleton about this "dreadful winter." – I mustn't let Spring steal a march on me!

TUESDAY, 23ᴿᴰ JANUARY 1979

It's a quarter past eleven and the boys are not in yet. So it's hard to feel I am finally alone today. I will be disturbed. I can almost never achieve solitude; there's always someone here. It's my state of mind, no fault of theirs. When *they* see me at my typewriter, they tiptoe through the room with nary a word bar hello. Through the glass of two doors I can see that Madla is still reading in bed too. She is reading Karol's odd, Jewish – almanac, I suppose.

Karol Sidon was here this morning and brought the almanac, which is for the first quarter of the year. I leafed through it and was unable to make out what was serious and what was for fun. In most cases the names of the various contributors are not given, or there are only initials. It is nothing but horoscopes, the Cabala, mysticism and such, alongside essays about anything and everything. "How many copies of it are you making?" I asked in pencil. He wrote me back a reply and chuckled at the paltriness of his output. I should like to send this curiosity to Šimečka in Bratislava, but also to keep one for myself, and I cannot get another copy. "You can write something for it too," Karol said. "A simple soul like me?" I asked in surprise. "Precisely!" said Karol. "You'll appear very exotic in such company!"

He told me that Dienstbier's flat had been searched. Immediately I started sorting out what I had at home: Černý ready for binding, a parcel of author's copies of *The Crime of Rebellion* for Jan Trefulka, several piles ready to be wrapped, in each of them a copy of Patočka's essay "The Writer and his Cause." And a number of manuscripts for reading, the most sensitive of which are Tatarka's *Jottings*. And where will I hide this diary of mine every night?

It is midnight. Our Jan has come in. I ask him where he was. Helping the Administrator paint his flat. The Administrator of the Orfeus puppet theatre is convalescing after an illness and yesterday his heart acted up, exactly the way mine did, according to Jan, when I was doing the painting before Christmas. "How did you make out with the cops?" Jan asked. "The same old threats," I said dismissively, and I will not talk or write about it here. I will reduce the whole business to insignificance. Jan will come back this way again – in pyjamas, with his pockets full of apples.

Madla has turned off her light. Every night she gets into bed with the comforting thought that she is another day nearer retirement. Today she came home from work angrier than usual, because on top of everything else she had had to clean the office. Some time ago the director came up with the idea that the institute's employees should assume responsibility for cleaning the building. Madla refused, and just to be on the safe side, I specifically forbade her to. "Why doesn't he want to take on a cleaning woman?" I asked. "How should I know?" she snapped. Then she said: "He wants to shore up his position at the top and his power-base below. At the top he can brag about how much he has saved on wages and below he can hand out bonuses." – "But he's still spending the same money." – "No, he isn't, that's the point. The bonuses are supposed to differentiate the psychologists' performance, but he uses the money for cleaning instead." The older women refused, but the prissy young ninnies agreed to do the cleaning for four hundred crowns. And the building is filthy again. And why? Because the sort of things that a cleaning woman will do after a fashion you will scarcely find doctors doing, because they are too fastidious. And all you hear is how terribly tired they are, and they still complain about having no money. And they leave their dirty crockery behind them in the kitchenette – who for? The cleaner? The fridge is in a disgusting state and the ash-trays are always full. Who's supposed to clean them – the cleaner? No, the person who can't stand to look at it any longer. And so, ever since the employees started "doing their own cleaning," those who are obliged to make up for them, by working harder at their real jobs in the institute, receive lower bonuses. "But I'll bloody well make sure it all comes out when my time is up and I take my leave of them!" said Madla. – "Well, what did you do the cleaning for, then?" I asked in astonishment. – "Because she is doing a post-grad course, and she's not very clever and really can't cope, so she called in sick, and if she doesn't do it, who will?" Madla spat the words out. "So you're not too clever either, then," I said.

It is one o'clock. Ondřej is back. "What's up?" I ask. He explains to me that his firm's new director refused to sign a reference for his university application, even though the previous director had promised to do so when he took him on. "Why?" I asked. – "He says he doesn't know me, and needs to get some background material on me." – "Aha," I said, "in other words he's got plenty of material, but he needs to get some instructions." – "A really vexatious case," said Ondřej. "Good night."

It is half past two, because I stopped writing. The thought of having to go everywhere sorting things out and the likely repercussions made me start tidying things up so they would not be here to be found. I had intended today to write a commentary to be included in *Dear Classmates* as a separate chapter, but I didn't even start it. Apart from that I want to write a feuilleton about this winter that would mark a change of mood in my present series. But there is no way I'll be able to consign this daily writing to a separate track where it won't occupy my thoughts or distract me from more important work. It's no joke.

WEDNESDAY, 24TH JANUARY 1979

Another afternoon gone to waste running around because of books. One package to take over to an author for him to sign the title pages, insert photographs and then take all the copies himself to be bound in such and such a place. I ask him when he will have it finished. Well... as soon as he has done the photos... I realize that the fellow can't afford the supplies and I give him an advance of 600 Kčs. Then I take a tram to the other end of the city where I am supposed to pick up the bound almanacs today. A glance at the clock tells me I won't make it in time, because I am supposed to be in front of the Rudolfinum presently to meet Zdena who is bringing me some more things she has finished transcribing.

I walk to the Rudolfinum – it is bitingly cold. I am walking up and down when a green car pulls up alongside with Zdena in it. "It crossed my mind that you might have some more errands to do, so I took the car." Quite, and she means that the time saved will be for her. She's wrong, at least for today. We drive through the centre of Prague. There is little traffic in the well-salted slush-covered streets, so I have no great difficulty keeping an eye on the cars behind us. "How did you make out?" I ask. Zdena took a day off work today for her doctors. She emits an expression of disgust and slaps the steering wheel. "I tell you what – we won't talk about it. I'm alive!" she declares with enthusiasm, and points towards the traffic lights as if they were a flowering meadow. In her case, though, such outbursts of euphoria could easily give way in a matter of minutes to a sullen silence if I insisted on asking her: So what did they say? We are driving to the bookbinders' for the almanacs. Zdena is just right for this particular job since R., who delivered them to the binders, for some unknown reason, gave the fictitious name and address of a woman. And if I, who am known to them, were to come to pick them up, such subterfuge might unsettle those innocent people.

We pulled up a short distance from the workshop. I gave Zdena the requisition slip and two hundred and fifty crowns, and off she went. I had a good look round: no other car had stopped anywhere nearby. The package was good and heavy, and worth over two thousand crowns – plus the two hundred and fifty. It would not be a good idea to take it home after yesterday's warning!

We therefore stopped at M.'s, where I stored the package, and agreed that I would come tomorrow afternoon and M. and I would organize a handicraft session. Seeing how smoothly and quickly it all went, I now regret not having brought Černý's *My Years in Dijon* with me for binding. Instead the copies are lying at home under my desk. But I was reluctant to handle two precious things at once. And I also thought it unwise to set the lady at the binders' puzzling how it was that no matter whether the name given was Václav Černý or Alena Nováková, I'm the one who comes to collect everything.

Zdena asked me where I wanted to go now (at least 20 Kčs for petrol to add to the price of the almanac!) and I directed her to take me to Jiří Gruša's at the Novodvorská housing estate. Jirka was reading his German book, of course, and looking for translation errors. There were apparently few serious ones, though a good number of minor slips. Zdena talked to Ivanka in the sitting room, with the dogs dashing all around and their little boy Václav – whom I have deliberately christened Walter (lest he become another Good King Wenceslas, as Jirka ambitiously plans for him) groping around the flat wreaking havoc: breaking the radio aerial, slopping tea onto the writing desk, etc. etc. Meanwhile Jirka and I completed some business, which we conducted, as far as most of the proper names, numbers and certain verbs were concerned, with pencil and paper; for the most part my friends mock me for acting this way but I have already managed to make them think twice. It was evening by now and I decided to pay one further call: to Otka Bednářová who lives almost opposite. But there was no one in. I have a feeling that Otka is annoyed with me, and I know why. I went back to Jiří's for Zdena who then drove me home. Jiří wanted me to tell him what the StB had asked me about. I told him briefly and I ought to do the same here, but it's the last thing I feel like doing.

Our Ondřej took his driving test today. It'll be nothing unusual if he flunks it – they apparently fail half of the candidates – but it would hurt him rather more. Jan, for his part, was summoned to the director's office for a talk. He was there with five other trainees who had passed the necessary exams and they were all treated most affably: they are to be recommended for university study and they will even receive a scholarship from their third year onwards if they agree to remain with the firm. The whole family is stupefied: we all fear we know something the firm doesn't know – that they won't be allowed to put Jan's name forward.

THURSDAY, 25ᵀᴴ JANUARY 1979

We have a house in Dobřichovice, but we cannot live in it. A modest but fine house, it dates from the end of the last century, and would be comfortable were we allowed to reconstruct the interior to suit our needs. It has no bathroom, for instance. It has six rooms, but we have the right to only one of them. In the rest there are tenants. When we bought the house six years ago, we naturally gave them notice to leave, but that is meaningless unless the local authority is prepared to rehouse them. And since we cannot expect any favours from this state, our boys have started to build their own place as part of a self-help housing co-op. It entails putting in about a hundred and twenty hours' work a month, Saturdays and Sundays. The idea we had was that as soon as the boys had their flat ready we would move there and swap the flat I am sitting in at this moment for some place in Dobřichovice for our old ladies. We have three old ladies: Mrs. Kopecká with her two cats, Mrs. Rohlenová with her scores of grandchildren from spring to autumn, and Mrs. Hermerková with her dog. There's the rub: they may be just three persons but they are three separate households and they need three separate replacement flats. And that is bearing in mind that someone might die (me, for example), but when?

Some time at the beginning of this month I made up my mind to call a meeting to seek expert advice. The topics: (i) The feasibility of moving the old ladies to a single – minimum three-bedroomed – flat seeing that they now live in a family house that is divided into three flats in an equally notional fashion; (ii) whether the authorities might have a trick up their sleeves enabling them to take the boys' flat away from them once they have built it; (iii) whether it might be advisable to have Jan or Madla registered as joint owners of the Dobřichovice house, which was bought in Ondřej's name. My being the owner of anything is something inconceivable both to the state and our family. As experts I invited Jiří Gruša, who also works in a housing office and knows the sort of trickery that might be used, Pavel Rychetský, because he's a lawyer in a similar co-operative, our lads, and Madla, of course, because she considers it possible that as soon as the boys have built the flat I will move into it with some woman or other.

The meeting took place at Pavel's, and Jiří failed to show up. We are not allowed to move three old ladies into one flat, but taking the boys' three-bedroom apartment and giving them a one-bedroom instead – if the boys are not married at the time of the final inspection – that's allowed. The next day I asked Jiří why he had not come. He said it had slipped his mind, adding with a grin that it was a Freudian lapse of memory because he was cross with me.

In December, I wrote my "Remarks on Courage," dedicating them to Karel Pecka on his fiftieth birthday, with the request that he let me have his

And that is bearing in mind that someone might die
(me, for example), but when? (p. 13)

comments, as I intended to circulate them. For my chosen topic – the meaning of courage for exceptional individuals and for the mass of normal people – Pecka seemed to me to be the best qualified to pass an opinion, having spent eleven years behind bars and being an unpretentious man free of all hatred, neuroses and affectation, one whose lifestyle more closely resembles ordinary people's than does that of other equally well-known opposition writers... He came to see me with a lot of reservations. Some points I was able to explain to him, others I changed; there were others that just dropped out of the text by virtue of that well-known law of nature that when we seek our opponent out, his very readiness to consider our criticism attenuates it.

Subsequently, everyone agreed with my text and some even congratulated me on it – from Madla and Kosík to Alexandr Kliment and Helena Klímová. In sorrow and trepidation I sent the text to Brno, but I have heard nothing from there yet. Jiří Müller, Jan Tesař...! My text caught Petr Pithart working on his own formulation of certain similar sentiments. In a roundabout way I heard tell that deeper within Charter 77 it was a cause of contention. At the Pitharts' I was apprised of a phrase quoted from some gathering: "...before Vaculík was demoralized by Martinovský..." The StB are bound to have read my article at that time too and I trembled lest some unforeseen smart alec among them should realize his opportunity. Otka took a copy, bore it away, read it – nothing. And then: "Listen, my friend, some people have got serious reservations about it and quite rightly, too!" Last month she told me that even Gruša had taken umbrage and was writing a riposte – and that it already ran to six pages.

When Jirka told me he was Freudianly cross with me, I knew the cause and wanted to talk about it. He told me he had started to write a reply but had then torn it up, because it's not right, he said. "What's 'not right'?" I asked. – "That the two of us should..." I had to finish the sentence for him: "... bicker under the eyes of the StB?" We were talking on Malostranské Square while waiting for a tram.

I said that once we had defined ourselves as free people – by signing the Charter among other things – it was up to us to act freely within this territory. We could not stay silent about certain matters just because the secret police were listening in. Jiří agreed, but said there was another reason why my article was unsuitable for open discussion: it was incredibly deceitful. He had subjected my text to a purely semantic analysis and could demonstrate to me how I employ the basest journalistic techniques, identical to those which *Rudé právo* had used against me in 1977.

That really took me aback. I insisted that he give me a clue to the basis of his criticism – off the top of his head at least. He pulled some papers out of his bag – we were already on the tram – and started to read from them *sotto voce*. I observed that he had three beginnings: "Dear Ludvík!" And lots of crossings out. What I recall of it, more or less, is the following: that I slander the young Pecka, and from the relative immunity of my exalted position I fail to see how today's youthful Peckas are again being jailed, and being jailed in my stead; that in my text I employ indefinable terms whose meaning I gradually modify so that by means of seemingly logical phrases I concoct a lie. For what are my "band of heroes" whose actions become incomprehensible for "sensible people"? Apparently I should not have spoken about heroes but gone right ahead and said "a handful of self-appointed has-beens," and the sensible, normal people I spoke of are no more than the "honest working people led by the party". And when I advocate "courageous honest work," what is it but the "honest cooperation" required by the state and the police..? That was it, more or less, and I am endeavouring to reproduce it here because I don't know whether he will ever let me have his ideas in writing.

I told him that I would very much like him to try and put down his comments on paper, all the same. Only he should try and do so without indulging in insults that would sour our relationship, give pleasure to the StB and summon up evil spirits. It was not my practice to speak that nastily about anyone, not even the secret police! If he would make an effort to express all those sensitive points in words that even I might be able to read, then he would probably find himself confronted by the same task as I had been, particularly if, like me, he tried to limit himself to three pages. He replied that he would not be writing anything now that he had said it to me, and my error might have been that some things just ought not to be said in three pages.

It sounds plausible, I thought to myself on the way home. But length depends on the genre. And everyone knows my genre, and it was obvious in this case too. And the very choice of genre implies certain assumptions on the part of author and reader alike.

That evening, I thought to myself how magnanimously I had taken it and how resilient I was. But then in the middle of the night came the usual awakening for no reason and a sense of anxiety about lack of success and being under pressure, because I wouldn't even manage to complete *The Trip to Praděd* or the book about the Indians and I would have nothing to justify myself with. The main thing is to complete *Dear Classmates*, because it will cover everything from birth to eventual death. That is the main priority. But my most urgent theme, the one that really haunts me, is what is happening to me now. And in my case the best state of mind for work, as I have discovered again and again, is agitation, fear and rage, plus a feverish *fuite en avant* until the final culminating sentence.

It's a quarter to four in the morning; I can't believe it. I should have written this this morning, but I needed daylight to photograph diary entries for *Dear Classmates*. Then this afternoon I glued in birds at M.'s and cut out circles for the *Hour of Hope* almanac. This week I wanted to deliver my feuilleton about the present winter. Quite simply, from the moment I look at my ugly mug each morning while shaving, I feel like shaving off the moustache as well, thereby returning everything to its original form before all the things that have happened and grown on me. Another thing Jiří told me: it is out of the question for me, all of a sudden, before people's gaze, to remove the outfit, costume or coat that I once donned of my own free will. I didn't do anything, and the apparel that others may have clothed me in is their business. People have to be grown-up enough to put up with it. But oh, the anxiety it arouses, the simple threat of losing friends!

FRIDAY, 26TH JANUARY 1979

My sleep tends to end in hectic dreams. They are action-packed and very seldom to do with emotional states. Mostly I feel nothing during them. I am driving along in a bad car which, though scarcely moving, reacts sluggishly to the controls, so that slowly but surely I crash into something. Or I am running away and it is not that my legs are too heavy for me to move from the spot, but they're too light to carry me forward. I courageously and adventurously climb rocks or constructions which tremble and drop away beneath me and I save myself by catching onto things, taking me further and further away from where I want to go: in other words, I save myself by placing myself in an ever riskier situation. Then I wake into broad daylight. I am alone in the flat, I can hear clattering from the street and from the kitchen the voices of our birds. Philip sings lustily; Catherine only clucks vulgarly.

Yesterday I finished the almanacs at Mirka's: I pasted birds onto the covers and cut out round holes in the dust-jacket so that the birds could be seen. The members of the household helped. I bought a litre of white Kamenáč wine for the purpose and added it to the cost of the almanac (1 Kčs apiece) – even so nobody else would have done it that cheaply. One reason I have to give up this work is because occasionally I get the vague feeling that people suspect I am making money out of it. You see, someone with a different personality from mine might say to themselves: he wouldn't be doing it for such a long time, otherwise! Year seven. Some of my subscribers are starting to treat me indulgently, as if I were a tradesman they were wanting to keep in business. Yes, and in the meantime my real trade is falling into decay. Madla told me the other day what our boys say about me behind my back, i.e. that it's shameful really – all the things he could be writing, instead of traipsing around Prague with other people's nonsense!

Today I was out delivering *Hour of Hope*. I did not get back until this evening so was not here when Otka came. She left me a letter from Mr. Václav that opens with the words: "Dear Mr. Ludvík," in which he takes issue with my "Remarks on Courage." Dated yesterday, it is already here, even though it obviously had to penetrate the police blockade of Hrádeček. Otka delivered the letter open into Ondřej's hands and specifically told him it was a "feuilleton." That was her way of telling me to treat it as such and do the necessary. She need have no fears on that score! Mr. Václav is also only pretending to have written me a letter. He is sure to let his friends have a look at it, but will leave it up to me how I classify it.

He wrote to me nicely: clearly and properly. And the tone is friendly. I am not even sure there is anything I could disagree with, were it not for the fact that it's extremely clear in my mind why I wrote the feuilleton. Mr. Václav's letter is a telling record of his bemused frown; he knows I know what he knows. "After all you know better than anyone else..." he says.

"After all you know better than anyone else that Gruša needn't have gone to prison over *The Questionnaire*, but Vaculík could have over *The Guinea Pigs*... At one moment it is more tactical to jail Gruša and thereby intimidate Vaculík; at another it may be more convenient to jail Vaculík as a means of intimidating Gruša... You can't have forgotten, surely, that you – like myself, incidentally – are still formally indicted on a charge dating back to 1969? And surely you must realise that precisely the two of us, for instance, could have spent the first half of the seventies in prison in place of Šabata and Hübl? Do you really think that miserable little text we both signed that time was worth it? Looked at that way, nothing is worth it. Neither leaflets, nor going to a ball, nor writing some novel. Let alone sending texts by Czech writers to exile journals! Was it worth Lederer's while? And he's lucky enough to have been one of those crafty heroes who enjoy only 'limited doses of repression.' After all, he needn't have been sentenced to just three years, he could easily have been given ten." – That is Mr. Václav's response to my view that the present regime's policy, unlike that of the fifties – when the aim was to raze society to the ground – is to jail its individual opponents almost reluctantly and for shorter terms, because among other reasons it has no desire to validate heroes. On the contrary, these days it needs to placate and even anaesthetise society. I go on to make the point that certain forms of resistance can actually foster greater cruelty in the regime.

"I am not sure what the intention of your feuilleton was," Mr. Václav writes. "I only know the impression it makes – on me at least. If you strip away its Havlíčekian, Peroutkavian and Vaculíkian elegance of phrase, what it seems to be saying in essence and in its implications is that decent people do not act the hero and are in no rush to go to jail – because there is something anti-social about being a hero; it isn't the sort of proper, honest labour that decent people like and that keeps society going; it is something that alienates and horrifies people. Moreover, heroes represent a danger in that they make things worse. After all, the cops are in general decent folk... the good fellows are only provoked into beating up women and dragging their friends off to the woods and kicking them in the guts! It is necessary to recognise their prestige and not keep on appealing in a provocative fashion to some international covenant or other, or even having the cheek to copy out writings by some Černý, Vaculík, Havel or other, which, as you surely know, is why three lads of your sons' ages are currently serving prison sentences in Brno. Some more heroes who only make things worse!" – Mr. Václav concludes with the statement that he does not resent it when people take a back seat – or even emigrate – when they have had enough. However, he does resent it when they (I) do not tell the truth.

It still strikes me that he managed to miss the main point of my comments and focused entirely on its "consequences." That is something I have heard throughout my life: the idea is one thing, comrades, its consequences are something else entirely! So when are we to expect a more opportune moment to express ideas regardless of their consequences? At that most favourable of times – 1968 – the consequences were the most disastrous. But Mr. Václav knows what I know, after all, and in passing – and only in passing, so that he may dismiss it – he hints at it: "Maybe you wanted to say that the discreet, inconspicuous humiliation of thousands of anonymous individuals is worse than when they jail one well-known dissident now and then. Undoubtedly. But the question is: why was that dissident jailed?" he asks, immediately returning to our dissident cyclotron of thinking and acting.

When I got home today, everyone in the family had finished reading the letter from Hrádeček. "He put it well," Madla said. "Yes, when you read it, you get the feeling that it all hangs together," Jan said. "I have yet to finalise my judgement," said Ondřej most elegantly of all. "Then I'm curious how you're going to cope with what I'm writing now," I said.

The only person that I am totally incapable of baffling and who believes in my good character would seem to be the ashenly menacing Major (?) Fišer who asked me in typical fashion last Tuesday: "So what are you up to now, Mr. Vaculík? What's this about us being murderers and about people being shot here?" And he held up between finger and thumb, like an asp, a copy of my "Remarks on Courage" typed on yellow paper.

MONDAY, 29TH JANUARY 1979

On Saturday we drove to Dobřichovice. I got a fire going in the tiled stove. Inside it was three degrees – above, thank goodness. Outside it was one degree higher. It was thawing. Three hours later the equipment was already recording fifteen degrees of heat in the bedroom. Madla helped it as usual by diligently ironing the clean laundry brought from home. While engaged in such activity – she ironing, I heating – we listen to foreign radio stations. I find it enough to hear once a week what is going on in the world. In addition, I managed to type a few copies of Mr. Václav's letter. It no longer struck me as so persuasive. I don't intend to react to it at all, only if there are more along the same lines.

There was nothing to be done with the garden, as it was too wet. I spent a few moments aiming snowballs at the trees. Our hare had gnawed white the apple-tree branches I had prepared, and even started to nibble the cordon.

Once more I found another hole in the fence and blocked it. We really are getting a rest from the garden this winter – but then it'll take off again! A proper winter at long last! I ought to write about it.

On Sunday, I cut a few fresh branches for the hare, I chopped some wood and we sorted over the apples in the cellar. I leafed through the apple atlas. When I peeled away a flake of twisted bark on the pear tree, grey plant lice started crawling away under it. And we have had temperatures of minus twenty this winter!

We returned earlier than usual to Prague, as I intended to make a few stops on the way to deliver the almanac. But no one was home. Yet again that sense of a miserable waste of time and this morning the itchy feeling that the dapper fellows were already coming for it, that they were already on their way up, two in the lift, one on the staircase (lest we miss each other!), while I stand here shaving. I finished shaving, got dressed and rushed out of the house without breakfast, carrying a bulging bag. It was almost noon, as I had got up at ten. I had spent the night reading Tatarka's manuscript.

Tatarka's Manuscript: that would make quite a good title for the manuscript! But more about Tatarka's manuscript later, depending on what the author decides, and I should so much like him to decide in favour. Meanwhile I am savouring him bit by bit, all by myself and in total privacy. We have never known anything like this here before, and distant Dominik surely wails in torment that he must have been deranged to relinquish it at all. He has words there that are not even to be found in the six-volume Slovak literary dictionary, and I have no idea whether they are mistakes or neologisms... The manuscript was selflessly typed out by one of our local Slovaks whom I do not want to name: Ján Mlynárik, a former historian, who did not feel like constructing the Slovak circumflexes out of a grave and an acute accent on his Czech typewriter, so those little roofs are absent from the entire work! Five times a page I get up and grumblingly reach for the (six-volume) dictionary. I think by now there will be a few circumflex accents too many in the text, unless I give it to Zdena. She was at university in Bratislava.

Today Alexandr Kliment celebrated his fiftieth birthday. A whole lot of us came for the party. Even good old Karel Kosík put in an appearance with Marie. I saw Zdeněk Urbánek for the first time in ages. I sat next to Standa Milota who looked sad to me. On the other side of the table sat Jan Vladislav who makes fun of me and I of him, but in such infantile fashion that it does not even produce a quotable joke. ("Your whiskers look upswept somehow today!" – "And your hair's downswept!") I asked Jiří if he had finished writing his execration of me; not yet. Eda Kriseová was wearing yet another fine dress. Petr Pithart was there but no one broached the controversial subject of our two articles. We're celebrating. And we have so few celebrations these days that everyone treats them with deference. Only Ivan in the corner started getting political – though in a low-calorie fashion. Every now and then I could hear his: "I'm not altogether so sure of that."

We discussed briefly the "symposium" held by Eva Kantůrková last week on the subject of her *Lord of the Tower*. She had invited people who liked the novel to explain why they liked it to those who, like me, did not. But only the critics turned up to the soirée: Jiří Pechar, Gruša, Vladislav, myself... it was almost silly how the book's advocates failed to put in an appearance. Ivan's attitude was so strongly dismissive that he sent his apologies instead. Sergej Machonin also found it better to send a letter. Jiří and I knew beforehand what it contained. It was dreadful and we sat in apprehension. Eva placed the unopened letter behind her on the window-ledge and entertained us. The letter unnerved me. Her husband Jiří shared her suspense. In the end she opened it, read it and then said: "We won't wait for anyone else. As a good opener for the discussion I propose to read what Sergej wrote me." Then she asked what else we wanted and went off to the kitchen, "to give us time for reflection." Jiří Pechar said: "Well, I have to hand it to her!"

To spend three years writing something and fail to achieve the desired effect is awful. Eva thinks she will put the novel to rights by means of deletions. Hardly likely. Pechar thinks it was an irreparable mistake for Eva to have committed the blasphemy of tempting the Devil and having Jan Drda bring the news of Jesus' crucifixion, not to mention committing fornication against the scourged Christ. The thing is that Pechar believes authors to be as responsible for the acts of their characters as for their own, and that retribution for them will be exacted within the week or posthumously. It beats me how some people managed to see Drda in it at all, but Ivan, for instance, is absolutely convinced of the fact. I do not like literature being deciphered in that way. My own objections to the novel are, by and large, that it is tediously descriptive when it deals with reality and coyly naive when it tries to fantasise. That apart, authors have the right to deal with anything; what counts is whether they do so successfully: success justifies everything. But Madla is always scolding me for this. She argues that in a society as demoralised as ours, true artists will be those who give people new hope, rather than picking holes in the little that remains. However, all she has read of the novel is the sample chapter in *Spektrum*, and she maintains – heatedly – that that is quite enough.

We had scarcely finished discussing *The Lord of the Tower* when Eva and spouse entered. At that moment I was sitting on the sofa between Marie and Helena D., so Eva greeted me in the following manner: "Ludvík among the women again of course," and only she found it funny. What's this "again"? I have forgotten what we went on to talk about. Alexandr was in high spirits. His wife Jiřina was magnanimously affable, even towards me (after our recent altercation at the Kosík-Mozarts), but our toasts were a disaster (ceremony phobia). Being among the first to leave, I felt a twinge of regret for better days now gone and a desire to invite some of our old friends over one day, though it will not happen. We gave Alexandr a collection of essays for his birthday. They were supposed to have some sort of connection with him. Ivan organised it. And what about me? A fortnight ago I dealt my Swiss publisher the final blow. Last year I declared that I would write a little book about my American Indian games from the time when I used to drive the goats to pasture. I have looked forward to writing it one day for as long as I can remember. When I took the first step by reading through my childhood diaries, I sat there as if I had been hoaxed: there it was – ready-made! Penned in my childish language, it was authentic and true to life, while I had been about to construct something artificial.

I followed it up by reading my "worker" and "student" journals and, lo and behold, I had written everything already. And at just the right time. All I have done in my writings since is to vary and illustrate my attitudes and opinions. I have never been wiser or cleverer than I was up to the age of twenty. Everything has come true: my worst suspicions were fulfilled, while my therapeutic hopes were totally groundless. It was as if I had written into the script not just my future successes but also my failures, failings and disasters and then proceeded to play them out.

After reading all those things through once more, I conceived a project entitled "Dear classmates and teaching staff!" and sent the following message to my publisher: Nothing for you, nothing for the Germans or Americans – sorry. All for the motherland: thirty copies. Once I've brought out my book in Padlock, that'll be my lot.

On the days I get up and find myself alone at home, I spend about an hour on housework. I wash the breakfast cups, clear away the bread and wipe up the crumbs, water the plants and clean out the birdcage: sunflower seeds in the feeder, a slice of apple and fresh water. From time to time I also sweep the floor and give the hall-floor and the passageway in front of our door a wipe over with a wet cloth. Only then do I put the kettle on, take out the bread and bread-knife again, and a tea-cup, and have my breakfast looking at the birds or out of the window.

Our birds are called Philip and Catherine. Philip is a cross between a canary and a goldfinch, which means he looks like a goldfinch, of course. Catherine is a canariess. Their cage hangs from a chain in a corner of the room amidst the plant life that blocks all access to the window. As I eat, the birds observe me, flying round me in circles or pecking the bread, buns or strudel on the desk. They do not venture closer to my hands, on the dining table. But were I to turn away for an instant they would be there on my slice of bread. When I have finished my breakfast I wash my cup and spoon, clear away the bread and the bread-knife, wipe the table and go into my room to write. Through the door I then hear the birds: Philip is starting to sing to the coming spring; a month from now, Catherine will start laying eggs. On gloomy days I do my writing in the kitchen. I do not enjoy writing; I regard it as hard labour. But I willingly read over the things I have written and improve them until they look as if they were written with enjoyment.

I do not go out in the morning but try to keep to my work schedule. That is why people have become accustomed to calling on me in the morning. When the doorbell rings it is generally Otka Bednářová, who comes for feuilletons or books and brings me other things to read, or Mojmír Klánský, who comes out of habit, or occasionally Luboš Dobrovský dropping by for a smoke between two shop-window-washes. Even when they come at a bad time, I am grateful to them for not being someone worse. I entertain visitors in the kitchen, where it is usually warmer and lighter and where one is even permitted to smoke with decorum. When I am not in the mood, or do not have the time, or someone sits around too long, I tell them to go home. When the phone rings, I let it.

Today at about eleven o'clock the doorbell rang. I was thrown into an unpleasant state of apprehension because Otka had already been to see me this morning, Mojmír is due tomorrow and Luboš is currently washing windows out in Prosek. I opened the door and it turned out to be Mrs. Helena D., which came as a pleasant surprise. Admittedly I had told her last week to stop by, but could see no good reason why she should. She looked very good framed in the doorway. She could almost have been a mistaken caller but for the eager tone, at once curious and timid, in which she said that she was stopping by – for a moment – if she wasn't disturbing me. She wore a pleated skirt that came to below the knee; she was very slim in the waist, and bareheaded; altogether too lightly dressed, in fact, for such cold weather, apart from her knee-high boots. Her top half was clad in a sort of short furry jacket on which the hoar-frost from outside was now thawing. She was like a bird fluffed up from the cold, though undoubtedly warm underneath.

I led her into the kitchen and made tea again. We conversed. She sat at the side of the table where the cage is; Philip was so put out by this that he started flying almost aggressively low over her, until at length he alighted on Vaculka's painting of a jolly Moravian swain. Catherine was scratching at the soil in the flower-pots in search of pieces of straw and thread that she bore off to her nest. Mrs. D. asked whether Catherine would have chicks. I told her that she would lay eggs, about five in number, but that nothing would come of them since Philip, being a hybrid, was infertile. Consequently Catherine would throw the eggs out after three weeks and lay some more, though fewer this time, again fruitlessly. Then one last time, only two now, until at last she would tire of it, forget about it and give up. Yes, it was almost heart-rending to see the maternal instinct operating irrepressibly and without fail in such a creature – and in the end to no avail. Mrs. D. was outraged by this: couldn't we find a new mate for Catherine? I told her it was out of the question because it had taken long enough for them to become accustomed to each other; two male birds could not be here together and Philip was a very fine bird who was cheerful and clever, and we had got him first. It was only last year that he had received Catherine as a Christmas present. And I asked Mrs. D. whether she had any children. She hadn't either. I asked her how old she was. Thirty-seven next birthday. I told her that one possibility, and one I was considering, was to put eggs fertilised elsewhere into Catherine's nest.

She wears her hair short and has an unruly fringe. Hanging from a cord round her neck was a little silver hand which in the summer will get lost in the grass. Now she was playing with it, winding the cord round her finger and putting the hand to her lips. She has a clear voice and occasionally speaks very fast, though always thoughtfully; she is abuzz with ideas, observations, objections and conclusions while maintaining a healthy composure, without which her face would not be so deliciously proportional. She has blue eyes with sharply defined irises. I asked if I might photograph her. When she agreed, I did so straight way.

It is surprising how much one can observe in a single sitting if one has the talent.

WEDNESDAY, 31ˢᵗ JANUARY 1979

Only now, after going through my childhood diaries for so many months, am I beginning to perceive them as the work of someone else entirely. And I must say I have a liking for the lad. Long ago, when I first took them out, there were passages that made me cringe and I felt should be left out because I took them personally. Now I have come to regard them as entirely in character with the subject under investigation. Coyness and a temptation to expurgate what I wrote will arise, I expect, as I get to the more adult years when the opinions and statements of that young man will be more obviously related to my present persona. It's a funny business, role models: for that little lad in the Indian head-dress I might well be a real somebody; yet I wish I were like *him!*

I was in town today; I felt a need to speak to someone. I called in on Vlasta Chramostová's Standa. When he opened the door, his loneliness was plain to see. I asked him what the trouble was. He said that the times had quite simply got to him all of a sudden. He had first noticed it when Vlasta was taken from their apartment off to hospital with that very same diagnosis: the times. The times are unbearable and I can think of nothing to advance as grounds for hope. My own hopes are groundless. But when I project the present state of affairs into the future, I have no wish to live in it. Young people live off stupidity. Or maybe they know something about the future that I no longer do. Traditionally older people are regarded as more knowledgeable. Well, nowadays the opposite is true: the older you get the less you know, and your predictions become more and more short-term until even tomorrow is a mystery. The new-born, on the other hand, know everything, because everything is equally possible for them, everything can still happen to them. They might even succeed at everything.

"I don't understand all the controversy over your feuilleton," Standa said. "It seemed plain enough to me." – "And doesn't it seem so any longer?" I asked. – "Now I'm beginning to get a slight inkling why it is some people might find it demoralising. Don't you see? Some of those who were accustomed to getting a boost from you are missing it all of a sudden." I told him that was the reason I could not take the usual compliments very seriously, since they were not the expression of considered agreement. According to Standa, Vlasta defends me as follows: So far, I have always managed to pinpoint a problem long before it came to a head, so I am bound to know what I am doing this time as well. Some people say I am being a brake or "dropping anchor"; Vlasta does not agree with that, though. – Well, it's not hard to put one's finger on today's problem. But it's a risky business to take a standpoint on it. "I find the kind of confidence in me that Vlasta expresses," I said, "as embarrassing as other people's suspicion. They both curb my freedom."

The apartment in which we were sitting seemed odd without Vlasta present, like a scene from an interrupted play: the art nouveau armchair covers, the white wood, the antique lamps. Physically and spiritually angular, Standa seemed almost ludicrously out of place here all on his own. I decided to tell him something, but it would be for his ears only. I had no wish for it to be used anywhere in my defence, as I wanted the controversy to run its full course unabated. I was aware of all the statements that were then causing some people offence: it was the jailed youngsters in Brno who were chiefly in my mind when I raised the matter of what it was worth going to prison for, and I realised that one day I would meet them and it would be up to me to say something to them. The purpose of my article was not entirely confined to what I wrote: it was to break out of the "dissident" circle. I wanted it to get through to the people who somehow manage to put up with the times, but were disgusted by them: the ones who had a bad conscience, but suppressed it. What earthly good would it be to have a brilliant handful of indomitable warriors on the one side, while on the other, society as a whole went to rack and ruin. Our survival depended on what would be preserved in the community's consciousness and morality, not on what would be preserved in literature. How many people had the strength to be dragged downstairs by their feet? Unattainable models increase the depression of the rest. Someone should give the millions absolution – for not having burned themselves to death like Palach, for not having gone on strike, for having taken part in the elections, for not having signed Charter 77 and for not having the capacity to resist violence of various kinds. But at the same time they should be told that all their other duties remain.

I had deliberately taken a step backwards towards those whom we had, in terms of courage (courage?), left behind. I had taken the liberty of talking about "heroes" the way I did, because people counted me as one and I did not want them to. I was lacerating myself as well. We pay with our skins anyway, but who exacts the payment – only the secret police! Over the years we have evolved ways of behaving during interrogations, making off with documents and smuggling information. We have developed strategies and tactics for dealing with the State Security, but do we have them for dealing with the lords and masters? After all, the StB is no more than a cudgel in the hands of the lords and masters. We – the free dogs – gnaw away boldly at that stick, while the lord and master is scarcely aware of us. I wanted nothing further to do with it; I was turning my back on it!

Besides, what if more people left the country and more of us ended up in jail, myself included? What would happen to the activity of those Chartists left, with nothing to do but assert their existence in a clandestine circle? What would remain of the original objective? Shouldn't we be thinking about constructing a second, numerically stronger, line of defence?

I think that sums up what I told Standa; I unfortunately let myself get carried away. But all the time I was ashamed to be talking. And I even felt nervous about doing so much talking. I haven't done any speaking for several years. Maybe it was more of an attempt at putting into words something I will eventually want to write about. But I doubt it.

I walked along Wenceslas Square. The afternoon was almost spring-like. The snow is going from the streets. There remains a grey coating of dry salt, that the spring rains will have to wash away. At the Akademia publishing house I asked why the *Astronomy Yearbook* was not out yet. I was told the printers didn't have electricity. But I was in a good mood. I had a yen to buy something interesting. Normally I would look for something like that at the stationers' or the photographic suppliers. On this occasion it was a necktie, but that shop was closed. I bought myself two volumes of Gebauer's *Dictio-*

nary of Old Czech. I looked forward to getting home, making a nice cup of tea, putting my feet up and having a good think. In the tram it crossed my mind that, after all, I would like a real bow and arrows one day.

THURSDAY, 1ST FEBRUARY 1979

Madla comes home from work, takes the bits and pieces of shopping out of her bag, looks round to see what we have done and left undone – whether I have vacuumed for instance, or our Jan has taken back the bottles. Then she sits down at the table, in her coat, and skims through some reading matter or other, which is her way of relaxing. Then she gets changed and starts cooking. For that purpose she takes the television out of the cupboard and switches it on. "Must you always have that box on?" "I need to know what's going on in the world." I leave the room in disgust, with a despairing wave of the hand and a quotation from Váchal: "The world is moving fast up the Devil's arse." – "All right," she manages to say to my retreating back, "but you need to know precisely when it's going to get there, in order to have time to duck."

Looking at the date at the top of this page I realise that today is the day Pastor Jan Šimsa is due home from prison.

I spent this afternoon somewhere, sticking slips with Kratochvil's signature into copies of his now ready-bound book, because I did not get them in time. I arrived home to find a slip telling me to collect a letter from the State Security at the post office. A familiar chill travelled from my chest down to my feet. With different eyes I perused the things I had on my desk and round about. I immediately made two parcels: one for Šimečka, the other for Kadlečík. I shall send them off tomorrow, before I go to collect that poisonous missive. I marked on them the intimidatory sum of 1,000 Kčs, as they contain Patočka and Hejdánek, among others.

Ondřej has decided to circulate his feuilleton about builders. I dutifully warned him against doing so and recommended him to sharpen the moral should he do so, regardless. Madla is not pleased. It could well be, she says, that his problems in the building field are due to the fact he writes. But why discourage him, seeing that he might not be allowed to advance any higher up the ladder in the building field anyway.

Madla fell asleep reading Šotola's *Saint on the Bridge*. She enjoys properly printed books. She finds our ones suspect. She scolded me about *Lord of the*

*I dutifully warned him against doing so and recommended him to sharpen
the moral should he do so, regardless.* (p. 29)

Tower. Why me? I told her that it would not be appearing in Padlock Editions in that form anyway, but she was still cross with me.

I have still not written my feuilleton about this winter. Tomorrow?

FRIDAY, 2ND FEBRUARY 1979

I went to see Jiří Gruša at work. The builder told me he had left already. I went to Zdena's. She was sitting smoking, drinking coffee and reading something. "Jiří has only just gone. He left you something." She passed me what she was reading. It was entitled "Dear Ludvík." I said: "What's it like?" In perversely intellectual style she said: "Well, I think it's a well-founded semantic analysis." That needled me: "So how do you justify the fact that you also praised my feuilleton?" I read through those pages, once, and stuck them in my briefcase without comment. Jiří had apparently stressed that it was for my eyes only. For my eyes only, and meanwhile he had already given it to Klíma and Lopatka to read. Everyone knows he is writing me something and they are all eagerly waiting for me to skedaddle with my tail between my legs. I read it once through and it makes no sense to me. I'll leave it for some other time. And have copies of it made!

Zdena went on to say: "It seems you also acted preposterously at your meeting on Tuesday." – "What's that supposed to mean? I didn't have a meeting with anyone." – "I'm only repeating what Jirka told me. He's pretty fed up with you because of it. You called a meeting in someone's flat, but when you arrived, all you did was have a drink, and before the discussion even got under way, you apparently said you were going swimming with the boys, and left. Seemingly it shocked everyone because they had had to make time after a full day's work, while your time is your own."

I have no idea how many negative thoughts, words and incidents Zdena manages to filter, adjust and conceal from me – plenty, I should imagine. But some of them she tells me with obvious relish, albeit in the tones of an impartial rapporteur. Now that she has that job in the factory, she insinuates more frequently that my time is my own. So I am getting it in duplicate.

What annoyed me most of all was the fact that Jirka had actually talked out loud in Zdena's apartment about such a meeting. Even if the names of the people, the venue or the agenda were not mentioned, it was letting on that something clandestine was afoot. What it was about I shall call "D.,"

31

and the persons working on it shall be A., B., C., and – seeing that it is now out – dear little Jiří G. It is no business of mine. I merely know of it and somehow I have been allotted the responsibility of seeing that the various phases of the work are completed on schedule. But I am not the one doing the work; it is not my job; I have no say in it and I have neither the right nor the desire to play the foreman. I happened to have taken part in a few working parties, but only to see how the work was progressing and because I enjoyed the company of the people involved. The work which started at a good pace is beginning to drag somewhat, mainly on account of B., with whom it is difficult to agree upon deadlines. And even then he does not respect them. I have my own personal problems with him: he wants me to set aside all the Padlock titles for him, but he never comes to pick the books up, and when I go to see him he is usually out and he pays no heed to the notes I leave him.

Last week I asked J.G. when they would be ready with something or other. He started to berate B. who had apparently managed to evade him for a long time, but had now solemnly promised to come to A.'s for a meeting on Tuesday at five o'clock. I could come as well if I wished and find out what I needed to know straight from the horse's mouth. I went there, maybe chiefly out of curiosity, in order to find out what A.'s place was like, not having been there before. Being a non-essential person, I arrived about half-an-hour late, as soon as I could manage it. Only A., C., and G., were there, B. having sent his apologies that he would not be able to make it before seven o'clock. I had been sitting around there for half an hour or so when they asked me what I would like to drink. I asked for fizzy lemonade and told them that I would have to be going as I had a swimming appointment with the boys. They said it was a pity and went on with their waiting. In the end I did not go swimming with the boys because the pool has restricted opening hours owing to a fuel shortage. It was to have been our first swim in all the years we have been living next door to the pool.

Just what is going on? Why are my neutral actions acquiring such unpleasant connotations? I never worry much whether my words can be taken otherwise, and I myself take other people's words at face value. Cooperation among people when there is no institutionalised hierarchy is a very specific testing ground and classifies people with precision. Gruša is an excellent partner because he is capable of working on someone else's good idea as effectively as on his own. He keeps his word, has a sense of humour, is a fast worker and lacks complexes, which means he does not begrudge anyone either money or status. The *Hour of Hope* almanac was Milan Uhde's brainchild, but since he was unable to do very much with it in Brno, Jiří and I undertook it jointly. Jiří did most of the inside work here; I took charge of outside contacts. It didn't even occur to me that our relationship was lopsided. Or had I unwittingly elevated myself?

I am not even able to write about it yet. I'll have to read Gruša's article more carefully. Certain war-loving folk (people who like to see a scrap) are beginning to treat me as if I were someone who was losing his friends: first Václav Havel, now Jiří. I shall bide my time and none of my friends shall manage to become an enemy of mine.

It was three years ago or thereabouts that I first took Jiří with me to Pavel Kohout's place on the Sázava River and introduced him to the society there. Silly Pavel made a funny comment that he subsequently repeated on several occasions to satisfy his need for theatrical success: "That's Vaculík and his latest young man!" Jiří and I laughed it off because we were able to, but it was not the nicest of things to say. When they arrested Gruša last May, some of my friends treated me as if I should be the one suffering: they'd jailed my Gruša. A bit further away, out of earshot, others put it slightly differently: they had jailed Gruša in my stead.

I do not consider it decent to go looking for hidden motives for friends' actions apart from the overt ones. So I might well have been responsible for misunderstandings or done people wrong. In contrast, it is almost comical the way Jiří revels in both probable and impossible combinations of motives, relations, links and causes when assessing people's actions. Among other things, he always takes into account the sexual aspect and what the devil might be up to.

So before making a serious effort to decipher what he is proffering with his "semantic analysis," I think first of all, and for the first time, I shall have a look to see what the devil is up to.

SUNDAY, 4ᵀᴴ FEBRUARY 1979

In point of fact, Monday 2 a.m. I just wanted to have a quick glance at Jiří's text before I have it transcribed. And it turns out to be neither as complex nor as good as I feared. Semantic analysis! I never even give a thought to these academic aspects of my writing. All I do is try to express my thought properly and succinctly, using emotional, logical and hyperbolic effects in turn. I do not claim my thoughts to be the truth about the matter reflected on; they are the truth about my reflections.

"Believe me," writes Jiří, "I too accept that a text designated as a 'feuilleton' operates with a certain degree of licence and simplification. Nonetheless even in such a text certain relationships ought not to be distorted... a globe is not the earth, but even on a globe, North is at the top."

Gruša knows how to write. He is witty, spirited and reputable. The very fact he chose me as a target came as rather a surprise for people. For me too, I must admit. The fact is I thought we shared the same opinion about the matter dealt with in my article.

I had written: "When some threatened group of people decides to redefine its internal structure and tightens its rules, it cannot expect widespread sympathy. On the one hand, the demand for unity intimidates free individuals, while on the other, the prudent majority comes increasingly to regard the ever more heroic actions of an ever-dwindling band of warriors as the latter's own affair." – I was sure it was plain what I was talking about: the risk that the Charter might evolve into the nucleus of some new iron-disciplined party, suitable perhaps for "people of a special calibre," but no longer for the likes of me – or Gruša – and that at the same time its efforts would become unintelligible and unattractive for ordinary people. Gruša homed in on that passage with such violence that he got me rattled and I started to check it through with apprehension. I wanted to find out how Gruša thought things ought to be, and what did I discover? Nothing! Straight away he takes me to task for the word "group," then "internal structure," then "cannot expect" and finally the "ordinary people" that he ironically designates as OP. But words of some kind have to be used and I tried to find as neutral ones as possible. The point is I am talking about the Charter and I have no intention of playing into the hands of the cops or government propaganda by using expressions like "organisation," "organisational structure," "find itself isolated," "discipline" or "the mass of the people."

Gruša's criticism of me: "Let us allow that the noun 'group,' albeit hackneyed, is harmless enough, even though the fact it is 'threatened' is almost tantamount to posing – at least potentially – the question of whether it is also 'threatening'... (Why, for fuck's sake? That was the whole point of my article! – L.V.) "… let us allow that 'redefining its internal structure' makes some sort of sense, though it is hard to conceive of an 'external' structure…" (Such an external structure is quite easy to imagine, though: 'an informal community' always represented outwardly by three spokespersons, concealing local and regional branches!) "… however, what is serious is the manipulatory way you say it 'cannot expect.' I'd have hoped for at least some hint of a reason why…" (Well, because a sect with strict regulations, disciplinary proceedings and sanctions ceases to be something for ordinary people, Gruša! But I can't say it in so many words when I have the Charter in mind, can I? – L.V.) "… Unless it can be demonstrated that it 'cannot' expect, then your sentence simply means the imperative 'don't expect' (Why should it mean that, for God's sake? – L.V.) again voiced solely by you, but this time on behalf of our OPs as well, with whom you apparently have some tacit agreement. However, in the process our OPs are transformed (my underlining – L.V.) into free OPs, for who else could be afraid of uniting with some group that is redefining its rules – i.e. making them more rigid, rigorous, restrictive, and less free. Our OPs have thus grown up and transformed themselves into some sort of perverted Supermen, or better still, Between-men… But those particular individuals are very well known to us, aren't they? They are none other than our 'simple,' 'honest,' 'popular,' etc., working people who "won't sanction," are "not to be deceived," "won't surrender," etc. – they are the actors of all those appeals in the name of the majority, the magic majority of the journalistic fakirs."

Just like that. Erudite and stylish.

But I refer back to what I was talking about: that a sect does not win over a) free individuals or b) the mass of ordinary people. The formula would be written (a+b). But for his purposes Gruša, in one sentence, arbitrarily transforms the OP into free individuals, whereby he foists a formula on me (a=b). He does the very thing he blames me for. I have found about six similar examples. I shall quote just one of them:

In my article I make the point that some forms of resistance are actually capable of perfecting oppression: turning the censor into a dictator, the dictator into a murderer. I was prompted by the question: What if, by taking part in the Railwaymen's Ball en masse, the Chartists had provoked the roughing up they received? (And anyway, if one is thinking in higher terms than mere political expediency, account must be taken of the slave's responsibility for his master's behaviour.) It was a totally general point I was making, though I realised the risk involved in a very specific situation, which is why, on Karel Pecka's suggestion, I added the sentence: "But where are the decent bounds of such considerations?"

Gruša writes: "But as soon as you start knitting there is nothing to do but to go on to the next stitch and then the next... there tend to be two sides, and they are mutually capable of provoking the other; however, by bringing up the OPs you make it look as if only one side is doing the provoking – the non-normal side. And as if you sub-consciously realised the depth of the water you were entering, you let slip in Freudian fashion 'where are the decent bounds of such considerations?'"

He thrust a needle into my hands and then proceeds to knit with it: he realises full well that the point I am making is intended as a general one, but acknowledges this by declaring ironically that I write as if I were talking about Iran. Precisely! Carried away with his own wit and his determination to wipe the floor with me, it never occurs to him – being tainted by Freud – that the words of reservation in that seemingly casual sentence might be the outcome of reflection and discussion. In fact he failed to notice how well I had written precisely what I wanted to write! What kind of conscientious writing is this: "A globe is not the earth, but even on a globe, North is at the top"? The point is that *only* on a globe is North at the top!

When I asked Alexandr Kliment last Monday what he thought about my argument with Gruša, he said: "I'd say that, first and foremost – leaving aside the point at issue, which I'd first have to study carefully – it is a young man's rebellion against – well – let us call it authority." I just gaped.

MONDAY, 5ᵀᴴ FEBRUARY 1979

One thousand, nine hundred and seventy-nine – that's a sizeable figure already!

Ten years ago, in June, we were on holiday in Norway. It has turned into an impossible dream. "When will we go to Norway again?" our Jan said after glancing at the calendar that hangs on the dresser. Every year we receive a Norwegian calendar from Mrs. Blekastad of Oslo. In the mountain village of Geilo the girl in the reception pronounced Oslo "Ooshloo.." I think I would be able to make better pictures for a Norwegian calendar. That company prints the same banal images year after year: January – ice in the mountains; March – thawing snow on heathland; June – midnight sun... *I* would take photos of rocks and the sea, low mossy crags on the shore. And maybe I would not even take photos, but would retreat to the heathlands among the mountain lakes near the earth's curvature and there I would rot.

When I saw Jiří this afternoon he was his usual cheerful and sincere self, so it was a mystery to me how I could ever clash with him. "So, have you read my pamphlet yet?" he laughed, rubbing his little hands. – "Yes, but you've no cause to be so pleased with yourself!" Jiří is a fine sight in his building office: director and democrat in one. There is another young fellow working there with him that I know from my days at the radio. He treats me with genial affability but every time I go there he leaves after a few moments. "You see?" Jiří laughed. – "I have decided to persuade you that I have to have your pamphlet circulated," I said. "A lot of people have already heard about it and I don't want them thinking I am seeking to hush it up." He sort of half agreed, and I had half decided to do it anyway. So I gave it for retyping today, though not to Zdena because I have already written comments on it. I intend to goad her into thinking about it independently and then saying who she thinks is right.

I got a letter from Alžběta R. "Dear friend, I have started to pen something here and already I don't like what I've written. I expect my hand will start to ache in a minute..." She had read Mr. Václav's letter and it struck her that it might have upset me. Her purpose is to reconcile parties whom she would not like to see in dispute. "Yes, maybe your sentence about people having to act in such a way as not to have to give even a thought to prison was too audacious, and possibly tactless. It might have been true somewhere on our planet at some time in history... But that was not the point of your original feuilleton, or at least that is not the impression I get. It does not devalue the actions of those who are sent to prison or suffer persecution. On the contrary, all it does is contrast them rather wistfully with the mass of the population we represent and forces us to confront them... By now everybody has got too accustomed to the absurd situation of the past decade in which it has been impossible to share one's thoughts with other ordinary people (OP... J.G. would slay her – L.V.) and your feuilleton is a sudden break with the practice of only writing for a narrow circle of like-minded individuals. It addresses the rest of us and appeals to people's personal courage in their everyday lives."

Last night I found myself in a large room of some kind, such as at someone's country place. There were lots of people there, apparently friends, though I knew none of them and the person sitting next to me was a cat. She was a young woman with a nice little elongated fox-face, and she was all covered in brown fur, so that she looked just like a fox though they all treated her as a cat. I asked her husband – or father – what she lived on. "Does she eat mice, for instance?" – "She loves mice," the man replied and the cat happily nodded her agreement. "And moles too?" I asked. "Moles aren't to her taste," the man said. I turned to ask the cat herself and to accommodate her likely tastes I worded my question as follows: "And how about worms; do they suit you?" – "Soothe me!" the cat gaily assented.

I love peaceful mornings like this when I am at home on my own. I carry my typewriter into the kitchen where it is warmer and there is more light from the yard. I have finished my cup of tea, cleared away the washed and now dry dishes from the family's breakfast, and given the bird-life fresh water. I feed a clean sheet of paper into the typewriter and look forward to no one ringing the doorbell. The phone rings, but I do not answer the phone. So – what shall we get our teeth into? There goes the doorbell.

"Good morning," she said in a clear little voice, and it struck me that she accompanied it with a very slight bend of the knee that might easily have turned into an ironic maidenly curtsy but did not, and maybe I only imagined it because of the manner of her greeting. "May I come in for a moment?" As I was taking her fur jacket, I immediately realised the origin of last night's cat. She was making straight for the kitchen after the birds, when she caught sight of the typewriter, and stopped short. I moved it away to Madla's side-table by the couch. "Coffee, tea?" "No, no. Nothing at all – if it's all right with you…" – "Then at least let me relate to you the dream I had last night." – "Oh, yes, please." – "It's about a cat." – "Ah, if I still have a choice," it was a game of etiquette at an empty table, with gestures above the table-cloth, "then no cats, thank you all the same!" This said with both hands raised defensively. – "Well, as a matter of fact it wasn't actually a cat. She looked like a fox, they only called her a cat." She put her head on one side reflectively. "Well… all right, but do be careful. A fox, you say? Well in that case, yes, that's fine."

*I feed a clean sheet of paper into the typewriter and look forward
to no one ringing the doorbell.* (p. 38)

When I told her the dream she expressed surprise and said: "Funnily enough I have a bit of an odd occurrence to relate. Actually it hasn't yet materialised. It might be better to call it a pledge of something that might materialise." Then, realising that so far she had only been giving me the dry outer layers of her news, she boldly tore it open: "I'm going to get a job for the first time in two years. It's..." – "Don't tell me!" I said, passing her a pad and pencil. She wrote it down for me. Then she spoke. "So I came... I'm not sure why... maybe I just had to tell someone. So forgive me. And now I must fly, I'm just on my way to make the first moves, as it were." – "But we should at least drink to it," I said standing up. "Oh, no," she said, getting up from the table with what was left of the fox, "I'm here with the car."

I did no writing after that. I sat and pondered. I reflected on how I was to write this work, what belonged in it and what did not. Dreams, naturally. I failed to record this morning's visit and only realise the need to do so when making a fair copy of the manuscript in February 1980! Dear reader, a fat lot you know! All those deceptions that writers practise on their readers! I, however, as you can see, am not out to deceive; admittedly I cannot be sure that the visit described took place precisely today, but occur it did, with the same subject matter, around the time of someone else's visit which I can date with certainty from a strip of negatives on which those two faces appear on successive frames. I was jerked out of my musing by the door-bell.

"Hi there! My goodness, the cold weather you have here in Prague cuts right through you! Where we are there's a nice warm frost and loads of snow!" I relieved Josef of his winter coat, thereby releasing a horsey smell. I gave him some slippers for his feet and ushered him into the kitchen. He went straight over to the bird cage, at that moment minus its occupants, who were perched on the radio and the picture; he cast an admiring glance at the vegetal decor in front of the window, flared his nostrils and sniffed: "Ludvík, you've had a woman here! A different one!" – "Damn it!" I replied. Josef said: "What are you up to all the time? Come with us and the horses to Romania this summer. What d'you say? The Transylvanian Alps!" – "Ha! Ha! Ha!" I said. – "What's so funny? At least you'd manage to learn Romanian by July. It's more than I could do," he declared, shaking his head sadly. We clinked glasses of slivovice. Water was heating on the stove for coffee. "That's not the problem," I said. "I'd master Romanian in a week. But I don't have a passport!" – "Geddaway! *You* don't have a passport?" he gasped, and only then did I realise he had been pulling my leg. We spent half an hour reminiscing about our trip to Mount Praděd thirteen years ago. Then I asked: "What made you come?" – "To ask you if you'd come to Romania, of course, and also to see if I could find a Christmas present for the wife." – "For next Christmas, already?" "No for the one just gone! The fact is I haven't had my December salary yet, but I'm expecting some money to come in." Josef Zeman from Bezejovice heads an equestrian team and is his own employee. We sat for a while longer and then I accompanied him into Prague. As we walked through the streets I gave him all the latest bad news. He expressed astonishment. We had not seen each other in a long time.

When we parted, I went to pick up *My Years in Dijon* from the bookbinders' and made a trip to Professor Černý's for him to sign them. I found him as usual working on the manuscript of his next volume of memoirs. "So tell me!" he said. – "What am I to tell?" – "The latest news, of course!" But I had no news, apart from the fact that Dr. Danisz, the lawyer, has been convicted and given a suspended sentence for "assaulting a public servant," on account of something he said in court when defending a Chartist, and for which they want to sack him. But I was in no mood for such chat. "I don't have any news, Professor." – "Ha! You never have any news, old boy. If nothing else, then are you writing something at last?" – "Something, yes." – "And naturally you don't want to talk about it. That also goes without saying, of course. A fat lot of good you are! So at least tell me what people are talking about. You have no news of Kohout?" – "None at all." – "Well, do you think he'll come back, at least?" – "I know he wants to," I said. – "Ha. What Kohout wants is beside the point. Do you think they'll let him back?" – "I would hope so. And not merely hope," I suggested. He exhaled the smoke from his cigarette through funnelled lips, and inhaled it back up his nose. "You're naive," he said. Then he asked: "What do you think about the new spokesmen?" I said: "If they've the courage to do it, then they'll have my loyalty." I wanted to indicate certain reservations about those people without having to say it in so many words. But he said unreservedly: "That Benda... d'you know him? No? No of course you don't. Well, that fellow appeals to me. He came to see me. And that Tominová lassie seems to have a bit more pluck than the singer woman." I must make a point of passing that rare tribute on to her.

The next few minutes he spent berating Václav Havel: "Did you see all the printing mistakes in my study on Masaryk that came out in Paris, in *Svědectví?*"

I expressed surprise that this had anything to do with Václav Havel. "Well, they took the text from the Dispatch series, didn't they? And that's run by Havel, who always has to have something extra, as if Padlock Editions didn't suffice." I explained to him the difference between the two book series and from that he concluded: "Oh, all right, all right! So you don't think I should send the Charter leadership a protest about the way *Svědectví* garbled my text?"

I was lost for words in the face of such powerful magic from the Good Old Days.

WEDNESDAY, 7ᵀᴴ FEBRUARY 1979

"You haven't even asked how I made out with the cops today," I reproached the boys at supper. "How did you make out with the cops?" our Jan asked. I nodded in Ondřej's direction too. He said: "Please tell us how you made out with the cops today." – "You'll be surprised," I said.

As surprised as I was. I was expecting them to take away my driving licence again and then keep me waiting two months before I could re-take the test on the highway code, and then fail me on at least three technical check-ups. I had enough of that last year. In the course of the most recent intimidatory sessions, the fragrant grey man with the heavy gold ring dropped several dark hints whose import I have been trying to deduce for myself. I have no desire to write about those "chats" for the time being, but if that grey man with the heavy gold ring raises the matter again, I shall be obliged to. In case he starts thinking I don't take his words seriously enough.

The harmless, considerate, uniformed traffic cop riffled through the tickets, found mine and read out: "'6ᵗʰ December, badly parked at the corner of Veletržní and Janovská street. Failed to observe statutory five-metre distance from the intersection.' That'll cost you a hundred crowns." I paid up and rushed out joyfully into the street. A normal fine for a normal traffic offence! It was a real pleasure. I walked down the hill, overcome with a desire to buy something (in order, I expect, to have the feeling I had got something for my hundred crowns!). I thought about what it might be and hit on some developer-fixer as I needed to do some photos for Šimečka's *Restoration of Order*. Only afterwards did I come up with a less inept retort: "You wouldn't have anything cheaper, would you?" That was after I noticed the fronts and rears of badly parked cars sticking out at every road junction.

As I entered our building I bumped into Jan Mlynárik. He had been looking for me. "Hey listen," he said, "it'll be Tatarka's birthday in March. He's
coming to Prague and it'd be great if his book were ready by then." I replied:
"Find me a Slovak typist then, seeing that you weren't even capable of drawing in the circumflex accents!" – "That won't be necessary, Skácel is prepared
to translate it into Czech." – "What nonsense!" I said. "It's untranslatable!"
But in the end I promised to have the book ready.

The trouble is I have not finished reading the manuscript yet. I am afraid
of it somehow, and a trifle shy. Besides, there are manuscripts here that have
been waiting longer: Ruml's documentary pieces and two new things by
Božena Komárková. One of them I asked Eva Kantůrková to read for me,
but she refused, saying that it would disrupt her work on *Lord of the Tower*.
The other one I pushed in Ivan's direction; he said he would do it as soon
as he had finished writing something. So it was up to me and Gruša again:
we took one each. Gruša has a tendency to go in for real editing – he made
substantial alterations in Sacher's *Bloody Easter*. But we can't do things like
that, for heaven's sake! All I do is correct mistakes, unify the spelling of foreign words, change the word order here and there, put a couple of question
marks in the margin and give it back to the author to sort out. We are not an
editorial board. We would be at it all day and everyday otherwise, and we
get not a penny for it. They do say that when a Padlock book finds its way
abroad and some emigrant does some clever wheeler-dealing, a single volume
can fetch as much as a hundred marks.

I took a trip to the Tuzex shop for tea, coffee and whisky (silly me: now
it looks as if those hundred marks came to me!) and there in the queue I met
Alexandr Kliment. As we stood waiting together for a shopping-trolley, we
chatted about his party and how nice it had been – almost as if we were living
in normal times. But these are not normal times at all, as Saša unwittingly
reminded me with a vengeance: the commemorative volume that we had
given him for his birthday had been a great success, so I had determined to
embellish the gift, as it were, by having it recopied and giving a copy to each
of Saša's old colleagues at the next meeting of the erstwhile *Literary News*.
Zdena had managed to type it out over a single weekend, to my astonishment.
She refused to accept payment, saying that she had done it as a gift to an
author she revered. But what would be just right for a commemorative edition
like that would be a picture of the birthday boy! I had asked his sons, both

43

of whom do photography, to produce the requisite number of pictures. They had both told me they had no time to do it. When I now broached the matter with Saša, I asked him to borrow a negative from one of his sons and I would print the photos myself. And then the truth came out: he thinks it would not be a good idea because both of them are due to sit some entrance exams.

Once again I felt that shiver, emanating inexplicably and incongruously from some disordered part of my body, perhaps. On the journey back – Saša drove me home – I was unable to speak, even. Back home after our customary friendly goodbye (I was fortunately alone) my sense of humiliation gradually gave way to one of outrage: were those boys of his really more precious and special than my own?

Then Madla came home from work and noticed that something was up. I told her about it, fearing she would scold me again as usual for lacking my friends' common sense. I must have seemed pretty devastated, as her habit of contradicting me took the following form: "Oh, come on, you must see that these are exams, after all... just on account of some photo?" – I know it was detestable self-delusion on my part, but I could feel her conciliatory attitude to the matter doing me good, so I would not have the doleful duty of complaining about a friend.

There was a group of people walking along the road to the mill dragging a sledge on which a man was lying. He was alive. Behind the sledge strode a large, coarse fellow carrying an axe with which he kept striking the prostrate man. This left pale, gaping, bloodless wounds on the man's body. I said flatteringly to the axe-man: I'll carry your axe a little way for you. Hesitantly, he let me take it and I set off with the axe at a wild, loose-limbed sprint. I dashed behind the barns and through the gap between them and I was home, my sister was there. It was in Brumov. I told her to hide the axe and crawled under the table. From the distance an enraged bellow was slowly coming closer. Perhaps they'll pass our cottage by.

THURSDAY, 8TH FEBRUARY 1979

At eleven o'clock this morning I was supposed to meet Drahomíra Pithartová (hereafter Mrs. P.) who had given me her "Exercise in Callousness" to read. It purports to be the notebook of an introverted woman who feels herself wasting away in a world spoiled by men who have instituted nylon and crimplene in place of silk and wool, police violence in place of politics, and the art of drinking, smoking and gossiping in each other's flats in place of social life, so that in the end men are no longer men and women no longer women. It is absolutely true, the whole thing! But it might well incense those Prague men and women who will say Pithartová ought to be the last person to complain, as she is at home with her children, and her husband even puts up with this kind of writing. It struck me that the manuscript's author needed to eliminate the neurotic tone that jars with the "callousness" she seeks to convey, and she ought to paint Pithart's household in even truer colours, particularly seeing that Petr has probably gone as far as a man can go today, and what she writes she gives him to read, so it is not just a case of conflict but also of cooperation. Yesterday I noted down my comments and gave them to Madla to read this morning. She had also read the Pithartová and said nothing bad about it. Hmm. "It's quite right what you've written her," she said, "but you shouldn't start fooling yourself that you can be a husband-substitute for them."

This infernally short circuit riled me, but I still asked her calmly: "For whom?" – "For whom? Vlasta Kavanová, for instance, and that Pithartová!"

Having worked for years in that social infirmary for the poor, created by the state that also created the infirmities, Madla has learnt the art of snap diagnoses. They are always correct, apart from minor details. But those minor details happen to be that delicate layer of relationships, interests and emotions that are the fragrant lubricant of everyday life. Without it the wheels of work, culture and society would not turn; it would be no fun for people to make theatre or watch it; to write or read; or to associate even. But she knows that as well as I do. The only problem is that the seeds of future tragedies all take root in this soil, it is the spawning ground of vice, according to Madla, particularly mine. For I have a date today again in a bistro with Pithartová, haven't I? And one thing leads to another, doesn't it!

I tore my notes for Mrs. P. into tiny pieces and threw them in the bin. I went and fell on the couch; I felt unwell all of a sudden. I wanted to render myself worthless somehow, so as not to be of interest to anyone ever again and not be penalised because someone holds me in esteem or respect. To hell with them all! But that sort of escape into sensible peace and quiet is death, or at the very least a monastic retreat. I can readily imagine my sort of retreat: writing, and leaving the finished sheets in a pile somewhere, whence they would be taken away by messengers whom I would never meet. And in the early phases going about in disguise until people forgot about my existence. Karel Kosík has that sort of retreat, or rather he had, before some woman wormed her way into it again. So is it possible at all? Or not?

Madla retrieved the pieces from the bin and put them in an envelope before coming to me to announce: "I'll send it to her with a letter merely describing what you did after my one simple sentence. It's about bloody time they knew!" – "Who knew?" I roared. – "All the ones that look up to you." And she calmly left for work.

I could not bring myself to move. On the contrary, I just felt myself growing stiffer and stiffer the nearer it got to eleven o'clock and then noon. I mustn't accept – God, how many times have I told myself – I mustn't accept any further responsibilities. I mustn't interfere in other people's time. I mustn't make any further dates! But for the time being I have to get up. I can't just shift my burden to the totally unsuspecting person behind me. I got up, didn't go to that bistro, of course, but straight to Mrs. P.'s. It turned out that she had not reacted hysterically in any way: she had waited a while, then gone off to an exhibition. On the way back she had looked in to see if I was there, and then gone home. "And it was only then that it crossed my mind," she said, "that they'd pulled you in. I was just wondering how to find out."

I now owe it to so many people to get myself arrested! And I still can't make my mind up.

I explained nice and methodically my opinion of her "Exercise in Callousness" (after all I had made proper written notes!). She took it all calmly, almost without comment. She happened to be in a quite different role: that of a totally contented woman whose children are at school and her husband at work, a woman who has finished her housework and cooking and is sitting down to read. I treated myself to a couple of spins on their revolving armchair, drank up my tea and left.

I left for Jan Lopatka's in Vlašská Street. There was a youngish fellow sitting there in a winter coat. Lopatka wanted to introduce us, but I told him Mr. Hejda and I were already acquainted, and it turned out to be Stankovič. The whole time he sat there in his winter coat with his briefcase on his lap. I asked him why he was sitting there like that. He said it was so he wouldn't leave anything behind. I squeezed three hundred crowns out of Lopatka for literature delivered. I apologised for having to do so. At this particular moment I have seven thousand crowns sunk in books on the go and have no money left to pay for new things; seven thousand metres is the height of the Petřín Tower: bit by bit I am getting it back. Lopatka poured me a glass from a bottle of Becherovka he received today by post for his thirty-ninth birthday yesterday.

I wandered in slow contentment up Nerudova Street. I stopped at the shop that sells porcelain coffee sets. They had some lovely gilt cups in the window for sale singly at prices ranging from fifty to sixty crowns. I would have bought one, but had no money on me and it would have meant dipping into the "firm's" money from Lopatka. So I continued my walk, looking upwards to see if I could make out the terrace from which I had looked down on Prague in summer 1968 in the company of Comrades Dubček, Husák, Smrkovský, Hájek... This description will appeal to Milan Šimečka, who once told me that he relished the thought of a book by me in which I just walk along, look at things and meet people. Today's entry, at least, I will dedicate to him. The book as a whole is promised to Jiří Kolář, who pushed me into it before leaving for Berlin. Since that day, i.e. 7th January, I have not been back to his table at Café Slávia. The castle guard was just passing through the Matthias Gate at a perverse gait when I turned off to the left. My boots slid on the slushy snow. Kosík was either not at home or not answering the door. I rang Zdena at work from the telephone booth in front of the Military Museum. It was the first time I had done so in the whole three months she has been working at that factory. "What an honour," said Zdena, "and I don't even have anyone to brag about it to, as I happen to be here on my own."

I decided to go where the first tram took me. It was a number twenty-three, so off we went to Mirka Rektorisová's. No matter where I am, there is something for me to attend to. I rang the doorbell and listened to her coming to open the door. Her asthma ran several paces ahead of her like a faithful hound. "What have I caught you in the middle of?" I asked. "Philately. Nothing, in other words. I'm glad to see you." In that particular household philately is no hobby but gainful activity on behalf of *Philatelic Horizons*, or whatever the magazine is called. "Had lunch yet?" Mirka asked. "Because, if you haven't, you're out of luck." – "I'd like to wash my hands first." – "Please do. The bathroom is through there, but don't get yourself dirty in the process. I'm turning over a new leaf tomorrow." I tendered my apologies: "I wasn't intending to come here, I was on my way to Kosík's but nobody answered the door. You're only a secondary target like the British bombers used to have each time they set out on a raid, so that even the Baťa factory got damaged." – "There you go," said Mirka, "that'd make an excellent beginning for something, and put those slippers on so you don't dirty your stockings in here."

She brought me a plate of cold pork knuckle, rolls and a glass of wine to the table in the living room. I said: "I bought you a great big bag of coffee in Tuzex of all places. But I didn't know I'd be coming to see you." – "You would go to such an expense? I tell you it didn't please me in the least. And I still can't get over it. How about you?" – "What are you referring to at this particular moment?" I asked. – "That, of course," she said, placing in front of me a pile of Gruša's transcribed pamphlets, before asking: "What do you intend to do with it – leave it unanswered?" – "That's all I intend to do for now. I'll answer it in good time." – "Tsk, tsk. And all the same, I know very well he's fond of you. What's got into the lad?" – I said: "It's already crossed my mind that it's because we like each other that we can afford something of the kind. That we're the only two in Prague who can." She said: "I couldn't make much sense of it – though in a way I could. Believe me, I'd have no idea where to start if I had to reply to it. Have *you*?" – "At first I lost sleep over it. I was bowled over the day before yesterday when he said, 'Well, have you read it,' and gleefully rubbed his little hands together like this. That made me realise that it was all just words." – "I'm an old woman already and much have I seen. What about our other friends, how do they talk to you now?" – "The suggestion I have received from specialist circles is that I should have these three bottom teeth extracted." – "Get along with you. And will you?" – "I'll wait and see how the X-ray turns out," I said.

I had finished eating and we sat drinking Three Graces. "Would you like a Ritmeester cigar?" I asked. – "Do you think it might be just the thing for my asthma?" We both lit up. She held up the slim cigar with its plastic holder and asked: "Are you going in for these from now on?" – "No. I got them in Tuzex. Sometimes when I'm in town I try and find something to buy for myself, something with real distinction, and I never manage to find anything of the kind. And these little saucigars took my fancy." – "They're dainty," she said, inhaling by mistake and exploding in a fit of coughing. – "I'll leave you another one then. And one for Franta." – Oho! Franta!" she laughed. "He had a bit of a turn the other day. Some guy made various indecent suggestions to him and he came over all disgusted, would you believe? Grandpa,

I said to him, you ought to be glad that you're still so sexy at seventy-plus. Mind you, the fact is that the other fellow was not entirely sober. He spent the night here on that sofa. The next morning he got up fit as a flea and all innocent. But when we were making the bed and deciding who was going to sleep where, Franta says to me: 'I want to sleep with you.' This place hasn't seen the like for I don't know how long!" "What do you say about that Iran business?" I asked. "I think those fellows are asking for it," she replied. "Who do you mean?" I asked. "Search me. I can't make head or tail of any of it."

We drank up and I told her I was going home. "Will you have enough of them?" she asked, indicating the pile of Gruša's pamphlets. "I won't even take them all," I said. "I'll have copies made elsewhere as well. Give them out to friends." "I don't relish the idea," she said, "but on the other hand, seeing that we're supposed to be meeting next week I'll take them copies so they'll have some clue about what's going on." As I was putting my boots on in the hall, I said: "You're taking my side, by the look of it." – "Oh, I don't know what to think."

When I got home I found letters in the mailbox from Jan Šimsa, just released from prison, and Milan Šimečka, plus a further contribution to the debate from Luboš Dobrovský. I read the lot and left it on the table – as is customary in our household – for the others to read. Madla came home from work, took the envelope with Mrs. P.'s scraps out of her handbag, and said, "I won't be sending anything." I threw it in the bin again. Then she read today's letters one by one. Šimsa's letter begins: "I am writing to you first with overwhelming gratitude for your feuilleton 'An Attempt at a Different Genre...'" Šimečka writes: "Regardless of the arguments, I agree with you because I made up my mind to long ago, when I discovered what sort of a fellow you are." – Dobrovský: "And since Vaculík's standards continue as always to be beyond all reproach... I find nothing to fault in this respect."

When she had finished reading it, her face was the face of sarcasm.

I will do everything in my power to see it never happens again.

FRIDAY, 9TH FEBRUARY 1979

We were seated around a dusty table in an empty room from which all the furniture had been shifted out. The outlines of rugs remained on the parquet floor and the shadows of pictures on the walls. With me were Ivan, Alexandr,

Jiří and someone like Petr Kabeš or Karol Sidon. It was a fantastic refuge for our meeting, whatever it was about. All of a sudden a drop of water fell from the ceiling onto the dusty table-top and burst into those tiny balls that gently roll around and turn grey when you blow on them. Then another drop, and suddenly water started to stream from various places in the ceiling above the corner where we were sitting. For a while we sat gazing at it, but then Karol, I think, said: "They've gone and pinpointed us again." We made our way to the window which was too dirty for us to see out of, or for others to see in, I hope. We did not switch the lights on; there were only loose wires hanging down from the ceiling, anyway. And all of a sudden there was some woman with us; she was a publisher from Austria. She wanted us to help publicize our matters by giving a television interview or acting out a scene. Unfortunately, Pavel Kohout wasn't there, and he is the one skillful enough to organize nonsense like that without wasting time. We sat there looking stupidly and reluctantly from one to another. Then Ivan suggested that we conduct something like mini-interviews among ourselves in which we would be allowed to put only one question to the other person – the key question. Saša said: "Such as – how are you feeling, Ludvík?" Ivan said: "How are you sleeping, Ludvík?" Jiří: "Are you cross with me, Ludvík?" The publisher, who was unattractive and smoking, but more friendly and intimate than I expected, laughed and said in a delightful way: "But that will be absolutely titillating!" I looked at her, wondering whether I knew her; I did not and I cracked a pretty good joke, as I manage to do sometimes in German: "*Sie sind ja eine echte Freudländerin!*"

SUNDAY, 11TH FEBRUARY 1979

"We were in some house of ours," said Madla at breakfast, "and the rooms were all upstairs; downstairs there were just sheds of some kind. I was there with Jan. All of a sudden I see the wood is starting to burn. And I was incapable of putting it out or calling for Jan. I just couldn't move at all. So I just watched it burn." I asked her: "And where was I?" – "I don't know. You weren't there at all. And before that I had some baby and I just couldn't tell whether I'd given it a drink or not. And I said to myself, how could I forget? After all, I always used to be so careful. And you weren't there either. So each time I ended up going to the bathroom, twice. Didn't you hear me?" – "No." –

"But you had your light on." – "I must have fallen asleep with my fat head on the typewriter."

Our Jan said: "You two are always having dreams. I never do. What's my problem?" – "You're still wet behind the ears," said Ondřej. "You're not attentive enough," I said. "Come on!" said Madla. "He's a healthy boy who has healthy sleep. As soon as he wakes up he forgets his dream straight away." – "That's right, he's healthy and wet behind the ears," Ondřej agreed. "Try being attentive next time," I said.

My brother Emil and his Lina asked us to drive all the way to Vodňany with them to have a look at some cottage they were thinking of buying. We left at half past nine. "How long will it take you to get there?" I asked Emil. It was a trick question. "Two hours," he replied with confidence. "Then could you try taking two-and-a-half hours?" I asked. He drives so fast, with such precision and panache, that he irritates me. Even now I feel more tired than if I had driven there myself. On the way we talked about Vondráček's memoirs. Lina is reading the first volume, Emil the second. As she reads, Lina is bowled over by the first Czechoslovak Republic and Austria-Hungary: Europe viewed from Asia. "I realized it again that..." – "Without the 'it'," said Emil. "...I realized again that you were more like France than Bulgaria." By now she was getting on my nerves and my irritation remained with me till evening.

The cottage is beautifully situated but a virtual ruin. Emil is loath to buy it, realizing that he would have to do all the hard labor himself. Lina, though, is already relishing the thought of lying outside the cottage on a blanket reading of Europe. She is frail and refined, and she feels the cold, as one might expect of someone with a noble family name ending in 'dze'. On those rare occasions in the past when she made as if to assist us in the garden – such as picking currants – she would take each shoot almost fastidiously between finger and thumb and hold it for ages before laying it aside carefully, expounding all the while on the latest titles in Georgian literature. But she is mild-tempered, comely, gentle and hospitable. She likes Madla, but not me – just because. She used to like me before she got to know me better, in fact she used to boast about me. While we were exploring the house she took me to one side and asked me to put in a word with Emil to buy it. "That's right. Emil will toil away and in June you'll be charmingly huddled up by the stove in your fur coat!" She smiled endearingly and said, "Don't you think, Ludvík, that people can to change?" – "Without the 'to'!" I said.

Emil drove slower on the way back. Southern Bohemia is without snow, so the government can feel more secure there than in Prague. We saw birds of prey perched in the trees just above the road. At one point, a flock of them were wheeling just above the ground. Emil stopped the car and I ran to see. The birds flew off and a hare leapt out of a furrow. Had I saved its life? There is nothing I would like better than to drive through the frozen countryside, if it were not for the feeling that when the frost departs, all the destructive processes, only delayed by the winter, will be unleashed once more. Yellow stuff is even being spread on the snow, for Christ's sake! I see nothing good anywhere; everything seems utterly doomed. (Less and less store can be placed on judgements like that one; it just might be old-age syndrome.) It also annoyed me that throughout the journey Lina gave priority to chattering instead of looking out the window. As we neared Prague, Emil declared: "What did we go there for? You won't even advise me whether to buy it or not!" I said: "Well, Emil, if you fancy doing something really exciting and utterly stupid, then I warmly advise you to buy it!" From the back seat Lina said: "Thanking to you for nothing!"

I have been gone the whole day and I ought to go to bed. But I still feel like doing something more. The blank sheets of paper lure me to set off along them, free to capture those fleeting impressions from my past that have started to flash through my mind again recently. Yes, they come to me at very long intervals – years can elapse between these brief periods, sometimes lasting only days, when my momentary awareness seems to make something like lightning incursions into the deeper strata. I receive impressions such as of snow blown in through the gap under the door, or doughnuts being fried, our parlor and Mother in the kitchen – Shrovetide revels, sliding on the ice, Thursdays off school. Or I read a perfectly ordinary sentence about the movement of leaves on trees and I obtain not a visual image but a complete and entire sense of going up and down hills, including my thoughts about what would be waiting for me when I got home from my wanderings.

MONDAY, 12TH FEBRUARY 1979

It's morning. My dreams contained no events of consequence. In one of them, the same three-digit number – that I could not subsequently recall – flashed on and off a board in front of me. It was composed of green numerals written in the ungraceful script of transistorized computers. Or I was shoveling ash into a heap with an iron shovel and I found it astonishing that it included the ashes of distinguished people: the word "distinguished" recurred over and over again and referred to Jiří Kolář.

Our Jan has no lectures till this afternoon. Now he is sitting in the kitchen by the telephone, making one phone call after another. He has made some tea and invited me to join him. "On your instructions, I had a dream today," he said. "I was walking through the streets on May Day, I was wanting to go to Dobřichovice..." – "How do you know it was May Day." – "Because the trams weren't running and the streets were filled with all that trash, people who are late for the parade or are just absconding from it. I was waiting for a bus at Palacký Bridge, and every time it looked as if one was coming, it turned out to be a group of people with a banner. In the end a trolleybus arrived – backwards." – "Trolleybuses are particularly good at that," I said.

Otka Bednářová came. I invited her in. She accepted the invitation, as well as a cup of tea and a piece of strudel, but our conversation was stilted. I have fallen out of favor with Otka. Only three years ago she still held me in esteem and, in fact, did the lion's share of the work on that amusing publication LN (Ludvík's News) for my fiftieth birthday. Ivan Klíma told me the other day that Otka's relationship with me was a text-book example of how adoration turns into its antithesis. It can't be helped. The cause is Zdena, etc. Just a few years ago they were on speaking terms and even paid each other visits; on one occasion she actually gave me a lift in her Trabant to Zdena's at Rochov. Well that's the way it is. I didn't even notice when the change occurred. When Vilém Prečan held a farewell party before emigrating and I was at his place, he took me out into the yard and said he had a question to put to me that he could no longer keep to himself: Otka had warned him that I could not be trusted any more because Zdena had been planted on me – could I disprove it? I said I could not, I could not disprove it. I could not even disprove it in my own case: there is no such thing, I said, as negative evidence. However, I told him, such speculations were not new to me and by then more or less everyone, including Otka, had been subjected to them. I quite simply refuse to countenance such talk. But I am cautious, to varying degrees, about every-one. There is just a handful of people I trust one hundred percent and they are aware of the fact. I never tell Zdena any more than is necessary for her work on Padlock Editions, and above all no advance information about any projects. It's for one simple reason: to protect her from blackmail. Not only do I want her to know nothing, I also want them to know that she knows nothing. And by now they know. (Martinovský once said about me to Madla: "He doesn't even trust Zdena.")

Otka now lives for the Charter and Lederer's daughter Monika. I have already disappointed her on several occasions for failing to do what she thought I ought to have done for the Charter. Either it was too remote for me, such as the so-called Patočka tribunal, or I was working on something more important, which, however, I did not tell her about, such as the *Hour of Hope* almanac. Until one day we had a real row, but I will leave it at that for now.

I am alternately reading Ladislav Klíma and Škvorecký's *Book of Self-Praise*. L. Klíma has previously managed to elude me and this is the first time I have ever read anything of his. At the time when people were always talking about him, I had never heard of him. Now I am reading in his autobiography about all the things he wrote, started to write, or burned, as well as what he lost or of which only fragments remain, and I could not help laughing. It reminded me of the heroic failures of Jára Cimrman. I had a similar Cimrmanesque feeling when reading Comenius's life story: all the things he was interested in, discovered, intended to learn, the things he rushed into and why he forsook them, the things that went up in smoke. I read it out loud at dinner and the boys laughed as heartily as I. Bohemia can boast two or three syndromatic national figures: Švejk (but not Hašek), Kafka (but not Josef K.), and apart from them such rare birds as Kondelík. I believe that the figure of Jára Cimrman has yet to be properly understood: it is not just the chance creation of two fun-loving intellectuals by any means! The phenomenon of total incompetence, failure and ill-luck – a buried talent unearthed a century on!

The *Book of Self Praise* is, in the opinion of some, tasteless, shameless and something else as well. As far as I am concerned, since it's a book of self-praise, there is nothing wrong with it. Apart from what always irks me: Škvorecký's obsessive incriminations against the Communists and the secret police. If I lived in Canada I would not give a damn about them any more. It is a question of health – just as it is here. It could be that Škvorecký believes, unwittingly even, that he is under an obligation because he emigrated. Under an obligation he undoubtedly is, but a rational one, with the wisdom of detachment. It is another, more powerful Škvorecký who talks about literature on Voice of America and must abandon his Dannyesque anti-Communist tics in favor of reasoned argument. While I share his view that a writer always writes about the same thing and he will therefore go on writing Danny, I do not agree and do not like it when he acts as if Danny and he were one and same person still.

Even before my fifteenth birthday I started making sure that no grown-ups should see me donning my Indian head-dress and creeping under the jetty in shorts, carrying a bow. My chosen role had such enormous inertia that I never renounced it. But I could no longer go on dressing up the way I used to. I must say I have made good use of my Indian chiefdom throughout my life since. I was looking through some photos recently and turned up one I took when I was thirty-seven. At that time I received a state award for my work in radio. I adorned my naked body with the medal on my chest and nothing else. Looking at it now with a moralistic and skeptical eye, I would agree that the picture calls for a few strokes of the retouching brush: to paint in three feathers in my hair.

TUESDAY, 13TH FEBRUARY 1979

Today I resumed dealings with the dentist after a two-year break. I had bumped into him before Christmas. "I have a bottle at home for you," I said, "and it won't be a bribe, because I haven't needed you once this year." He replied: "Then it will be a normal fee as in ancient China. There they used to pay the doctor when he wasn't needed." Mind you there is always someone from our family visiting Dr. Kurka throughout the year.

He ordered me to climb onto the horizontal chair and pumped it in such a way that my feet ended up almost higher than my head. He gave everything a good poke and asked me when we would finally take out those three dead incisors at the bottom, which were already wobbly anyway. And at the top left it was perfect for a bridge: we'll do an X-ray. I reminded him that we had already X-rayed it. But, Mrs. Krumphanzlová read from the card, that was two years ago. I said that nothing was hurting me and I had come for the sake of good relations. He scraped away at something or other of mine and said to the assistant: "Get me a temporary dressing ready." Then he said: "Rinse." But as I had my feet higher than my head, this was impossible. First he had to lower me to a more suitable position. "There you are," he said, "that's what happens when patients have to rinse out for themselves." I expressed surprise that someone else was supposed to rinse out for me. The nurse said: "It's supposed to be the assistant's job." Doctor Kurka said: "What's supposed to happen is this," crossing round the back of my head and standing on my left. "The assistant is supposed to stand here, and here, as you can see, is a sort of hose. While I'm working in the patient's mouth, the assistant is supposed to suck it all out straight away. It has quite some suction." He pushed a button and the hose started to hiss. "And when the patient needs to spit, a funnel is pushed into the end of the hose and he spits into that. But we are unable to achieve that standard here as the personnel is lazy." – "And it's the same all over," the assistant said. We went to do the X-ray.

In 1969 I received a summons over "Ten Points" and was expecting to go to court. I was terrified at the thought of all my teeth starting to ache in cold concrete surroundings. The dentist we had before Dr. Kurka was not very well known to me. When he read my record card he asked: "Are you *that* Vaculík?" – "Yes." He gazed at me for a moment and then said: "Forgive me, I know it's not the time or place but such things interest me, how old were you when you joined the party?" – "Twenty." – "Open wide. So, from the age of twenty you worked for us to have the Russians here today. Now let's have a look at you and make sure we deliver you to your jailers in good shape."

At that time I was in good health and hence strong as well. So was Czech society – virtually of one mind, divided only in its estimates of how long this might last. Over those ten years we each have had to retreat further into ourselves and act with ever diminishing support from outside, and in the face of ever increasing sanctions. That takes some strength! Sometimes my ear-trouble gets so bad my head aches. My glasses have got stronger, my gall-bladder acts up and I even ought to go for a heart test. But not till next week.

In trepidation I went to some semi-subterranean metal workshop to take back a faulty bullet. The bullet was the size of a thimble, i.e. short and fat, made of dull grey metal, i.e. lead. The fault was clearly in the manufacture: there was a small hollow bubble on its perimeter. Badly cast. A dark, dangerous fellow in a leather apron examined the bullet in mute annoyance – and then without a word gave me another one. Superficially it was perfect, but it was clearly of a smaller caliber. – And it's the same all over, as Mrs. Krumphanzlová at the dentists' said.

As she was leaving for work this morning, Madla asked: "What will you be doing?" – "Whatever I want. It's my life," I said. – "That's precisely the problem, damn it!" – "Do you want me to give it to you?" – "At least half of it. It wouldn't be a bad idea," she said, putting on her fur hat. "What if I come to call for you at work this evening? From home!" I said. – "That would be nice. But it's not necessary." She pulled her gloves onto her small hands, opened the door to the hallway, turned again and said: "You won't swap me for a mess of lentils?" – "No." – "I'm oats." – "What's that supposed to mean?" – "There not as good, but they're necessary."

I loaded my briefcase with books I have been setting aside for the elusive B. and set off by tram on a long journey. The last time that I failed to find him home, I left a note for him to come. He did not. Fine, so now I am making this one further obligatory attempt, and if he is not home this time I shall happily cross dear B. off the list. I have to start somewhere. And that pleasant young author who was supposed to have some photos done for his book (600 Kčs), insert them in the transcriptions of his manuscript, and then simply take them to the binders', has also not bothered to do so yet; I shall not even bother to ask why, I shall just cross him off. And so on. My days will soon abound with free time.

I took a slim volume containing Šimsa's study on Havlíček and Mezník's on Jeroným Šrol to read on the tram. Mezník is unknown to me. I don't think I have ever met him. I was immediately taken with his writing and his style of argument. He is writing about a political man of the Hussite period who managed to protect his property, status and power throughout every phase of the revolution, while all around him many disappeared, some of them even on the execution ground. In reply to the question as to how this was possible, Mezník paints three different, but equally plausible views of the man: either he readily pursued a course of treachery for the sake of his property, family and career; or he cunningly and justifiably steered a tactical path, rescuing as much as he could while sadly and humbly, fully aware of his sinfulness, "staving off the worst." A third possibility is that he was an entirely honorable and truthful man insofar as he was never taken in by anything, but had the insight to grasp the reality and act in accordance with his convictions, which evolved in line with the movement and the times.

I did not find B. at home and I hereby give him notice that I am done with him. I went over to Zdena's. I was greeted by an explosion of black, furry passion – Bibisa. Zdena was not yet back from work. I put my bag down and went out with Bibisa. She jumped all over me and her yelps were almost human. Then she flew off down the stairs with a dainty clattering of claws, turning her head every now and then and looking up at me where I towered high above and I found her frenzied joy almost painful. Bibisa is a Pekingese, all black, and her big bulgy eyes lend her the appearance of a little imp.

We went round the block and Bibisa did nothing. I took her to the park where there was snow, and still nothing. I let her walk through the snow to clean her paws and then carried her home. I knew what I was to look for and where, and found it, pushing Bibisa's impish face into it and symbolically smacking her rump. She rolled her eyes at me and her sheer terror almost made me laugh. But I also noticed that one of her eyes was bloodshot. I caught sight of a bottle of boric acid on the table, along with eye ointment and some cotton-wool. I washed her eye and put some ointment on it. I had a look round the adjoining room to see what was new. I found a new bill for three hundred crowns from the legal advice center and the transcriptions of three articles that I left here last time: "Dear Jiří Gruša," "Dear Luboš Dobrovský" and "To my dear friends Vaculík, Havel and Pithart." Our controversy continues, with love. Zdena transcribes it all, but I have not managed to make her choose between Jiří and me. "I can't help it," she said, "when I was typing out Jiří's thing I couldn't help laughing. I can't take either of you seriously." A witty escape, all things considered. Then I had a peek at the number on the page in the typewriter: she has been belting through the Tatarka! Let's get it out of the way as fast as possible. They're bound to come and take a look at her desk once in a while, and being a Pekingese, Bibisa is all too symbolic a dog.

Shortly afterwards, Zdena arrived (explosions of affection from Bibisa), her right wrist in a bandage because of arthritis. She is having a course of injections for her left arm. She is supposed to be going for a stomach X-ray and for back exercises: all in all, hers is a clinical knot of counter-indications whose loose end might possibly be found after lengthy rest in peaceful care, free from agitation and typing. Padlock Editions is to blame for her back, and her stomach and nerves were the result of the police offensive against Padlock that culminated last August in an original form of terror: they interned Zdena in the V.D. clinic and forcibly examined her for venereal infection. She was kept there for three weeks, banned from using the phone, writing letters or receiving mail, and that was not all.

"I felt so bad today," she said, "I just sat at my desk and struggled not to faint or scream." – "You managed to smoke, though." – "Only eight cigarettes! The whole day!" – She really must have been in a bad way. "You shouldn't type so much. Why are you going so hard at the Tatarka?" – "Listen, my darling, they've pushed me into that factory to stop me making transcriptions. That's why I type, even if it'll be the death of me." She took out a cigarette and offered me one too. I took it. "Unfortunately," she said, "I can't manage to get as clean a result as I'd like. My Slovak has gone a bit rusty, after all. And you went and added," she broke into noiseless laughter until her belly started to shake and she had to stop and grip her stomach, "you added a hundred and fifty accents too many!" I said: "You should charge fifty hellers extra per page, naturally." She pointed at the table where the lawyer's bill lay for her unsuccessful suit over last summer's terrorist attack. I said: "I noticed. I can give you an advance for the Tatarka. You've almost finished it." I gave her four hundred-crown notes. "Thanks," she said. – "Don't mention it, it's your money." – "I really enjoy typing it. I find it, er, stimulates me," she said. "Where?" I asked.

Having finished her hors d'oeuvres (a Sparta cigarette), Zdena had a paltry snack (attended as usual by Bibisa's affection). Then we had a coffee and decided it would be best to take Bibisa to the vet's. "She had a temperature yesterday and the white of her eye was bloodshot, but now the whole eye is turning opaque!" At the casualty clinic at Říčany we waited about half an hour. Bibisa took the injection without flinching. The examination and treatment came to only thirty-three crowns and I paid the bill. Zdena will have to go there again tomorrow evening. We drove back to Prague. She wanted to take me all the way home, but I asked to be dropped at the terminus of the 29. In the tram I read Šimsa's study on Havlíček. If I happen to come across a pair of unencumbered female hands, I shall have the thin volume transcribed.

Madla did not get home from work until ten. "How was it?" I asked. – "I really worked like hell today!" – I did not catch what she said (my bad ear) and she repeated the sentence. I said: "I hoped I'd heard: 'I really gave them hell, today!'" She helped herself to a piece of crisp-bread, took the quark out of the fridge and sat down at the table. "I did eight admissions today." – "How come *you* did?" – "I was there on my own." – "They are leaving you there on your own again?" I said in surprise, because for the past year Madla has not been left alone in the room, in case she spoke to a client that might happen to enter at that moment. And here she was admitting patients! She gave me a filthy look and hissed: "Do you have to go and say that here?" – "You just said that you'd done eight admissions, for heaven's sake!" I unplugged the telephone from the wall (how stupid) and she told me about them.

Then she asked: "And what did you do?" – "This and that," I said with a shrug of the shoulders. – "Did you have lentils?" – "There wasn't the time," I said and refrained from adding that there had been neither inclination nor hunger pangs.

I wish myself a good night. I was planning today to write something else I owe myself. But it would not come. I shall take the Ladislav Klíma to bed and read some more of another horrifying tale, that of Sider and Orea.

FRIDAY, 16TH FEBRUARY 1979

It's one of those fine mornings. I am at home alone. The temperature fell slightly below zero again last night. The roofs opposite have a fine dusting of snow. There are a hundred things I can do. I traced the sketches in my diary that I want to reproduce. I touched up two old photos that I have to get copied. I have no idea who took them. I cadged them from my godmother about fifteen years ago, though it was a mystery to me what they represented; I just liked them for their mood and tone. They turned up again just recently and I have finally deciphered them.

One of them depicts a lane lined on each side with linden trees. Beyond the lindens is a row of barns, each of them with its own little wooden bridge over the ditch. The lane bends away behind the tree trunks, so one cannot tell whether it is already standing there or has not yet been built – our cottage. A little boy in a white peaked cap is squatting in the lane: probably my cousin Ludvik Kozáček. Since Ludvik is four years older than me – if it is him in the photo – our cottage was not yet standing. It is an odd feeling – almost as if by magic I can see our lane as I wrote about it in *The Axe,* when it no longer looked that way, when it was only a memory – at a time when I had no inkling that such a photograph even existed. And all of a sudden I have it.

Cousin Ludvik Kozáček is in the second photo too, and some geese; but they are nothing to do with him; his people did not keep geese. The action – Ludvik sitting on the close-cropped grass alongside grazing geese – is taking place just below Katrmajer's flour mill and sawmill to be seen on the left. On the right is a wooden barn, now gone. The lane winds between the barn and the mill toward Klobucká, which was common land where cows or goats were grazed. It was along that lane that I first chased Ajna; she would not be ruled by me and every now and then would butt me with her bumpy head; Dad had deliberately taught her to butt – she used to be docile before.

Ladislav Klíma's horror stories have no more than a poetic effect on me. I can read them last thing at night and then have a nice peaceful bureaucratic dream. Such as about them giving me back my job at the radio: I am entering our office, they show me to a desk in the corner; I recognize it by the stains, the dust and the scattered paper clips. The drawers contain empty folders and files, yellowing blank sheets of paper, not a syllable of anything to be seen anywhere. I am surrounded by unknown youngsters – regime dupes. They turn away: they are forbidden to speak to me. I am supposed to write something; I can write what I like! But not a word of it will be broadcast. And this is offered to me as a magnanimous solution; this way they have given me a life sentence of liberalized conditions. I wake up with relief. What does a dream like that mean? I am not a believer in the prophetic nature of dreams, but I am convinced they have a diagnostic value. So does it mean that one by one I am eliminating dead ends into the future? Which one will eventually be revealed to me as a solution or a necessity?

I made thirty prints of Dominik Tatarka with a cat on his shoulder. From Brno I received the negatives of several pictures of Professor Komarková; I selected one of them, but I will pay to have them printed elsewhere. I am afraid I am not getting so much enjoyment from making photos any more; when I finished the ones I had to do, and was able start on my own, I riffled through some negatives here and there, but nothing took my fancy. The only one I found and did was "Age 37." Painting feathers in would only make it look scruffy, I thought, so instead I cut out feather–shaped holes above the head and backed the print with red paper; the effect is terrific. The feathers glow above my head like the flames of the Holy Spirit, except this time they would be the Devil's.

Yesterday we went to a presentation of Oldřich Wenzl's poetry sequence "Scattered Daisies" at the Orfeus Theater. Orfeus is not in fact a theater but a travelling company *nolens volens*: every time they set up somewhere and the public discovers them, they are given notice to quit. The theater is run by Radim Vašinka, and the man's a magician. Years ago I found the contrast between his robust appearance and the inappropriate softness of his delivery rather disconcerting. What I saw in those days in his theater seemed to me over-demure and confirmed my view that poetry was something soft and unbecoming of a man. Recently I have seen two of his productions: Gilbert's *Pirates of Penzance* and this Wenzl. Vašinka is the same as he always was – and his theater is splendid and riveting! So I was probably a bigger fool before. Vašinka has hardened by sticking to his method and polishing his delivery, which enthralls me. His theater makes no use of scenery, only a makeshift platform under lights. The very first thing to be said is that there is something to look at – a bevy of variously charming girls. The other is that the author's text constitutes scarcely half of the spectacle; the rest is supplied by Vašinka: he transforms the words into a bizarre ballet and parlando-opera. Wenzl's verses, rhymes, aphorisms, homilies and calumnies would be scarcely audible or visible on paper. Vašinka accompanies them, plays them for all they're worth – or more even. Wenzl would have had found it great fun.

Wenzl is not having fun any more, though. Wenzl is resting in a grave at Chloumek near Mělník, having spent the previous quarter of his life lying in bed. Yesterday's performance was the last: they have been given notice again. When I asked Vašinka why, he replied that sooner or later his past catches up with him in the shape of his wrong answer to the question: "What is your opinion about the entry of the troops in 1968?" So why do the scoundrels ask the question, when they only expect one answer? It seems an awful shame to me that people will be deprived of this theater once more, even though it is something uniquely beautiful in this world.

And a good day!

We are having breakfast at ten thirty. Last night some more brilliant ideas came to me, all I needed was to get up and write them down. But it is out of the question for me to start something new. So I stared into the gloom, walked round the darkened room, looked out of the window and felt good. It is clear that my plan is the right one: gradually to hand over everything – all the things, and leave myself just my thoughts. Will I be blessed with a bit of peace at last, for this year at least? In the course of the coming few months, and by summer at the latest, I intend to publish sections of *Dear Classmates*: the early Indian Book, the Worker Book, the Student Book, the Journalist Book (possibly extending as far as the 1967–68 period) and in the autumn, the last one: the late Indian Book. (I really am so disciplined that I'm not even deleting this balderdash as I retype the final text in 1980!) If only I had someone who could search out documents, transcribe them, round out the bibliography, copy photos and duplicate them.

Ondřej has gone off somewhere with Marta. Jan is planning to develop some photos from his summer trip to Slovakia. Madla and I are going to drive to Chloumek near Mělník to pay Wenzl a visit.

It is evening again.

Wenzl dwells in a corner of the forest cemetery under the sign of the Blažej family; they were all lawyers.

"I am sorry
To have talked so much about myself in this book
But a few months ago
I suffered a mild stroke
And my mouth twisted up
I couldn't eat or drink
I'm better now
Nevertheless you were right, dear lady
When you gave me the brush-off
But on the other hand I wouldn't have demolished your house
on Wenceslas Square
And we would have brought up a child or two
And they wouldn't have gone naked or in rags

But there's no forcing love
And we were hale and hearty
You were right, dear lady
To have given me the brush-off about twenty-five years ago
I have trouble walking now
But otherwise I look fit
And no one would know I was ill at all
When I die
I want to lie in the tomb at Chloumek above Mělník
It's peaceful there and only birds fly over the graveyard sometimes
I don't care whether I'm buried or cremated
I wouldn't want lengthy visits to my grave
A silent remembrance will do…"

And so we only stopped for a moment, walked round the graveyard and left. The cemetery is very comfortable, though small. A corner site is advantageous and I felt a twinge of regret that I would not get plot No. 55 at Brumov. "The other nuisance," I said, "is that the one of us who dies first will have to wait so far away for the other." – "I don't know," said Madla, "do you think we ought to give up our option at Brumov?" – "My mind's made up. There's no sense lying in a grave in Prague." – "When I die," Madla declared, "a lot of people will come to mourn." She's right.

I didn't fancy driving back on the usual old Mělník – Prague route. Madla said: "I must agree that you have rather over-used it." She had in mind my trips with Zdena. "Just leave it at that or I'll deliberately drive us into a tree," I replied. We drove through Mšeno where the streets were lined with blackened battlements of scraped-up snow, but the road was mostly dry by now. Flocks of ravens rose up from the flat white fields that glittered dazzlingly in the sun. The hares had gnawed white the lowest branches of the trees and those that bent downwards. Here and there trusses of hay were stacked up in the fields. The lanes were empty. What could everybody be doing? Zdena is bound to be bashing out Tatarka on the typewriter. And I had told her: "Make sure you go out for a while on Sunday!" But she won't, just so she'll be able to tell me she didn't.

We passed through Byšice and arrived at Kostelec nad Labem. It is a low, flat, grey, backward town. The main square and the streets are all dug up. They are renovating the sewers. But there were some footballers rushing around the slushy playing field and a few youngsters looking on. I pulled up in front of a dismal-looking one-story pub. Via a dark gateway and a door in the massive wall we entered a friendly-looking tap-room and went through into a low, somber room with two small windows. Around the edge there were several square tables, at each of which sat elderly people, one or two at most, apart from the corner table by the window which was occupied by a fat old man and two soldiers. The table by the glowing stove was free. I hung our coats up on a hook that was fixed so high I could scarcely reach it. We sat down by the stove and looked around. On one wall was a large wooden pike holding a smaller fish in its teeth, and beneath it two trophy heads of pikes with sharp teeth and shriveled gills. In the middle of the wall above us hung a diploma, conferring honorary membership in the Fishing Association on Mr. Zurynek for invaluable services. At each side, in gaudy frames, hung a colored print: one of Hus in the Bethlehem Chapel in Prague, the other of Žižka on a war cart. Opposite was a mirror, and stuck into its frame were seaside postcards and a notice saying one hour's play on the billiard table cost 2.80 Kčs. Two packs of playing cards lay on a shelf alongside a wooden abacus, a grubby notepad of some kind, a pencil, some chalk and an ashtray. In the middle of the room – attracting the gaze of all the solitary clients around it – stood a billiard table. Two army conscripts were in the middle of a game; the two at the table in the corner with the fat old man were their companions.

We ordered coffee and a soft drink. We sat there watching for about half an hour. The coffee was good. It was quiet in the pub with only the click of the colored balls. The old wind-up clock hanging above the mirror gave the same time as the watch in my pocket, but it did not tally with the time outside. I had no desire to go out into that time at all.

MONDAY, 19TH FEBRUARY 1979

It was still half-light, only about half past nine in the morning, when Ella Horáková came and made a bright splash here with her red suit. Under it she wore a white semi-transparent blouse with stitched pleats.

I led her into the living room. I don't think Ella and I have ever sat together in the kitchen, and only now do I wonder why. Most likely because I have always wanted to lend her visits the character of an official audience taking place at her request for the purpose of discussing professional matters at a socially acceptable time. And the reason for that was because she scared me, I think. She is a woman who provokes man and woman alike – each of them in opposite ways, of course. She is, or rather was, a woman with a woman's reputation that was based not so much on what was said but on what was not said, and the motive for the men's silence was different from the women's. She turned up year after year in every "dissident" literary circle, where her guarantor against any doubts about her bona fides or affiliation was Václav Havel, for whom she acted as executive editor of Dispatch Books. On each occasion she was always amply surrounded by men, so I avoided her, not wanting to be attracted by what interested other men, as well as me. Over the years I should not think I have willingly exchanged more than a dozen sentences with her on such occasions. When I started publishing collections of feuilletons, Ella also brought me a few and most of the time I would have to return them for reworking, sometimes more than once. I found it humiliating and thought to myself it was the last thing I needed, but she was persistent. What I found impossible to explain was why they failed. Each text invariably contained an interesting idea, an original perception, several witty phrases, but she failed to build on them, and somehow the piece would just overflow lengthily in another direction. Quite simply it did not work as a feuilleton. When I argued with her about them, and she defended them, she would generally express her idea much better. "So write it that way, for heaven's sake!" When I subsequently "accepted" some of her feuilletons, it might well have seemed – and some women's circles actually accused me of it – that I had been motivated by her *je ne sais quoi*, but it is more likely that after those arguments with her and the explanations I received, I was the only one who understood her texts the way she intended them. When I read her excellent contribution to the symposium about the origins of Czechoslovakia, I realized that she ought not to be writing feuilletons at all, that she ought to be writing something else. So why did she write them? Anyone who has enough self-esteem and is fascinated by certain issues needs to frequent those places where such issues are debated – and such places simply do not exist at present. In normal circumstances, a person like Ella Horáková would make a fairly rapid name for herself and would not be obliged, at every stage of her career, to leave behind an unnatural pile of natural droppings. – I sneaked in this whole lengthy paragraph as an addendum a year later, because this is a manuscript with feedback.

"Mr. Vaculík, I have to 'give in' at last." (p. 68)

The moment she arrived I was surprised to see a sort of world-weary expression on her face. "Mr. Vaculík, I have to 'give in' at last. What you prophesied has happened, so I've come to ask you if you'd be my witness." – "Why doesn't Mr. Václav do it?" – "There's no chance of getting in touch with him soon enough and besides... I'm not sure he would." – "Why wouldn't he?" – "But you know very well what they say about me..." Of course I do. But how is it she does? She should not. "Oh all right," I said, "but if Mr. Václav gave you away, he'd rid himself of you at least." She smiled thinly behind her glasses: "Why don't you ask who I'm marrying, instead?" – "Well a few names did occur to me," I replied cravenly. "Well it's none of those," she declared with a resolute wave of her hand. "It's Pavel K." – "He's here?" I exclaimed in surprise. "Since Christmas. And they say they won't let him leave the country again unless he marries me. And he's got contracts and deadlines over there and he'll be in dire trouble unless he starts shooting very soon." – "Will you be leaving with him?" – "I'd rather not." – "How can they force you?" – "The same way they did him. They've already given me back my passport and it only took them four days to give me an exit permit. Look." She handed me her passport. "What's your explanation for it?" I asked. She replied: "We can't come up with one. We can't sleep because of it and spend our nights being vile to each other." – "It's bound to be some dreadful trickery or other," I said. She said: "And we won't ever be able to explain it to anyone. Our friends just seem to have disappeared into thin air. I could put up with anything from the other side, but when it comes from your own side too... I can't take any more. – Will you do it then?"

"I will," I said. – "Thank you so much. Pavel said you probably wouldn't, because you don't like him." – "How could he tell?" – "He just felt it." – "It's not exactly true," I said. – "Surprise, surprise, eh?" she said. With relish almost. I said: "It'll be the ruin of you, but he's the only fellow you ever loved." – "How could you tell?" Flattered, I said: "It came to me again when I read these poems of yours." – "What poems? Show me! These aren't mine." – "So whose are they, for goodness sake? Well, well! And when Kabeš tried to give them to me, I told him he didn't get them from me. But Gruša also said I had given them to him. And for the life of me I couldn't remember who gave me them and tried to deduce it from the content." – "And you were able to deduce that I'm in love with K. You're a marvel!" I thumbed through the anonymous little collection of verse: "There's one here that talks about a distant lover. Juráček. Do you play chess?" – "Yes." – "There you are. I recalled seeing a game set up on your table. Here, 'Come, the chess-men are set up.' And here's something else, 'But should you want me very much, I could have an earlier bath.'" She laughed softly, her hands clasped around her knees. I said: "I was beginning to feel sorry for you, and was terrified of the moment you'd come and I'd have to tell you that Kabeš and Gruša didn't want them published in Padlock." – "Jesus, I'm glad I didn't write them!"

Even though a year has gone by, nobody has been to see me about the verse collection. As I leaf through them once more, I am beginning to like them; they just need sorting out a bit. So I appeal to the lady who wrote the following to contact me:

> I'll draw on my drawers
> pop the sun on my head
> for my feet battered boots
> that have been through the hoop
> and I set out merrily
> On my back a little sack
> with bread and honey
> a little money
> A short bus-ride
> then I'll glide
> down the hillside
> through the meadow to the shore
> I'll wash my drawers
> and hang them high
> out to dry
> and doze naked nearby

WEDNESDAY, 21ST FEBRUARY 1979

"I'm already wondering how people will find out." – "They won't." – "Things like this are destined to come out into the open sooner or later." – "Why should they? It's up to us, after all." – "Precisely. In the end I'll write about it myself." – "Oh, for God's sake!"

The game is almost up.

The landscape is a white cracked bowl under an azure bell. The sun is melting the snow on the edges of the ditches and verges. Dry and grey, the paths make surprising twists to reach their destinations and often miss them completely. All around there are hundreds of thickets, piles of stones, lines of boulders between fields, and below the little churches the glistening eyes of frozen ponds. And everything is deserted, not a soul anywhere, just like after a good healthy battle when no firm government has yet been established and good news could be on the way.

"I might invite you to lunch, but I'll have to check my wallet first to see what I got out of that exchange."

Last night I had a totally inappropriate and unwarranted dream. I was sitting in a restaurant with some American who wanted to help me out by changing money with me instead of at the bank. He is giving me four hundred Deutschmarks and wants six hundred crowns. But I have only three one-hundred-crown notes and some change, so he keeps on offering to take less and less, and a circle of people starts to form around us. A few of them throw in some two- and five-crown pieces so that I should have enough for this advantageous deal. All of a sudden I realize that at any moment someone is bound to come and arrest me. I quickly rake the cash together into a pile and thrust it towards the American, taking from his hand what I estimate to be just two or three banknotes.

Now as I looked in my wallet all I found was one eighty-crown note. And at first I really did feel disappointed in view of what I had expected. But then I immediately felt a sense of relief that those troublesome foreign banknotes were out of the way too.

THURSDAY, 22ND FEBRUARY 1979

It is nine o'clock in the evening. Madla is at a concert. She put on a long dress and had me put her earrings in. No word was spoken. I have not been home for two days. I have a feeling of lost continuity, rupture, even.

Today I was the witness at Ella Horáková's wedding. It took place at the Old Town Hall. The presiding official was comically formal. Realizing, however, whom he was marrying, he left out the spiel about socialism and state welfare and it was briefer than usual. Ella had the ceremony recorded on a cassette. O.S. took the photographs. The other witness was – right now I can't recall his name – a friend of Pavel K.'s from film or television: a smooth fellow with a dark complexion, whom I found both likeable and suspect. We four were the entire wedding. But I have no wish to write anything else about it.

I said to Zdena yesterday: "I am going to be Horáková's witness." – "Why didn't she ask Havel?" – "The proper thing would be to ask who she's marrying, don't you think?" – "I've a fair idea who she's marrying: Ruda, isn't it?" – "No, you're wrong: it's K. They say they won't let him return to Germany unless he marries Miss Horáková," I explained, and at that moment it sounded even more daft to me than it did on the first occasion. – "So she's getting married on the orders of the StB? I wouldn't mind giving in to that sort of pressure. Other people get thrown into prison or kicked out of their jobs. Ella is forced to get happily married and then gets sent off to Germany. Isn't it fishy?" – "I don't see why she should refuse to marry the only fellow she ever wanted, just to spite the secret police." – "But that is exactly what she should do. Something else is going on, everybody's turning away from her and she solves the problem by running away. It's an admission on her part." – "What is she admitting to?" – "Oh, for goodness sake. Didn't you hear about that Charter document that the StB could never have got their hands on except through her? " – "I did, but I have no way of verifying it." – "Other people have verified it! People just as dependable as you. So it's not just talk." – "You ought to remember all the things that people could say about *you*." – "Except that in her case some people have actual evidence." – "It's only rumored that they have," I said, intending it as the last word. "But surely you accept," she said regardless, "that every Tom, Dick and Harry in the Charter slept with her?" – "Well *I* didn't get round to it – and tomorrow I'm giving her away!"

It was not even a quarrel, just a quicker-fire exchange than usual; Zdena does not quarrel. After my last word she chuckled: "But you still have time – a nod from you and she'll bestow you her wedding night!" And she went on to add that million-dollar line from the silver screen: "I bet she'd be really nice to you." – "I'll come and tell you all about it afterwards," was all I could retort.

In a little while she said anxiously: "It must be obvious to you that you're only there to repair her shattered reputation." – "Yes, that seems quite likely. But I don't know what I'm supposed to do about it." – "Don't go." – "I told her I'd go. She didn't have enough time to find anyone." – "And you were ready and willing." That was the last straw. "Listen, she came and said she was getting married at nine twenty. I happen to be free at nine twenty, so I'm going." – "Yes, they're right when they call you a good old Czech sucker." – "I'm nobody's good old sucker..." – "Careful! I did say 'Czech'" – "I'm not a Czech sucker either. I do what I want for my own particular reasons."

Everyone minds that I am not a sucker solely for their use. Or rather, no one would object if I were a sucker for their sole use. They wouldn't even notice.

Jan has come in from somewhere and is warming up some soup in the kitchen. I went and joined him. "Jan, my singing isn't up to scratch lately." – "How do you mean?" – "I've noticed it over the past fortnight. I find myself having to clear my throat all the time, I'm not happy with my intonation, and I just don't like the sound I produce. It sounds to me rather like a moron singing." He gave me a long look and then said: "Oh, I should think it's just a passing phase, that's all! Something to do with the humidity." – "No, my breathing's bad too. I can judge it by this phrase that I used to sing in one breath, and now I have to break it in the middle: "When I die, just bury me beneath a mound." I sang it to him and I really did have to take a breath in the middle. Jan gave it some thought, went on eating and then said: "That Tonda fellow, the one who typed out Hrabal just for himself and it didn't even occur to him to make a single copy, well he's gone and bought himself a cabin in the Jeseník Mountains that he saw advertised, and he's moving there for good." – "Why?" – "He says he's fed up with everything in Prague."

I went back into the room. I took a deeper breath, found a more comfortable pitch and managed to sing the whole phrase in one go. "When I die, just bury me beneath a mound..." I sang it a second and a third time, but it still sounded like a moron singing.

FRIDAY, 23ᴿᴰ FEBRUARY 1979

Yesterday such a weariness came over me that I just had to go to bed and was unable to read, even. This morning I did not wake up till noon, almost. It was ten o'clock. Mojmír Klánský came, and did not even want to sit down when he saw me, and I was glad because we would certainly have ended up talking about his *Albatross*. I washed, shaved and left for my ECG. There I suffered a fiasco: no ailment detected. Great. But why, in that case, am I unable to mow a whole strip of the garden with the scythe in one go. February snow, barns overflow.

On the way home I bought a chicken and put it in the oven, planning to do some writing while it roasted. But Luboš Dubrovský came and I sat him down because of his excellent defense of me against Jiří, which he had penned under the title of "Dear Jiří Gruša." He looks like a small boy who has been prematurely saddled with adult cares. The birds flew about above our heads. He brought me a commentary on our controversy by Jan Příbram that Luboš did not like but I did, and I told him I was losing interest in our puristic dispute. Luboš said that this was all he needed to hear, that I was probably right, and that he would throw away his reply to Příbram. Then we talked about the international situation, a good topic with Luboš, who, as a former foreign correspondent turned window-cleaner, always has his own peculiar insights and prognoses. But what he said on this occasion I am unable to recall because I am becoming increasingly nervous over my inability to escape from topics like this. I am reluctantly reinstating (it is February 1980) some deleted lines about Trinkewitz because by reading ahead I have discovered that later I have a conversation with Trinkewitz about it in the street. Trinkewitz also took issue with me on the grounds that heroic deeds are sometimes necessary, which I know, of course – consciously-chosen death as an extension of the right to life, etc. He included quotations from Camus, Sartre, Eysenck, Exupéry, all appropriate. I now told Luboš that Trinkewitz's piece was well-written but that he too had missed the point, and Luboš said that it was not even well-written because the same authoritative quotations could be used to support precisely the opposite case.

When we were driving from the Old Town Hall out of Prague, Ella said: "Do you know why you enjoy publicizing those attacks on yourself?" – "Do tell me." – "Out of vanity, Mr. Vaculík. Sheer vanity." I had accepted an invitation to the wedding lunch, having seen the mournful script for it that had been approved. The lunch was supposed to take place somewhere just outside Prague. Costume: Ella was wearing a floor-length dress made up of large vertical blotches of color, predominantly red and blue. Flowers: sowbread; a meagre bunch of about ten of them, but as they were with some asparagus fern, let's call them cyclamen, at least! "Oh!" sighed the bride, "as a young girl I dreamed of marrying in white with a wedding garland." – "Well you should have thought of that earlier," I said.

We drove alongside the Vltava and somewhere uphill to some village or other, where the car skidded on the icy roads like a sledge; I suppose K. is a good driver, at least. It's true I do not particularly like him, but it isn't his fault, it is just his physical type. Maybe if I got to know him I would make an exception in his case. We pulled up by the pub and he ran to tell the manager he was just married and would like to have lunch there. It was about half past eleven. We drove through the village and into a forest where there was a log cabin; I am unable to remember whether his or hers, I wasn't paying attention when they were showing me round and telling me about it. I stopped paying attention when they started to tell me how it had once been a sort of wine-restaurant for day-trippers on a cliff overlooking the Vltava. I was suddenly overcome by the paltriness of the times and what sort of life it is that has no place for a wine-restaurant on a cliff overlooking the Vltava.

At two o'clock, we returned to the pub where the other wedding guests had arrived meanwhile: Ella's parents and Máša, the screenwriter, with whom I myself once had some dealings – about a film! It was called *The Submarine*! It was a witty piece of nonsense which ceased to have any point the moment that the Spring of '68 suddenly arrived and it no longer made sense to employ allegorical language. So it died a death. It was a very strange gathering: Mr. Máša who is making films, K. who is not allowed to, except perhaps in Germany, where he will only be allowed to return if he takes with him Ella Horáková who is not allowed to do anything, and I. After all, Máša should not really be talking to me! And *did* he, come to think of it? Seated in the pub were several fellows in track-suits or overalls wearing knitted woollen hats, plus one tipsy gamekeeper and the local police-informer. Lunch: aperitif (Georgian cognac), excellent bouillon, liver Frankfurt-style, wine, coffee, and Neapolitan ice-cream topped with whipped-cream.

I sat opposite the bride's mother, so I could not help perusing her the whole time, overtly. And I have not been able to get her out of my mind for the past two days. Ella's parents both struck me as pleasant, reserved people. They give the impression of being sympathetically remote from their daughter. Have they renounced judgements about the difference between their world and hers? I cannot tell whether they realize the position she is in and I would not like to be the one to explain it to them. Because she should have been The Daughter. Still, they do have another. Mrs. Horáková – possibly in her sixties – is beautiful with a delicate and weary noblesse. Next to her

Ella appears coarse, semi-masculine and prematurely aged, which I say as an indictment of the horrors that women have to choose from here, and which they choose. They actually choose them! Here, I felt, was a woman from the days before the women's movement, although she is said to have been politically active in some way: a German anti-fascist. In her scanty conversation at table, with its little errors of grammar, I heard a vanishing emphasis on matters other than those that occupy our minds. It is not my wont to interest myself in the fate of other people for no good reason. I do not observe people at the theater or at concerts. I do not expect to find them inspiring in any way. I endure it as a punishment – and I know what for – when I am obliged to listen to someone's story. It's always a tale of normalized ill fortune, prescribed cheerlessness; they arouse no pity in me; they are nationalized destinies and fit only to be rejected!

Outside the sun shone fiercely. The snow and ice were thawing. I was suddenly gripped by the awful realization of an entire day lost: I had intended to go straight home from Town Hall and now it was three thirty. What am I doing here?! I got up and took my leave of everyone. They gazed at me in alarm and offered to drive me to Prague, finding it hard to believe that nothing had happened to me all of a sudden. They could well have still been shaking their heads over it as I stumbled out of sight down the icy path. And when I was out of sight I not only stumbled but fell, and away flew my three bags of books, sliding down the ice. After all I did say that I was intending to go about my business after leaving Town Hall! I slid down to the road by the Vltava and set off in the direction of Davle. The hillside across the river shone in the sun; this bank was in frosty shade and just to serve me right, my gloveless hands were freezing. I still did not like Pavel K., but in a vague way I was beginning to feel sorry for the two of them.

A bus came towards me, swerving to miss a crumpled scrap of paper. A private car behind it did the same. I fixed my eyes on the paper and walked over to it, fearing that someone might end up squashing it flat. It was a cat. Its eyes could still see and there was a drop of blood on its nose. I touched it with my foot and it rolled limply onto its stomach but some spasm caused it to twist to one side. I picked it up gingerly, afraid that it might think I was the culprit and bury all its claws in me. It was like a forgotten dream. As I carried the cat, alive and warm, its breath in the icy air came out as two separate little puffs of steam. I carried it as far as the first cottage in Davle and pushed it into the yard through the gap under the gate. The house was inhabited, but it looked as if the people were out at work. If somebody took the cat in straight away it might survive. It was ginger with grey stripes. I felt hatred.

I can't help laughing when Ladislav Klíma writes: "An utterly false vision of things is the condition for being a poet." He says that only an artistic pigmy respects reality. There you are, what did I tell you? What will you make of that, dear diary, you old chump?

Good Night!

SUNDAY, 25ᵀᴴ FEBRUARY 1979

I was watching television this evening while Madla did some ironing. I was then about to go and write up the last two days when disaster struck, as a result of which I'd sooner tear everything I've written so far into little pieces – were it not pointless, as there exists a copy to which I have no access. Yet again I'm like a swine turned ugly side up, split up into destructive pieces only: a thing that ought to be destroyed, not scrabbling up onto public platforms, of all things. It has always been like that, and it has always taken me some time before my self-esteem is restored somewhat. But it's not entirely clear which of my self-assessments is more authentic. Perhaps my writing activity is based on self-deception and an overestimation of my better side. Maybe what I fully deserve, instead, is to be clothed in rags cleaning sewers somewhere, with nine hundred crowns take-home pay so that I can't afford anything, and to come home from work battered and covered in filth as becomes me, so that I have neither the possibility nor the desire to go anywhere and so that no one would seek me out or invite me in. It would be one way of achieving the requisite innocence and modesty.

MONDAY, 26ᵀᴴ FEBRUARY 1979

I have to record a couple of things for the sake of continuity – without enthusiasm.

On Saturday afternoon, we took a walk across Letná Park to the Castle and then to St. George's Convent and its art gallery. It was lovely inside, by which I mean warm as well. It is worth looking in for just one or two pictures and a coffee. "I'll come here regularly when I retire," said Madla. I consider the adaptation of the old building for its current purpose as one of the fine achievements of the present time. There are several of these, so one should no longer say that nothing has been created that will outlive the regime's paltriness. I resolved to note all the good things, which is why I mention it here. I wanted us to call in on the Kosíks, but Madla did not want to. She never wants to go anywhere and her aversion to pleasant improvisation – her virtuous reserve – always wrecks my mood too.

In the evening Jan Šimsa came to see us. He brought his little boy, who, though quite small, spent the whole evening with his eyes glued on his distinguished daddy, and I was amazed how he managed to sit and listen to us intently from seven o'clock till midnight.

Šimsa is looking well. We talked about all sorts of things but I am losing the inclination to belabor the typewriter over it. He enjoyed the status of a prominent prisoner, partly because he suffers from an exclusive ailment – he is allergic to cold and his condition's unpredictable course slightly worried the prison authorities – and also because of the popularity of his case. He regards it as good fortune that the burden fell on him, once it became clear that someone from his family would go to prison. In his view, young people – up to the age of thirty-five, say – should not go to jail if it can be helped, lest they damage their personalities. He spoke again about "An Attempt at a Different Genre," the feuilleton I had written about him, and I was astonished to find that he had not properly grasped its point. In it I write that "like our brother Jan in Špilberk prison," it was up to us to seek the original guilt in ourselves, and not always in those who oppress us or banish us from the land. Let us not expect our efforts to "find their reward" or to be victorious, or even to go down in the annals as a sacrifice. Our enemies constitute the entire left side of our work: "Without the symmetrical composition of a proper martyrdom with an uplifting moral, we felons on the right would not emerge so radiant and our Savior Himself would be deprived of an opportunity. Amen."

He took this paragraph simply as a literary tribute to his Christian humility, which I speak of earlier, coupled with a vaguely didactic message. But in his view I thereby disrupt the earthy humor and common sense of what I am saying. So now I was unfortunately obliged – and even more unfortunately because it was in Madla's presence – to explain that that paragraph was a true expression of my present level of cognition. It contained the real meaning of the article, not simply that Israel could no longer endure those insults before the Lord... As we pursue the struggle, some of us at least must realize that not only can we not win, but that victory is not even desirable. The evil vanquished outside ourselves would straightaway take root within and coalesce with us. I was happier to see it objectively outside myself, so that I could distance myself from it, rather than have it in my very tissues where I could vanquish it only through suicide. What we were now undergoing was an auspicious phase of our struggle. A vague social awareness of the need for socialism ("a better world") had finally given way to two separate levels of cognition: a higher and a lower. I found it unacceptable that our decade of resistance to state oppression should remain in intellectual stagnation. And it was not, I maintained, only a matter of the last ten years, but of a much longer period, for example since the death of Šimsa's father Jaroslav in Dachau. Had the "evil people" that Jaroslav Šimsa wrote about from a concentration camp been defeated? Could they be defeated? If not, could one contemplate a world *with them*? What if it meant our having to acknowledge their existence as something fixed, given and permanent? "The question," I said, "is whether, by rejecting the blows, we are not also rejecting part of God." – I put it that way in an effort to draw closer to Šimsa and it was not intended as a personal statement about the existence or nature of God, or about my relationship to Him.

Šimsa did scarcely more than display mute amazement. Then he said that if that was the case he understood better my "Remarks on Courage," which would seem more as a continuation of the ideas enounced in the previous feuilleton "An Attempt at a Different Genre."

I said that my aversion to wooing the reader, coupled with my inability to express myself with perfect precision and my need to undermine every slightly daring idea the moment I voiced it, made the final paragraph appear no more than a literary device. But everything I write I believe – at the time.

TUESDAY, 27ᵀᴴ FEBRUARY 1979

This morning I found a note from Madla on my desk. It said:

"I'm sorry everything has turned out the way it was bound to. I don't intend to go on playing a false role, and anyway, I have the feeling you can't bear me in any shape or form. It's known as 'the devaluation of all spheres of matrimonial coexistence.' It is how the equation W/M x M/F usually turns out."

The black menace of Plzák's psycho-algebra. What was the "everything" that had turned out that way? The past days or the past thirty years, even? I stare at that unintelligible equation: the M would seem to be me in both cases. In the one I dominate, in the other I am dominated. Twaddle. But useful in again putting any thought of writing out of my head. She left another note on the kitchen table: "As proof that I care about Mr. Pecka, I have baked a strudel. Make what you like for supper." I had invited Karel Pecka over for this evening, but apparently she doesn't intend to play a false role in front of him.

I packed my briefcase and bag methodically, and went into town. First of all I delivered Tatarka's *Jottings* to the binders. Mutely, the woman in charge took a block of order forms and wrote my name without comment or smile. I have yet to strike up any sort of relationship with her, and therefore have no idea what she thinks. When I told her once that I did not require an order form, as a way of suggesting that she do this on the side and pocket the money herself, she coldly passed me the form to sign. Now she said: "Express?" – "Yes." – "Color?" – "Olive Green." If someone is waiting for the first pretext to harm us, here they have it. I went to Kampa and stuck Mlynárik's original of *Jottings* in his mailbox. I was in no mood to ring doorbells or talk to anyone. I walked slowly across Kampa to the house where the Pitharts live, in order to leave them, in similar fashion, the Ladislav Klíma I had borrowed. However, I discovered that they share their mailbox with the people with whom they also share the toilet, and I had no envelope in which to put the book and address it, so I went to the tram stop. If I met Petr on the way he could ask me, "Hallo, coming from our place?" and I could reply triumphantly: "No I'm not."

In the tram I turned over in my mind what else I had to do before I could shut up shop for good. I shall get someone to pick up Kohout's *The Hangwoman* from the binders and I shall have to sell it. I still need to take Rotrekl's poems *Town without Walls* to be bound; they've already been typed out and he's a Brnonian. I'll get the Mezník-Šimsa transcribed once more, seeing that the first batch seemed to go rather easily somehow. And Šimečka! I'm supposed to pick his thing up next week, then to get rid of it fast. And when I get back the three thousand crowns that are tied up in Eva Kantůrková's *Black Star* I'll add it all up, make an inventory and go bust, or hang up a sign saying "Closed due to illness." However I have started to read the Božena Komárková: the second part of her study, "The Gospel in a

Secularized World"; I have to complete it, there's no other way! I started to consider a trip to Brno. I was already relishing the thought of taking a train somewhere and being away from here. I got off the tram at the stop before ours, to give me time to think up something for supper.

I had invited Karel Pecka to supper even though I do not cook. Pecka left a few moments ago and I have thrown open the windows to get rid of the smoke before Madla returns from work.

For supper we had chicken paprikash that I bought at the take-away snack-bar round the corner. We both enjoyed it and Karel promised me that he would sing paeans of praises about my cooking to Kostroun, who is sure to be peeved at the thought that someone in Prague might be a better cook than he is. He will be bound to rush over straight away and ask how I made the chicken. Karel brought a liter of red wine from a cellar in Moravia and we were soon discussing the rights and wrongs of the war between the Chinese and Vietnamese. I said, "We and the rest of Europe will end up having to go to the aid of the Russians, and we'll be only too happy to, Karel!" Karel agreed with me. I asked him: "Do you know what Gruša says?" Karel replied: "How could I, mate?" – "Well, Gruša says that China is a country with a riparian culture, based on land cultivation, in other words, its culture is intensive and entirely introverted. Your Chinese isn't by nature an aggressor, unlike certain others." Pecka nodded his head and then said: "Well, well, well, hmm. The trouble is that once your Chinese has squeezed in as many paddy fields as he can, he needs another river." – I must pass that on to Jiří.

"If I had a wife and children," said Pecka, "I'd send them abroad now." I said: "You'd have to send them right out of Europe." And I told him about Olda Unger, who wants to take his family to Canada. However, his application to leave the country has been lying around somewhere for the past five months. I told him how Olda was selling things and they were already sleeping on the floor. "Where would you go?" Karel asked. "Me?" I said. "If it came to the crunch, I'd head north too." And because the wine had warmed me up, I went for somewhere really northern: Labrador. "What does Unger want to do there?" asked Karel. "He doesn't even know himself," I said, "and he's no good at anything apart from recording birdsong. I used to work with him in the radio, you know." Karel said: "Well there's no reason why he shouldn't start recording birds again, they're bound to have different ones over there." And maybe because my cigar was burning well, I warmed to my subject and said: "How right you are! It's not fowl song but foul lies they broadcast here nowadays!"

I then went on to sing Karel Pecka the song "Cigarettes are truer than a maiden's lips and more intoxicating," and he left for the U Pešků pub.

THURSDAY, 1ˢᵀ MARCH 1979

March is here. This afternoon I was walking along a narrow road that winds above Troja, and there were too many rooks clustered in the fields. Helena held my briefcase while I looked for a stone. The moment I went to throw it, those birds all rose into the air and flew a bit further away. My next throw went only a third of the new distance. I said it was perverted and thought to myself that I would have to come here earlier tomorrow. – Unfortunately, as I type this out in fair copy I have no idea what that last sentence meant. I went nowhere tomorrow.

I came home, put down my briefcase and popped out again to do some shopping. As I approached the grocery store in our street, a black car with the government registration AA pulled up outside. A woman got out and the driver parked the car round the corner. I said to myself: Let's have a look at what you intend to buy! She wore a fleecy beige coat; slim; a light-brown fur hat; a surprisingly expressive face with fine features. I watched her having difficulty negotiating the turnstile: she was trying to take her shopping-trolley with her, which is impossible: you have to push it through a different entrance. What are you doing here anyway? Why don't you go to the official shop? First she dithered at the bread counter. Unbelievable! You intend to eat bread from sprayed fields like the rest of us? Then she put a copy of the humorous weekly *Porcupine* into the trolley. But of course – Idiots of the World Unite! Then she took some butter from cows who have never even had a glimpse of the regime's own green meadows in their whole milking lives. As I trailed her I also took some bread, a copy of the evening paper (another idiot hooked), and an imitation Camembert. Then I stopped looking at the woman, put in two bottles of beer, two Amara sodas, and looked to see if they had some Tokay wine should I need it. When I went to pay, the AA woman was at the next till. She still had the bread, the *Porcupine*, and the butter in her trolley. As she rummaged in her purse with normal hands, her head bowed, I felt a need to exonerate her. I decided that she was the wife of the chauffeur.

Back home I took out a map of Indochina, sat down in an armchair and began to read the war report in the evening paper under the incensed headline: "CHINA MUST LEAVE!" The main battles are being fought for control of Langson, the capital of Longson province, from where a successful Vietnamese counter-attack has been announced. I could not get over this: We in Bohemia are used to the capital of Luxemburg being Luxembourg!

Madla came home from work and an hour later we went to dinner at the Administrator's. I cannot even recall the last time we were invited to someone's for dinner. This was an invitation we could not turn down; our boys love the Administrator and it was they who arranged today's visit. I was not on my best behaviour. I was simply in no mood for conversation. However, my reticence could have been interpreted otherwise. We talked about Brno, the theatre – or rather about theatrical texts, because what is actually being done in the theatre scene is terrible. Zdena Tominová is an up-and-coming-talent in the Administrator's view; he has read her book in Padlock Editions. Thus I saw how our work was seeping through natural cultural pores well out of our sight and it gave me great satisfaction, particularly in the presence of Madla who is very sceptical about all women's writing. The Administrator was unable to recall Tominová's name and only knew that she was now one of the Charter 77 spokesmen.

We also talked about children, but tactfully, as a calamity occurred here last summer: the Administrator collected some mushrooms that poisoned him; he survived, but one of his children died as a result and now they have only one. His wife has the appearance of an Italian *Madonna Nuova*; she obviously likes children, but after what happened, she gives the impression of being traumatised for life. She cooked us Brussels sprouts *au gratin*, and served it with a salad of cucumber and spring lettuce. It was very tasty, and the Administrator brought some beer from the pub in an enormous jug. Madla praised the meal: "I see you go in for healthy cooking." I remembered those fateful mushrooms and said: "I don't think I'd quite put it that way." – How could I?

FRIDAY, 2ND MARCH 1979

My cousin Ludvik was apprenticed as a cabinet-maker to his father Ludvik, who was my godfather. As his test-piece to become a journeyman – or maybe

82

on some other occasion, I do not exactly remember – he was required to make a puzzle. It consists of six pieces of wood ten centimetres long and with an eighteen-millimetre square cross-section. They slot together in pairs at right angles and in three directions to form a sort of star. Whoever thought up how to get the six elements to pass through each other at the same point must have had some powers of imagination! Each of the pieces has a different shaped hole cut out of its centre: no two are alike. Cutting it out precisely according to the plan is certainly a test of joinery skill on its own: the rods fit together tightly with no spaces left in the middle. When Ludvik first gave the puzzle to me as his younger cousin, it took me several days to assemble it. The finishing stroke is bewitchingly simple: a smooth stick, without any cuts at all, is merely inserted into the hole formed by the rest. When it is withdrawn, the whole shape falls apart in your hands.

I have no idea what set me thinking about the puzzle, in the frontier zone between sleeping and waking. In my dream I had been assembling a puzzle out of metre-long rods. I took one of them and dragged it out onto the meadow under the trees. Until I brought the next one and all the rest, it would look meaningless – just a piece of spoilt wood. Awake, I suddenly realised I was thinking up a story out of parts that were meaningless and unintelligible of themselves and could be assembled in many wrong ways and only one right one; only when the final episode had been tightly inserted would it make total sense.

The manageress was not there. A superb, tall, dark-haired woman emerged from the rear of the workshop, a bright apron round her waist. She took the chit from me, went round the back again and returned carrying a proper parcel… and behind her another woman peeked through the door and then yet another had to come right out to the desk and take something from it. Fascinating – the majority of the bindery workers are young or middle-aged women. What happens to the old ones? Do they boil them down to make glue? These women had been telling each other about me and could not resist coming to have a look at me, the client who brings in jobs the likes of: "You wear no panties I see" (Dominik Tatarka: *Jottings*, 1979, p. 71).

I paid the amount, which, when rounded up by fifteen crowns, came to six hundred, and plunged back joyfully into the bustle of the street. Now to deposit the parcel somewhere. Take one copy to Jan Mlynárik; let him send it to the author for him to proof-read it and send us any errata.

"They say you almost married Mata Hari," said Mrs P. – "Would that bother you much?" I replied. – "What truth is there in the story that he threw the cake at her during the reception and that she threw the passports out the window?" – "During the time I was there they were getting on fine. That must have happened later." – "So you think there's no truth in what they say about her?" – "What do they say?" I asked; let me find out precisely what at last. – "That she's working for you-know-who." – "Yes, so they say. Do you think I shouldn't have gone to the wedding for that reason?" – "Of course I don't! What did your wife say about it?" – "'There's bound to be some political calculation in it somewhere, but you could hardly refuse.'" – "But apparently she really is working for Them. When Mlynář was emigrating, he specifically said so. And Irena said she was a top-notch concubine; she even knew which of the notables had a finger in the pie, and how much money was involved. And she didn't even say it nastily – it was more out of respect, really, meaning that she was too good for this system." – "Well I'll be damned! I'll try to see her again." – "But she's supposed to be leaving any time now." – "But you just said she threw away the passports!" – "She went and found them afterwards, of course!" – "One thing's for sure," I said, "she's going to have a hell of a life. Certain deeds incorporate their own dire punishment." – "That's one of your sayings, Ludvík. And you wrote that it was your wife who said it." – "That's right, she said it about me." – "Would you like a drop of sherry?" she asked, putting her feet down off the couch. Her son David was tearing round and round the room. "Is Petr writing anything?" I asked. "You can take a look," she said, pointing at the desk.

Petr's desk is an exhibition-ground of respectability, whose comicality is evident to its owner. On the shelf above the desk-top there is a reproduction of a film subtitle in Slovak: "He left behind heaps of manuscripts." And the entire surface of the desk is covered with writings in pedantically neat heaps like so many piles of army blankets. Even the latest, still unfinished, manuscript, with its many corrections, sits there so meticulously neat that I dared do no more than lift the top sheet. The main title and the sub-heads were very interesting and topical, and that is as much as I may say, as I don't know which audience the text is intended for.

I pulled a handful of papers out of my briefcase. "Give this to Petr. It wouldn't fit in your mailbox." – "You mean you weren't even intending to call in?" – "That's right." – "Why ever not?!" – "I want to sulk!" – She laughed heartily at this. "It's already rumoured you're avoiding people, anyway. Except for Mata Hari, of course. David!" She scolded her son who had come in again and was once more circling round the room. "Quite right, David!" I said. – "When are we going to read something of yours at long last," she wanted to know. "Not long now! In a year!" – "You're not even a writer any more." – "I never even wanted to think of myself as one. It was not until the StB forced me to say it, in order to know what to put me down as. *You're* writing hard, though, aren't you?" She raised her eyes to the ceiling in an ironic grimace: "It's awful!"

SUNDAY, 4ᵀᴴ MARCH 1979

Suddenly the snow is gone and spring will now take wing! I swooped on the hedge and started to prune it with a hacksaw and pruning shears while the ground was still frozen, so that I would not go stamping all over the awakening vegetation later. Mrs. Kopecká's eranthis and hellebore are already in flower, along with Mrs. Rohlenová's snowdrops; ours were uprooted by something, Mrs. Hemerková's dog, most likely. Then I left the hedge and set off toward the masts of the trees. My interventions this year will be carefully premeditated and few in number, but bold. I cut the whole central "stalk," as thick as your leg, out of the Princess Louise apple-tree. I saw straight away that it was good: the tree opened out like a chalice.

I had a feeling that it must be noon already. I went upstairs to our quarters and found Madla in a splendid atmosphere. The tiled stove was burning warmly in the tidy room. Madla was typing out Solzhenitsyn's Harvard lecture while listening to dance music on the radio: perversion number one. It was one of Prague's foreign broadcasts and they happened to be announcing in German that some former Sudeten German had requested some music from the Böhmerwald and they would play it for him: perversion number two. Admittedly the band played only the melody but I joined in with fervour: *Es war in Böhmerwald, wo meine Wiege stand…* I then went and took over from Madla at the typewriter so she could prepare a quick lunch, as the Kosíks were due to arrive any moment.

When they arrived, Karel was unusually pale, while Marie was her usual rosy-cheeked self. The hares had been gnawing the bark of ten of their young trees and Karel asked what he could do about it. On this occasion good advice was cheap: dig them up and throw them away. – But saplings could not be had for love or money! I told him we would help him get something; two I promised for certain, though I haven't the foggiest idea where I'll get them. But he needed to hear something quite positive and encouraging at that moment. He was intending to take two trees out anyway because he did not like them. And another one had to go whatever happened, as the row was too crowded. "So that's five of them already, and you might still manage to save one of those," I said. "So that means you only have four of them to write off in your mind." He laughed and said: "Well, now that you've helped me sort it out like that, I feel quite relieved." I said: "There's still one thing we could try. We'll cut them down low and they might start sending out shoots again from the bottom. It happened with one of mine that I felled – before I got round to rooting it out, new shoots started growing all around the trunk. Would you like to see it?" – "I certainly would." We went outside to take a look. Karel perused the marvel. Marie laughed and said to me: "He's getting his colour back a bit now, but he was in a bad way." – "I'm glad," I said, "but on the other hand, Karel, you can't go reconciling yourself with it too quickly. It was ten trees, after all!"

We got in the car and went for a short drive to have a look at the surrounding countryside. During today alone, the snow has completely slipped from all the south-facing slopes. It's time I did my spring feuilleton. What's it to be about this time? I didn't write anything about the winter in the end.

MONDAY, 5ᵀᴴ MARCH 1979

Mr. Václav is back at his Prague flat. The cops have planted themselves in front of his door and are not letting anyone visit him and he is not even allowed out. He has written a letter about it to the Minister of the Interior, which I've read. "The officers guarding my flat even told me they didn't care if I starved to death at home, and that they would gladly obtain a coffin for me."

It is as monstrous a horror as war. The mere fact that it is on a smaller scale is not the main indicator. After all, a regime's character is determined not by the way it treats ten million obedient citizens, but how it behaves towards one disobedient one. That is what indicates its attitude to ideas, the human personality and the rule of law. Having revealed its bad character, it is clearly capable at any moment of widening its hostility to any number of people, so it is only some mysterious administrative reticence that stands between us and a mass grave. It seems to me that after Pavel Kohout they have now singled out Mr. Václav for meticulously conceived mental terror. It could as easily have been me. And it still could be at any moment; it depends on me.

This morning, Otka came. I was in the middle of writing. She brought me something and took something else away with her. "I don't want you saying anything about me anywhere," she said, "about what I do, why I come here, and what I'm involved in!" – Why is she telling me this? I wondered. The answer was not long in coming. "It's just as well I never met that Ella Horáková. I always made a point of avoiding her, from the moment I heard of her existence." – "You used to avoid her even before there was any reason to?" I asked. – "I am ready to trust anyone so long as they don't let me down," she said. – "What's on your mind in this particular instance?" – "Nothing. Nothing at all." – "How do you want your coffee, ordinary or instant with milk?" She went for milk. We exchanged a few table messages. It is a mystery to me how they select candidates for rough treatment. Do they persecute Otka because they have correctly gauged her importance or because they have gauged it badly? She now lives permanently on the run between her flat and other places, always on other people's business. It is an unhealthy life. She has become very hard over the past two years; she is invariably miserable and sulky these days.

When she was putting her shoes on in the hallway, ready to go, she said: "Pavel Kohout sent me a postcard: 'Get me some seed potatoes!' That means he intends to return soon – now!" I instantly put my finger to my lips. "See how thoughtless you are?" I whispered. Pavel had based the plan for his return on a sudden, surprise crossing of the frontier, well before his twelve-month permit expired. Seed potatoes, eh? Please God, let him come and plant them! Before turning to go, Otka said: "I'm telling you for the second time – I don't even want you to tell anyone what sort of cap I'm wearing!" Well, on that score, dear diary, I won't oblige our friend: the cap she was wearing was of green corduroy, and had a peak.

I loaded my briefcase and canvas bag and set off for town. It is weeks since anybody has visibly tailed me on foot or in a car. Are they trying to lull me into negligence? There are, however, plenty of suspicious-looking fellows on every corner. It could be that there is such a network of them that they visually

*"I don't even want you to tell anyone what sort of cap
I'm wearing!"* (p. 87)

pass us on from one corner to the next. By the time I reached Smíchov, my bag was already empty, bar one Čivrný that I was taking to Eva Kantůrková. She was not home, though, and the fact that there was no note on the door saying "don't ring the bell, our dog doesn't open the door" meant they were out together. I set off up Xaverius Street in the direction of the cemetery, where I might bump into them. On the way I bought myself some salami and two rolls and ate them with enjoyment as I walked. In Little Xaverius Street there are rows of anglo-bizarre cottages that are stuck together almost by the skin of their occupants. They were steamy with body heat; it was running out from underneath them. – That's as far as I feel like going. Tomorrow maybe.

Zdena recounted me her latest dream: "I drove to Rochov and went into the house. I was carrying Bibisa in my arms. I don't know how it happened, but the house looked the way it did when I first started working on it. The ceilings were collapsed, the floors torn up, piles of bricks and earth. One feeling I can remember precisely, that it could not be true, that I must be dreaming. I had already got the house into a fairly decent state, hadn't I? Do you get it? I dreamt I was dreaming. I put Bibisa down and walked slowly through the entire house, absolutely stunned – a total disaster zone. Bibisa kept a couple of paces ahead of me. All at once she stopped, looked back at me, lifted her little black face, bared her white teeth and spoke. She was able to speak. Quite distinctly she said to me, Don't cry! And then again, Don't cry!"

TUESDAY, 6TH MARCH 1979

On two successive days, yesterday and today, I've had dreams about Josef. Yesterday he was the director of an agricultural college, like he used to be. In his Sunday best, he hovered around the horses in the yard, giving orders about how they were to be shod. And I was urging him to give it a rest, for God's sake, because our coach was moving off round the bend between the trees, becoming smaller and disappearing, and I was filled with a dire panic because something was leaving me behind forever and it was Josef's fault. – Today, in a field camp, pitched on the edge of a forest, I welcomed Josef, who had laboured up the hill in muddy wellington boots and a hideous old black raincoat. He handed me a piece of typewritten paper which said he was being given the sack, and it surprised me that it should upset him so much, seeing that he had always been indifferent to his dismissals in the past. I told

... our coach was moving off round the bend between the trees,
becoming smaller and disappearing ... (p. 89)

him not to worry because it didn't matter anymore, because I – and I looked around the wood in which the flickering shapes of men could be seen as they walked among the bonfires – I can easily sort it out for him.

My daytime powers, on the other hand, are virtually non-existent: I have not the faintest idea how to induce B. either to be at home when I visit him or to come and visit me when I stick notes through his door to that effect. I have already convinced myself that task "D" is no business of mine, but today I received a justly urgent query from the publisher about what was happening with it. And who will deal with it? If only I could corner him, I would tear it all from his grasp and give it to anyone to finish. And even if somebody else were to finish it now, this very minute, the typists would still sit on it for several weeks more, so the delivery date of end-March is already out of the question.

Jan Mlynárik came to tell me that he would not have the time to send Tatarka the book for correction so he had read and corrected it himself. And he handed me a list of about thirty minor errors. So I have to open thirty books thirty times and write in the corrections in ink. Who else should I ask to do it? He also informed me that he would soon deliver me a selection of Tatarka's political articles from the years 1968–69. "Fine," I said "but deliver me a Slovak typist with it. Then we can talk business." With bear-like familiarity he gripped me by the lapels and said, "Don't be crazy, Ludvík! You know very well there are only the two of us here: You and me!" On his way out he gave me a nonchalant wave of the hand: "Oh, you'll manage somehow." We conducted our business outside in the hallway, of course. I fell into an armchair and started to check the mistakes. Seeing that they have a president, several ministers, a host of officers and prison-warders in Prague, couldn't they delegate one dissident typist, the bastards? For their Slovak God's sake!

Last Sunday, Karel Kosík declared that the time had come for us to start telling the younger generation the plain truth that the present situation was going to last another fifty years at least. So what was required of them was fifty years of consistent, purposeful, small-scale endeavour. But I should like to know something about goals too! Karel said he would be quite happy to arrange some discussions for a small circle of old friends, for which he, or someone else, would provide an introduction. I told him to rule me out as far as introductions were concerned. I don't know anything.

And then Mrs. Helena D. has to turn up here. Our boys are already grinning about what I have found. "That universally likeable lady of indefinable age was looking for you," Jan said. "His kitten," Madla said, and had in mind a fluffy little creature, not the playmate of an elderly gentleman, otherwise she could not have resisted prophesying that I would end up like all those other pathetic old men – in the admissions office of that social infirmary of hers. Never!

Today, when Mrs. D. was showing me photos of furniture which she had designed and will now go into production, I said: "So, as well as being familiar with the material available on the market, manufacturing standards and technical feasibility, you also have to have some idea of how parts are crossed and joined, whether to use a tenon or a screw, and so on?" She doodled all over a piece of paper with a pencil and without taking her eyes off her drawing she said: "That's right, of course, although I get things wrong as well and people point them out, but it shouldn't happen, it really shouldn't!" And because I am never inclined to believe in women's engineering talents (as in the case of my sister-in-law Lina), I got up and fetched Ludvik's wooden puzzle. "That's what it looks like," I said, showing it to her from all sides but not letting it out of my hand. "Have you had a good look?" Under the table I took the puzzle apart and then held out my palm with the six blocks before putting them together again. "Make a drawing of it, if you like," I said. – "No, no, I don't really need to. It's clear enough," she said and I made the following decision: "Try to solve it yourself and make a drawing of it. Bring it to me next time!" Her fingers wandered about the table top for a moment, and then she took the paper and started to fold it into smaller and smaller squares. "I see... homework! Now I get what you're up to! If I understand correctly, I'm not to show my face until..." and she laughed.

It is inconceivable, in my view, that she should solve it.

WEDNESDAY, 7TH MARCH 1979

I took my brown plastic briefcase with its reflectors to ward off dangerous motor-cars, loaded it with Tatarka's *Jottings,* and then spent three-quarters of an hour fuming in stinking and chaotic traffic travelling the mile over to Malá Strana. I rang the Mlynáriks' doorbell. "Listen, Jan," I said, "I'm not doing it all by myself!" But I didn't actually say this until his wife Edita had managed to roll him off the cushion where he was sleeping after a night-shift in the boiler-room where he works.

And he had already suspected as much and had a table of corrections written out in quadruplicate. We all sat down: myself, Jan, his wife Edita, and some young woman who was visiting them, and we corrected all thirty copies in two hours. Edita brought each of us a mug of tea or coffee while we worked. We had already started when the doorbell rang. Edita looked out into the yard. "There's some elegant young man down there," she said. While Jan pounded slowly down the wooden staircase I hastily gathered the books together into my briefcase, ready to disappear loftwards with them. But the matter was dealt with downstairs in the doorway. Jan came back with a summons to a meeting tomorrow. Purpose: requirement of clarification under paragraph such and such.

And now I was able to see from the outside what I am very familiar with from inside: Jan brandished the summons and chucked it on the window-sill. He wobbled off in his dressing-gown of heavy towelling into the next room, dipped his old pen once more in the ink-stand and went on correcting mistakes. A minute later he was back again, standing at the window studying the summons, trying to squeeze more out of it through closer perusal. He turned to me. "And you have no idea what 'clarification' might be required on this occasion?" He mixed Slovak words in with the Czech. "The only clarification I know, my son, is under para. 19 of the national security law. This paragraph is new to me," I said. "Fuck them. What can they want after seven years!" – "You haven't been to see them for seven years?" I gasped. – "Of course not. Do you go more often?" – "Every month," I said. Jan stuck the slip of paper in the pocket of his dressing-gown and went out.

Wherever my eye alighted on the text, I found it comical. Mrs. M. asked me what I found funny. "Look at any two or three words in a row and straight away they're suggestive." She moved her finger down the list of errors, wrote in a correction and said: "Worst of all, while we're sitting here doing this, his honour the author is sure to be boozing somewhere in Bratislava!" The young woman chuckled. "You're too young to be reading it at all" I told her and Mrs. M. said: "No woman should read that all by herself!" "And a man can?" I asked in surprise. – "Well, a man can cope with it because he doesn't have such inhibitions."

The floor started to shake. Jan pulled the door-curtain aside and stood arms akimbo, plunged in dark contemplation. "Hey, do you think it might actually be on account of those Germans?" – "You're involved with the Germans?" I asked. – "Not at all. I mean that article in *Svědectví* that criticises the expulsion of the Germans." I recalled it: "You're right, I have heard they've pulled in some people over that," Mrs. M. said: "And what business have you with the Germans?!" – "Me? Not a damn thing at present," he replied conciliatorily, "but the question is whether it was right to expel them." Mrs. M. waved her pencil: "Oh my God! What do you want to go writing about them for? They're not here any more!" – "Ach! They can kiss my arse!" Jan turned and disappeared. Edita whispered: "I slipped a sleeping pill in his coffee and he doesn't know."

We finished the job. Then I calculated the price in front of Jan. When we have given the author a complementary copy and one each to the typist, myself and Jan, the price of a single copy will come to eighty crowns. Just as I was on my way out, Mrs. M. barred my way and steered me towards the dining room. She placed before me two plates of halušky: one with brynza cheese, the other with cabbage. They were hot out of the pan and with fried bacon on top. I left the books there.

I arrived home and anxiously opened the mailbox: inside was the cyclostyled monthly programme of the Moravian Slovak Club in Prague. I changed, vacuumed the carpet, read a few pages of Kerouac's *On the Road*, got dressed again and left to go to the cinema at five o'clock with Zdena.

They were showing an English film called *Lion from the End of the World* or something. The trouble is it really was only about lions. I started to get drowsy and Zdena said she had already seen three similar films by the same people, so we got up and went off to have dinner at the bistro in the Black Rose arcade. I was expecting it to be packed, but on the contrary it was empty: people these days celebrate International Women's Day at work or in social clubs. Brass band music was belting out from just such a celebration at the Teachers' Club on Příkopy. We ordered a schnitzel and I remembered to ask: "How did your X-ray go?" Zdena answered: "My gall-bladder filled and then emptied, so there's nothing wrong with it. It still hurts." – "At this moment?" – "Now that you ask, it doesn't seem to. There are moments, like now, when I'm completely all right." – "It's nerves," I said and it crossed my mind whether she was making it all up. When we had finished our –

rather dry – schnitzels, I gave her two of the tablets I always carry around with me.

"I'm beginning to smell a rat again," she said. "Ever since I've been working there, they've been promising to send me on a seven-day in-service training course, one now, another one in the summer. And the moment I was supposed to go, the boss told me there was too much work. So when I asked him for the work on Monday, he said he hadn't had time to get it ready for me. And now it's Wednesday." – "Maybe he got orders to keep you in a state of ignorance," I said. – "That's precisely what I think. Another thing, it used to be my job to order theatre tickets. Now they've taken it off me and they told the colleague who's doing it now to let them have the list of people who order tickets. I think it's only because of me." – "That's possible," I said. "They probably objected to the fact I went to the theatre with you that time." She rocked back and forth in mirth and said: "Yes, because you were able to say good evening to various people from our department, and that caused some excitement."

On that occasion I had done my best to play down the event by going in a brown suit, whereas Zdena had dolled herself up in an evening gown so that everybody stared at her. It had really annoyed me. She said calmly: "People dress according to how important the evening is for them. This is how important it is for me." And she insisted on standing there, ashen – nay green – with nausea, puffing away during the interval: but every inch a lady.

But at this moment she was nicely pink, probably from the half-a-glass or so of schnapps with which she had washed down her gall-bladder pills. I drank the rest. It's only our second evening out this year. Apart from ourselves there were two other couples, one of them male. "Did you watch the Turgenyev on television yesterday?" I asked. – "I put it on too late. But I did finish reading the Škvorecký and I really think he's great. Why doesn't anybody here write a novel like that?" – "Other people are writing other good things here, aren't they?" I remarked. – "Yes, but – if you wrote anything as good as that I'd... I'd break it off with you!" That magnanimity is a standing offer of hers. I laughed; Zdena was radiating old world charm. It had taken just a glass of schnapps and two Febichols to dislodge that bubble of heavy, deep-seated sadness. "Damn it, you've really whetted my appetite, I'm going straight back to read that *Engineer of Human Souls*!"

The waiter doused the main lights. They're closing; it's eight o'clock. "Shall we go?" She put on her coat and said: "Jiří Gruša phoned me at work to say he'd got permission to visit his former cell-mate in Bory prison, but they had fixed it for seven in the morning – probably on purpose. He asked me if I'd drive him there." – "Why you?" – "He's already given his father the old car and he hasn't got his new one yet." – "Why should you drive? You could lend it to him." – "That did occur to me, but I expect he doesn't fancy travelling there on his own. Three of us would be going, including Danisz, the lawyer." – "You'll need to leave by five at the latest." – "Precisely. Jiří suggested that I sleep at their place on Friday night, because," she laughed, "Ivanka won't be home, he says." – "So what do you want from me?"

We walked to the tram-stop in the middle of Wenceslas Square. I took a tram down, she took one up.

THURSDAY, 8TH MARCH 1979

I walked out of the farm's arched gateway. The land sloped down in a lush lawn to the village square, empty and clean. On the right-hand side stood a group of mighty lime trees and beneath them the white statue of a saint. A group of tourists was straggling towards me from that direction. Lightly dressed, they had left their coats in the bus. Among them I noticed one particular man, almost bald, wearing a grey striped suit with pressed lapels, sleeves and creases, and a shirt-and-tie. The man had a boyishly chubby, ruddy face, with sweet little pouting lips like Aškenazy or Auersperg... it *was* Auersperg, of the Central Committee of the party! And when he recognised me also, he made as if to come over to me, but when he had almost reached me I realised he was looking over my shoulder as if I weren't there, craning his neck and smelling of perfume. But by this time I wasn't going to let him ignore me. I say: "Come on, don't be scared, come a bit closer and don't let on. There's no one following me." Beguiled by my words, my will, and – last but not least – the way I walked ahead of him without looking back, he trotted along behind me. We took a footpath into open country. I waited to let him catch up and walked along at his left. I said: "I've nothing against you, if only I could understand you. For the time being we are waiting to see what your intentions are. Do you have any rescue plan? I realise that you can't talk to us, but say something now." I stood opposite him looking into his face so that he should fully sense my longing for understanding. His agitated expression gradually gave way to one of boyish shame and he declared: "We can't do anything at all. No one in our shoes would be able to do anything. Do you believe me?" I longed to hug him. But all of a sudden, at the side of our path, though there was nothing there before, there now appeared an iron pipe which was leaking water into the field. Leaning over it was a group of three plumbers. One of them had fixed the pipes in our flat on a number of occasions. They looked up, and the plumber I knew assumed a clownish expression in anticipation of some fun, but at that moment he noticed Auersperg and his expression changed to one of astonishment. The other plumbers also started to look at us – even me – with distaste. Auersperg slowly raised his hand and covered his face. I stepped in front of him protectively and said: "It's all right, lads." – End of dream.

I have always been haunted by a yearning for reconciliation. I'm not quite sure what I ought to regard it as. It's not the best trait for a warrior. There have been times I have worried that it might let me down. But I just can't imagine a life of irreconcilability – towards anyone – though I may be obliged to live that way. It must be dreadful to live with the duty to vanquish the stronger opponent, and since this is usually out of the question, it gives rise to the twisted, poisonous hatred of the cripple, which probably has an even greater capacity to poison the atmosphere than the moods of the oversated lord. My constant readiness for conciliation refreshes my powers: all right, if you don't want peace, you'll find I am against you today as energetically as yesterday. My resistance is calculated to last until the evening; that's my limit. And tomorrow – with the same provision – again, and again, and again... If someone had told me, then, that it would last until now, I doubt if I would have made it even this far.

My assertion would be self-deluding sophistry, and nothing else, but for the fact it clearly works. However, my devil whispers in my ear that I have never held power. Isn't my virtue in fact a beautifully written diploma for those who never managed to wrest any material prize in the race?

I have no understanding for people who regenerate their integrity by continually rejecting old components of themselves the moment they no longer fit. It irks me that I did it also – just once: during my military service in 1952 when I mechanically filled in the form to say that I was leaving the Catholic church. I wasn't a Catholic anyway, so what sort of idiot was I to leave? But our every deed counts. In other words, every resignation counts and so does every enrolment. Everything that people do counts; all those who are foolish enough to screen their past will lose their wits; those who refuse to acknowledge all their parts will become schizophrenic. By opening my arms as wide as I can, I will try to embrace everything that was ever mine and I will stay sane. And so I hope and pray that no more terrible fate awaits me than to lie on the bed that I have made for myself over the years.

The ringing of the doorbell mechanically roused me from my sleep, without telling me where I was, what day it was and what was up. I made my way to the door, my mind blank, gesturing to those I'd left behind me to wait – I'd be right back. I opened the door and there stood Havel Minor, Mr. Václav's younger brother. He was wearing a coat with decorative metal buttons such as for a very congenial uniform. "I woke you up," he apologised, "but I was told this was the most convenient time." – "It's all right," I said, echoing my last words to the plumbers. – "I see you're not quite steady yet," said Havel Minor. "Do you wish to react straight away or should I wait a few moments?" – I enjoyed these words immensely, this was Mr. Václav's brother without a shadow of a doubt. "I'll react straight away," I said, "but think carefully about what you say here," and I pointed at the ceiling. – "What I want to tell you," he stated with precision, "they already know. I heard you were intending to visit my brother. I have come to tell you that I tried to do the same, but unsuccessfully, even though I am his brother."

FRIDAY, 9TH MARCH 1979

The X-ray showed that the roots of the teeth pointed inwards from right and left deep into my head, where they almost met. But I was prepared for an operation and was not afraid of anything. I just found it odd that Dr. Kurka was not there. Instead there were two unknown doctors who had not yet reached a consensus. But for the time being I had been given an anaesthetic injection. One of the doctors was more congenial and I turned to him for a hint that he knew me, but he was unwilling to make any sign in front of the other. Now and then one or the other would go off to make a phone call. The one who remained with me would examine my head with his fingers. The less familiar doctor seemed to be mutely astounded that I wanted the operation. Meanwhile I started to shake automatically, without fear. At last the supremely favourable moment for the operation arrived. The only part of my head I could feel were my eyes. At this moment there was a sort of commotion above my head and someone rushed in and the doctor standing by me said: "It's not to be done." He unfastened the belt across my chest that had held me down to the table. I stood up and went out wordlessly with my face numb. I was upset that it had been postponed.

I shaved, took a shower and put on my dark brown suit, the one I bought twice from Josef for a hundred crowns each time. He had been left it by his father-in-law, who was an army vet during the First Republic. For that reason I find the jacket a bit tight over the shoulders, while the trousers are too baggy, particularly in the crotch. But when I tug them on all the way, they almost reach up to my armpits. Madla is appalled whenever I put it on, but the material is good quality and I wear it out of consideration for Josef and the First Republic. I forced the second hundred crowns on Josef by making out I had not paid him the previous month.

I gave the birds fresh water, did not make myself tea because I did not feel like breakfast, and packed my briefcase. I estimated how many crowns I should need to pay for the Šimečka at the binders, but I shall have to ask Mirka to go for me, because R. gave a woman's name again. I was putting my shoes on, ready to leave, when the doorbell rang. It was Mojmír Klánský, and I had a sour pang of conscience. He too was unpleasantly surprised to find me on my way out. He had brought some tickets for a concert, attached to a page of meticulous details about the orchestra, the conductor and the composer. I told him I was just leaving, which was just as well as we could talk together outside. I just had to bite that sour bullet once and for all. Mojmír had offered me his story "The Albatross" for Padlock, but it had not been liked by any of those I had given it to read.

It is the story of an army officer from the First Republic who goes off to join the resistance during the Nazi occupation and when he returns after the war finds himself not promoted but the opposite. Eventually, after 1948, he is arrested. Advancement is possible only for unprincipled and weak-minded individuals. Our hero had been fond of horses as a young officer and even raced them. An episode around a magnificent horse brings him into close contact with a magnificent woman. Things are just getting exciting when the war comes. In the story those events are related in flashback. The actual plot in the present tense starts with the officer setting out on an enforced leave, whose denouement he senses, and running into the woman on the train. One thing leads to another – there's no other way of putting it – and instead of going home to her husband she goes off with the officer and stays with him a day – or two? At last, everything between them is almost as it should have been before the war when each of them was young and between their thighs there raced a horse, by which I mean that sensual magic which ought to be in the story, *Istenem,* but is not, unfortunately.

Outside I told Mojmír the lot. He exploded: "I couldn't give a damn what your friends say! At first you told me you liked the story!" – "Yes. And by that I meant how much better it was than the original version. But we have a principle that each manuscript has to be supported by two or three people." – "Well my case is the first time you've ever implemented that principle." – "Don't be crazy! Kantůrková was adamant that her book was ready. She was furious and maybe even wept in private. In the end, though, she took it like a man and is reworking the text." – "And what did Klíma say?" Mojmír bellowed, as a roaring file of cars passed within a yard of us. "I'm sure he can't stand me!" – "I didn't give it to Klíma to read." I was bellowing also. "I deliberately asked people who had enjoyed your earlier book. So there!" We stood waiting at the pedestrian crossing. The traffic cop took ages to change the lights. Mojmír said: "You haven't even the faintest idea what I've written since then, and you'll never find out!" – "Why?!" – "So I don't cause you difficulties with your friends and also so you don't have the awkward duty of smuggling me in among them or explaining their attitudes." – "You're a touchy fellow." – "I'm not." – "You are, though."

We eventually got across the road and onto the tram. Once aboard, Mojmír explained to me that he intended to be a loner in that case. "I like that," I said, "I'm a loner too." He laughingly dismissed the idea with a wave of the hand. "It's all my fault, Mojmír. I failed to tell you right away what I didn't like about it, and instead I tried to give you positive guidance in terms of what I liked about it. And there's another thing, you're always giving me your things to read so that by now I am so used to your style it doesn't bother me any more." – "Have I really got so much worse since *Banishment*? – "You haven't changed. But just try and remember what I told you straight out that time. About your language being bland and lacking any aesthetic tone. It's an austerely informative style. In *Banishment*, by lucky chance, it turned out to be an asset. It looks like something intentional on the part of the author, as if he were an impartial observer of one man's terrifying fate, and it generates incredible tension and emotion." Mojmír said, "So why did you put the kibosh on Fischer Verlag bringing it out in German? I don't mean you, I mean whoever did!" – "What do you mean? I was under the impression that it was coming out soon!" – "Oh, for goodness sake!" he scowled. "You must have read that sentence, the only one in the letter, 'Why is the Klánský not to be published?'" – "I don't recall that and I know nothing at all about it. It could be that Filip screwed it up – unintentionally perhaps," I said. – "So why didn't you want me to be published in Switzerland with the rest of you?" – "Oh, come on! Why wouldn't we? In fact we were desperately seeking a replacement to join us in our calamitous enterprise after Šotola dropped out!" – "But it was you who referred me to Filip!" – "Me? It was he who contacted you of his own accord. You came and asked me what you should do and I advised you to write him a normal letter and send it by official post, asking for a contract to be sent. Or am I wrong?" – "No, sorry, you're right. And then you told me I ought to phone him." – "And did you?" – "I did. But there was no reply." – "Oh, for Christ's sake!" I exclaimed in despair. It was beginning to get to me. I said: "Besides that, you wanted to join us at Buchers' at the very moment Mrs. Bucher was selling the firm and we were about to leave them. Braunschweiger was launching his own publishing house and didn't want to start out with unknown names. He wanted new books from his established authors, which is why he held off Trefulka for so long, until the latter received a better offer from Fischer's. That's how it was!" – "I remember that," said Mojmír.

We got off at the Rudolfinum and before we parted company, Mojmír said: "But Braunschweiger wanted me in your almanac, and I didn't get in." – "That was your own fault." – "Not at all. Gruša ditched me." – "Don't you believe it! It was I, *I*, Mojmír, who ditched you, because when we were having tea together once, if you remember, you really pissed me off! You started to talk to me about it openly in our kitchen. You wanted to know the details, and these days if someone wants details and isn't trusting, then he can't be in. It seemed quicker to me to take you out than to prove to you what Gruša had done for you. You just rejected all his suggestions, that's all." – "But you didn't even tell me it was Gruša. For me it had to be some mysterious authority." – "Why should I have told you at that stage. I was the one dealing with you. But you needn't have any regrets, you spared yourself a couple of interrogations." – "Let's forget it. He's an arsehole." – "Why?" – "Because of what he just wrote against you, of course." – "But that didn't bother me in the least. He didn't even want to publish it. That was my idea." – "I know, you don't have to tell me. You want to play the Good Samaritan. So long, then, and don't forget that concert!"

I took the metro to Mirka's, where at last I had a breakfast of tea and bread and butter, and Mirka went with me for the Šimečka. I waited in the park. Then we went back to her place again and bought a cake on the way to have with our coffee. I added it to the price of the book, which is something I never do. We drank coffee, ate the cake and Mirka said: "How'd you like to take a look at that Idi Amin Bubu Hugo fellow?" – "Here, show me," I replied. She leafed through the Austrian press. There was a story there about him loading his 80-member family into a Boeing and sending them out of the country. He left himself just one *Liebesfrau*, and gave her a medal for killing a lot of soldiers bare-handed. There was a photo of her. "So that lady celebrated International Women's Day yesterday," said Mirka. "And I'm supposed to share a celebration with her? Not likely!"

From her place, the best plan seemed to take a walk up beyond the National Museum to see whether Standa Milota might be in. I received a booming thespian welcome from Vlasta Chramostová, who had been allowed home from the madhouse for the weekend. "But darling, Joey will be thrilled. Joey!" she called to Standa. And she explained to me what she was planning to do when they let her come home for good, and she explained it so loudly that I was amazed – at the power of her voice, that is. "But of course you'll have a major role in my plans too. You've been assigned one already, little do you know..." she crowed. – "Hold it, Joey, you'll spill all the beans," Standa said sternly. "Perhaps Ludvík fancies a bite of something." – But I did not want anything. "When are they letting you come home?" I asked. "It'll be some while yet, darling," she said. – "How do you feel? Any better?" – "Better? Not in the least, I'm afraid," she replied very deliberately and Standa shook his head silently in the background. It was a sign for me to have a closer look at her eyes.

SATURDAY, 10TH MARCH 1979

I am sitting here tending the fire in the tall white-tiled stove. Madla is out in the garden digging in the rockery. It is usually the other way round: I am outside while she is steadily poking in more fuel until the temperature in the room – five degrees, say – has risen to at least twelve.

"How's your new one?" I asked in the car on the way here. – "It's getting her down," Madla replied. – "What is?" – "Well, for a start she had no inkling just how many cases roll in every day, one after the other." – "She's already seeing clients then?" – "Not on your life! She just sits there, and is terrified at the thought that she'll be obliged to offer advice herself one day." – "What did she expect? What made her take the job, then?" – "She said to me: 'Mrs. Vaculíková, I thought I was ready for it after ten years of study and reading.'" – "Where was she working before?" – "In a library. 'I'll never have your experience,' she says. 'You will,' I tell her, 'but you have to use your personal experience, study and professional experience just aren't enough.'" – "Who does she sit with?" – "She's with me in reception for now, but when individual psychologists are dealing with cases, she goes to their rooms. She says: 'I have studied them all – alcoholism, arguments over children or money, infidelity, aged parents. But the tragedy behind every one of those cases comes as an awful shock.'" – "How old is she?" – "Thirty." – "What's her Christian name?" – "I couldn't tell you. I think Olga would suit her." – "How's the Phantom taking her?" – "He's rather non-committal. I get the feeling, though, that he's beginning to think she might be some old friend of mine. But that's because she is so trusting in the way she seeks my advice. He's never pleased when any newcomers come under my influence. But he has to put up with it as I'm the best person to show them the ropes, and he knows it." – "And how's she taking the Phantom?" – "Well, he manages to impress everyone by playing the thoroughly modern boss. The right manners, the suit. This one – 'Olga' – strikes me as being unsure of herself. I get the feeling she still has some unspoiled natural instincts." – "All right, but for goodness sake don't go telling her anything about him yourself!" – "Of course I won't. There's no need for me to. A while ago he was drawing up the duty roster and it turned out I'd be doing the afternoon shift in reception on my own. The Phantom turns to her and half-jokingly says, 'So you'll take the afternoon and keep an eye on Mrs. Vaculíková for us.' Afterwards she says to me, 'Was that a joke?' – 'No, he's serious, I'm not to be left on my own.' – 'And you put up with it?' – 'I'm used to it by now,' I tell her. 'But they need you, from what I can see. They're even afraid of you'" – "And what did you say to that?" – "Nothing. And then she says, 'Do you think the Phantom does it on his own initiative, or is he under instructions?' – 'I haven't discovered yet,' I say." – "Jesus Christ! And you said all that in the office?" – "Not on your life. We were talking over lunch." – "Does she know the place is bugged yet?" – "I didn't tell her, but over the past year we've developed such a particular manner of talking, discussing and not saying things that you only need to be there a day to get the message." – "What gives it away, do you think?" – "Well, for instance, the Phantom can't stand it when two or three people just talk about nothing in particular. Straight away it's 'No congregating, no congregating!'" – "'Congregating' – that is practically secret police terminology. That's their greatest nightmare, people talking among themselves." – "But that's what I don't get. You'd think the Phantom would be interested in finding out what people say – about him, for example, whereas it looks from this as if he's afraid that something might crop up there that someone else would have to deal with over his head. It was the way he behaved that first convinced me something was installed there. As if he himself were trying to call our attention to it." – "But I thought you said, when the building opened, that there were cameras, TV screens and microphones installed so the director could monitor the consultants from his office, to see the way they work, assess them and advise them." – "Yes, of course there are, but nobody's used the equipment for that purpose yet. And that's the other reason."

What Madla is trying to figure out at the moment is whether the Phantom is a freemason with the intelligence agency or an intelligence agent with the freemasons. It's three thirty, the sun is shining gloriously out there but the wind is icy. Straining every muscle, Mrs. Hemerková is bringing Don back from his walk on a short leash – lest she get it in the neck again for those enormous paw-marks among the budding tulips. I'll go outside.

SUNDAY, 11ᵀᴴ MARCH 1979

Snowdrops and winter aconite are in flower. Flakes of snow dance in the air. The light is dim and full of promise: there is bound to be a brightness beyond the curtain. Today, yesterday and a week ago, I dragged together enormous heaps of tree and shrub branches. I stand amidst them axe in hand like at camp. I chop them the easy way, on a high chopping-block. The pile of sticks grows and I feed a steady bonfire with heaps of small twigs. It is a rare treat after a decent, long winter. Work like this also unleashes thoughts that lack any particular purpose. The rest of the time they slumber somewhere. I think they are something like budding thoughts; when their turn is too long in coming, they dry up and are brushed out of the head in the form of scurf, without ever influencing one's other ideas, opinions or behaviour. And everything then strikes one as properly thought out. It is all logical and correct and proceeds along its well-planned course to a bad conclusion because some thoughts just failed to materialise.

For instance, I can only surmise with trepidation how crippled I am as a result of not being allowed to travel. But I counter it with the thought that people only blunt their senses and judgement when they drag themselves all over the world. They suddenly take everything so much into account that nothing is definitely good anymore and there is nothing to be done about anything. Immobility through mobility. And as I go on slowly chopping this wood, I come to the conclusion that it is not right to do too much travelling in one's youth. Young people only need to discover that the world they know is not the only one, and nothing else. They should then stay put in their own country until they have developed a firm commitment to it and only then go off somewhere again in order to view their commitment from a different angle. When little children are dragged off to Yugoslavia like pieces of luggage, then, as teenagers, they hitch-hike to Bulgaria, and after that are always heading off somewhere with some travel agency, not to mention dull, single-purpose, official trips on account of their jobs – that is not enriching them, it is making them hollow. Wherever you look all you see are imbeciles, row upon row of them, particularly on television. But why should I care?

I also spend a few moments thinking about Škvorecký. I got a parcel of books from him and a Honda motorcycle from Japan. One of the bits of scurf that I combed out of my hair as a young man was the hunch that we should never have been taken in by any sort of communism. Or: communism should never have taken. I leave off chopping because I remember that I'm supposed to cut several grafts from one of the apple trees for someone. I'm just back from sticking the grafts into sand.

There don't seem to be many birds around. They can't have frozen to death, surely? That little one with the reddish belly would normally be hopping around about this time. As soon as I did anything with the soil or the bushes, he was always sure to be there. There's not a titmouse to be seen, and even the blackbird is a rare visitor. Like last year, I have again decided not to spray the trees. Perhaps his joyful pose is just for the benefit of the female world and he's maddeningly faithful to his wife – old Škvorecký I mean. What sort of effort – an effort quite different from any we have ever known – does it take for someone to keep going in a foreign country? Mention of Škvorecký's name is an opportunity to write something about Major (?) Fišer, but I won't. If it will gain me a little more peace, I shall desist for the time being. I can bear to be without him. "So long as you don't try to foist yourself on me as a subject, I'll ignore you," I told him, when he asked whether I intended to write about him. I had the feeling that he regarded what I said as a contract. But he made no comment; what else could he do?

If ever it happened – if, on the orders of certain influential circles, the Dobřichovice local authority were to give our ladies alternative apartments, we should be obliged to move here. How my life would change. One never knows whether one ought to put ideas in their heads, or not. I expect I'd travel to Prague about twice a week. What would I manage to do in that time? Almost no one would come here to see me. I'd know nothing, get no new ideas, have no chance to sort out my views in discussion. And I'd start to have truly original ideas at last! I would just keep a diary and before long I'd comb that whole regime of theirs out of my hair.

MONDAY, 12TH MARCH 1979

I unlocked the door, went in and Bibisa did not leap out at me. I continued through and looked round the corner. There was something lying in the bed – Zdena. The room was scarcely smoke-filled.

She considers it degrading to talk about her illnesses since her health is so crucial to her. For that reason, it was difficult for me to find out what had happened. Her coyness about complaining amounts to: what's the point of your asking when you do nothing to help? On Saturday, it seems, she had to go to the urgent treatment centre. The woman doctor on duty expressed surprise at something and called the surgeon, an old doctor, who examined Zdena. They then discussed whether to have her taken straight to hospital or whether to wait and see how she was on Monday. The duty doctor expressed astonishment: "You mean you go to work in that state?" She answered: "Yes. I've even been X-rayed, but they say I'm all right."

"You ought to have said," I said, "that your cow of a factory doctor won't let you stay home even when you have a temperature because your cow of a factory doctor is mostly worried about herself. I hope that they've forbidden you to smoke, at least." – "The subject wasn't even mentioned." – "Great! So we'll light up then?" I gathered up the matches on the table top. She gave a weak movement of her hand: "I don't enjoy it somehow…" I sat there and wondered what to do. She said: "Worst of all I can't even sleep."

Bibisa was being looked after by Zdena's son for a few days.

TUESDAY, 13TH MARCH 1979

Today I made one last attempt to meet B. for a talk, but again he was not at home, even though his colleague at work told me he wasn't there. I knocked at the neighbours' to see whether he had picked up the parcel of books I left for him last time, when I had also left a message in his mailbox to that effect. He had picked up the books.

I bought some food and went over to Zdena's. She was asleep. It seems she is sleeping all the time, reading a bit and doing scarcely any typing. She is continuing with the feuilletons – last year's – and in the meantime this year's are already waiting to be typed. I am now putting them together and wondering what to write in the preface. And who I might get to type them.

I went to Mlynárik's. Tatarka is supposed to be celebrating his birthday tomorrow, so what's afoot? There was no one home. I then called in at A.'s to discuss with him what action to take against B., but A. was not home from work yet; he is working different hours now. Just as I was talking with his wife, the phone rang and it was him. I borrowed the receiver and in clumsy code we agreed to something for the day after tomorrow – I'm curious what.

I came home and Ondřej was there, just back from military training: I forgot to note here that he was away. He asked whether we had gone to pick up his approved university application from work in his absence. We had; Jan went there – but it had not been approved!

WEDNESDAY, 14TH MARCH 1979

I am aware, of course, what ought to be done. In random order: reward uniformed Major R. who allowed himself last August to be manipulated into using terror tactics against Zdena. As they were driving her home distraught, one of the ordinary uniformed policemen said to the other: "If someone did that to my wife I'd kill him." Watch out, though, Ludvík! She could easily have put that into your head. She was right, though. Secondly: go and have a closer look at that pig of a director in Ondřej's firm. Thirdly: think twice and then do the last deed regardless. Last September Milan Šimečka travelled from Bratislava to pay me a visit, but they came and picked him up while we were having dinner in a pub, and bundled him into a train home. I sent a complaint to the Prosecutor General but have yet to receive a reply. Just let some cheeky bastard ring that door bell again! Just wait until I open the door and find four guys standing outside! Just wait until one of them shoves a paper supposedly signed by the Prosecutor General under my nose! "Come on," I'll say. "Prosecutor General? He doesn't exist, you swindlers!" I say it so vehemently that some of them tumble out the window into the yard.

THURSDAY, 15TH MARCH 1979

In fact it is Friday the 16th; I am writing up yesterday – i.e. with distaste. This morning (yesterday) I got up at the diabolically early hour of six o'clock. I took the car down to Malostranské Square where I rendezvoused with Messrs. A. and C. at around seven a.m. Not realising it was a weekday, I pulled away and turned into Letenská Street, as if it were a Sunday, and I got stopped by the police right away. I got fined a hundred crowns, the penalty was marked on my licence, and they even put me down for re-testing. Why that progression, I need not explain. Meanwhile Messrs. A. and C. sat inside like timorous mice. Even though that hundred crowns is a bit stiff, at least it's for breaking a traffic regulation. The rest I got for failing to regard policemen as my superiors. As every year goes by you can see that outfit turning more and more from enforcers of public order into a bloated higher caste.

With heightened care I managed to drive to our destination. We got out, went into the house and banged on the door – the bell there does not work. A drowsy B. came to the door and his astonishment was unfeigned and massive. I explained why we had come and I insisted that we take everything from him without any song and dance; after all we know how it's done, we've all been through the routine ourselves. Apart from that, I felt that B. owed me the hundred crowns I had paid for the fine. I have no desire to elaborate; my two companions let themselves be talked into extending the deadline to the end of next week. I no longer care. In a week's time I shall merely ask them: yes or no? The lot of you can go and jump in the lake for all I care.

I got home at ten and found Karel Kostroun standing by the lift. He had come to ask me how I cooked that chicken for Pecka. "Well, what could you have put in it!" he said in amazement. "It couldn't have been anything but herbs!" First of all I told him I had bought it at the snack-bar, but then I came clean and told him Madla had made it. When Kostroun left I washed the window. Madla is often saying: "What do you do around the house? Not a thing. You just try keeping a record and you'll see." This is a record that I washed the window. And that's already my bit towards the Easter cleaning – so take note!

I had a quick shower, got dressed and intended to set off for Hradčany, where a certain lady was holding a lunch to celebrate her thirty-seventh birthday and I had accepted her invitation. ("Do you have the solution to the puzzle with you? You haven't." – "No, I certainly haven't, not yet. But seeing I have this birthday, couldn't we have a short interval and then your severity could resume afterwards, if that's possible. Please!") So I still need to buy some flowers. As I left the apartment, the lift stopped at our floor and out stepped Tomin who had an urgent need to speak to me. We walked together through Letná Gardens. He explained to me a discovery he had made which had something to do with my controversial "Remarks on Courage." At the end of the plays in which he criticised the Athenian regime, Aristophanes suddenly wrote the word "Peace." "Then it hit me!" Tomin shouted, the way he does. "It was something that one should have realised sooner, of course, from the time-sequence of his plays, if one wasn't so bloody stupid. After years of struggle, Aristophanes – either from exhaustion or a re-appraisal of the issues (but this is precisely what I'm not sure about yet) – suddenly exclaims: "So do something to make life in Athens a bit more decent, please, and I shall stop attacking you!" Tomin had started to write a study about it. It will have five chapters, of which the first is finished. He wants to give a reading of it and would like me to attend. We continued through the park full of mothers with babies, and pensioners with pensioners. Tomin was speaking very loudly, the way he does, so I assented without further ado, in an effort to sweep this exotic subject off the public table. But it didn't work. "What was the melting pot in which Athens could be transformed?!" he shouted, and kept on stopping all the time. "Why, theatre, of course!" Theatre.

As a result I forgot to buy the flowers. And it turned out that no one else came to the lunch. "It was churlish of me, and besides, when would I have got to see you?" I said out of a lack of confidence in women's engineering prowess. And in order to assist her, handed her one of the six sticks – the one with the most cuts. She turned it round adroitly in her fingers and almost knocked me out when she said: "Aha! I was assuming that they all have to look the same. Whereas only this one can look like this!" And she tossed it into the leather handbag hanging from a corner of her chair. After lunch and a walk downhill, a stop at the florists – mistake corrected. Otherwise, though, I made no progress in drawing closer to my intended virtues. I shall have to start all over again tomorrow.

FRIDAY, 16TH MARCH 1979

I sleep well, except that whenever I wake up in the night, things I have not done start crowding in on me and I rearrange them in order of importance. It's a strenuous task, like shifting a pile of logs. What bothers me most at the moment are Madla's work records: she is not keeping any, even though she resolved to do so on several occasions. I keep reminding her, but she comes home so exhausted every day that all she can do is recount the latest stories and events, which gets it off her chest. And there it rests; responsibility for recording them passes to me and I have neither the time nor a system. And yet her experiences seem to me more important than my own – at night. Then I get up next morning and something else seems important.

I woke up feeling edgy but could not identify the cause. Yesterday's episode with the traffic cops, maybe. What worries me most is the thought of having to go for testing again. "I don't make a habit of breaking the highway code," I said when they marked the penalty points on my licence, and they expressed surprise that it was clean. When they put me down for re-testing on account of my insolence, I said: "I was re-tested three times last year!" They could not square the two statements. Here I am again with a nervous reaction that I neither want nor understand. While I am shaving or tidying up I find myself going over the incident again and again, breaking it up into its component parts and proving to myself that it was no more than a traffic incident.

Alternatively, my edginess and reluctance to leave the flat at all might result from my apprehension about what will happen at the dentist's. Surely not, though, because when I break the event up into its anticipated components, I have a sense of satisfaction that something important will be resolved at last. After all, allowing one's teeth to be extracted when they do not hurt is an exhilarating exercise of free will.

Doctor Kurka showed me the X-ray. It clearly showed that two teeth had to come out for sure and possibly the third. I was not happy about it but Mrs. Krumphanzlová said: "I'd go ahead and take out that third one while we're at it." I rounded on her fiercely: "Well you'll have to pull it out yourself, then!" She was taken aback. "Me?" – "It's not hard making decisions about someone else's teeth, is it?" I said. The doctor handed her the pincers. She shrunk away. He did pull the three of them, of course, and when he looked into the chasm that was left he must have given some inaudible instruction; Mrs. Krumphanzlová took hold of the back of my head with her warm hands and he pulled out a fourth one, painfully and with a crunching sound. He showed it to me, saying: "For your information, when it was uncovered from one side, barely two millimetres of it remained in the bone and we'd have difficulty getting a crown to stay on."

Before he pulled them he gave the teeth next to them a scrape; the cast he had ready from last time. Now he worked with his mixing bowls for a quarter of an hour and shortly afterwards I was on my way out with a mouthful of brand-new crooked teeth. "You know, doctor, you could easily construct a whole new imitation Vaculík," I said. – "Do you still go there?" he asked. "Every month. But I haven't been this month yet. I'm expecting it any day."

On my way from the dentist I bought a chicken, roasted it and rushed off to collect *The Hangwoman* from the binders. It is one of my longest outstanding debts. Now to get rid of the three Komárkovás and shut up shop. No one believes I'll do it. "You don't mean it seriously. Padlock mustn't finish!" But it won't be finished. "It's not Vaculík who publishes Padlock Editions, they're put out by loads of people," one of the Brno lads rightly declared in court. The first letter has arrived from Pavel Kohout. He confirms he is receiving the feuilletons, goodness knows how, and for my benefit he confidentially injects an interesting note into our controversy: "You'll never become a private individual, so give up hoping. Maybe when you're getting old, but by that time you won't yearn for it so much. You'll seek company, more likely – even among heroes…" Of course I shall become a private individual when the fancy takes me. However, I know it would mean holding my tongue and keeping my thoughts to myself…

There is another section of the giant puzzle lying on the meadow. The way it is cut makes it totally different from the first one.

SUNDAY, 18TH MARCH 1979

It is nearly midnight. My hands are heavy from digging, sawing and chopping and it strikes me that I am losing sensation in my left hand. To test it I took out my fiddle. I had scarcely played a couple of words – "The neighbours they have an old bitch, She sleeps with her arse in the ditch…" – when Madla came in, agitated. Whenever I take my fiddle out she thinks I'm love-lorn. I tell her I am just testing my hand. It must be a year since I last played. "Aha! You're afraid of losing your concert form!"

The boys had spent the weekend on their building site. By assisting Ondřej all the time, Jan has become not just an honorary builder but his presence is virtually indispensable by now. As the apartments gradually reach completion, the co-op members tend to shut themselves up in them and start fiddling around with the minutiae and there are fewer and fewer of them to tackle the joint tasks. It means that nothing gets done on the house in Dobřichovice, where a lot of work also needs doing in the garden. And on the odd occasions that the boys have a free Saturday or Sunday, Ondřej goes over to Marta's and Jan pokes about inside Švácha. Švácha is an Aero coupé of 1946 vintage bought for fifteen thousand from a Mr Švácha. Herzen is our two-year-old Škoda, bought as new, already slightly rusty, from Tuzex and she got her name because when they were small the boys secretly nicknamed me Herzen, since he was a writer too. I had to chop down – new paragraph.

I had to chop down a huge cherry tree that had gone wild; if I'd waited a week, I might not have had the courage to. Its fine twigs, enveloped in rosettes of swollen buds, look very strange on the unlit bonfire! We have two chopping blocks, one low, one high. I first trim each branch roughly on the low block and then I turn southwards and chop it up on the high one. When I was at it last week I thought about Canada's five frontier lakes and tried to work out their sequence; so now, every time I turned southwards with my branch, I could not help thinking about those damned lakes and it really annoyed me. And those lakes stayed in my mind and only cleared off in disgust when I hit on the song about the old hobo gazing into the waves of the Niagara: "Niagara so sadly roars/ All day and all the night/ A man whose heart with love is sore/ For him there's no respite…"

I have now read Škvorecký's *Engineer of Human Souls*. There, over yonder and without the rest of us, that fellow has managed to do something that at least five people over here, who consider themselves especially qualified for the job, are currently toying with: write the great Czech novel. Škvorecký has succeeded in uniting the Czechs' sundered destiny. There is a new story on every page. He has managed admirably to steer a different course from Egon Hostovský, who was bewitched and endlessly obsessed by the intimate horror of an all-pervasive "universal conspiracy." Škvorecký seems to have said to himself that he must provide the ninnies of the world with an object lesson in what that horror means, as attested to by his own destiny and the destiny of all those he has ever held dear. Finely chopped destinies spill from his grasp and, though seemingly scattered without any great skill, they form themselves on the ground into an almost monumental picture. I think it will be his best book ever and that everything he wrote before was a prelude to it. All his usual smirks, poses and displays are suddenly put to proper use and are incredibly effective.

I would love to know if he gave anyone the manuscript to read beforehand (apart from Mrs. "Santnerová") and in general what he thinks about editing manuscripts. He has things in it that I would have advised him to drop. Blažej/Blažek's jokey letter-writing style was already getting on my nerves in his earlier book *Card Game in Reykjavik*, for instance. Even the hepatica –

Even the hepatica and crocuses are already out and all sorts of primroses are beginning to flower. It now looks for certain that the small birds have frozen to death because they are not coming back to life.

MONDAY, 19TH MARCH 1979

In the gloomy corridor with its darkened wood panelling there were a number of doors. I went from one to the next reading the nameplates. Zdena's name wasn't on any of them. Even so, she suddenly emerged from a door with a sheaf of important papers in her hand and walked ahead of me into the light of the front hall. A figure. I heard her say to the man, who had eagerly risen from his desk: "I just have to give these in" – she waved the papers – "and in five minutes we can go." I was embarrassed to have overheard it and returned to the gloomy corridor where I waited by her door. When she came upon me, she said: "Oh, hello. I'll have to stay a bit later today, so don't wait about for me." As I left the building, the man was slowly pacing up and down outside. I knew precisely how I ought to be feeling but it just made me grin, without a trace of anything of the kind, and I said to myself: Yes, it's right for her to be aware that she can still decide what to do with her own time.

Achieve an equilibrium, attain a life of wonderful peace, get rid of objects, problems, complete my study of abandoned themes, and write them up. Discover and invent something completely different, something that will be extremely effective because no rapid retaliation will be lying in wait. And do it out of the unknown! Do it as a nobody! That would be something!

Today is St. Joseph's Day and I did not even send Josef a card. I will put that right. And in two day's time a new spring. I am supposed to write a feuilleton and am squirming at the thought. It is bound to take me a week again. I might as well get on with this writing instead. And another beam with cuts has been dragged to the woods. ("I spent hours trying to figure it out yesterday. I think it would have been better if you'd not given me that stick. It actually misleads me. I should have tried it unaided.") Today I asked about the astronomical year-book, but it is not out yet. A whole quarter of their heavenly phenomena they can now stick where they like. I wanted to buy myself some shoes – the sort they used to have for ninety crowns, then for a hundred and twenty and last time for a hundred and forty. But I have not found them anywhere. I can't even find a bow. I went to the House of Sport. They have kids' bows for 52 Kčs. It's years since they've had adult-sized ones. Just for fun I decided to ask in the hunting shop. "It's ages since people hunted with bows, sir!" the elderly assistant whispered discreetly. "Yes, but hunting with bow and arrows was the healthiest way," I said. "Hmm, yes…" he mused, "but otherwise it comes down to the same thing. And anyway he still got caught by Maid Marian." Can you believe it?

It is afternoon, the surrounding streets are jam packed with trucks. There's a cold wind blowing. This evening we're going to the Kosíks.

For the second time I received about five hundred Tuzex vouchers from some firm in Stockholm as a remittance from Franta Janouch. I thanked him and asked him what they were for. The first payment was apparently for some feuilletons of mine that were published somewhere, the second was from the Swedish PEN-Club for no particular reason, simply to encourage my work on the Indians. Franta asked whether he should not try offering an occasional feuilleton of mine to some magazines. Yes. Why should my life be just work and interrogations?

For years I have been burdened by the awareness that instead of working I walk around, carry things, talk, glue things in, cut things out. Instead of writing I read others' concoctions, edit, correct and negotiate on behalf of authors who don't even know whether at the end of a piece of direct speech the punctuation should precede the inverted commas or vice versa. And when I do write, it's not some nice thick tome but instead some piddling little commentary in jester's garb, apologising to myself at the outset for injecting some drops of a more hopeful hue into the stuffy atmosphere. And my time and strength are running out.

Walking down Belcredi Street one day, I suddenly realised: And so what! It's my occupation, isn't it? I myself evolved it. I came home and proclaimed preventively as I opened the door: "That's it! Nobody's going to go telling me that I ought to creep about with my head low just because I don't have a rubber stamp in my identity card! I am engaged in my rightful employment!" The boys stared in surprise from the table and Madla said: "But we know that!" I went off to my room in a temper. I'm an editor and journalist; I just lack a newspaper. But I know that if I felt like it, I could write for any newspaper in the world. Whenever I've tried to, I've succeeded. Don't talk to me about borders, censorship or fear. After all, I don't have to write about the Russians, the secret police or repression in general – not in so many words, at least. And if I managed to convey to people elsewhere in Europe the feeling that their vital nerves stretch as far as here, then I'd have hit the mark!

Two years ago, with that in mind, I tried to persuade my friends that we should deliberately occupy pages in the leading European newspapers. Nobody fancied the idea apart from Pavel Kohout. We already had one newspaper: Hamburg's *Die Zeit*. The idea appealed to some fellow there and he launched a "European Column." However, only Pavel and I wrote for it, each of us twice or thereabouts. Then some Icelander wrote something for it, and then a Spaniard. It finally folded on account of the Italians, French and Germans, who are an unreliable bunch just like my companions: disloyal, disinclined, incapable of meeting deadlines. Either they've no inspiration or they don't need the money enough, I don't know. So it came to an end, but I'm convinced that if they put their mind to it, five Czechs could damn well teach the whole of Europe how to read properly! And from here – from Prague!

At the Kosíks' yesterday evening there were the Kliments, the Mlynáriks and Marta K. On the programme was their beloved Mozart: all sorts of keyboard music. Madla is astonished by the choice: entertaining strumming she calls it, all very pleasant, but no real depth. Kosík did not sit down for an instant. He was constantly offering something: wine, tea, haricot-bean soup, and finally his own special goulash. And beforehand we always decide that there will be no refreshments, because the demands of hospitality end up placing an intolerable burden on such get-togethers. But then the hosts relent and programmes start to escalate through soup to elaborate roasts. Nobody smoked.

Massive Mlynárik is mad about Mozart – as much maybe as about Dominik Tatarka. There is not much he can do for Mozart anymore, but he is proposing Tatarka for the Nobel Prize. He regards his *Demon of Consent*, for instance, as a supreme achievement because Tatarka took the lid off the cult of personality long before Solzhenitsyn. I told him that I had my doubts. Dominik, I said, was a marvellous fellow and a great writer, but I had my doubts, all the same. It so happened that I did not even like *Demon of Consent* all that much, and as for taking the lid off the personality cult, there was some Latin American whose name I had forgotten who had written a book on that theme which was as lethal as a gunshot at a dictator: its title was *The Great Burundun-Burudá is Dead*. Yes, I was curious about Tatarka's political essays, for which Václav Černý was writing a preface, but I want a Slovak typist – end of argument! These exchanges took place, of course, during the intermission and Mozart remained unsullied.

Mlynárik listened to the Mozart standing up, a glass of wine in his hand, moving his ears gracefully in time to the music, in which one could tell he was totally immersed along with his big trousers that flowed in abundant folds from his waist down to below his knees. He knows everything about Mozart: dates, conductors, biographies, and the stories of the different compositions. He stops the gramophone in order to draw attention to interesting passages before playing the same piece in a different recording. And you wouldn't believe it to look at him. I was astounded. Mrs. M. said almost nothing. Afterwards Mlynárik had a bit of a dig at me in the next room: at his interrogation (yes, it was on account of the Charter document about the German expulsions) those gentlemen had cited me as a good example of sensible behaviour. I had not read the document about the Germans, only Hübl's criticism of it. Jan replied that Hübl got on his nerves. "Just imagine, he said he still respects Husák!" There was no comment I could make. "But that's speculation!" I am not sure, but I am not of the view that people who have been imprisoned or let themselves be jailed earn the right to a place in a better government. (Better?) But I've already noticed there are certain individuals who have a need to envy other people – even their imprisonment; hence their tendentious interpretation of it. It's half past two again; is my writing becoming a bit confused?

Then I asked them to give the Mozart a rest at last and put on something completely different. There was immediate speculation as to what I might mean thereby: folk music, chanson, jazz... I had nothing particular in mind – just something else. Jan had a look and fished something out. It started with a beautiful rustling as soft notes were swept towards us from afar, in ripples, like the wind tossing the first sprinkling of rain into the treetops. Schubert's *Unfinished*. All conversation ceased at a stroke. Afterwards Karel Kosík said: "Gentlemen, explain how it is that a romantic should sound so dramatically contemporary to our ears? Or maybe you don't think so?" It hit the nail right on the head: the whole time I had been exchanging greetings with the *Unfinished*. Is that you? I recognise you, but do you know me? Where have we been all this time? Karel asked what it was that made Mácha write what he wrote and die young; Schubert wrote what he wrote and died young, too. Is an early death written into a person's fate?

The tea I drank was probably too strong. It's three o'clock. I can't find the *Great Burundun-Burudá* book anywhere. While I was looking for it I came upon the minutes of a meeting of young people on Žofín Island in November 1968. I've just re-read what I said on the occasion. At that time Pachman, Zátopek, Hochman, Sekaninová, Martin Vaculík were also there... I don't know whether I was clever or stupid; my oratory now strikes me as skilful, truthful and adventurous. But I don't think I had too much success with it that time. These days I wouldn't even be inclined to open my mouth. We were handed up written questions from the audience. Young people wanted to know how to behave so as not to feel guilty for cowardice later. I quote my answer from the minutes:

"The question of cowardice and courage – young people raise this question because they regard it as a value *per se*. I myself am not so sure, because courage must be related to some specific issue. To ask oneself whether one is brave or cowardly without reference to context or goals is to distress oneself and goad oneself to act before reaching understanding. That's why I am unable to answer the question as to whether young people ought to demonstrate or not... The threat facing young people again and again and in every generation is our own fanaticism, which is the very thing that happened to our socialism. I would say that you can be sure of an action if you're ready to risk the hostility of your friends on account of it...

"We all tend to congregate with people whose company and conversation we enjoy. At this very moment you'll find a particular sort of people in one meeting place, while on another premises they'll be quite different. It's all wrong. We are quite capable of working ourselves into a state in which we'll be convinced that we are actually free because there is no one depriving us of our freedom. It's vital that we take the disagreeable step of making contact with people whose company we don't relish. There is one thing that afflicts people throughout their lives: the constant censoring of their acquaintances and the weeding out of their friends. The need for harmonious coexistence in society drives people to create their own private societies instead of solving the problems of society as a whole."

THURSDAY, 22ND MARCH 1979

The camp was laid out on an enormous arable field that sloped down gently towards the west. There were no buildings, just tall wooden posts joined at the top by a mesh of wires. From a distance it looked like empty hop-fields in the spring. From nearby I could see that wire cages with one-metre-square cross-sections were hanging from the upper horizontal wires. They looked like the boxes used for growing individual tomato plants. Most of these crates were empty, but here and there, at a distance from each other, people were squatting in some of them, one to a crate. I approached one of the occupied crates and examined the arrangement. There were no guards and no one complained about anything. I noticed that the soil between the rows of wire boxes had been raked in criss-cross fashion and I got a sudden fright that I might have left some solitary footprints of my own.

Today and yesterday I worked on the spring feuilleton. I still haven't got the punch-line right. I'll have a look at it tomorrow morning. Then I shall type it and hand it out tomorrow too. I am late with it already, but oh, how I didn't want to do it at all!

The difference between my feuilletons and what I write here is as great and strenuous as the difference between two opinions. Here I only reflect my feelings and my thoughts; there I am obliged to express them effectively. There I think about the reader; here about myself. Should readers of my feuilletons happen to read this diary, they could well be disgusted – so which of the pictures is valid, and which one am I? There is only one of me.

It was Mojmír who disrupted my writing this morning. He came to tell me not to take seriously what he said about my friends and above all not to spread it around. That's disagreeable. I cannot help keeping such records. I shall have to start calling him Dalibor here.

People might well be amazed at the liberties I take. When I describe my own actions here, I have either carefully considered them or disguised them anyway. As far as Padlock is concerned, it is all common knowledge. When this work comes to be published, I will not be doing it anymore and other people can tackle it the way they like. If someone protests that I have failed to give a true or faithful rendering of their words, it is my wish that his or her version be given preference and greater credence. For reasons of courtesy, if nothing else. I don't care. I cannot see any other way of producing an authentic picture of the present day, and a more favourable situation might never occur again. If people start avoiding me, I shall not be surprised or offended, and, anyway, in time everyone will forget about it and things will be the way they were. I am the one I threaten most: I am giving the police spychologists something to get their teeth into. But I know that by coming to terms with myself, I am better prepared to come to terms with God as well.

Today was warm and sunny. I went over to see Jan Vladislav. I gave him some books and got some others in return. Five or six years ago or thereabouts I did not know him. It hardly seems possible. He's a tough cookie. The day they cut him open they will discover his annual rings are narrow and close together. When I came to him with my Padlock that time, he welcomed me with his Quarto Editions. He had started his even earlier. We swap books and mutually adopt some of the other's titles. His wife, Maru, always offers me something to eat – chidingly: "Well? Do you or don't you?" If I hesitate, she reminds me that even Professor Patočka was sometimes wont to eat at their table, though he too had to know how to make up his mind. In Patočka's place, albeit lacking his breeding and intellectual depth, I end up eating things I do not even like, because by then I must. If I fail to appear for a long time, she sends me a note by post: "Why haven't you been here for so long?" They both tell me what they heard on the radio, but each differently, and they then proceed to argue about it in brief, 15-second bursts. On my way out, Vladislav always makes me sit down on a low bench to put my shoes on, because he made it for the purpose. His books of fairy tales are being sold abroad by the Artia state publishing house at enormous profit – minus his name.

Someone smuggled out a letter from Mr. Václav. He apologises in case his reaction to my feuilleton offended me, and lets me know that the questions I had in mind were by no means foreign to him. "On the one hand, I realise that I can scarcely do anything else but what I'm doing, that I have no alternative, even if it means having everyone against me. But on the other hand, what never ceases to depress me is the thought that I am basically an extravagance as far as the majority of citizens are concerned. What's the answer? I don't know. And your feuilleton didn't give me one. Maybe your feuilleton goaded me for precisely that reason: that it seemed to be giving the answer, but in fact it was the wrong answer... Perhaps it's a theme for a novel, perhaps I'll try to come to terms with it in a play, perhaps it needs a philosopher like Patočka. In all events a feuilleton debate won't provide the answer. This present one seems to be barking up the wrong tree entirely (and that includes my own contributions). However, the fact that the topic was broached at all – albeit clumsily; I'd even say idiotically – is a good thing and extremely important. And to hell with Ella Horáková. – Best wishes and a friendly hug."

Madla came home from work in the evening and told me what people are saying: that Pavel Kohout is working for the secret police along with sixteen others. "Sixteen people for the whole republic or just Prague," I asked. "You didn't hear about it?" she said. – "No, and I don't plan to, either."

I was asked a question: "Do you think I still have plenty of years to live?" – "Ever since I've known you, you've maintained that you won't live long and I have counted on the fact," I said. "Are you frightened all of a sudden?" – "No, I'm not. I just find it odd that my remaining life," at the words "my remaining life," I looked at her more attentively, "might no longer be counted in years." How strange! How odd! But I was right to surmise she was enjoying life! And now the plant is frost-bitten. "What sort of welcome did you get from the factory doctor?" I asked. "A very friendly one, would you believe it? I had some caustic words ready for her, but she was scared out of her wits and asked why I hadn't gone straight to hospital." – "Most likely she'd already had a dressing down from the district health officer," I suggested.

Zdena has to go into hospital on Monday. She was given a probe to swallow but it registered nothing and she is no better. They therefore intend to continue their tests in hospital. "And seriously, please don't come to see me!" – "Great!" I said.

Madla heard from someone that a few days earlier there was apparently something on Voice of America about Zdena's adventures of August last year. As I do not inform her of such events this was the first she had heard of it. "You got yourselves into a pickle again, the pair of you," she declared with a virtuous smirk. "*We* did? *They* did, you mean!" I said. "On the contrary, they can be pleased with themselves," she said, "that you took the bait. It would have been cleverer of you to keep quiet about it." – "On the contrary. They probably counted on us keeping quiet, and assumed it would be too delicate a matter for anyone to take Zdena's part. I can hardly thank enough those women who wrote that letter to Husák. – It was my friends who disappointed me." – "I expect they have more sense and taste than you have."

The delicate nature of the case first became evident at Hrádeček last September. I had gone there for the regular annual gathering at the Havels', firmly convinced that the ball was now in my friends' court and it was up to them to make a move. My friends now had to prove that there was some direct link between themselves and Zdena, not merely a roundabout connection. She had typed out books for all of them. They had all accepted her. She had been working on Padlock from the outset and in recent years had literally become a professional, declaring her activity to the local authority and paying taxes on it. The State Security ordered her to be investigated for parasitism: How do you support yourself? How much do you earn? Who pays you? In the end, I felt it would not be such a big mistake if she were to name a number of authors who had recently ordered work from her and paid for it. The authors agreed, but Zdena was reluctant and got her lawyer (Dr. Danisz) to explain to her all about parasitism, and how the law stipulates that even whores have to be treated properly, which proves that it is quite simply a case of intimidation and blackmail of the direst kind. It would be too costly to prosecute. So one sunny day they called her in again, shouted at her (in Slovak as it was Major Rybár, but they still won't let us have a dissident typist!) and when she failed to give them any names, they carted her off.

At Hrádeček, Pavel proposed that we set ourselves up officially as a literary partnership – which did not strike the rest, or me, as wise – with Zdena being declared as our secretary or something – I'm not sure exactly – whereby we'd have supposedly provided her with a cover. (Wrong: we'd have exposed her to every kind of coercion.) Two friends, I don't recall who, expressed the view that the attack on Zdena was actually aimed at me, and that – to tell you the truth I forget exactly what they said; I registered nothing except that it was only to be expected and I just had to put up with it, and in fact it *was* my business. It was embarrassing for me, but I was obliged to tell them that both Zdena and I were counting on the sort of support that any member of our community of friends or Charter 77 signatories might expect. The hesitancy that then manifested itself was unbearable both for myself and Mr. Václav: he withdrew for a moment and returned with the text of a statement that was intended to be sent somewhere, I don't know where, and don't even know whether it was sent in the end. About a week later, Zdena Tominová started to organise a women's protest letter to the President. I don't remember now how many signatures she obtained, but I know of two that were absent because of the delicacy of the case: even though such protests were by now more or less a routine, those two women were unable to disregard their friendship for Madla, and were quite simply incapable of reconciling the two things.

That experience taught me two lessons: first, that I was not to entertain illusions, and second, that I had to find a way of exercising responsibility for Zdena and no longer rely on anybody else. I would not have her typing just anything. I would not swallow her pretence at being someone stronger than she could possibly be. She wrote a complaint to the Ministry of Labour that she was unable to obtain employment (but that she refused to take work below her qualifications!) and she received an incredible reply: the offer of a post as mathematician-analyst in a firm; she was escorted there – kindly almost – by some official of the local authority. "I wish to point out that I have been expelled from the party and that I signed Charter 77." "That doesn't interest us," came the reply, at the very time when another signatory, Dana Němcová, was being forced to leave even her job as a cleaning woman at a school. A ploy of some kind? She joined the staff in November; it is now March. Never having studied mathematics, she scarcely understands the sort of work they will be wanting from her one day. They have given her lecture notes, regulations, text books and instructions how to write computer programmes, and simply ignore her. A kind of internment? It is seven minutes' walk from home. "Now you don't even have the time to commit an offence on the way to work or back," I said. Salary: 2400 crowns gross. There is one thing she has realized already: the equipment around her could transcribe Padlock all on its own, non-stop.

Yesterday Madla said: "The word's going round in Prague that you're giving up Padlock because Zdena can't type it any more." – "Who told you that?" I asked, but Madla never tells on Otka. – "So I'm asking," she said, "whether you'll still be doing Padlock when I retire." – "Don't you worry." – "But I don't want to type out every piece of nonsense." – "Don't you worry. I won't be giving you the thing I'm writing now." But Zdena won't get it either, by the look of things.

As a rule, I remember and record here only one dream per night: either the most striking or the closing one. Naturally, I have also had on several occasions that pathetic dream of all men in my situation, in which the two women are engaged in friendly conversation. Each time I quietly slip away: Let them have their fun! But I won't talk about it here; that would be bad taste of an almost literary variety.

SUNDAY, 25TH MARCH 1979

Today was the first proper spring day. I grafted apricots and yellow plums on to the plum tree. Whereas I have been successful at grafting apples and pears, I only get about fifty percent response from the stone fruit. I therefore did everything in duplicate. Yesterday Madla told me that nothing gave her pleasure any more, but apparently it is better today. This morning, we went over to Všenory to see Kosík but he had not arrived yet. I left him a copy of my feuilleton "Spring is Here" under a stone inside the gate, along with a message for him not to chop down the gnawed saplings; we would graft them with their own grafts. Several times during the day, Madla left what she was doing and came to me with questions like: what was I thinking about, how was my writing progressing, was I waiting for her to die, whether we should transplant the azalea that is too close to the juniper, and whether Hejdánek might not think I'm starting to lose my nerve.

I don't know what Hejdánek thinks, apart from what he directly wrote about me, but even that gave me no pleasure. They all write to me things that I could equally write to them. I too am aware that the honest labour of the working people helps hold up the regime, but I dislike the idea of a bad regime plus bad workers. I too share the hope that in prison there is a possibility for self-improvement and refinement, so why do people think they have to write to me about it? Without heroic deeds, humanity's spirit would have never come into being. Even Hejdánek's answer in *Letters to a Friend* is a defence of the group spirit, the spirit of a group that includes me. What I tried to do, however, was to take a bit of a sideways step. Whatever happened to imagination, humour, wit and tolerance? I have stuck to one main theme throughout my life. What I do is to orbit around it and take the liberty of publishing reports from my orbital position. I am also capable of looking at it from the opposite side, and I have the right and indeed the obligation to do so. I can sometimes have two or even three opinions about something, depending on my mood, state of health, circumstances, or most recent experience. At a particular meeting where the establishment of a "Patočka Tribunal" was discussed, I said that I tend to have more than one opinion about things. That made them laugh and Hejdánek gave me a bit of a drubbing. People who are not capable of having more than one opinion do not think, they just go straight ahead. I fear that what people regard as thinking is often no more than the ordering of new knowledge and perceptions in such as way as not to disturb those that are already filed. Hardening the stone. People can't stand it when you fail to live up to their image of you. Their inability to accept you is interpreted as a defect in your character, not in theirs. A case in point is Pavel Kohout. He has on his conscience the stupidity of a million or so Czechs! Joe Citizen sees two things and they do not seem to be connected in any way;

it's obviously a mistake that has to be put right; so he immediately starts to concoct a theory: Hübl must have ambitions to be President!

I dug over the potato bed. It is a debased manner of reading. It is now the trend to read every text with a political eye. Any essay that has any depth at all is immediately treated as if it were a draft parliamentary speech, an exclamation of annoyance becomes a sharply-worded memorandum, a joke is acceptable only if it can be interpreted as satire. A text of aesthetic merit is only acclaimed if its subject-matter happens to be – at the very least – human rights, spiritual valour or resistance to the mighty. But it is also possible to write with the intention of teasing people, provoking and confusing them, and pulling the rug out from under them! And lastly, I can also talk about politics anti-politically. ("That'd be right up your street, Ludvík, wouldn't it?" – Z.M.)

Afterwards I chopped some branches for a while. I had scarcely placed the trimmed branch on the high chopping block when I was assaulted by the song: "Niagara so sadly roars, all day and all the night..." and it gave me no peace until I switched over to Škvorecký. Danny's conversation with Marie and her daughter Daniela is a delightful gem of amorous dialogue. At our place last Friday, Ivan Klíma declared that he had not particularly liked *Engineer of Human Souls*. He says *The Swell Season* is better. He feels that the torrent of anecdotes is a sign of indiscipline and long-windedness and that Škvorecký has done something quite frightful with language. The book's language – dreadful slang and a mixture of Czech and English – exemplifies something I too have always found repulsive and criticised. Here it didn't bother me. (I have two views on it.)

Once she came to me to ask: "Isn't it striking that the ones who are most offended are those who have been to prison, but not for ten-year stretches?" This is also a concoction – but a nice one. I gave it some genuine thought before saying: "Well, maybe those who have served ten-year jail sentences have nothing more to learn and they don't read any more."

MONDAY, 26TH MARCH 1979

I went to bed last night at four o'clock this morning. I woke up at eight o'clock, for no reason. I found it odd; I am coming round to the view that there are clever autonomous organs inside each of us that take measures for our good but have no way of explaining it to us. One should quite simply heed them. So I started to act as if a house search was in the offing. A lot of things I destroyed, but I also left something for them to take away; they are only human too; they can hardly go back empty-handed to their base with the shameful report: there wasn't the tiniest scrap of paper for us! Half-an-hour later the doorbell rang insistently. But it was only friend C., bringing me the first and larger half of completed task "D" from friend B. We savoured it over coffee and a slice of bread.

I met Trinkewitz today on Charles Square. "What are you up to?" I asked. "I'm packing," he replied. "What does that mean," I asked with fake curiosity and he was suddenly covered in confusion. "Oh, I'm moving to Hamburg. Hadn't you heard?" – "No I hadn't," I said in feigned surprise. "It's your affair, but I wouldn't have expected it after your article." My friends can testify that I am often boorish, though they believe me when I say it's not intentional, just awkwardness and lack of breeding. This time it was intentional. Trinkewitz's warlock features underwent a strange transformation, as if a solid, finely-chiselled wood-carving was starting, of its own accord and without the touch of a knife, to lose shape and disintegrate. In order to halt this destructive process I said: "You see, I was very impressed by your decision to go about with a dagger under your coat." – "That still applies," he said and patted his jacket.

I had met him near Café Slávia a couple of days after Medek was assaulted; we talked about it and Trinkewitz said: "I carry this around with me now," and pulled the dagger out a short way. I thought to myself that it was an extremely proper move – if done by a big, strapping fellow like me. In his case, I could not reconcile it with his black-and-white frailty, but you never can tell.

Now we boarded the same tram and of his own accord Trinkewitz gave me his condensed life-story: a half-Jewish child during the war; after the war the son of a small businessman, and hence ineligible for study or employment in the field he had set his heart on. A brief period in the sixties when he could draw and write. Publishing activity forcibly interrupted. His efforts to find a living resulting in the confiscation of his studio. Reasons enough for leaving the promised land – promised to whom? – without reproach. Apart from all that, when we were sitting in the tramcar I was able to observe from close range the edge of the thick black beard surrounding his mournful mouth and could see that to a distance of three millimetres from the skin his beard was grey and the razor's edge had heaped up skin and blood among its roots. "Do forgive me for getting on at you in that way," I said, "but I can't help feeling that every departure weakens me." – "It does," he admitted, "but I don't intend to let them off the hook when I'm over there!" I pondered this and then said: "I don't know precisely what you have in mind, but when someone leaves here, they are gone. They shouldn't send us their imprecations. People here don't appreciate them very much anyway. It's better to fit into the culture over there and mix some of our experience into their stew. I like what Kristofori does – his semi-abstract pictures remind people there of the horror they fear irrespective of us." He said: "First and foremost I expect I'll complete my studies there, and then I'll see." I wished him all the best and we parted.

I met Vladimír Karfík. "I'm so relieved!" he exclaimed. "It's not true about Kolář!" But I didn't know what wasn't true: that he had died. "He phoned me yesterday," Vladimír said. – "How is he?" – "He says he's beginning to do a bit of work." Trefulka would soon be fifty, I told him; might he not write something about him, perhaps? He said he had not read Trefulka's latest pieces and did not have them. I shall lend him them. Vladimír is a literary critic but has been working as a water surveyor, living in a trailer somewhere; he is already fed up with it and has given in his notice, but has no idea what he'll do next.

I made a quick visit to Zdena's empty flat to find out whether we were of one mind about what ought not to be left lying about unattended. Everywhere spick and span, the carpets swept, the refrigerator switched off, the typewriter – its firebox now cold – covered as if she had no intention of typing for a long, long time to come. I bought the last rose they had in the shop and set off for the hospital, six minutes' walk away. It is a small, old hospital, quite cosy inside. There are only three beds to a ward. The corridors were full of old men and women. Although it was not a visiting-day, they called Zdena for me. We went down to the basement so she could have a smoke. "You look a bit too calm somehow," I said, "did they give you something?" – "Not so far. But I am calm, because I am here at last. Yesterday – yesterday I was too pissed off with your whole family." – "Yes. Naturally." – "You don't have to come here. Look in on Bibisa sometimes instead." Bibisa is quartered at Gruša's with her Pekinese comrades Cézanne and Diana. "Apparently Jirka has already written twenty pages of his new novel. How many have you done?" – "A hundred and twenty. But that isn't what counts. What counts is quality." – "Won't you tell me anything about it? Not even here?" I shook my head. Then I said: "You'll all be unpleasantly surprised." – "That doesn't matter," she said. "But does it have a happy ending at least?" – "I haven't a clue." She speculated about the possible meaning of those words. Over her light-blue pyjamas she was wearing a long, red, quilted dressing-gown with a white collar.

TUESDAY, 27TH MARCH 1979

The grey walls of the canyon opened up cinematically before me as in my childhood. In places the rocks crumbled down almost to the track along which I was heading north on foot. Down here there was a deathly silence, but from the swaying of the trees at the edge of the canyon above, I could tell that a desolate wind was blowing over the landscape. I looked back over my shoulder from time to time, in hopes of catching a glimpse at last of that southern sun, but I kept going north! I wasn't carrying anything. Views of the surrounding gorges opened up between the rocks, but I didn't dare go into any of them. Now and then I passed a tree. Each time, its trunk, up to my eye level, was grey from mud, and there were wisps of old grass in its lower branches. Had a torrent swept this way? But there was no stream here. "I wanted to lie down with you," suddenly Ester said at my side, even though no Ester had been there before. "But there was nowhere for us to go. So I went to my friend's to borrow the keys. She happened to be sitting at a table with some man. She gave me the keys and left. I don't know how it happened but the next thing I knew I was in bed with him." – "Do tell me more. It's good for me." – "Maybe I shouldn't have told you at all?" – "Why are you telling me?" – "So you'll find it easier to part from me. I'm leaving." – "Where to?" – "Hamburg." Suddenly, at those words, a river was flowing north to the left of me. Four unbelievably real white swans were flying above it, with long necks stretched northerly. "You see," I said sorrowfully, "the key should have been for me. Now you're leaving for Hamburg and the two of us didn't even get to the letter H." I let her walk ahead of me, so I could weep behind. It was like a dream within a dream. The river was really racing along! Dark ephemeral eddies rushed along it like balls of the blackest sorrow from crudely sentimental songs, but it was true. "I don't believe it," I said, "what's that you said?" – "It's already happened." – "Well you'd better be ready not to find anything anywhere. Run along!" She walked ahead of me dejectedly, her legs passing each other like a woman's legs, and I was very sorry for them, sor-ry, sor-ry, sor-ry... I strained my eyes, something strange was coming nearer. It was a shack nailed together out of logs and planks. Some kind of rigging stuck out of it and it was surrounded by logs, old pots and pans, ladders and other old junk. It was like a dream within a dream. Below the eaves were nailed three enormous heads carved out of wood: a black one in a white hat, a yellow one in a straw hat, and a red one with a feathered head-dress. All round the shack there stood dry, rotting tree-trunks; on the highest trunk, which was forked, there was a multi-storey dovecote with many holes. Wonder-struck, I moved closer and said to myself with relish: Now they ought to start shooting at me; why aren't they shooting? No one is allowed to come here; defend yourselves! Why aren't you defending yourselves? But the Yukon shack was deserted – dead; only the three masks looked stiffly over my head at the rocks, because – I turned round – the river wasn't there. In its place there glistened a cold, oval lake shimmering slightly. I also have somewhere to run to, I said loudly.

But I should, it strikes me only now, have looked around me; somewhere there must have been a sort of small mound of weathered stones.

WEDNESDAY, 28TH MARCH 1979

The Lucerna was only about two-thirds full. There is flu about. We were seated – Madla, Ondřej and I – on the second balcony, in other words, up near the ceiling. We felt a draught on our backs from somewhere in the darkness. I was sitting directly over the violins and could see their scores, and so could follow the progress of the music. The programme included Dobiáš's *Sonata for piano, strings, wind quintet and timpani*, followed by Schubert's *Mass in A flat major*. For some reason or other, the organisers changed the programme sequence and half the audience left after the Schubert. Mojmír (Dalibor) did not come; I expect he is ill.

I placed both fists on the rail, supported my chin on them, and amused myself by experimenting with the different musical effects to be gained from moving my head to right or left. When I turned my left ear to the ceiling I could only hear the high voices of the red-robed women's choir. With my

She walked ahead of me dejectedly, her legs passing each other like a woman's legs ... (p. 129)

right ear I was able to hear the entire polyphony, but it bounced off the ceiling as if from an over-modulated speaker. When I had both ears balanced I could hear in marvellous stereophony: the music emerged from the entire hall below me. From the platform beneath me came the sound of the violins and the back row of the audience were playing double-basses. I was afraid of dropping off to sleep, being tired. But my tiredness only expressed itself in the well-known phenomenon of seeing double: when I wanted to scrutinise something I had to strenuously merge the two images.

What I wanted to scrutinise carefully was the violin part of the Schubert Mass just below me, at the moment during the Gloria when the entire string section was engaged for ages – half-an-hour perhaps – sawing out semi-quaver seconds, up and down, in slow moderato, with an unchanging, even intensity. At first I accepted it as something quite normal, but suddenly it struck me as singular, whereupon I ceased hearing anything else. What the chorus and the rest of the orchestra were doing I now perceived solely as a kind of background music, while for me the main message and affirmation was contained in the wave-like rise and fall of the notes, which, on the contrary, were perhaps originally intended only as a background to the divine Latin communication originally with God. I should really like to know if Schubert wrote it like that or whether it was first perpetrated by today's officiating priest Václav Smetáček, or whether it was just my mood today after the incident with the northerly flowing river and the swans above it; the elated submission to the Glory of God was punctured from below by an unsubmissive rage that continued and pumped itself into the prayer, to such an extent that I was unable to think of anything else and I too started to rage: against our fate, our enslavers, and the brutishness whose priorities would have made sure that some little Havel never built this hall, and I started to wish that the whole Lucerna along with me and the philharmonic would sink into the past – the earth – leaving behind just an abyss full of stagnant water with a couple of rotten planks floating on it, allowing the cholera to behold its own beautiful face in that water!

I said half-an-hour; in fact it was only a couple of minutes, but even so it was almost an entire page of the violin score, and I cannot be sure they were semi-quavers; they might have been quavers seen double. And the conductor officiated like a priest; I clearly saw that neither his coat-tails, nor his hair, nor his cheek-pouches billowed in theatrically polished gestures, but instead he stood there bolt upright as rigidly as in a stiff chasuble and his dignified gestures truly conveyed liturgical exaltation and benediction; I almost saw a chalice and a monstrance, but each time the conductor would remember where we were and the movement of his outstretched arm transformed itself into something else at the last moment and ended with the entry of a new instrument or a bang on the kettle-drum.

After the intermission, half the people left. After the Mass no one had any desire to even hear the Dobiáš, whom they did not trust. I felt sorry for him. He died last year. He also wrote a couple of political numbers, so the public was obliged to criticise him now to give him a lesson. We, of course, stayed. Dalibor actually obtained us the tickets on account of him. I cannot say anything about the sonata; it is modern music, seemingly out of keeping with the Schubert, but I think not. It is a mighty song, loud on the ear like a celebration of some kind, but in reality tragically mournful. A chorus of silent, lonely people is singled out; the truth is revealed.

I too have always wanted to play or sing somewhere. In 1971 or there-abouts, Dr. Excellovacuous took me to St. Giles, where they were in need of an extra violin. He used to pipe there on an oboe. I went there twice without my fiddle to see whether I might be able to cope. When I was beginning to get the feeling that I might, the choirmaster had second thoughts and did not accept me because they might ban music in the church altogether on my account. He was quite right and Dr. Excellovacuous was more devastated about it than I was. I heaved a sigh of relief that I would not have to go somewhere three times a week. In the Baťa School Symphony Orchestra I was absolutely reliable and I would not have skipped rehearsals.

THURSDAY, 29TH MARCH 1979

Today I drove with Karel Kosík to his garden to graft the gnawed apple-tree saplings for him. I had to lie on the ground to do it, or I would not have been able to see.

Karel's garden is on a steep slope. At the bottom there is a small flat area with a wooden cottage. Then narrow terraces rise up to another flat area at the top where Karel enjoys visits from friends under two mighty trees: a walnut and a cherry. They have to get all their water from the stream, their beer from the pub. He is not happy with the shape of the terraces. He is reshaping them and buying topsoil for the purpose. My work finished, he invited me to the pub for lunch. I felt like a proper expert. Karel praised my latest "Spring is Here" feuilleton. I said: "You are praising me out of a sense of duty." – "Not at all, Ludvík. No one knows how to voice people's feelings the way you do." – "Voicing what everyone knows is no great achievement," I said, fed up because I should like to come up with a new idea, a brand-new one! "I don't agree with you there," he said, "because people often don't realise what they know, and only when it is explicitly stated does it become obvious to them. Words are even capable of creating a new reality."

Now I am even more curious about what Karel is writing. What if he ends up discovering all on his own that the world arose from the Word!

In Prague, I let Karel off in Smíchov and drove on to see Mrs. Bookbinder. I parked in a different street, and as there was a little while left until the appointed hour, I went and rummaged in the second-hand bookshop. At five o'clock I rang the doorbell. Her daughter, about fifteen years old, answered the door; it is a mystery to me how old her mother is. Her mother works in the bookbinding workshop of a government agency that would prefer to remain anonymous. She takes books either one or two at a time in her handbag, first to work and then home again. It means that binding takes a long time with her, but it is a safe place for titles that would feel unsafe elsewhere. On this occasion I was coming for the annual volume of feuilletons for 1977/78. The workshop does not have suitable lettering, so I have had a stamp with interchangeable years made in a metal workshop. It is also safer for Mrs. Bookbinder that way.

But Mrs. Bookbinder is not afraid. In fact I was the one who got a fright when she once showed me her own book collection, also typewritten. I bought from her a beautifully bound copy of Solzhenitsyn's *The Oak and the Calf*, and it was a long time before I went back again. But then I found myself in a tight corner and I sought her out once more. Everything she binds she also reads, and I suspect that is why the work takes so long. Sometimes she says: "When will I bind one of yours?" or "Are you bringing yourself for binding?" She is a working woman, no more nor less, and I often think about what working people used to be like: proud and quick-witted. It is also a mystery to me who she lives with.

She loaded the books into my bag without a word, and sat down, thin and pale, in an armchair; I sat in the armchair opposite; she lit a cigarette

"I don't agree with you there," he said, "because people often don't realise what they know..." (p. 133)

and sat in thought as if getting ready to say something momentous, until at last she said: "It's all a waste of time." "What is?" I asked, out of concern for my books. With her cigarette she pointed in the direction of the window and through the window to the world in general: "All of it." She propped her chin on her palm and then leaned into it, so that her long dark hair fell forward and she remained sunk in thought for a long time, her eyes on the floor, until at last she looked over at me, indicated my bag and said: "Those horrors of yours convinced me of it." I sat there for a while. I am never sure whether it is more appropriate to get up immediately after paying or to stay for a few words. The fact is that I would like to speak to her more, but I do not want her to think I am only going through the motions. I got up. Wordlessly, she accompanied me to the lobby, where she said: "I won't be able to do anything for a while." I said: "That's a pity. We're just finishing another year's collection of feuilletons." She stood leaning against the wall. She reflected a moment and then said in a flat voice: "Bring it over then." I have even wondered on occasions whether she would be as cold and mute in an embrace. "I'll bring it then," I said, "along with a bunch of flowers, madam!" She gave a half smile. "There's no need!" Maybe that struck her as rather too blunt, because she immediately added: "...Unless," and she surveyed me with large, ironically dark eyes, "you wait for the autumn crocuses."

I drove home repeating to myself: autumn crocuses, autumn crocuses! *Autumn* crocuses!!

At home I did a bit of reading: just some sci-fi short-stories by some Pole. Nothing very perceptive, but there was one sentence in a story that takes place on Mars in the twenty-fifth century that was very good: "Psychologists are coming to the conclusion that children of a certain age shouldn't be taken from the Earth."

FRIDAY, 30TH MARCH 1979

Philosophy and all other branches of learning are increasingly becoming halls accessible only to delegates with increasingly expensive credentials. But I still hold the view that an entirely new and startlingly truthful discovery is more likely to be made by someone totally outside those halls. – That thought rankled in me yet again when I read in the astronomical magazine an article about how it was impossible to exceed the speed of light. Yet again they failed to disprove my idea that the speed of a moving source must either be added to the speed of the light that it emits or be deducted from it. What if the speed of light is not the movement of photons? What if there is no such thing at all as the speed of light? And what if there is some other state of which the speed of light is only one aspect?

I packed my briefcase, took my umbrella and set off for town. In the street everyone was in a rush and the cars were throwing up spray. I enjoyed watching the rain wash the smoke straight down the drain. I quite like rainy weather, so long as it is not unpleasantly cold. These past few days it has been. The first relief I afforded my briefcase was at Kléma Lukeš's, and while I was there I placed an order for some wine. Kléma asked me when I was going to write something and whether Pavel Kohout would return. I said I didn't know and rushed away because I had a date with Mrs. Helena D. Today she was handing in her first work in two years and she had invited me to spend some of her first money. We sat drinking grog in the Alfa. "I can even afford to buy something from you," she said with her gaze fixed on my briefcase. "Do you have anything interesting?" – "Well, I just might have. Incidentally, are we to be on first-name terms?" I asked. – "I don't know, you decide," she said. I hesitated and then broached the incident: "At the Kohouts' Turkish Soirée that time, you came and sat on my lap. It was in the presence of my wife, so there is almost grounds for familiarity." She shook the confusion from her hair and hands and said quickly: "Oh, that. I must have been drunk, mustn't I? Oh dear, if only I could say I was drunk! But I wasn't!" – "I don't think you were," I cautioned her. "So what was it all about?" – "Oh, but that happened two years ago, didn't it, so what makes you suddenly recall it, or why only now, now that we are – talking – together – again, for a while?" – I replied: "I, only now that we are somewhat – acquainted – am taking the liberty of talking about something that you, prior to our acquaintance..." – "But you're mistaken there!" she interrupted me. – "Sorry, it's just that I suddenly feel elated," I said. "Whenever I'm walking around these particular streets – Wenceslas Square, Národní and Příkopy – I am in a constant state of depression at the thought I won't meet anyone I know! Only five years ago, I would be bound to bump into someone. They've all gone." – "What do you mean? Where?" – "Either they're lying low, they've left Prague, or they've emigrated." – "Do you really have such a strict attitude on emigration?" she asked. – "When it's people I don't know, it annoys me. When it involves my friends, it grieves me. I feel it as a threat." – "Yes, you're bound to..." she said uneasily.

She had a childlike expression. In fact, she always has a sort of charmingly boyish face and boyish figure – above the table. But her gestures and facial expressions, particularly when she is, as now, slightly perplexed, are sophisticatedly feminine. She has noticed I am observing her. "But you, that time, at that – Turkish Soirée, as you called it – did you think very badly of me?" – "Did it worry you?" – "No. I mean, yes." – "I didn't think anything bad. But I found it a bit puzzling. I solved it by coming up with my own diagnosis, that you have a low threshold of presumption." – "Is that a very adverse assessment in your book?" – "Not in the least. It just makes for suspense. One would find out nothing more unless one was ready to cross that threshold." She firmly said nothing and stared into her glass. I left her alone. She shifted in her seat, raised her eyes, looked down again, then raised them after all and asked: "And did you want... that is to say, did it strike you?... I mean, that time! That you'd care to cross that threshold?"

It strikes me, dear diary, that you're beginning to let your imagination run away with you! There could not have been such a debate: it's beginning to look like something out of Škvorecký. And yet my factual memory tells me that we did indeed talk about that! I replied to the question I had been asked and then drew out of my pocket another slotted block. She looked at its indentations – a trifle wearily by now – and wordlessly put it in her handbag. "Do you know what that means?" I said. "What, sir?" – "That we shall see each other three more times." – "And what then?" – "The end." – "Well, well!" she laughed. "Not bad! Not bad at all! And why, may I ask?" – "It's not possible." She was absolutely, but absolutely, astounded. No – more, even. I felt odd. I added: "We are hardly going to start seeing each other, are we?"

Now she was paying the bill, getting up from the table, backing away, and dodging me; she was dashing off ahead of me down the stairs. At the bottom, before we went out among the people in the arcade, she turned and said: "And does such a misfortune loom – from your side – or mine – and would it really be such a misfortune, anyway?!" It would, and a great one too, I thought to myself.

Out on the pavement, I unfurled my umbrella; she came and joined me under it and walked along at my side without asking anything, almost resignedly. "I still have to call on the Chramostovás. Come there with me!" –

"Oh, that's super, I certainly shall!" and a spring entered into her step. We were just below the Museum when there was a sudden sharp gust of wind and the rain lashed us. First my umbrella turned inside out and then my cap flew onto the roadway where a score of cars and a dozen lorries immediately drove over it. I had to laugh. Helena stepped into the road, hooked up the cap with her fingertip, brought it back and waited. I was standing holding the bizarrely misshapen umbrella, with water running down my glasses. We ran on like that.

I vaguely hoped that only Standa would be home, but Vlasta welcomed us as well. They let her out yesterday. She was pale, but otherwise pretty well. She greeted us with a happy whoop and no amazement. But Standa remained mischievously silent as I related my mishap, and then he said: "That's OK, that bit I understand, rain, wind, an accident. But that still doesn't explain to me how the two of you come to be together." Vlasta snapped at him: "They had a date, stupid!" – "Thank you. That's perfectly in order," said Standa. "That's quite sufficient explanation. And I must say that it's a great idea of Ludvík's to strike up relationships with young women who won't have a chance to take things too far." I did not follow. Helena blushed. "What do you mean?" I asked. – "Oh, I thought you were in the know too. Our Helenka is emigrating, of course!"

Later, when I had repaired the umbrella, and my sodden cap had dried slightly in front of the electric stove, I accompanied Helena to the tram stop. I won't speak another word! She also maintained an appropriate silence. When the tram was already in sight, I said: "We might as well say our final farewell here and now, then." – "I understand," was all she squeaked. We shook hands. She boarded the tram, her face a mask. I still feel bad about it, even now. I don't know when, where, nothing. Why do I feel deceived?

But the houses stand here just as they did before; my bag has not let itself be bamboozled by anything and like a well-brought-up thing is pretending that it heard nothing and saw nothing, that nothing happened.

Zdena looked all puffy from sleep or drugs. She spoke faintly and list-lessly, and as she walked she touched the wall for safety's sake. "Have they done anything with you yet?" – "I've no idea. I have the feeling they just keep taking blood samples." – "No results?" – "I don't ask. Yesterday I was literally crawling about on my knees. They gave me an injection and a Vítek tablet, but they wouldn't give me a second dose." – "What did they give it for, and what is it?" – "A kind of tablet, for the spine. I was crawling about on my knees from the pain. But they say it's no good for the stomach." – "You've got it from the typing." – "And from those beams in the barn, remember?" Seven years ago the two of us took apart the roof of an enormous barn and used the timber to repair her house. We rolled the beams to the house on wooden rollers, but there was some lifting to do as well.

"As soon as you get out of here, we'll go away somewhere for two days," I said. – "Oh you. Say three, at least!" – "Three, then," I said. She started to laugh, taking care not to move: "We'll do it the tried and trusted way. You'll go on Monday afternoon, spend Tuesday away and return home on Wednesday afternoon. In fact it'll be two days, but I'll count it as three. You know me, I'm generous that way."

SUNDAY, 1ˢᵗ APRIL 1979

We were waiting for the stove to start heating up. Madla said: "I came back from an errand and I found a man sitting in the waiting room. He was stout and oldish, a working-class type. 'Who are you waiting for?' I asked. The lady doctor. I went inside. Olga and Líba were sitting there. 'Where's Marcela?' I asked, 'there's someone waiting for her.' – 'She's on study leave,' Líba said. – 'So why are you letting that fellow wait out there?' And they told me that Marcela said she might drop by. I asked them if they knew what the man wanted. They didn't. So I went and asked him. He had already had a number of previous appointments with us and Marcela had given him some tests to do. But then she didn't tell him how they turned out, and the results didn't interest him. Now his wife was divorcing him and using the results of the tests as an argument in the divorce suit. He wanted to know what they showed. I went and found his file and asked Olga and Líba if one of them would read it to him as I – officially – wasn't supposed to know anything about the files, or deal with clients. Líba said, 'I'm not sure if he's allowed to know about the tests, though, seeing as it's a court case.' I told them it was his test, after all. And I went and read him a note that said he had been invited to attend the preliminary session and he hadn't turned up or excused himself. 'You might be right there,' he said. Then he thanked me and went away. When I returned to the office the two of them were complaining to each other about how unfair it was: Olga had met Hatoňová on Purkyně Street, and she, as a dentist, was earning almost three thousand, whereas they, as psychologists, only made two thousand six hundred, even though they have to work with the whole person. What would you say to that?"

"They are young, state-owned livestock," I said.

It was cool today. April weather. I gathered up the wood I had chopped during the winter; there was so much that by now it had sunk into the earth and was beginning to rot. Then I transplanted three two-year-old grafted saplings, but it was hard to find room for them. Madla was doing some sewing; she had no wish to come out; she was not feeling too well. Exceptionally we had the boys with us. Ondřej was replacing a rusty exhaust on Herzen, Jan was putting Švácha's gear-box back together. He has hardly driven it, but is always renovating it. I said to both of them: "You treat them the way the Cimrmán troupe treats the National Theatre. When the value of that junk reaches forty-five thousand, the price of a new car will be zero."

Multicoloured clumps of primulas are beginning to spread charmingly all over the Kosíks' terraces. They invited me to tea; I did not want to detain them or myself; Marie brought the cups and the tea outside and we drank it standing in the wind. I took the opportunity to ask Karel whether he had ever given any thought to the top speed of light. He said he never had and it did not even interest him. As I would not like to distort what he had said about the relationship of the word to reality, I brought it up again. "Last time you said that words can create a new reality. What sort of reality do you have in mind? Social, cultural..?" I did not want to give away my deliberate trap immediately. – "Not just social or cultural," he replied straight off, leaping over the trap. "I also mean the real surrounding world, and I don't maintain that words create it. What I have in mind is that people use words to define other aspects and characteristics of the world, whereby it broadens for them, and opens up, as it were." – "You're lucky," I said, "I was planning to catch you out." – "Go ahead. Tell me. I'm interested." – "I wanted to bring you round to the Word in the beginning." He replied: "It all depends what one means by the Word." – "Karel, I'm on tenterhooks already about what it is you're writing."

When I go to bed late, like yesterday, I get up at nine, like today, and before I get myself moving, have breakfast, and feed the bird life, it's ten or later, like now. What shall I see to? Writing the introduction to the completed feuilleton annual, or adding the commentary to the Indian book? But I have still to write up one interesting visit from yesterday. Catherine laid three eggs, as small as the nail on my little finger; blue-grey. Each time, she clucks like a hen; the tone is different of course, but the resemblance is touching. We're all amazed. Catherine is sitting on her nest and does not fly away even when I have to lean across her to water the plant behind the cage. She just moves her head, ruffles herself up and is so scared that a chirp actually escapes her, but she holds firm. She drives Philip away. She permits herself scarcely a minute away for a peck and a sip. She is beautiful.

We have a new typist, a retired lady. Yesterday, I picked up her first job: Patočka's essays on theatre. She even got it bound herself, and pasted the titles on the spine. It was perfect. However, when I opened one copy in the tram, I at once noticed "stund" in place of "stand." It's annoying: I shall have to make it very clear to the typist that that this will just not do; it means I shall have to read the book through again. I could really do with the assistance of some younger patriots when it comes to this kind of work.

I found Zdena yesterday in a much improved state. On Sunday, she had a visit from Ivanka Grušová and Dr. Danisz, who... "And he brought me an orchid! Imagine!" – "How many blooms does it have?" – "Three." – "Three times twenty-five is seventy-five. Hmmm!" I said appreciatively. We were sitting in a dark passage by the boiler room. Zdena praises the doctors and values the service, but the rest of the patient population gets her down. She told me how she had heard a lamentation from the lavatory: St. Joseph, Holy Mary, St. Joseph...! Some old lady had fallen behind the pedestal and could not get herself out. Zdena had pulled her out, carried her into the corridor, and supported her on a bench. There she took a rest and then lifted her up and carried her to her bed; meanwhile the nurse was searching for the mislaid wheelchair, warning her loudly: "Stop that at once! You mustn't!" I said: "You always were a work-horse, and one day you'll die a work-horse. The cart will roll over you." – "I'm already under the cart. All I'm doing is winking out from there." She was in such better shape that I made bold and asked: "What with?"

I came home and put my accounts in order, wrote some letters, and in various other ways put off the moment when I would have to start reading up on the Highway Code: the incident from Malostranské Square had been followed up and tomorrow I have to go for re-testing and "to present the vehicle for technical inspection." "It's interesting," said Madla, "that you always end up getting something even though you claim you don't drive. Our Phantom drives and doesn't get called in for re-testing." – "Your Phantom probably doesn't commit any traffic offences. Either that or he gets away with them because he's one of theirs!" Listlessly, she took herself off to the kitchen where she stuffed into a saucepan a lump of beef bagged on the way home from work, lit the gas, curled up on the couch and fell asleep. Josef Císařovský called in.

Josef Císařovský (henceforth J.C.) called in and asked me first of all to come out into the passage where he enquired when the deadline was for the Jaroslav Seifert birthday volume, as he would like to contribute some of his "lithographs" to it. The reason for the quotation marks is that he prints them on glass plates, which he sand blasts, using glass technology. However, I knew nothing about a birthday volume and asked where he had heard about it. "In Café Slávia today," he replied. "Well, if they're talking about it in the Slávia there was no point in our coming out into the hallway!" I have not set foot in the Slávia since Kolář left for Berlin.

We went back inside. He did not want coffee, tea or anything to eat. I had a smaller-sized, slightly broached bottle of Queen Anne and this I placed, more out of indifference than any desire, on the side table. We each sat down in an armchair and both put our feet up on a chair placed in between. "What are you up to?" J.C. asked to kick off the visit, and he chuckled for no particular reason. – "I'm reading the Highway Code." – "Are they hassling you again?" – "On this occasion, it was my own fault," I said. We clinked our first glasses. J.C. said: "I've already given up bloody driving, I've sold the car, and couldn't give a damn about it anymore." J.C. lives in Northern Bohemia, where he has a cottage in the middle of nowhere. He would really need a car, but they confiscated his driving licence straight after the Charter. But the way they confiscated it! They took it away from him at home: the car was not even anywhere nearby. In other words, out of sheer wilfulness. He wrote ten complaints, but only got two replies, both the same: We see nothing at fault in the action of the officers. At the present time, a Gypsy acquaintance of his is negotiating the purchase of a donkey for him. J.C. is equipping a two-wheeled cart and it will be fine.

He was now in Prague to enquire about the possibility of a bargain hernia operation. "What do you mean by a 'bargain operation'?" I asked. – "Well, I've got no money or insurance! Ever since those bastards kicked me out of the union, I'm not allowed to sell my stuff or exhibit. I've got no income. In fact, it's only the meadow, those sheep and the dog that keep me going," he chuckled. "And the chickens, of course." – "I was under the impression," I said, "that everyone had the right to medical treatment." – "I was told that operations aren't covered. Only first aid." – "And how much would an operation like that cost?" I asked. – "According to the tariff, five thousand. But if I could get a doctor friend to do it, then nothing." – "Well I'm not entirely sure, mate..." I said, "but I have a feeling that doing something for nothing might actually be against the law nowadays!" – "Quite right. It'd have to be secret or those fucking bastards would kick the doctor out of his job." – "That's for sure," I said. We talked about it for a little longer over our drinks. It struck me that as long as J.C. paid for the anaesthetic and the waxed thread, there need not even be any legal obstacle. But do people risk committing a good deed these days? After all, they investigate anyone who helps prisoners' families!

"And how did you manage to do it, for goodness sake?" I asked, pointing at his belly. – "My own stupidity! An anvil of mine was about to fall off the chopping block. I managed to catch it and pushed it back on the block while I was still bent over. And it weighs four hundredweight, the sow!" J.C. is as big and strong as a boar and all overgrown with ginger stubble, so he managed to push the old sow back up again. But since then he has been unable to do any heavy work. And on a homestead like that! "That must cause you difficulties in other areas too, doesn't it, Josef?" – "You bet! But anything's possible with a bit of skill and imagination – you know what I mean." We started to compare different positions we knew. In one case we were not entirely sure whether we each had the same thing in mind; J.C. tried drawing it, but in the maze of lines the essential information was illegible. That made him angry: confronted with unsuspected impotence in his own field! "Do you know I'm going to have to do a few sketches at home," he said, "to see how the two materials roll against each other at this point here." – "Sketch it? Maybe try it out first, instead," I said, as it seemed awfully artificial to me, and J.C., critically observing his sketch, said: "You're right there, you know. The fact is it wouldn't make a very good hernia position!" We burst out laughing. Little Queen Anne looked discomfited. We poured out the last glass, with the words: "Here's to that then!" That put paid to her.

I picked up the sketch, tore it up and took it to the lavatory. From the kitchen came the smell of boiled beef. I went to turn off the gas, but it was already off. This was an indication that Madla was not in the mood for company. She does not like meeting new people. Then J.C. noticed on the side-table some physics notes, lent me by my brother Emil, that I had left lying there. "You do physics?" – "Not likely, I was just looking at them now. The speed of light is getting on my fucking nerves," I said, so he would understand me better. – "Why?" – "Because it's supposed to be finite. What's your view?" He sighed and said: "Nobody knows in the final analysis what old Einstein took with him to the grave. He apparently wrote in his will that he had made some revolutionary discovery that was best not to know. And not long ago some fellow turned up in America – by the name of Benda would you believe – who refutes the whole theory of relativity. At first I was excited. Then I came up against an impenetrable wall, and ever since I've made do with just a taste of those things, and try to paint accordingly, and that's about it." That's great, that's something that Kosík should hear, it strikes me as I write this. I replied: "I have confirmed, through my own experience, that people's ambitions are greatest in fields where they are least adept. And that goes for me too!" I roared. – "You'll have to come to terms with it," he said, "we're both over fifty. We won't manage to screw all the women we fancy anymore." And I think he's right there.

At that moment, Madla came in, her face fresh and beautifully smooth. She greeted Josef with a smile; it was their first meeting, She had only heard about him up till then. I asked J.C. for news of a dispute with an erstwhile pal of his, who is now apparently a fucking bastard. "It's a right fucking mess, I tell you. Fuck it, I say," he replied with a laugh. "Because either I live and paint a few more pictures, or I do battle with bastards. I've chosen the former."

Back in 1968, when many of us had high hopes that life was just beginning again, J.C. suggested to four of his friends that they jointly set up a workshop, studio and artists' association in his back yard. He gave each of them a notional fifth of his property as a gift. When the Russians came in it became clear that such a splendid idea was unfeasible. J.C.'s association sensibly broke up and it was clear that each of them would have to seek his livelihood elsewhere. Their senses restored, the friends came to view their project as a dream of madmen and Josef's gift as a nice joke. Except for one, who insisted on it because he was a socialist realist; Josef paid him his fifth in cash and their association came to an end too. Mr. Raban, for that is his name, of Jankovcova Street 94, Prague 7, seized the opportunity and went full steam ahead. Not satisfied with his fifth, he wanted the house, the barn and the yard. He took the case to court and lost it at the first hearing and on appeal. But as the bastards started to become established in their posts, he managed to obtain a new court hearing. The judge opened the proceedings like a normal human being and during the first half it was clear that he intended to try the case according to law. Then there was a recess, and as J.C. tells it: "During the recess I heard from the back a very loud conversation, almost shouting. After the recess I witnessed the total transformation of a man into shit. The judge who came back was broken, crushed and humiliated. He just stared at the floor. Then, will you believe it, in unbelievable contradiction with everything that had gone before, he ruled that in addition to the money, I had to surrender the whole barn and part of my land."

At one moment during this evening it struck me – I am referring to the speed of light now – that something might come clear if I looked at it the other way round: i.e. if the speed that light travels was regarded not as a property of light but of space – as in the case of sound, incidentally. At that moment, the speed of the source clearly would not affect it. But then, of course, space is itself matter; space does not exist outside of matter; to place matter into space is nonsense, because space is only a dimension of matter, and all the enormous events in the universe, which are sought out, observed and measured so strenuously, are no more than internal processes within matter.

That was what was going through my mind while Madla asked J.C. all about it, from the very beginning, and listened to him spellbound.

THURSDAY, 5ᵀᴴ APRIL 1979

Things went well for me yesterday at the cops. They know me more personally than I thought, addressing me by name and treating me in exemplary fashion. They just gave the car a friendly jiggle. They did not even look at my identity card or driving licence. As if to say – after last year's shenanigans: If it were up to us, that's how we'd behave. Or alternatively: If only you were to stick to traffic offences, Mr. Vaculík.

Today it is rainy and cold. Nothing is going my way. I needed to speak with about five people, but I did not catch anyone at home or find them anywhere. Instead of life becoming simpler, it is becoming more complicated. Again I have three new manuscripts here to read. One of them is a history text-book! Are we really going to start typing out text-books as well, so that ten children at a time will retain an archival awareness of how things really were?

I put the remaining pieces of the puzzle in my pocket and went to take the bus to the place in question. No, it wasn't OK last time. She opened the door and stood dumbfounded. I had never before seen someone's face, covered at first in a mask of stony determination, change so many times beneath it in the space of one or two seconds. I forgot what I was intending to say, did not even say hello, and, forgetting myself entirely, could not help exclaiming quietly: "My, you're awfully distraught!" She looked as if she was falling and about to collapse. I crossed the threshold, naturally. After a few moments she at last spoke. She passed her hands over her face and said resentfully: "Does it really show that much?"

FRIDAY, 6ᵀᴴ APRIL 1979

The weather is foul. It makes it nice to be sitting at home, a clean sheet of coarse-quality paper, the kind I like, inserted in the typewriter. In the yard, the chestnut tree – horse-chestnut to be precise – is puffing itself up, and Philip and Catherine flitter over my head from time to time. But I must get dressed and go to buy a chicken. A topical riddle: What is long, moans and eats chicken? A queue for pork. – But we could not care less.

I have to go and pick up the bound Hájek and the wine ordered from Kléma Lukeš. I shall leave the Hájek till Monday, but the wine cannot wait: they would drink it. I am supposed to be delivering Patočka's essays on theatre, but those typing mistakes annoy me. A moment ago Eda Kriseová brought me her *White Lady* bound. The book has been guillotined a bit too close, and part of the picture on the frontispiece has been lost. Eda notes the fact wearily; she speaks about the book with a kind of reluctance – for her it is something three years old. I sense she has more recent things to worry about. I think I know what. We talk in the doorway, as best we can; she didn't even take her coat off; there is no point inviting her in. As we say goodbye she smiles with effort; she is on her way out.

In my typewriter I have a piece of paper with the page number on it, the kettle is on, the doorbell rings. It's an acquaintance. He has received my message about the hares gnawing Kosík's saplings and has bought me two. He has brought me them here. I am so taken aback that I forget to ask how much I owe; the man overloaded my grey cells with so much important information that I must not confuse. The tree saplings have an English name: Golden Spur Delicious. Karel will naturally want to know what the word spur means, but that happens to be something I have known for a long time! Karel will congratulate me once again on my rapport with nature, how important it is, how it helps improve my mind, and how Czech intellectuals must grasp the unique opportunity they now have, because everything is turning them inwards. That's true. I am drinking coffee and gazing at the paper in the typewriter. I have an urge to write something really good, but it is now time for me to go out on some errands. First of all to get a chicken, which will have thawed by my return. And it would be marvellous if I could manage to roast it so that it is cool by the time Madla comes home, and she won't know how long I've been gadding about.

I am back from town. It is evening. I was at Vlasta Chramostová's. I gave her one copy of the Patočka at discount and in return she will read it, spot the mistakes, make a list of them and I will take it to the typist so that she realises that it won't do, because I read everything after her! No one fools me! I bought the astronomical year-book, but a quarter of the annual ephemera they can shove somewhere. I only just made it in time for the wine – Pecka was getting ready to take it.

The Vltava is so full of brown water that the weir at Štvanice is nearly level. I went to the store next door for some razor blades. Two old-world shop-assistants work there. When you want washing soap they ask: "Will the Schicht soap with the stag do?" They have all sorts of slogans that I remember from those enamelled advertisements of the First Republic: *Radion* washes for you. *Obé* gives you a shine divine. I said I wanted some razor blades. "Ours or the English ones," the old assistant asked, and the other one mumbled from the back: "Oh, he won't want the English ones. What if they were found at his place!"

A postcard came from Jiří Kolář in Berlin. On one side is the Kurfürsten-dam, on the other the message:

It's Friday and spring
A strange unease
Has settled on me.

I had at least four dreams last night. The first of them was about a woman reader who came to the editorial office for some wooden bowls she had lent us. I accompanied her round the office, which was a workshop full of wire, mortar and battered barrels of lime; we stumbled over various tools; I pushed aside sheets of metal and boards leaning against the wall, in my search for the two bowls. I was terribly embarrassed and in the end offered the reader compensation of nine hundred crowns for each of the bowls. Then I opened the door to the adjacent room, which was my mother's old kitchen in Brumov. Madla was there, and when I told her what I was looking for, she pointed to the bench, where two wooden bowls were standing, one containing poppy seeds, the other beans.

In the second dream, I had come to Josef Zeman's to help him make a deserted cottage habitable. But Josef looked different; it was not really him, and the cottage was not the main thing. Alongside the cottage stood a small deserted factory; it had no roof, the windows were all knocked out, the equipment dismantled – all that remained of it were the cross girders under the ceiling and iron catches in the wall. Some of the walls were tiled and bands of dust on them indicated where the pipes used to run; it was a chemical works. The man I was supposed to help in the cottage came out of it and was climbing all over the factory on a ladder, cleaning walls, sawing off the protruding iron catches and indicating to me with hand gestures that all that was needed was to put on a glazed roof. I saw that it could make a very bizarre but cheerful studio. I just looked on in wonder that someone should take on such a formidable task single-handed.

The third dream was about the radio station, which I was leaving again, but the radio building was not situated lengthways along Vinohradská Street but at right angles to it and it had only two storeys. The corridors were full of hurrying people, none of whom I knew any more. They were all on their way to the canteen. I went along too. A long, wide table had been prepared there. They were just covering it with a white cloth, because a performance was due to start. The performer was supposed to be Dr. Ferdinand Smrčka's secretary, but when she appeared in front of the table she looked different: she had long hair, and a boy-like figure, without any bust. She was wearing a shiny white ballet dress; she was supposed to dance on the table. She took a run in order to jump up on the table, but she failed to jump and her stomach collided with the table top. She repeated this three times. I said to myself she must be bleeding by now. Then they helped her, fainting, onto the table, but I could not bear to watch. When her routine was over, she wended her way to me through the grey-suited audience and asked me why I had not watched. It had been a farewell dance for my benefit, she told me. In a state of agitation I walked along the corridors to the rear of the building where there was a row of editing booths; I opened the door of one. Inside there was a small table, like the folding ones in express trains, and at it two small chrome chairs with red plastic seats. On one of them sat Zdena. She told me that she was unable to leave and if ever I wanted to speak to her I would always have to come to her here.

The fourth dream was about my organising a mock funeral with a few people – actually there were a lot of them, but I was only supposed to know one or two. We were walking through a colonnade along a shiny marble floor in time with funeral music. Two men were carrying between them, under their arms, an empty open coffin. The funeral had a political significance. It was intended to represent the end of something and a victory. I had a minor role to play in it: I walked among the first three and was to see to it that the parade wheeled in orderly fashion. But wheeling, as everyone knows, is done about the flank man, either on the right or the left. And the right flank-man spoiled it: he did not know he had to mark time while the trio turned round him. It was "young" Bakonczyk from the 10th brigade at Baťa's.

I woke up to discover it was half past nine. Madla was still asleep too, while Mrs. Hemerková was already coming back from her second walk with Don, whose barking had woken me up. I put my oversleeping down to daylight-saving time and Voice of America's new broadcasting schedule: their programmes now start at ten p.m. Incidentally, they mentioned yesterday that the US Supreme Court had decided that traffic cops are no longer permitted to stop cars for random checks but must have a specific reason to do so. They may, however, put up a road block and stop all the cars: that is not interfering with the individual citizen's privacy. What we would give to have worries like theirs!

I did some grafting and pruned the frost-bitten climbing roses – altogether I have no idea what I did the whole day. I pruned the roses section by section, starting at the top and looking for some sign of life. But I always ended down near the root. Madla was washing the windows – it will be Easter in a week – and she has been reading about rock plants. Jan was doing something with Švácha again. I helped him install the universal joint and half-axles in the gear-box. I was amazed how anybody could invent something like that in the first place, and then produce drawings and manufacture it with such devilish precision. We would have to regard it as an enormous waste of time on Jan's part, if it were not obvious that only once in their lives do people have sufficient enthusiasm, patience and strength to take a real car apart and put it back together again. He had to get some of the cogs made.

The Kosíks did not come today at all. I had to push the Golden Spur Delicious saplings into the compost heap. I had been rather looking forward to confounding Karel's philosophy with my sentence about space and matter.

MONDAY, 9TH APRIL 1979

I woke up and my first feeling was that something was nonsense. Interesting. I focused my attention towards the source of the radiation and I discovered my breakthrough – that space and matter are identical. In my refreshed brain a suspicion started to flicker that I had read something on that very subject a long time ago. I did not even have to get up. From my prone position I slid back the glass door of the bookshelf above the couch and took out Albert Einstein's book *How I See the World* (published by Československý spisovatel in 1961). Well, well.

"Since it would have seemed utterly absurd to the physicists of the nineteenth century to attribute physical functions or states to space itself, they invented a medium pervading the whole of space, on the model of ponderable matter – the ether, which was supposed to act as a vehicle for electro-magnetic phenomena, and hence for those of light also... Physical space and the ether are only different terms for the same thing."

So I've discovered ether! Admittedly my more advanced colleagues have abandoned it in the meantime, but I found it all on my own, by simple thorough reasoning. I now have fresh proof of my old tenet: "If, my dear young reader, I were to get down to study in earnest, I must inevitably discover every hidden thing, all on my own unaided. Every hidden thing by thorough concentration. There are certain ideas that are bound to be discovered by everyone if they put their minds to it" *The Guinea Pigs*, Toronto 1977).

I leafed through Einstein's lectures and articles. In an article on Russell, I suddenly spot an incredible sentence: "The belief that it is possible, solely by contemplation, to discover everything that is worth knowing, was fairly widespread in philosophy's infancy"

Would you believe it? That book trifles with me sibyl-like. My philosophising has reached infant level. Ah well, it can't be helped. I got up and went to pour myself a glass of VAT 69, something I never do, or the fact would be recorded here. I went into the kitchen. Philip immediately started diving at me, telling me he wanted something. I could not see Catherine anywhere. She was not to be found. I went to wake Jan, to ask him if she was in her cage last night when he came home. He told me she was. We started to move the furniture away from the walls. When we moved the wash-stand, Catherine fluttered out and up to the ceiling. Birds can fly but they cannot get out of holes on their own.

I then sat for a while reading Einstein. The doorbell rang. Jan, in the kitchen, was nearer to the door and came and nodded to me that I had a visitor. There stood Mrs. Helena D. all in a fluster. In her open palm she held a square box, which she handed to me with that ironic suggestion of a little-girl curtsy, and a smile. I took the box and opened it: there was the puzzle assembled. To its topmost face was taped the first of the yellow flowers – a coltsfoot. We just slightly pursed our lips at each other from a distance and she left.

Zdena is home from hospital, and gives the impression of wanting to commence a more joyful existence. She cannot decide what to do first: start typing or do the round of the hairdressers. For the time being, she has decided to hold a miniature celebration of her restoration to life. In the grill bar a hundred yards from her apartment we each drank a large aperitif. The pale yellow light and the raucous unchanging wail of the muzak immediately gave us the impression of being out somewhere.

That young patriot, Vlasta Chramostová, read through the studies on the theatre over the weekend and drew up a list of corrections. There are almost sixty of them. When I arrived home, I washed the kitchen window for Easter, because I had silently promised Catherine I would if I found she had not flown away or nothing had happened to her. Then I spent about two hours correcting the books on the basis of Vlasta's list. Being my own psychiatrist, my own Einstein and my own young patriotic assistant is a bit demanding. But it's fun.

In the kitchen, Madla is cooking, lying on her back on the floor, vehemently kicking her legs in the air to the rhythm of the Moravanka brass band as it plays and sings:

> Oh, lofty juniper tree
> You're as tall as me
> Leap o'er it, sweetheart mine,
> I'll be your Valentine!

There is so much joy in the singers' voices and the sound of the brass that we sing along with them. I now have a real urge to visit Brno.

TUESDAY, 10TH APRIL 1979

The spring dust blew across the flat upland fields and I could not detect whether it was posthumous or prenatal. Those feelings alternated. I was able to rock from one to the other as I liked. There was no one left to love those dusty fields, but the skylark continued to flutter above them, faithful as an aching memory of the joys of youth. The sun glowed above the west, yellow as a million years hence, and it gave little warmth, as if the Earth was one orbit further from it. Oh, when I return, how pleased I shall be with that which still remains to me!

But from out of the shallow slopes of the dry, yellow fields a hill rose alluringly, like a cold crater above the regolite plain. Beneath my steps, the crumbly earth was moving backwards, but the hill was retreating! Thus scrutinised in detail by my walking, the plain revealed its furrows and cultivated gullies. In them lay terraced fields of old grass, cosy and enclosed like cells. They were deserted, however. Above them stood abandoned houses with their windows turned towards the yellow sun. With an uneasy feeling I arrived among them and caught sight of a stranger. Startled, I greeted him, but he did not respond. As I left the last house behind, the cold hill, so long distant, loomed sheer before me!

But when I had clambered up the dry rustling grass to its crest, something else became clear: that everything I had passed through so far was only the windswept floor of an enormous volcano – *that* had been the crater. I was looking down through one gap in its perimeter at a living planet. Far into the distance, forests rolled forever onwards, until they formed thin lines and disappeared beneath the bright haze that rose above the horizon towards its source, the sun. The sun brought everything back to me and I fell. And as if I could return to earth through a woman's womb, I pressed myself to the dead, dry grass. But there was no woman's womb there.

I went back across the dusty plain treading on my shadow. At my back the sun's light was dying. I stared at the cold, silvery body on the horizon before me and my last, lingering feeling was nostalgia for my mother, who was still able to keep the horrors of cosmic space outside her life's boundaries, and only referred to it in passing:

> Beyond the hills, beyond the woods
> The silvery moon shines bright
> Oh, how I yearn to know for sure
> How fares my love this night

It suddenly struck me that one day I would not believe it, so as proof of my journey I picked up a small round pebble to look at later. But I do not have it.

TUESDAY, 12ᵀᴴ APRIL 1979

I woke in a weepy mood but I had no opportunity to indulge in it as Olda Unger called. I got dressed and went out into the street with him. He had come to ask me whether I had forgotten that he has a packet of letters of mine. I had. What letters? He could not say; I had given them to him ten years ago. They might be letters from Zdena. The Ungers are winding up their affairs: packing some things and selling others; but they have not received written permission yet. There is no response to their reminders. "What makes you think you'll go at all?" I asked. – "We have no choice now," he laughed, "because soon we'll be sleeping on the bare boards. We're living off what's left and famine will break out any day now. Maybe they want to starve us to death." – "I'll come for those letters next week," I said.

We went our separate ways in front of the church on Štrossmajer Square, and my initial mood from this morning returned to me with a vengeance. That betrayed its origin. I feel as if some misfortune is looming, one I am reluctant to talk to people about, in case I compound it and actually set it in motion.

A short while ago I came up with the idea of proposing to a certain Well-heeled person, who is allowed to work and earn money, that he establish a literary prize. I would give him all the better manuscripts to read and he would award a prize to any that particularly took his fancy. The sum awarded could be ten or twenty thousand, and for the time being he would give it anonymously. He could give it any name he liked, and later, when things start to return to normal, his name could be made public. Or we could do it the other way round: he would read all the best writings of the past years and he would decide from which author he would like to see something new. Maybe – and this would be very sporting – he could organise a writing competition on a given theme.

Last week, I put all those suggestions to my W-hee-per. It surprised him. He said he would think about it. Today I went to hear the reply. It's not good. Mr. W-hee-per doesn't think there are any outstanding authors. The money would first have to be put aside before he committed himself. He might be able to donate it, but it's not certain; all sorts of intrigues were going on around him so he's not sure whether he'll go on earning the same sort of money. Moreover he and his wife unfortunately have a joint account now, and giving such a sum for such a purpose would seem scandalous to her. Yes, he would let me have the money straight away if I needed it, so that I could finish writing *Trip to Praděd*. I replied that that would be a slightly different venture from the one I had in mind.

I told him that the present state of affairs could be regarded either as something really awful or as a primeval chaos, in which those with foresight could sow the seeds of their own new order. Our literary colony was beginning to come back to life, contrary to the wishes of the authorities. Governance of our affairs was starting to return to us in a rough and ready fashion. With a touch of unsentimental romanticism, one might regard it as a return to the

Today I went to hear the reply. It's not good.
(p. 154)

days when European society took care of its arts, all on its own in the person of its most aware members, while the state worried its silly head over taxes, wars and religion. With those words I managed to unsettle Mr. Wheeper again. We all had a need, I said, for excitement, praise and presents, however small. Where was it to come from? Wherever it could be found. – All we agreed was that I would send him interesting manuscripts from Padlock via someone (which does not sound so menacing as: I will bring you). Why didn't this occur to me years ago?

I found Zdena at her typewriter. She is typing out Mr. Havel Senior's memoirs: the history of Barrandov and the Lucerna, the family history, and his portrait of Prague society in the inter-war years. I went to visit the old man a little while ago in search of news about his son in police encirclement, and when I observed the frailty of his step and his anxious, though controlled, expression, when I saw the documents he was working from laid out on his desk, I had a twinge of time panic. I had promised him that Zdena would come and see him, but she had fallen ill, only now had she managed to see him.

The weather was fine. I prevailed on her to leave the flat and we drove a little way out of Prague to Počernice Pond. A torrent of water was pouring out of the flood gates; enormous tree trunks, their tops bare, exuded a pre-festive air and the yellow fronds hung from the weeping willows like long hair after washing. Bibisa ran left and right in front of us, drank from the pond and forded the stream, with no fuss. The combination of the weathered walls of the old houses and farmyards, the trees and the water, helped restore my composure. Forty minutes later we were back in Prague and I still had time to go looking for some Easter meat.

FRIDAY, 13TH APRIL 1979

I was going to water the plants, feed the birds and start writing. I was going to tidy my desk top, and sort out what needed throwing away and what I could pass on to somebody else. I was quite simply going to send the whole world to blazes and get on with my own business. After all, we were not dead yet, even if we did not have too long to live. And I was going to make myself a nice cup of tea.

But the doorbell rang – it was little Mrs. D. She was bringing me a hatchet. They were in the first stages of liquidation. The camping hatchet would be just right for my car, she thought. "Why don't you take it with you?" They wanted their move to be as cheap and easy as possible. I don't belong among people like that, people who are able to exchange one thing for another without batting an eyelid. Helena wants to tell me something, but outside. If I had some errands to do, she could drive me. I needed to go the Municipal Library, to Hradčany and to the bookbinders'. She waited in the kitchen with the birdlife, while I changed.

"What have you to tell me, then?" I asked in the car. – "You know the different workshops. Have you any idea who'd repair a leather-bound Bible?" – "I have. Is that all?" I said. She drove absent-mindedly, I was obliged to point out traffic lights to her and tell her to stay in her lane. She suddenly said: "I expect you reproach us for emigrating – in fact I know you do. You have only to tell me something along the lines of, Don't go, because it's a rotten thing to do or because... I don't know, whatever words you'd like to use." – "That *I'd* like to use? Never on your life!" I looked at her from the side. I sensed something strange. "Or are there certain words," I said, "that might cause you to change your mind and not go? Have you any particular words in mind?" I had to point out to her that the lights had turned green. She drove off and said: "Yes." I didn't dare say anything. Then I said: "Even if it would ruin your husband's departure?" – "Why should it? He could leave on his own." I didn't dare speak; she said: "Look, I've just received another offer of a job. I just can't tell," she said, thumping the wheel with her fist, "whether it's a refined form of torture, or coincidence, or whether things are maybe on the turn. I've got a chance of working with a girlfriend of mine on the Svatá Hora site near Příbram, where they had that fire. We've already been to have a look. It's something I've only ever dreamed about. I'll hardly get offered jobs like that over there." I said: "It's either coincidence or a refined form of torture, things aren't improving at all. Quite simply, someone is not aware that you're banned from working. As soon as they find out, they'll put a stop to it again." We drove on a little further and I returned to the sore point: "Are you asking my opinion as if I were something like your father?" She replied artfully: "Do I seem like a daughter to you? Do you have fatherly feeling towards me?"

"No," I said. Starting a new paragraph, I added:

"But you remind me that I don't have a daughter. And I wanted one."

The precise sentence that would have halted her flight I will not now tell her. The critical moment is past. She is leaving, let her go. She'll be as good as dead as far as I'm concerned.

EASTER SATURDAY, 14TH APRIL 1979

Catholic News wrote that the little church at Lhotka had some new Stations of the Cross, sculpted by Stádník. We drove over there to see. It is an unusual sight: the stations are formed either of figures in deep relief or statues emerging from the wall, and they represent the final scenes not of Jesus' life but of humanity's. The flagellation – a scene on a slave galley. Then follows the Thirty Years' War, a concentration camp, the atomic bomb, and so on. We weren't able to decipher everything; we had no wish to disturb the pious folk who had come for the Easter vigil. How did such an experimental work come to be in some small church on the outskirts of Prague? These days there is no way of knowing whether it was to the credit of an enterprising priest who was ready to take the risk, or to the shame of a panicky church administration which, on the contrary, had not risked installing it in some more prominent church. Madla said: "There's no such thing as great and small when it comes to churches."

Built into the altar is a fragment of the Marian Column that used to stand on Old Town Square. The history of the church on the wall by the door describes the siege of Prague by the Swedes and their retreat; the inhabitants' gratitude to God's Mother for saving the city; the erection of the thanksgiving column; the subsequent repeated attempts to demolish it. With suppressed indignation, the history's author writes that the column was bound to fall after deputy Šťastný incited a socialist mob with a demagogic slogan linking the defeat at White Mountain with the Marian Column. The mob went off to the Old Town Square, and no one knows who threw the rope. It happened on 8th November 1918 during the first days of Czechoslovak freedom; and it is not surprising, therefore, that the latter suffered its subsequent fate – so says the author, albeit far more delicately than I, of course. That tickled me pink and I felt a gloating sense of agreement. I still think that a nation which, in an effort to improve its character record instead of amending its character, goes round knocking down monuments which reflect the different moods it felt in earlier times, deserves to be obliterated.

Apart from that, the church history incorporates some charming pieces of hearsay, which is what always fascinates Madla most, wherever she is. And indeed – it states – the Holy Virgin punished the authors of that crime: they either fell gravely ill or died. Deputy Šťastný, for instance: his son was to earn dismal notoriety as the perpetrator of the first political assassination in the "free" republic: the murder of Minister Rašín. "I thought I was cutting down a statue," he said afterwards.

Madla has a unique filtration capacity, unmatched anywhere, allowing her to take in only that information which fits her idea of a particular matter. She has her own history of humanity, her own history of literature, her own religion, her own network of Soviet spies. As we were leaving Lhotka, she declared in stupefaction: "Did you notice?" – "What?" – "That they were all punished. Doesn't it ring a bell with you?" – "What?" – "Surely Seifert has a poem in *Umbrella from Piccadilly* about Holan having at home the head of the Virgin that he, Seifert, had previously seen lying about on the Old Town Square. Those two were there as well!" – "So what?" – "Well, Holan can't walk and Seifert has difficulty." – "Holy Mary!" I said.

I am now leafing through Seifert's poem, "The Head of the Virgin." I quote:

(…)
Just as I entered
Holan slammed shut the book
and asked me rather crossly
whether I too believed in life after death
or something even worse.

But I did not hear his words.
A female head of iron
upon a low box near the door.
My God, she's familiar!
She lay there on one cheek
as if beneath the guillotine.
It was the head of the Virgin
From the Old Town Square

Pilgrims toppled her
on their return from White Mountain
Just sixty years ago.
(...)

A moment later Madla said: "But what about Braunerová?" – "What about her?" – "She laid a green wreath at the site of the column, didn't she? She was expecting the mob to tear her to pieces, but people only looked on in amazement. And how about Myslbek? He denounced revolutionary crimes of that ilk."

That's the point, isn't it: there are always amongst us one or two just individuals – albeit a number far below the divine threshold. On the other hand, though, some of those sinners sing about their sins so sweetly that the Good Lord is at a loss what to do with us.

EASTER MONDAY, 16TH APRIL 1979

It's night again. My whole body aches from digging. We were sowing spuds (we should have done so a fortnight ago) and transplanting strawberries (ditto ditto last August). So we arrived on Saturday to do the garden and a real festival of resurrection awaited us. Our forest glade was full of anemones. The rockery was bright with the pointed flowers of botanical tulips. The foxtail lily is emerging from the soil, and everywhere we come across further new spikes of the local wild lilies. Only my grafts are keeping mum for the time being. On Sunday there was still no sign from the currants; on Monday they were in flower. The gooseberries will be abundant again this year.

Madla brought the washed laundry from home and dried it outside in the afternoon sun. And in the evening while ironing it she related to me how the Phantom had called her in for a "disciplinary chat." He accused her of misusing her position – "But you haven't got one there!" I say – for the purpose of political subversion. "How?" I ask. He says she spreads the word that he's a stool-pigeon. – "But he is – that's the point!" I say. He also says she is not as dedicated to her work as she used to be. "What does he mean by that, the rotten blighter?" I ask. He says that previously she would never have just handed some poor client an appointment with one of the psychologists, without comment. "But it was he who banned you from talking to people!"

That is what she told him, but he just brushed it aside: But both of us know, Mrs. Vaculíková, that you don't abide by it. "And anyway, how does he know how you talked to that client?" He said he happened to catch something she was saying on the phone. "He *happened* to? He's a stool-pigeon!" I roared. "How come you didn't give in your notice on the spot? I'll go there and kick the whole thing wide open. I'll tell him who's the political subversive. Before long they'll start to think that their ideas have weight, that their attitudes are normal and that they're in some way our equals! State-owned shits in the pay of the enemy!"

Whenever I get really overheated like that, Madla starts to argue that it really isn't so important – that she has no illusions on the Phantom's score, naturally, but that she also knows he is not necessarily the worst of them, and it could well be that he does it reluctantly and under duress almost. She has already noticed that these crudely threatening "chats" always occur in April...! She pulled out her last year's diary, leafed through April and showed me her entry: "Phantom – disciplinary chat." Thus the ironing ends with the discovery that most probably it does not represent a mysterious new offensive, but simply the stereotyped implementation of the original, still operative, schedule of moral terror.

But I still imagine myself going to see Madla's boss and tackling him like this: "I would remind you that we are the ones behaving properly, not you. Your duty is to look after people, not the state. You and I both know that my wife is better than you are. Not only do you pay her badly, but you also insult her. If you don't start treating her better, she'll stop coming here, I'll forbid her to. – Silence! I'm the one to decide! I've come to draw your attention to the original and proper state of affairs. I have you under surveillance and I'm keeping a record of everything."

Last night I was woken by whimpering. It's nothing new to me, she has always done it: someone was taking away her child, or she saw me falling from a cliff, or snakes were crawling over her, or she had lost an arm or all her teeth. I stretched out my hand across the gap and touched her head. I said: "It's gone now." She woke up and in a calm matter-of-fact voice said: "I was surrounded by murderers." – "How did you know what they were?" – "They had special masks."

When the night is at its half-way point, such as now, at half past one, I either have to finish because I don't want to write any more, or I am at a loss how to continue, which takes the form of thirst, for instance. I invariably go to the kitchen and turn the light on. In the cage on a perch, or on top of the cage, sit two feathery balls, heads under wings, their shallow breathing causing them to swell gently. On the couch, Madla is breathing, stretched out most frequently on her back or her stomach. Depending on what it is like outside, I either close the air vent or open it a bit. But the gap must not be more than a couple of inches, otherwise when the birds start flying their impetuous, morning-fresh spirals, one of them might whiz straight out the window. They do not venture through gaps narrower than their wingspan. (They are capable, when landing badly, of falling behind the furniture.) I wake Madla with a mundane phrase in an ordinary voice as if she were sitting at the table. "Aren't you cold? Are you thirsty?" As if she were not asleep, she replies through lips half-covered by her elbow: "No, I'm not." Or: "Is there some unsweetened tea there?" Then she wants to know the time. It is two o'clock, say, as it is by now. "That's good," she luxuriates, "I'm sleeping like a log."

That's the usual pattern. Let's give it a try now.

I switch the light on. Philip on the perch, Catherine in her nest on the eggs. Madla on her back, one bare leg out: "What's the time?" – "Two." – "That's good." – "Thirsty?" – "I wouldn't mind a little apple." She receives an apple. I look to see what I might have myself. Madla: "Don't touch the meat, it's for Ondřej's sandwiches." I just have a drink of beer. "Good night," I say. I turn off the light.

TUESDAY, 17ᵀᴴ APRIL 1979

It's turned cold again. There is nothing in Prague to look forward to. (And whenever my thoughts turn to a certain thing that I might look forward to, I feel utterly wretched. Away with it! "Good luck has he who deals with none!") My work on *Dear Classmates* is dragging; I am stuck on the commentary, which ought to be witty, convincing and timeless. I have altogether too much work.

Friend C. came to see me with a further section of the work on project "D" from friend B. He looked glum: I took the pages from him, glanced at them and my blood boiled. It was the very same part that B. had already given us, but entirely reworked and with fresh information added. "What's going on?"

I asked. – "I don't know," said C., "maybe he's bonkers." But B. is not bonkers, he is a literary scholar through and through, which almost boils down to the same thing. "According to him," says C., "now that something like this is being done at last, it has to be one hundred percent right. He came across some new details and wants them included." – "But why doesn't he push ahead with it instead!" I said. Friend C. shrugged his shoulders plaintively. I poured him a glass of VAT 69.

Our Jan is taking the Czech literature section of his matriculation exams today. The topics were not as daft as one might have feared. Jan chose the influence of children's literature in the formation of attitudes or character, or something. "You wrote about *Little Bobeš*, didn't you," I said. Pleva's Bobeš was the favourite reading for each of our three boys. "I worked in *Little Bobeš*, *We Were a Handful*, *Pussy Blue-Eyes*, and also mentioned Jules Verne and Trosek." – "Trosek! That was a great idea!" I said. "And Engineer Zababa?" I asked. Janek got up from the table and smote his forehead: Oh, the ingratitude! "That's really dreadful, how could I be so stupid?" When Pavel Nauman, the author of stories about locomotives and Engineer Zababa who built them, died recently, our boys asked whether they ought to write to the family.

Over the last few days, I was starting to think about the fact I had no money when – lo and behold! – I received three thousand francs from Mrs. Bucher, a publisher in Lucerne. Today. In addition, I received an invitation to an interview with Major (?) Fišer tomorrow. I am trying to guess what it might be about: either my spring feuilleton or my reply to the questionnaire about 28th October. Alternatively, I will be left guessing what is on his mind.

There is nothing to look forward to and no happy events in the offing. I have no friends with a premiere or a private view. Chance invitations to celebrate someone's personal success are still not coming my way. Since Pavel Kohout left, we do not even observe our *jours fixes* when you had a real hope of meeting someone in particular. There is no chance of good news: they are bound to turn down Jan's application to university and the next telegram our family is going to receive will only be sad tidings about our schoolmistress. The only piece of good news I have is for Karel Pecka and I look forward to being able to tell it to him, but he is not to be found. Madla is looking forward to her retirement.

FRIDAY, 20TH APRIL 1979

"Adolf Hitler wurde am 20. April 1889 in Braunau geboren…"

Yesterday comprised two events: the interrogation in the morning and the lecture at Tomin's in the evening.

Major (?) Fišer had a younger colleague with him this time, but I have a suspicion that the latter either is or soon will be his superior, being brighter, more vigorous and more ambitious. They wanted to know why I wrote the feuilleton "An Experiment in a Different Genre," where I had obtained the background information for it, how it had come to be published in *Listy*, and whether I was being paid a fee for it. The interrogation lasted three hours. All I said was that I had written the feuilleton out of sympathy for Jan Šimsa, and that I had obtained the information from the indictment and the verdict and from what his family members told me. Otherwise those three hours were an exchange of monological statements about the Constitution, the law, freedom of speech, Charter 77, etc. etc. – as usual. And exceptionally – a unique opportunity! don't miss it! – an exposition by me of the symbolism of the cross and the two thieves. Major (?) Fišer looked on in swarthy silence, an expression of ponderous weariness on his face, whereas the young man, after listening to me avidly, stated: "I don't deny what you say. But we aren't Christians here." I believed him one hundred percent.

Whenever you correctly spot an opportunity it is always rewarding. I do not intend to write any more about the interrogation, though there is more I could tell. Unless they call me in again. I certainly learn more from them than they do from me. They said, for instance, that they had already seen O.S.'s photos of Ella's wedding, which I myself have yet to receive from O.S.! There was one moment when the young non-Christian declared, looking at his watch: "Your son is just now taking his Russian exam." I did not react. Also significant, without doubt, was the comment that it must be distressing to have a house and not to be able to live in it. If it were vacated, would we move there? I replied that we bought it with that in mind. "Then you wouldn't be able to spend the whole day running round Prague organising people, gathering information and distributing Padlock!" – "There you are, you wouldn't have so much bother with me." – "Why didn't you let us know?" the young non-Christian laughed. "I was amazed that you didn't figure it out of your own accord," I laughed also. – They even make you afraid to want things you would normally want

I spent the evening at the Tomins'. Last year, Tomin wrote to a number of European universities about having to work in a philosophical wasteland, and asking colleagues for assistance. For a long time there was nothing and then – lo and behold – a professor arrived from Oxford. The subject attracted me: the identity of the person. Tired out from my morning's impressions, I fell asleep before supper with a book on my belly, and when I awoke did not feel like going anywhere. But the thought of Tomin's pleasure at the professor's visit got me out in the end. I went and was rewarded.

The first pleasant surprise was that something so young and feminine – while voluntarily sage – could work at Oxford; the second was that I was able to understand the professor all on my own. (Tomin provided brief translations at intervals.) Her lecture contained nothing unprecedented, and above all, no exact data apart from some anatomical and neurological information relating to the function of the cerebral hemispheres. What I hadn't experienced for many years, and what was entirely unknown to the students attending, was the freedom of a discourse conducted without obedience or acquiescence to any doctrine, school syllabus or so-called educational goals. The teacher took her examples from literature, philosophy and psychology, treating them as material with which to build something of her own design.

She began with a quotation from Hobbes: If we swapped the brains of a prince and a cobbler, who would then be the prince and who the cobbler? To the identity of memory one had to add the identity of the body. To the subjective standpoint, the social: because regardless of what each of the victims felt, we would be obliged to ask their wives which one was their husband? The body's cells are renewed several times during one's life; only memory remains, though it suffers regression. The human "I" changes; in fact we have several "I"s at one and the same time, depending on place, function and purpose. The one continuous lifelong "I" is made up of partial "I"s which overlap each other: memories are followed by memories of memories. The unity of a person is like a cord of strands spun from desires, aspirations, moral principles and so on. The longer the strands of one's personality, the stronger the personality. The personality must be consciously cultivated and kept in order if it is to resist the influences that seek to destroy it. Thus, rather than being something permanent and demarcated, the personality is a constant striving for a stable unity. It expresses itself through its own development.

The lecture ended with an example from literature: The son of a rich Russian farmer declared at the age of twenty-one that if it was up to him, he would distribute the land among the *muzhiks*. He had an affidavit drawn up requiring his young wife to carry out his intention even against his will, should his present high-minded plan no longer appeal to him once his father was dead and he had become the owner. That indeed came to pass thirty-five years later! The new landowner fiercely resisted his youthful ambition. – The story remained unfinished, as a riddle for the reader, and now for us.

People here will be thinking to themselves: What on earth is this comrade teacher teaching these youngsters? In the end she topped it off in the discussion, when she stated that speculation about the identity of the person, as we had proved today, would always be to a certain extent no more than a fascinating intellectual game. The discussion was almost as long as the lecture. What fascinated the audience most were the examples she cited of thrilling and sometimes almost comic experiments concerning the relative independence of the two cerebral hemispheres. When, following an admonition by Principal Tomin, the debaters subsequently turned their attention to the more abstract aspects of personality, I found it interesting to see that those youngsters returned most frequently to the moral principles that ought to constitute or govern the personality. That provoked me into offering them a very experimental example: We all knew a person who was consciously aware of himself, who had always been socially committed to a major degree, and had been quite consistent and integral throughout his development. It always amazed me how many people failed to realise or understand his stability, and how much pettiness and intolerance they displayed towards him. I was speaking of Pavel Kohout. He was someone entirely true to himself in his striving to discover reality and in his conscientious effort to act accordingly. As far as certain components of his personality were concerned, the scope of his activity as a young man had exceeded the level of his knowledge. He had continuously eliminated the inconsistencies between those two components, and thus renewed and asserted his identity. Only a misapprehension could lead one to describe his as a case of discontinuity and maintain that Kohout had done a somersault. The moral criterion struck me as the least reliable of all because, were it applied from outside, it might differ from the criteria recognised by the person in question. In my view, the main thing was to strive for the truth and act accordingly; morality would issue from it of its own accord, and not necessarily at once.

The students seemed to me rather surprised at the choice of example and apart from Bednář, who mumbled something, they remained silent. The professor congratulated me. (Tomin interpreted for her.) She wore black trousers of a shiny fabric that made sharp creases, and a matte grey blouse with surplus material on the bust and shoulders. She looked like a young girl in cap and gown!

Today's television news included shots from the statewide teachers' conference. For a while I sat incredulous until disgust overcame my amazement. A speaker with as unthoughtful a brow as I could possibly conceive declared that only a teacher dedicated to the principles... as concretised in the decisions of etc. etc. ... can educate a generation of people that will also etc. etc... The camera recorded a few of the brighter morons writing down that startlingly new idea.

"... but his soul goes marching on."

SATURDAY, 21ST APRIL 1979

Walking along a firm forest road, which had been moist and shady, we came to a place where a trickle of contaminated water ran into the ditch. It created a muddy puddle with oily blisters and clods of some decaying matter. An enormous boulder had been thrown into the puddle, and two battered posts joined by laths were supposed to assist the leap across to the other side. A woman dressed in dark trousers and a black coat gave a mute signal that this was the place and jumped across easily. I was just about to follow her when I realised that she was looking at my crotch in embarrassment, and she even made a sort of warning motion without actually moving. I got the message, covered myself slightly from below with both hands, and leaped after her. Above me I heard the rumble of wagons, below me ran the rails. I had quite a safe grip on the wheel truck; what worried me was something else: how to maintain my hard-on until eventually she – who? – returns from – Oh, God! – emigration.

Excuse me ladies.

The gloomy red sky is covered in opaque horizontal smudges; a bluish sandy plain approaches from the horizon with something ludicrously red dancing on it; it looks like a wavy triangle or an upside-down top. At the bottom it has little thin legs sticking out and with its little arms it is holding its two lower corners like a skirt. Its body is also a face, in fact it's an executioner's hood! Cut out of it are three smiling holes, two eyes and a mouth. It's cheerful. The top of the hood is decorated with a little gallows in place of a tassel. The outlandish creature is approaching the foreground of the picture, threateningly, almost filling half the left-hand side. In the background, two tiny progeny are coming closer with the same flapping dance movement. The plain darkens from the rear, becoming almost black, and in the dark field immediately in front of me tiny white flowers are growing.

And since the painter is always painting such pictures or something similar, it occurred to me to have her paint my portrait. What will someone who sees things that way see? She accepted the challenge and I have been going there about once a month since last autumn. So far, it amounts to a pile of charcoal sketches, as realistic as can be. But soon the time will come for her to put them aside, forget them and make up something about me! I am curious about her inspection, and if eventually she manages to come up with something, it looks as if I will have cause for trepidation. One can usually see inside the heads of her figures; trees spread their limbs, people have roots growing into the soil. In February, a four-legged rooster with a bloody comb is being pulled along on a leash by a naked man. A woman is pegging a sheet onto a washing-line; above the sheet we can see her head and extended arms, below it her bare feet, but the thighs, belly and breasts hidden behind the sheet are projected onto it X-ray fashion as long bones, a pelvis and ribs. When the painter draws me, I sit and look at her, trying to figure her out, and neither of us says anything. I lack the courage to ask about anything. That is to say, I dare not speak about what is, after all, stated overtly by the paintings all round.

When I turned up here today for the first time in more than six weeks, she made a sort of scowl of impatience. But I had not come to be drawn; I came to invite her to spend one of the May holidays with us at the garden in Dobřichovice along with her husband and children.

That happily-married couple, the Ella-Horákovás, sent a card from Munich confirming that they are already there, and apparently she goes out demonstrating for women's rights. We have more than enough of those over here, so why did she leave? When people are kind enough to repair to another, better country, why don't they politely keep their traps shut for at least ten years? But I thanked her for the greeting.

Mr. Václav sent an Easter card in which he thanked me for the spring feuilleton and books I sent him. From Brno, Mrs. Müllerová, Jirka's mother, sent me excerpts from his prison letters. He had been inside two years already when he wrote, for instance: "In its way, prison is a form of monastery. The cell resembles a cell. If you are calm enough, not bitter and are able to concentrate, the opportunities for contemplation are invaluable. In many ways I have the feeling that I am growing up a second time. I am grateful for this opportunity... Prison helps you know yourself and mercilessly examine your assumptions about yourself..." – It is the mildest discussion contribution I have received to date. A shy comment from backstage.

I had to go and perform my smile for Dr. Kurka, who is expecting puppies, through the agency of his boxer bitch Aura. For that reason he is taking a holiday and wants his gobs shipshape before he goes. He offered me one of the future puppies. No thanks. I shall ask Dalibor Klánský, whose boxer Philip died two years ago. Dalibor has not been to see us in a long while! Is he cross? It is my turn to go and see him.

"How many puppies are you expecting?" I asked Dr. Kurka. – "She's capable of having as many as six. I'd want about three of them." He has two bitches; they always wait for him in the car by the church; sometimes he walks them to work and back – and he lives out in Troja! He took the other bitch to some competition or other; she got high marks for behaviour and a slight minus for her appearance, because she is a centimetre longer and her jowls hang about three millimetres lower than the judges like. With his index finger in my muzzle he explained to me how they test a dog's character. It was very painful, and even brought tears to my eyes. Up to about five years ago, he would talk about nothing but new drills; he used to go to exhibitions of dental technology and keep specialised catalogues. He was considering moving to some country where fresh breezes blew through dentistry, but he would far sooner just be allowed to travel to symposia and have the opportunity for once in his life to see a different consulting room from his own. In the end he had to content himself with getting a proposal through the local trade union branch allowing the metal door frames, windows and heating pipes in the entire dental department to be painted a strange shade of dark blue that he personally mixed according to a foreign catalogue.

When I came out into the fresh air, I felt in my mouth that my "s" had shifted slightly. But I shall put up with it until the birth is out of the way and at the end of May I get the – no doubt perfect – finished set. I did a detour round St. Anthony's church until I found the red Zhiguli and looked inside. Aura – heavy with pup – gazed at me languidly, without even raising her head from her paws. The other one approached the window and precisely in accordance with the norm for a well-bred dog of her breed, as I had now learnt, she uttered her one, compulsory, gruff woof.

TUESDAY, 24TH APRIL 1979

I have that packet of letters from Olda Unger. There are more than fifty of them. They were sent to me in 1967 after the Writers' Congress. It is only a section of them, which probably Madla put aside, the rest – almost two hundred – remained in the *Literary News* offices. They are all marked "replied to" – I was conscientious. I read them through; it even occurred to me to copy out some excerpts and quote from them here, but it's not possible. It is a single explosion of fellow feeling from many quarters that was dangerous for me at the time because it placed me under a serious obligation. Had I subsequently wanted, in 1968, to establish a new movement, or at least a political party, it was there for the asking. It was a veritable popular outburst. What comes to me from those letters, wafted on a now forgotten spirit – is that these were informed, thinking and well-read people. Everything was crystal clear to them. They had their fingers on the pulse, they were in tune with the times. Even though the editorial board was unable to communicate with them openly in any way, they were all around us and did nothing but read. The paper's enormous print-run (around 300,000) was a clarion call. They still included people with a republican literary ethic, a democratic historical awareness and a good old Sokol-style readiness to believe yet again in personal honour and to march forth! There were working-class sceptics. There were well-read peasant sages slowly recovering from the effects of decimation, outnumbered by their well-bludgeoned offspring. There were pensioned-off teachers and a lot of new ironically-voiced chemists and technicians demanding proof, proof... and only then – maybe – some tasks. The Czech cultural community.

I shall have to get rid of the letters again. Maybe I should get them transcribed to preserve them as evidence. They include Šimsa's first two letters; that is how we got acquainted, he wrote to me about *The Axe*. And there is Tytl's invitation to Borová near Polička, where I did actually find refuge later, when Prague got too damned hot. That week at a Protestant manse in an upland village was the last time that my time was truly my own and untrammelled, when I was totally alone in the landscape, and could, as of old – as of young, in other words – come to terms with my inclinations. Since then, I have had the feeling that my work, my duties, my stubbornness and my commitment to the things I have said have pushed me to the forefront of people and events; the siren-voice of fame alerts me to my possible downfall. I do not know, and it will never be established, whether I would have managed to remain independent from my success. All I can do is declare faithfully that I would have, and divulge that our family descended into clownish mirth when, the following spring, friends of ours started talking in terms of my inevitable, and perhaps mandatory, political career. By then I was already racking my brains how to demonstrate that I intended to act publicly in a purely private capacity, and that my speech at the Writers' Congress had merely been intended to show how I thought everyone should be talking. Anyway, at that time – I was forty-one – life had led with a fairly high heart, and there was nothing to do but trump it with an ace of diamonds, and the name of the game had changed. Only now does it strike me: I did not want to control politics, I wanted to destroy them. And I might conceivably have managed on my own, by my own means, but there was someone around who saw I was badly in need of assistance and could not withhold it from me: the Soviet Army.

I smile every time I read in so many of the letters the kind words: "Should you ever need anything..."

WEDNESDAY, 25TH APRIL 1979

I wanted to put more in yesterday's entry, but it was too late and I left it to today. Now I am reading what I wrote yesterday and I have half a mind to tear it up and throw it away. Of course I should write as much as I can about certain older events while I can still remember anything at all. But I would rather not. When you're walking along and you twist your ankle so that it hurts to walk, you deliberately tread in such a way as to avoid the painful spot, and sometimes you don't even have to limp. In time, when the pain has gone, you find yourself walking normally again and you cannot recall since when. Whenever by mistake – or experiment – I touch on some of the events of my past life, I feel that it still hurts. So I desist and expel them from my mind. Maybe I'll enjoy returning to them one day and I won't have any trouble dreaming them up again. That is how proper memoirs are made.

Time must really be flying! And I have the impression it is standing still. 1968 seems to me both recent and long past. That it is probably quite a long time ago is something I have to bear in mind whenever I read historical essays about it. And I always find it a trifle insulting how they manage to evaluate everything, and how historians are already able to come up with such objective and astute analyses – and whole documents, even. It strikes me as impudent and callous: we are still alive and crawling around our still smoldering Troy, and they are already excavating their Hisarlik while we are still there.

We are going to Dobřichovice because Madla is obliged to take a few day's leave still owed to her from last year. At last we shall have a chance to observe more thoroughly how an early spring like this develops. Apart from reading-matter, we are also taking with us a packet of letters that Madla wrote to me and I back to her when I was on military service in 1951–53. I have asked her to find among my letters one that she would consider typical of my topical commentaries of those days. I want to include it in *Dear Classmates*. Yes, she will manage to do that all right. But I bet she will not manage the second task: finding one of her own letters that would illustrate the circulation of influences between the two of us. I can tell already what will happen: she will find all her own letters silly and in a hysterical outburst she will call herself stupid. And for all I know she might stuff all her letters in the stove. My own letters will be all right, of course: I was clever and sensitive and I longed terribly for her, it's a pity I went to the dogs. I will be tempted to stuff my letters in the stove.

In front of the window the mighty cherry-tree was just coming into blossom when we arrived yesterday. Today it's in full bloom. It hides its dark figure behind a white veil. The cherry-tree resembles a bride, and I am the one who will clamber all over it in June. I know its every limb and groin, I can gauge the degree of deflection of each bough under weight. I have firm footholds in which I wedge myself to pick clusters of cherries. I am amazed at the tree's fertility and I feel I am respectful and grateful. But unhappily, I become bolder each year, moving further and further along the boughs, and the older I get the more riskily I put my trust in the cherry-tree, so that come the moment of total surrender, I shall fall and that'll be that.

The apple trees are only just beginning to divulge how much each of them intends to blossom. But flowers are not much use if the bees aren't flying. It is cold and today it was wet and drizzly too. Last year all the trees flowered resplendently and afterwards there was a meagre crop. The weather was like it is now, grey and damp, and the bees were not working. I recall doing the rounds, looking up into the trees; it was already late afternoon and the white veil of blossom was softly glowing when suddenly I heard from somewhere a mighty buzz. I looked all around and then I caught sight of them: two solitary bumble-bees, Buzz and Fuzz – stomping on the white lace like gum-booted labourers and fertilising the ample apple-tree with masculine growls. And they must have been successful because it was full of fruit afterwards.

But I must leave off writing, it is time for Voice of America.

SATURDAY, 28TH APRIL 1979

Someone had left me – possibly Ester to Hamburg – and in my misery I went into some apartment or other where a young dark-haired woman took one look at me, gestured oh dear, and without a word, like a good old-fashioned remedy for desperate cases like mine, started to strip. There were two beds there, side by side. I was getting her ready. I turned her round across the side of the bed, slipped a pillow under the small of her back, and popped myself into her pod. I look up and what do I see – a young man coming into the bedroom. He glanced at me, tiptoed to the bookshelf, took down a book from the highest shelf he could reach, and then went out, having thrown me another apologetic glance. What I did next was a trifle deliberate, to teach her a bit of a lesson: I popped out again, sat back on my heels, and gestured her to her feet. Then, as she stood above me smoothing her hair in astonishment, I said, looking up into her face between her swelling breasts, "What's going on here?" But she was totally in the dark, she had seen nothing and it had nothing to do with her. I understood straight away even before she spoke, from the shape of those breasts, and the expression of her belly. It was most cruelly etched in her furrow, still present but now closed for good. The square resembled the one in Hradčany. One side of it was entirely taken up by a red-brick cathedral. I entered a two-storeyed house, and on the ground floor there was a room that was a cross between an office and a café, and Madla was sitting opposite me at a small table. A fellow came in dressed like an army clerk and started doing something under our table. I took a look afterwards and saw that it was a little box with wires coming out of it. I immediately realised what was up; I rushed out into the square and at that very moment it all started to happen: the palace opposite seemed to lift a yard off the ground before quietly disintegrating, and then another one on my side rose and collapsed. By now I had that agonising insight into the inevitable outcome of my dream: whatever I thought of would happen. No sooner would I look at a building with trepidation than the bastards would blow it up and it would collapse. Not the cathedral as well, for Christ's sake! I looked towards it, and its two red spires (Copenhagen) were already toppling. Now I started searching about me with the strange feeling that there was something missing. Madla! I looked towards the house where she had remained, and immediately the two buildings on either side of it started collapsing. But that one still stood – of course: that was where the detonator was. I ran towards it, but at that moment a troop of horsemen appeared from a corner of the square. They were mounted interrogators. The first of them was wearing the St. Wenceslas crown. All of them were dressed in rich raiments covered in jewels and they brandished swords. So they've made kings of themselves, I thought to myself, and waited until I could run across to Madla. I was the only person there and I realised that I would be the only one capable of bearing witness to it all. I dashed into the house, but there was no one there anymore. I took a look under the table. The box was there and something was purring inside it. Madla had gone. I rushed into the next room, and there she was: on her knees scrubbing the marble floor. It was so typical of her that I lost my temper. "What do you think you're doing?" I roared, but she didn't hear me. I ran up to her, grabbed her by the shoulder, turned her towards me and yelled into her face – slowly so she would understand (the air no longer carried sound): "They've made kings of themselves; they're running amok and knocking everything down. What the devil are you up to here?!" She recoiled in shock, more on account of me, I'm afraid, than because of the news. She screwed up her face in horror and started to fall to the ground. She slipped out of my grasp, slowly collapsing on to the marble, and, with a fixed expression and pose, she actually started to sink into it, flattening out, becoming thinner and smaller. I went down on all fours and roared into her face, "Don't go turning into a picture on me!" She was young and slim, and was wearing the same blue-print dress she had worn twenty years ago when we took the path through the woods from Brumov to Starý Hrozenkov, and she wasn't moving any more.

I woke up to the sound of my own extraordinary words: Don't go turning into a picture on me. I stretched out my hand across the gap.

"Wha-what's the matter?" she said in alarm. I switched on the light. "I had a horrible dream about you," I said. "So did I about you," she retorted. "Tell me yours first," I said. "We were in London, in some hotel or other, the two of us, and all of a sudden I see that you've got some woman with you in bed, but this one has dark hair. I started to trample on her face and ran out into the street. Then came the most terrifying part – I didn't know where I was and just went on running. I got myself lost and didn't even know what the hotel was called. All of a sudden a young girl came up to me and said, "Ludvík says you're to stop acting the fool and come back. He says it's only the wife of that historian Mikeš and you know her, so there's no harm in it, is there?" – "Did you go back?" – "I can't recall any more."

I told her my dream about the dark-haired woman and her husband – apparently the historian Mikeš – and how he only went to get a book, as well as about the palaces being blown up. After the don't-go-turning-into-a-picture-on-me scene, she said, "I've never come across anything as dreadful as that."

WEDNESDAY, 2ND MAY 1979

That's the holiday over. Prague, late morning. I can see there's a whole pile of books on the shelf again with slips of paper sticking out of them. It is time I did a delivery and I have too much on my plate. Where is all that peace and quiet I had planned in order to get down to some untroubled, painstaking

"Don't go turning into a picture on me!"
(p. 175)

work – work that may not be visible for a long time, but is all the worthier for it?

The week in Dobřichovice sped by and I don't even know where it went. All I managed to do was cart away a pile of clay I had dug out, and even then I did not take it all. I used it to build quite an interesting tumulus, covered it with some nice topsoil and sowed it with grass. On one of the days, we went to the market in Beroun and spent an awful lot of money. On our way back we stopped off at Hostim, which is just a couple of cottages in St. John's Vale, and clambered up some enticingly bare crumbling cliffs. We found ourselves in a natural rock garden. I collected about fifteen kilos of interesting stones, Madla boldly scraped off a clump of moss containing a few bobbles of houseleek. Clusters of flowering alyssum hung from the rocks and bells of windflowers tossed in the wind. It was bleak, chilly, empty and grey, but that is precisely how it is, the eternally prayed-for lee in the historical tempest. I sensed a whiff of Old Bohemia and shuddered. They don't even have a village square of any kind – there is no room for one in the narrow valley with its turbulent stream. There was scarcely any sign of movement among the cottages below us during the few hours we spent scrambling here and there over the rocks above their roofs. The pub was closed – for good.

I had with me a manuscript that Míla Semrádová had pressed into my hands. Reluctantly, I started to read it. They are her reminiscences about and for her exiled son. But I was pleasantly surprised! Previously I knew her only as a journalist. We used to bump into each other at the radio building. Here she is writing about her youth, and her political escapades and love affairs in the years right after the war, as well as about the dreams she has nowadays – bad dreams that merge with reality. Who'd have thought it? And she has written it better and more succinctly than I ever could. After that I didn't feel like sitting down at the typewriter, and I didn't either. Mind you, Semrádová is a perfect example of a sinner caught red-handed, and she describes her transgressions in the most charming manner, in the expectation of absolution from her God the Son. I would not be so quick to forgive: there were other youngsters in those days who did not feel the need to ride the horse of revolution and trample people under foot! It was she who drove her son out before she even conceived him. The manuscript ought to be published.

I wandered round the garden, looking and doing the odd bit of weeding, pruning and planting. I used some saltpetre concentrate to try and get rid of a rank speedwell with delightful tiny blue flowers. I chatted over the fence with the neighbour about the earthquake. When it rained we sat and read by the stove. After a few days like that Madla was in a condition not just to put up with visitors, but actually to welcome them. My painter came with her family. They looked round the garden. It was she who came up with the idea of not dumping the clay: if it were hers she'd sculpt it into a shape and sow it with something.

One evening the Kosíks came over and we sat drinking Kléma's white wine. We sent him a postcard about it. Karel started talking about Deml and continued throughout the evening, resisting every attempt to get him to change the subject. He has great regard for Deml's courage in breaking with everyone and admires his far-sighted attitudes and his utterances on all manner of things. Mind you, in between I came in for a bit of praise too: apparently I have something of Deml's unique grouchiness. "Make up your mind, Karel," I said, "who is it I remind you of – Havlíček, Neruda or Deml?!" Because I won't manage to play all of them. In his husky voice and with slow gestures he mused about the wealth of personalities and characters we had during the First Republic, even though there were only a handful of truly great figures. He said he had managed to find out which of the villas in Dobřichovice had belonged to Šalda – and apparently we had been walking past it for years! It amazes Karel that anyone like Šalda actually lived, walked, talked, had human intercourse, and so on, and we lack all record of it. We are without any record, picture or vivid account. We are unable to visualise it. And yet people wrote about people in those days. The correspondence and reminiscences exist. These days there is nothing! All the trouble Šalda had with his maidservant! The time she ran off and left him and he was obliged to clean his own shoes and buy food... What relationship did Pavla Kytlicová actually have with Deml? And what about Rosa Junová? – A normal one! I commented naturally enough. – By no means; Karel says Bedřich Fučík denies it (though admittedly he is a devout Catholic). Whoever will establish the truth now? "And do we have to know?" I said. – "Oh, all right, but that's not the point," said Karel, "can't you see? The point is how seriously, in that case, can we take what those people said about the world? What were the deeply concealed personal experiences behind all those opinions, theses and judgements?!"

Most of the time, Marie remained silent. Madla seconded Karel. "Nowadays everyone thinks they can write," she said, "but on what basis, about what, for whom?" – "Quite right," said Karel, and Madla named some of the principal superfluous titles published in Padlock Editions, and I asked Karel, who never reads any of them: "Have you read them?" – "No, I don't need to. My dear Madla, allow me to compliment you on your perspicacity and taste – I totally agree with you," and he gave his Marie a slap on the hand to stop her biting her nails all the time. "What's up?" I hissed to her across the table, and she charmingly turned her hands to me: the nails of all ten fingers had been bitten down in truly exemplary fashion. We exchanged smiles.

I really don't know whether I understand what Karel is getting at precisely – what he is querying, or the point he himself is trying to make. Damn it, I'd like to read what he's written at last. Seeing no outcome to our discussion, I suggested we make a trip to Deml's grave at Tasov during the summer. That is bound to give us more of a clue – though to what, I am not sure. The only thing that counts for me these days is the spirit of the landscape and buildings, what I can deduce from foundations, streams, the patterns of fields – and from graveyards.

Only the last day was warm and sunny. We planted some dahlias. There was no time left for my military service letters. I checked the grafts we had made in Karel's garden and it looks as if they will take. It was warm enough for the bees, but the wind was quite strong again, which meant that they would not stray far from the hive. Only Buzz and Fuzz, the bumble-bees, circled the garden, and even they kept close to the ground on account of the wind. In other words, they stuck to the dandelions. I chased them, clapping my hands and shouting "Up you go," but to no avail. I shall have to see about getting some honey bees.

Don got away from Mrs. Hemerková again and raced in and out of the lilies and tulips, his leash flying. I saw red. The whole house stinks of that dog. Sometimes she ties him up by the woodshed where we have our compost heap. I went after him. He took fright and leaped at me. I took fright too and almost smacked him round the chops. But when I look into his face, I cannot help liking him. I am just afraid he might do something to Madla.

We didn't talk about her job. She did not have to think about it for a whole week, and that was the best rest she could have had. I had been intending to question her about it and record it here, but she was too happily ensconced in Deml's letters, Šalda and the First Republic. And probably I was in no mood to get rattled either. Madla has the following plans for when she retires:

put the household in order, read, go to exhibitions, spend more of her time at Dobřichovice, pay a visit to her old teacher in Brumov, go to exhibitions, read, work in the garden, read, sightsee in Prague, spend as little time in Prague as possible, get a good night's sleep every night, cook interesting dishes, read – and write. These days everyone wants to write!

Every time we go there, we get the garden straight and then, when it is looking its best, we leave. The tulips from the bulbs that Petr Pithart gave us last year came into flower during that final afternoon. Overwhelmed with gratitude, Madla picked several of them and we stopped at Kampa on the way home. Madla actually went inside that house and the flat. That only goes to show what a good rest she had.

THURSDAY, 3RD MAY 1979

I went to see Jaroslav Seifert. His wife opened the door and seemed not to recognise me. She shook my hand limply. She is discreetly ill, sadly beautiful. Her husband, on the other hand, looked better than last time. He had lost weight, but got up painfully from the table. "How do you do?" I greeted him in English fashion. – "I feel lousy, thanks all the same," he responded in proper Czech fashion. He wanted to hear all the news so long as it was good. I had nothing of the kind to offer. He had a bouquet of flowers on the table. Another enormous bunch stood in a vase on the floor. He had been given them for his name-day.

I handed him a letter I had written in advance at home: "Your birthday is coming up. If the times were different, leading national figures would come and visit you, bearing bouquets and decorations. It would be on the film and television newsreels. Some friends of yours would like to do something of the kind in a more modest fashion. Would you agree to a filmed interview?" He resisted the idea, but I convinced him with the following argument: "One day the younger generation could reproach us for having lacked even the sense and presence of mind to photograph, film or record certain people." With a feeble wave of the hand above his huge baggy trousers, he said: "Oh, all right then."

I then asked him if he was still waiting for them to publish his memoirs. He said that he wasn't and had decided to release them. He had agreed on it the previous evening with Vladislav, who would edit them. He said this with a guilty look on his face, as he had been promising me the memoirs for the previous two years. "On what sort of terms are you with Vladislav?" he asked. – "The best." – He told me with discomfiture that, although he had signed several dozen transcriptions of *Umbrella from Piccadilly*, the official publisher *Československý spisovatel* now wanted to bring it out. "Isn't it dubious?" he asked. – "Who for?" – "Both parties." – I replied: "Not as far as we're concerned. It's the reason we operate Padlock Editions, so that the publishing houses finally realise that even without them books still come out. And it's no problem as far as they are concerned because they are always able to outdo us in terms of output and quality." – "I'm relieved you look at it that way." – And then I got down to the main business.

"There's a poem in your *Umbrella* collection about the destruction of the Marian Column. What is it you actually saw then?" – "What did I see? I saw them knocking it down." – "Can you possibly remember who, exactly?" – "Who? Franta Sauer, of course." – "But tell me, please. How did he do it?" – "How? He threw a noose over it and people pulled it over." – "Were you with them?" – "Of course, not." – "You don't recall whether Holan was there, do you?" – "You must be joking! I was seventeen then, and he was four years younger. He was a child still." – "Aha, aha." – "You know how it is. Anything can happen in a revolution – and that was supposed to be some kind of revolution." – "And what about Sauer? Didn't he die some complicated death soon after?" – "Not on your life! He died quite a contented death at quite a respectable age." – "The way I see it," I said, "monuments should be left alone – all of them." – "Of course they should!"

On the way home, I stopped by at Jan Vladislav's. I hadn't noticed that it was nearly mid-day. They were having baked noodles and Mrs. V. invited me to join them. It was good. "I just happened to be passing by," I apologised, "I was at Seifert's." Jan beamed and said: "What did you find out?" – "That you beat me to it, you rascal!" – He laughed, but even without that he would have looked comical with his wispy hair slicked forward on his forehead, almost into the noodles. "And are you cross with me?" he asked sweetly. – "I can't be when I'm eating at your table." – He told me that Eva Kantůrková had brought him a collection of my feuilletons for transcription. I expressed surprise. True, she had spoken to me about it last year. It was to have been a critical selection, to which she wanted to write the foreword and Gruša the commentary. But that idea had been abandoned and since I can see no good reason for a mere collection of feuilletons, I am against it. Jan took note and Mrs. V. was miffed – she wanted to type them out.

FRIDAY, 4ᵀᴴ MAY 1979

I had to go to the Slávia to speak to Professor Černý, who is a regular visitor and now sits in Kolář's old place. Whenever I join them at that table I feel out of place: it is meant for the likes of Hiršal, Boštík, Pechar, Vladislav… I never used to go around with artists and poets, and it is an outcome of the present irregular situation that we all huddle together nowadays. Admittedly Kolář made me welcome, and so do the others, but I prefer it when each of us sticks to our own enclosure. One reason for my sense of incongruousness is doubtless my briefcase, which I am always obliged to leave yawning wide open while I remove things from it and hand them out. There are books to be submitted to their authors for signing and I no doubt look like a smuggler, a middleman or an agent. And all the while I can sense with my dorsal nerves how we are being observed by the police-spy from a corner table that affords him a view of both wings of the room: I have dubbed him the corner cop.

By the Rudolfinum I happened to bump into Helena D. She was also on her way to the Slávia, where she hoped to catch Gruša. She was happy for me to accompany her as she had never sat in the Slávia before. I found that admission almost unbelievable, as unbelievable perhaps as others will find my assertion that I bumped into her by chance. We walked together along the embankment and she laughed to see the water foaming at the weir, and the chestnut trees on the island turning green and ready to blossom. From her neck hung a tiny brown-leather pouch scarcely capable of holding more than forty crowns – just like a schoolgirl. "You should be able to advise me. Our old professor has his eightieth birthday coming up and I've been chosen to propose the toast. What shall I say to him?" – "But I don't know the man. What has he done?" – "He designed the offices of Prague Transport, for instance." – "Well, say you have some good news for him, they're demolishing the entire embankment by Hlávka Bridge – and his building is the only one they'll spare." – "That's a great idea!"

And then, as we were walking along, who should come towards us from the opposite direction but a well-known press photographer. We said hello, smiled, and passed each other by. It occurred to me to turn round and I found the woman already looking back at us. I took a couple of steps towards her and she put her camera to her eye calling: "I know, I know, it struck me too, but a bit too late." I said: "I've got a special order for you, though: one snapshot of Hradčany for a lady emigrant." – "What's that?" the photographer exclaimed in surprise, and went on flashing away, taking several shots of us. At my words, Helena scowled disapprovingly. She was unwilling, but I thrust her in front of Hradčany; it looked as if there might be tears. "OK, but another one with the two of us together!" and I went and stood beside her. Here we go again: it's like being alive and conscious and calmly arranging one's own funeral. That was the feeling I had – have. Can she possibly not realise?

In the Slávia we sat at a good distance from Kolář's table. We ordered coffee and I went and took a peep round the pillar to see who was there. Hiršal was there with Dr. Danisz, who was also waiting for Gruša. What did we talk about, Helena and I? I didn't note it down, and now, in March 1980, I don't recall any more. Outside the window, the carved figure of Trinkewitz was walking along the pavement. A moment later, as he passed by our table, he said: "I've brought some farewell presents," and departed in the direction of Kolář's table. The next to walk by were Vladislav and Jiří Gruša, who embraced Helena. At two thirty I asked Professor Černý to accompany me to Žofín Island.

On the way, I explained to him the plan to film an interview with Seifert, and I asked him whether he would conduct it. The script is being written by someone I shall call Slavík. "Do you know Slavík, Professor?" – "Naturally, he's that booby." – "He's no booby, Professor. He's an intelligent, reliable and courageous man. What makes you call him a booby?" – "What does he do, then? Why have we heard nothing about him?" – "There are people who don't let on about themselves without whom those of us who happily let on about ourselves would be scarcely capable of doing anything. Such as making this film, for instance." – "If you say so. And it has to be me? You have no one younger for Seifert?" – "We've got several possibilities," I said airily, "but it was Slavík's idea that you would be the best one for the job, as in this way there would be two outstanding personalities in one film. As members of the same generation you would be better suited as conversation partners, bearing in mind, of course, that the film is being made to mark Seifert's birthday and that he should therefore have the larger role, which it would be up to your adroitness to achieve and Slavík's job to ensure. Should you decide to undertake this task, Professor, I would ask you to defer to Slavík." – "All right, all right, but I wish you to understand that I am undertaking it on the basis of your confidence in him. Most importantly, you've spoken to Seifert about this?" – "Yes, and he agrees." – "He agrees, you say. I'm surprised."

We had now reached Žofín Island and Slavík rose from a park bench to meet us. I introduced them, and Slavík, brandishing an open copy of *Literary Monthly*, declared: "I've just been reading this issue on *Aryan Struggle*, where they also mention you…" Ten minutes later I left them sitting together in the sunshine and went back to the Slávia, but Helena had left.

THURSDAY, 10TH MAY 1979

I would sooner be picking out a few songs on the piano than writing. It's after midnight. I could do with taking a trip somewhere on my own too. But who'd believe I was there on my own? Would I be sure of it myself, even?

My last three days off I spent with Zdena in Rochov. That enormous stone house has eleven windows, most of which look out from habitable rooms. The shutters of rough boards are hanging off as the nails are coming loose. The heavy shutters will have to be sawn in half. The house is austerely beautiful and splendidly situated. The plot surrounding it is unfenced. Zdena is trying to get a hedge to grow all round. In front of the house there stands an enormous apple-tree – a withered old golden rennet – alongside a mouldering, half-alive walnut tree covered in splits and cracks, and a plum tree with fine red fruit, whose trunk has been eaten away by the ants and is only held together by the thick bulging bark. Beneath the apple tree, a deep stone well towers towards the centre of the earth. The north side of the property is enclosed by the walls of neighbouring farm buildings, while to the other sides there are unbroken views, particularly towards a small hill on which there stands a church and a famous cemetery.

Either the news that I was there had not had time to reach certain circles, or they were short-handed during the holiday period: no one came to observe us and we had to make do with surveillance by local informers. I inspected the fruit trees and pruned them. I tied up the gooseberry bushes and made incisions in their bark to allow them to swell as they grow. I grafted some budding twigs into the trunk of the morello cherry – the buds being at the same stage of development as on the host tree. It is totally against the rules, but we shall see what happens. I mowed the abundant patches of dandelions with a scythe still sharp since the previous autumn. Over the winter, the gateway had sunk because one of the stone pillars had tipped sideways. I repaired it after a fashion.

A crack runs down the narrower side of the house, from the top down to the foundations, via the window frames. There was even a draught from it in my cell on the floor above. Three years ago I added a thick stone wall to that corner in order to weigh down the foundations, and it looks as if the menacing crack has not grown any bigger. We decided to preserve it so that it would be clear even to a dunderhead that the house was about to fall down at any moment. "Maybe that's the only reason they didn't take it from you," I said to Zdena. In the wake of the Charter, certain circles had stirred up the villagers against Zdena. In my cell, I poured some liquid cement into the gap from inside and then whitewashed the room. It is a room beautiful in its starkness, with a window on the sunny side of the house overlooking the hill on which the church and the famous cemetery stand. The floor is of unplaned boards that I pulled out of a ruined inn years ago. The ceiling is held up with sturdy, fissured, black beams. There is nothing here but a table, a chair, a small marble-topped chest of drawers, a heavy bed that I built out of logs, and an iron stove with a long stove-pipe into the chimney. Zdena imagined that now I had a perfectly simple room here, just the way I wanted it, I would no longer give the others preference. It did not happen and she still does not really understand why. She thinks it is because I lack the courage to change my life. The one occasion, some years ago, that I tried to live and write here, I did not write a thing because the house interested me far more than anything I might think up.

The way into my cell is through a square room with four windows to the south and west. Originally there was a hole in it down to the ground floor and it remained there for a long time. It was only when Zdena started to make a ceiling from below that I was finally obliged to put in a floor, turning it into a lady's bedroom with ceiling beams painted light blue. The paint was left behind by the original inhabitants: Germans. Zdena later used the same paint on the wardrobe, bed, table, chairs and dressing-table that she inherited from her parents. But she never sleeps in that room of hers, even when I am not here. I have the impression she only combs her hair there.

A tall young man with a deep velvet voice came here and gave me five thousand crowns. I passed him a note asking what it was for. He wrote one back saying it was up to me: for Padlock, for people in need, for myself. I shook my head but he gestured over the paper with such determination that I took the money. Half of it I put aside for him and will give him books in return. Some of it I will use for giving reductions on more expensive titles to certain people, such as Ivan Kadlečík, and I immediately took six hundred for myself and used them to buy from Jan Lopatka the three-volume selection of Deml's works that have been edited and "published" in typescript by VBF. Jan Vladislav brought me a message from Jaroslav Seifert that he has had second thoughts and no longer wants to do the film interview. I was relieved. Pavel Kohout sent his friends a postcard with a text that people are interpreting as a message: "I'm bound from the Labyrinth of the World to the Paradise of the Heart." Meanwhile Helena is dismantling the paradise of the heart: Gruša will get the bookshelves and I can also have a piece of furniture if I like.

I said: "Who's going to look after your graves here?" – "We haven't any," she replied. And yet her father died in January, her mother a few years ago and her brother even earlier. "How come?" I asked. – "We've nothing, not even urns. My parents were against it. They just wanted their ashes scattered any old way, without any ceremony. That's how it was done." It strikes me that this is a family trait: casual farewells. "A low threshold of presumption", I said. – "Are you in favour of ceremonies, then?" she asked. – "I want to be laid in a grave in Brumov, with a band and maybe a priest – but I'm not sure of that yet. It'll depend on the sort of government there'll be." And it crosses my mind that Šimsa might be quite willing to do it for me. "Well I hope you expire from homesickness, so you won't be able to return." – "You really want me to expire?" – "Just so." – "And no mercy?" – I reflected a moment and relented: "Well die decently then and have a proper burial, and I promise you, Helena…" – or maybe I said Mrs. D. – "that as soon as they give me a passport I'll pay my respects to you during my first trip to Vienna."

I said: "Who's going to look after your graves here?"
(p. 186)

I said to Madla: "When they were knocking down the Marian Column, Seifert was seventeen, Holan wasn't there at all, and Sauer, who started it all, died a normal death. What do you say to that?" – "What do you expect me to say?" – "You came up with the theory of divine retribution." – "I didn't come up with it. It was written in that church." – "But that said nothing about Holan or Seifert. You were the one who said that." – "You haven't gone and spoken to Mr. Seifert about it, have you, for heaven's sake?" – "What do you think I am!" I reassured her.

It looks as if the grafts I did in Kosík's garden are all stirring, apart from the American Mother – but then the tree it comes from is also a bit on the tired side. Karel is spreading tons of topsoil on his land, a whole load for 200 crowns. We talked about the Mrštíks, how they all died quite young, and Karel declared: "And take Karel Čapek. He was four years dead at our age!" Madla started to surmise that two things had hastened Čapek's death: the cloudburst at Strž and Olga Scheinpflugová.

We walk to the Kosíks' garden along "Šalda's Trail" past his villa. On the way home, Madla told me that she had quite enjoyed herself in my absence: a lot of people had visited her – Pecka, the Bartošeks, Rudolf Slánský Jr., and another day the Mlynáriks had come. "And I had a chance to give them my attention without feeling nervous. We had some lovely chats and I discovered that without you I am more self-confident and even witty. I'm my own woman."

From outside the door I could hear the sound of splashing water and the clatter of crockery. Professor Machovec was at home. "Good morning," I greeted him, then pulled down my lower lip and told him, "Another four false teeth." – "That's fine," he waved me in with a wet hand, "do go through to the sitting room, Maestro." – "First of all, Professor, I would very much like to view your Ella Horáková section, if I may." – "But of course you may, though I fear you know it all already," he said motioning me into his study. – "Not so, Professor, you've got two new ones here," I called back. He wiped his hands and came to join me. "Quite right," he said, "I had those done by the professionals."

They were two 240 × 300 mm coloured photographic portraits. "May I have a closer look," I asked. He reached across the furniture to the wall and passed me one of the photos. They struck me as very good photographs whose colour and tone placed them somewhere between realism and romanticism. Unfortunately, I didn't ask who was responsible – not for the idea but for its execution, which seemed to me both subtle and witty, whimsical and nostalgic: two smallish pale breasts in semi-profile whose nakedness is not so much proclaimed by the tightened nipples as whispered by the gently scattered freckles; surmounting it all a bespectacled serious face, whose expression you may interpret – according to your own private inclinations – as either a reflection of restrained sensuality or the projection of a penetrating intellect. I have the good fortune to perceive both. I took off my glasses and brought the picture up close to my eyes. I marvelled at the subtle way in which the skin tones had been developed, how the pigment seemed to contrast differently in light and dark areas, and in particular how the freckles receded away from me over the slope before flattening and finally overlapping onto the other side, like on a drawing of the lunar seas at the point where the illuminated and dark sides meet. That brought me back to the reddish tone of her hair, which, after all, I could have noticed ages ago but which had never really struck me till now. I quickly hung Ella back up again. "She didn't look like that last time, though," I said.

"She was pretty exhausted," I said more accurately. Professor Machovec gestured despairingly: "She ruined herself for good, that one. Her life, I mean. Her talent, her promise. You may well say that it is the delusion of a loving gaze, but believe me that whatever happens I have still retained enough objective judgement. She could have been the woman of the century. Seldom does one encounter such penetrating reason, even in a man. And she falls for some ordinary fellow in such a hopeless fashion." He covered his eyes. "And she knows he'll ruin her, but she just can't help it because he makes her go all weak at the knees!" – "That's the way it goes!" I said.

Professor Machovec excused himself, saying he had to go and finish the dishes, and left me in the room. I scrutinised all the Ella pictures: at the ages of twenty, twenty-three, thirty…portraits, nudes, fancy dress. Apart from Ella, Professor Machovec also collects pictures of Naďa Urbánková, though in her case his collection suffers from a lack of good personal connections, so that they are only agency or magazine Naďas. In addition, there are pictures of women from mythology and female saints. It seems – I ought to have asked him more precisely – that he is interested in the phenomenon of women in the history of humanity. When I came here years ago and saw it all for the first time I was stupidly a bit open-mouthed, being unable to reconcile it with the stature, name and character of that professor of philosophy. However, over the years I feel I have maybe gained the humility to understand.

He re-entered with the words: "I've already forgiven you for it, Maestro." – "For what?" – "For having gone as her witness. You couldn't have acted otherwise. But don't be taken in by what she said about having to get married – she told me that one too – the fact is that just four days before the wedding she assured me the cops wouldn't be able to force her into anything. Mind you, the truth will turn out to be quite different, and I doubt we'll ever know for certain. I wouldn't discount the possibility that it was precisely the other way round, that she suggested to the StB that they finally force him to marry her." – "Really?" I said in enormous surprise, mostly at the fact that such an idea had not occurred even to Madla. And yet it was just as likely an explanation.

"You played a thankless role, poor fellow. You really ought to have realised. But on the other hand, you succumbed to her womanhood and she knew very well why she came to see you of all people – because she despised you. Maybe I shouldn't tell you – though why shouldn't you know? As far as she was concerned, you – and it applies to me too, of course – are a primitive, a peasant, a yokel, one who is O.K. as a punster, but the only man of her calibre is Pavel Kohout, a man not only of world renown but also a man of the world who knows how to behave, present himself and act with style. You – and it applies to me as well, of course – you and I were miserable wretches to her: pathetic creatures, of no account."

"At her wedding I was much taken by her mother," I said. "I'm even considering going to see her. What do you think?" – "My dear friend, you're not the only one to have fallen under her spell! It's the Moravian in us. But you won't find what you're expecting. I don't mean to imply – heaven forbid – that the woman lacks the qualities that attracted you. It's just that you'll find out, as usual, that appearances can be deceptive." – "In what sense, for instance?" – "In the fact, for instance, that she is a German – and a rigid Saxon to boot – who entered this nation and has absorbed absolutely nothing from it – nothing! No sense of humour at all…"

Finally I asked Professor Machovec to accompany me out into the street where we discussed the matter I had chiefly come to see him about.

PRAGUE, MAY 15, 1979

Dear Jiří,

Thanks for your card from Berlin. I also read the letter you and your wife sent the Vladislavs. It grieved me to read that you feel it's more peaceful there. In a way I would sooner the greater peacefulness were here. Goodness knows whether you'll ever want to return here if that is how you feel…

I have been to the Slávia twice since then, though I haven't been staying away on purpose. It simply became clear that when I don't have anything to deliver you, I find no reason to go there, nor the time, apparently. On the occasions I have been there, the place has been extremely full. Even your seat was taken. You'll have your work cut out to get Him back to His own chair.

There's nothing new here. The weather has warmed up a bit at last. Trinkewitz is going around giving away his works as souvenirs – he's on his way out. This whole business of departure has weighed heavily on my thoughts in the recent period. People are almost laying bets on whether Kohout will return or not and the assumption is that he would like to and she wouldn't. She apparently received a decision from the prosecutor's office that she would be liable to psychiatric examination. That's probably intended to whet their appetite to return.

I am now writing almost every day, as you told me to, and when you come back it will be waiting for you. So come back. I have given up writing feuilletons and am giving up Padlock Editions gradually. Otherwise there's nothing new to report. Everything is available here if your expectations are not too high. I got a haircut again – for spring. New titles include: Klíma: *My Merry Mornings*, short stories; Komárková: "The Secularised World and the Gospel"; Pechar: "Man and Truth"; Kriseová: *The Woman of Pompeii*; and Jiří Hájek: "Human Rights, Socialism and Peaceful Coexistence." Everything has been put in the agreed place.

They had Klíma in for a – very amiable – chat: they talked to him about the possibility of giving him a passport and a telephone. They called me in too, about three times. With me it was worse, but equally inconclusive – if I'd be a good boy everything would be all right. They've demolished everything at the Holešovice end of Hlávka Bridge; it's probably an oversight – the proper target was on the opposite bank slightly upstream. Our level of organisation still leaves something to be desired, as you can see. I'm reading Marquez's *Autumn of the Patriach*. He's the one who wrote *A Hundred Years of Solitude*. It's in the same style – it's excellent – but duller; less happens. Of course I read a bit of the Deml, but didn't I tell you so in January? Kosík's reading him at the moment and he talks about it every Sunday when he comes to see us.

Alexandr Kliment told me that Kleť Hill (where he has his cottage) had prophesied to him that things would change for the better. And he believes it because one evening he saw boulders and flames leaping out of Kleť and lava flowing, and there was an earthquake in Yugoslavia afterwards. Kleť Hill only makes minor geographical errors apparently.

Hiršal commits major faux pas at your table (...) Another regular has joined the table – Danisz, who has received a further summons: for a "verbal" – he attacked a public official again. We've got a proper lawyer there, eh? Whenever I see him there I say: "Doctor Danisz, go away!" But he's already been given his notice at work. Gruša sits there arguing with Pechar, who defends Marx. Hegel caught it in the neck too. At one point in the argument Pechar says: "What do you think about it, Professor?" – "I have my own opinion, but I've no wish to get involved in this debate." – "Silly debate" he probably means, and just sits there with the smoke going straight up his nose. And then they start talking some vague nonsense about how apparently they actually threatened Kohout in Vienna by telling him they'd confiscate his flat because a Charter meeting took place there. Nobody has any real information and they just go on speculating until in the end the Professor says: "I see I'll have to get involved in this, because I'm completely *au courant* with this affair..." Boštík says nothing and Vladislav wears a blue jacket. But there's one thing I must tell you – tips are shrinking! I actually saw Pechar, when she said "four crowns" to him, give her four crowns! I can imagine the staff passing one another and whispering out of the corners of their mouths: "I can't wait for him to get back!"

Yours,

Ludvík

Surprise: Messrs. A. and C. came and saw me to hand over completed task "D." It's an odd feeling: it is no business of mine; it's simply that the responsibility for the two-month delay has been shifted onto me. But it will be a good job. No one is expecting it.

It's a fact: when I don't push anyone or anything, padlockery abates. I leave bound editions uncollected for a week and it's not the end of the world. I have not yet delivered my foreword to the feuilletons and no one has asked for it. I have a growing pile of unread manuscripts and the authors say nothing. I am beginning to resemble a state enterprise: the second part of the astronomical year-book with information about space research has not come out yet either. Tatarka has not given permission for his *Jottings* to be released. And all the fuss we had with that!

Our emigrant son, Martin, has written to us. He had not written for nine months. He explains his silence as worries, work and an inability to finish the letters he starts. And finally he declares: "I haven't written because I would have felt like giving vent to one particular emotion. That emotion is a feeling of aggression towards father that has a thousand and one causes. It might conceivably have done me some good, but not him. It strikes me that the way he brought us up did more harm than good, but since at present the harm is more obvious to me than the good, I am not a good judge, by any means..." He goes on to say that he has difficulties with people in authority and the root cause of his problems he sees psychoanalytically in me.

I did not bring up Martin any differently from the two younger boys. The only difference, and one I could not help, was that a man becomes a father gradually and later, unlike the mother, or so I believe. I had a couple of very simple and essential guidelines that Ondřej and Jan found easier to accept than Martin. Those guidelines were: from the age of two, you tidy your toys every evening; from six years old you get yourself off to school on time; from age twelve you wash your socks in the evening, make your bed in the morning, and bring your homework for signing. Apart from that there was total freedom of speech, movement and action. It was mostly Madla's job to implement those guidelines – the ones she agreed with; the others we would argue about. And sometimes I would have to argue in favour of the boys' freedom of movement and behaviour, because she would sooner have had a well-ordered flat, whereas I thought there was no reason why the boys' room should not be a menagerie, a workshop or a chemistry lab. (Everything tidied up in the evening, of course. Every game starts afresh each and every day! So if it takes someone more time to tidy up his toys than to play with them then it's his own – stupid– fault, and no one else's!) But Martin had the bad luck of the first-born. He had to put up with all his parents' initial energy. The other boys practically reared themselves on their own, and Martin himself had a lot to do with their upbringing. He also writes in his letter how the violin came to haunt his dreams so much that he finally gave his instrument away to a friend. His violin was a trial for all of us, but nobody forced him to play! All I wanted him to do was either to play or to stop taking violin lessons. His ambition prevented him giving it up and his stubbornness prevented him improving: of his own accord he would play just one piece for as much as an hour, but with the same, recurring mistake every single time. And I was obliged to listen to it. So how dare you criticise me for it now, all the way from France, you stupid boy? Do you want a clip round the ear?

Our Martin is explosively clever, hardworking and trustworthy. The only thing is he doesn't know how to economise his time and effort – I don't know about money. We didn't drive him to emigrate; it was his own decision, after the ministry prevented him from finishing the course in France which they had given him permission to take two years previously. Now we argue about him again from time to time: Madla maintains that our Martin is worse off than us; my view is that he does not have it easy, but he is better off than we are because he has a choice of how to act when the going gets rough.

For last Christmas we sent him a tape with a recording of us telling each other stories and having fun at the supper table. About that he writes: "Listening to your family tape almost made me physically sick. You seem so harsh to me. Your sense of humour is utterly black, merciless, verging on the demented. What's happened to you? Have you gone mad? It puts me on edge to listen to it. It's so reminiscent of *The Guinea Pigs*. Only Mother projects serenity and kindness. Do bear in mind that you're deranged and spare her. If you can't stand it any more, run away from there."

No, we haven't gone mad, my dear Martin, we have simply developed a mode of behaviour that is probably the only way of surviving with honour in our climate. Our climate is harsh, un-Czech and conceivably lethal.

It crossed my mind that now I had a telephoto lens I could try photographing Arizona from the hill opposite. I used to have a go at it every year, but in the overall panorama of the landscape Arizona looked small and insignificant. And whenever I came right up to it I was unable to get a whole shot of it from any angle. Its obvious demarcation from its surroundings was lost, and it quite simply ended up looking like any old meadow. People might have wondered why I was so attached to it.

Even in the days when I herded animals in it and lived like a creature of nature, I was aware of its specific character and I tried variously to describe it in words which have still been preserved. I also made drawings of it, but those I no longer have. I also liked making detailed maps of it for the benefit of our tribe, but then we would all tear around in it from memory. My maps depicted every individual tree or copse by species, as a matter of course. They also indicated a pit of mysterious origins that still exists at the junction of two woodland paths and into which everyone fell at first, and all the major ant-hills. Even though in reality the terrain does not exceed thirty metres in altitude, the map's large scale provided scope for using all the specialised map-making colours, from the joyful green of the lowlands to the exciting grey-beige of the prairies and the red-brown of the impenetrable mountain ranges. I did not go as far as to pretend there were glaciers, because they never appealed to me.

I woke up to find I was alone in the flat. The schoolmistress and Madla had probably gone shopping. I took my camera and went out. The sun shone golden in an unblemished sky. On the way, I took my customary photo of the castle and brewery, as well as one to show the progressive devastation of our former street. A factory has bought up the entire left-hand side of it and demolished the wooden houses. Last year, they were still there! Then, from the bridge, a shot of the stream overhung with willows and alders. On the level area where the poorhouse once stood, there now stands a block of flats of eight storeys or thereabouts. My godmother was looking out of the window of the house opposite and I took a photo of her too. And then I walked in the direction of the non-mill and non-saw-mill – where I thought they still were! – and the two wooden barns I mentioned earlier when I wrote about some little lad – most likely my cousin Ludvik – sitting in front of them among the geese. And I went on up the hill where, on a miserable patch of goat-nibbled, sun-scorched grass amidst hard prickly junipers, I used to catch crickets, and where there once grew tiny white, pink and red flowers – cats-foot that flowered at precisely this time of year. But I did not find any. The vegetation has changed, possibly even the micro-climate, the regime certainly. Flowering now were silverweed, crosswort, and the kidney-vetch known as *bolhoj* – paincure – that I refer to disrespectfully as *holboj* after the Holba boys I used to go out herding with. And in the damper hollows, whole clumps of comfrey were glowing yellow. The junipers have disappeared without trace. I sat down under a cherry tree and spread out my things. On the opposite side of the valley, in the faint glow of the sun, lay Arizona.

I took aim and held my breath. Like a living being – a woman, say – it danced in the dewy light in all its now vanishing beauty. As always it struck me whether there was anyone else living here who loved it enough to want to preserve it. I noticed with disgust that someone had already established the first little field there. I could see the original trees. I shall go and look at the orchids. This evening perhaps.

On my way back from the hill someone called out to me from the eight-sto-rey block of flats: "Come on in!" I looked up and counted how high it was. As I got out of the lift, the flat door was already open and the man greeted me with the words: "Welcome, Chief!" We meet each other almost every time I come here, but this was the first time he had addressed me in this way, as if aware of my present concern: my chieftainship. I went in. "What were you called?" I asked. – "Mes-haba," he said. I was disappointed, I was hoping for a better-sounding, and above all slightly human name, such as Whistling Arrow, though I do recall giving someone some such name at that time. This is him? – "Ai doraka manya hane..." he chanted, as if wanting to prove his credentials. – "All right, all right..." I said, "I've been to photograph Arizona as usual." – "And still no luck?" he sympathised. "I'm trying it with a tele-photo this time." – "Is that so? Send a *lunokhod* there for goodness sake!" he advised me. "No," I said, "I'm sending a *lunokhod* into the past."

His wife brought in a bottle of red wine. Mes-haba opened it. We drank it. "How come you're both at home in the morning?" I asked in surprise. – "He doesn't work at all," she said indicating him, "and I won't go to work till this evening – if I feel like it." It turned out that Mes-haba has some kind of semi-job which seems to entail him working overnight in the winter while in the summer he only works a few hours a week. In the summer he chiefly grazes his fifteen sheep. "Why don't you come over with your wife this evening when I go out with the sheep. I've got a ranch in Čertoryje." – "Orinocio," I corrected him. – "Orinocio. That's where I've got a sort of... well a... ranch." – "But what do you live on," I asked. "Partly my wages, partly those sheep..." Mes-haba replied. – "And partly we are eating the proceeds from the cottage," his wife said. The factory had paid them a fairly decent sum for the old cottage it had demolished; money had no future and there was no sense in working your fingers to the bone for your pension. "Who'll give us a guarantee that we'll be drawing a pension for ten years?" The only thing that had any point was living: going for walks, grazing sheep, reading books. "Hey, bring me the... fetch me the... you know," Mes-haba gestured to his wife from his armchair. She went to the bookshelf and brought me two books to autograph. The wine must have blunted my otherwise excellent judgement so, like an idiot, instead of writing Black Panther, I signed them as if they were a police statement. "Here, by Jiminy, do you remember," said Mes-haba, "how we ambushed that train?"

I was thus reminded me of a dreadful incident which – Well I never! – I actually failed to enter in my diary at the time, and mostly likely forgot all about. I can still feel the amazement I felt then, that a well-meant plan could go so horribly wrong.

I spent several years building up an Indian tribe, starting afresh every spring because over the winter my redskins would all revert to being their parents' fearful little boys again and amuse themselves with banal mischief-making. Every summer I came nearer to my vision of a true Wallachian Delaware Indian, and when at last we knew how to do it all and had all the necessary props, when we were known and people started to be a trifle scared of us, I took a good look at myself and those Delawares and suddenly I felt a trifle stupid. Particularly after I had ruined my eyes reading about Indians and had to put on my first glasses.

Once, on a hot summer afternoon, a Sunday when a humid silence still reigned above the Rocky Mountains, Arizona, in the valley of the Little River, I went to my hide-out and applied my warpaint and then bedecked myself in my entire rig: bow, a quiver of arrows, several loops of cord round my waist, a knife in my belt, my head-dress, my *wahgun* in my left hand, my spear in my right, intending all alone, as a solitary Indian – unspeaking, silent, untiring and fleet of foot – to traverse the whole territory and make sure that it was still mine. I would have to cut across an open highway and then melt into the woods on the other side. The moment I stepped onto the white sole-searing road and ran a short way along it, two figures emerged from the bend ahead. They were two old men from Návojná or Nedašov returning very late from morning mass. My first thought was to turn tail and run for it, or dodge into the field and squat among the corn. But that was out of the question! On the other hand I did not feel capable of jogging on towards those two old people, because it was such an uncertain encounter.

I decided to go and stand by the trunk of a (Maid of Bohemia) apple tree, lean on it, relaxed, and with a firm and keen gaze observe these two outlandish white men, let them pass me by while I maintained a proud silence. This I did. I realised I was already big enough to admit to being an Indian. With noiseless, faltering – but persistent – step, they came nearer, their iron-tipped sticks smiting the stony road. When they saw me, they stopped conversing and just focused their gaze on me from the shade of their black hats. I felt like running away, but now it was impossible. The two *Tarahoons* – our pejorative name for the upland villagers – pattered almost noiselessly towards me on their thin bow legs. On their feet they wore white coarse-woollen slippers with red trimmings, on their legs, white trousers of the same coarse material, with red piping, and from their embroidered purple waistcoats there protruded the well-worn sleeves of their linen shirts, which were tied with a string at the neck.

I stood the test – in my full rig. And as they passed by me, their heads turned in my direction; not a muscle moved in their tanned and furrowed countenances, not even an eyelid. They passed on, tapping with their carved sticks, and when I saw them from behind, their studded belts hanging ingeniously low on their backsides in a gentle loop, I knew that my days as an Indian were over. That I would never again be able to live it, but only play at it, maybe.

But before things came to that pass we had performed several real deeds: because a well-fashioned arrow is made to be shot, a sharpened lance to be thrown. One afternoon, I ordered the members of my tribe to get ready and dress themselves up, as we were going to ambush a train. In some of their faces I detected surprise, in others fear, but most of them displayed the artless human joy of the redskin. It was early evening and the sun was dipping towards the horizon: the time when goats graze best and most calmly and

*"... do you remember," said Mes-haba, "how we ambushed
that train?"* (p. 197)

they require neither effort nor attention. I would have preferred the freight train, of course, but it did not run on Sundays. I painstakingly and repeatedly stressed that the effect on the passengers was to be entirely psychological – it's debatable, of course, what words I actually used – and that immediately after charging out from the prairie, as the train was passing below us, we would yell right into the windows, and at that moment they must release their arrows to fly just over the top of the carriages. I say *over*, but I also say *just*!

It must have been an uncommon surprise for the Sunday travellers leaning out of the windows of the good old slow train when the ten or thereabouts of us – but why not say fifty – rose up out of the prairie and rushed yelling towards the train, and a cloud of arrows whistled just over them. We were still celebrating, after retrieving our arrows from beyond the track, when a blue uniform appeared in the prairie. On the subsequent report the names did not appear as Whistling Arrow, Cawing Crow, Lame Dog, Mes-haba, Black Panther… but as Lorenc, Kozáček, Vilímek, Ambrož, Klok, Loucký and Vaculík.

"I plainly said that you were to shoot over the train," I now told Mes-ha-ba. – "Me?" he said, pointing at his navel, "I shot over the train! But you should have taken into account that Lame Dog was too clumsy to pull his bow properly!" Lame Dog. Yes, I was fond of him. He was a very clever lad, a real bookworm, with a good singing voice. But he was left-handed, sickly, and had a limp in both legs. I could not exclude him.

I told Mes-haba: "Best not say too much about that train. It might occur to them to use it against me!" – "Don't you worry. I know what you're up against. And seeing as we're on the subject, what's the story of those photos in *Ahoj* magazine?" – "Those photos? That's the very same story."

We talked and drank wine at the top of the poorhouse. From the window I could see the water shimmering in the stream.

WEDNESDAY, 23ʳᵈ MAY 1979

It's the kind of weather we won't have in the summer: fourteen degrees from early morning developing to twenty-six at noon. The sky is monotonously blue. Last night's storm cleaned the distant views, freshened the lawns and washed the dust from the streets. Yesterday I had a fine old headache just behind the eyes – from the sun and from sadness. Not to mention a dose of conjunctivitis. "It looks as if I'll have to wear dark glasses," I said at the supper table, "and look ghastly like Martinovský." – "Funny you should mention it," said our Jan, "I bumped into him in the tram." – "Did you say hello?" asked Madla. I had also bumped into him: first a fortnight ago, and then again yesterday. The first time I was the one who greeted him, yesterday he greeted me: "Good morning, Mr. Vaculík!" On each occasion, it was at the same place. I'd love to know what we're both up to there. I think he'll soon figure it out.

Yesterday, Eva Kantůrková came looking for me and left a message that she would be waiting for me by the tank monument at ten. I left home on time but the trams weren't running. In a panic I took a taxi and got there only five minutes late. But she would most likely have waited even longer as she certainly wanted to be seen: she was in a long red dress that reached the pavement and was open to reveal one leg. It suited her, but nice she wasn't: "I've brought you my *Lord of the Tower*, but you're not going to like this one either, so it's pearls before swine." – "I'll make a note of your dedicatory words," I promised.

Then we discussed my collection of feuilletons that she wanted to have transcribed. She was already aware that I had put a stop to it at the Vladislavs. She asked why. I said: "Your original plan, the one you approached me with last year, was different from this year's. You were wanting to show that I continue to write the same way and hold the same opinions despite the vicissitudes of the times. On the radio, in the press, before 1968 and afterwards. Is that how it was?" – "Yes, but I realised it wasn't a feasible idea." Aha! I said to myself, you just don't feel like giving me a testimonial like that that any more. Out loud I said: "But I didn't ask you to do it. The idea was all yours. You've decided to withdraw it, enough said." – "But that would be a shame. Your feuilletons are really good, and besides, I've already put a month's work into them!"

We wanted to go somewhere for a cold drink, but were unable to find any restaurant open. On the way we both grumbled. About the émigrés too. Mlynář, said Eva, who had it from Hübl, was apparently beginning to see things through German eyes, regarding Sudetenland and the expulsion of the Germans. I had no view to express on the matter, as I had not read any of it; I never get to see anything. Eva asked if the Hostovský Prize had reached me yet. Nothing has reached me. It is said – underlined – that I won last year's

Egon Hostovský Prize for the first annual collection of feuilletons, which was subsequently published by Index. I know nothing about anything, but it will be unfortunate if the feuilletons' authors think I have kept the money for myself. A thousand dollars. In the end, we went to the Black Brewery, where there was someone who showed us a transcript of secret instructions for the traffic police. They are to keep a regular check on drivers, passengers and any luggage in cars whose numbers were given on an attached list. There were more than six hundred cars there, and Herzen, registration number AO 19-77, was among them.

I got home to find a message waiting for me from Helena to say that the Finnish publisher Keijo Immonen had arrived. He would like to have a word with somebody but she had been unable to contact anyone. She would be sitting with him at four-thirty on the terrace of the Parkhotel. I vacuumed up the dust in the bedroom and the kitchen, had a shower, made myself a coffee, read a bit more of the correspondence between Deml and Šalda, and then walked over there.

It was pleasant on the terrace, which was by then in the shade of the building. A balmy breeze ruffled the orange linen table-cloths. Helena was wearing a charmingly ridiculous girlish dress of yellow cotton. The Finn greeted me as if he knew me: we had apparently met at the Kohouts' place in Sázava, on Pavel's birthday, where he claims I made a speech. Out of the question! All I did on that occasion was sing the Water Sprite's aria from *Rusalka*: "We're all children of one mother…"

We ordered ice cream. The young lime trees in the nearby lawn waved their translucent green gowns; another summer storm was taking place somewhere else in Bohemia. I thanked Mr. Immonen for publishing my *Guinea Pigs*, though it turned out to have been another publisher. We exchanged apologies for that faux pas, but I think he had greater reason to apologise. He asked if I was writing anything. I said I was. He asked whether I would let them have it. I said I would, willingly, but was afraid that they would not find it interesting enough, even though, for my part, I actually enjoyed reading books that took me into the intimacy of a strange environment in such minute detail as to make it virtually incomprehensible for me: banality transformed into fantasy. Mr. Immonen said there were five publishing houses for literature in Finland and they had all agreed to support Czech writing. What was my new book about? – I told him – whereby he became the only person to know: about things, people and events. "Is it about Helena too?" he asked, smiling at her. "Of course," I said, "and as of now it's about you as well."

Helena said little. There was a dark area on the left side of her upper lip that hinted at an eruption of domestic bliss. I admired the aplomb with which she wore it there on the Parkhotel terrace in the company of a Finnish publisher. And now he was inviting her to a concert tonight. It sounded so nice and quite natural, since the two of them had become slightly acquainted that time at the Kohouts', when I had registered neither him nor her. Is it possible? And now she will depart. Every night there will be a concert with a different man, anywhere in Europe, maybe. My eyes were on her.

Helena understood his invitation and asked me to excuse her, which I did gladly: "*Sie darf nicht abends allein ausgehen.*" – "*Warum, ist sie so leichtsinnig?*" he asked with a smile. I answered with a pun such as I occasionally manage when the German invites it: "*Nein, aber ihr Mann ist so schwersinnig.*" Before we took our leave there was another question for me: "When will you come to Finland?" – "As soon as I can," I promised.

Helena and I went off towards the tram and I was just wondering whether I ought to tempt her into walking a short way with me when she set off for Stromovka Park of her own accord. We walked along in silence. The sun was still doing its job up in the dense, mighty crowns of the beech trees, but the ground beneath them already exhaled the dampness of evening. After a little while Helena said: "I already know you love me. It's sweet the way you love me." A couple of hundred yards further on I stopped and told her: "You know what, I think you'd better go now, lest you get another one at home!"

SATURDAY, 26TH MAY 1979

I was just trying to work out today's date when Woice (typo) of America told me. It is apparently a hot day in Vashington. Like it was in our garden. A government commission is investigating a plane crash in Chicago, the Soviet government is relaxing its policy on emigration, and Jaroslav Hutka is on a performing tour of America. Madla is getting ready to do some ironing and the Israelis ceremonially handed over the town of El Arish to the Egyptians today.

And what's our reaction here in Czechoslovakia to all that? I think it is right that terribly heavy aeroplanes should crash, for whatever reason, in the same way that terribly long tankers quite rightly break in two. There is just no excuse for three hundred people to be transported at once and at high speed from one place to another. Their collective desire is harmful. From time to time the Soviet government lets a couple of its Jews go to the Promised Land, and the good-hearted Americans nearly have kittens over it. The fundamental human right is to live freely at home, not to be free to run away. What happens to a country that irreconcilable people run away from? What sort of people remain and what can be expected of them? Most importantly, what are they are up to in such a country, for heaven's sake?

I am very, very tired. Madla has had a change of plan and gone to bed; she will do her ironing in the morning. "They were all at the meeting yesterday, except for me." – "How come?" – "The Phantom said it would be a supervisors' meeting, and I'm the only one who is not a supervisor." – "They're all supervisors? Then where are their subordinates?" – "It looks as if I'm the only subordinate." – "That's great!" – "They're all supervisors of something, supervisor of the statistics section, reception supervisor, supervisor of the trade union section. They are subordinate to each other, but are all supervisors." – "Other times you attend the meetings." – "Precisely. That's what made me think it might be a meeting about me. The other day he asked me if I was serious about wanting to retire." – "Whatever makes him think you might want to stay there a day longer than you have to?" I said in astonishment. – "I don't know. I just don't know!" – "And did you get the impression he wants you to stay?" – "That's just it, I can't tell. It's obvious that he needs me and makes use of me. When I've sorted things out in reception, he sends me up to the office. When I've done everything there, he sends me downstairs again, because the stoolie down there has done nothing but mess things up again." – "Then why doesn't he kick her out?" – "I already think that if it were up to him he would kick her out, but he's not allowed to," Madla replied. – "And haven't you got an inkling by now at least whether he's a spy among the freemasons, or a freemason among the spies?" But Madla doesn't know. A little while later she brought up the meeting again. "One thing's for certain, he's already wondering how he'll cope without me. But it also crossed my mind that they might be having a meeting to discuss what they'll give me as a present." – "But they've a whole six months to do that!" – "But what if they needed to make a decision to deduct five crowns from each person's salary to buy the present?" – "Oh, my poor wee lamb!" I said.

The main feeling I had after listening to Hutka's interview with the Woice of America reporter was regret at the injustice done to the nation that remains here. Hutka is right. The moment he realised that he could not be himself while staying here, he left. But who do I become when first one, then two and then thousands leave? I will not be able to stay the same if Pavel Kohout does not return, for instance. Will it be the same nation, if *they* see to it that only *they* remain? Doesn't that worry them at all? – Just lately, I have felt a desire not to be here. Almost a desire not to be at all. I banish it for the sake of Madla and the boys who are – and here – so naturally at home, as if they were safe, and they would not let themselves be dragged away. They will go on putting up with an ever more limited existence and squeezing the life within them into an ever harder stone.

This morning I watered the roses, which are looking very promising. Then I mowed the grass, but only in those places where it is coarse, because scything in this heat wave would otherwise expose the soil and it would scorch. I do not really regard the dandelion as a weed. It has a fine flower and even afterwards it has those downy globes. The saltpetre that I hoped would destroy the speedwell is having the opposite effect – which is excellent: since I put it down everything has grown prolifically – speedwell and grass alike; but since the grass is taller it serves to suppress the speedwell. I mustn't cut it. I painted the garden chairs. In between I hosed myself down and the only bit of planned reading I managed to complete was Mrs. P.'s latest story. The feeling I get is of a new authoress charmingly putting herself through her paces behind a pillar in a corner of the hall of literature. Her story "The Lorelei" manages to convey an extremely vacillating, vague and hesitant emotion in an unexpectedly specific and eloquent manner. It is cruel, contrived, true, ironic and rueful. And although the setting bears only a tenuous resemblance to the present-day world, it is strikingly contemporary. "If you don't like it, I won't like you!" its author told me. So I like it.

I am waiting to see if Karel Kosík will come and see me of his own accord without my going to him. Otherwise I will not find out the latest about Karel and Hynek and Mácha, or Šalda and Deml, and more importantly about our grafts. They must be suffering, poor things, in this heat without any shade. We are in for a drought again. The lilac is in flower and its scent reaches me from the dark through the open window. I would much prefer never to return to Prague.

When I cut the grass again this morning, the sun was not as glistening as yesterday. Meanwhile Madla was upstairs reading "The Lorelei." I knew when she had finished because she immediately dashed down to scold me: the story was stupid enough for a woman's magazine and I was turning into a coffee-house lounger; if anyone still respected me, then it was only for my past – all I could do now was ruin my reputation; the book's author was a pampered madam who could see no one but herself; and the Anton in her story, the one with the moustache, was no doubt me; *et cetera, et cetera*. So there we are.

Let people read things or not? Why not?! This time I surpassed myself – I did not argue. I made myself a coffee, took it down to the white table under the trees, and sat watching the grass and the leaves and the flowers, how they just *are*, and wondered to myself whether I too have the courage – and whether I am allowed to have the courage – quite simply to be, without worrying what I look like? What about this book? I have still six months to go. But as soon as the end comes in sight I shall start to squirm with fear. What else am I going to write? And who will give me their seal of approval?

Ivan will probably say that what I am doing here simply isn't done. Eva Kantůrková will say I've gone off my rocker, and if anyone else were to write about me the way I write about others I'd come to a bad end. Gruša? He'd say I've got the jitters and am lashing out in all directions for fear I'll never write anything else... No, on the contrary, that's what Kantůrková would say, Gruša's would be the other. Mr. Václav will say I've spilled the beans about everything and everyone. Zdena will notice that I didn't do justice to her life's sacrifice. The literary critics: "But is it creative writing?" The psychiatrists and cops – can get stuffed. (Let's be our own psychiatrist and policeman!) My boys: It looks as if we'll have to wait till we're older, but so far so bad! The schoolmistress must on no account read it. I can't even be sure of Brno. Only Šimečka in Bratislava and Kadlečík way off in Pukanec are remote enough, and have sufficient emotional detachment from the things described, to be able to think that what they are reading is as good or bad as if I had made it all up. Madla: "I haven't the slightest wish to read what you're writing. There's only one thing I'd ask you – be so good as not to even mention me!" Ha!

I thought better of it and went upstairs to make her a coffee too. She was ironing; she had "The Lorelei" open again on the bed and was just making sure that its author was indeed hopeless. "Switch the iron off and come on downstairs," I said.

The thermometer on the pear-tree registered twenty-four degrees Celsius. The blackbirds swooped down low in among the bushes. The grass mowings were fragrant as they dried. "See how it's impossible to talk to you about anything," I said. "You turn everything into a conversation about me." – "You'd sooner be sitting here with someone else. I know." – Since everyone has their proper place, I said: "If I want to be with someone, I go and find them. This is your place." From the wall of the house, the goddess Mnemosyne looked over the glade at us with her dusty eyes.

We looked in at the Kosíks' garden in the evening. Karel was varnishing the parquet floor in the cottage, Marie was gathering up watering cans, rakes and things. The grafts are drying. The terraces are doing well. I helped Karel give the grafted trees a proper soaking for good measure, then we all embarked and drove in a line of cars all the way to Prague. Straight to Hradčany, in fact. Marie invited us in for what they call "iced coffee." While she and Karel were making it, I managed to read what was sticking out of the typewriter. The page was unnumbered, so I don't know whether it was the preface or afterword of his by now possibly one-thousand-page philosophical treatise. Judging from what was there, it might be fair to say he was starting from scratch again. For on the paper was written something along the following lines:

"To deny the statement that Being is deduced from social being does not imply that we take nature into account or that Being is composed of social being plus nature, or that these two things merely exist here together. But neither does it imply that Being is composed of the two of them plus art..."

I made an effort to remember the sentence, but it is obvious to me now that I cannot vouch for it. When Karel returned with a cup of iced coffee I said: "I have a suspicion that you are headed for God." – "In fact that's just what I'm trying to avoid," he replied remarkably, and then, as if I had finally touched the right nerve, with incredible readiness and of his own accord – and succinctly – he explained to me his endeavour: "I want to say that there is no God, and that people's belief in God actually conceals a yearning to know Being." – "And doesn't it strike you, that's precisely what the Christian philosophers might have had in mind? Only they employed the accepted terminology of their day?" – "Could be." – "So one might say the God of

"To deny the statement that Being is deduced from social being does not imply that we take nature into account or that Being is composed of social being plus nature, or that these two things merely exist here together. But neither does it imply that Being is composed of the two of them plus art..." (p. 207)

the philosophers is the provisionally achieved form of your Being?" – "That's about it."

Marie who had been attentively following with her eyes what Karel was saying to me and vice versa, now said demurely: "Sorry to interrupt, but would you like a bite to eat?"

FRIDAY, 1ˢᵀ JUNE 1979

It is already June, the month of grass. The ripening grass is sparse and wispy in the scorching sun. In the meadows along the railway track there are rings of harebells, ox-eye daisies and some pale mauve flower. Yet another reason for weeping after the weirdest of nights.

When I was leaving home all those years ago I felt as if I was taking leave of my life. I placed myself at the mercy of my misfortune. I accepted it meekly. My childhood was losing me and I no longer cared about anything. But it turned out that I was dying into a new, long life, the one that gave me what I have. But that horrible experience of leaving virtually everything behind remained with me, and that sense of disaster could be evoked by all kinds of unlikely events, and hence I proved incapable, for example, of throwing away a chestnut once I picked it up. The upshot is that I prefer to leave things where they are.

Last night – a feast of mourning and grief. A carnival of leave-taking! A marvellous party of absent friends where all their chairs and armchairs are empty, no one moves, no word is spoken, no puff of smoke is emitted. And the crowds that used to be here! All those words between esteemed friends! All those esteemed words between friends. I executed several dance-steps. "Put on some music," I commanded, and put a record on. The sound of guitar chords emanating from some coffins, followed by Hutka's unaffected, almost subliminal singing that elicits his listeners to join in the chorus. I joined in and sang through my breast bone. I twirled around and transparent figures slid past me. Would you believe it? Which of them knew then that it was the last day? To know the last day, to recognise it! Now I could move the limbs of the dead: I could bend their arms this way and that. I sang into the skull resting on my breast: the whole night ahead of us! Dead funny, gentlemen! You bet!

Alas and alack, the grey dawn was just breaking outside the window when I raised my head from my pillow. At that very same moment my briefly tranquillised "grief" resumed. And there was no way of halting the new day, the first day of my next death, and there was no more life-generator to help me oppose it in any way.

In the morning the sun shone. With the heat the river started to dissolve into the air, and the grass on the meadow once more quietly started to pop. The harebells, the ox-eye daisies, the pale-mauve flowers. Dew under my feet. "Do boys have the Body of Christ too?" – "What do you mean?" – "Like Christ, I mean."

SATURDAY, 2ND JUNE 1979

I intended to record my encounter with Ludwige Van but changed my mind and got on the bike to go and see Karel Kosík. Like an idiot I managed to fall off twice on the way, because I am used to a bike with a coaster brake and also because when I wanted to jump off I would forget to take my feet out of some paraphernalia on the pedals. It was Jan's bike and has all sorts of nonsense on it such as a derailleur gear. Karel treated my grazes with alcohol and a disinfectant spray and only after I had suffered these indignities did I get a chance to start questioning him about his philosophy. It is my duty to state that what I wrote or will write here about his opinions is unlikely to be valid. I would have needed a tape-recorder. It is more likely a record of the sort of discussion I should like to have with him. There is nothing for it but to wait until he has finished his treatise.

I had been planning to put to him a serious objection: How was it that a philosopher with such an appalling attitude to the speed of light could aspire to any kind of understanding of Being. He replied that it was a prejudice and error of the last century if we understand the task of philosophy as being analogous with that of mathematics and the natural sciences. Philosophy has its own specific problems and procedures and bears no responsibility for the truthfulness of knowledge in other disciplines. Nor is it subordinate to them. The independence of philosophy goes right back to Ancient Greece, he said. Meanwhile he put another bottle of wine into a bucket of cold water, leaving the previous one there, and was annoyed when the bucket overflowed. "Take out the one that's already cool, then!" I advised him. "Now would any Greek philosopher with the slightest notion of Archimedes' principle do something like that?" I said. Karel has to carry the water from the stream. The temperature today was around thirty-one degrees, and even now, around midnight, it is twenty-six degrees in the bedroom.

It was a hot day in Vashington too, almost summer-like; Pope John Paul II is in Poland; President Carter is off to Wienna and here they arrested Charter 77 spokesmen Benda, Dienstbier, Havel and Bednářová, along with several other people. It must have happened on Wednesday, when I left Prague. It was the day Madla suspected that someone had tailed her to work, though she could not think why. When I arrived home, I found an already-expired invitation to an "official discussion." I wonder when they will send me a new one, or whether they will come for me directly. That's the way they arrested Gruša and Roubal just a year ago.

Silent moths fly in my open window. It is becoming pleasantly cool and so I start to picture myself with scarlet Ludwige Van. We were at a concert on Tuesday. Madla brought the tickets from work. It was given by the Hamburg Radio Orchestra. We sat bang in the third row on the right, so I had a good view of the proceedings, which were not split in two this time. And I could also hear extremely well, the right hand side of the orchestra even better. They played Dvořák's A minor Violin Concerto and Bruckner's Symphony No. 0 in D minor. Meanwhile the streets were full of promenaders; Prague looked for once as if it were part of the world; I am sure Dienstbier, Benda and Dana Němcová were unaware they would be arrested the following day, in the same way that I don't know about tomorrow. Things are going from bad to worse. They are probably five times worse than in the summer of 1879 when Dvořák started to write his violin concerto – i.e. exactly a century ago.

The violin solo was played by Edith Peinemann. She wore a scarlet robe tied at the waist with a green ribbon. Her brown hair was cut straight, shoulder-length, at the back, and she had a fringe half-way down her forehead, and she gazed from beneath it brownishly, now businesslike, now seemingly abstracted, free of all coquettishness, and her movements were devoid of the affectations that are so off-putting in women soloists. She could have been thirty years old and she had a violin made by a man, of course – something so obvious to me, incidentally, that my curiosity started to be aroused: I wonder what you are intending to do with it! I had never seen a woman play a violin before and have no idea how numerous women violinists are. I don't count women who play in orchestras: they are something else entirely – indistinguishable – such as in the tramcar or at the post-office when there is no man available to do the job, which is always preferable.

She started to play. I am absolutely certain that Dvořák never expected anything of the sort. It is altogether debatable whether women should interpret music by a man – a male solo – at all. No one will convince me that Dvořák wrote this concerto for some "violin *an sich*" irrespective of whether it is held by a man or – for want of one – a woman. He wrote from within himself – from within a man. And as a man. What will happen to a man's music in a woman's hands? When a woman plays a male role on the stage it has to be a joke, an emergency or part of the genre. I am not enough of a connoisseur to judge Edith Peinemann's performance of the solo violin part of Dvořák's Violin Concerto. I do not know how it is generally played or how others have played it in the past. I listened and also watched with equal attention, to see whether I would discover the identity of this woman. She seemed to me relaxed yet matter-of-fact, like someone who knows what he's about. There were none of the artificial trimmings, hallowed tics, winsome gestures and posturing. She started off frowning slightly at her fingers and the strings. During pauses she stood relaxed and almost a little sloppily, with a childlike unselfconsciousness. Then gradually the piece started to engender a more impassioned expression and I, noticing her beautiful wide mouth, which from time to time she would purse stubbornly, Beethoven-like, and then open slightly for breath while her eyes did not look outwards at all, only inwards, thought to myself: Dvořák really ought to be here! Here he has aroused passion. But is it passion of the masculine or feminine kind? What would he hear?

And what is it I hear? I hear a woman, see her, imagine her. Dvořák does not enter my thoughts at all, that's for sure. Otherwise I was aware of the hall and the streets outside. Prague like the city of an oft-visited nation. A festival of music. They come, they play and go home to their hamburgs. Fiddlesticks! – I started to react to that woman with an angry indictment.

SUNDAY, 3ʳᵈ JUNE 1979

The summer is now. In summer it will be cold. From early morning it is eighteen degrees in the shade of the pear-tree; it will reach thirty by noon. I fill a hip-bath with cold water and soak in it. As I run the water the hose tries to straighten out and keeps jumping out of the bath so I stick the end into a heavy glass vessel and stand that in the bath. Madla is astounded: "You're a genius with your brain!" However, a moment later she adds: "But they'll write about you that women were your downfall." She is still reading F.X. Šalda's correspondence with all and sundry, it's all just opinions and ideas, and that's bad for Madla. "Why should anyone write about me," I said, "and who will? I don't intend to leave any letters behind."

She exaggerates about the women in my life, I almost have nothing to do with them, and even that is an exaggeration. It is wrong to make too much of affairs like the one I had with Mrs. P. last Tuesday when I, as a notorious café lounger, had a tryst with her on the terrace of the Praha Expo restaurant to talk about her story "The Lorelei."

I am looking out of the window into the crown of the cherry tree; we shall only get about a thousand cherries. There is nothing for it but to start keeping bees. Our boys are at the building site again. I fear that Ondřej will announce a marriage. That would be the end of our family. The lads don't even have the time to go bathing in the Berounka River by the weir. Jan came yesterday for half a day, did something with Herzen and Švácha and then left. One thing he did manage to do was repair the hose connection on the tap and frighten Mrs. Rohlenová into thinking we were moving in. When she is not cross with us, Mrs. Rohlenová talks to us copiously about life and plants. Mrs. Hemerková takes Don out for a walk twenty times a day. I was doing some watering. She went past just at that moment and said, "Water that mound too," where she had sown some nasturtiums in my lawn. "Yes, I will." Then when I was watering the mound Mrs. Rohlenová said: "Water the yucca too." It stands by her steps. "Yes, yes," I said and laughed. She got the point and apologised: "My leg hurts again, it's all swollen." – "Rheumatism," I said. – "Poppycock!" she replied. – "All right, poppycock," I conceded. – "Rheumatism in heat like this?" she continued. – "It must be summer poppycock," I concluded.

Mrs. Kopecká goes visiting her children at the Karlík cemetery. She grows all sorts of flowers for them in order to have some at every season; she is always watering them and in the process she sprinkles our potatoes which are already nice and big, thanks to her. All around can be heard the sound of motor mowers; I do not understand why people turn their gardens into a singed semi-desert. I mow with a scythe, and then only the shaded places. I leave the daisies be; we have a meadow of daisies here. I want Kosík to see it, not to mention other people who will never the see the like in their lives. I am going to fetch Kosík here in an hour's time and we shall return to Prague the back way via Karlík Valley.

I'm not looking forward to Prague; I am frightened to learn the news – how many people have been arrested and for what. "They won't arrest you yet," said Madla, "you're a VIP. When they send you to prison it will be for good, and things will get even worse. Brezhnev will die, Husák will resign and (expurgated) will take his place. Then at last you'll all discover how well off you were today." That could well be true, mind you. As an illustration of her assessment of the status quo, i.e. that it is not that bad, she reads me Šalda's letter to Machar: Prague is a nasty little hole, the Czechs are riff-raff who always begrudge outstanding individuals their virtue and success; it's impossible to make any headway or undertake anything; pettiness everywhere, slander and denunciations flourish... Written in 1907. In another letter, Šalda writes that when things were hardest for him, he was bucked up by the words of the noble-minded Růžena Svobodová, who restored his belief in the value of his work and gave him strength. "What could she have said to him?" I said, and immediately visualised it: "Oh come to me, my poor little diddums!"

So everything was probably the same as today, except that Russia did not extend so far into Europe. And that makes an enormous difference!

MONDAY, 4TH JUNE 1979

Ten arrests so far. They include Otka, Mr. Václav, Petr Uhl, and Jiří Němec and his wife Dana. I went to see Petr Pithart and then with him to Gruša's and Ivan's about what we are to do. But nobody knows the terms of the indictment. We would be able to say nothing more definite in their defence than release them! So we share Ivan's view – though we did not manage to catch him at home – that there is nothing to be done for the time being. As always my mind turns on the unenticing idea that I, personally, at least, should do something. But I have been avoiding solo performances and I am afraid to jump back on the hateful merry-go-round now that I have at last managed to find the time and concentration for writing and wider reflection, and now that I have so many unachieved goals. Only now am I recovering from my winter dejection which, in retrospect, I can see was enormous.

On the other hand, there is another thought that also crosses one's mind: the dragon has got his princess. Isn't it now safer for the rest of us princesses to go ahead with preparations for our summer festivities?

It's thirty years ago today that my love and I were wed. The event was commemorated, as it is every year. On this occasion, by a larger than usual gift – a picture by Vlastimil Beneš. It depicts the grassy banks and rocks at Hlubočepy, a place we used to go on walks with the kids, as described quite interestingly in *The Guinea Pigs*. The picture was painted in 1974, when I did not go on many walks with Madla, very few in fact, and she used to go to exhibitions and monuments on her own, or occasionally with Mr. Beneš. When I brought the picture home, she was not back from work yet. I unwrapped it and the boys asked me why this one in particular. I replied: "Your mother lay as a model for this picture somewhere round here," and pointed to a the spot where a gentle green hillside ends abruptly in a terrible, suicidally sheer cliff.

JUNE 7, 1979 (FROM AN UNSENT LETTER:)

...I'm worried about you. The whole day, and particularly this afternoon when there was a big storm and everything went dark. I've had the feeling that somewhere you are calling to me for help. I am deaf to the things being said around me and can think of nothing but the suffering I have caused you. I'm not sure what I am more afraid of – that you'll decide not see me again or what you'll suffer if you decide otherwise. It is now entirely up to you and the decision you take will govern your future life even if you live it elsewhere.

Yesterday's meeting with your husband on the square (you did right to send him) I did not find particularly shocking or humiliating at all. Instead I was astounded by the discoveries I was making. Setting our case aside, I can't help thinking about what sort of life you've had and will have... and that some day you'll have to put things in order as a woman if you are to salvage any ideas or any feeling for your work or for other people.

Being a violent man myself, I am hardly in a position to get hot under the collar about someone being violent to a woman, but I do think that one ought to be forbearing too and not begrudge one's partner a full life and self-expression. One ought to enjoy the privilege of giving. And there's play and cuddling when the mood takes one. I can't tell what it is you have; you'll have to add it up yourself. If it comes out entirely on the credit side, don't hesitate and don't be ashamed (on my account) to cleave to such a man.

...a gentle green hillside ends abruptly in a terrible,
suicidally sheer cliff. (p. 215)

He used extremely coarse and insulting language with me, but I remained strangely calm somehow. It all sounded so peculiar – here was I being sworn at by some husband. I put up a very weak defence, for two reasons: firstly, I couldn't use anything that would betray any knowledge of your private life, because he would have taken it out on you; secondly, it was as if you were there or could hear it from somewhere, so that I found myself incapable of saying any of the things that traditionally form part of such charming disputes among gentlemen, and which would have only caused further injury and humiliation to your husband. Because it's not easy for a woman to live with a humiliated man. Besides, there was no telling in which direction your favour might have swung. So all I did was treat an infuriated man to some thoughts of mine that had been valid, as it were, on some other occasions, but were wasted, as I realised, on this, in the hope that he might recall some of it one day. He responded with ridicule, but this had no effect on me because I was too horrified at the thought of the punishment you must be taking. Only two things offended me: his conviction that if you didn't see me for two months I'd cease to exist, and his statement that he had disliked me from the very first moment he clapped eyes on me long ago. Why those things in particular, I can't really say. But I expect his feelings and actions are more natural than my recent efforts to get to know him better for your sake, in order to understand the nature of your relationship. My request that he deliver you my bouquet – admittedly by then made for research purposes and as a literary exercise – came to grief. "A scruffy little bunch of flowers – for all that?" he exclaimed. It's a marvellous exclamation, implying as it does that there is something that deserves an enormous reward. But were that the case I can't imagine what I would have to give you. (...)

I want to go on seeing you – how is entirely up to you. And I shall wait for you only as long as I can stand it and then I'll come for you myself. If it is to be the last time, then I must hear it from you alone.

MONDAY, 11TH JUNE 1979

Today, at last, I am able to do something again: read and write. Since last Wednesday I have been going around with what I hope has been a granite expression. And I am not sure whether it is permissible to let any of it seep in here. But what sort of book is this? When I started in January, I had no idea what its main theme would turn out to be; I did not even know all its future characters and had no purpose in mind. So now that my main theme is here and tormenting me and the characters have presented themselves, am I to deny or disguise them? How do I know what any of them will do and what will be the point of it all?

I wrote her the letter with a feeling of helplessness such as I have not had in a long time – a dreadful state – but it was no help to me, as it just lay here and I had no idea how to get it to her. It gave me a better appreciation of a hostage situation. The moment I try to do what I have to – bang. I didn't know where she was at that moment; I suspected all kinds of harassment. I felt amazement at what had happened and a fidgety anxiety that I either ought to be with her and taking her away, or to apologise deeply and drop the whole thing. Why, though? I didn't think I was acting so badly. I was old enough to value the things that were still possible, and I was serious with my offer to that man: let her speak to me, speak to me and see me, and here's my hand on it!

Relief came only when I hit on how to get the letter to her. I recalled the name of a friend of hers. I phoned her this afternoon, and to my surprise learnt that Helena had just been there – with her husband, mind you – and had managed to leave a letter there for me. I asked her friend to open the letter and read it to me. All it said was: "Sorry. The whole afternoon my hand-bag has been under surveillance, as if you didn't have enough worries. I had to promise that I wouldn't see you now, but I have to talk to you. Are you willing? The families are being used as a threat. Do take care." I'm to collect the letter tomorrow. I want to see the handwriting. I unstuck my letter and added under today's date: "And God gave us the freedom to choose between virtue and sin, otherwise virtue would be worthless; and if we make a bad decision then let us suffer for it! Fear not, I'll send you to Austria myself if that's what I feel you're fit for!"

We spent Saturday and Sunday (yesterday and the previous day) on an excursion with the Kosíks and it was stupendous. Karel has had Marie for about seven years or so and had yet to visit her parents. He says he hates travelling, that he sleeps badly in strange surroundings. So now we set off there on a sunny morning early. Louny, the panorama of the Mid-Bohemian volcanoes, the delicately drawn-out pantile of the Ore Mountains (Erz-gebirge), the distant smoke-columns of the chemical works, the coal dust and gas of ill repute. Kadaň's deserted square, painted and arranged like theatre scenery for a historical play that has not been staged in a long time. Maybe it was because I had to concentrate on driving that all the yesterdays were blacked out in my mind. I only registered the agreeable present, as I expect a horse does when it is being ridden. I enjoyed everything.

I ought to say something about Marie's parents, but it would take too long. Her mother is a German, her father a Slovak from near Košice. Hence the children are one hundred percent Czech. It aroused my admiration, my laughter and a brief permitted burst of something akin to love of my country. I got her mother, still a fine young woman, to write out for me two genuine Erzgebirge songs in dialect, and during a gentle stroll uphill among the blueberry bushes and birches, her father told me about the occupation of Košice in thirty-eight, his service in the Hungarian army, captivity by the Russians, his arrival in the border zone after the war, and his vain attempts ever since to grow a few decent apple trees here.

That evening, we watched on West German television the Pope's holy stampede in Poland, even though the picture was both elongated and double. One thing led to another and Marie's father, a manual worker, remarked to me and Kosík: "You shouldn't have shot your mouths off so much in sixty-eight!" – There was a 'shush!' from the mother, and the father started, very unwillingly, to squeeze his face into a semi-apologetic expression and we had to talk him out of it. Early on Sunday morning he was again coaxed to apologise, but he didn't want to. And in the end it's just as well, because if we accepted the apology in principle, it would be as if the two of us, Kosík and I, were to blame for it all!

On Sunday, we went on a walk through the little town and then kept on upwards alongside a brook in the direction of the border. The town gradually petered out, giving way to meads and hillsides. Healthy insects buzzed in the tops of the maple trees and there was the sound of birds in spite of the scorching heat. In the brook, small fish violated the border with the GDR. The white line in the middle of the tarmac road was still there when we reached an iron barred gate. There I stood flabbergasted at the sheer artificiality of it all: about two metres-fifty centimetres beyond the gate the town of Klingenthal with its three-storey houses began. There stood a pharmacy, a news stand and a sweet-shop, and a motor-cycle was crossing the intersection. It was as if we were in a menagerie looking out into the world of humans or in the cinema watching a foreign film. I could not tear myself away. But it was nearly noon and we were getting hungry.

Lunch was followed by leave-taking and a drive to Cheb for ice-cream and coffee. Too hot for walking! Sculpture exhibition. Upland plain, green, wind, grass, trees, sun and mountains all around. On a narrow footpath we stopped and listened to the breeze.

> *Auf da Barch, do is so lustich*
> *auf da Barch, do is so schie,*
> *scheint die Sunn am allererschtn*
> *scheint sie a am längstn hin...*

Karel commented: "What if you were to move here? Do you think they'd leave you in peace then?" – "Here, yes. That's if I ceased to want anything," I said. – "That's what everyone here has done," Karel said.

On Friday morning, I received an ethics lesson from Major (?) Fišer of the gold signet ring. I had made up my mind not to say anything about them, but to do so if they didn't leave me alone. "What did we agree on last time, Mr. Vaculík?" – "I don't think we agreed on anything." – "I asked you whether you were writing another feuilleton, and what did you say?" – "That I wasn't, that I was writing something else." – "So what's this supposed to be?" he asked, showing me a photocopy of "Spring is Here." I replied like a reprobate schoolboy: "I'd written that already." – "Why didn't you tell me?" – "I don't see why I should. It's not intended for you." He started to read some sentence out of context, haltingly, as one unaccustomed. "What's a cont?" he asked. "That's supposed to be coat," I said.

I switched over to automatic. I'm hardly going to defend myself for real, get riled up, argue. I will just sit here for the next two hours. He has to say his piece while also training this young fellow sitting here with us: We won't allow law and order to be subverted. Every state takes action against subversion. If only you used your work to create something worthwhile for society. What have you created, in fact, over the past twelve years? Write as much as you like, so long as it's for this republic. What's that cowshed supposed to represent? Who are the cows meant to be? And those weeds freezing to death like dormice – who do you have in mind, us? There's always the last straw, you know. Are you suffering any injustice? So why are you bothering your head over those people? They were committing an offence and now they've been nabbed. After all, you're over fifty – life is too short, isn't it, or don't you think so? I don't get it. Can you explain it to me? You're not going to say anything. At a given moment, given laws apply. Why do you need to be in some committee for the defence of the so-called unjustly persecuted?... There was a flash from the glim lamp of my automatic pilot – Aha! That must have been the one important question I was supposed to react to and declare truthfully: "But I'm not in any committee!" I stayed silent. A pause. I smiled, his lips twitched too. I can't remember now when it first struck me that they collect sentences like those and string them together like beads, so that at some later date they can use them to build a picture of me to present to a ruminant television audience. "What's your rank?" I asked. "It doesn't matter," he retorted dismissively.

It's still warm but sometimes at night we get a healthy storm. The dried-up corn is being ploughed under. It is summer now and a pleasure to walk around Prague. But ice-cream does not tempt me very much. I found not a thing in the astronomical year-book about that awful catastrophe of quasar 3C 273 that *Rudé právo* wrote about in January 1977. I can't get any sandals, or a bow. When I opened the door today, Bibisa rushed up to me and we went out together. On the stairs she kept on rolling her huge eyes at me. We came out in front of the house and she started to lick her scorched paws in surprise. I picked her up and carried her across the road into the shade. Her mistress didn't come. She is taking part in exercises out on the gravel in civil defence uniform.

When I got home, I took a shower, found the transcription of that German song and am now working on a stylistic translation:

Oh, it's merry on the hill
On the hill it is so fine
The sun it comes up earlier
And shines here longer too

TUESDAY, 12ᵀᴴ JUNE 1979

I was coming to meet her friend and from a distance could see how distraught she was. "I haven't got the letter. I destroyed it. I'm only a beginner, you see, and stupid too!" – "What happened," I asked. – "A couple of seconds after you called, the phone rang, I lifted the receiver and said hello. That wasn't enough, the man on the other end wanted to know if I was so-and-so. I said yes, as if I were mesmerised, although I should have slammed the phone down. What do you want? I asked. And he answered me in sort of a casual, flirtatious tone: Oh, nothing, just to know whether it was you. What do you need to know for? I asked. You'll see. We'll meet soon. So then I started wondering how soon was 'soon' – ten o'clock that same evening, or six the following morning?" – "Hmm," I said. – "And now I want you to advise me how I am to talk to them when they come." – "Try not to say anything if you can possibly help it." – "That's what I feel too. But even so – do I know you? I can't deny knowledge of Helena." – "You don't know me." – "Do I know there's anything between Helena and you?" – "Why should you, for heaven's sake?" – "Yes, I agree, it's just that they heard the letter she wrote you." – "But they don't know it's me, do they? I was calling from a phone booth in the street." – "Of course! I see now," she said, slapping her white forehead in that premature summer. I said: "I've written Helena a letter. In the circumstances, should I give it to you ?" – "Give it here. I'll cope from now on. It was just the initial shock." – "It never stops being a shock!" – "Give it here," she said with determination, "there's nothing political in it, so what?" – I said: "Dear friend of Helena! They run a network of stations the length and breadth of the republic where the demented populace is supposed to go with such matters for help. Family rows, adulterous relations, that's their bread and butter." – She reflected a moment in a pleasantly coquettish way before replying: "What a delightful thought!" We walked a few steps further as I awaited her decision: "Give me the letter. Helena's coming to see me mid-day Thursday. I can't say whether she'll have her retinue with her. So it's up to you." – "Many thanks, I'll return the favour some time!" I said by way of farewell. The smile on her pale face and the sideways shake of her head meant: "Ah, well!" One of the things I could not help wondering at that moment was why in such cases almost no one sticks up for the marriage partner.

Prague's 1979 lindens are getting ready to blossom.

WEDNESDAY, 13TH JUNE 1979

I don't know what to write or what direction to take it in.

"You have a new picture, I see," I said. A dull red sky weighs on a horizon of sea, the sea arches in virulently green waves. Along them a light is approaching us. It is a ship shaped like a nutshell with a candle burning in it. It is not a candle, but a white figure, its hands clasped above its head. The gleam radiating from it outshines the dull twilight beneath the lowering sky. "Hmm!" she said with her arm. She told me to turn my head more to the left. I wanted to know why. "Because," she smiled, "that's the way I did the preliminary sketches all those times you didn't come. I'm just adding the detail now." – "Haven't you enough now, if you don't mind my asking?" – "I have to have it precisely in my mind's eye before I start painting." How stupid can I get, I thought to myself. In less than a quarter of an hour she was done, and annoyed. "Problems?" I asked. – "I've finished. I only needed to put in the detail." She turned the paper round for me to see and I jumped. I am unmasked!

THURSDAY, 14TH JUNE 1979

It's raining so hard the water has come through our kitchen ceiling. We'll have to fix the part of the roof above our apartment ourselves. We'll fall and get killed in the process. Anyway, we're not getting anywhere with writing; we're not enjoying it. We're also beginning to have strong doubts as to its quality. The fact is we haven't read a word of what we've written so far!

But I can't just sit here. I went to see my intended patron and took him a change of reading matter. This time I brought him all sorts of essays and memoirs of a literary and philosophical kind, of which he is fond. Fiction bores him; he calls it derivative and devoid of ideas – it's no great tragedy that it doesn't get published. The pity is he's read everything by Balzac too many times over already! Prague is becoming a monstrosity, nature has been wiped out, Europe has been carved up by tricksters, and he feels weak, he's always sweating and even the sauna doesn't help. He has already decided to work less in the future, as he is simply accumulating money to no purpose. But he can't do less work except by proceeding slowly from one project to another, and this means his output just grows and grows! What happens, for heaven's sake, to all the value that must inevitably be produced every day if all the workers work as slowly as he does?

Ondřej and Jan always come back fuming from the building site. They have the impression they have fallen among thieves. Stock keeps disappearing from the warehouse, and no one dares provoke an investigation because the culprit's identity is known. The thief would have powerful means of revenge: blocking the supply of material. Our boys have the feeling that by now they are the only two left working there, apart from a couple of the dumber members of the co-op. Those whose flats are more are less completed fiddle around in them while the other side of the building still lacks a cement staircase. Jiří Gruša is not home, nor Ivan Klíma, nor Petr Pithart. To hell with it, I'll go somewhere too. But where to? And how can I go anywhere now? Josef is inviting me to Romania. He came looking for some gasket for the car. I went round town with him. Finally, as we walked aimlessly down Celetná Street, across Old Town Square and up Národní Avenue, I felt free and easy and realised how happy I used to be in those days. ("Good luck has he that deals with none!") I told him what had happened to me. He stopped and stood facing me on the pavement before saying: "That's fantastic, man! Who's the lucky one then?" He shook his head from side to side. "I don't envy you!"

We popped into a hot-meat shop for pork knuckle and mustard and a beer at the snack counter, and then somewhere else for a stand-up coffee. The hour approached when he had to go for his bus. "But you haven't got your gasket yet," I reminded him. "Not to worry. I don't even know which one I need to buy anyway! I've no idea where it's leaking from, to tell the truth. I mostly came to find out if you were one of the people they arrested."

I promised I would send someone to repair his car.

THURSDAY, 21ST JUNE 1979

I went to the post-office to send a parcel. I exchanged last year's telephone directory for a new one and paid the telephone bill, which amounted to just four crowns fifty in addition to the standing charge. I took the opportunity to get some fifty-heller pieces in change so I could make some phone calls on the street while I was out. Then I went to the dentist's.

As Doctor Kurka sat me down in the chair, he said: "Notice how agreeable Mrs. Krumphanzlová is today. Can you guess why?" – "No." – "Because those seven hundred crowns you paid in advance for the new denture went straight into her pocket." – "But I paid it through the post office!" – "That doesn't bother her, does it?" – "No, not in the least," said Mrs. Krumphanzlová. – "Really?" I marvelled and it was the moment for me to open my mouth. Doctor Kurka removed the temporary bridge and put in the new – gold! – one. He handed me a mirror: "Well, how do you like it?" – "It's splendid," I said, relishing my new "s." "But tell me in all honesty if there's not someone I particularly ought to reward for this – the laboratory technician, perhaps." – "No, not at all. Call her in, Mrs. Krumphanzlová."

A moment later I heard quietly from behind me: "Hello." And then a graceful, pretty young woman was standing at my side. Doctor Kurka said to her: "Just so you can see how well-fitting you've made it. And you've done a marvellous job on the colour-match. And that incisor, look how you've made it just that teeniest bit lop-sided so it recalls the dreadfully crooked one that was there before – that, too, is perfect work, don't you think?" The technician looked in my mouth, said "hmm" modestly and smiled with her perfect set of teeth; her face, and no doubt her shoulders too, bore a tasteful summer tan, in no way overdone. "Are you pleased?" Dr. Kurka asked her. – "Well, the main thing is that the patient should be. So, healthy chewing, then," she said and left. – "There you are," Dr. Kurka declared, "see how wrong you can be. It's not money that people need so much nowadays. They need praise and job satisfaction." Mrs. Krumphanzlová interjected: "Or maybe you'd like to bring us something nice that you've been writing." And Dr. Kurka said: "Quite so. And don't forget to write that Mrs. Krumphanzlová pockets the money." I didn't forget.

On the way home I called into the bookshop and bought the two-volume German-Czech dictionary for Helena, who sent me a message via her girl-friend that she would be dropping by to see me at two o'clock, but gave no guarantee. I did some reading and writing, put Padlock in order, had some tea and let the time pass. No Helena. I turned over the possibilities in my mind and smiled mirthlessly. At half past four, when it was clear she was not coming, I decided to go shopping. In the mailbox I found a note saying that she would be, i.e. was, in Café Savarin at three o'clock.

It's half past one – in the morning. It is the shortest night of the year: the sun, which set yesterday evening at 20:12 and will rise this morning at 3:50 Central European Time, will set this evening a minute earlier and will rise tomorrow morning a minute later. And still nothing.

(The end of spring)

I came out of the house this morning and stood in the shade looking up and down the sunny street. Our street is now quiet, as quiet it used to be when we moved here in 1956. In those days this was its normal state; now it's in a state of emergency, caused by our being cut off from the embankment, which is being reconstructed. If I had any influence in the matter I'd have the acacias that were once here replanted, or rather, if they gave me both permission and the saplings, I would dig the trenches and plant them myself. Whenever I start to look at things in a favourable light, I forget how unfavourably I am perceived by the city fathers and I hanker again as of old to prove myself a good citizen, do voluntary work for the community and set an example of modesty and diligence. The cool summer air through one layer of clothing gave me the urge to break into a cheerful jog, but I controlled myself.

I walked slowly. I turned the corner by the florist's and straight away I was in a street full of cars and people. There were vehicles parked right up on the pavement and men were unloading tin tubs full of meat, rolling off barrels of beer, carrying boxes of freshly-washed carrots and unloading packages of laundered linen.

She arrived all in a rush and out of breath, pressing her palms to her temples as if to assuage the pulsing blood. "Will you still want to see me?" she exclaimed in a hushed voice. "Will *I*?" I replied. It took her a few moments to get her breath back and then she said: "It was awful what I did to you, wasn't it?" She had not done anything awful to me at all; I looked at her and tried to discover whether she was saying this to me as a woman or as a child, and noted with regret that however equal a relationship may be between a man and a woman, the man, if he is so much older, as I am here, is still bound by that ordinary primitive non-sexual responsibility for a younger person. No enchantment can excuse me here. I ought to have known, as indeed I did!

"You didn't do anything awful to me, Helena. Whatever are you saying, Helena?" She gazed at me searchingly. "I expect it was up to me, unfortunately. I ought to have regarded you in rather a different way." – She probed me with her eyes, trying to fathom my meaning. Then she blushed and said: "But-but-but... but that can't be quite right either!" – "Why?" I asked, surprised that she might really have fathomed it. – "You see me as a little girl." – "No comment. But I wouldn't mind seeing you when you think you're being the most grown-up of women." – "But that's exactly what I do think! And no one else made me doubt it except you. And my father." – "There you are," I said, mocking her in jest but myself for real. Her shoulders slumped wearily, defencelessly. She was disappointed! So I said: "But if I had a daughter like you, I'd take her to bed, have no fear!" She thought for a moment and perked up. "And I do believe you would," she said. – "Why's that?" I said, puzzled. – "Because you say so."

I wanted to hug her, but instead we took hurried leave of each other on the street in front of The Prince restaurant. And went our separate ways.

SUNDAY, 24TH JUNE 1979

We came up with the idea of erecting a stone wall between the house and the ruined shelter. It would give us a bit more privacy. Once the rear is secure it will be possible to devote oneself more to the view of the countryside and the hill with its church and famous cemetery. It will also put a stop to locals wandering through here because they are too lazy to go round the property. That age-old building technology of stone and earth appeals to me. Each stone must be turned around as many as five or six times before it fits. Then it must be bonded lengthways and breadthways to prevent the wall subsiding under its own weight. I was too engrossed even to eat.

If someone enlisted me to build a few hundred metres of stone wall, I would do it, for a small wage plus board and lodging. But it would have to be a wall in some peaceful spot where there were few passers-by and no one to disturb me with chat, no one to ask questions or remind me of things. It would also have to be wall for a good purpose, naturally. If it got too hot I would sit in the shade or go down to the stream. I would grope for fish among the tree-roots. And soon be raring to get on with my wall again.

I went up the broken-sided stone stairs to the first floor. A warm coolness wafted through the house and there was a scent of wood, stone, the smoke of ages, and my straw hat. I donned the latter in my cell and went over to the window. But all I could see was the mighty green walnut tree. I inspected the cemented-over cracks in the wall; there had been no movement in the wall since last time. I turned away from the window towards the white room, now suffused with the green gloom of midsummer. The rough floorboards were freshly waxed. By the stove stood a full box of coal in case the sun should suddenly cool. There was nothing else but the enormous hand-made bed, the

Everywhere it was peaceful, from somewhere came the scent of lilies. (p. 229)

chair and the desk. And that's how everything has stayed, waiting, for years. The desk was suddenly tempting.

Yesterday, we climbed Sedlo (726 metres). We carried three Chinese palace dogs, named Bibisa, Diana and Tsar, and one child, a little boy whom I suggest we call Walter. We trailed through the cool shady forest in quite a long line: Zdena, her son Ivan, his fiancée Alena, Jiří Gruša with Ivanka, and Dr. Danisz. Visibility was not brilliant, but the impression was monumental all the same. I don't know what we talked about. Would I even recall a single sentence of it? It was an armistice: a slice of normal time. In a battered pub at Levín we lunched off warmed sausages. Everywhere it was peaceful, from somewhere came the scent of lilies. We were, it occurred to me, slightly wonder-struck, comparing our lives back there in Prague with our state of mind here. It was something beyond the power of words, so we spoke more with the dogs than with each other. After coming down from the hill we went and bathed in the pond near Liběšice. There we also competed at stone skipping, except for Gruša, who dozed on his belly. I didn't manage to throw them very far. Then the Grušas and Dr. Danisz left, and after our return to the stone house I went on with the wall. Bibisa lay in the cool grass in the shade like a goner.

On our way back to Prague in the evening, today, we stood for quite some time in front of the gates at Hoštka. Zdena smoked constantly. She had nothing on her feet; she worked the pedals barefoot. It made me recall one of our compacts from many, many years back. I now felt unsure about one of its clauses: "I'm not sure whether I'm right about this, but didn't you say I was to bury you without a coffin? The dirt straight onto your face?" She nodded.

MONDAY, 25ᵀᴴ JUNE 1979

My outward life is busy again. Again I have no time for peace and quiet and my third-party affairs keep me running around the city and its outskirts. Eda Kriseová asked me discreetly whether her *Bat's Collarbone* was being processed and I could not even recall whom I had given it to for typing three months ago. Zdena had it but had forgotten because she has no time for typing. She also had the third Komárková, which I took away immediately and will have to give to someone else. I want to deliver the Professor her three books at the same time; two of them are now ready. It will not be long before we have production delays like the state printing house. There are too many manuscripts.

Eda signed *The Woman of Pompeii* and then we sat together on the steps of St. Nicholas' church. People cheerfully passed by below us on their way to the pub or one of the little theatres. The clock in the tower chimed the fine evening hour. We talked about Ivan Klíma. Could I say something about his life and writing? Was it possible to say that an author was writing his own destiny in advance. I left Eda sitting by my packages, so that I could make a quick call, unencumbered, higher up the hill where Lopatka dwells. Being extremely conscientious, Lopatka comes to see me almost every other day to inform me that he has not finished writing *it* yet. When I rang the doorbell, the curtains at the window above the staircase were drawn back to reveal three little white figures: bigger, smaller and smallest. The smallest one — only her nose could be seen above the window ledge — said: "Daddy and Mummy went to buy some featre tickets for us." The two older girls laughed indulgently at this mighty aspiration. "Do you want to leave a message?" asked Veronika. – "Just say I came and that you were being good, especially the littlest girl." – "It's not a girl, it's a boy," said the middle one. And the bigger one, to prove it, lifted her little brother a little higher above the sill. "You'd have to hold him up the other way," I said. Two night-dresses fell about laughing. When I got home I found a note from Lopatka saying *it* is not ready yet, but he would soon be able to give me a bit of it to read.

I don't even seem to be dreaming, which probably shows that my outward life is uncomplicated and I have no harassing thoughts that need confronting in my sleep. Alternatively they have yet to attain the sleep stage. The last dream I recall was about trying to climb on a huge grey wind-smoothed rock with the help of an enormous carpet that was draped across it. I scrabbled up the folds of the carpet and as I drew nearer the top, the threadbare carpet would start to rip and slide down with me and I would quickly grab another fold which in turn would immediately give way. I knew full well that it was a silly dream and I could not give a damn how it turned out. When it realised I didn't care, the dream just came to an end.

I would not want to say it for certain about Ivan, but it looks as if I for one am writing my destiny in advance.

I needed to get something typed. I went to see Mirka. "Sorry, old lad, I am off on holiday and I'm beside myself with joy because I shall be heavy with child there, i.e. I'll have two delightful grand-children with me. But they'll be climbing trees all the time, so no time for typing!" – "You mean you're intending not to type a word the whole summer?" I asked in surprise. – "For heaven's sake, this godsend won't last that long, just a fortnight, in fact. But can you imagine how hectic it'll be? Breakfast, snack, lunch and so on and so forth... until at last that adorable moment of 'Granny, tell us a story.'" – "Martin wrote to us that he and Isabelle are expecting... we're supposed to guess what. He say's he's forty percent happy about it. So they're finally getting married and Isabelle wants to come and visit us." – "But that's great news, isn't it? I bet Madla at least sees it as a boon to the family, doesn't she?" – "She does. But I see nothing wrong with it either. But there's one thing, I'll not have anyone calling me Granddad." – "Oh ho! What then?" – "Mr. Vaculík." – "Well, well. And in this here rag," she indicated some Austrian newspaper, "I've been reading that the public is shocked at the behaviour of President Carter's armed guards in Vienna. So it's six to one and half a dozen to the other..." – "Well," I started to comment, but she guessed and immediately corrected herself: "I know, the difference being that the fellow over there took them home with him afterwards. That's what you were going to say, wasn't it, you rascal!" She gazed at me, her legs firmly straddled, a cigarette between her fingers. "What a ninny I am! Had your breakfast?" – "Yes." – "Wait, I'll fix you up with something. It's only bits and pieces left over from yesterday. That's a nice red shirt!" – "Yes it is. Only it's not..." – "Yours?" – "It's mine, all right, but it's not cotton as I thought, but some synthetic. I thought it might be, seeing as it had a Kashmir design." – "Aha. And did you hear they're collecting money for relief aid again – for Sweden this time?" – "No I didn't." – "Yes, the Raskens on television had another cow die on them."

WEDNESDAY, 27TH JUNE 1979

Eva Kantůrková came: "I'd like to sign that protest," she said in velvety tones. – "So would I," I said. – "You mean you haven't got it? But everybody says you wrote it." – "I didn't. When I'm running around with the one thing,

I can't be running around with the other." – "Alright, but," she said aghast, "you mean you're not going to do anything about it? After all, they're friends and colleagues, decent innocent people. Three of them are women and one is a mother of seven children." – "I have read three drafts and would sign all of them." – "Hold on! One of the texts admits their guilt…" – "That wasn't my impression," I said. – "Have you been invited to lunch at Vladislav's too?" – "I happen to be on my way to Vladislav's but I don't know anything about any lunch."

On the street Eva said: "Ivan Klíma has blocked the publication of my *Black Star* abroad." – "What do you mean? You've got a contract." – "Yes, I have. But why, in that case, hasn't it come out yet! Someone must have blocked it from here. Jiří Gruša also thinks it was Klíma." – "But that's absurd!" – "Well, he doesn't like me!" – "But you don't like him either!" – "But I'd never do anything like that to him." – "But he didn't do it to you." – "How do you know?" – "And how do you know?" – "It's what Gruša thinks. He'd had enough of it and it just spilt out." – "I'll make a point of asking Jirka." – "Ask away. You always stick up for your pals, it's a well-known fact." – "That's nonsense, Eva. I know very well what Ivan's position is on such matters. The very most he would say, if someone were to ask him right out, is that he doesn't like the book. But he'd never say that if it were a matter of publishing it or not. On the contrary, I know how concerned he is that as many things as possible should be published outside. But I will ask him about it." – "You won't ask him the right way. He'll deny it anyway and be even more annoyed with me." – "He couldn't be more than he is. There's no need to get upset." – "What did I tell you? But I just don't see why." – "I do. He says you scribbled all over a manuscript of his." – "But he lent it to me for my comments." – "That's really monstrous! When I read your *Black Star* I handed you a list of my comments on separate sheets. In the text itself I only marked the places faintly in pencil in the margin. You made yours in ball-point – right in the text. You ruined one of his copies." – "And that really annoyed him so much?" – "Of course it did. He was spitting mad." – "Well there you are. But he had some absolutely inadmissible sentences in it. That's all I corrected." – "You want to correct Klíma's sentences?!" I shook my head so violently that the tram we were in swayed from side to side.

We arrived at the Vladislavs; it turned out to be Jan's name-day. He hadn't invited me as I was supposed to be coming anyway. We were having lunch when Gruša arrived. He didn't eat anything, though: he's on a diet. After the meal I said: "Jirka, Eva says you told her…" – "Hey, there's no need for that now, Ludvík," Eva said. – "Eva says you told her that Ivan blocked the publication of her book." – "I told her what?" – Eva: "Cut it out, lads." – Me: "Did you talk to Ivan about her book?" – "Not at all. But I know his opinion of it. What was it I told you, Eva?" – "It makes no difference any more." – Jiří: "I said that Ivan didn't much like *The Black Star*. And he might have imparted his view to someone else, that's all." – "So what's the truth of it?" I asked turning to Eva. "Stop it, will you, it's so offensive. You really think you have the right to manipulate people!"

Vladislav pleased Eva more: he had the transcriptions of *Lord of the Tower* ready for her to sign. I immediately bought two copies from her. Then we argued, I rather half-heartedly, about Pithart's article "A Tentative Homeland." In it, Pithart has recourse to Emanuel Rádl and Bernard Bolzano in scraping the grime of oblivion off the idea of the state-homeland, as a home for all nationalities dwelling in a particular territory, as opposed to the "biologically" national state which, Pithart maintains, has neither proved itself nor sustained itself here; witness the present situation in which people are "divorcing themselves" *en masse* from the nation, disengaging themselves from their duties to the state – duties that we still owe regardless of its wretched nature. However churlish it might sound, says Pithart, we ought to know how to tell people that they must cultivate this, the only state they have, and by good work and a reform of the general ethic, they must bring old civic virtues back into currency and display goodwill and tolerance towards everyone – everyone, even "regime people."

That irritated Jiří so much he decided to attack the author. Eva also said that it might be true for Pithart but it was hardly something one could expect of people at the present time. Jan said that the body of the nation instinctively defends itself against violence in the only possible way: by ignoring plans, tasks and stipulations, and by the concomitant withdrawal into private life, accumulation of advantages, corruption, racketeering, the whole "pearl strike," as he called it, whatever that is. I walked about the room just listening to them.

Olda Unger came by to invite us to a farewell party. It ended up the other way round: Madla invited the Ungers to our garden next week. We chatted. Olda brought Madla a present: tapes of bird recordings. What should I give him? When he was leaving I came out with him to the lift and he said to me: "Treat Madla more considerately. You're dreadful." I said OK.

THURSDAY, 28ᵀᴴ JUNE 1979

Today our Jan had his entrance exam and interview for the engineering faculty. He did all the calculations correctly and got the general questions right. He had a top grade in his matriculation so he is unlikely to get in. The interview featured the following exchanges: "What does your father think about 'socialism with a human face' these days?" – "I don't know, we don't talk about it." – "What do you think about it?" – "I think that the very concept of socialism implies a human face." – "But what do you think about it as the right-wingers' slogan in 1968." – "Nothing. I was too young." – "Was your father expelled or suspended from the party?" – "I don't know." – "But you must have put it in your curriculum vitae." – "I didn't. It's *my* C.V." Ondřej bought a cake.

We drank tea and ate the cake. The conversation turned to treasure seeking. "Funnily enough," I said, "even when I was a boy the thought of buried treasure – at Brumov castle, say – never really caught my imagination. But I recall that some of the local lads did go digging with that in mind." Madla said: "Buried treasure didn't tempt me either. What I wished was for my mother to help me pick that big pot full of strawberries. Or to make me a dress." – "And did she make you one?" Ondřej asked. – "No. It was something I wished for when she was already dead."

SUNDAY, 1ˢᵀ JULY 1979

Here we are in July. I have started on the cherry-tree. It is not a big yield (the bees didn't fly) but the cherries are fine and sound, and there are just enough for eating and giving away. I was at the top, whistling and thinking to myself: Here I am cherry-picking again, it only seems like yesterday. I have the same feeling when I'm hanging decorations on the Christmas tree that I took down only about a fortnight before.

There is an evening concert on the radio: mournful Martinů, and it occurs to me that Mojmír might be mournful too. He always gets us tickets for concerts. And now he is sitting there alone in his little cabin, not so very far from here in fact, and what's he up to? Lazing about or vainly writing, with only cigarette-smoke for company.

Today I cut the grass – with a hand-mower – in the part of the garden that is lived in. I weeded the currants and pruned the roses. I enjoy inspecting the grafts to see how they are looking. I put a bit more saltpetre on the gooseberries to keep them going and help them nourish their terrible burdens of fruit. I actually took a nap in the afternoon. From time to time I read Lenka Procházková's manuscript. Yesterday I went to bed at nine o'clock and woke up this morning at nine without dreaming anything. I expect I have low blood pressure and I have an ear-ache. I ought to go and see Dr. Soukup with it, but I haven't the time, so I expertly prescribed myself penicillin. The barometer, having dropped slightly during the day, is rising slightly now in the night, I notice.

Being with people all the time, I am no longer capable of being on my own for a couple of days, which is why I kept waiting for Karel Kosík to come. If I don't go and fetch him he won't come of his own accord; this experiment has been going on for the past fortnight. I want him to see how our cabbage rose (*Rosa centifolia*) is flowering and to have a look at that new rose – "Diamant" – that we bought together last year. The Jessica is also magnificent this year: firm and sturdy. Jessica, Jessica, I pronounced the word to myself and tried to see what sort of woman the sound conjured up. Queen of Bermuda so frost-bitten that she had to start again right from the ground, and it looks as if it did her no harm. I use no sprays on anything. There is none of the mildew that was so prevalent last year. The world is outraged at Vietnam driving the Chinese out onto the sea and everything possible is being done to give them somewhere to land. But my view is that any government under which so many people are unable to live ought to be punished. How crazy it is: by the time Europe and America eventually adopt a wise and conciliatory attitude towards all living creatures as being manifestations of the Spirit, Africa and Asia will be just reaching the stage of loutish nouveaux riches who want everything and go around beating people up. It makes me chuckle to hear how the Soviet press are warning the American Congress not to have the temerity to reject what the Russians have just agreed on with the President. Their idiotic amazement that the top official is not the Big Boss too!

I talked to Jan Procházka a fortnight before he died. He said: "It's OK now. I just need to get my strength back a bit." His daughter Lenka – how old she is I do not know – came to ask if I had read her *Pink Lady*. Previously she gave her things to Pavel Kohout to read. He, I suspect, lent a hand with the family after Procházka's death. There are several children, I am not sure how many exactly, and the amazing thing is that they seem to have grown up and reached adulthood under their own steam, without society showing the slightest interest in them. Most of the people I know were at a moral loss, so to speak, when it came to Procházka: a writer, a member of the Central Committee of the Czechoslovak Communist Party, someone who associated with President Novotný... His writing displayed unalloyed rural common-sense and feeling, and his life a similar rural respect for the Castle. Naturally! It has always been a well-known fault of the Castle that it lets us country people down. "A proper Čapek to his Masaryk," was someone's perceptive observation, but even then I did not think it told the entire truth. Something happened between Procházka and me that I will always be ashamed of: he was more open with me than I with him. He already regarded me as his friend while I was still scrutinising him from a distance.

"When I write a novel," Lenka told me, "they reject it as being too much like a film script. The film people tell me it's a novel. I gave the children's publishers something; they said it was quite good but someone else should have written it." She is nut brown and skinny as a rake; a kiss-chaser. A big kid just beginning to behave like a woman. But from her face with its oddly coarse features, there gaze out enquiring eyes that are much older. At page sixty of the fairly-well-typed manuscript I suddenly realised that the novel already had four pairs of characters of different ages and backgrounds whose lives were in full flight and I was eager to know what would happen next. It involved me. Her language is not developed, however, and she lacks a distinct voice. I expect she doesn't worry too much about it. She probably thinks that the story-line is the most important thing. I hate the thought of having to say something to her about it. I don't know what, how or why. It's a nuisance. But I will ask her some questions and get a better look at her.

This bedroom has a nook with a small skylight. The nook is curtained off by a linen screen, embroidered with probably Slovak patterns. It is where Madla has her bed and she is already asleep. On the table she left a letter she wrote this afternoon to the schoolmistress.

"I've just started a fortnight's holiday. We've shifted to Dobřichovice, because the cherries, currants and raspberries are now ripe. (...) There was excitement all round last week. Martin wrote to us that they're expecting a baby, and it's due in January. So they're getting married in July, and at the end of July or the beginning of August Isabelle will come on a visit. So we all started to rejoice straight away. Friday evening L. and I went to the post office to phone them, so as to talk to Isabelle as soon as possible. But Martin informed us that she was in hospital, that she had a miscarriage. His voice was odd. His intonation was like an actor parodying an American. For the first time he sounded like a complete stranger to my ears.

"Jan has finished his exams. They're bound not to accept him, yet again. You can tell from such details as the fact that the moment he arrived they told him his application had been mislaid, and he would have to obtain a duplicate reference, which is an awful nuisance. (...) Ludvík is furious and says it might be an idea for Jan to go and study abroad. But he's probably just saying that. I can't imagine where we'd be without Jan. He's such a pillar of the family.

"I retire six months from today."

It's true I said Jan should go and study abroad, but I don't really give it that much thought. What I do think about is how best to exact revenge when worst comes to the worst, as we expect it to.

MONDAY, 2ND JULY 1979

Whatever would I write about if I really ended up living in Dobřichovice? I made a plank fence along the top of a low red-brick wall and enjoyed it. In the evening I was cherry picking when Mrs. Rohlenová came and asked me if I had change for fifty crowns. "I've no idea," I said, "but even if I had, I happen to be cherry picking at this very moment." – "But I don't want you to come down." – "Oh, yes you do. Why else would you ask me?" – "Well, you could also say that your wife is up in her room and send me to ask her." – "No I couldn't, because she isn't there. What I can say is that somewhere upstairs there's a purse, so go and have a look yourself."

She probably took umbrage, as she said nothing more. She comes accosting me the whole day long, always dreaming up something or other. She's lonely. It will stop when at least two grandchildren turn up on holiday. Then she will totally avoid me so as not to give me an opportunity to complain about how the grandchildren get on my nerves, how they're always rushing around, how I have to put up with interminable screeching from somewhere.

Weeeah here, weeah there. To spend the whole winter working here in the garden without let-up and then have others come in the summer to do the relaxing while we are still at it – pulling out the nettles, trimming the edges of the path, watering, mowing, cleaning, clipping. And then when everything is perfect, we leave and they enjoy a peaceful week without us. But *we* never get peace from *them*.

"A penny for your thoughts," I said to Mrs. Hemerková as she sat by her shed in the shade of the elderberry tree talking to her dog. – "Save your money, this blessed Don is the only thing on my mind. I can't even go to Prague and I'd dearly love to." – "That dog owns you," I said.

Mrs. Kopecká weeds and waters her miniature flower-beds to have something to liven her children's graves. The walnut in front of her windows is full of fruit. For a long time it was unfruitful – it's a young tree – and Mrs. Kopecká wanted me to fell it, saying it simply robbed her of light. I felt sorry for it. Then the next winter I suddenly saw that it would one day be a mighty tree and sap several fruit trees behind it, as well as cast a shadow on the only sunny spot we have for growing vegetables, strawberries and potatoes. I declared accordingly that I would cut it down, and Mrs. Kopecká started silently to weep. She came to Madla and said: "I am scared that if you cut down that tree, Světlana will die." That I understood perfectly, of course, and immediately cancelled my plan. Světlana did die the next spring, anyway, but the walnut-tree, which had heard it all, took such a fright it put on fruit that year and has been giving more and more ever since.

Světlana has been dead two years. She was twenty-eight. When her brother Pavel was lying in his bedroom on the north side of the house or at very most playing one of his intermediate exercises on the piano and I was cutting the grass, I was afraid to sharpen the scythe beneath their window and always moved further away. Though I doubt if any of the Kopeckýs had read Jirásek's *Crusaders*, and if they had, they would hardly have recalled the scene where Daniela is dying and from the meadows comes the sound of scythes being sharpened, which is actually only her hallucination. Pavel Kopecký has been dead four years. He was twenty-six. Madla says she would never move into any of the rooms after the Kopeckýs.

I would. I would turn them into an office and gallery with a view of the garden. The ground floor on that side is set high above the landscape. It would afford a view of the Berounka Valley, the steep hillside opposite, and the mouth of Charles' Vale. There is a niche between the windows in the wall containing a symbolic statue of a woman. Professor Patočka once diagnosed her to be Mnemosyne – Memory. She is covered in a layer of grey dust. Her dusty eyes are especially charming in their effect. Ondřej cannot wait for the day when we shall repair the facade at last and paint the niche a different shade than the statue. If I lived here, it occurred to me, I would give Olbram Zoubek the chance to turn our garden into an exhibition of his cement sculptures. I'd invite people here. When Laďa Vaculka was still alive, the year before last, I considered commissioning from him a bronze statue to stand permanently in the glade below the house.

Laďa Vaculka also died of the regime, one might say. Any time we went to Brumov we would stop off and see them in Uherské Hradiště, and they would visit us in return when he and Ida came to Prague. On account of me, Laďa had troubles with the official brutes. He received fewer and fewer commissions, exhibited less and less, and was forced to quit the art school. His output was not academic or merely for exhibition, the objects he made served to decorate the world, in the same way as a fine gateway, a gable, a porch, a wayside cross or a carved wine-press. His statues, mosaics, tapestries and canvases are in many places in Moravia. He was a collector of coins and doors: soliciting the latter from villagers when they were converting their cottages into something uglier and more modern. He kept his door collection in the school, about fifty items all told, or maybe twenty, I can't recall now. Once he made an enormous sculpture out of chrome-plated steel for an industrial works in Zlín. It resembled an enormous eye or a cell of living tissue or some fantastic creature from outer space. First it stood in front of the managerial building, then they sawed it off and carted it away into storage, before another enterprise got hold of it and it stands now at Malenovice on the right-hand side of the road when you are driving towards Zlín. He was not a pensioner for long. One day, he received written notification that he had been charged with major fraud: he was drawing a pension while earning more than six hundred crowns a month. His home was searched, and it was clear that it was something else they were interested in. They also interrogated him about me. The indictment surprised and amazed him: it came as news to him the he had no right to a pension if he earned over six hundred crowns. What genuine artist does not earn at least that? What sort of artist would give up his creative activity for the sake of a thousand-crown pension? And

"It's the same story everywhere, nowadays,"
Laďa said. (p. 241)

if he did, what sort of artist would he be anyway? And if he chose to give up the pension, what had he been paying towards all his life? The crass stupidity of the whole business is obvious. Laďa Vaculka had a better argument in his defence: the artists' union had informed its members that in the case of artists, a pension and remunerative activity were not mutually exclusive. Laďa came to Prague in a temper. He went to the union, and came back to our place that evening and showed us the official notification: This is to notify Comrade Vladislav Vaculka that the union's lawyer Dr. So-and-so, now retired, misled all the members of the union. "Would you believe it?" we marvelled. "It's the same story everywhere, nowadays," Laďa said. He arrived home, suffered a heart attack, then a second one, and then died. About a month afterwards, the family received a ruling that the indictment was quashed, as it had been a misunderstanding. In smaller localities even pathetic little pimps have greater power.

The nethermost cherries, the ones that can be reached from the ground or from a stool, we do not pick, so that the house's residents can help themselves. And anyway, the ladder is left standing among the branches. I tell Mrs. Rohlenová to get one of her sons to pick some for her, but they never have the time. Sometimes I shake a few out of the basket for Mrs. Kopecká. Mrs. Hemerková's dog can climb the tree for her for all I care, the pair of them get on my nerves. A basket of cherries – about seven kilos – has taken about an hour to pick this year. Who does an hour's work for me?

I have finished reading Lenka Procházková's *Pink Lady*. – Hmm. My bet is that the author yearns for her own life to start moving towards a happy ending, like Kytka's. Maybe she'd like to find an older man that she wouldn't have to explain anything to, and then have peace and quiet. How old can she be?

WEDNESDAY, 4ᵀᴴ JULY 1979

Pressing engagements obliged his lordship to return to London. So I too, unfortunately, had to leave the garden and go to Prague. It was necessary to pick up the book of feuilletons from the binders, reach some decision about *Jottings*, buy some creosote to coat the plank fence, negotiate something with friend Slavík, show myself to Dr. Kurka, sign an appeal to the President, buy some creosote – I've already said that, and then go and check out how

Mrs. Helena D. is absorbing the realisation that she is leaving me and the homeland and might see us both no more. No more – that's not as proverbially menacing as Nevermore…

So yesterday I picked a basket of cherries, washed myself, cleaned Herzen's windows, said goodbye to my wife and drove to Prague. At home, I emptied my pockets of everything but my identity card and went to the Tomins with the cherries. Dispassionately and without a word of greeting I thrust my identity card in the faces of the two policemen serving the working class in front of the Tomins' front door, and rang the bell. "There's no one in," said one of the stout young men. I put the basket down on the step: "Well, no one will steal it from here, will they?" There was no hint in their voices that they understood the joke when they told me that two others would be relieving them at some point, so to avoid any possible confusion it would be better if I left the basket with the neighbours. I therefore rang the neighbouring doorbell, a man took the basket, closed the door and I heard him trying to calm some frantic little kid: "No, we can't! They're for Mr. Tomin!" There is not a cherry-stone to be had in the market, you see.

A warm evening breeze wafted down Veletržní Street and I was struck by the summertime shortage of townsfolk and cars. A nice time to be in Prague. I took a walk over to Professor Machovec's, but he wasn't in. I went back, climbed into Herzen and set off for Jiří Gruša's, but he wasn't in. I drove on to the Klímas' and there was nobody in. (A foreigner would ask: But why doesn't he telephone first?)

Irritated by such results – it was almost ten o'clock – I drove to Zdena's. I found her dressed and with her hair done, sitting at the table in front of a cup of cold coffee, her right elbow supported on her left arm, a cigarette in her right hand. "Surprised, eh?" I said. – "On the contrary," she said, "I was surprised that you hadn't shown up yet." – "What are you up to?" I said, looking round. – "I was just thinking to myself how incredible it is that I put together quite a complicated programme for the computer, and it accepted it, which means it was fault-free." – "I've got a piece of good news for you, too," I said. "I signed a protest to the President on your behalf." – "Excellent! Are you going to stick around, then?" – I shook my head gleefully and declared sweetly: "No-o, my darling." – She repeated after me on a smaller scale my gesture and tone: "Of course it's no-o my darling. But there's no harm in asking, is there? Do you want a cigarette or one of your little cigars?"

And another piece of good news: when we were seeing who could throw a pebble furthest at the pond, and Jiří was lying on his belly, Zdena got up, picked up a pebble, threw it, roared out loud and fell on the grass, doubled up in pain. Two days later it was discovered that she had, luckily, managed to tear apart a pleural adhesion, so she is now breathing more freely than she has for ages.

THURSDAY, 5ᵀᴴ JULY 1979

Jan Mlynárik is mightily enamoured of Dominik Tatarka. As of a brother who is the pride of the family. Dominik is worried his *Jottings* might jeopardise a certain lady in France. "How, for heaven's sake?" I asked in astonishment. Mlynárik said: "The French Bolsheviks might take it out on her." – "Nonsense!" I said. Mrs. M. turned towards us from the table where she was slicing us some bread and bacon, and tapped her forehead in scorn. Jan said: "And here's some money he sent you – two thousand crowns." – "What money?" I asked. – "The money you invested in it." He showed me the back of the envelope, where there was written in Dominik's hand: "Ludvík mine! Jano will explain you my concerns. Do what you like!"

I said: "If it's 'do what you like,' then this is what we'll do. You return him this money and we'll sell the *Jottings* outside Padlock." – "That means what?" – "That means it won't be counted as a Padlock book. It will be a manuscript which, in its duplicated existence, will be deposited with qualified subscribers who'll be willing to pay for the privilege of being its custodians, lest it be lost to posterity." – "Hey, that's great! Did you hear that? What do you say, wife?" Mrs. M. turned towards us, shrugged her shoulders, and said with a flourish of her knife: "That's your affair, boys." I went over to her, took her by the elbow: "Well there you're wrong, Mrs. M.! It concerns a woman." She said: "Pshaw!" I understood: A woman like that, pshaw! "Hold it now!" I protested. "If a woman's good for a fellow, she's good, ain't she?" She stayed sarcastically silent, before banging the board with sliced bacon down on the table: "Do something useful – eat that!"

From alongside me at the table I hear: "But Ludvík, you're not listening to me!" Jan had been reading me something for several moments. – "I am, I am!" – "This'll be a literary bombshell!" Jan declared, turning over a heap of handwritten sheets. They were letters Dominik had exchanged with some

243

friend who addressed him as Gadjo. – "Who's going to decipher them and type them out, for heaven's sake?" I grieved. – Jan brought his enormous palm down on the file of dusty old paper. "This is correspondence from the first republic…" He started, laughed and repeated the last word, with a capital letter this time. "Republic!" Dominik always writes republic with a capital letter. "Re-pub-lic!" we declaimed, both with a capital letter. "So let's drink to his big R," I said, and we all three clinked glasses.

I ambled along sunwashed Karmelitská Street, which was idyllically peaceful because they have pulled up the cobbles and are laying new tram track. The track is already down, pinned here and there with concrete panels and with stone chippings poured in between. But along its entire length not a soul to be seen. From time to time the track reverberates, which probably means someone is working somewhere. And round the corner, in truth: five Republicans of the darkest hue here available were walloping iron, mixing cement, carting earth. I am wearing new sandals and I can feel how well I am walking, maybe I could walk to that exhibition of photos from Sudek's legacy.

I rang the Pitharts' bell. "Come with me to an exhibition," I say. – "Don't you want a cup of tea? Or coffee?" she says, wrinkling her nose. Then she says slowly: "I won't come. Yesterday, Petr said something about how you're always coming here." – "Fine, well this is the last time then," I said, drinking up my tea and leaving. On the bridge I am stopped by a party of foreigners. A lady is holding a street-plan. She points at the bridge we are standing on and then across the river towards the Castle. "How do we get there?" she asks in Romanian. I could almost speak Romanian once, in 1966, when the editorial board of *Literary News* wanted to send me on an exchange to some Romanian literary magazine. But I immediately forgot what I had learnt after my trip was banned by Auersperg, it must have been, of the Central Committee. It struck me the simplest solution was to backtrack a bit with the Romanians and guide them as far as the Old Castle Steps. I desperately tried to remember something in Romanian, but all that came to mind was what I had learnt at school at the time of the Republic, when we had a Little Entente with Yugoslavia and Romania. I pointed at myself and then held my hand about one metre twenty above the ground, to show how small I was at the time, and said "la scoala" and sang: "*Traiasca regele in pace si onor, de care iubitor…*" Agog, is the only way to describe their reaction, and they looked about themselves warily. It was the royal anthem.

Afterwards, as I was walking back across the bridge again, I sang to myself at walking pace the other one: *"Naprej zastava slave, na boj junaška kri, za blago očetnjave, naj puška govori!"* I thought how much it would fascinate Dominik, but *you* wouldn't know anything about that, silly Pithart!

FRIDAY, 6ᵀᴴ JULY 1979

Yesterday evening, Madla arrived from Dobřichovice with her hand in a bandage. She had cut herself on a sickle. At Bulovka Hospital, instead of sewing up the cushion of her thumb, all that a young surgeon could do by then was to excise the flesh. "Whatever made you go all the way to Bulovka from Dobřichovice, for heaven's sake!" – "First I went to Radotín. The doctor there, another young fellow, said, That needs stitches, madam. We don't do them here." So from the accident to the eventual treatment five hours had elapsed. Fuck them! Everything gets worse, only the surveillance improves. Able-bodied young oafs keep watch on a single philosopher in three shifts, and the housing authority lacks a fellow to do emergency repairs on the roof above our kitchen.

I sent Josef someone – Jan – to repair his car, and he has been there three days already. The fault would seem to be escalating. But it is equally conceivable that he has no wish to leave the place: horses, water, forest and the biggest attraction of all – Josef.

Madla has just been to ask who I'm writing to. No one! Her head is in a whirl with the Šalda, Deml and Růžena Svobodová letters – and I just about managed a couple of lines to Milan Šimečka because I have found myself thinking about him more and more over the past days for some unknown reason. I write to no one. It is nothing to be proud of, but these are hard times and these days there is no way of cultivating intellectual finickiness in one's letter-writing. Betray one's top-secret personal thoughts to the employees of the Department of Intrigue? Besides, I do not feel like writing anything at all these days. I am writing these lines with distaste. I don't know how much of it will endure, time will tell. Eva Kantůrková has written to the British Prime Minister, asking her to intercede somehow on behalf of our prisoners. "You're not going to write to anyone?" she assails me. "But they're your friends too, after all!" I don't think I shall write anything. Who to and what, if I am not to end up feeling like some figure-skater on television?

245

Jan Trefulka wrote to me saying he had just recovered from a heart attack. "I tell you, my dear Ludvík, it's just heaven in that heart unit in Brno. Not only do they feed you well (literally!) and all the rest, but in addition they have a team of nurses there who'd grace any beauty contest. They didn't let me stay very long because the demand was too great and anyway the surroundings weren't so marvellous afterwards and sometimes I could not help thinking of my old theory that I was a real idiot in 1968 not to have procured some suitable capsule that I might use should I ever need to escape the clutches of medical care. Because beyond a certain stage all medical care is just a fucking waste of time. But things haven't got that bad with me yet and a doctor friend of mine explained to me afterwards that even if I had obtained such a capsule, what was in it would have decomposed by now and at best I could have..." (expurgated). "Briefly: no thoughts on Czech politics this time, anyway nothing of the kind exists, nor can it. Above all I must finish that new book. Please tell the lads in Prague," and I expect this is the main point of Trefulka's letter, "not to be cross with me if they don't find my signatures where I suppose they ought to be."

I had no luck at the dentist's today. I waited there about half-an-hour and then the nurse came out and told me the doctor was in the laboratory displaying his dogs to his colleagues. I could not wait as I was meeting Helena. The message is beginning to seep from her brain into her body that – alas! – we won't ever see each other again.

SUNDAY, 8ᵀᴴ JULY 1979

One of my hobbies here is a fir stump about a yard high and two feet across. I once stripped the bark from it and was intending to polish the cut to bring out the seventy or so annual rings. Before I got round to it, the stump had weathered. Moreover it had not been sawn off straight, so I said to myself: As soon as I have someone to do it with, I shall cut it again lower down. Our boys have no time for such trifles, so I waited for a visit from Emil at some opportune moment. But all he does is take some apples, pick some cherries or plums according to the season, and wash his car with the hose before disappearing again. He finally slipped up yesterday and came earlier. "Emil, old chap, we're going to do some sawing!"

Emil is a fairly willing sort, and extremely kind, almost too kind for his own good. He does all sorts of things around the home – not like me! The fruit he picks here he will preserve at home, and so on. Catch me doing that! He and Lina are both engineering graduates, and the work they do is of more or less the same importance, but whereas Emil takes it as it comes, Lina is a go-getter. She is gifted and successful, but she unfortunately has an inconvenient name at the present time. She wants to do a Ph.D. and has written her thesis, but her employer would not let her defend it. She gave in her notice and left. Amazingly, she got away with her proud and rightful gesture; she got herself a post elsewhere and they endorsed her candidacy.

I fetched the saw and greased it with vaseline. Then we got started. Before that we had drawn a line round the circumference of the stump. At first the saw kept to the line. But little did we know what we had let ourselves in for! When the whole blade was in the trunk, it started to behave of its own free will and the two ends stuck out at such an angle that they could not be part of the same saw. "I think," said Emil, "that if ever we finish cutting this, two saws'll fall out the other side." – "Do something then. You call yourself an engineer?" I taunted him. We gave about ten tugs like that and then had to rest. Eventually there was so little of the saw to manipulate with that the sawdust could not even get out – we just tugged it back and forth inside, grinding it ever finer. "What does it need to be cut off for?" Emil asked, too right but too late. – "I'll polish it up really well, treat it and then varnish it, and I'll make a calendar of events during the life of this tree." – "So there'll be the Battle of White Mountain too." – "Are you soft in the head, or what, Emil?" – "I must be, or I wouldn't have come here today."

It took us almost two hours to gnaw through the thickness of the wood. In the process I got two enormous blisters and tore them off straight away, though amazingly enough I have new skin on them this morning, probably thanks to the penicillin course I am taking for my ear, which it has not helped a quarter as much. The fruit of our efforts was a wooden cake about four inches thick. I gave it to Emil for him to make a calendar too. "Don't forget 1620," I reminded him.

We went upstairs and found Madla and Lina drinking tea. Madla seemed irritated to me and she immediately laid into Emil: "And why don't you make a career for yourself?" – "What are you talking to him like that for? What's a career supposed to mean?" I intervened. Emil said: "A career to become a

247

dolt? I am one already." Emil has publications and a couple of patents to his credit already, but his inventions come into being as a sort of by-product, almost against his will, when he encounters some obstacle at work. First he has a dilatory look to see if it has already been described, solved and tested, and if it has not, he is obliged to do it himself in order to proceed. Lina is a different case entirely. Lina is a Soviet person, Emil is a Wallach. On the table there was a cutting from the Russian edition of *Evening Tbilisi* (yes, it does exist!) where, under the title "Far from Tbilisi" (how else?) there was a story about the family of Emil Gvenetadze-Vaculík in Prague, all about how the walls of their home are covered in Georgian woodcuts, how they have Georgian pottery and literature on their shelves, how they both studied in Leningrad, where they met, how they started at Nižná on the Orava, and now live in the famed city of Prague, where Mozart and Einstein lived, and where Charles Bridge is, how Lina is engaged in academic work and will shortly be defending her Ph.D. thesis – which is the reason why the entire piece was written in the first place. The author is some influential friend of Lina's who was here on one occasion and was annoyed at the local practices. He said it would be unthinkable in their country for a person to be harassed because they were related to someone. – Great! But can we believe it?

When Emil and Lina left, Madla said: "Do you know what she told me? That she had to sign a statement about her relations with us. She wrote that she only had family contacts, and chiefly with me, less with you, and that she doesn't know your friends." I said nothing for a moment and then: "It galls me, admittedly, but she wrote the truth. She also had to help the people who wanted to help her." We talked about it for a little while longer until we finally came to terms with it, more or less. It cannot have been easy for Lina to tell Madla. But nevertheless Madla did say in the end: "All the same, I'd sooner not be anything." – And she isn't.

In the evening, Karel Kosík at last came over – alone and clearly woebegone. Marie had gone off to her parents for the weekend. "I expect I'll go to Prague, I don't feel like doing anything," he said. Mourning over Marie, we thought. "I accompanied Luboš Sochor to the airport yesterday and I feel as if I've been at a funeral," he said. Sochor, the historian, was literally forced to emigrate. This regime is inimical to the human heart and mind. (Even as I subject this text to critical and dispassionate corrections in March 1980, I feel unable to renounce this sentence.) For a while we spoke about Šalda, who is suddenly beginning to find favour with Madla: "He must have been an odd patron, but he had a real mind. His life was literally a service to Czech literature. But why did he have to fall prey to that Svobodová woman, when Benešová, who worked alongside him quietly and unassumingly, was so much greater!" – "Ah well," said Karel dejectedly. – "So what's blooming for you, Karel?" I asked. "At the moment, that *Pariser Charme*," he replied with difficulty. – "And finally he ended up with a philosophy of centrism. I like that. It's always necessary to build a synthesis of Left and Right, to marry progress and tradition." – "So we'll come over and see your *Pariser Charme* tomorrow morning, alright?" I said, trying to brighten his future slightly. – "Would you, really? I would like that very much. I am, as I said, post-funebrial."

This morning, that is to say, nigh on ten o'clock, we took the Šalda Trail to Všenory. We did not find Karel, the cabin was locked up. He had not held out. We retraced our steps. The leaves of the acacia saplings right and left were yellow and singed. At the side of the wood, there were panels with the proud message: NO ENTRY TO FOREST! CHEMICALLY TREATED. I needed to go to the toilet. I side-stepped off Šalda's Trail and squatted down, Madla walked on. I called to her: "Do you think I'll poison myself if I wipe my backside on the grass?" She laughed as if I were joking, but I meant it seriously. Anything's possible in this country now.

MONDAY, 9ᵀᴴ JULY 1979

The Ungers were here. They have left and taken Madla with them to have her dressing changed. The Ungers will depart in about a month's time. I asked Olda what he was seriously intending to do in Canada. "I've no idea. Lumberjacking is probably out, they have pros who are much better at it." (After several days in someone's constant company these are my first moments alone; I wonder how best to use them. I'm off now to try taking a nip of some so-called brandy. – There. But it's not much good.) I took Olda on a tour of the garden and he said: "I understand now. If I had something like this, I wouldn't think about leaving either." – "I wouldn't think about it even if I hadn't," I said. But that is not entirely true, I have already given it thought, but I always come to the realisation that I mustn't. The fact is I have no other weapons left in my armoury apart from staying. I said: "Once you've settled down and had a look round, try and find me something too." – "Like what?" he asked. I pondered. I discover that I have no plan for an alternative existence. The fact is I have no wish to do anything apart from what I am doing now. But if I had to – then some basic human activity: a farm, some herds, corn, timber… Olda said: "This country is now a write-off as far as our generation is concerned. Even if you locked yourself up in your house and told yourself that none of it concerned you, it would come looking for you, some mischief – from the local authority, from the school because of your kids, not to mention your job. There's not a single little thing that you have any control over. I want my kids to be whole people, not skeletons picked clean by the state, the way we are." – "The worst thing about it," I said, "is that no one wants it. I don't think the government does, even. " – "You're still the same old…" Olda laughed. But I am convinced of it: it must be as hard for the people who have actual responsibility for this state as it is for us, or at least for some of them, sometimes. That is why I have sympathy for Pithart's attitude. One's assessment of the status quo is one thing, how one acts within it is another matter entirely. It provides food for thought, whereas absolute rejection leaves no room for any kind of reflection at all: its upshot is resignation or escape. Iva Ungerová was delighted at being able to eat strawberries here. In the end, we did not actually say our farewells.

The barometer has fallen and it is beginning to drizzle. I will not manage to get all the cherries picked now. I will leave something for the blackbirds – at least it will keep them off the currants. These have been boiling days for Madla: fruit and jars. We never eat all the preserves, and they accumulate over several years. Last year I took a trip to Ruzyně Prison on account of Gruša. I had to change at White Mountain, and on my way to the bus stop I saw a garden hedge with some Soapwort (*saponaria*) in flower. I pulled off a couple of heads that were going to seed and rubbed the seeds out near our fence. I have just noticed that there is one little plant growing already.

Madla has a bandaged thumb. When she was washing this morning she said to me: "Wash my hands, please." I soaped her little hands and said: "Where did you get yourself all grimy again. You have to go touching everything. You're not capable of walking straight home from school. You have to run your hands along the railings and swing round every lamp-post. Do you have to bring in every speck of dirt from the street?" While I was saying these words, my heart lost a beat as I observed with amazement the effect of this make-believe: her face assumed exactly – but exactly – the expression of a little kid. As she was drying her hands afterwards – for herself now – she declared: "I see now. I must have found my mother in you." And a moment later she went on: "Poor me." I look round to see where the sudden scent is coming from, and it is a cabbage rose in a vase.

It is dull and miserable, and the trees sway in the wayward wind. Soapwort I love because of the stream where we used to herd goats. The low-hanging, supple willow-wands always had a bitter smell and taste. I was chewing a twig. There was a storm circling all round us yesterday but it has come to nothing. I am going out to see.

THURSDAY, 12ᵀᴴ JULY 1979

We were sitting on the café terrace in front of the Hotel Ambassador on Wenceslas Square, drinking coffee and looking at the crowds moving past us on the other side of the coloured fence. I am able to now. Only three years or so ago I would never have been able to sit here as if on show. What has changed? I am more indifferent to myself. I do not think about the effect I am having, I just have it. It is everyone else who is on show for me. I just make sure I am properly buttoned up and I sit. I expect the next stage of relaxation will be when I shall sit improperly buttoned.

"So make up your mind, then," I said. "I am happy to go on sitting here. I'm seeing it for the first time in my life, in fact." – "We ought to find out whether they've got any tickets first," said Zdena. I went to a phone booth and called the Flora cinema to ask them if they had tickets for an English film: *The Medusa Touch*. They weren't answering the phone. So I thought we should see *A Hunting Accident*, but Zdena said she did not feel like Chekhov. All right, we wouldn't go then, and we went on sitting. Then, as dusk started to fall, we went to the Black Horse for dinner. The lighting was dim, something I dislike when I am eating. Or maybe what annoyed me was that she had not wanted to see the Chekhov: it's a story I like. I started to get upset, realised it and knew I had to get over it. Zdena always wants more from each moment than she can get; we have not been anywhere since March (IWD). It's her evening out – what does she get out of it all?

We ordered a schnitzel. It was dry, more crumb than meat. "Our firm paid thirty thousand for working out the June wages on the computer," Zdena said. – "They'd have done better to divide the money among the workforce,"

I said. – "But it could be an exception, because no one knows how to write a programme properly yet." – "For God's sake!" I said. "None of it of it makes any sense to me. What does the machine do with those wages? Seeing they each have to be dictated separately into it anyway because individual outputs and earnings are different every month, employees come and go, some people go sick, and some are on holiday!" She tried to tell me something about it, but I understood less than a word of it. "Come on, we'll go and a have a drink somewhere else," I said, when the question of drinks arose after the meal.

It was nine thirty summer time; it was still only just getting dark and the street lamps were not even on yet. And Wenceslas Square started to empty. "This is a capital city at the height of the tourist season," she remarked. – "I can do without tourists," I said. And I sensed that I could equally do without something to drink, which is what we were ostensibly seeking as we walked slowly past the shop windows. Zdena's pace was almost demonstratively slow. Had I asked what she found so interesting when there was nothing interesting in them, I would not have heard the end of it! "I never get out. I've not been here in the day-time for the past nine months. All I do is go to work and come home from work. Out with the dog first thing in the morning, out with the dog when I come home, out with the dog before I go to bed, the same thing day in day out." – I asked: "How about that wall, has anyone continued working on it?" – "No one's laid a single stone. I don't have anyone to." Now, as I write this, I have started to feel really sleepy and I imagine myself waking first thing in a wide bed in a black-beamed white cell and going straight off to build a wall!

She had some French wine at home that the professor had given her. "I had a dream about you the other day," I said. "You were living in a single-storied house, an abandoned cowshed, in a room like a stable, full of all sorts of old junk – packing cases, boxes, sacks of things, barrels. You had a bed in one corner, and it wasn't made – grubby sheets strewn about, dust, rubbish and dirt. But you weren't there. I went out into the yard to look for you and there I caught sight of you. We said something to each other and suddenly there appeared at your side a real swain, one of those robust flaxen-haired country lads with blue eyes, bony features and a wide mouth. Clever but ingenuous. Alongside each other, the two of you looked like a lady and her groom. He was clearly very devoted to you, and he was looking at me from the other side where he was standing with you." – "The other side of what?" – "Of nothing. Of where I was standing." – "How old was he?" – "He was young – thirtyish. And I asked you, You sleep there? Yes. And we all went over to the house. And he sleeps – where? I ask. And you, in your usual matter-of-fact way, which is only feigned and is a sign of utmost resistance on your part, you say with indifference, Where else would he sleep? There, as well! – And guess what I did then." – "I can't wait to hear!" – "I said to myself very clearly in that dream, Aha. This is nothing new, it's exactly the same situation as with her agronomist that time at Rochov, and I'm supposed to be incensed, but I'm not. How come? I saw you in all your spaciousness and could vividly imagine you cradling that lad, and I didn't begrudge him you in the least!" – "You're vile!" She punched me and said: "Yes, in your dream I have to lie in a cow-shed on a filthy bed with a groom!" – "And all of a sudden it was as if the groom had never been there and you were leading me into the cowshed. You opened the gates and this is what it looked like inside: a bed-stead, cast-iron, on the same spot, but beautifully made up with white linen. And the whole stable was full of stools, tables and cupboards, and on each of them was a vase, and in each vase a tall yellow flower. We walked down an aisle of yellow flowers, all of them standing at different heights. And that was your reply and I was ashamed and felt miserable, and still felt bad the following day."

"I feel like saying some really nasty things to you," she said. – "What would they be? Go on, tell me." – "I can't." – "Have a go." She laughed knowingly: "I won't. Because when nasty things are said to someone above, they always fall back on the person who says them."

FRIDAY, 13TH JULY 1979

This morning I went to buy some meat. There was a woman trying to get something better out of the butcher, something lean: "I'll tell them in Brno the sort of stuff you sell here." Obvious blackmail: can't you take into account that I'm here on a visit? The butcher (butcher! "distributor," more like) replied: "Yes, you do that, lady. Please tell everyone in Brno. It'll be more worth your while there." I took what they had. It's all the same to us.

This afternoon we were at a French reception. I would not have gone but for the fact that Kosík persuaded me. He promised Madla (who had never been at anything of the kind before) the Buquoy Palace: there's no other way of getting to see the inside of it. I had been there twice. The last time was two years ago. It was eight o'clock in the evening when we arrived, and Kohout, Kosík, myself and others of our ilk found the company already well-oiled, as the reception had started at six. They had invited us for a later hour lest we clash in some way with the "regime people." This offended some of us, but it was all the same to me. Last year I didn't go and this year Kosík said: "I think we ought to go, seeing that the ambassador has recognised that it was in poor taste and he has invited us for six o'clock this time."

We arrived there and saw that the rest had been invited for four o'clock. Without moving a muscle in his face, Karel bristled. It was all the same to me. And not the Buquoy Palace but the garden. It was lovely and warm. I have no idea how many hundreds of people were standing around or wandering about the lawn among the roses, glasses in their hands. There was no one I recognised, but then I had not recognised anyone ten years ago either, when people like myself, Kohout and Kosík had made up half of those present. Shortly we caught sight of Saša Kliment with Jiřina, which meant there were six of us, and then Bartošek made it seven. Madla enjoyed observing the company. Bartošek, already a trifle inspired, kept introducing me to different people in French. Thus I was even able to say hello to M. d'Harcourt, the ambassador, who surprised me: he told me he had been expecting me, and that he had a present for me, a book from M. Ehret, the former cultural attaché, with whom I was wont to speak rather more (in German) ten years ago. He knows Martin.

In fact that richly varied company on the green lawn was a splendid sight. We were able to inspect, for instance, all the various uniforms, foreign and local, ranging from threadbare legionaries' garb of the First World War and the more up-to-date World War II uniforms, to the theatrical glitter which they are planning to wear for World War III. Marie Nováková (Kosíková) was beautiful in her white dress, but her feet were sore because she had come there straight from work and had therefore been wearing high heels since the morning. Saša and I agreed that he should sign the title pages of the next transcription of his *Boredom in Bohemia*. Someone there introduced me to someone else, who introduced me to a third person until I eventually found myself amidst some friendly veterans of some kind who were just then agreeing to restore Greater Moravia. They extended me an invitation. I said: "It's just talk, gentlemen, come and see me when it's for real." For the time being, we have agreed that a year from today at the same place we will discuss further details.

I received the first letter from Ivan Kadlečík in a long time:

"Do forgive me, old chap, but my grass never stops growing and when I finish mowing at one end, I have to start again at the other. This is my way of telling you that I've not written for at least three years, in spite of my gratitude to you. I expect I've received everything. My family hasn't managed to branch out any further in the meantime, but I've got ten hares, four hens, a dog and a cat that died. So far I've no bees or friends. Apart from that I cultivate vines: twenty roots that I planted out in my garden last spring. In a couple days' time I'm off on my holidays (on foot) to my own garden – I don't expect I'll rush off anywhere else. What for? The body should not displace itself too much in space, it should only move about more or less in the one place. There are plenty of plums showing, not so many apples. And I'd like to see you too sometime, Ludvák. It's a pity I don't write anything, I'd like to have something good to read some time, even something of my own. I've gone silent, as if I had time a-plenty. Who knows? The poet has gone silent but the grateful country or nation won't forget him; the writer has laid aside his quill and in his rubber boots is turning over the compost that smells far sweeter than the state (of Denmark)... Fraternal greetings to our friend, the living Slovak historian in Prague, to whom I also didn't forget to write, even though I didn't write. Listen to some Mozart but don't let yourselves get carried away! I've just received some books and am reading Bartholomew's thoughtful couplings. There was no letter with the books and I'm not very surprised, so be so kind as to write me a few lines. I've got some notes but what I'll make of them and when I can't say."

Prague is full of the scent of linden blossom. I like the linden tree but only the ordinary European kind (*Tilia europaea L.*, *Holländische Linde*) or the large-leaved variety (*Tilia platyphilia*, *Sommerlinde*), with the simple flower. But I find the scent of the linden with the heavy, fat blooms (?) suffocating. It was wafting about the streets yesterday evening when I was waiting for a taxi or a tram. Three women came out of somewhere and for a long time their indistinct conversation and laughter got closer and louder through the darkness, and as they approached me one of them said: "Come on, let's cuntilate him." But they didn't, they just burst out laughing and went their way. And I really had to escape the clutches of those stiflingly pungent linden trees. If Ivan had been with me he would have suffered a hay-fever attack straight away! That word they uttered I had never heard before, I didn't even know it really existed; I thought it was one of my inventions. I had asked Ivan, or maybe he had volunteered, to deliver some books to Rychetský, but when I met Rychetský and asked for payment he knew nothing about it. I can't even rely on people to do little things like that, which is why I'm packing it up. Then there's Petr Pithart who makes my blood boil each time by expressing surprise that the books are so expensive. Eva Kantůrková, who, when she paid me, did not have a five-crown piece and joked about Vaculík going broke because of five crowns. And there's confounded B., who has owed me 305 crowns for the past three months, so I've stopped putting books aside for him. It's no good! I just can't achieve a situation where I no longer have any responsibilities. Now Šamalík has published *Thoughts on the History of Czech Politics* on his own. I've started to read it – it really ought to be transcribed! Money has finally come from Index for the feuilleton collection and from Japan a Honda motor-cycle: I shall share it out – and that'll be that. But no sign anywhere of the Hostovský Prize. I am amazed when I recall –

I am amazed when I recall how we used to pull down any little tree, such as an alder sapling, because it is so brittle, just to get a long straight stick for something, or those long hazel wands for arrows! I hadn't the slightest perception of nature's separate existence, it was there entirely for me and because of me. And we would flatten every patch of grass... "Hold on, do you really mean it?" – "Really and truly." – "But you'll come after the holidays, won't you?" – "No." ... on the meadows and break off branches from every bush for the goats, and when my parents sent me for linden flowers, it was understood that I would climb up the tree with a saw and crop it, apart from the very top branches (afterwards it shot upwards!), bind the sticks into a bundle and drag them home. At home on the veranda they would be stripped and the flowers put up in the loft to dry; the goats would get the branches. Everybody did it like that and the linden trees were indestructible. And we had flowers in abundance – for sale. In fact we counted on the income from it! As much as 60 pre-war crowns, I recall! And every summer the trees were abuzz with bees once more and the light, sweet scent wafted over the meadows. Those were maiden-like lindens, not these fat floozies of the town with their suffocating perfume.

On the other hand, it is also true that when I was as big as I am now, merely lighter and more supple, I imagined being captured by three women somewhere up there, high above Brumov, somewhere below Bare Hill. What their faces and voices should be like I was unable to conjure up, however. And how to reconcile their behaviour with my exacting requirement that they should be not just charming but also intelligent is a problem I am still grappling with!

TUESDAY, 17ᵀᴴ JULY 1979

Madla's thumb earned her a week's sick-leave. She is in Dobřichovice while I had to come to Prague for various things: dentist, book-binder, watchmaker, Bibisa… As I was leaving, Madla impressed on me that I was to take some currants to auntie, stay at home, write and, if possible, buy, roast and bring back with me a nice little chicken. "Why do you call it a nice little chicken, for God's sake?" – "Because it needn't be a big one." – "That's a lie! The reason you say it is so I'll think it entails less work!" – "Yes, I think you're right there," she giggled. "But I only realise it now that you tell me."

I always open the apartment door in trepidation at what awaits me inside. When there is no message lying there for me and no mail, I am relieved. In the kitchen, a cup with tea still left in it; in the sink, a plate, two cups, a knife and a spoon; on the draining board, several items of clean crockery. Catherine had scattered it all with poppy seed which she gets from a cup above the sink. In the sugar, tiny indentations from her beak. I warmed myself up something to eat, washed the dishes I had used and put them away so that I could say to the boys when they came in: "What's all this crockery everywhere?" – "But we haven't the time," they'll answer if it's Jan. "Hmm…" Ondřej will reply and start clearing it away, whereby the discussion ends up a blind alley. To Jan, on the contrary, I'll say: "It all depends what you consider part of the eating process. When you're eating you have to open your mouth and shove in the spoon. If you didn't consider removing the spoon part of the eating process you'd end up accumulating spoons in your mouth." – That'll put paid to him. "Er–er–er…" is all that will emerge from his engine-room.

"The doctor's gone to buy the dogs some meat," said Mrs. Krumphanzlová. "Take a seat for a few moments." I didn't feel like it, I'll come back tomorrow. My new teeth are in place, but they are not cemented in yet. As I passed the pharmacy I remembered I had a prescription for Febichol. "We haven't had that in for a year, sir," the pharmacist told me. Yes, people tell me there is a growing shortage of medicine. Such talk depresses me, it sounds like a presage of far worse things to come. A shambling old gent told me outside on the pavement after I had held the door open for him to come out: "An age-old Russian remedy for when you're sick, inhale chlorate of lime from a little bottle." – "And they sprinkle it on you if you don't survive," I added. – "I've seen a few places in my time!" he said, and shambled off.

The way I use Febichol is to carry a few of the round pills on my person in a little bottle, mixed with some other pills, some flat, some round. I just carry it, that's all, and it works. It's my "medicine." (Be your own medicine-man.) I don't think I've needed Febichol for three years now. I swallow one now and then, however, just preventively, when I eat Chinese food with doughnuts or a gateau crumbled in wine. In the case of a serious bilious attack I still have some Aristochol granules from my publisher and friend, Braunschweiger of Lucerne, who fancies that only a heavy gall bladder can keep an active author from completing a book, no matter what kind.

The latest instance of Febichol use was Kosík's "cherry party" last Saturday. He bought fourteen pork chops and some fish or other, and held a "cherry party." It was raining. I discovered the company under an awning stretched between two trees. Karel was in the best of spirits! A delicious smell was coming from the grill; the smoke from it wafted heavily over Všenory. Karel Bartošek was there with his daughter and his friend Čutka, whom I didn't know. Then there was Saša Kliment with Jiřina and several motley items of youth. Plus Rudolf Slánský Jr., who had taken the invitation literally and wanted to bring his mother back a basket of cherries, of which there were plenty on the tree. But as fast as he picked them, Bartošek, who was already slightly inspired, would take them and put them in his own basket. "I thought Madla looked very elegant at the French reception," said Jiřina, as if wanting to be pleasant for a change, "but I was surprised she came." – "So was I," I said. Saša intimated that over the years she had been working at her present job, Madla had acquired a more accurate perception of her own worth, and hence greater social aplomb. Madla did not attend the cherry party; she wanted to do some reading and assumed that it wouldn't happen if it rained.

Marie offered me a piece of fish on a fork. "What is it?" I asked suspiciously. "Hake," she replied. "I know a dog called Hake," I said, and kept the rest to myself: Hay–key, Hay–key! Helena calls and blows on a scarcely audible whistle that her dachshund Hake can apparently hear. "And how about you, Ludvík," Jiřina says in my direction, "how's your little romance coming along?" That really made me jump, but it turned out she had in mind the novel I am writing. Novel? – I wonder. "I'm writing away," I replied.

All of a sudden I realised I was alone among the women and children; the gentlemen had withdrawn down to the cabin. As I entered they were just starting on a bottle of wine and were talking about mistresses, or rather, the mistress as an institution. Bartošek, whose French wife is on holiday in her homeland, felt the need – I had noticed it previously at the reception – to mention her all the time. And so he mentioned her on this occasion too, telling how his Susette had put paid to his mistress. She had given him no hassle, instead: it's O.K., it's O.K., all smiles. Then: why don't you invite her home, we're rational people aren't we, I'd love to meet her. The mistress came – apéritif, hors d'oeuvres, dinner, petits fours, and over coffee Bartošek's delightful Susette says to the woman: "So let's get down to business, shall we? What are your intentions weeth my Bartošek?" Oh, my gawd! We all clasp our heads in our hands. And Bartošek explains gratefully and with nostalgia how embarrassing it was for him. But she's some woman, eh?

I had a yen to sing, but Karel doesn't, Saša joins in half-heartedly, Bartošek fools around, Rudolf Slánský doesn't look like the singing type, really, and Čutka started to intone: "Diddly diddly doo, there's fuck all we can do." Then the Kliments discreetly disappeared, I don't even know when. By now Karel, Marie and I were hoping for a few moments alone, but the guests deliberately missed one train after another. Bartošek is the most irritating one in that respect. – But I must be off to the bookbinder, continuation this evening or tomorrow.

Yes, it's this evening still: This afternoon a sharp, cold shower swept through the streets. It was not unpleasant – just so long as it does not stay around till November! When summer came in with a vengeance in May, I said to myself, what will nature do in the summer? What will it find to do with itself until autumn? We all hope that it will continue to be warm and bright. The linden blossom is falling. I noticed from the tram that the soil around the lindens on the embankment had been freshly dug over. I was surprised, and immediately turned a kindlier gaze towards the Castle.

When I came in, the washing-up had been done, the crockery put away and both the boys were gone again. Ondřej came back just a moment ago. "What's new at work," I asked. He replied: "At work? We work slowly and steadily. Work today faltered mainly because of talk about that new epidemic in Slovakia and the price increases. Tomorrow the conversation will be about preserving fruit." – "And how are you getting on?" – "I'm getting on fine." – "Would you like a Gardavský for fifty crowns? I picked it up from the manufacturers' today." – "Who is he?" – "He isn't any more. He died last year." – "What does he write about." – "Educational freedom." – "What did he die of?" – "The status quo, you might say."

Tomorrow I have a date with Helena, one of the last few.

WEDNESDAY, 18TH JULY 1979

Evening. We made ourselves some tea. "What's new at work?" I asked Ondřej. – "The main item on the agenda was the price increases, particularly on petrol. Our driver, who goes round with the Robur truck, was boasting he'd already managed to pinch fifty litres." – "What's the Robur got to do with it," I asked. – "It's the only truck that runs on petrol. That's why it's been withdrawn from use and is only brought out when some vehicle is off the road. So all the drivers see to it that one vehicle is off the road all the time. They've even managed to introduce some kind of fair rotation into it."

"And what's new at your place?" I asked Jan. – "Today I potted my first plant. It's a Wandering Jew that I acquired by opening the engine-cover of a bus where it was growing in a permanent puddle of water. I transplanted it into a bowl of soil. It's a centimetre tall." – "But I shouldn't think," said Ondřej, "it'll grow. It's been used to the dark." – "Where do you think you'll find light in our workshop! It's bound to grow well." – I asked: "And how are you coping with the work? All right?" – "I'm coping all right, but I'm held back all the time. Party members were told at a meeting which prices would be increased and they immediately spread the news among the ordinary people, so the items on today's agenda were cholera and price increases. Mr. Loula called over to me, 'Forget the work, the cholera's coming anyway.' And they've banned me from drinking milk, the lads. One of the workers said, "Fellers, the one who survives erects a plague column, O.K.?"

Ondřej said: "Actually it's quite normal and commonplace, there have always been price increases and cholera." Jan said to Ondřej: "But they said on TV that it isn't cholera, but some new strain of jaundice, and they've got plenty of drugs." – "There are plenty of drugs," Ondřej agreed, "but they're not effective. Where does a new strain of virus come from anyway?" That was a question for me; they both waited to hear what I would say. I knew the answer: "Science has succeeded in cultivating it, of course. But boys, I don't like it when you conform to the regime by adopting the workers' psychoses!" – "Who's conforming?" They looked at each other. "We only report it to you, when you ask." – "I'm working properly," said Ondřej. "So am I," said Jan.

"And now tell me what this is," I said, reaching into my breast pocket and placing a chain on the table. – "It's a chain," Jan answered. Ondřej went on: "And more specifically, a flat chain, 60 centimetres long." He looked down at the chain from above as if it were a worm. Jan took hold of it, examined it more closely and continued: "With links of alternate metals, looks like copper..." he broke off, scrutinising more closely the long flat links of highly polished grey metal which seemed to have some fine copper wires pressed into it. "How've they managed that?" he mumbled. – "Show me!" Ondřej took the thing out of his hands. "I expect they're only etched in – no, they really are wires pressed into the surface of the material. But if we examine it more closely, we discover that the chain is extremely worn in places and here it's actually broken." – "That's the reason I'm asking you," I said. "Do you think tin solder would work on it?" Jan took the chain back, examined it and said: "I'm not sure whether you could solder that grey material with tin. But if we were to snip out a grey link we'd have two copper ones next to each other, and then you could." Ondřej said: "But I'm sure Dad doesn't want two copper links next to each other, does he?" – "In that case we'd have to cut out another copper link." – "But Dad doesn't want the chain to be so much shorter, because..." he leaned over to Jan and whispered something to him. "Oh, yeah. Oh, yeah. Oh, yeah." Jan said in succession, and, imitating Madla's intonation of wonderment, said: "How did she dare!" I reached for the chain with the words: "No, no. She was wearing it round her neck. I was taken by its sheen and its colour. I asked what it was made of, and she took it off. 'Anyway, I was worrying about what I'd give you, Ludvík,' she said." Ondřej nodded, Jan gaped at me and then they both said: "You mean you're on first-name terms already?"

We were sitting in Café Savarin on Příkopy, by a window, and she was afraid that her husband would be able to catch sight of us through the net curtains. "Is it still as bad as that?" I asked. – "Yes. So I've decided to leave as soon as possible, on my own, before him, as soon as I'm not needed here." – "And it's all because of me?" – "You're never mentioned overtly."

She was wearing a light green blouse, probably of poplin, with a long pointed collar and long sleeves. Over it she had a dark-blue short-sleeved pullover. It is inconceivable she was unaware of the critical combination of those two colours, it was bound to be deliberate. The black-blue-green pleated skirt is her most frequent item of clothing. Stockings of a greyish shade, black shoes with flat heels. A silver chain wound tightly three times round her left wrist, a thin wedding ring on her finger, around her neck two loops of chain with oval links made of some polished material the colour of grey steel. She seemed thinner in the face and I was yet again aware how pure she is – pure as ordinary water from a brook. We both ordered Becherovka.

"When I left the house today," I started to say what I had decided in advance to tell her, "it was raining. It's such a dull day, I said to myself, now I'll make my way there through the streets – I've got an umbrella – I'll arrive at the café, I'll sit down here and you'll either come or not. You came... And you're lovely." (That bit was improvised; she quivered.) "But one day you won't come. Again it'll be a day like today – in October or November – and you'll be in Vienna walking along an almost identical street and you'll feel lonely. And that'll be our date. It almost amounts to the same thing, doesn't it?" She gazed at me clearly, striving to understand not just the words but also their motive. She had the solemnity of a child for whom it wasn't quite usual yet. She said: "A few days ago you were talking about the grave. I heard what you said but didn't understand. Now I'm beginning to feel it terribly! All the preparations for leaving that we are making at home are a kind of final reckoning. In retrospect, I'm beginning to realise that you have taken leave of me already." She fell silent, clasping and unclasping her fingers unconsciously on the edge of the table, her eyes downcast.

I said: "Yes, Helena, I have buried you. I now have your death behind me, but to my glorious surprise I discover you continue to exist for yourself! So look after yourself and your husband, drop me a line from time to time, and when you come to Prague one of these days we'll see each other. We're going to go on meeting each other, aren't we? It's just that a few years might elapse between our dates, that's all. Is that so bad, Helena?"

She shook her head uncomprehendingly, and covered her eyes. "That is precisely what crushes me, the fact that you can come to terms with it, and that we're just letting it dissolve into nothing. It's that! Don't you understand?!" – "Damn it, who's leaving – you or me? I'm grown up already, you're still young. Besides, you still have plenty of time. Do you really think I ought to be saying: Come away with me for a day, two days, a week? You'd be too scared to anyway! But even if..." – "No, Ludvík, don't say I'd be scared. Don't say it..." – I knew what she meant, I knew all too well. She was right: "You're right, it's not a question of fear. But even if you weren't just about to leave, even if you weren't leaving at all, we would either not allow any of this to happen, or we'd be obliged to take one particular step that would shock everyone around us. But in all events, we've come this far, so just keep playing the game and don't run away before the final whistle. That's one thing I forbid you to do, because it's me you'd be hurting if you did. And what for, for heaven's sake? Should I speak to your husband?" – "On no account, for God's sake! Wh–wh–wh–whatever could you want to tell him?" – "To let you go out and make your farewells. That I would see you on your way in a sound state of mind."

That was when I got engrossed in that chain and she gave it to me, tension released, joy from sadness, from feelings, from perceptions. In a fresher voice she said: "Have you thought up any assignments for me yet? What could I do for you there, for all of you?" – Well that was out of the question, she does not seem to realise that she will have plenty to do for herself. "But you've already got two assignments. No, three. Make Binar's acquaintance, in order to have some friends, but do not fall in love with him." She winked and a silent pleasure escaped from somewhere inside onto her lips. "Then you have to deduce from the terrain where the yard and the chateau in Stifter's *Nachsommer* were located..." – "Hmm, that shouldn't be too hard. I've already discovered that there's a Stifter Museum and I've already found it on the Vienna street-plan. I expect they'll have everything there." – "But your job is to visit the places and describe to me what they look like now." – "That's two. And the other?" – "You're to become a subscriber to Sixty-Eight Publishers. As soon as you earn enough!" – "That goes without saying. But listen, Ludvík, will you write to me?" – "But I am already!" – "Are you still writing what you spoke about?" – "I am... what's the matter? Is something wrong?" I look around. The blood left her face.

"No, no, nothing! I had a... an odd feeling, all of a sudden. As if I'd lost my past and had no future, I've just this moment realised it – all there is is the present, this disproportionately huge present. Who am I? Who for? What for? Should I be scared of what you're writing?" – "Oh, yes, you should be! Because the moment you take off, I'll start to think up the most awful things about you, absolutely freely and with relish." – "Tell me what – tell me!" She gripped my hand across the table. – "I'll start to elaborate our story as it would have developed had you not gone. I'll become your public bed-fellow, there'll be a dreadful scandal and your husband will send me a protest through diplomatic channels..." – "Oh, yes, I had a dream about you – us!" – "Out with it, another one for my collection!"

"We were – excuse me – lying down and he came and shot you, like this, from above, in the back, if you see what I mean." – "From above, in the back. Yes, I see. And then?" – "I tried, in vain, of course, to shield you everywhere with my hands. Well anyway, he fired, and nothing. You got up and your were just full of holes. I forget to say we own a shotgun – or rather he does. But he shot away something important of mine." – "What – like your eye?" – "Like my eye, yes, but both my eyes were still intact. Just a feeling that, you know, something had been shot away." Of course I knew what: me. But I said: "I think I know what, your *kep*." – "What's that?" – "*Kep*, masculine noun, the vulva, marked in present dictionaries with a cross as an archaism, but in Jungmann's it was still without the cross: 'A keppish woman,' 'Why art thou standing there, thou kep?' 'Three letters to thee!'" – "Wh–whatever are you going on about, Ludvík?" – "I mean, the word had three letters, so instead of using it, a polite person would say threateningly, 'Three letters to you!'" She laughed so heartily that people turned round to look. I went on: "I had to laugh though, because the Poles would have to say: Four letters to you, because in Polish it's *kiep*. In other words, to sum up: 'Three letters to you – or four in Polish!'" She laughed, but I knew how to put a stop to that: "In German it's *Scham*, I looked it up especially. How many letters is that – five, and how many sounds – three. It's not funny in German. See where you're going to?" – "Oh, God. Are you starting that again, Ludvík?" – "I'm just helping you. You have to study it. Study it!" – "But I'm studying it all the time. Go on, test me." – "How do you say..." I tried to think of something basic and practical, "how about damn it!" – "Dammit!" she blurted out almost tearfully.

THURSDAY, 19ᵀᴴ JULY 1979

There is a song that has been buzzing in my head since about last autumn. I heard it sung – playing it was forbidden – in Zlín during the war. It was of Hungarian origin and it was subsequently banned because officers apparently used to shoot themselves out of nostalgia when it was played.

> Sunday is sad and it seems never-ending
> The romance is gone, all that's left is our yearning
> But I've now forgotten the rest of the song
> I'd love to recall it, it's not very long
> The lamps are now lit and I feel their sorrow
> I'm sat by the window, no thought of the morrow
> Lalala lalala dusk is now falling
> In my heart all that's left is sadness and yearning
> No returning
> No returning
> There's something quite drastic about it to boot
> and it's dreadfully mournful, especially verse two:
> He kissed my sad lips just once and so fondly
> The sweetness of love I tasted once only
> But our love was dying with each passing day
> And all that remained was dull and mundane
> Dadada dadada dadada da dame
> Quenched in my heart is that lovely flame
> Only dreaming remains
> Only dreaming remains

I went to the Hungarian cultural centre to enquire whether the song had not perhaps been unbanned since and even recorded. As I started to give an approximate rendering, all the saleswomen recognised it and started hunting for it in Hungarian: "*Szomorú vasárnap, szomorú, vasárnap,*" they said to each other. But sadly they did not have it, not even in sheet-music form. I went to the Šiktances' to ask Mrs. Š. – she is Hungarian – whether she knew it. She knew bits and pieces of the Hungarian text. It differed quite a lot from the Czech version. Most importantly, it is all spoken by the man: Come to me, I'm waiting for you, you'll find me, I'll be lying like this, six tall candles burning round me... Now that would be even more likely to affect the trigger finger. Then I almost forgot about the song, until yesterday, when Karel Šiktanc told me that Hradský had given him the original text and he and his wife had tried to translate it. But the translation still sounded too kitschy for their taste. I said: "Karel, for goodness sake, don't let that put you off. It has to sound kitschy! It has to be romantic sob-stuff, that we pretend to sing as a parody because we're ashamed to take it seriously, when in fact we mean it awfully seriously!" – "I expect you're right," said Karel Šiktanc, "I'll have another go then. Hey, I hear Tatarka has written something erotic – you don't have it by any chance do you?" I immediately went home and brought him a copy of *Jottings*. He asked how much. "Gratis, if you translate 'Mournful Sunday' for me." – "Well, thanks very much, you can count on it."

I bought some meat, fed the birds, watered the plants and drove to Dobřichovice, because Josef Zeman was due to come there today with his wife. When I arrived they were already sitting with Madla round the white table beneath the apricots. Josef's car is running again and he thanked me for Jan's assistance. We left the women sitting there and went up to the room for a chat. But Josef caught sight of Ondřej's mandolin, picked it up, and started to play it while I sang: "If you're looking for the generals, you'll know where to find them, Oh, yes..." I asked Josef to help identify a particular plant of the order Asteraceae. I have been searching for the past two days in the plant guide and I never get any further than *Buphtalmum* or *Telekia*, or something else. It's a tall plant with lanceolate, coarsely serrated leaves and its dark yellow flower resembles a Rudbeckia. Josef immediately suggested elecampane, but the shape of the petals is wrong. After this tiring research, Josef picked up the mandolin once more: "What shall I play?" – "Play *Boleraz*, that's a good old faithful," and straight away we were back in the days when I used to go and visit him at the agricultural college where he was the principal. Then we went outside and Josef found fault with the way the blade was fitted on the scythe. "Why don't you keep bees?" he asked. "Read up about it and start a hive!" – I replied: "I did something about it, and I discovered why I can't start keeping bees yet."

I was always afraid that with age Josef would become irascible and cantankerous and would be unable to concentrate on anything. But on the contrary he is calmer. He is looking forward to retirement. He is thin and I'd say he weighs less than sixty kilos. A fortnight ago he took part in a show-jumping competition after the woman who had trained the horse fell ill. He won the competition! We agreed that things did not look good for Khomeini, or Iran either, for that matter.

We joined the womenfolk who were still chatting away about the same things as when we left them. And meanwhile Josef and I had discussed so many different things. Madla took the opportunity to ask Josef about the birds we see around here. Josef confirmed the spotted woodpecker and the kestrel. Madla suggested a walk to show the Zemans where Šalda used to live. On the way we sight-saw all the gardens and villas. Josef was staggered by the ignorance of people who are capable of putting up their uninspired little boxes right alongside older houses of richly varied design. "Who's the bastard that allows it?" I was astonished at his astonishment, and when we reached Šalda's villa, Madla started to expatiate about how a single good prostitute, probably from Dejvice, had managed to ruin half the country's pre-war literature. Josef did not understand what she meant, so I had to explain to him that Madla was simply repeating some nonsense that Jiří Gruša had told her.

"What are you reading?" I asked. – "I bought a biography of Corot." – "Who's Corot?" – "He's a painter I like." – "Josef, I wish you'd start taking photos again." – "When I retire," he replied. He asked what I was writing. I gave a vague reply and promised him I would let him read it. At that, Madla said that Kantůrková had written some good feuilletons, but only recently: Didn't she realise earlier where those policies were leading?" – "Hard to say," said Josef, and I said: "Take no notice, she's just rehearsing our quarrel for the twentieth time, for the benefit of guests." Madla said crossly: "What are you on about? It's nothing of the sort! I'm not saying she isn't right! It's just that it's obvious to everyone nowadays – the destruction of the countryside, the demoralisation of the people, the economy in a mess... Why doesn't she write about something that will become a crisis in twenty years' time? Why isn't she ahead of events? If people aren't capable of saying any more than what everyone knows already, they shouldn't write at all!" – "Why not?" I said. – "All right, but I don't need to read it!" she said. Josef didn't understand – he didn't know what I knew: that this was also a form of warning directed at me.

When the Zemans left, I picked up the plant guide and made a fresh start at trying to identify that yellow plant. I think it will turn out to be a *Telekia*. As I gazed at its magnificent flower – the dark centre and the deep orange petals arching in a crown all around it – I thought to myself what a good model it would make for an artistic goldsmith. Maybe I shall have a go at it myself one day. When I retire.

FRIDAY, 20ᵀᴴ JULY 1979

Total disaster. I spent the whole day messing about with an acacia log, saying to myself all the while: I'll just do this and then I'll go and do some writing, and the moment I was really ready to go – visitors! Four people. I was not even able to control myself. I shook hands and then started to rush about the garden as if I were looking for something. I think I am catching Kosík's disease: unannounced visits can actually make my hackles rise. But why? My flexibility is failing. I hate it now when someone disturbs my plans and state of mind. So I left the people sitting under the Apricost (that's a genuine typing mistake that speaks for itself) with Madla, and I am here.

The log came from the acacias that grow over the path just beyond our fence. One of them was toppled in a storm, actually smashing our gate. The foresters chopped it down and sawed it up. People dragged away the thin branches and three sections of the trunk are lying here. Were lying. The log is a metre long and eighty centimetres across and what makes it a rarity is that it is not a single trunk but about five smaller trunks that have grown into each other and joined up but are still separated by their bark. I am gouging out the now rotten bark. A sinewy tangle of fragrant wood. What I shall use it for I have no idea.

Mrs. Rohlenová walked past and said: "Time fliest like a deer with an arrow in its rear." I corrected her verb ending and determined not to react further. She must want something. In a little while she came back again and said: "I don't want anything, my question is purely academic. Now that there's a fuel crisis and there's no coal at the Řevnice depot, even though summer's coming to an end, it means I'll have to drag wood from the forest like old Hermerková. Where am I to store it?" – "What sort of academic response do you want?" I asked and went on gouging. – "Well, somewhere here in the garden." – "In no time it'd be like a Gypsy encampment," I said. "What's wrong with your cellar?" – She went away and was back a moment later: "But if I put wood in that cellar, it's like, well, storing sugar in a pond." – "Or in a cellar," I finished her thought for her. "But seeing it's a purely academic question, come and show me where you think you might store your wood. Mind you, it'd have to be somewhere only you would have to look at it all day, and the rest of us wouldn't." We went round to the southerly side of the house in front of her flat, where she grows roses, raspberries, wild strawberries, old pots, preserving jars and a broken wooden chair. There, behind the trunk of a yew-leaved spruce, having pushed aside the overhanging branches of *Philadelphus* and lilac, I pointed at a heap of rags, glass jars and flower-pots, saying: "An ideal spot, Mrs. Rohlenová, isn't it?"

She stood behind me, dry and diminutive, hands on hips, large eyes in a furrowed face, and said: "I admire your ingenuity. So be it. All it needs is to knock in four posts here and put some sort of roof on top. Do you agree?" – "That would be the best plan, Mrs. Rohlenová, so long as you don't mean we should do it." – "No, no, no! I have three sons, after all!"

I departed for my acacia shape. Mrs. Rohlenová came up and, facing my pile of various poles, logs and sticks said: "You don't mind having a Gypsy encampment here, then?" – "No I don't, because I want it here," I said calmly, but I immediately saw red. "Because this is a work corner shielded on all sides by trees and bushes. This is where I do various jobs, and say to myself all the while that I am your labourer, gardener and maintenance man. This is where I fume at you, but I never go and tell you about it and I'm only telling you now since we're engaged in a purely academic conversation." – "All right," she said, "and what'll that be for?" she pointed at the log. – "I don't know," I replied. – "It could make a good stand for an enormous plant," she suggested. – "I've already thought about that," I said. – "But where will you put it?" – "In the summer-house for now, and one day it'll go in the greenhouse." She departed.

The greenhouse is a sore point for Mrs. Rohlenová! It stands alongside her flat and hence she uses it for growing cactuses and in summer she has lunch there with her visitors. The trouble is a greenhouse must be kept in repair. The iron frame rusts, a roof pane occasionally breaks, the tiled floor subsides: who is to pay? Madla has asked me again and again to wrest the greenhouse from Mrs. Rohlenová. But I don't want to. It seems silly to me.

"I'm sorry," came from behind me. I turned round. "I'm aware of all that and I don't want anything from you. But I was in Řevnice at the dentist's and you can see into the coal depot from there, and all they have is a pile of coal dust." – "That's all right, Mrs. Rohlenová, that coal dust frightened President Carter too, so I fully understand." – "So you're not cross with this silly old granny." – "Not in the least," I said.

SUNDAY, 22ND JULY 1979

Yesterday evening in his garden, Karel Kosík broached the subject of virility in politics. As late as the 18th century, he says, a man who wanted to influence the world was capable of backing his decisions with his words and even his life. This is no longer the case. Men have become effeminate – in ordinary life too. In the same way that women have lost their femininity. Dubček wept, Husák moves himself to tears. Carter started by writing to Sakharov and ended in Brezhnev's arms. He is a clown. He should have been a preacher.

Karel Pecka did not agree: To have induced Egypt and Israel to sign the Camp David accords was an act of firm will, determination and political skill. To have told the Americans the situation they are in today and start to take steps accordingly is a risk worthy of a man. Men are tested differently nowadays.

Kosík said: Only a madman or a fool, who'll never learn anything, could have ever signed SALT II from the American side. It's a great victory for the Russian Empire, one such as we would never have imagined back in 1946.

Pecka: That kind of thinking takes into account only two factors – Russia and America. But now there are at least three. Or four, more likely. China had a better measure of the Russians when it moved against Vietnam. What did the Russians do? – There is a conclusion to be drawn there if one were clever enough, and what is signed or not is not so important. SALT II was signed quite simply because it suited both sides in the short term.

I did not say much, only that I couldn't see how Kosík's demand for virile firmness could be reconciled with the requirement for politicans to have tactical skills, as he had advocated on other occasions. Is Carter supposed to interfere with the democratic order and force the Americans to negotiate beyond the extent to which they feel threatened? American society as a whole would have to suffer disillusion and start to be afraid. – Pecka supported me in this: America is England before Churchill.

Madla raised the matter of whether what we were saying could not be heard in neighbouring gardens and cottages. Both Kosík and Pecka said that by then it was immaterial. Her concern was a trifle belated after having held forth herself for almost three hours already about how the same forces which had wiped out the peasantry in the fifties, corrupted the working class in the sixties, and marginalised the intelligentsia in the seventies, were now engaged in trying to break up families, transfer people's existence to supervised workplaces and in general abolish human privacy. She only hoped she would live to see the day when this revolution would overtake Europe from coast to coast. – The two men gazed at her with awe and respect, but only I knew that at that particular moment Europe was taking the blame instead of me.

At ten o'clock, when it was already dark, we saw Pecka to the station and went home. At night I dreamt that I was climbing down a terribly steep slope overgrown with soft grass like Kosík's terraces, with the help of a rope stretched over the road, the railway and some high-tension cables. I cannot understand why I did not glide down as on other occasions in similar situations. Madla had a dream about some fellow shooting me, very artfully: he drew the pistol, fired, missed and threw the pistol in my direction, drew a second one, fired and missed, again threw it away and only when I went to reach for it, he shot me with the third pistol. It was a lovely –

It was a lovely sunny morning. I took some coloured transparencies of flowers and things. The mood of the sky and the air changed several times before evening: from summer to autumn. Madla has acquired Prague-phobia: after three weeks away she has no desire to return. Nor have I. I still had to finish picking the summer apples from the heavily-laden tree. We picked the last of the currants and enjoyed the first of the dahlias. On the juniper there sat a spotted woodpecker – four spotted woodpeckers! Two adults, two young ones, pecking away at the cones. The racket they made was as if we had some fellows in to do a job and they were putting their backs in it while we were around so that we would go away easy in our minds. As we were returning to the gate and taking a farewell look, Mrs. Hemerková bent down to Don by the wood stack and whispered, "Hold on, they're about to leave!!"

Back home I found a summons for the morrow, signed by Major Fišer: "For an interview about a serious matter." No, this time I have no idea what he might want me for: either he has already seen the feuilleton collection, even though there were only ten copies of it, or he wants to get my agreement not to attend court on the day the VONS members come to trial, or maybe he would like to know what is my relationship with a certain prospective woman emigré – or it is even possible that he knows already and would like to make use of it, or he wants to offer me a passport to travel abroad as well, or he wants to caution me against enemies, friends, fiends, spouses, mice and lice! The best opening gambit I have thought out theoretically is: Q. "I expect you know why I asked you to come." – A. "Yes, you want to tell me who Zdena Tominová's attacker was."

Now I'm cross: I didn't want to write about them but they keep on making me.

MONDAY, 23ʳᵈ JULY 1979

There was a jam kolach lying on the table. When I came in Catherine flew off it, circled round the kitchen and landed on the cage. I pushed the kolach to one side and cut a slice of bread. I made myself some tea. I ate my breakfast though I had no appetite. A little way away, Catherine boldly breakfasted off the kolach. Philip just complained noisily, but did not dare come to the table. I still had an hour, during which I went through the papers on my desk, selected a number of them, took out a plastic bag from the cupboard, added the papers to it, tied the packet up and took it into the courtyard of the house next door, and hid it under a bin of sand left there in case of fire. The bag contains nothing illegal, of course, only things that could create difficulties with existing projects and harassment of other people as well.

When I had finished I felt an incredible sense of relief, so that I almost felt cheerful. And on examining my state of mind closely, I discovered to my surprise that I was not afraid any more. I really am not afraid of them, not even if they keep me there this time! How nice and simple to be in prison at last, if that is your lot, when they have nothing serious against you. You just hold your peace, for one month, two months, three months, a year, while their difficulties simply go on mounting! And when it comes to trial, the same tactic again: say nothing, don't react at all: You don't exist as far as I'm concerned, you call yourselves a court? – That's my plan.

America is England before Churchill. (p. 271)

What bedevils and terrifies me is my incomplete notion of the movement and behaviour of things in my flat, and what they might mean, or be made to mean in relation to things in other flats. Always the same question: should I keep them here, since I insist that everything is legal, or should I assume that the law is of little value now? It's an adventure story about nothing. The hero bravely conceals himself, fearfully holds his head high – meanwhile his adversary is quite unaware and might not even have any plans for him. In the end, the hero is brought down by an illness. But on the other hand, they must be investigating something. When they have convicted the ten under arrest, what will they do then? Lay off staff?

Major Fišer was waiting for me with a young man – a different one from last time. I shall not describe our exchanges in detail. I do not enjoy writing about them anyway, and only do so because that is the way it has to be now. Mr. Vaculík, you're at it again, adding your signature to something. What are those people to you? You won't help them and you'll just harm yourself. You've got a gifted son in Jan: top marks on his graduation exams, an excellent employment record, an award as a model trainee of Prague City Transport, an excellent character reference. So it's a shame he couldn't get into the engineering faculty, in spite of the fact that there was not a lot of competition for places, because it's a strenuous course, and one for which he is amply suited.

I expressed surprise that he already knew Jan had been turned down, when we ourselves had not yet been notified. It was his turn to be surprised: we ought to have been informed a long time ago; after all, Jan would be sure to lodge an appeal. I said that he would, of course, and that I also would take some action. After all, you yourself have just said that Jan is well suited for study. He told me not to issue threats but instead to display goodwill so that the child shouldn't suffer on account of its parents, something he also was opposed to. I said: "Don't use my child to put pressure on me."

Major Fišer is slightly older than me. My guess is that he is also looking forward to retirement, and he behaves decently. He exercises greater self-control than I do, and I have discovered that some things are best said to him with no holds barred: he then finds the motives for my behaviour more understandable and it is as if – in human terms – he even accepts them. I know, I know! So I said it was more important to them that Jan should get into university, for policy reasons. If they did accept him, it would actually complicate my decision-making, since the demarcation line between our family and the state had been clear till now. Besides, the university was so full of dross these days that it might even do Jan more harm than good. – He looked at me triumphantly: "There you are, you'd sooner sacrifice your son, just so you can display your stubborn attitudes." I replied that it was easy enough for them to overcome me.

The conversation also touched on Pavel Kohout, Klement Lukeš and Jiří Lederer. An odd aspect of these interviews is that they still expect us to display some sort of Communist solidarity with them. We were expelled from the party, but if we feel we suffered an injustice we ought to go on behaving as Communists, and not like Pavel Kohout, who in the old days used to wave his little rhymes about like Mao's *Little Red Book*, and now where is he? I said I found it interesting that they should criticise Kohout for views they shared with him in their Communist youth. He replied that he didn't criticise him for the views he held then, but for having run away from them, whereas he, Fišer, had remained loyal to them. I said that, on the contrary, we were the ones who had remained loyal to our principles whereas they had abandoned them. "I wonder if you'd have dreamed thirty years ago," I said, "that even after the class structure of this society had been totally transformed, some kid would be discriminated against because of his parents, or that you'd be trying to persuade me not to concern myself with my imprisoned friends, colleagues and comrades." He said that I was entitled to my views, but that I must think carefully about where they would inevitably lead me. I ought to do a bit of soul-searching; time wasn't standing still. "Yes, I will do a bit of soul-searching – today's the perfect day for it," I said.

He nodded to the young man to show me out of the building. But as I was going out the door I still asked: "Have they discovered who attacked Zdena Tominová?" He replied: "Not yet. But we're bound to find out in the end."

Catherine was plucking the fringes of the floor carpet, Philip was nibbling at the kolach. The doorbell rang; it was a birthday telegram from my publisher in Lucerne, containing the hint: when would I deliver *Trip to Praděd*? Shortly afterwards the doorbell rang once more. It was Helena; she gave me a kiss and a rose and rushed off. Karel Pecka came and we drove to the Two Cats for lunch.

I related the morning's proceedings and we discussed what their real significance might be. We agreed that it could have been reconnaissance to see whether I was willing to pay for Jan's studies. Karel Pecka said that it was unbelievable – that we lived in a wonderland. "For ten years in the camp we yearned for the moment when we'd emerge and take those drills we used for drilling uranium and go after the Stalin monument. And then one day they literally booted us out into freedom without any explanation, we go after Stalin – and they are drilling into him and blowing him to smithereens themselves! What's it all about? The prison is theirs and so is freedom. They steal our actions and put them into practice instead of us, in a distorted way. Answer me this, Ludvík, and sincerely – do you feel hatred towards that Fišer of yours? You can't, it's obvious! They won't allow him to beat you up! He negotiates with you! Where are we, for goodness sake? Take Kosík yesterday. I said to him, What's your problem? You sit here at your ease drinking Hennessy, even though you're not allowed to publish or teach. You ought to be in a labour camp! They are and they aren't, at one and the same time. You call that Stalin? – It's Fišer, I tell you!"

TUESDAY, 24ᵀᴴ JULY 1979

But I'm glad, mind you, because that's the only hope I see for any improvement in the world: the world can be improved only as far and as fast as the worst section of humanity improves. I refused Pecka's invitation to a stand-up glass of wine in one of the lanes of the Old Town and we went our separate ways. There were several things I wanted to get done by four o'clock but did not manage to: the watch-mender is on holiday, Klement Lukeš is not in Prague, Karol Sidon does not answer the phone and three shops refused to repair my glasses. I turned left off Celetná Street into Štupartská and bought Jan a would-be baroque bedside table in the antique shop, as a reward for his exam scores... It only cost three hundred crowns.

At four I was waiting under the Astronomical Clock. Zdena arrived with a bunch of carnations, fed up, she said, because she had no present for me. She finds present-giving a difficult chore unless she is lucky enough to come across just the right thing. It is no easy business buying me something: how am I to introduce the thing into my household? ("Are you taking the umbrella you got from Zdena?") Whenever we are out walking in the street prior to some anniversary, Zdena keeps note of what I look at in shop-windows or any comments I make about things; so I have to take care. Now she was in a bad mood because she had not managed to get a copy of *The Prehistory of Bohemia*, which I had recently mentioned. "Thank goodness you didn't buy it! After all, I said I had to have a look at it first, in case it's some of the usual nonsense they put out nowadays! I'll get hold of it myself, and you know what you can buy me sometime – a bow." She stopped in surprise. "I mean a full-size bow, not a child's one," I added. – "But there's a bow bigger than you hanging on the wall at Rochov, isn't there!" She's right, for God's sake! "I never knew you'd be interested in it." – "But I want a strong bow with a blood-release at the bottom," I smiled at her feminine simplicity.

We walked round and round the streets in search of a table at which Zdena could wine and dine me. Everywhere was full, of Germans, mostly. Zdena was wearing a beige suit – a skirt made of some fine shaggy material, and a jacket made of the same material with knitted trimmings. She now wears a grey rinse, but is planning a pink one next time. Her legs and breasts hurt. Finally we found a table and she recovered suddenly: "Choose whatever you like!" – "Fine. But why do your breasts hurt?" – "Oh, stop it. I expect it's because I can't invite you home."

The waiter put the flowers in water for us. We ordered liver. "How are you?" I asked. – "That's a most unfortunate question at the dinner table. You know full well I shouldn't be in Prague in July. If I don't get a certain amount of sunshine now, when there is some, I won't be fit next winter." – "How are things at work?" – "I'm just sorry for our manager, Mr. Matouš. Otherwise I'd give in my notice." – "What would you do instead?" – "I'd go back to typing." – "The whole lot – as before?" – She shrugged and then said: "Mr. Matouš and you. I know how you're relaxing, now that you're not shouldering" – she pointed towards her breasts with the knife – "the whole burden."

Then she went and got on a tram while I walked home across the bridge with my bunch of red and pink carnations. It was getting late. It was like an evening in the far north: a grey stillness. As if it had nothing to do with any sun. Summer time, politically enhanced into the bargain. Prague actually looked like a human city for humans. I reached the end of the bridge, leaned over the stone parapet, and gently dropped the bouquet into the Vltava. It spread-eagled itself on the slow dark water, as one killed suddenly, though tied indissolubly at the waist. At that moment it had all my love. It had the appearance of a sign, an explosion, a letter in word of supplication.

"Oh God, if only I live to see my retirement!" (p. 279)

Only the boys were home; Madla had gone to work on the afternoon shift. When she came back, she sank exhausted onto the couch and looked around her. She is trying to guess what I have been doing from the things on my desk, the way the papers have been moved and the position of the chairs. "Who did you get the rose from?" she asked. – "From Helena." – "Any news?" she asked further. – "Old Mr. Havel, Václav's father, died." – "How old was he?" – "Over eighty already." – She picked up books absent-mindedly and put them straight, mechanically. "I wonder if they'll let him attend the funeral," she said. – "Václav? You're joking!" – "You really think they wouldn't even let him go to the funeral?" she said, in what seemed to me obtuse surprise. I asked: "And what kind of reception did you get at work today after such a long time?" – "Not bad. But they don't take much notice of me there any more. Oh God, if only I live to see my retirement!" – "Is there something wrong with you?" I asked. – "Oh, nothing."

At the table I described my conversation with His Excellency the Socialist State about Jan's studies. The family endorsed my approach. "I was told," I said to Jan, "that I don't give enough thought to you. So I went straight out and bought you a present. Go and pick it up tomorrow," and I gave him the receipt from the antique shop. At that moment I regretted I hadn't bought the other bedside table for Ondřej; there had been two of them. Ondřej said: "My bricklayer colleagues were talking today about how much cheap petrol each of them had managed to get in time. Ten litres, one of them, another fifty." Madla said: "For goodness sake, how much did they save that way? They'll use it up in no time." Jan spoke slowly, with careful deliberation: "If they don't pour it straight in their tanks but mix drops of it with the more expensive stuff they'll make the benefit last that much longer!" At that Ondřej said: "Today I told our Nepustil he reminded me of that Soviet cosmonaut Remek and he took offence!" – "Whatever made you say something like that to him?" Jan asked. "I would have taken offence too. So would Dad." – Ondřej said: "All I wanted to say was that their faces were similar, from a certain angle." – "What a nasty lot you are," said Madla. Jan said: "And perhaps we could eat Dad's ice-cream cake now."

Madla handed me the book she had bought me. It's a handbook for identifying shrubs and garden plants by their fruit. I asked her to write something in it for my birthday. In the matter of present-giving, Madla is calm, collected and prompt. She buys a thing as and when she sees it and it then serves as a present, or fulfils a need, or she finds someone somewhere to give it to. She is never caught napping. I have started to follow her example: I already have a Christmas present for her from the antique shop – a large mirror in a carved frame.

This is precisely the age at which my mother died. If I go by Dad's longevity, I still have four years left.

WEDNESDAY, 25ᵀᴴ JULY 1979

In a palace room without carpets or pictures, groups of people were standing about or moving to and fro. I looked around and suddenly saw Pavel Kohout making for me. He was fatter, with an unkempt, almost colourless moustache, and he walked with a shakier gait – all in all he resembled Ota Filip, but it was Pavel. It was equally obvious from his voice, his gestures and his facial expressions. "So?" he asked confidentially as we moved away to a window-bay in the sturdy palace wall. There was a view out onto old factory buildings. It was amazement I felt, rather than pleasure. And guilt. Guilt for having given him misleading information, and for having deceived him out of a purely personal and selfish desire for reinforcement. How will he live here? Either they will send him to prison or he will have to withdraw into the forms of existence of those of us who remain.

I awoke to a clear realisation: if Pavel returns, it won't be a simple question of "he went and now he's back," it will be a bold act. He will find Prague more humiliated and our numbers reduced. What advice shall I give him? I find it hard to imagine that they would leave him alone; they will have to find some place for him as well. Some people they send to prison, others they pacify in all sorts of ways to render them inconspicuous, and a third group they try to lure into a modicum of loyalty. He will have to choose how they will treat him. It will be up to him. I'm extremely curious to know what misconceptions about the situation and his own possibilities he will come up with!

It rained in the night. The patch on the kitchen ceiling is once more shiny with moisture. If the damaged area were accessible from the attic we could repair it ourselves, but it is in a walled-up corner. It's ages since I have played anything, such as the fiddle, or even tickled the piano keys. I have whole packets of manuscripts here once more, but it never occurs to anyone to slip me something really nice to read. I enjoy mornings like this when nobody comes, but when I decide to go into town I would like to call in on someone, but on whom?

The doorbell rang, I open the door. "Is it O.K.?" Helena whispers. She's just a kid. "Hold on," I sit her down in the kitchen and lend her a picture book – about shrubs and orchard plants – and I go into the bedroom to change. Today we're off to the National Gallery for a permit to export some paintings. We have black-and-white photos of them and a list; the official is a friend of ours (he will call on us later to look at the originals). It will be a smooth and pleasant formality, the official deals with hundreds of similar emigrants every year, he talks about it as if it were something quite normal. At last we have someone who is capable of looking calmly at what we're doing: after all there's nothing shameful about people changing their place of residence. Then we'll hang up the pictures in our new flat, make ourselves some tea and joyfully step out into the street having made refreshing love on our old divan – hey, look what they've got here! We'll take a trip to the mountains and over the mountains. We're perfectly happy at last. We've taken the last, remaining step to our happiness after all.

We walk to the embankment. Helena is afraid to go any further on foot: there are too many cars, someone might see us from one of them. We take a tram. I hold onto the pole, she onto my arm. She makes such a face that I am obliged to say: "Think of it as if you were off to the nearest big city! It doesn't matter! Think about what you'll find there!" – "I-I-I know, I know…" – "And stop stuttering! Speak slowly and calmly!" – "Sorry. I'm talking calmly again. Do you – love me?"

A red seat has fallen vacant, she sits down and takes my well-laden brief-case on her lap. The tram whooshes across the bridge, to the right can be seen the weir and above it Hradčany. That's as much as I know.

I want peace and quiet and everything sorted out. Now nobody is answering the phone at the Procházkas: *Pink Lady*. I go to the typist who is transcribing *Boredom in Bohemia* to give her the blank sheets signed by the author for the title pages. She has a surprise for me: the job is already finished and painstakingly wrapped up. I'll have to take it home, unwrap it, type the title pages myself and exchange them for the unsigned ones. This is the last book I am doing this way. And I'm fed up with Saša Kliment; I am fed up with everything and everyone. There's Šiktanc who never comes to see us and I have to take books to him, and when he has no money, he does not make a point of coming to pay me, I have to go looking for him again. There's Vladislav who isn't here and I've got things for him. There's Karol Sidon who wants to emigrate to Israel as he has nothing to live on here. ("Our Karol?" – Madla was shocked. "My favourite Jew!") And I am even fed up with poor old Havel Senior for having gone and died before completing his memoirs somehow.

I am glad that some time in the early spring I heeded my anxiety and went to ask him how it was proceeding. And when he told me that he was completing the seventh part of his *Memoirs* and he would be only too pleased if Miss Zdena would come for them, I sent her there: "Drop everything else and type it for him." – "But I'm typing Klíma's stories. You wanted them quickly." – "So put them to one side." – "But I dropped Trefulka on account of Klíma." – "Put it all to one side and go and see him." – "Whatever you say. I'll be only too pleased to. He's the most gallant gentleman I know."

THURSDAY, 26TH JULY 1979

I have an ear-ache again and my arm hurts. My arm from brandishing a brush all over the ceiling, my ear from the inevitable draught. I painted Zdena's ceiling and then she and her son papered the walls. I had to scrape off the entire ceiling. Dark stains had appeared from previous layers of paint; there was no way they could be painted out, and I knew it. It's ludicrous but it's only fair: at home I do everything I can to avoid painting. But Zdena has a crafty way about her: she just starts the job and then what am I supposed to do?

Even as I walked from the lift to our door that evening I could hear the tap-tap of the typewriter. It was Jan:

> Dear Comrade Rector, I feel almost obliged to appeal against your ruling as I simply cannot understand what conditions I fail to fulfil; I think that my rejection is more likely to be a mistake on the part of the faculty. I accept, of course, that in the written part of the entrance examination there were some questions where I might have made some errors and that during my school career I was occasionally given a B, but I trust that account might be taken of the fact that I am an industrial worker, a trained motor mechanic, and that I graduated from a vocational school where facilities for study are not as favourable as at grammar or technical schools.

"Our Karol?" – Madla was shocked. "My favourite Jew!"
(p. 282)

As far as my world view and moral qualities are concerned, I am sure that they are not in any way at variance with the needs of our society. And I trust that my attitude to work and my achievements at work and school are the best evidence of this. I respect my superiors and I do my best to fulfil their requirements without exception, and I get on well with my workmates. I conserve energy and resources and do not take materials home from work. I respect social norms and traffic regulations, do not resort to violence, do not smoke or drink.

It is possible that you have certain reservations about my father's social and political activities in recent years. I do not think we inherit our parents' attitudes to society in the way we do such things as a tendency to obesity; we form them in the course of our lives on the basis of our own experience. But if, nonetheless, you attribute such great importance to my origins, I would only recall that both my grandfathers were ordinary unpropertied workers, and Communists, and that they both came from poor rural families, as did my grandmothers also.

I think that if in spite of this I do not fulfil the conditions for university study, then I must be guilty of something very serious. But what?

It's a brilliant appeal! I would not have put it better myself. I was surprised that not even Madla had seen the inexpediency of an appeal worded so excellently. When Jan gave me the letter, typed out in its final version to read, all I could say by then was: "It's excellent, lad. Keep it up!"

We were chatting after supper about the state and its idiots when the telephone rang. I was lying on the floor. It was Martin. He announced that Isabelle the Childless would be arriving on 7th August, that she was a bit afraid of us and did not like caraway seeds. I had them ask, on my behalf, if she would be arriving as a married woman. Martin replied that he did not know yet. The reason I asked was that she would probably make it here under her maiden name, but was unlikely to with our notorious surname; I could not say so, though. Martin was a very long time on the phone. When he spoke to the boys he expressed surprise that they had not had a summer holiday. "We don't have a holiday, just a fortnight's leave, and we have to spend that working at the building co-op." Martin thought they were building a family house. "No way," said Ondřej, "it's a great big block of flats." When Paris found this astonishing he said: "That's the way it is here now, my dear Martin." Martin probably said it was terrible. "One can't say that so categorically," Ondřej protested. "Admittedly it's backbreaking work for us, because we're stupid, but on the other hand, it's very kind of them to let us do it." – "Anyway we can't be certain yet," Madla started to prompt him, but from the floor I immediately stopped her: she was going to say that we could not be certain that they would let them have the flat in the end. Why put that idea into their heads through the telephone? Martin apparently asked about me. Jan explained that I was lying on the floor and did not use the phone on principle. Why? "It would take too long and cost you too much – stick to the point," said Jan. – "You'll probably be interested to know," said Martin, "that I'm learning to surf, but keep falling over." – "That's OK.," was Ondřej's response.

Madla and I have already had several arguments about which of them is worse off, the ones who are here with us, or Martin abroad. Madla always thinks it is Martin because he is abroad. I think the opposite. It might be harder for him in the sense of being more strenuous, but he can decide his own actions, he is free to choose a solution. He continues to do what he likes. We don't.

We hung up and Madla said: "So we'll have to paint the kitchen." I said that it would be silly to do it while the ceiling was still leaking. Jan was of my opinion: it would be like painting the walls and then making grooves in them for the electrical wires. Madla started to scold us all for our lackadaisical attitudes. Ondřej said: "So I'll climb up on the roof and mend it." I leaped up from the floor and roared: "That's a bloody perverted idea! And what if there are no spare tiles in the loft? You think we'll go to the brickworks and make them ourselves?" In the end I quite simply forbade anyone to repair the roof. Let Isabelle see the real state of things here – at least then she won't be so silly. Because it looks as if Isabelle probably is indeed silly (*a la française*), seeing that she could write me a letter in English suggesting I write to our Mr. President and tell him to intervene with the French Mr. President to award our Martin French citizenship. I think that, apart from the ceiling, there is nothing wrong with our kitchen. "But the ceiling is the main thing!" Madla raved. "The French are notorious slobs!" I replied.

In the end, the boys both said they would help me somehow with the painting. "Yeah, we'll go and paint the place up and then they'll refuse her a visa," I said as hope died. "Well, at least we'll have the painting done,"

Madla shrieked. No, I'm not happy with it. Besides, I feel as if I painted it only the other day!

SUNDAY, 29TH JULY 1979

It was raining this morning; the rain murmured in the leaves of the trees and dripped from the overhanging spruce branches outside the small window, so I got up late. I lay in bed reading Tatarka's *Wicker Armchairs*. At first the book seemed to be simply toying with language; only towards the middle did the poetry and wit start to appear. It's a delightful little book and more suitable perhaps for foreign-language translation than *Demon of Consent*; Ján Mlynárik reads literature politically, not aesthetically. But who could possibly draw the attention of a foreign publisher to such a book? Milan Kundera, perhaps, except that he doesn't give a damn about us any more. (The last sentences added in March 1980, in annoyance at Kundera's interview about our culture's demise!) The narrator of *Wicker Armchairs* calls himself Bartholomew Teardrop, which gives the story a somewhat tearful undertone that annoys me. It annoys me in *Jottings* as well. Such a formidable fornicator as Bartholomew can hardly have such a feeble name!

It was warm, the clouds unfolded and the sun came out. I took off my jacket, then my shirt, trousers and shoes. Summer Part II on its way, maybe. The birds are bringing out their young, the trees and bushes are full of birdlife. The blackbirds have finished the currant-picking for us. Summer apples lie in the grass; there are so many of them we cannot find enough people to give them to. Tomin, since he is incapable of returning the cherry basket, shall get none.

The dahlias are beginning to flower; it is the high point of the holidays. I love dahlias. My mother's garden used to be full of them. The beautiful unscented smell of them. Later my father introduced highly scented phlox; I like them too. There are mushrooms in the woods but we have no time for them. The Indians, too, are thronging without me, somewhere, maybe. People who cut their grass with a power mower, like my neighbours to right and left, regard it as dust on the floor. I examine carefully what lies beneath my scythe; this year there is lots of wild thyme. I ought to find someone to explain its chemical significance to me. Although it has been wet enough, all the plants and flowers grew small this year. The May heat wave inhibited them. Hence the grass is scarce: I would usually have done my third mowing by this time.

On Thursday, we were at the Klímas. Helena Klímová had come back from Yugoslavia with their daughter. Helena is always strong on hospitality. Ivan is missing his friends. We went outside and there he confided in me his peculiar situation: his son had enrolled in university without problem, they had allowed Helena to make a trip to the seaside, and his particular StB man had friendly chats with him and had even invited him to go mushroom-picking in a military forest. "I won't go, of course," Ivan said, "but it did strike me that I might go if they invited you too. I'd go if you went." Ivan has the impression that some kind of dynamic element has appeared in a situation long static, and he is tempted by the thought of finding out more. We talked about it for a while. I said that if the offer was repeated he should tell the man that he would go with me. But I doubt he'll agree. They would be obliged to alter their entire plan, and I am dealt with in a different category from Ivan.

I told Madla about it on the way home, and she became irate: "Do you recall the way Ivan lectured me for going to a café with Martinovský that time? How I ought to refuse on principle, how I mustn't run away with the idea that I might learn more from Martinovský than he would from me, how I mustn't play along with him!" I said I did recall it. But if Ivan wants me to go with him, I will.

Old Mr. Havel's funeral took place on Thursday at the Strašnice Crematorium. When the side doors to the hall opened, Mr. Václav was among the bereaved who entered. He took his place along with Olga, his brother Ivan and Ivan's wife in the front row, the rest of the family behind them – at the prescribed safe distance. There were no guards on view, but they were undoubtedly there, dressed in deepest mourning, down to black ties, which no one else wore – apart, perhaps, from Standa Milota and Dr. Kriegel. Who was going to deliver the oration?

The doors opened a second time and a slender walking stick entered followed by a grey-haired lady. She unfolded some sheets of paper and started calmly to recite the life history of the deceased: the sort of man he had been, the things he had done; how, during the First Republic, it had been his initiative to build the temporary student halls of residence, which went on being used for the next fifty years; how he had organised the construction of a permanent hall of residence that was completed and fully equipped within two years; how he and his brother had founded the Barrandov suburb with its film studios; how he had built the Lucerna Palace... Václav Havel Senior's legacy continued to serve, as we could all see. He had raised his two sons to be honourable people.

That unadorned account spoken in the direction of the coffin aroused and moved us. Music, strings, and finally the hymn: Oh Holy Wenceslas, Prince of Bohemia. When the doors and the curtain opened, the people queued up as usual to offer their condolences. As we shook hands, Mr. Václav whispered a few words to me, of which I caught just two: "our controversy."

Outside, I asked Dr. Kriegel who the speaker had been. It had been Dr Anna Kavinová-Schustlerová. He introduced me to her and I thanked her. Two policemen emerged from cars parked outside the crematorium, went up to young Kyncl and Bednář, and confiscated the film from their cameras. If I know those two young men, they had by then substituted blank film. Zdena took time off work to attend. There were many people there, including Karol Sidon, whom I asked: "Is it true you want to leave?" He replied: "I'd like to, but I won't. I will one day, though."

I was mowing short sparse grass containing an abundance of wild thyme and pondering what Mr. Václav might have said: the end of our controversy? a contribution to our controversy? we'll revive our controversy? Everyone was speculating on the significance of the generous gesture: They had a twinge of conscience, said some. Now they'll use it as a psychological weapon against Václav, others maintained. They were simply boxing a bit more cleverly, was the view of the rest. Only Madla thinks it was just normal – anyhow she knew beforehand. What else is there left for us to complain about? – That's right, they did it for Madla's sake. But that's fine; one must take all their positive features into account. Furthermore, I have a thesis about this: the world will improve only as far and as fast...

I was sweating. In a concealed corner behind the currant bushes I removed the remaining fabric I was wearing and climbed into a bath of water, as a result of which a nerve in my right hip joint has started to ache.

It was really fine – warm and humid, and the ground was warm under my feet (I go barefoot in the garden), the evenly mown slopes of the domain reflected the sunshine in various shades of greenish-gold. I was sorry that Madla was upstairs ironing and could not see it. What's more, it was about time she called me in for something to eat, for mercy's sake! At that moment she did appear and uttered certain words. They are words which are guaranteed to make me leave home. I got dressed and took the train to Prague. It was two o'clock when I arrived in the city. I was hungry. I got off the tram at Charles Square and had lunch in the Black Brewery. I don't expect it took more than twenty minutes. I came out onto the pavement and peered from the shade into the glare of a summer Sunday afternoon. I was astounded at how marvellously empty and quiet the streets were. I considered which way to wend my steps. It crossed my mind to pop into the Botanical Gardens and check whether what we had was an *Inula* or a *Telekia*. But I did not relish the thought of dragging myself around there in this sultry heat. I took several steps in a homeward direction, when it struck me that if I were able to ascertain it, I could record it here. So I went to the Botanical Gardens. Ours is a *Telekia*.

I felt quite, quite good. ("Good luck has he that deals with none!")

WEDNESDAY, 1ST AUGUST 1979

At night it rains, the days are pleasantly mild and warm. The streets are empty, calm and clean. As I was walking with Petr Chudožilov across the park in Vinohrady late this afternoon, I got a yen to do some painting or photography: beneath the low-hanging branches of the trees, the thick, short grass reflected lushly and with sweet languor the radiance of the sun as it gazed gleamingly at the city from below. Summer is on the run, time is disappearing and my autumnal dejection is coming closer.

I painted the kitchen deftly, quickly and, I think, well. When I am obliged to do something and am able to hold my own, I even enjoy it. At four o'clock Auntie Cilka came to do the cleaning. By nightfall, most things were back in their places. Ondřej climbed out onto the roof, while Jan held on to him with a rope. The greatest risk was that he might drop a fragment of tile and it would fall the five storeys and hit someone in the street or the courtyard on the head. The silly thing is that in the end they were unable to discover where the leak is; most of the tiles are out of line anyway, and the mortar has crumbled out of the joints. They changed about twenty tiles, as many as they found in the loft, but they could have gone on scrambling like that over the entire roof.

Almost as disgusted with the painting as I was were Philip and Catherine. They had to weather it in the children's room, where they spent the day perched just below the ceiling, neither eating nor drinking, lacking both strength and sense of direction. When in the evening I finally set out all the plants on the window-sill in the kitchen, hung the cage among them on its chain once more, and opened the little door, they flew out in agitation, circled the room screeching, had a drink of water from the sink, crept beneath the enormous leaves on the roof of their home and went to sleep.

I also slept soundly. I woke up with the feeling that something was being spoilt for me, that I was losing something. It occurred to me to take a holiday and make a trip into the unknown all on my own!

During the morning I gave Madla a bit of a hand tidying things up before sitting down to write a couple of letters, including one to Binar in Vienna, though I had no good news for him! I put a folder with Tatarka's articles in my bag and set off for Mlynárik's to tell him that it wouldn't work – someone would have to edit them! As I walked down Mostecká Street I noticed an open window at the Pitharts' and remembered that Mrs. P. has a birthday somewhere around this time. I bought a bunch of flowers and gave them to her little girl as her mother wasn't home. I had started to walk back up Mostecká towards the square when we bumped into each other by chance. She was visibly wilting in the heat and told me to come to a little celebration this evening and bring Madla with me. I replied that the invitation would have to come from Petr, and that I wouldn't come anyway. She said... and that's crossed out. Because when, last December, I let her read the pages where I mention her so she could tell me what she thought, she forbade me to use any of this particular entry and her comments about several others were something like: "You are so silly when you write she had her legs tucked up on the couch – whatever will people think?" – "That you had your legs tucked up on the couch, won't they?" – "You're vulgar, inconsiderate and vain, and for the sake of your novel, or whatever it's supposed to be, you spare no one, so if your deranged realism doesn't even let you use the slightest degree of imagination and you lack the slightest notion of how to sublimate reality, then be so kind as to leave me out altogether! That's a request!" She was perspiring slightly, incensed, exquisite. OK, OK. So I am crossing out today's entry about her. It is 15th March 1980 and I have been through all the earlier entries and checked them carefully and found nothing objectionable, and as for that part where she was sitting with her legs tucked up, silly goose, I have added, out of innate tact, the sentence about her son David wheeling

I replied that the invitation would have to come from Petr,
and that I wouldn't come anyway. She said... and that's crossed out.
(p. 290)

about the room. Who says I'm incapable of using my imagination? I'm sure that the reader didn't miss that sentence.

But I mentioned Petr Chudožilov. The reason for our meeting was that he wanted to ask my advice. For eleven years he has been trying to change his career. If he is not allowed to publish, so be it. He'll stop considering himself a writer or journalist, he'll stop thinking about it. He'll simply forget about it. He doesn't want to be a dissident either. He wants to fend for his family, have fun with his children and repair his country cottage. For some time he has been taking various temporary jobs, but he isn't getting any younger. What is to become of him? When he got a job on an archaeological dig for the National Museum, he decided OK, he'd become an archaeologist and do the necessary study. It was an interesting and civilised occupation. However, it turned out that he was only allowed to be a digger and had no hope of a career. And so the backstage directors of our lives confronted him once more with the question he had determined to forget: shouldn't he be a writer?

"The question I want to put to you, Mr. Vaculík, is as follows: I'm thirty-seven and it's high time I decided what I want to be. Can I make a living if I devote myself entirely to writing and, with all the risks entailed, start publishing abroad? If you tell me I can't, then I must emigrate to Canada. Here, they want to make a Czech writer out of me. What if they're right? What if they know better than I what I'm suited for?" I asked: "Why are you coming to me with this?" He replied: "Because for the past eleven years I have been engaged in a mental quarrel with you. I ridicule and curse you at turns." – "Why?" – "Because you give me no peace. Without knowing it, you have been the main boulder in my path to success from the very beginning, when I brought my first article to you at *Literary News*. You could have thrown me out with it or printed it. But not you – oh, no. You started to say it would be fine if only I reworked this and that, and you sent me back to the scene again to take a better look before writing about it. You sowed in me the seeds of permanent discontent and doubt. You ruin any enjoyment I have from my writing. And furthermore, you have been destroying me the whole time by the things you write. Either it is so good that I say to myself, Petr, you could never write like that. Or it is such crap that I say to myself, Petr, you could do much better yourself. So what's your advice now, then?"

I said: "In that case I guessed rightly at the time the reason for your boorishness, which has lasted many years. You've got an inferiority complex." –

"I was an adolescent." – "And you aren't any more? Only last year you told me that my feuilletons were crap and I should give up writing them." – "I still think so, Mr. Vaculík. I'm always saying to people, Mark my words, that Vaculík can manage a sentence or a paragraph, but never a whole book." – "I can't give you an answer to your question until I've seen what you're writing." – "I've a number of manuscripts, but I won't give you any of them to read: not *Fat Bog Pig*, nor *Left Cardiac Chamber*, nor *Murder in the Tomb*." – "Why?" – "Because I haven't the courage. I need to work on them." – "But someone will have to read them, Petr. So choose someone you can trust and afterwards I'll ask them their opinion." – "I'd go for Karol Sidon." – "OK then, give him all your manuscripts by the end of the week," I said.

On his living-room wall Petr Chudožilov has a framed original photograph from the end of the last century showing the embankment and the building where our editorial offices used to be, and the little park with the odd pseudo-gothic tower minus the emperor who once stood inside it. It is ten years already since I tried to wheedle the picture out of him, even offering to buy it. He refused. He said it would have to be a gift from him to me – but on one condition: that they send me to prison. Now I stopped by the photo and said not a word. Petr observed me with a smile – a smirk? – and then said: "If they held you for just one day – and after all, that's absolute child's play for any Chartist – the photo's yours. Don't you find it odd, Mr. Vaculík, that you still haven't spent even a single day in custody?"

I said: "Tell me, Mr. Chudožilov, wouldn't it be so much simpler in the end if you just emigrated to Canada? Come to think of it, why don't you just go to hell?" – He smiled, saying: "Last year we bought that lamp for the table. We said to ourselves, Well, now we can't go. Then I managed to get some tiles for the kitchen. We have to get some enjoyment out of them first..."

Later, as we were walking across the sun-drenched park, he reminded me of an occurrence I had forgotten. He had wanted to emigrate as early as 1969. It was a Friday afternoon in the editorial offices. He told me he was leaving for Vienna the next day. "And you know what you did to me, Mr. Vaculík? Even though I had clearly told you that I was going to Vienna the next morning, you said to me before we went home that day, 'Petr, come over to our place tomorrow!' – And I fucking blew off Vienna."

I'm damned if I'll try and hold on to him this time. Let him go. Let them all fucking go! Fuck off! Just leave me alone, for God's sake! Let them just disappear without my knowing. Then, when I get a card from them at Christmas, I'll say to myself: Well, well, can she be there already?

FRIDAY, 3ʳᵈ AUGUST 1979

It rained again last night and it's a beautiful morning. The sky is blue and a fresh breeze is blowing from Stromovka Park. But I hear they want to build a highway through it. That ought to be halted by massive protests. But I have no idea what truth there is in the story and no one will tell me. No one will tell anyone anything at all. In the Ostrava region it seems that miners have been taking slovenly, disorganised, impulsive and sporadic strike action against price increases. The workers are foolish: they only notice the symptoms of the plague, and then only the ones that erupt on their own bellies. But I started by saying what a fine morning it is. It is.

Eva Kantůrková sent me a message to come over to their place. She showed me a letter from the British Prime Minister which the ambassador here had passed on to her. It states that the British government will keep our prisoners in mind and speak up for them. "Now they almost won't send you to prison," I told Eva. – "Have you written to anyone?" she asked. – "No, and I don't intend to," I said. – "You're chicken," she said. I didn't feel like talking. I said nothing. But the main reason she asked me was a letter from Ota Filip. He tells her how difficult it is to promote Czech literature in West Germany. He says the prevailing attitude there now is that it's time we gave it a rest and stopped snivelling and demanding that someone should come and blow on it to make it better. After all, nothing really terrible is happening to us; if there were, we'd make rather more noise about it and Kohout would actually speak out instead of just swanning around the West as if nothing was up. Nobody's interested in the Prague Spring any more. There are worse things happening in the world: Palestine, the Vietnamese boat people... Three million Palestinians move the world, fifteen million Czechs and Slovaks keep their lips buttoned. He says that Czech literature plays around with such private issues as people's relationship with God, the individual conscience, private honour and I cannot remember now what else he mentions. A forthcoming bestseller over there will be a book about the status of women in the Muslim world.

"Ota's got a point there," I declared to the astonished Kantůreks. We really ought to pay for a situation report like that. But I would like to hear comments on it from other, more clear-headed people like Prečan or Vladimír

Blažek. The sentence about Kohout is crudely misinformed: in what he does, Pavel is guided by deeply-held convictions, and he would disappoint us if he allowed himself to get carried away. "If what Ota says is true," I said, "it means those Germans are lagging behind us again."

But not even that was the main reason Eva invited me. Ota is reviewing her *Lord of the Tower* for Fischer Verlag; he would like to recommend it, but he has misgivings and reservations, precisely in view of the aforementioned German attitudes to us. And he asks whether I might send him a few lines about Eva's book... I promised her I would, but goodness knows what I'll write.

As a further illustration of the prevailing disgust with us over there, Ota describes a debate in some club at which a young Czech emigrant uttered a sentence that apparently set German society brooding deeply: "Since 1618, there has been no such thing as Czech history, from then on all they did in Bohemia was..." and now I can't recall exactly what he said, but what it boiled down to is that we have done nothing here but snivel.

Yes, we already have a hunch how it will be: many of them will conceal their lack of knowledge or understanding and above all their unwillingness to live through it with us, by means of such would-be witticisms. But it's ridiculous! At certain moments in history it must become clear in every society that one just cannot bring about new developments by military or guerrilla violence without incurring appalling damage. We are entering an era of maturation within the collective consciousness. The historical events engulfing Africa and Asia are bestial havoc, and if they do not grow out of it soon, they will destroy us all. Nations were happy during chapters of history when nothing was considered unsuitable for under-age viewers. I would abolish the under-thirties' right to vote, all over the world, because it's preposterous!

Helena should have put in an appearance, but she hasn't. I expect she is not allowed to. I suggested to her that the two of us should disappear somewhere for a couple of days, but the idea terrified her. She believes that if she leaves here in an orderly fashion, with proper permission from the various authorities, they will allow her to come back for a visit at Christmas. But she is wrong. I doubt we'll ever see each other again.

I looked in at the Slávia yesterday for the first time in ages. I caught sight of Standa Milota there and we went and sat by the window. None of the rightful regulars had yet arrived at Kolář's table, so it was unbecoming to sit there. Standa said: "Do you come here much?" – "Not often," I said. He is also here exceptionally and gazing at him there with his plebeian looks – a typical guy from Žižkov – I realised he didn't fit in here too well either. I don't know why he happened to come today; I forgot to ask. "The other day I'm talking to a… sympathiser," he said, hesitating over the expression. "And he says to me, 'I've got you Chartists figured out. There's the Havel group, they make a lot of noise and get locked up. And then there's the Vaculík crowd – all they need is a minor pogrom and they'll all scuttle off with their tails between their legs and sit quietly in a corner fiddling with their Padlocks. But what I'd like to meet is the brain, the brain behind the Charter!'" – "Interesting," I said, and felt contempt and anger welling up inside. Standa went on: "And then I told him that the brain of the Charter was made up of those two groups plus others that he could no doubt find insulting descriptions for. "Tell me," said Standa, "what do those people want? How dare they? And they are the so-called… sympathisers!" He said the word with a curl of his upper lip like a dog when it is becoming riled. He knocked the ash off his cigarette. "Give me a cig," I said to him.

The waitress came up. I ordered myself two glasses of apple juice with ice, Standa ordered coffee. Trinkewitz passed by, making for Kolář's table with resolute step. Standa lit my cigarette and said: "The interesting thing, though, was that straight afterwards he asks me whether I had some new feuilleton of yours, saying they were great and that it was a shame you didn't write more of them. So I say to him, Listen, have you ever done anything for the cause, for heaven's sake? Have you ever copied out a feuilleton, for instance, or donated a couple of crowns, or even a fifty-crown note towards the cost of paper? And now – and please don't be offended – he pulls out his wallet, takes out five Tuzex vouchers and tells me to give them to you. So I brought them for you. And then I say to him, There you are, now get into the habit of doing that for every single thing you read and appreciate." Standa took a sealed envelope out of his pocket and handed it to me. I tore open the envelope and stuck the vouchers in my wallet.

Shortly afterwards, Jiří Pechar, the lawyer Dr. Danisz, and Jan Vladislav arrived in succession and joined us at our table. Our conversation became louder and disturbed the mournful Trinkewitz, who realised he was in the wrong place and came over to us with a smile. I made room for him on the seat. "How come you're still here," I asked in surprise. "It's dragging on because I'm taking too many things with me." Vladislav and Pechar chatted about translating Proust; Dr. Danisz, in answer to Standa's question whether the VONS members could expect high or low sentences at the end of their trial, said that both sorts were conceivable. Pechar suggested that the instigators of the trial had got themselves into a pickle and would sooner it had never happened. Someone said that it must have been planned in consultation with the Russians, and someone else could not see why it would be. Someone said that Carter's speech made things worse for the defendants, and someone else that it didn't. A large part of the conversation was devoted to speculation about whether the prosecution of the ten VONS members was an isolated action or even an aberration, or whether it was instead the start of a broader campaign. Both are possible. Standa took a pessimistic view; Pechar the opposite. I don't know anything, but the interesting thing is that the pessimistic view never surprises me whereas the optimistic one always does.

"Have you got a job yet?" I asked Dr. Danisz. – "It looks as if I'll soon be starting as a night cleaner in the metro." – "But they say that's well paid, and you have to bribe your way in." – "I don't know about that," said Dr. Danisz, "I'm getting in through connections." – "But you ought to be treating us to an exemplary legal battle for the right to do work for which you're qualified," I said. – "How right you are! Don't forget, though, I'm still under suspended sentence. But don't you worry, I don't intend to take it lying down."

Then Petr Kabeš arrived and just sat there quietly smoking. Next came Eva Kantůrková. She expressed surprise at seeing me. "I haven't written it yet," I quickly retorted. – "I won't mention it," she said. The café was half-empty, clean and airy. It didn't even look as if the corner cop was here. "Dog days," the glorious days when nothing happens. Eva had not been sitting five minutes before she had to go and say to Kabeš: "I'll get even with you." – "For what?" he grumbled, turning to her sullenly. She said: "For blaming me for the trials and the fifties last time. I've just been reading your first verse collection and you're not without egg on your face either," she said with a smile. I went rigid. Kabeš said to her rudely – more rudely than is his wont: "Kindly refrain from talking about something you don't understand!" And she laughed with her chin raised. Someone remarked that some foreign journalist or other was expected at any moment. That rattled me. "I'm off," I declared. For some time now, I have found foreign journalists even more unpleasant than I used to. It is as if I had a broken arm in plaster and people came to stare at it and tap the cast. Not only are they not doctors, they lack even ordinary sympathy. I never have anything to tell them. I realised, of course, that a slightly different interpretation could be placed on my fright and decision to leave, but I could not give a damn about such things any more.

I said goodbye and Eva got up saying she would accompany me. On the way we scarcely spoke to each other. Then I said: "If you go on behaving like today, you'll make yourself unbearable to everyone. You're just absolutely wrong about Petr, you must have dreamed it up. He's never written political verse. He's written intimate and existential poems, and if they have ever contained some element of social criticism, then it has been extremely veiled and from a political stance diametrically opposed to yours." Eva put up a rather feeble defence. While I was waiting for the tram, she said: "I've been observing you – in fact you're very unsure of yourself, but you play the tough guy, Ludvík. You are always playing the tough guy." I said nothing. I couldn't give a damn. "You're better than you make yourself out to be," she added, somewhat incongruously.

SUNDAY, 5TH AUGUST 1979

This morning I sallied forth into the garden with the scythe. I mowed under the greengage, which is already beginning to shed small yellow leaves that drop quietly onto the grass; the scythe gathers them together and I forget where I am and when; it is not me mowing but some uncle, and I am a little boy looking at him as he swings the scythe; he gathers up the golden leaves along with the grass, leaving behind soft, smooth turf which I tread barefoot.

A few moments ago, they were talking from abroad about how Kosygin is supposed to come to Prague to sort out a leadership dispute over how to deal with opposition. Husák, apparently, is for a more moderate approach, Biľak for a tough one. "There you are!" said Madla triumphantly. She still believes in Husák. But Biľak scares me too. "It amazes me," Madla said to Ivan, who wasn't here though, "that anyone can think that a mere shuffle in the leadership could mean an improvement!" That is what Ivan said when we were last at their place.

Several times during the day I twiddled the knob on the radio in search of some festive music. And when I found some it always turned out to be on an Austrian station. They have a good time, the Austrians. This evening they had a live broadcast from the Salzburg music festival. During the interval between two acts of Mozart's opera *La clemenza di Tito*, two gentlemen chatted for twenty minutes about the circumstances surrounding the opera's composition and the meaning of its plot, as well as about antiquity and its virtues. Their discerning tone, their concerns, and their characteristic German seemed to me distant, ancient and nostalgic, like tales from a normal world. Like those yellow leaves in the grass that I have to cut; I can't play with the leaves any more. When someone decides to emigrate, what sort of decision is it, in fact? Binar stated it clearly when he wrote that he would always be a foreigner. Binar emigrated for the sake of his work as a writer, which is also the form his loyalty takes. But what about all the other breadwinners?

Two days ago, I was waiting for the tram when Helena's husband happened to drive by in his car. I was in for a surprise. Unintentionally, even before my brain had time to give any thought to his sudden appearance, I felt towards him a strong aversion. I say aversion because it wasn't jealousy! I can't help being amazed at what is already perhaps the wisdom of my consciousness: that in a split second, before it even started to think anything, it screamed out its disapproval – objective disapproval, quite irrespective of our "case." At that very instant I knew that if this misfortune – their departure – could be revoked, I would willingly unknow Helena! Stay and live here happily with your childlike face of yore! Yes, I was surprised to find that I felt no jealousy. That is why I think that if she were not emigrating, if there were not this catastrophic atmosphere that accelerates expressions of affinity and loosens the tongue, we would be bound to come together in friendship. Because I am becoming mature enough for friendship with women. Throughout my entire life women did not exist for me... yes, it's true! The fact that I lived throughout that same life with one woman is another matter: it choked my responsiveness towards them, so that I did not hear, see or feel them in their multifariousness. For a long time it was all just a kind of collective womanhood – with the exception of my wife. – But enough of these speculations, I am starting to go on a bit. Some other time. And better.

After he had driven past and my brain had traversed those various states, it suddenly realised that Helena was therefore now at home alone! And that

I could see her! I set off for the bus stop... and stopped before I got there. My aversion – albeit to my regret – had extended to Helena as well. Good riddance to all of it! Why did I have to acquire, on someone else's decision, this new and very distinctive pain? So I merely walked one tram stop. And the regret with which I rode in the opposite direction from the one I ought to have taken was my contribution to her successful departure.

But time to pick up cheerfully from where I left off! I had such a well-honed scythe that it even cut the short, soft grass in the recently-mown parts. Because Isabelle is coming and for the next fortnight I shall not have any time for the garden. I had a dream that Martin and I were supposed to meet in a big department store. I looked for him there but could not find him for the crowds. I'll call out to him, I thought: Martin! Straight away there was a muffled answering call from somewhere. He was sitting squeezed up in a telephone box, which had no telephone in it. We hugged each other. He was younger and smaller than he must be now, still attending grammar school. I asked him where he had Isabelle. She'd gone off on holiday to her parents, he said. I was so disappointed that I sat down on the steps and wept. How silly can you get?

Mrs. Rohlenová has three grandchildren here and they really get on my nerves. They tear along the paths round and round the house, they are always pulling at things, climbing up the stack of planks under the eaves, and screeching. I am fed up. What an effrontery, I say to myself, to leave these three brats here when they have nothing to do with us – it wouldn't be so bad if one of their fathers were to paint the greenhouse, for instance. Vengefully I started to think about raising the rent when it struck me that – damn it – I will have to raise it, revenge or not. It was fixed twenty years ago. These days I could not even get a can of enamel paint and a paint-brush for it: Mrs. Rohlenová pays about thirty crowns a month, Mrs. Hemerková about twenty, and we lose part of that to the "Residents' Income Tax." *Non*-residents!

I mowed and raked the garden. Madla helped me cart the grass to the compost heap. I pruned the roses that had finished flowering but left the new rose-buds, because they are beautiful. Madla hoed round the roses. Now everything is nice and neat for another week and we're off. Happy leaping, brats!

When we arrived here yesterday and took a walk round the garden, I noticed some flattened grass. I'll give them what for, I said to myself. "What's been going on here now?" I said severely. They gazed at me mutely, and then the biggest little girl said quietly: "We were catching butterflies." Hmm. Of course, what else? Classic. "It's hard to mow the grass afterwards, you see," I said. "Then we're ever so sorry," whispered the little girl. "That's all right," I said and stroked her head. Dammit. I cut the grass strewn with the first yellow leaves from the trees and my mind boggled, just boggled as I remembered the dreadful way we always used to flatten the whole of Arizona!

MONDAY, 6TH AUGUST 1979

The landscape has just two colours: deep gold and deep green. Green has progressed from all its delicate shades into a single dull tone: the beets, the maize and the leaves of the fruit trees all have the same, slightly misty radiation. It is harvest time, in fact. The horizons are hazy, sultry. In the sky, the clouds, portly and bloated with water, mix together like dough. Humidity is a constant seventy. In the lush grass on the meadows where the cattle graze, mushrooms ought to be growing. From the sultry waves of the wooded landscape the spires of churches emerge. The Romanesque church is surrounded by a crumbling stone wall. In the old cherry orchard it is twilight.

The motorway permits a speed of a hundred and ten kilometeres per hour, but Helena drives at eighty, nostalgically. There is plenty of room between us and mostly silence. She would like to keep on driving like this forever, I sense. I know too that this homesickness will stay with her always, and it will leap out, like a wild animal, straight under her wheels, whenever she finds herself in just such a hilly landscape of fields and meadows. On every one of her future (now totally unknown) journeys. I am afraid of her killing herself then. I cannot speak at all. I fear every word. I know that I, I still have someone to drive with like this, someone who will also enjoy the trip. But afterwards I will have to recall this silence too and there will be no way of talking about it. In life, silence grows, time shortens. I will say to her, let's spend a few days together. No, I won't, because she's suffering enough as it is. I will place my left hand on her right, skirt-covered, thigh. It's done. Her face, looking forwards at the road, undergoes a remarkable transformation and becomes a beautiful feminine life full of children – though I am not so crazy as to think I have a patent on this miracle; it is simply love, ready and waiting for the right hand to come, and sadly all I can do now is wish it for her wherever she lives. I take my hand away and put it back again, but more lightly and flatter this time, and looking sideways at her face and her journey I am astounded to find that it works as precisely as in a laboratory, and as delightfully as in bed. I have to cover my face; she can't. She just mouths mutely: 'Oh Jesus!' over and over again.

In a country town I walk with her to the main square, where she has some official matter to attend to. I sit on a bench in the shade. I do not mind waiting and do not understand why she apologises to me afterwards. I find everything confusing. It really is as if she is sorting out some business of ours, as if the two of us were setting things straight in advance this way. I say, now we'll go for lunch, and it seems to us like a wonderful plan with the fantastic prospect of coffee and then another drive. She is ebullient, almost jumping up and down, the corners of her skirt swirling round her knees. Afterwards she wants to buy me something, I am to say what. I tell her to buy me a watermelon, the biggest they have. I don't like melon. I will take it home to the family; they will eat it in an instant without suspecting that I am throwing the bird to the cat because I cannot bear the way she is fluffing up her feathers at me! Let it finish if nothing is to come of it!

In the distance, tractors are turning over the first stubble. The water is twenty centimetres warm and three metres cold. In the sky the sun is mixing the heavy clouds like dough for some happy future, but without me, and the spire of the church juts above the forest, the church is surrounded by a crumbling stone wall, and in the old cherry orchard there is a green darkness. I'm a sentimental old madman and this is a hard-hearted young person. She gets up, adjusts her skirts at the back, her eyebrows in the front, and she's off! She is leaving, and who is to lay flowers of mourning here every sixth of August?

I brought home the melon, the heaviest they had. I put it on the floor in the pantry and, shaking my tired arm, went into the boys' room. "Another handful?" asked Ondřej. "Yes. A heavy melon," I said cheerfully. "So we'll help lighten it a bit straight away," said young Jan. As they sliced the melon, Ondřej held forth: "Today I was rendering a wall and it was pretty tricky. For a rough stone wall you use a cement render but you have to cover the wall first with metal mesh, since nothing will hold on the stone. It's the only case where concrete is used for a facade." I listened to his explanation attentively and with relief. "The concrete is meant to be two centimetres thick but the wall is so rough that in places the mesh is as much as five centimetres away from it. So in those places I had to put on five centimetres of cement. What if it comes off?" I replied in all responsibility: "It won't come off."

"A miserable looking fellow came to us," said Jan, moving to the next item, "to have the valves on his bus adjusted. He's got his own bus for a puppet theatre. He was so unpleasant that the lads charged him a hundred crowns for a twenty-minute job. I was supposed to share the profit, but I refused." I was surprised: "He has his own bus and a puppet theatre?"

"That old guy from last year is back," said Ondřej. "But he's much weaker this year! He can't manage anything now. It took him the whole day to move a tiny pile of sand that high." He showed us above the table-top. "In addition to which he has the unpleasant habit of telling those of us who are quietly getting on with our jobs what we should be doing. Now lads, we'll have to move that thing over there, this'll have to go here, and now we'll dig this out. It's driving them all crazy, they've started to twitch and get in one another's way, and it's slowed the work right down." – "So why do you have to have him there?" I asked. "He has a mobility scooter, and to get a fuel discount for it as a pensioner he has to work a certain number of days a year."

The phone rang. Jan took it; it was Martin. Isabelle got her visa and would be arriving tomorrow. He asked what the weather was like and what she ought to wear. Jan replied that it was warm and would be cold. I gathered there was a question about whether she should come in jeans or a skirt. I called to Jan to say that I didn't want her coming in jeans. I gathered that Martin was vexed and was saying that she wasn't *my* wife. I repeated that I simply didn't want her coming in jeans.

WEDNESDAY, 8TH AUGUST 1979

High over Prague there hangs a full moon, with warm, wet clouds drifting over it. It is a delightful sight and totally different from the way it would appear to a voyager aboard the American space probe Voyager, which reached Jupiter about a year ago. The last issue of *Universe* has some photos from its voyage. The first one is of a muddy red planet with darker edges, with the little ball of the moon Io stuck onto it. Twenty-eight million kilometres away. The next shot is a close-up of a terrifyingly convincing ball made up of fire, ash, and gases that include helium, ammonia, sulphur, typhoid and smallpox. Above it all, two of Jupiter's satellites hover irrevocably; they even have one side in shadow, just like benign little moons. But let us take a closer look: they are six of one and half a dozen of the other. They are both the colour of clotted blood with blisters of black mould and greenish pus in which we can imagine the germs of a political purge. It could be a highly magnified cell of the inferno, or a follicle of Czechoslovak Television's cloaca, a fabrication, or a nightmare. – I think I might send this issue of *Universe* to my painter; it is like something from her palette of horrors. And I will write her a nice letter – I should like to see her.

I was walking with Isabelle along the street at night when a fellow who is familar to me from night-time trams came sauntering along from the opposite direction. Slim, dressed in light-coloured clothes, about sixty-five. His face shone like an angel's and, with arm upraised, he was singing the song he sings in the night tram: "... small but beautiful, oh God, preserve it, there I spent my young years, there was my home..."

Isabelle just went on smiling and did not ask anything. I told her he was always singing in that beautiful and innocent way. We speak together in English, but our Englishes are taking longer to get acquainted than we are and do not yet understand all the other's sentences.

At the airport I recognised Isabelle straight away. For one thing she was the last out and for another she was already smiling at me from a distance. She is tall and slim with dark hair cut short like a boy's. She has a darkish complexion, a distinctive nose and a sharpish chin – bird woman. No extro-vertedly delightful Suzette this, but a taciturn, watchful and reserved Isabelle. She entered our world responsibly, as if determined not to make herself out to be something she was not, and, during her stay, to be both unshockable and non-judgmental. It was the bride coming to introduce herself. Only after looking her up and down very carefully and generally taking her measure did I start to suspect that our Martin has probably grown up. It's strange.

I used the trick of driving her straight from the airport to Hradčany. She was taken by Prague unawares and I could see she was overcome! I decided not to say anything at all to her in advance about the way things are here, only to answer her questions as and when they occurred to her. We walked down Nerudova Street, and then through Malostranské Square and across Charles Bridge. From the Rudolfinum we took a tram back to the Castle and had lunch at the Loretto Restaurant. Only then did I take her back to our place, where nobody was home, and then to the student residence hall two streets away from us. That is where she sleeps, in a room to herself. She joins me, Catherine and Philip for breakfast. In the evening she has dinner with us and after dinner we chat. So she virtually lives with us. Today we were at the Vladislavs' because they speak French and we wanted to get some proper news at last about her and Martin.

She permitted herself her first critical comment today: "All the houses are dark." – I asked: "How often do they paint houses in Paris?" – "Maybe once every ten years." – "But damn it, this street was painted the year before last!" I said. Damn it is my translation of *kruci*; *žloutenka* I translate as hepatitis. Isabelle has learnt from Martin the words *doprčic* and *blbečku* (*merde* and *petit idiot*). Jan once baffled her by using the expressions *blbec* and *blb*. We had to explain to her in a very tortuous manner that *blbec* is a momentary state of idiocy, whereas *blb* lasts from cradle to grave. *Blbec* could describe me at this present moment perhaps. *Blb* is an office of state. Isabelle goggled at us and her bosom heaved with incredulous silent laughter. All this was much to the annoyance of Madla. Pointing to the three of us she slowly enunciated: "*Blbí*, id – i – otic!"

THURSDAY, 9ᵀᴴ AUGUST 1979

She is twenty-eight years old and has been teaching mathematics at the lycée for three years. She actually supported Martin on all those occasions when his student grant was held up or while he was looking for work. Employment was a problem for him because he was not naturalised, although he had been there ten years. He couldn't discover where was the glitch. It has only just been settled. He is to go for his papers and immediately afterwards he and Isabelle will be married. Madla asked what Isabelle would wear for the wedding, but I thought it was a silly question and refused to translate it.

Isabelle's parents were killed last year in a motor accident. Hers was one of those so-called "better homes," to judge from the photos she brought to show us. Apart from three siblings she has a grandmother. Her grandmother used to manage ten cinemas; now she has only one left, in which she is gradually frittering away the family fortune because she has always steered clear of trash and pornography. She was apparently quite a well-known personality in the film world and even attended the Karlovy Vary Film Festival once. For a long time the news of Isabelle's slumming with Martin was kept from

Jan once baffled her by using the expressions blbec *and* blb.
(p. 305)

Grandmother. Then they had to make out that Martin was from a fairly well-to-do home: when he went on holiday with Isabelle, she gave him the money in advance so that he could pretend he was paying. Last year's misfortune brought understanding and assent. I bought Isabelle a map and a guide and she will go for walks around Prague on her own, as soon as she dares.

I am reading the Čapek brothers' letters to Stanislav K. Neumann from the years 1910–18, and they are fantastic! They reveal a different Neumann and different Čapeks, quite unlike the popular images of them. Those two young men regarded Neumann as a fascinating figure, one who fired their imagination and their activity. They were free-spirited and assertive and had a very clear idea about their work, combined with acuity of judgement and firm determination. They were very strong young men! Most of the letters they wrote jointly. Thus, when one of them had made his point, the other would continue with the next paragraph while the first would reflect further and pick up from where his brother left off as if they were his own words. When they outline to Neumann their idea for a new literary journal, the project is precise, sound and bold – original for the times and topical even today! Compared with what we have now, the situation of literature during the First World War, and the publishing opportunities that they decry so bitterly, was a golden age of Czech literature. A Golden Age!

Šalda does not emerge at all well from their correspondence; I shall have to tell Kosík. And the brothers' beloved Neumann is beginning to infuriate me, even though his replies to them are not included in the book. The lads both look after him, send him money to live on, try to find him work in Prague, hatch a scheme to keep him out of the army, take an interest in his every little verse, send him journals and then look after his wife when he finally is conscripted. And they are constantly inviting him to stay! Three times in one letter: you'll stay with us, of course; you can sleep on the couch; you've got somewhere to sleep. They invite him and wait expectantly like children. Then, disappointed, they put in a letter all the things they were intending to tell him, and elicit his opinions, whose substance we can only surmise from the way they then discreetly contradict him… Such expectations, admiration and respect could never be satisfied anyway. It was beyond Neumann, and that's why he infuriates me.

But the greatest surprise of all is today's news that, on appeal, Jan has been accepted to the engineering faculty. I wonder what my friends will say to that.

I am now completely disenchanted with Neumann. I read, in that same book, the letters he wrote to Viktor Dyk during the same period. He writes solely about himself and his own matters, his verses, his debts. There are none of the ideas, reflections or friendliness as in the case of those two students, just dry matter-of-factness. In almost every letter he wants something from Dyk, but almost every time he apologises for not sending anything for the journal Dyk edited. – Be assured of my loyalty to *Lumír*, but I had to send my verses to *Lidové Noviny* because they pay better.

I was in the Slávia today and took Isabelle with me. They all welcomed her nicely and she already had her own acquaintance there: Jan Vladislav. I told her something about each of them, and then Vladislav briefly interpreted our debates for her. She looked fine there. Eva Kantůrková arrived too, which reminded me I have to write to Ota Filip. I have therefore done so, just now. I didn't refer to *Lord of the Tower* as such, but rather to criteria that should *also* apply when assessing new manuscripts.

"...to superficial gaze: woe, boredom, nostalgia and self-pity; in the eyes of a decent psycho-sociologist and literary connoisseur: a stage of promising remorse (=repentance), individual self-examination presented as a sacrifice to a collective b(B)eing, i.e. a contribution towards understanding the national conscience or creating one, for in its absence nations are B(b)loody stupid, and just scream and shout, overthrowing one thing, setting up another, filming things right and left, putting people to death, driving far too fast, wasting fuel and polluting the seas and the air. A society which, under the influence of crude oil and Khomeini, is acutely interested in – for example – the status of women in Islam and publishes bestsellers about it, is not interested, in fact, in anything! Once again f...ing Westerners understand nothing and fall far short of our own level of understanding. Oh no, we don't feel at all impoverished compared to them; we are not expecting pity; our present sin is rather different: we are observing them with malicious enjoyment, saying to ourselves: Keep it up!"

(I belted that into the typewriter – complete with typing errors – in a state of annoyance, but reading it now, in March 1980, I could not put it better than I did then!)

There was one objection to Kantůrková that I could not help including, however, counting on the fact that communicative Ota will certainly pass it on and it will come to the attention of others who merit it more, because when all is said and done, Kantůrková remains here with us: – "Communists shouldn't go writing about questions of faith, and if communism has burnt itself out as far as they are concerned, they should show greater modesty if they want a place at another hearth."

Isabelle left the Slávia to go for a walk in town and I popped over to Zdena's. We were due to meet up again at seven o'clock on the ramp in front of the National Museum. Isabelle turned up three-quarters of an hour late, and I was beginning to get worried. She told me that when we separated she had gone home for a shower and a change of clothes. Then she had correctly taken tram twenty-nine. Suddenly the driver said something, half the people alighted and the tram set off in a different direction. She had worked out her location from the street guide and found another tram route, but the next tram had not followed the route on the map either. "I am happy," Isabelle said like someone rescued, "to find this museum here, at least!"

TUESDAY, 14TH AUGUST 1979

B. came here out of the blue and bold as brass looking for some books from Padlock. "You have an outstanding debit to settle," I say calmly, "before we can discuss anything else." Oh, yes, of course. Certainly! And he readily pulled out three hundred and five crowns. I crossed off his debit, saying: "And now we're quits. I haven't put anything aside for you and I won't give you anything from now on." He could not believe his ears. But it was true. It's a pity, of course, and it irks me most of all. Who, if not he, should have everything? He is a literary scholar. But I'm not a doormat. Things are beginning to go my way at last, and soon I will have almost no more extraneous business left.

B. evinced the interesting opinion that task 'D,' which we had considered closed, required corrections and additions. I got hot under the collar. I told him that no work was ever perfect, but there came a moment when it had to be declared finished. He smiled and said: "That's all very well! But something like this gets done once every ten or twenty years, so I would have thought it worth our while to delay it for a couple of months!" I clasped my head in my hands.

I get the feeling I am descending into oblivion. Now that I go hardly anywhere and people are out of the habit of coming here, now that Saša Kliment has moved more or less permanently under Kleť Hill and Mr. Václav is in prison, now that Jiří Gruša is out of Prague and Ivan has no telephone, now that Otka no longer visits us because she is in custody, now that Karol has become a missing person and I have stopped visiting the Pitharts, now that Šiktanc never comes and I have to go to them instead (and so I am too offended to visit them), and now that Mirka is away from Prague for the whole summer, I feel alone and unknown on the street. Why not go off somewhere too? – But I am constantly waiting.

"I'm in a bad way, it's almost physical by now. In fact I don't know if it's my mind affecting my body or vice versa," Helena said this morning. I said: "You ought to think more about the good things that you might be going to see there, the things you'll discover and experience. Think about work too. I'm telling you, Helena, you will have to become somebody there! If you're leaving here because you're not allowed to work, then when you get there, show what you're capable of when you are." I force myself to adopt this didactic role, but I'm beginning to realise that she listens to me when I do; she takes notice of me and would actually take my advice! I am almost made dizzy by this frightening thought. She fell silent and then said: "I already know when we'll be flying out – on the Friday of next week." I started to feel slightly ill.

Auntie Cilka wanted to meet Isabelle, so I invited her to come along for this afternoon's walk with Isabelle. "How does she like Prague?" Auntie asked. – "I've no idea," I said. – "So ask her," she said and pointed at Isabelle. – "I won't. What for?" – "Have you taken her up to Petřín yet?" – "She chooses for herself where she wants to go." – "But she'd find it great fun, in that maze with the crooked mirrors!" – "For goodness sake, Auntie, she's a grown woman!" – "Young and old alike have a good laugh there," Auntie said.

We were walking along Revoluční Avenue past a shop with some coats or other. Auntie slowed down so that Isabelle could look in the window. No reaction. "Do you think fashion doesn't interest her?" Auntie said. – "I've no idea," I said, "but I should think they look like cast-offs to her." The truth is we have not yet ascertained what actually does interest her, whether architecture or music, or painting. People, maybe. Influenced by tourist propaganda or out-of-date information from the period before the present state of emergency, it occurred to Isabelle that she might buy some jewellery with Czech garnets. It is her one and only specific desire and she brought plenty of money with her for the purpose. She went for a walk yesterday and in the evening announced that she had not found any goldsmiths anywhere. It turned out that she mistakenly considers our goldsmiths to be jewellery shops: they have no gold anywhere. As I found this hard to believe, having sometimes caught sight of gold in shop windows, we set off for Rytířská Street. They actually had rings in the window, but they were only wedding rings, and inside there was a queue: the shop had just received a delivery of some gold. Isabelle found this surprising. "Meat is delivered twice a week, gold once a month," I explained.

Afterwards we found a nice place on a café terrace for a coffee, before walking round a few more streets. Auntie took the tram home and Isabelle and I made our way to St. James' Church for an organ concert. "Tell her at least," Auntie Cilka entreated me, "that it's the best organ in Europe." – "Bullshit, Auntie," I replied. Or rather I didn't, but it would have been appropriate. Because I've caught myself in the throes of feeling ashamed of everything. To what Siberian waste do all those famed "fruits of Czech industriousness" go?

In Celetná Street we suddenly encountered Helena coming from the other direction. Dressed all in white, with a flared skirt, she came smiling at me from afar in that shady street full of leisurely moving crowds. We merely exchanged hellos. Auntie immediately wanted to know who it was. I told her, but without superfluous detail: nothing about having spent the morning together at the zoo where we had had to give the big-cat house a wide berth (even though Helena saves spiders from the bath by letting them climb up along her naked arm), nor about my unbearable thought that never again would she and I meet like that: by chance on a crowded street. The grotesque absurdity of meeting her – and walking on past her.

In St. James' Church, people were by now sitting on the floor or the steps of the side-altar, or were leaning against the walls and pillars. Isabelle and I found a spot on a stone step. The church went on filling up to an incredible extent for another half-hour. They were mostly young people; some had small children with them. There were lots of foreigners: they were the ones with maps of Prague on their laps. Isabelle shook her head in amazement. Somewhere behind a pillar were Helena and her husband. When there was no space left on the floor slabs for even one foot more, the concert commenced. They were compositions for trumpet and organ. Two hours flashed by while time stood still. I merely listened without feeling or emotion or any change of mood or thought. I emerged lame in knee and brain.

FRIDAY, 17ᵀᴴ AUGUST 1979

Today, on March 18, 1980, I reached a critical point in the editing of my manuscript. From mid-August, my writing went to pieces. For a whole week there was no entry and it was only a feeling of responsibility towards Isabelle that led me to sit down at the typewriter on the evening after her departure on 20ᵗʰ August and give a retrospective account of what we did. The record is confused and disjointed. For simplicity's sake I am dividing it up and inserting the trip to Karlovy Vary in roughly chronological order:

It was a fine, sunny day. The spa's only main street, alongside the stream, was cheerful, bustling and clean as if it were not just the northern province of Wonderland that we had arrived in. Straight away we had a coffee at the – where was it? the Beautiful Queen, and then promenaded slowly up and down. We wanted to buy Isabelle a present, in fact we were duty-bound to buy a wedding gift and, a week late, I translated Madla's question about what Isabelle would be married in. She replied that it depended on the season. Madla was disappointed and had assumed, as I had, that it would be before the snow came. (They then got married in September.) Isabelle had taken a fancy to the Zwiebelmuster porcelain in our kitchen. We looked for it here without any luck. She came upon some cut crystal aperitif glasses, but all they had was the one glass in the window. We all laughed. I am talking about Tuzex, of course. In the normal shops they had nothing.

We also had a look at the gold counter – and there they had garnets! The bride wanted something to go round her neck; she wears neither bracelets nor ear-rings. The choice was between just two creations: one was a thickish affair in gold, not particularly imaginative or pretty, the other was a lighter, more tasteful thing in gold-plated silver. The first cost 700 Tuzex crowns, the other seventy-five. – Now I was curious. Isabelle wasted little time in thought: she expressed regret that the expensive item was not so nice and let them put the three little stars round her neck. A fine gesture of modesty and taste, I thought to myself, but what about the virtue of sincerity? "Isabelle," I said, "if the other thing had been as nice as that, would you have taken it for sure?" – "Of course," she said. – "And would you have accepted it from us as a gift?" – "Of course," she said with a crafty smile.

Then we ambled around again, went up to admire the view, had lunch and then ice-cream. I interpreted everything Madla wanted to know and they chatted away about women's matters. It was warm; the sprinkler wagons moistened the air, the grass and the pavements. While we were drinking our first coffee that morning, Isabelle had spotted a fantastically dressed lady pass by, and when we went for our ice-cream after lunch, the self-same lady was walking there, dressed fantastically but differently. After all, two hours had elapsed in the meantime. This elicited a wise and understanding smile from her. She was wearing a simple fifty-franc cotton dress with a pattern of small multicoloured flowers on a black background. Madla was wearing her light-brown speckled dress, as always.

Isabelle took the wheel on the journey back to Prague. She told us we had no brakes. When we pulled up in our street and got out of Herzen, a police car approached us and informed me that it had just left me an appointment for the morrow. So the next day I had to take the driver's test again. When the head of the traffic section was returning me my licence, he told me sheepishly that they had one other problem... Immediately I tried to think how I might possibly assist them with it, and it turned out to be a simple matter: all I had to do was let them change my license plate – AO 19-77. I came home with the news and Madla exclaimed: "I've got it! Now I know who! I know who it was I told in our office how to remember the number of our car: 'just think of Charter 77'!" This made us all laugh. Isabelle smiled too.

One day I took Isabelle over to have a look at the building site when Ondřej was there, and then the three of us went off for a swim in the pond at Kamenné Zehrovice. Isabelle didn't want to get in the water, however; she had no swimsuit. So we went back again on Saturday, with Madla this time. Isabelle has a nice figure. A bosom. I tried to imagine how someone like her, who can see the sea, the Alps and anything else whenever she likes, reacts to a little village pond like that, with its reeds, well-trodden banks below a pinewood, a concrete overflow into a willow-shaded stream, and there's a patch of grass where local people have blankets with naked children, and nearby, properly-kitted-out anglers with sun-hats and rubber thigh-boots keep casting and casting to no avail. All of a sudden, Isabelle ran up with agitated news: she had just seen an angler haul in a big fish, about this big – she indicated forty centimetres. Was I proud!

My account contains no record of how I took Isabelle to the sculpture gallery at Zbraslav. I know why I said nothing about it at the time, but I no longer consider it a valid reason: lots of beans have been spilt about it already, so these might as well be too. So I am adding the following on 18th March 1980:

On one of the days, I told Helena that I couldn't meet her tomorrow because I was going with Isabelle to the sculpture gallery at Zbraslav. She said she would like to go too, never having been there: the gallery had been closed for years. I was silently turning over in my mind the drawbacks of that idea when Helena immediately detected and dispatched them in the following way: she would invite a woman friend who spoke French to come along too. But that's splendid! Terrific! I could kiss you, Helena! I thought to myself, or said, or did, I don't recall now. So we went there. Helena's friend Ivana spoke French – how well I cannot tell – but they could be heard talking. Helena and I did not let on at all, because it was lovely anyway. We wandered through the corridors and rooms, all together or separately. Helena carried my canvas lens-bag dangling over her shoulder from one finger and was clearly thrilled by the powerful intimacy of it. So was I. I rounded on her sharply and admonished her severely: "Hold it properly, before you go and smash them to pieces!" And I was treated to the blissful sight of her stopping in her tracks, gazing at me enormously, and flushing blissfully from her forehead downwards, so that she almost dropped the spare lenses and smashed them to pieces.

The whole time we must have met no more than three other visitors – we had the gallery to ourselves. We started to mess around a bit and make fun of the national heroes. Ivanka, pale and frail, stood alongside the hard black sculptures, mimicking their expressions and poses, and her French improved by the minute. In quiet and cultured fashion we traversed hurriedly the different rooms, returning to make comparisons, and I told them all to choose some object and create a tableau or sculptural group with it. I photographed it. The old lady attendants trailed behind us from one room to another, observing us with unexpected indulgence, smiling. At my herd of young women, I expect, as it must have been a mystery who was who's what. Isabelle behaved a mite more respectably than we did, which was only proper, but she was clearly having fun and we all got simple enjoyment from the sudden freedom that had sprung from who knows where, protected by the old mansion of sculptures in which we were almost alone.

How did it happen, I ask myself? By the female element occurring in a conflict-free combination for once. None of us demanded from anyone else more than what was available to everyone in sufficient measure. And I had the extra thrill of imagining how Isabelle would impart it to Martin, what she would tell him about me and my women friends. And goodness knows how many! It was a superb afternoon, rather French!

MONDAY, 20ᵀᴴ AUGUST 1979

This morning, Auntie Cilka came with us to the airport, and Isabelle is gone. Martin acknowledged receipt a moment ago. Auntie wanted to see the airport for once. "Have you asked her," she said, "how she liked Prague." – "No, Auntie." – "I'd ask her." – "Go ahead and ask her then," I said, a bit roughly. – "How can I, when I don't know how?" Auntie Cilka said.

We had managed to show Isabelle Křivoklát Castle and the towns of Beroun and Rakovník. All the towns seemed empty to her. In addition, Jan had taken her to Karlštejn Castle and Archduke Franz Ferdinand's Konopiště, then to visit Josef in Bezejovice, and then on to Okoř. She would have found Karlštejn interesting had the guide not herded them along at such a pace that she had no time to see anything properly or read the French captions. At Konopiště, there had been such a throng of tourists that they did not even go inside the chateau. Josef had no spare horse for Isabelle, since it was the Saturday when the riding team's Prague members arrived. As the weather was unpleasant, he had at least made Jan and Isabelle a fire, and loaned – or gave them, I can't recall which – some sausages to grill. They had also gone mushrooming, but found nothing. "How do mushrooms grow where you live?" I asked. "They're also sparse," she said and added, "when we don't find anything, Martin always says: Czechoslovakia – that's where you find mushrooms!"

She's quick-witted, her sense of humour is considerate, somehow, and with the few words of Czech she learned here she succeeded in making meal times a convivial affair from the very start. I think we – our family – were the greatest attraction for her. She reserved for us a lovely, open smile. Madla is clearly something the like of which she has never seen or heard before. She observed her face and movements constantly, and any time voices were raised or there was disagreement, she would look to see if "Muzzer" wasn't being ill-treated.

"Is Martin clever, at least?" Muzzer wanted to know. I said it in English, but was misunderstood, so young Jan and I tried using the French dictionary. The dictionary is older than I am. "*Malin*?" Isabelle laughed. "Not at all! He always tells everything to everyone." We saw the problem and tried to get round it with another word. "*Rapide*?" she burst into laughter. "On the contrary! He is always an hour late everywhere." I threw away the dictionary and said apologetically: "Mother would just like to know something more personal about her son." She smiled and said: "He has nice legs." – The boys fell down laughing.

Isabelle was assigned Martin's old place at table. She enjoyed everything she ate, including the dumplings, but ate little. In restaurants we would always try to find her vegetable dishes, but they never had any. After the St. James' concert, I wanted to take her somewhere for dinner. No chance! Everywhere was full. At the Praha Restaurant on Wenceslas Square there were tables... because they were without a chef. "A restaurant with no chef?" Isabelle smiled. At the Golden Goose there was plenty of room. We sat at a table and the waiter came to inform us they were not serving because the cash register was broken. "What?" said Isabelle. "Cash!" I said in English, but she didn't understand and I had to spell it. Then she said, "Don't they have a pencil and paper?" I too felt as if I were in Wonderland. I'd really had no idea – it needed her visit to bring it home to me. In the end, however, we had dinner at the Alfa, albeit uneasily, in view of the queue of people outside the door waiting for us to wipe our chins and buzz off. It was my own stupid fault, of course – it would never have happened to Pavel Kohout. But I shall not act the man of the world, nor do I intend to serve someone something in a better setting than the sort we ourselves gobble up our food. The best food and service of the entire fortnight was in the town of Řevnice, opposite the train station. And in the end, what impressed her most of all was when the building manager at Okoř told her – in French – the story of the castle, past and present, and talked about the plans for preserving it.

When the plane started to taxi towards the runway, Auntie wanted to wait until it took off, but I didn't think my nerves would stand it. I could easily have taken a rest, of course, but the space vacated in me was immediately occupied by another aeroplane. That one had spread its heavy grey wings, and as I drove down into Prague, the road cool from an evening shower, it was pressing me closer and closer to the ground.

TUESDAY, 21ST AUGUST 1979

I am counting the days. I don't want to, but I can't get it out of my mind. I wake up at night and know straight away that it's five, four, three days away. As if I had it for homework. Before going to sleep, I have again taken to dipping into the astronomical year-book, which contains nothing that could possibly remind me of anything else, and then I am roused by something as if being taken to task: Remember that in a week's time Helena won't be here. But that year-book gets less and less readable each year. As exact knowledge of those worlds increases, they become increasingly incomprehensible for me. The best things are written when people know next to nothing. But this much I have understood: a supernova explodes in our galaxy every ten to thirty years and not, as was formerly believed, once every two hundred years. Better and better! That too.

I sat at a table in front of the Malá Strana Café, pondering as I waited. Two hours went by. Helena did not show up. I realised I was here a week late: I was either mistaken or had overslept a week. She is in Vienna after all. But people moved about the square as if she was suddenly supposed to emerge from the bustle. And at that moment she emerged. She saw me and smiled. My mistake: when I am sitting here a week from now, I shall again be staring into the crowd waiting for her to appear. And again the following week, and the week after that, and so on until I get out of the habit.

She smiled wearily. The packers had arrived two hours later than promised, they were finished two hours later too, and her husband had said: "Now you can go and leap into bed." – I asked: "So why don't you?" – "Because we're sitting here." – "Do you want to go somewhere else?"

We had fixed Thursday as the farewell day. I told her she could go away with me directly, now her packing was done, and return straight to the plane. It didn't matter anymore and nothing could happen to her. Out of the question, because of the dog. Of course, and because of the husband too. Forget it then. I asked what time it took off. About five. In that case, I told her, I'd be waiting for her at five in that little wine bar, the first place we ever went to together, last year – in November, wasn't it? She burst out laughing in true style, Of all the... well I'll be... and what if I did it? Do it, I'm serious. What would it mean? Try it, you'll find out. She laughed, Well I'll be...

In the end we went back to the idea of leave-taking on the Thursday. As I ponder on it, I gradually discover all the things I ought to tell her. It might almost be worth taking notes. First and foremost then: an authentic life is one that is lived, and it is nonsense to wait for it to arrive. It will do no harm for her to suffer a bit so long as her suffering is incorporated in her work, which will be the more beautiful for it. Secondly, arrange for life with your husband to be calmer and steadier than it has been here. Less artistic if necessary, maybe. "What do you mean by an artistic life?" she'll ask. Next: don't be cremated. The way I imagine our leave-taking is not in some hide-away but among people, on the street – in the Slávia, say, calling in at the Chramostová's if we take our leave in a southerly direction, or at the Kosíks' if we proceed northwards. I want to make our relationship something both permissible and possible! "And then forget me with the sorrow that gradually, gradually disappears and leaves no aftertaste," I shall say as point five.

In the mailbox for me when I got home was a packet containing Karel Šiktanc's translation of "Mournful Sunday." Added in handwriting at the bottom was: Dear Ludvík, this is my crack at it. So sing it – but don't shoot yourself, it's intended for Hungarian officers!"

> ...Day of rest dawns again, rosebuds and yearning,
> A swing now empty, forever returning...

So everything tallies exactly. I weep. (And again now, 18th March 1980.)

WEDNESDAY, 22ND AUGUST 1979

I have no distinct dreams at the moment, so I recall nothing in the morning. My life is so down-to-earth and practical that there would be no point writing about it – except that I have now got so far with this book that I must continue. But I am cornered once again by the question of whether I am to write about the most private aspects or remain silent.

For the time being, what I write I write without knowing where it will lead – either of its own accord, or under my guidance. I store the original of the manuscript in one place and a copy in another. All I have at home are the last few pages, which means I do not read over what I have written. The copy is kept for me by Richard Slavík; he reads it and so does his wife. About half way through the year I asked them both to tell me what they thought. I dare not record everything they told me, but some of it I simply must.

Richard: Wonderment that a single individual human life could be like this, that it could be so extraordinarily free while reflecting the unfreedom of life in general. Unsure whether the documentary edge of the record ought to be retained, or whether it needs softening with a touch of fiction. Who is to bear responsibility for the pain of the characters involved? The pain cannot be erased, or forgiven, but perhaps it might be offset slightly – says Richard – by the work's extraordinary "success." It is hard enough living with me without becoming the subject-matter of my writing!

Richard's wife: Moved to tears when reading it. (I am when writing it, dear lady!) Readers are accustomed to novels developing in a fair and just way, so they can sympathise with the hero and share his catharsis. Don't I have anything like that in mind? She is surprised, not disappointed, simply surprised that in reality I write differently from how I seemed to before. Only now is she able to appreciate the work that has gone into my sentences to achieve their adage-like pithiness.

I said I did not know where I would go from here; for the time being, I simply had to go on writing. I am tempted by both: the cruelty of the documentary and the magic of fiction. Catharsis? I get that from confessing. I confess that I live not from hatred of anything, but from the power of good things and from the strength of the people who have become part of my destiny. This is my final reckoning. Language and style? Even before this it was not my habit to dissemble, but it is true that I used to pay close attention to perfect presentation and to the reader. When I complete this thing, all I shall do is go through it quickly with a pen before running it through the typewriter once more in order to get rid of the roughest edges, and I shall not concern myself with the reader. And the public? (Because I also sense in their comments a certain regret that "the nation" might be disappointed.) Let the nation abandon its convenient assumption that someone else represents its virtues, apart from those whom it dignifies with ninety-nine percent of the vote. There are a lot of people in prison here. What does the nation do about it...?

Madla has just come home from work clasping an enormous bunch of roses. Fifteen altogether. We spread them out on the table and divided them between two pots. A flower messenger had delivered them to her at work. A card was attached with the words: With love and respect – No signature.

FRIDAY, 24ᵀᴴ AUGUST 1979

I have roasted a chicken. The time is ten past three. I expect Helena is being driven along some nearby street on her way to the airport.

Today I dreamed I was due to take my final exam at school. What chance have I anyway, I thought to myself? I couldn't care less. And I sat there apathetically in the waiting room, while Petr Pithart went on studying. "Show me." I stretched out my hand. He passed me his orange exercise book. The edges of the pages were trimmed and bore alphabetical markings like a pocket telephone list. I found the letter C: coffee. It gave the chemical formula for coffee, the places it was imported from and the different ways of making it in various towns of Czechoslovakia. The most interesting methods were from Benešov, Mělník and Votice, I thought. I'm damned if I'll take the exam! I said to myself, then returned Petr the book and woke up. In the wink of an eye I was in the depths of misery. And if I must write anything else about it, then it will have to be some other time.

It is four o'clock. I have to get dressed and leave. During dinner yesterday the last thing I said to Helena was: "What time did you say it takes off?" – "Just before six." – "I'll be waiting at five, Helena! Good luck!"

SATURDAY, 25ᵀᴴ AUGUST 1979

Saturday is still a few minutes away, but this entry already belongs to it. Friday received due treatment. I dragged it home almost unconscious.

But first I have to do something with those roses. One portion of Madla's fantastic bouquet we put in a tall, slender vase of Ida Vaculková's, the other in a rotund jug from Georgia. I will now describe the pots – this is important. Both are nominally from the same material: smoky black ceramic, matte on the outside, glazed on the inside. Ida's vase has the elegance of a blast-furnace chimney, the Georgian one has a ram motif girdling its plump hips. Ida's glaze is drab brown; the Georgian one mysteriously volatile, opalescent. The roses in Ida's vase are jubilant; in the other they hang their heads – all of them! And it was the selfsame water.

I took the wilting roses to the bathroom, laid them in the bath and ran just enough water for them to float freely. I shook the air out of the blooms under water. But really I ought to cut their stems again. So I am off to get a knife.

Now to what happened in that wine bar. I settled myself into a corner alcove that a group of fellows had just vacated. They left behind them puddles of liquid on the table-top and an ashtray overflowing with litter. A waitress immediately appeared. She wiped the table and took away the ashtray. Before she could return, the doors swung open letting in the noise and chill of the street, and Helena entered. "Good morning," she said in a warm, soft voice, even as she approached, drawing off her gloves. She turned sideways to me so that I could help her off with her fur coat. Then she slipped into the seat opposite with a distinctive movement, as if she were so slim and supple that she had no need to bend any limb, crease her tummy or even weigh anything. Curious, I ordered some wine or other and when the waitress left, invited Helena to come straight to the point.

"Well, first of all, I must describe our family to you," she said leaning forward. She articulated her words precisely, not slurring her speech-sounds after the Prague fashion. When she was excited her tongue would become tied somewhere in her mouth and then she would hurry to catch up. Her sounds and ideas emerged quantum-fashion, one might say. As she paused for reflection, her lips would remain ready-formed for the next word, and waiting for it meant observing her two large, clean, upper incisors. At that moment, those teeth assumed the character of a rather daring, albeit innocent, décolleté, something she otherwise lacked. She wears blouses with fairly high necklines, and long sleeves, often rolled up. As she spoke, her gaze was fixed on the index finger of her right hand, with which she wrote invisible signs on the blank table-top. Only occasionally did she raise her blue eyes to me.

"My mother died four years ago – from cancer, that is. My brother did too, earlier, when he was twenty-six. At that time, when my father saw there was no hope, he gave him, well," this stammering, "with the doctor's knowledge, that is – though on his own responsibility – something that allowed him to die without suffering."

I looked around. "If you don't mind," I said, "I think we had better change places." Now she was talking not into the room but at a wood-panelled wall. I was at a loss to imagine where I might come into it, and was a trifle apprehensive. Moreover, on account of the habits I had acquired in radio, I had started to follow what she was saying from the point-of-view of listener interest and the possibilities for editing. Technically speaking, editing would have presented few problems as she spoke clearly and naturally, and before I left the radio I had become skilled enough to edit between syllables, although that was neither necessary nor even possible if an exposition as condensed as hers was to retain its logical integrity.

"Then daddy had a stroke and was left partially paralysed a few years ago. He stopped going out and lost any opportunity for activity, and, that, if you knew him just a little bit, was the cruellest thing of all..." What sort of home surroundings does she have, and how come I have only ever seen her cheerful and uncomplicated? She continued. "Over the past six months it's been clear that things are going downhill fast with daddy, and I find it dreadful to see him in such a state. I'm so sorry for him... and I know how it hurts him for me to see him like that, when he was always such a strong father and fantastic guy. To cut a long story short, he's always asking me to render him the same service, and I've already got something for the job. Do you think I ought to do it?"

In the past two hours, the roses in the water have stiffened. I can take them out. I put them in a vase of pale greenish glass with metal ornamentation around its neck and across its bosom. Two hours on these few lines; I'm overcome with helplessness at my inability to find a form of expression that is adequate, faithful and succinct, but also as red-blooded as possible, besides which I have no idea what was the purpose of that event. Though it certainly had one! Why did she come to me with it?

I left my first question for later and asked first of all: "When does your dad make the request: when in pain, during some attack, in the heat of the moment, when he's depressed, or when he's feeling better?" – She replied: "The way we talk about it is that each morning, when I bring him his breakfast in bed, he asks jokingly: 'Well Helena, is it there yet?' – And I, his beloved and loving daughter, reply: 'It'll be there one day, daddy, let it come as a surprise.'" – "Who did you get it from and who knows about it?" – "From a good friend of ours, a family friend. No one knows about it." – "Who have you spoken to about such a possibility." – "No one, before you." – "Where is the thing, and does your dad know its whereabouts?" – "Well, strictly speaking, I've returned it, in case anything happened or I did something before I finally reached a decision. But I can have it any time. It's agreed and there are no complications. Daddy still thinks I have it, and I act as if I did, because it's good for him to know that he has the possibility of instant relief."

"What sort of opinions does your dad hold? I mean, does he believe in God?" I asked. – "I don't think so, that is to say, he has never acted – or rather, spoken – as if he did. As for his opinions, he doesn't like the Communists, but he didn't like Masaryk either. God? I don't know, probably not." – "And what about you?" – "I – I'm not sure…" she said, shaking her head and scrawling rapidly on the table-top, "probably not. But I don't really know." – "Then you don't," I said, "because those who do, know it." – She asked: "Do you believe in God? No, that's a silly question, isn't it, seeing you're a Communist." – "What sort of judgement is that?" I protested. "Do you use foregone conclusions like that in place of perception? – "I'm sorry, it was silly of me."

I said: "The reason I ask about your dad's faith is the possibility that he might now regard the service he rendered his son to be a sin, one with which he can't leave the world." – "You mean it's as if he now wanted to die the same way?" – "Yes, something like that. Even people who don't believe in God in the religious sense have a sense of balance, a settling of accounts, or whatever you want to call it, and feel a need to settle up." – "That would more or less fit daddy, admittedly, but I think the real reason is something else. He has lived his whole life, which has been both pretty hard and interesting, according to the principle 'all or nothing.' Work full tilt. Risk everything. And that means that it's now a case of live or die. He feels his present state to be above all a terrible humiliation, in front of me, his daughter, I mean."

"And yet it doesn't worry him to burden you with such a decision!" – "N-no. Because it's no burden, in fact. The fact is, if I decided to do it I wouldn't feel any remorse, because it's all part of the one decision." – "So what you're really concerned about is doing it too soon?" – "More or less…" she said and blushed. – "I don't believe you," I said. "The doctor could give a pretty good estimate." – "As far as the doctor is concerned – he's daddy's friend – there's no doubt. He says there's no hope. He could die tomorrow. Or now." – "Why don't you trust to providence, then?" – "Because he's my nearest and dearest. I love him so very much and…." – I laid my hand on hers, halting its agitated movement. That's the story of the first touch from my side.

Of course, I had already asked whether her husband knew. For the life of me I am not able to recall her reply.

In the end I had to give her some sort of answer. But before I do, there's just one other thing I'd like to know: "Now I'll ask you what is, for me, the most important question. The two of us have only spoken together three times in our lives. Why have you turned to me with such an important, and even dangerous, matter?"

It's four o'clock. I wish through some miracle I could see where and how she is sleeping, or what she is doing.

SUNDAY, 26TH AUGUST 1979

After a miserable and rainy day yesterday, this morning dawned so golden that when I opened my eyes I had the happy feeling that none of the bad things were true. But it only took a couple of seconds for me to realise what had happened. After my nocturnal unconsciousness – my best means of detachment – as it came into focus, I could see afresh the absurd, senseless cruelty of the thing and for the next hour I marvelled, motionless, at just how far one can stray away from oneself, and from one's yearnings and wishes.

But what if one returned, I add on 18th March 1980, and in rage and pity tore down the barrier one had erected to block a particular path? Would one find the thing that had grown into such a frantic need, or only what lay there calmly and sensibly before one lost one's wits?

I put on my boots and went out into the garden as into a foreign land. I had no desire to do anything, because every task, while it lasts, removes me further – from what? I have been deceived, beguiled and betrayed. I am disappointed and have betrayed. How much further will it go? The pine tree goes on growing out of the earth, beneath it the heather is blooming, the apples are swelling with juice among the wet leaves, the dahlias, red, purple and variegated, bow their heavy heads, exhausted by the rain. A branch of the plum tree has broken under the weight of fruit; that's one thing I must do at least: prop up those trees – those devoted, quiet, obedient and so very loyal trees. I bustle about, looking for props, but before I start trampling the grass under the trees I ought to mow it. As I mow I peel off two millimetres of earth with the grass. I'm scalping the garden! That's how skilled I've be-come after seven years of sharpening a scythe. I brush against a branch and it sheds rainbow-coloured rain. And all the time two lines from the ironic song which I made up myself to the tune of "Mournful Sunday" keep going through my head:

... Write to me Monday where you were Sunday
And whether, by chance, we weren't going the same way.

Once, a long time ago, I had a dream which my family found extremely amusing the next morning. I was at a conference and even though no one had invited me or expected me to, I stood up and made a speech. Some speech! It was no speech at all! Even as I took a breath to start I had no idea what I was going to say. But I did say something, after all, some nonsense that cruelly drew me onwards, so that I sauntered along, concocting a complicated problem as I went, and then immediately brandished a solution. My speech was only nine words long. But it was a knockout! The torture of it, though.

The gravel crunches: Madla is coming. She is gazing upwards at the tree-tops, her bare arms clutched across her chest. She has grown slimmer and younger over the past month, during which she has complained now and then of a touch of stomach trouble. "You're mowing?" She goes over to the dahlias and tries in vain to get their heavy heads to stay upright. She goes behind the summerhouse and breaks off some clumsy sticks from a pile of bushes lying there ready for chopping. I say: "I'll make you some props for them if you bring me my camera." She scurries lightly back with the Flexaret, which is loaded with a colour slide film: just one roll to last the summer. For I have decided, after past experience, always to go for just one of many tempting shots: the definitive one. Thus the twelve-exposure film starts with tulips (Oh, what became of them?) and ends – I am determined – with the yellow falling of leaves. I take a photograph from beneath the apple tree, looking through the hanging fruit at the bright flames of the dahlias in the background. The old, old question: what do I want in sharp focus, the apples in the foreground or the flowers in the background?

By doing a bit of mowing every week, I have no difficulty in keeping the whole garden smooth and clear. It reveals the micro-relief of the property. And the apples are beginning to fall. I collect them in a bucket. I pick up my camera and take a shot of Madla among the dahlias, without her knowing.

I set out the white chairs in a semi-circle like seats in a lecture-hall. I place a white table in front of them. I call out: "Come here, there's going to be a lecture!"

"Which row am I to sit in?" I point her to a seat in the second row. Where are the others? All our friends! "But you have to give your lecture!" she says and sits in the allotted place. I fix the camera in the tree, set the self-timer, go over to the table, lean on it with both hands, gaze fixedly into the hall for a few moments, and start an illustrious and celebrated lecture on my own special topic, the one at which I excel:

Why do
goats butt
gently?

Because
they're mostly
friendly.

MONDAY, 27TH AUGUST 1979

It is cooler all of a sudden. I have to choose some different outdoor clothes, and alter my travel routes and destinations.

Last week, Olda Unger was looking for me. He had come to say a last farewell. Madla told him I was saying Goodbye to Helena. The capital G is a typing error, but I'm leaving it. I set off this morning for the Ungers. A relation of theirs opened the door. She said they had gone off to say goodbye to somebody, and were leaving tomorrow at midday. She showed me round the pitifully empty apartment. Bare walls, empty windows. My old pal!

I went part of the way home on foot, on the off-chance of meeting him returning. To my left, across the river, the slopes of Barrandov stood unaltered, and ahead of me was the cliff of Vyšehrad. I passed a small church on the right; on a playground in front of it boys and girls were engaged in a noisy game of volley-ball. I looked around to see where I was, and when. I felt as if I was back in about 1960 when I knew almost no one in Prague, although the newsrooms were full of people, many of whom I soon came to know. And now, again, I know nobody there. And where have I seen a street

Where are the others? All our friends!
(p. 326)

as unfamiliar as this before? I know: on an assignment to another town where I found no one. It feels like being on an assignment again.

Three youngsters were coming towards me, one of them holding forth while the others guffawed after every sentence. I do not understand them. Maybe this is the sensation of a waning world that old people feel.

It is nine o'clock in the evening and there is no one home. I peeled some potatoes and put them on to boil. The first to come in was Jan, who told me how he had spent the weekend at Josef's, what he had done to tune Josef's engine to perfection, and how he himself had perfected his horse-riding. On Sunday he had gone with Josef to some equestrian event at Kutná Hora. Josef had taken two horses; on one of them he competed himself and came in third. When the announcer was giving the results he used the words: "the oldest participant in our competition." I asked Jan: "How did Josef look?" – He replied: "He'll never change. He can't, in fact, because there's nothing about him that can change. He's the essence of himself. On horseback he looked the best of all of them, with the grey hair showing under his helmet." – "Why didn't Hanka compete," I asked. Hanka is Josef's daughter, the pride and fruit of his equestrian pedagogy. For years he would roar at her in the riding-school: "Shorten your rein! Give him some rein! Don't sit on him like a pudding!" – Our Jan said: "Hanka was there, but she wasn't riding. The doctor told her she mustn't. She's very thin and her kidneys have dropped because of her riding. He says she has to put on a bit of weight first." – "How is she taking the ban?" – "She's acting as Josef's trainer. She yelled at him very authoritatively in her shrill voice: Shorten your rein! And after the competition she dressed him down: You were impossible! He's a fast horse, why did you ride him so slowly!" – "No mention of puddings?" I asked. – "No." – "How did Josef take it." – "He just smiled with his big wide mouth and said, Okay, okay, I'll do better in five years' time." He came third and won a little clay jug.

TUESDAY, 28ᵀᴴ AUGUST 1979

I had a pleasant dream in which nothing in particular happened. An apricot orchard, a field track leading from the back of a farm, a walk on level ground, a Sunday off after a strenuous week's work, a friend of yore whose mother was getting lunch ready for us in the meantime... I expect it was an echo of

Zlín and my visits to the Klajns at Kyjov – a walk with Jura Klajn up behind the village, while Jura's mother was frying schnitzels. The apricot orchard has been felled, Jura's mother is dead, and Jura – already a widower – looks as old as his father. At this year's reunion of Zlín ex-pupils he played a practical joke on those of his former classmates who thought they recognised him by introducing himself with the words: "I'm Jura's dad, Jura can't come." And they believed him and asked about Jura. I watched it from the staircase, having immediately recognised Jura, of course, and was overcome at the pity of it. I expect that was Jura Klajn in today's dream: a young, mischievous and happy Jura.

I got up refreshed, shaved happily, took an ice-cold shower, seeing there is no hot water, made a cup of tea, heated some water to wash up yesterday's supper things, and gave the birds some seeds and a lettuce leaf. And I drifted through the morning in a state of pleasant anticipation. Mind you, I did have momentary attacks of unease. Then Olda Unger came because he was unable to bear the thought that we had missed each other yesterday. We said goodbye to each other in two minutes with a handshake, standing up. He was on his way to the station. Then some young man or other brought me a summons to see Major Fišer tomorrow. I told him that tomorrow did not suit me and we agreed on Friday. Then a registered letter arrived from Ota Filip – a prompt reply to what I had written him. Ota writes that I greatly upset him, that he feels very much the same way, but that there, on the spot, one just cannot act according to one's feelings. "Here in the publishing house there is a sharp conflict between our ideas of what we'd like to do and what we are able to do. I will have to fight fiercely for every book originating in the Slavonic intellectual and linguistic world. Not with my editorial colleagues, but with marketing and the whole computerised machine that sells the books. Authors shower me with manuscripts and then demand: Now that we've sent it to Filip, it's his duty to see it through. So far I have regarded it as a duty, but on more than one occasion I have come to grief. It's not hard to write recommendations – using the very arguments you cited, in fact. But when I fail it can lead to lifelong enmities... Sometimes it almost drives me to despair. As far as *Lord of the Tower* is concerned, I really did get a bit frantic... My written assessment of it was my spontaneous reaction... Give me a bit of time to get over your letter..."

And then twelve o'clock came and the telephone did not ring. I was at a loss. An hour went by, then another and I can see I am still immature, that I am incapable of acknowledging reality when it humiliates me with the truth. Even though I knew how it would turn out, I still did not expect it to be like this. It doesn't fit the bill!

At four o'clock I thought it better to go out. I went to the Chramostová's, but they weren't home. I bought about fifteen spare bulbs of different wattages.

WEDNESDAY, 29ᵀᴴ AUGUST 1979

I accompanied Zdena on a trip to Rochov. She had to take a day off from work to obtain a certificate from the local authority that her house does not form part of available housing stock. I was coming along as a prop in the event of Zdena's collapsing at their refusal to give her a certificate. There is someone in the village or locality who would like to get his hands on the house and is using political means, under the slogan 'Expropriate!' For that reason, Zdena wants to make her son joint-owner.

As I approached her car, it seemed to me through the windscreen that she was smiling behind the wheel. She turned out to be crying. "Where do you have Bibisa?" I said. She broke down in tears. "These things happen," I said, but they hadn't. Bibisa had simply got lost, yesterday evening. The water was off in the house so Zdena had gone down to a lower floor to fetch some. Bibisa had run after her and automatically out into the street. It was black outside, like Bibisa, and she had been unable to find her. Nor this morning. She is feeling so bad that she cannot drive. I drove and was obliged to stop just outside the city limits: she had a splitting headache and felt sick. But she had no wish to go back, seeing she was already losing a day's leave. I am not much good as a comforter. I felt more sympathy for her than I was able to show, and anyway whatever I said would only irritate her all the more. Maybe she will calm down sooner the less fuss I make. And this turned out to be the case. Half-an-hour later we were able to set off again. I spent the journey in thought, as she objected to my speaking to her, and I considered the possibility that her explosion of misery over Bibisa was merely something like a fistula from a much larger centre of misfortune, which even she herself knows nothing about yet. It took about another quarter of an hour for Zdena, her stomach and her head to calm down enough to have a cigarette.

At the offices of the local authority she showed her title deed and a report on the house's condition and obtained the necessary rubber stamp to proceed with the matter at district level. She was surprised and thinks it is a good omen. Between ourselves, it does not mean a thing yet. But she immediately made an incredible recovery and was ready to weed and dig the garden, and help me build the wall. The latter still stands as I left it. It has not grown an inch; if anything, it is collapsing slightly.

We drove to Litoměřice. There she invited me to lunch and I bought her a catch for the vent-window of her car – only the left side as they did not have one for the right. She has both windows tied with wire. She went to the building department and handed in the papers, and then to the notary public for a form to fill in. She chose a court assessor and agreed to take him on Monday to show him the land and her buildings. "What do you think, ought I to grease his palm, and if so, how much should I give him?" – "Do you want a low valuation or a high one?" – "That's what I don't know." – "If you manage to pull it off, then a low valuation would be better, but if they actually did take your house, then you would need a high one." – "I know what," she said, "I'll put the assessor in the picture, from the very beginning." – "That'll be the best idea," I said, "and don't forget the cemetery." We laughed. She was pale and weak, but handsome. She was recovering the way grass does after a trampling. She was wearing a new outfit that she originally bought for her son's planned wedding. But now she is making herself something else for that. She is grey-rinsed.

We drove back towards Prague along a clear, winding road, Říp Hill rising above us to our left. "What are my chances of getting Bibisa back, do you think?" – "Even probability," I said, "but hope – ninety percent." The sun shone, pears fell from the trees, pears everywhere. "I can't keep anything," she said. "I lost that beautiful silver looking-glass. I lost the silver pendant that time. Maybe I'll lose the house too. They already stole two of my dogs, my goldfish died and now I've lost Bibisa. My honour is shot to hell. I can't keep anything." – "What about men?" I said experimentally. – "A man isn't my property." Devilishly cunning.

We turned into her street. Children rushed over to us, calling: "Your doggie is over there – that man found her." He had found her last night and locked her in his car for the time being. Bibisa barked, yelped, jumped against the glass, flung herself from the front seat to the back. But she will just have to wait until the man comes home from work. – So one loss, at least, is postponed.

When I got home and opened the door I caught sight of a vaguely familiar face at the kitchen table. The fellow was holding the telephone and talking to someone in several languages and he just waved at me wildly with his free hand. He is tall, blond, about forty-five, boyishly trusting, cheerful and sincere; a professor of economics in Bergen. He finished speaking, stood up and greeted me: "*Hallo! Kennst mich?*" – "*Ja freilich!* Rafto!" I said, because there's no mistaking this good fellow once you've made his acquaintance.

He was coming from Warsaw and had been waiting two hours for me. The boys had fed him and he had even managed to have a nap on the couch. Oh, how happy he is to see me in good form, Warsaw was fantastic, he had spoken to the KOR representatives, would like to talk to Hejdánek, Hájek, and him and him, he's bringing greetings – he showed me Newsweek with the title-page covered in faces: our prisoners. He wants to assure me that the Norwegian government... "*Wunderbaaar!*" I immediately exclaimed in a loud voice, and I gave him a pad and pencil, thus indicating that wir sind aber nicht in Warschau. He wrote me a lengthy message and I just went on repeating *wunderbar* and *herrlich* and rushed him out of house and home.

THURSDAY, 30TH AUGUST 1979

At nine in the morning the Malá Strana Café is transparent and clean. I close my umbrella and enter. I take a seat by the window so that I can see the tram stop. It is quiet and cosy here. I order two glasses of Becherovka and take a sip from one of them. The other waits opposite. From the back of the room, two waitresses observe me, leaning towards each other. Their smiles broaden when I drain the other glass after my own and order two more. Trams arrive at the stop. I watch who gets off: raincoats, umbrellas, bags, legs, hips, crutches, jeans male and female, shoulder bags, breasts and double-breasts, soldiers. The alien fabric of the city and nothing else. I wait and my serenity seems strange to me: maybe this is not even me, or maybe I have changed. I have a new l..e and it is only coming home to me now after all my denials, flirtatious games and sophistry, now that we have to part; this is our last day and the bell of St. Nicholas has just sounded its first quarter of an hour. I will come and listen to you, Nicholas, in a week's time, and see if I can hear the difference there will have to be! After all, I shall be poorer – and old maybe.

There was suddenly a familiar movement in the doorway. She had arrived from an unexpected direction. She rushed into the first room opposite and then the second, looked around, and I could tell from the nape of her neck how tense her face was. I came up behind her. "I'm here, Helena!" She spun round as if whipped and I saw the tension dissolve into unloosened sorrow, about which swam a reassuring smile and a greeting: "Hi, hello, been waiting long?" – "Well, since nine, but what's that compared with what it'll be like next week – and next year!"

I am tormenting her and will go on doing it. I gloat over the torments from the height of my sudden exhilaration that she has come! Her eyes do not see the joke, or they do not assent to it, and about her mouth there flickers a suffering whose expression has held me fascinated for four months now: it is like a delicate physical feat performed by someone who is not used to it and does not have the knack, so that there are no fine gestures and it comes to naught as a consequence, whereupon the performer becomes embarrassed and incapable of masking their embarrassment. There is something childish about it. For four months, as an observer, I have observed the process of her falling in love, and I am troubled by the beauty of it, as if I were under a mountain waterfall, which likewise would not be there solely for my benefit. But now I have found it I must accept and admire it and show it gratitude. I know that many another sceptic (I do not say *any* other sceptic) might have happened along this path, but that is the way it is: I am the one who is here and is involved, it is I who am aware of this feminine transformation, this "end of a gamine," I who must fear that it will cost her more than she thinks, and it is I who am actually scared of what I am doing.

I led her to the table. "It's all ready for me!" she laughed, seeing her glass. – "Had breakfast?" – "You know, I'm not sure," she looked at me with a strange, all-embracing, wide-angle gaze. This is going to be a phenomenal celebration! – "I have so much to tell you," I said. "I'll tell it to you bit by bit as the day proceeds." She started, then reached for her glass and raised it to me. "First of all, then," I said, "we won't mope, we'll make plans." – "I invite you for three years from next year," she said tersely. I was speechless.

"I meant plans for today," I said, shrinking back. She reached across the table and placed her hand on mine, saying: "I have to go home soon. You see... I made a mistake and told him I was going to see you." – "I'm glad you did..." – "So there was a scene and he told me not to think he'd walk the dog for me..." So it's the dog? The dog? – "I'll go there with you, you'll go in to get the dog, and then we'll take the dog with us everywhere, all right?" – "And at six... I just m-m-must be somewhere for dinner, at an aunt's. She's invited a dozen people along. And at mid-day," she hunched her back, "Ivana's expecting me, but she'll understand if I don't turn up. It's wicked and shameful the way I treat those girls, would you believe it?"

I'm an old fool and ought to be the first to see the funny side right away. But I too can show what I am capable of – for the first and last time. I had been under the impression that our plans were the same: to spend the whole day together, to cram many things into this day – talking, walks, visits, an exhibition, food; I would be very wary of lying down; to lie down together for the last time: a funeral! I began: "So this is our day, the one we have managed to salvage from the several we had originally planned? You don't seem to realise that I too could resort to violence, seeing how effectively it works on you! I don't have to let you go, you know, I could kidnap you. Am I the one who started all this? How dare you. I knew back in March when you said you were leaving that it wasn't worth walking to the end of that line of trees with you! You're a stuck-up kid. What sort of rubbish is that – invite me for three years? You know very well they'll never let me go anywhere! And I know, even if you don't, that we're parting and I said to you, remember, You mean you want us to say goodbye in a café? What did you go and do with that key that time and what are you to me? As you like. Why don't you go straight home, then? Go away! Clear off!"

Her face tautened into a terrifyingly controlled mask and tears welled up in her motionless eyes. "Helena," I said softly, "you know very well it'll be the way you want it. I won't make things difficult for you anymore, and I'm sorry for the way it's gone so far. I'll take you home as soon as you need to go, but the thing is you'll never even find out now how important today was for me. And the two miserable little hours that you have finally managed to steal for us are fit only for some... Okay, fine, but Helena, it'll be terribly sad! That's not what I wanted at all!" She does not realise that I shall never see her again and there will be nothing more. We each know something different, our minutes are of a different length and we each perceive the present in a different way.

"Have you had breakfast?" I said.

After breakfast it was already sunny outside. We walked to Charles Bridge and under the bridge-tower Helena suggested we go up it. I had never been up before. We wandered around the gallery and looked out in all directions, our feet slipping slightly on the rain-moistened pigeon-droppings. I started to take my shots of G-Day. But it did not feel like a last goodbye, more like an introductory journey above the lanes and roofs, in the sultry atmosphere above the Vltava, into which the sun trickled in celestial rays. The bridge below was inhabited by crowds – they almost seemed to be camping out. I felt like a visitor. Life is short: not long ago I used to cross it daily on my way to lectures at Lobkowitz Palace. There were tram-tracks across the bridge in those days.

We climbed down. I cannot recall what was going through my mind. Nothing. It was like when there are too many choices and I don't know which to take, so I end up taking nothing. What will I do with Helena if she leaves tomorrow? Am I to fall asleep? Forget her straight away or wait? I feel slighted – horribly! It's then I will forget and become an incorrigibly good husband. It's the end. We took photographs of each other with Hradčany in the background. I paid no attention to possible passers-by. We stopped at the statue of St. Christopher with the child on his shoulder. This is where we tossed a stone in the water last spring so that Helena should still have a baby during her lifetime, with anyone – whoever would oblige! We looked at the spot where the stone must have fallen. In all events it won't be mine any more.

I will disappear and she'll never hear from me again. That will be the best thing. I won't write to her at all! All at once I recalled the dialogue of the dying couple in Gruša's novel Mimner. "It's come, adimai. – It's come, kasimai." – Idiot. I once said a few words to him about Helena, and he, totally unsuspecting, commented appreciatively on that occasion: "Mm, I wouldn't mind having a go with her!" – Idiot.

On Karlova Street we drank – what was it? Probably wine or coffee. During the summer I had come up with an idea that she rejected: that I should buy her some clothes as a souvenir – nobody would be the wiser. She would wear them *ad nauseam* or until they fell apart. That would be the right pace and time span for forgetting. "You'll put them aside with the thought – My

335

goodness! And you'll shake your head in disbelief." She said angrily: "No! No!" So what does she think, poor thing? That's what she'll do with me in the end anyway. Vienna is full of clothes like that! I am the only one who can't – I'm incapable of abandoning anything once it's mine. So I end up with nothing but cherished fluff in my claws.

The gallery on Husova Street was closed. And I was in no mood to go any further, and I have a feeling I started a minor tiff, but I can't recall what about, but it's obvious we are not going to have time for anything now, apart from lunch! I had thought it would be right for her to say goodbye to the Chramostovás, I wanted to walk along Wenceslas Square with her, and be seen – be seen, damn it! What's the matter with me?

Yet another of my scenes over lunch in the Convent Tavern, but this time for real. It escaped from me against my will. Never in my life have I had such a deafening question mark in my head about what I would say or do the next moment. It started with the words: "Well, now that lunch is over, it's about time you were going." She said nothing, like a hardened criminal, thereby admitting she was on her way. All of a sudden my surroundings were lost to my gaze. I stared at her as I strove to lay bare my idiotic infatuation with a lovely woman. What is the truth of the matter? I asked in rigorous, scholarly fashion. You are an idiotic old man, I replied learnedly. A lovely woman (one of her exes actually called her Her Loveliness!) wanted to have another fling before leaving and you are simply a notorious clinical case. No one could help loving her. Calm down. As for her fate and career, she is not going to come to any harm, she will allow herself to be taken in hand again in her delightful way...

She gazed at me coldly for a moment and then said: "You've just been making up something vile about me. And I have no way of changing this day for another, even if I wanted to." Which means she did not really want to when she could have. I was seized with an unprecedented attack: an attack of furious immobility and silence. With those words she said it all – that she was not in such a bad way as she had made out now, nor had she been before. She's not even crying! What's worrying her now is that I'll mess up her farewell. After all, she'd intended to take her leave "as nicely as possible." And my mental checks have all broken down and, just like grain trickling out of a hole in a sack, my spiritual innards were oozing out on to the table-cloth in front of me. What would I be willing to sacrifice and what would I destroy in order to stay with her, here or there – all the betrayals necessary to such an end, all the shame and guilt that would result – what would happen if this moment of weakness should happen more often, if she were to sense it, and if she were gracious enough to spend another loving week with me? Or if someone else, diabolically unloving, were to discover me in this state of weakness! – But there's no longer any time for that to happen, she's leaving tomorrow. The enemy is surrendering by mistake, unaware that my ammunition is totally spent. Goodbye then!

The inwardly raging fit of immobility gradually passed, to be succeeded by a lassitude so debilitating that I almost fainted. And at that moment her expression changed. As if we lived together, she said with a mixture of astonishment, concern and tenderness: "Come on, what's up?" I could feel her compassion and that was enough for me to snap out of it. I reached in my pocket and said: "Here's that song I wrote for you." You see, I wrote her a song to the tune of "Mournful Sunday." I do not feel like including it here; I am no poet. It is vindictive and I wrote it to fit her. I had already sung it to her once before, the day before yesterday. She bawled during it.

> …Run home to your hubby
> Since you love him so much
> you've bought your Sunday
> And my bargain's Dutch
> I uncork the bubbly and then close my eyes
> I'm straight away back again deep la la la
> For it's Monday ma belle
> And you've gone to – (Vienna!)

"It'll be better to have our coffee in the Slávia," I said. She got up briskly, and left, walking ahead of me through the aisle between the tables. At the mirror in the passage she raised her arms to her head, I could see her from behind; the coast's clear, she turned to me in collusion. I walked at her side enjoying extensive powers. We came out into the street; just across the tracks and we're on the opposite pavement; at her flank in its loose skirt of coarse blue material, the teeny toes (and teeny breasts!), the fine silver chain wound three times round her left wrist. I remembered giving blood one time; I was light-hearted after what I lost, the way I am now after that fit. With other

337

women, whenever I was out, I was always afraid of someone seeing us and passing judgement. In other words, I'm getting old and silly, or something. Gimme a kiss.

We sat by a window overlooking the embankment. Kolář's table empty. Don't scoff now, Kolář, it's what you wanted! I'm writing it all down. "First and foremost," I started according to the plan that had already been well unhinged since that morning – angular Trinkewitz dashed back and forth through the café – "since you're going there because you can't work here you have to be successful and make something of yourself. Secondly, when you don't feel in the best form don't exert yourself. It's probably silly my telling you this..." – "I want to hear it! I need it! Tell me!" – " ...the way you rush about here, out of breath, you know, the way you'd always arrive to meet me all breathless, well don't do that there, for instance. Nothing, or no one, is worth it." – "Rest assured, there'll be no reason to there." – "We're not doing badly, are we? Next I've made the decision on several occasions to itemise what I like about you. I'll omit that. You have to walk the dog. But I've just decided to tell you the positive role you play – have played – in my life. There are five headings."

Out on the pavement I had to take out the umbrella again. She clung to my arm. We had shoved all her things into my bag and were waiting for the number twenty-two tram. In the tramcar I had to pull out her handbag, she needed a ticket. She held out the block of them tellingly – she had only three Prague tramway tickets left! The windows were dirty on the outside and misted up inside. We got off at the Malá Strana Café, where she said: "Hey, Ludvík, we've already been here, haven't we?" – "And fifthly," I continued, so that the fragmented speech and the matter should finally be linked, "in the winter my state of mind and spirit of enterprise were at their lowest ebb. I could see no purpose in anything."

Up at the panorama wall we stopped and turned towards the city – Nicholas struck half past five! – and looked out from beneath the umbrella. I tried to empathise with her last impressions at this spot. She said: "We've just the right weather for it." – "The weather's on our side," I agreed. – "A lovely day," she said, admiring the drizzle. – "I'm really pleased with our parting, Helena, it lacks nothing." We crossed the square, rang the doorbell at Karel Kosík's, but he wasn't home. Either that or his philosophising brooked no delay. We went down into the bar in the same building. "What'll we have?" Helena asked and immediately answered: "I don't think we'll start with anything new, but just carry on." She ordered a Becherovka. She paid for everything that day, enjoying the full value of her crowns. – "Had dinner?" I asked, repeating the refrain. – "I won't. I can't. Do you want a cigarette from the last packet? Because I promise you I won't be smoking there." – "Why?" – "I just want you to let me promise you something, I need you to. Go on, make me promise something – if you can think of anything." I tried to think of a promise that would not depress her too much if she broke it. Darling girl, do you realise what you're saying? No, I couldn't, it would be too cruel.

I said: "Be a good girl and sort things out with your husband... wait, listen. The fact is you can't do without a man, and if you were to find another one he'd erase me from your heart and I'd be finished." She rummaged in her handbag. – "Look at this beautiful letter they sent me yesterday. They don't know I'm leaving, they could have saved their energy." – She handed me an official notification telling her she had been expelled from the artists' union, thereby losing her qualification and insurance. "I'm glad they sent me it. I'll carry it around with me always, in case I ever have any doubts." It struck me I was holding an evil charm that lets us forget everything we once loved. "I don't want to see Prague again!" she blurted out. "I don't want to see it... for eight years!"

We ordered wine, Helena is going to be drunk. It's awful, and she'll drink there as well, and when she gets drunk... I started to get a headache. "Dinner's waiting for you, Helena, I hate to tell you." – "It's kind of you, Ludvík! Ludvík – Ludvík! Make me promise you something, please! Please want me to!" I hovered between pity and anger. I said: "Okay. Live the way you choose! Because I... can't ask anything of you. Or everything would have to be different. So live the way you choose, but for safety's sake" (i.e. so that I would not go on waiting for her like an idiot) "and out of friendship, let's say, write and let me know the moment you fall in love with someone."

She looked at me with a mixture of sympathy and derision, as if unable to credit what I was saying. Her blue eyes offered a view straight into her soul and her womb; I started to be afraid of the responsibility and the thought struck me that her eyes might be trying to tell me what her lips could not. "But you don't understand me at all," she said. "I was under an awful misapprehension – I thought you wanted me."

339

"Go and phone there, at least, to let them know you're on your way," I scolded her. She happily grasped the opportunity, but the phone box had been blocked by a dud coin.

"Sorry, Helena, just one more thing, the last one. We've spoken about it before, but some time has passed since then, and you've evolved, Helena. It's about the grave. I'm sure I don't have to explain to you, an architect, someone creating new life-styles, that cremation is an assault on European culture. It's part of a plan to reduce people to garbage both in life and death. Without a grave that you can think of as waiting for you, you'll never properly understand pictures or music. Without a grave we wouldn't have had Erben's "Wedding Shirts"! Don't you find it odd that governments support cremation? Take a look at the kind of people who spend their year transplanting flowers on graves and then at the kind who place wreaths once a year at anonymous monuments! There's a hell of a difference between those faces! Or compare the faces of people who put their parents in old-people's homes and those who care for them at home! You took care of your father right to the end and now you'd let yourself be vaporised? I just don't want it! If you're interested in what I think then I quite simply forbid you to! It is incongruous and a sin! You wanted to promise me something. Well that's what I want you to promise."

She answered: "You make a good case, but I'd have to make up my own mind. But I won't smoke!"

I went to pieces, each of which tumbled over to her. It was an overpowering weakness. I abandoned my stiff, unbending defiance. "Okay, I agree. Don't smoke. You're really prepared to place a solemn seal on something so silly? Okay, fine. But when I get a letter saying 'I'm smoking' I'll read more into it. It will relate to something that concerns me rather more – it will betoken a far more important lapse, Helena!" She gazed at me with emotion and then we shook on it.

An hour passed. She declared: "Once I'm there, maybe I'll find the words I'm wanting to say to you now but just can't." – I declared: "Forgive me this morning's scene, Helena!" – "Why? It was beautiful! I want to keep it!" – "But I was even unbearable at lunch-time, Helena," I pointed out. She said: "I think something slightly unpleasant had to happen if we were to go through with something like parting at all."

I said: "But seriously, now, you really are going?" She laughed, bowed her head over the table and put her hand over her eyes. "What time is your flight?" I asked. – "At a quarter to six." – "All right, at that time I'll be waiting for you in the wine bar where we first sat, when you told me about your family." – "I beg your pardon? Tomorrow?" she asked. – "Yes. Tomorrow you'll make your final decision," I said and ice-cold fingers ran down my spine. – "Ludvík, the matter has decided itself. You invited me," she suddenly said in a voice I did not know, "for three days. I'm inviting you for three years." – "That's what you say, and you know I'm not allowed anywhere. You can be bold because you know there is no risk of my coming." – "Ask for a passport. Give it a try," she said. – "I'll be waiting for you tomorrow at that place," I replied.

The next day, as you know, I was sitting in that wine bar. I expect it's ludicrous, but I thought it possible she might come. That would have decided the matter. But, as you know, she didn't come, and I was forced to admit humbly that I'm no judge of women... or men either.

We walked out into a damp darkness dried slightly by a warm wind; we might have a fine autumn. The public telephone on the square had had its receiver torn off, and the next two telephone booths we passed on the way to Helena's dinner party were not working. People were destroying public phones as retaliation for increased call charges. We walked across Charles Bridge once more, alone and at a very slow pace. "I'm aware," she suddenly said in even tones, "that this is the wickedest thing I've done in my life. Forgive me." – I said: "You once said that if you changed your mind and didn't leave, I was not to take it personally, that I would be under no obligation. So now I'm telling you, should you want to return because it's no good there, leave me out of your considerations and come back. That's the most we can do for each other."

The night was warm and balmy, the weir murmured, and beneath the street lamp the *sophora japonica* was showing its final flowers. A narrow lane, in which all the windows were unlit, led us, ineluctably now, to a house in total darkness apart from some first-floor windows, in one of which an elaborate chandelier was visible from below. The shadows of the guests who had come to the farewell party swayed agitatedly about the walls. One could also make out the top of a door that opened and closed from time to time. We stopped thirty metres away and from the empty street observed that powerful and imperturbable leave-taking mechanism. A distant clock chimed ten. Helena was small and feeble. It was a terrible thing that still remained for me to do. "Off you go then," I said, laying my hand on her waist and pushing her away from me. Why am I doing it? What kind of command is it? I stepped back a few metres, the better to see the door of the room opening again. Mutely, the shadows played on the wall.

I am not even sure why I don't believe I'll ever see Helena again.

Nevertheless I sit here at the table, looking out the window at the tram stop, and reject everything that alights. Nicholas has struck ten and his voice is the same as a week ago, even though everything is different. I drink up the opposite glass and leave.

SATURDAY, 1ST SEPTEMBER 1979

I took the typewriter out to the white table under the apricot tree, the first time I have had both machine and garden together. I fed in a sheet of paper and wrote today's date. Madla came to me, quiet in bare feet, and said: "Write, Dearest mine, sweetheart... it is to the sweetheart, isn't it?" – "Who do you mean?" I asked, just to be on the safe side. – "Helena, of course. You are writing a letter, aren't you?" – "No. I'm writing my book and you've spoilt my beginning."

So three hours have now elapsed since the lines above. In the meantime I have picked the apples on the Croncels tree, cut the grass with the lawnmower, watered the rhododendrons for the last time before winter, and I don't know what else. Writing in the garden is out of the question. The weather is glorious, the temperature 24 in the shade, the sky grey-blue, and calm. Not a leaf stirs on the trees, not a bird chirps. The layer of warm water in the ponds will last for a day or two more; then the water will forget about summer and us, and in the mountains the glacier will start to grow. The streets will be invaded by slush and I will have no reason to go outside.

But it was a long summer! Or rather – we were given a long summer this year!

Madla is cleaning up the strawberry bed. Until this moment she has been reading Kundera and taking him to task. "He couldn't even encounter a decent woman! He's so conceited, so complacent!" Against her notorious vice of confusing a novel's hero with its author, I defended the author in these words: "That's unfair of you. Trust for trust. He trusted you with something from within himself, something he wanted to come to terms with by writing about it, and you go and identify him totally with it. He's describing a coward, so what's he supposed to say about him?" – "Where does he find out so precisely what goes on in a coward?" She leafed through the book *Life Is Elsewhere* until she found the passage about each person choosing a death to his or her own measure: Hus let himself be burnt, seduced farm wenches end up drowned in the duck pond, Jan Masaryk ended his life by falling from a window... "What a bastard! That's really dirty!" Could it really be, heaven forbid, that Kundera accepts the official version of Jan Masaryk's death? I take the book from her hands and show her textually that it does not say he jumped, only that he ended his life by falling from a window. In that case, she asks, why is it included among reflections on voluntary death? Hus, Giordano Bruno, Palach... On account of a book which I myself have no desire to read after what I have heard about it, I nonetheless defend the principles of writing. "I would ban you all from writing and the only book I'd keep would be the Bible," says Madame Khomeini, taking the hoe and departing, leaving me sitting here at the typewriter. That's some judgement day a-coming! It might not be a bad idea to condemn myself beforehand.

Helena phoned me yesterday morning: It's terrible for her, particularly at night. But she's beginning to do some work. And she's spoken to Olda Unger! She can't write to me; she is tailed everywhere. She hasn't received my letter yet. She says she'll soon be seeing Pavel and Jelena. She hopes I have no mishap to report.

Then I went as agreed for my scheduled talk, which was certainly about something quite different, but as yet unknown. "We agreed, Mr. Vaculík, that you would give no more interviews and we would leave you alone..." Naturally we had agreed on nothing and naturally I had given no interview. I have no idea what he is talking about, and I do not ask. "There you are," he went on, "you were wrong again! Your son was accepted for university." – I said: "I'm pleased." – He leafed through some of his papers and then said: "What foreign contacts have you had?" I turned over in my mind what he was getting at: Isabelle? Or had he already heard about that nice chap from Bergen? Or is it about my letter to Helena... no, no, they will be careful to let that run its course and just keep fanning it gently lest it go out, so that in the end something fantastic should grow from it – for them! I'm waiting, I really am, gentlemen, believe me, in sincere suspense, for you to raise the issue.

"The foreign contacts I have, I have," I said. "If you really think, now you've let my child into university, that I'll be coming to report to you every month, then you're mistaken. You've accepted him for university – and you're the ones who benefit most. As far as I'm concerned it's one grievance less, but otherwise my attitude to everything remains unchanged..." I don't feel like writing anything else about it.

On the way home, I bought a chicken; I roasted it, then did a bit of writing before going off to a date with Professor Rafto, which we had agreed on that morning when he inaugurated, in our kitchen, a telephone information service about his Prague activities. He was waiting for me in a sun-drenched street in front of the Hotel Amethyst. He waved to me from afar with both arms, calling out how kind I was: "Nice of you, Ludvík!" he said in English. He was without shirt or vest and his pale northern chest was savouring our southern sun. He hugged me with the words: "What a lovely day. Let us have a drink." He led me into the hotel lobby where he greeted the staff right and left, and they returned him genuine smiles. "Marvellous people here. And none of them agrees with the way things are! They're all clearly expecting changes!" he rejoiced when we sat down in the dining room. A helpful and truly very pleasant young waiter arrived and asked us: "What would you like?" Professor Rafto said: "Ludvík, what wine will you have?" Well, in that case, I would like a dry Martini. "Martini secco, signor!" he translated for the waiter, "parlate italiano?" He himself ordered a fruit juice – "a big one!" he stressed, holding one hand high above the other. Then we had an omelette, followed by coffee and cake, and the – surprisingly precise – bill: 52.50 crowns. Professor Rafto of Bergen studied it cheerfully and loudly expressed his satisfaction, before setting out on the tray fifty-two fifty and waving sincerely with both hands at the departing waiter. "What a decent man, really," he continued to say in appreciation, even though he was already out of earshot.

We then got down to business. "Ludvík, tell me, what help can we give to you." I said the first thing that came into mind: "First, take better care of yourselves." He grew earnest. Yes, it could be serious; nevertheless what could Norwegian intellectuals do for our country.

I was almost stupefied to discover how, over the past years, I had lost all idea of what we can reasonably expect from abroad. I felt like a passenger who had fallen asleep on the train, and now people were shaking him and asking him where he was going. I did not understand. I had no idea, and I described it in detail to our excellent friend, Professor Rafto of Bergen.

MONDAY, 3ᴿᴰ SEPTEMBER 1979

I said to Jan this morning: "If Vienna calls, I'll make an exception and use the telephone." – He expressed surprise: "Professor Rafto has arrived there already?" – "Not Rafto, for goodness sake – Helena!" We were sitting drinking tea, with the birds flying about over our heads. When the phone rang, Jan got up and went out.

"How are you?" I asked. – "I think it's beginning to sink in now. The thing is, it's very deceptive, everything looks almost the same here. I'm able to phone you..." – "What were you doing Sunday?" – She has been commissioned to furnish a small shop for someone. She hasn't a permanent address yet. She hasn't received my letter and she hasn't written one herself as she hasn't the time, the space or the freedom. I asked her: "How are you physically?"

When she rang off, I reflected on how I would go about it if someone were to get me to furnish their shop. I would go and have a look at a couple of similar shops, to get some idea what was conventional and standard, and then do it in such a way that the client was satisfied that he had obtained something that was usual for that particular type, plus a little extra. I imagined, for some unknown reason, that it was a milliner's or a draper's. At that moment she rang once more: "Sorry, it's me again. It strikes me there was something wrong with our conversation, and I'd like the day to have a better start." – "It already has, now that you've called again," I said with great pleasure. "Tell me, what kind of shop is it you're furnishing?" – "It's a sort of haberdashery." – "I see. And are you reading anything?" – "Our things haven't arrived yet." – "If you think of any little thing you might already need from here, tell me and I'll send it." – "No, nothing but one big thing."

It's nonsense somehow. A momentous thing like that has happened and here we are exchanging small-talk. The whole pathos of our misfortune is being spoilt and the misfortune itself will start to pale. "Everything looks almost the same there," she's able to telephone me. She'll get over it like a minor illness. It's hopeless! I went to get on with some writing. Outside the roofs were damp; it crossed my mind to water the plants. In the afternoon I went into town. I opened the mailbox, aware that the letter I was waiting for was not even written yet. There was some news from Milan Uhde in Brno that Jan Trefulka had suffered a second mild heart-attack. That's another alternative to everything. I am amazed I'm still as fit as a fool. We'll see, though!

It was warm, the sky was grey and there was an occasional warm, clean shower. The streets are full of traffic again. It's September and the trams are packed. I wondered whether to go for the remaining books at the binders, but there are too many of them, I would have to take them straight home, and I don't fancy going there. What about that telephone? I got off the tram on the other side of Šverma Bridge, and stood for a moment in front of the airline offices, looking through the glass at the people inside buying tickets to somewhere. I could not think of anywhere, except Brno, maybe, to see Trefulka. I walked on, looking at everyday things in the shop windows. There was nothing unfamiliar or interesting. I have no date. Zdena is out of Prague. Apparently they have founded an opposition party in Poland. If it happened here I would not want to join anything. I do not feel up to a *coup d'etat* at the present moment; try me some other time. The telephone is a marvellously human institution, of course, but I can sense its insidiousness already – you call them up and you say something. The best or hardest things you cannot say anyway. The ardour of one's memory is dulled, unattainability remains. It is an aid to breaking a habit, I can already see that; I shall not be telephoning. I walked on further, and just past the travel agency something struck me and I went back to buy a week's holiday for two in the Bohemian Forest for twelve hundred crowns. The transaction took ten minutes, as easy as a trip from Austria to Germany, from there to Belgium and through France to Spain. It required nothing but a decision. I walked on, and as I went I read, aghast, all the details on the voucher for a week's holiday for two in the Bohemian Forest.

I could think of nothing else of importance for me to sort out. All I vitally need are sulphur candles for the cellar. Alternatively, I could go to the Rudolfinum and buy tickets for some subscription concerts of chamber music for the winter season. I did that. Going down Celetná Street I called in at Kléma Lukeš's, but he was not yet back in Prague from his country seat. The hunting suppliers were closed for inventory. I could nonchalantly pass by the shop that sells drawing requisites: Helena has promised to send me a metal ruler for cutting paper, which they never have in stock. I ambled, more like swimming than walking, across the Old Town Square, which was not white with summer's glare, but grey. I looked about me; no one heeded me and no one was there for me. I looked at the houses and the people, I was neither thirsty nor hungry. Charles Bridge was like a warm enclosure once more; the river, crossed through diagonally by the weir, was redolent of water; water radiated from the warm clouds that crammed the sky, but there was safety beneath them, the clouds hung firmly in thermal and static equilibrium, women were walking about in blouses with their breasts visible, men with their cameras uncovered, only the road-side artist was packing up his wares in panic. I gazed at the bridge-tower with its arrow-slits; there was no one there any more. At the request of Mrs. P., I am deleting in March 1980 a sentence saying how a corner window of the house beyond the bridge was open and the curtains drawn aside: an empty black rectangle. Then comes the florist, the record shop, the perfumery, the little shop with etchings, the handmade bread shop whose fragrance spills out into the street, the delicatessen with Tokay and champagne, and the square. More a hall than a square.

Via Sněmovní and Thunovská streets I climbed the steps to the Castle and sat down on a wall with my back to the city, looking at the windows of Pavel's apartment and failing to comprehend in retrospect why I had not gone there more often when they invited me. The first yellow trees on Petřín Hill reminded me of a business-meeting that some friends and I held under a pear-tree there, eating pears. Solar searchlights played on Prague, lighting up the gold on the steeple-tops. A glorious day, with the weather on my side, like last time.

I walked across the square and Karel Kosík nimbly opened the door to me. He immediately started to lure me upstairs, where he said he had three Mexicans. I resisted, but in the end went up. The Mexicans, including a woman of Indian origin, had come to get Karel to write them a preface to some book of philosophy. I made fun of them for thinking they would get anything from him and Karel actually agreed with me. One of the guests spoke excellent Czech: he has a Czech wife and studied in Prague. I took the opportunity to ask the woman of Indian origin about my old friends, the Indians of the Yaqui tribe. – Say the word Mexico and people automatically think of the Aztecs, but they never interested me because they had institutions and titles more or less the same as we Wallachians; I found that boring and never wanted anything to do with the Aztecs. But I really enjoyed being chief of a Yaqui tribe, living wild in the mountains above the Pacific Coast. What had become of them?

"The Yaquis?" the Indian woman brightened up. "They still live in the mountains far from civilisation and the central state authorities. They do not even understand Spanish and have refused to accept the white man's institutions. They have their own laws, which are very democratic in many respects. They refuse to cooperate and there are a lot of problems with them."

I said I was glad to hear it and soon left.

TUESDAY, 4ᵀᴴ SEPTEMBER 1979

In the morning I always read through what I wrote the night before. That way I find out if it's any good. But I never change much; I would be effacing the fluctuations of mood, energy, rhythm and truth. Jan came in and said: "Breakfast is served." We had breakfast and looked at the birds. Catherine has taken a bath and made her feathers so wet she is unable to take off and just runs around on the floor like a mouse. Philip is airing himself after his bath and drying in a ray of sunshine on the roof of the cage. Jan has a couple of days off before he departs for the introductory course for first-year students. He is taking his leave of his workmates and he would like to take them a box of apples from our garden. He enjoys the alacrity with which his comrades always grab the fruit. The Croncels took over without a break from where the translucent summer apples left off.

The telephone rings once and if it gives a long ring in a moment, then it will be Helena. "Hello, how are you?" she said. Jan moved away. "Fine, but suddenly much better," I replied. – "I'll be brief this time. Your letter has materialised and I have to collect it." – "How are you?" – "Yesterday we went to the theatre to see Pavel's play. Then we sat somewhere till quite late, so I'm a bit groggy." – "Tell me, you had a smoke, didn't you." – "Yes." I had a senseless rush of blood to the head. But why? What did you expect, lad? After all, you knew she would, so why the panic? But I could not help lamenting. Didn't I say so? Jesus Christ! "Are you there?" I asked, forcing myself to speak. – "Yes... sorry, but that made me go hot all over." – "Me too, Helena. But why?" – "Because of the awful misunderstanding, of course. Because such a misunderstanding can arise like that. What I told you meant just that

Eda surprised us with the news that things are even worse in Turkey than here. (p. 352)

and nothing else." – "Yes, Helena, I believe you. I just panicked out of fear, that's all. So let's start again, shall we?" – "Okay, fine. Ludvík–Ludvík... I'm sorry, someone's coming." – "Just one word, how was Pavel yesterday?" – "Very good – sorry..."

I wrote to the Brnonians letting them know there was no news here, then a letter of condolences to Stanislav Budín's family. I made up a few parcels and sent them off, exaggerating their value on the dispatch slip. I cleared up some money matters, bought some flowers for the evening, and prepared some fresh developer and fixer; we are going to Tasov with the Kosíks on Saturday in search of Deml, and I have not even done the photos from the Kraslice trip yet. I am fine and feeling lousy. I did not expect to. In such a mood I managed this morning to complete an article that I had got nowhere with during the previous two months. I expect it needed that outsized longing to knock some sense into my stupidity. I am also thinking about Trefulka, whose mind must be on death and writing.

If only I was able to identify and describe what it is that enables Moravian-Slovak folk songs to have words and tunes for every occasion! Most strangely of all, now that realities like green grass, scythes, water, juniper-bushes, and pathways are becoming extinct, the more poetic and even magic is the significance they acquire in the songs. The songs become deeper and deeper and also more exclusive, so that one day they could turn into church hymns, meaningless to the mob. I sit and marvel and now and then I have to slam the book shut or I would go mad. I sometimes get the urge to sing to someone; there is a bit of the performer in me, but it is a very delicate matter. It is something one can do only occasionally and then only among equals. Once I used to sing wholeheartedly with Jan Trefulka and Milan Uhde, and on other occasions, more frequently, with Laďa Vaculka, who died. I think I could make a good singer: "Oh my wee thoughts, where are you wending?" There was a time when Madla and I used to sing together. A lot. We still do, two or three times a year.

This evening I took the bunch of flowers and went off to Eda Kriseová's, as she had left me an invitation in the mailbox. I thought she was celebrating something, like a birthday, or that some book of hers had finally come out abroad. But it was just that she had returned from a holiday in Turkey where she has a doctor friend, a Turkish woman, I understood. It will probably be Eda's last trip; as soon as her book comes out in Germany, she will not

Jiří takes every opportunity to wave his brocade Catholic banner with the tassels, preferably embroidered... (p. 352)

be allowed to go anywhere. Jiří Gruša was there, along with Ivan Klíma. Saša Kliment is not in Prague. Eda surprised us with the news that things are even worse in Turkey than here. Whether she meant in economic terms, I can't say, I wasn't paying attention at that moment. She praised Islam as a nice religion, and that enraged Jiří: "Islam – but that's the Marxism of the sixth century!" I don't care one way or the other. Jiří takes every opportunity to wave his brocade Catholic banner with the tassels, preferably embroidered with the Virgin Mary, or if a male motif is required, with St. Wenceslas. Catholicism, he maintains, did the best job of building woman into its dogma. It is thanks to woman, he says, that in Catholicism the gradation of sins is worked out in such detail, so that the delight of the sin is followed by the bliss of repentance and the satisfaction of total absolution. The Devil is terrifying, but you just need to pay him a bit of attention and you'll get along all right with him. God is open and accessible. Catholicism made Europe what it was at the time of its glory. "But now they say," said Eda, "or so I heard, that there is one God for all religions and that Mohammed is one of his prophets." – "So Mohammed is a prophet, is he?" Jiří roared. And he said what Mohammed was as far as he was concerned, but I cannot exactly recall what now. I am trying to think what he might have had to say about him, and I am pretty certain that he might say about him that he arrived in Arabia in a sealed camel. Ivan declared that the Koran was a mess of a book. "Just look at the way they mucked up the Joseph story!" I have a Koran somewhere, but I can't find it. Eda's outfit suited her.

I enjoy seeing how self-confident Jiří has become in company since *The Questionnaire* came out and he completed his first course in Czechoslovak penology. To someone meeting him for the first time he might even appear pompous, but it is simply a game put on for show, a bit of verve necessary if he is to write. He related to us the adventures of the hero of his latest book, a certain Dr. Kokeš, and we all had a good laugh. Ivan badgered me to know what my problem was; I had immediately struck him as out of sorts and sad, and I marvelled how one's stuffing can really protrude as if from a rip in a teddy-bear. I just sat and observed them. It is all boyish merriment, a bit like it was with us boarders at Baťas' in Zlín. Ivan is writing something and he is pleased with it, but he is always pleased with what he happens to be writing. He talked about Saša, how he had first met him and how on long walks Saša would always describe in such delightful detail the plots he devised, and this

...Saša would always describe in such delightful detail the plots he devised, and this had always disconcerted him. (p. 352)

had always disconcerted him. "But then he always went and wrote something completely different," Ivan said. I said: "That would make a good sentence for his dying words: 'I wrote something completely different.'" Everyone laughed, except for Saša, who is out of Prague, and Jiří squirmed with pleasure at the thought of what else would happen to his Dr. Kokeš. Eda's two little girls came to say goodnight to us. From time to time Ivan would get up and walk around the room rubbing his hands like a little Jewish trader. He took a drink of tea to wash down some Aristochol that he held up suggestively and shook before my eyes. I nodded in collusion. He was trying to provoke me into telling him something about what I am writing. Young Jiří gave a knowing wave of the hand and winked at me, as if he knew but would not give me away. Eda laughed right out loud because she realised that Jiří did not know anything, whereas she knows something because I had told her certain things that evening on the steps of St. Nicholas. Ivan figured out what all the mimicry was in aid of and laughed at himself in a satisfied way: "She didn't give anything away to me, but it must be said that I didn't press her."

I can say that I write what I feel like. Now as ever. But I am very sleepy as I write this account of the evening and exhausted to the point of euphoria. I don't know whether it will survive the light of day tomorrow. So long.

THURSDAY, 6ᵀᴴ SEPTEMBER 1979

I entered the house and rang the doorbell. Mrs. Bookbinder was ready and waiting and I led her to the car. "Tell me where to," I said. – "Take the Jilové road," she said. When we had extricated ourselves from the city, she asked with relief: "May I smoke?" Then, holding the cigarette in front of her mouth for rest of the journey, she said, "I'd never have thought you'd remember that – autumn crocuses!" – "I have to, once I've said it. Anyway, it suits me." – "Eh?" she asked. – "It suits the situation and mood I'm in," I replied. A lengthy silence and then she said: "Great."

We walked through a pine forest in which an old-established colony of wooden cabins was concealed. Some of the buildings were built in bizarre shapes inspired by the Wild West of pre-war days. Now, at the end of summer, all the cabins, fences, sheds and privies were freshly painted or stained, the shutters padlocked and each water barrel chained to a pine tree. The dry forest crackled all around us.

She was wearing black trousers, tough boots, and a light green blouse over her hips, and her dark hair was held together at the back by a wide clasp of the same green. At last she stopped at a structure wildly overgrown with brambles. The rotten gatepost was attached by wire to the trunk of a birch. The fence was lost in nettles. The wooden steps up to the veranda were broken. Doors and windows nailed up, making it uninhabitable. She took out a cigarette and lit it. She stood there staring impassively. I moved away. She took a few steps, looked behind the cabin, stood for a moment and then came over to me. "When were you here last?" I asked. She stared at the ground as she worked it out: "The girl is fourteen... twelve years ago." I waited, not wanting to be the one to determine when we should leave the spot. She pointed uphill with her chin and set off, with me a few steps behind. She stopped, unable to leave me without an explanation of what I had seen: "He went to court over that, so that he could let it rot."

She left the path and we made our way through bushes out onto a meadow. It sloped down towards where the sun hung fiercely in the west above the toothlike hills. "Would you wait for me?" she said. I sat down on a dry patch of turf pushed up by a pine root. Slowly she walked down the meadow until she disappeared behind a billow of grass.

I became aware of the wild song of thousands of grasshoppers and, among the branches above my head, a motionless cloud of mosquitoes, which suddenly moved a short distance and hung there stationary once more.

She returned half an hour later from somewhere higher up, skirting the forest. Her face was calm and motionless, different somehow from the one she had come with – she was triumphantly elated. Loosely in her palm she held a naked clump of pale mauve flowers. Supporting her hand against the green fabric below her breasts, she carefully separated a section and almost smilingly said: "I picked some for you too."

We drove back.

FRIDAY, 7ᵀᴴ SEPTEMBER 1979
Before I let the young woman take the stage, I have to make sure she really knows her recitation. In a small room at the back, amidst packing cases, packages and rolled carpets, I tell her to start, and listen to her with arms folded, leaning on the corner of a battered packing case. I do not know the

woman, or her poem. I cannot recognise the author and she did not announce his name. She recites in a monotone, and I am here to make sure she does so: no pathos or emotion, just calmly from start to finish. The young woman has precise articulation, but her lips move informally, as if chatting, not performing. She looks through me into the distance, her arms hanging freely; she wears a white blouse and a navy-blue skirt. All of a sudden something goes wrong: she grips the hem of her skirt with her dangling right hand and fiddles with it nervously. Then she starts to half-sing two verses in a strangled voice, so that the melody is almost indistinguishable:

> Bohemian speech, Bohemian song
> No more shall fill my soul...

Immediately she returns to the correct text and delivery, and at the back, behind the packing cases, I can hear muffled laughter from the hall as when a child whom everyone is wishing well makes a charming mistake. My attention is no longer on the reciter as I desperately try to remember where that couplet comes from. It eludes me, and then just as I am beginning to get a glimmer, I start to wake up. With surprise I realise I am in tears, albeit reciting, or rather saying, without pathos or emotion: Shine thou golden sun upon this last step from my land... I am awake, and cross.

This morning I was sitting writing; the (golden) sun was shining outside, and I was just savouring the peace and quiet when the doorbell had to ring – no news is good news, so I went to the door with trepidation. But it was Mirka Rektorisová, whom I almost hugged in apology, much to her amazement. She has spent the whole summer out of town, where she is always looking after some grandchildren or other. "Don't be alarmed," she said, "I've got some good news, we've got two new states – Kiribati and Redonda." I invited her in and offered her coffee and Gauloises: "They're from Isabelle for you." – "No, really? Well I'll be blessed!" she said in surprise. She immediately opened the packet, lit one and said: "So tell me, how's the grandchild?" – "There's none yet." – "So it was a false alarm." – "It was no false alarm, it didn't live to its birth." – "Tsk, poor thing! We'll just have to live in hope, then."

I put a sheet of paper on the table and we sorted out our business matters in writing. "I can't say I'm not looking forward to coming back to Prague," she said, so I didn't know whether she was or not. "On the other hand," she

"I've got some good news, we've got two new states –
Kiribati and Redonda." (p. 356)

went on, "I've had more than enough joys. The bigger of the two is Little Clarrie, a crafty little devil who's more often up a tree than anywhere else. I find it a bit too much to cope with now. I was used to having males around and there was no difficulty telling when they needed a good hiding. But with little girls what can you do? All of a sudden one starts bawling for some unknown reason. It was a long time before it came out that the other one had been given her tea in a bigger cup. And they can have as much tea as they like, mind you. Would you have thought of that?" – "What you're trying to tell me is that you did nothing the whole summer?" – "I was coming to that, but it looks as if you've guessed it yourself." – "Well, do you have to look after them all the time?" I asked. – "I could happily do without, but you try telling that to Little Miss Crafty, now that she's taken such a fancy to me! She says: I wanna be with granny, because she says 'shit and damn'! – Though I never say it in her hearing." – "Oh, she probably reads your thoughts," I said.

After Mirka left, I washed the mugs, cleaned the ashtray, and destroyed the paper we had used for our messages. I got dressed and went off to the Slávia. But I was too early, so I took a walk along Národní Avenue and back, looking at the people. On one side of the street the (golden) sun shone, the other was in the shade. I met no one. I do not know where I shall go from here; I feel at sea somewhat. I feel like making myself scarce. I am crossing the intersection, on my own, and have nowhere to deflect the rage that suddenly wells up within me; I confront myself alone once more. Everything has been and gone, there is nothing to come.

In the Slávia, Professor Černý was sitting by himself at the table. As I entered his better eye's field of vision, he raised his arm in greeting. "Good day, Professor," I said. – "What news do you have?" he asked. – "None. How about you?" – "Did you hear they've offered Václav Havel an exit visa to Broadway?" – "Who has?" – "'A representative of the foreign ministry', is the way I heard it." – "That means it was a representative of the interior ministry again, in disguise," I said. – "Quite so," Professor Černý agreed and went on: "But he refused it, apparently, until that trial has been settled and so long as the others are still in prison." – "That was a proper response," I said. I am sure Professor Černý smiled and said: "You didn't expect anything else, surely?" It was an uncommonly good assessment; in fact, it was the first time I had ever heard him say anything so unambiguously positive about anyone. When I told him Budín had died, he said: "Oh."

I asked: "Do you smoke Gauloises?" – "I should think so!" he replied and he stuck the packet I gave him in his pocket. I had another one for Hiršal, but he never came. Then Dr. Danisz arrived, still jobless, followed by Kabeš, Trinkewitz and Vohryzek the translator, who said: "I had a meeting with Professor Rafto at the Hotel Amethyst just after you. When I came out into the street a police car overtook me and checked my papers. How about you?" – "No, they know me from memory," I said. Apparently they then arrested Professor Rafto and escorted him to a northbound train. There ended his top-secret mission. He shouldn't have used the telephone. Where did he think he was?

Otherwise I have no idea why they were at the Slávia. Kolář supposedly wants to extend his stay in Berlin by six months. I gazed through the big windows at Hradčany across the river. I wanted neither to go home nor stay. As I was leaving, Professor Černý declared: "Go away then. You're no use to us here anyway. You look today," he said, fixing me with his better eye, "as if you've lost a pound and found a penny."

TUESDAY, 11ᵀᴴ SEPTEMBER 1979

I am picking apples: up, down, up, down… I sort them according to size and quality, although there is no reason to. The rotten ones I throw into a bucket, but I take a bite out of each one first, because the apple-tree is watching. The Croncel would seem to be at the height of its womanly fertility: such large and flawless fruit it has never borne. I could exhibit them. I have started to give the trees the most up-to-date treatment: none at all. No spraying, and throughout the year I tread on the leaf-roller moths that fly out languidly from under my feet when I am mowing in the morning. I cannot tell – and I always wonder – which I affect most: the males or the females. Minimal pruning: I have to find out at last what sort of figure the tree itself hankers after. I have not even used any manure this year. I am never going to do it scientifically, and seeing that I cannot tell what there is in the soil and how much remains there each year, let the trees use up the surplus, i.e. lick the bowl, or else let them go refreshingly hungry, for once. Besides, trees are also male, so let them exhaust all their seed and know the painful satisfaction of an emptied sac. And then sleep and sleep. And know nothing until definitively good news of spring returns.

The local radio is starting to play a tramping song, which I don't think I have heard in twenty years: Hey buddy, tell us what's wrong, and why we've not seen you so long... Madla is in the sun scrubbing the fruit boxes with a soda solution and putting them out on the grass to dry. There are lots of them – it is a job I would not like. And she is about to preserve some plums, another job I would not like. As a matter of fact, even this apple-picking is beginning to pall on me; there are too many apples. What would I really like to be doing at this moment? Sleeping and sleeping until definitively good news of spring returns. Today I dreamed I was playing at stalking with some unknown boys in rolling grassland. We were hurling stones at each other. Life is short. It no longer makes sense to change anything in what there is left of it, or to start anything new. Summer seems so very long to me this year! I wonder what the informed Pavel Kohout will tell me, and what I'll retort, when he comes back from Vienna – as he is expected to – at the end of the month? Ella Horáková sent me a card from that city with a single sentence: It's almost like Prague here. – Interesting. It's not almost like Vienna here.

Madla came once to ask me if I was sad, and once again to ask if I love her a bit. The answer to both questions is self-evident and genuine.

Whatever she does, she does properly and with enjoyment. Over the next two days the grass will be leached in the place where she is washing the boxes. The world is desperately trying to work out the significance of two thousand new Soviet troops in Cuba. The Americans regard it as a threat. I do not. The Russians say that there are not two thousand new troops – they were there already. The Americans are poring over bleached old photographs, wondering how it is they did not see them before. I think that the Russians could invade Romania, for instance, and recall those two thousand troops from Cuba. It would have a sure-fire effect – the Americans would stand back grinning with relief. Or something of the sort. I assess my physical condition according to how well I cope with the step-ladder: sometimes I have no trouble pushing it around, sometimes it makes my joints ache. At present I find it light, but soon I shall be laid low with an illness, as I promised someone.

We spent last weekend on a trip with the Kosíks, so the past two days in the garden have been overtime to make up for it. We left on Saturday morning at nine-thirty and by noon we were in Velké Meziříčí. There my brother-in-law Pepek from Spešov was waiting for us; he is Madla's sister's husband and famed in his locality as an amateur tourist guide. He guided us to Tasov, and this was clearly not his first visit. We talked to a number of people who had known Deml and whom we would never have met but for the brother-in-law. We saw Deml's house. Karel Kosík and Madla found everything very interesting, I less so. I seem to be a bit jaded. I was quite palpably aware of the present – the abandoned garden and the bench under the linden tree where Březina used to sit with Deml and a tame roe-deer called Susie – but I was unable to make the time-leap back to Deml, and in fact I wasn't even tempted to. On the other hand, the pleasant thought crossed my mind, more than once, that I would not be having to write about this trip or even to bring back a reportage on tape for broadcasting. It used to be dreadful! Dreadful. But radio teaches one to ask questions briefly and to the point. "Forgive me," I said to the man who is curator both of Deml's house and of Deml's "bright memory" – an unavoidable function since he lives in the house – "but I am simply unable to reconcile Deml's cantankerous treatment of people with his moving outpourings to nature. What was it really like to know him?" The curator had declared himself to be a relative and friend of Deml's and so was the right person to ask. But I have forgotten his reply. What shall I broadcast?

From Tasov we drove to nearby Jinošov, from whence Marie Rosa Junová, who must have been a bit of a minx, used to write to Karel Čapek on Deml's behalf, calling him a thief. (Or maybe it was from somewhere else? But she was a great name-caller!) This is also where Březina started his teaching career. In the cemetery there are two carved tombstones by Bílek. We were walking round the outside of the church when we were noticed and hailed by a jovial fellow with a slight limp. He was wearing a straw hat and well-laundered off-duty overalls for early evening wear. He was pushing a two-wheeled hand-cart, on which there sat a child so shy of us that it hid its head right down between its legs. He was a retired teacher, with merry, ironic eyes and a slow, fascinatingly rounded manner of speaking. As a young man he had actually held in his hands the class record book from Březina's time as a teacher and read the poet's comments, fully aware what he was holding: "His class discipline wasn't up to much," he said with an understanding smile, "and the pupils spent the whole year singing 'Spring is Coming.' The whole year." We found that amusing. I did in particular. At that moment I slipped out of the present for just one second.

That evening, brother-in-law Pepek took his leave of us, after furnishing us with all sorts of suggestions and advice for the morrow. The only one we followed was to make a stop at the gallery in Jihlava. The gallery is housed in a Renaissance building that is not much to look at from the outside but is enterprisingly arranged inside – the rooms are on different levels and the cosily furnished staircases are held up by slender pillars. Paintings by Špála, Čapek, Fila, Medek, John, Matal… but in the mood I was, I was most taken by Chitussi, the Mánes brothers, Slavíček, Preissler… What's this superficial rot I'm writing? It's night.

> Unloose my thoughts from pull of gravity,
> At the speed of light through space let them soar,
> Over the green sea and the realm of clarity,
> Then to fathom volcanoes and Earth's burning core;
>
> Let me flash through the gulf into night eternal,
> Where fiery throats spew scalding springs,
> To the weeping caverns whose tears primeval
> Petrify in a dream beneath baldaquins.
>
> (Otakar Březina: "Evening Prayer," 1895)

WEDNESDAY, 12ᵀᴴ SEPTEMBER 1979

Two days in Dobřichovice have flashed by again. We are back in Prague. I have so much work here, I don't know what to begin first. I climbed down from the tree (this afternoon) and went for more boxes. Madla was talking to Mrs. Rohlenová, who was standing on the top step of her disputed greenhouse and holding forth. I was not intending to take any notice of them, but she addressed me: "I had a poem from him, Mr. Vaculík, a short one." – "That doesn't matter," I said. – "But you haven't asked who from – from Tagore. If I can remember it, I'll say it for you." – "No thank you, Mrs. Rohlenová. What sort of sentence did your husband get?" – "Life." – "And how many years was he inside?" – "Six." – "That's not bad," I said. – "And that bitch he married afterwards," said Mrs. Rohlenová, "took away all my books with dedications by the authors. Including the one that the poem is from. You surely recall that Tagore was in Prague, don't you?" – "Of course," I said, but I don't remember a damned thing. – "Wait a moment, how did it go, now?" Mrs. Rohlenová said, searching her memory. "Aha! The lotus blooms and gives its all, loath to

The lotus blooms in the sight of the sun, and loses all that it has.
It would not remain in bud in the eternal winter mist.
(p. 364)

stay a bud in the endless winter mist. – I always used to wonder what it could be about, and that's how I came to remember it. And I think I've hit on it now. Better late than never. Try and guess what the poem's about." – "I don't know. You'd have to recite it to me again and slowly." – "Pay attention then:

> The lotus blooms in the sight of the sun, and loses all that it has.
> It would not remain in bud in the eternal winter mist."

"I couldn't tell you," I said, with the feeling that someone had been frightened of death, "it could be about all sorts of things." – "Not at all. There's only one thing it could be about." – And what's that?" I said. – "About a woman! He fancied some woman and enticed her with that argument, the eternal winter mist!" – I said: "That's possible."

THURSDAY, 13TH SEPTEMBER 1979
I got things ready in the bathroom to do a few photos for Dear Classmates, but some water splashed on to the negative, so I had to soak the whole film and dry it again. I therefore did some other photos – Arizona from the summer – in a particularly bad mood, and that was the last straw. My lenz (yes why not? lenz!) has too soft a line; everything merges, landscape and vegetation alike, and all the more so on document paper. I gave up and went into the kitchen, where Madla was again getting some food ready for the boys to take with them to the building site and for us to Dobřichovice, and she had the television on. They were showing a Bulgarian "detective film." I came in at the moment when the hero, seated at a radio receiver, took off his headphones and turned to his comrades with the words: "We've been given the order to be ready for anything." Immediately I understood what it was about. Only a general staff of towering genius could issue such an order. Cool and collected, I went out and was at a loss what to do. I inserted this sheet of paper into the typewriter, wrote the date, and did not feel like writing anything else, so didn't manage a single line. Yes, that is a fact, because I am writing this the following morning.

And moreover, yesterday evening, when Madla finished her work, she came to tell me that Dr. R. sends me her regards. She sends them so often that Madla does not even bother to convey them to me any more. But on this occasion it was worth it, as Dr. R. also expressed her disappointment that I was making telephone calls to Vienna. She had apparently said sadly: "Women will be the death of him." That really needled me. If any women will be the death of me, then it will be the ones that are here, not those that have gone. However, before getting upset, I purposely asked Madla for her own opinion. She chose for the time being to adopt an attitude of smiling forbearance. She replied: "But I'm all too aware that it's your greatest failing!" I said that the decision had been forced on me. Why should I have to distort every aspect of my life, just because of the damned secret police! It was debatable what was strength and what weakness. It was also an act of strength to choose a crucial exception to the pattern. I said it was odd how in the end people went for a dogma that suited them, instead of acting freely. What right had Dr. R. to judge me? These supporters and friends were a millstone: it mattered not that you had nothing, the main thing was "don't let us down"!

Following my fierce and, of course, exceedingly reckless defence of my decision, Madla started automatically to talk as if I were not speaking on the phone with Vienna, but sleeping with it. I agreed and therefore defended it as sleeping, which in fact it also is. She said she had long ceased to care, and had had to come to terms with who and what I was. I was suddenly seized by a cold anger, directed not at her but at everything in general: all the things I have had to wrestle with, in both myself and my surroundings – until it has made me ill! My ten non-writing years are a record of vain attempts to square the circle, until it has finally come home to me that there is no point in trying any longer! All I have is all I am, and those who don't like it, let them leave me alone. I, for my part, do not intend to wrest myself away from anything again.

Doctor R. also said, Madla added, that for women I was nothing but a parasite. What women? Where are they? How many does she think there have been in my life? A lot less than in the lives of most men I know – as God (and Madla) is my witness. I asked her: "And what do you say about this parasite business?" She replied: "I think she's right."

If only I had a little hole of my own to creep into, but I never made myself one. I never thought I would need it.

There is an evening concert on Radio Prague – something by Britten. Outside, a cold wind is blowing, the sky is studded with very cold stars that shiver. And according to the latest news, the Small Magellanic Cloud is being penetrated by some other galaxy, though I can see nothing with my eyes. I can only hear the first leaves flying through the air. I think that winter will not be long coming this year.

It was a sunny day, but when I went out into the street at noon, the cold took me aback. I have had a headache for several days now. On the way to Zbraslav I was astounded by the sharp visibility and clarity of the horizon. I lit some sulphur candles in the cellar and went out to tackle a tree. Which first, the Maid of Bohemia, the Princess Louise, or the Raspberry Red? The day is bound to come when I shall no longer be able to go climbing trees. The skins of the walnuts are beginning to crack too. It is as if the birds have completely abandoned the garden. Where are they? My ear aches.

I have finished reading Eda Kriseová's *The Bat's Collar-bone* – her oldest manuscript. I read it years ago, but do not recognise it: I like it much more now – a lot, in fact. It is the story of a girl who, in the end, is ready to fall in love with anyone, but she is too demanding. Nobody wants her and she does not suit anyone the way she is. Eda uses here a language she subsequently abandoned or transformed: it has a separate existence and scarcely needs a precise story line. In her more recent books she has moved nearer to a functional language that serves her plots and opinions. I will have to ask her why the change. There is a phrase that is repeated refrain-like throughout the book – at first it has nothing to do with the text, but later the connection grows until in the end it fills it entirely: "And tomorrow morning they'll find you dead by the brook." The difference between this book and the later ones is obvious: here she is talking about herself and making appeals on her own behalf, in the stories and in *The Woman of Pompeii* she is talking about other people and judging them. It is the transition from a poem written out of an irrepressible urge to a professional decision to write about this, then about that, and also about that.

Madla is reading a collection of documents about the fate of writers after the so-called victory of the working class, entitled *I Accuse* and compiled by Antonín Kratochvil. It is her wont to inflict on me an occasional excerpt of what she is currently reading, much to my annoyance. But sometimes it is the only thing I get to know about certain books. On this occasion she had to read to me about the case of Zahradníček, which she has always found moving. She read me a passage about his return from prison, how the doctors got him back on his feet again and he was in quite good shape... suddenly she stopped reading. I looked and she was crying. Her eyes had jumped ahead two lines to where Zahradníček died. I was on the verge of tears as well, though I am not really sure why.

"I can't wait," she said in the car on the way here, "to choose the people I want to spend time with. You haven't any idea, because you've not been employed for years, that the most intolerable and degrading thing these days is having to talk to people you wouldn't even look at normally, and having to listen to them." I asked: "What people will you choose?" – "Of the women it will be Piranka... sometimes Kylieska, maybe, Dr. R. certainly, and in small doses, Vlasta Kavanová." – "And what about the men?" – "Mr. Beneš, Spunar..." – "I thought as much. And it doesn't bother you that those gentlemen don't look you up any more?" – "A little bit. But I know it's out of fear of you, or because they disagree with you." All right, I know. "I shall also pay greater attention to your guests," she continued, "the ones I usually don't have time for. Professor Černý would interest me, for instance – a great deal. I'd have just the right questions for him, and I would always keep a record of it." I thought for a moment about her plans and inclinations and then said, "It'll be horrible. I won't have any privacy with you around. I'll lose my morning security." – "Don't be so scared all the time. Half the week I'll be in Dobřichovice."

Yesterday I asked Zdena if it struck her that I was taking advantage of her. I did not feel like using the word parasite. "I'd be really offended, if I didn't know that a question like that could never have come from your head." – "Tell me, though." – "A question like that can only occur to someone in a particular situation. I don't feel as if I am in it." – "What if it's because you don't really perceive your situation properly yet? The day may come when you'll see it that way and you'll judge our entire past that way retrospectively." – "Is something the matter?" she said.

Once more the boys are spending their days-off at the building site. They are plastering the interior walls and feel they are on the home stretch. It remains to do the inside work: plumbing, floors, fitting the bathrooms, kitchens, dark-rooms... They were a person short and were almost tempted to call me in, but in the end they have persuaded a friend of theirs. I was actually supposed to go there last week, but they changed the plan and this week the garden is already calling me. And here, inside our house. nothing gets done. Today I inspected the cellar to see whether I might not install a lair all to myself. In the workshop, maybe. But there is all that dust, and the floor has dry rot.

The evening concert has finished. I switch over to some other station where there is some old-time sentimental piano – just the way I wish I could play myself – backed by strings and percussion. The announcer's German is silkily intimate.

FRIDAY, 17ᵀᴴ SEPTEMBER 1979

I have recently been having trouble remembering my dreams. Last night I had such a clear dream, and even in the middle of it I thought to myself that I would have no problem writing it up, but when I woke up, not a thing. My nights are strange. I sleep as if it were a task I'd been given. In other words, I waste no time in falling asleep and then rush through to the morning, waking an hour earlier than I have been accustomed to in the recent period, as if I had something to see to and was afraid of oversleeping. Then I get up, have a quick wash, make the bed, quickly tidy up in the kitchen if need be, set out things on my desk, get my briefcase ready, all in great haste, as if expecting someone or having to be somewhere. But I am expecting no one and am expected nowhere. There is nothing going on. When I realise this, I slowly start spreading things out again and either take the typewriter into the kitchen, where it is warmer and there is more light, or I stay in my room when I feel like being more secluded amidst my books, dictionaries, pictures and papers. That fact is I do not have to go anywhere, and when it finally dawns on me that I have no one to expect, I will even stop going to the door – I shall be a Kosík.

Only now can I see all the work I had in connection with the annual feuilleton anthologies. People told me, when I stopped editing them, that it would be the end of them. It struck me as silly at the time, but there really do seem to be no feuilletons. It is ages since I received a Charter document or any news. Is there nothing happening, or am I just out of touch? If it is a case of nothing happening because ten people are under arrest, does that mean that the nation consisted of precisely ten people?

I have not taken Otka on that drive in the country as I once promised. There has not been the time and we have gradually fallen out somehow, almost imperceptibly. First she used to expect some more significant political activity from me, then we had an altercation over Zdena, then she thought I should be more active in what was going on at the time. But I have never been governed much by what is going on at a given time, particularly when I have had some work of my own in hand. Otka, for instance, must have gained the impression back in the radio days that I am some kind of warrior with a well-conceived plan, who asserts his own view and approach in conjunction with others, or at least in concert with them. Only now am I beginning to see the reason for a misapprehension that has existed between myself and many other people: since the time I started to be a bit adult, I have never been assertive; that was something I gave up in the "unquiet house." Two years of military service then provided me with an opportunity to deliberate on how a free and intelligent person can come to terms with orders, coercion and discipline, and to try it out in practice: and I was a pretty good soldier, and had no conflicts with my commanding officer or with the lads. Since then I have believed that is possible; you simply have to make it work!

I have a tendency to respect my superiors and chiefs, even the government – particularly when I consider what people are like and what an awful task it is to govern them well. It is only bad experience that eventually leads me take a stand, and I am ready to desist as soon as there is some improvement from above. One has no other measure of whether things are right or not than one's feelings and conscientious experience, and some notion of the possible. Programmes, rules, ideological canons and ethical prescriptions are a particularly bad measure. I will never – if I live to get the chance – join any party!

So I did not assert my own opinion or approach. It would be more accurate to say I exhibited them. But because they corresponded to what others were asserting, I was taken as one of their number. People were then unable to grasp why I was unwilling to draw further conclusions from that correspondence. Luděk Pachman – though his is a rather singular case – almost went into a rage when he could not enlist me for anything. I was not even in the Central Committee of the Writers' Union, for instance. I felt in that company like a schoolboy invited home by his teacher for curiosity's sake.

Having joined something, I would immediately feel an urgent need to cocoon myself against those who were there already. With a personality like that I would have done nothing, made nothing of myself, and achieved nothing but for the tremendous luck I had with people: both in the radio and on the staff of *Literary News*. At the radio, they (Dr. Ferdinand Smrčka, Dagmar Maxová, Josef Kleibl, Jarda Pour, Jiří Lederer...) understood me, helped me and rescued me from potential disasters. I regarded it as something normal and the general rule everywhere. When people talked about vice, deceit and corruption, and how nepotism and cliquishness were rife everywhere, I had no idea what they were talking about: I had never come across anything of the sort! Nobody envied me and I envied nobody. I had no enemies as far as I knew. I even have pleasant recollections of Karel Hoffmann, then the director of the radio and now a pillar of the regime. With the radio censor, Smolík, I had a relationship in which there was human respect on either side.

I would compare my situation in those days to that of a physical particle on the narrow boundary between two oppositely-charged poles, either of which can instantly destroy it. But since the particle is equally aware of both the poles, it is able to keep itself on a narrow course and fly upwards as if propelled by the two opposing forces.

It was Karel Misař who one day gave me the first signal that mine was a baffling course. Things like the following used to happen to me: One afternoon I received from the hands of I don't remember whom a state award "For Excellent Achievement." That very evening they broadcast a programme of mine that caused me to be disciplined by the party and packed off to reform myself at a shoe factory at Zruč nad Sázavou, where, as a former footwear worker, I was accepted as one of their own. I was allowed to work in the factory's radio station. I got to know the problems of the plant, and when I left a month later I put out a broadcast which, according to the firm, damaged their interests and reputation throughout the republic. They therefore filed a complaint against me, and I can still see old Dr. Smrček, whose sole desire by then was for a bit of peace and quiet, supporting me at a meeting of that factory's party committee and explaining – far better than I ever could – the loftiness and propriety of my intentions, which could not be assessed objectively from the standpoint of a mere factory. I felt very humble.

I liked Karel Misař for his absurd sense of humour and his book *All Quiet Over Here*. I went out with him on several reporting assignments, and we had a lot of fun travelling the country and meeting people. But he suffered from a sort of self-inscrutability that prevented him from incorporating his witty judgements and slightly sardonic philosophy into his actual programmes. When he was editing what he had brought back and had to write a commentary, he simply could not cope. He once asked me to listen to something of his: he played me a twenty-minute tape, edited with blanks in-between into twenty incoherent statements, and then said: "It's fucking useless, isn't it?" It was. From somewhere inside him there erupted a laugh that traversed his gullet like a bubble, blew up his cheeks and seeped out in a hiss between his pursed lips – sssss! "And now listen to this." He changed the reel and played me what he had cut out: it was the same! "What would you say to that, then?" We chortled like a pair of idiots.

If that had happened to me, I would have donned my mildly subversive head and solved it by using what was staring us in the face: our laughter. I would have targeted the programme at the brighter minds of the "young republic" of the day in the following way: If an interviewer asks you what you want in life and then separates the recording into usable and non-usable parts, what does he hear? Then I would play them something from each of the parts and conclude with the words: So before you can achieve something in life, your ideas and your stupidities have to differ somehow.

What Misař did with his edited report that time I do not remember. In the autumn of 1965, I left the radio for *Literary News*. At one of my last editorial meetings, Daša Maxová made us listen to one of Misař's programmes; she thought it was too bad even for transmission. She counted on me to give her my opinion, as usual – surely the fact I was leaving did not mean I was taking leave of my critical judgement? I saw it otherwise: here am I on my way out, surely I am not going to say something bad about those who are staying? In the end, of course, I told her what I thought and the programme was rejected. It must have been about nine o'clock in the evening when Misař phoned me at home to say he was sitting in the Derby, the nearby wine bar, and would like a chat with me. I went there. He told me I was a bastard and that he had finally seen through me. Before he joined the radio he had heard I was a rebel and an angry young man, and that was one of the reasons why he took the job. When he arrived there, what did he find? – The rebel was winning prizes at radio festivals, was getting state awards and was hand in glove with the bosses. I was a celebrity – it was all right for me to make audacious programmes when none of my mess-ups ended the way they would for any other editor! Work was no hardship for me, with female technicians dancing round me as if I was a star. No problem for me to get a car and a driver when I came up with some bright idea; everyone had to alter their recording frequencies because Mr. Vaculík did not make it in time, and when my wet nurse Maxová shoved my programmes in front of the censor at the last minute, he would be faced with a *fait accompli* and the risk of a break in transmission and would give the okay to things he would never let others get away with. He would even allow the transmission tape to be edited.

I cannot recall my response. He was absolutely right. But all it meant was that the heads of our section were indulgent toward programmes that interested them more than average. Things were beginning to look up and people were no longer trying to be inconspicuous or choose the comfortable path of mediocrity. All the technicians in the radio knew what I was going after and wished me well, so that even that holy terror, the most feared of the shift technicians, 'Scatalogical Soukup,' grudgingly granted me a quarter of an hour before transmission and did the one thing that was absolutely prohibited in Czechoslovak Radio – he edited the transmission tape.

But I was not the only one with that sort of status; every main section had at least a couple of cases like me: on another floor of the same building, Otka Bednářová was just such a one. It was the early sixties.

Back to where I was: I therefore think that the assertive course, particularly with the help of organisations, is a disaster. Even where the rules are democratic, it is a conspiracy against the rest. If the conspirators are few in number they get jailed; if there are too many of them, they jail the rest. We can only regard a well-ordered system as permanently established when it is translated into good habits and behaviour throughout the community. It is not hard for rulers to throw ten enlightened individuals into prison or even a thousand revolutionaries. But when a million obdurate subjects start to act determinedly in a particular direction, the rulers are virtually suspended. Someone – Petr Uhl, for instance – is bound to say that a million people will never agree on any question and that it needs "people of a special calibre" such as ourselves. And we could start the debate all over again.

It was quite late in the afternoon when I arrived at Zdena's, but she was not home yet. I took Bibisa for a walk. Bibisa is very beautiful. As we go downstairs she looks back with her head raised so high her eyes almost pop out. She jumps up at a me and when I lean over to stroke her, she wriggles on the steps and rolls herself into an affectionate ball. Out on the pavement she dashes like mad to the next street corner and then waits to see if I am coming before tearing off again to the dustbins and a pile of sand. We cross the street in exemplary fashion: we stand side by side, and I, being the taller, look both ways, and when I say "Go!" she glides across the street on her shaggy legs, close to my heel. I said "Go!" today as usual. She took off, making for a gap between two parked cars on the other side of the street. At that moment one of the stationary cars started to reverse! Bibisa was running towards it, was a metre and then ten centimetres away when I at last managed to shout out. She sat down on her bottom, ducked her head and the wheel passed just by her face. The whole street and the people in the public gardens went rigid and stared to see what had happened. We walked to the telephone booth where I usually transact my affairs while Bibisa runs here and there; today she sat next to the glass of the booth and did not stir an inch. When we got home she once more welcomed Zdena wildly. I sat in an armchair to read. As usual Bibisa jumped up on me and let me ruffle her fur, occasionally taking my hand in her teeth and licking it. Then she jumped down again and started to vomit. I did not tell Zdena the likely reason. It has only just occurred to me.

TUESDAY, 18TH SEPTEMBER 1979

I cut an oval board out of wood, stuck various moving figures on it, and showed it to Kosík. He was on his way out somewhere in a terrible hurry, but the mechanism took his fancy. He mounted it on an even bigger board, where there were even more amusements of a similar variety. Everything moved and lit up like a model railway, and in addition it said something, kept repeating that the best part was mine, and Karel Kosík stood in his raincoat ready to go but unable to tear himself away. He smiled at me and said: "Well, there you are!"

Later I am on a shady forest path, which is, however, illuminated by beams of bright sunlight from the countryside. I saw several snakes. They were quite short: thicker at the head end and then abruptly tapering. They crawled and wriggled about the path and I thought they were nice. I hoped they would come to no harm. Some of them changed colour from purple, through red and brown, to grey. I watched them as they looked for their holes in the earthy bank above the path. There were lots of attractive, clean holes like that, crawled smooth, and I said to myself: "So things aren't so bad with the snakes here, after all. There are still some left!"

Then I wanted to take something from my hiding place and discovered that someone had found it. They had rummaged in the papers, apparently taken something and then covered it up carelessly. Anxiously I went through the things in an effort to deduce the principle by which the thief or the police had proceeded. A lot of the papers I immediately discarded and destroyed: the ones I thought belonged more in a literary archive. And with the rest I scurried helplessly here and there. All the time I had the nasty feeling of being watched.

The whole afternoon I sat and pondered on who it might have been, what had led him to the hiding place, what would happen next, and what was the best thing for me to do – preventively if possible. It is too late for that. And since it's impossible to rid oneself of a worry without taking some sort of decision, what I decided was to ask the boys about it in the evening. Tactfully, though! I was not able to write, or read. I didn't even have lunch. From time to time I would get up and go to rummage in some other place that I remembered. In the process I was surprised to turn up from somewhere a transcription of Hájek's study: "International political aspects of the year 1968 in Czechoslovakia," which I could have sworn I had returned to the author; however, even that inspection failed to unearth the two volumes of Božena Komarková's *The Gospel and a Secularised World* that I had put aside to present ceremoniously to the author when she completes the third volume of her work *The Origins and Significance of Human Rights*. I am supposed to go and see her in Brno and I just cannot find those books, so I shall have to give her my own copies. Such phenomena are ludicrous and awful.

But I have to go out, at least. I looked at the thermometer outside to get an idea what to put on and waited another quarter of an hour in case the phone rang; it didn't, so I spent the next fifteen minutes plucking up courage, telling myself that I must not be dependent on a thing so notional as something female in another country, and I left. In the tram I read in all humility Einstein's article "Geometry and Experience." Yes, that's you all over: unable to understand something that interests you most of all. And I realised that the whole summer I had culpably neglected the speed of light and here was retribution!

Karel Kosík sat me down and said: "The First Republic spawned whole pleiads of gifted personalities. When we were at university there were also lots of interesting, original and bold individuals, weren't there? Where are they now, Ludvík? I know some of it was no more than youthful enthusiasm. But there's simply no one as far as I can tell! When I meet them, they are just wrecks, drivelling on about how long they have to retirement, about their gall-bladder trouble, about their recent divorce, about looking for a flat for their grown-up children, moaning about the way things are, living on the news they hear from foreign radio stations – what will they leave behind? Nothing." – "I think..." I began. – "Hold it a second. Tell me, Ludvík, were they gifted people, or was it just an impression? What do you think?" – "I think," I began again, "that there were gifted people among them. But the idea of Socialism destroyed them. The idea, not the practice! As soon as their thinking and feelings came into conflict with politics, the most conscientious ones, being honest, asked themselves: 'Aren't I a prejudice-ridden individualist? Aren't I an egotist? Don't I lack humility and discipline?' And from the contradiction between reality and themselves, they came to the wrong conclusion – they condemned themselves. Instead of destroying the reality, they destroyed themselves. They turned into dross, into nonentities." Karel nodded in agreement: "I expect you're right. But hold on, what is our duty then, as the ones who saw through it?"

That's Karel's perennial topic – which never gets beyond the question stage. I always say: "When will you finish writing your philosophy, then?" – "I don't know, Ludvík. But now I know what I want to say and it is something completely new. I am in such a state of euphoria that as I write I can see the whole structure of the thing. But you seem sad to me. Ludvík, you're sad, aren't you? Why? The same thing still? Isn't there any way I can help? Of course I can't." Meanwhile he kept smiling and smiling until at last he said: "It hurts, I admit, but isn't it fantastic?"

WEDNESDAY, 19TH SEPTEMBER 1979

Searching everywhere for my lost things I found the Koran. I read the Joseph sura, the one that Ivan objected to. It truly is a muddle, and the story and the sense of it develop in a very rambling fashion, though I cannot recollect too well what this sura looks like in the Bible. Trusting that these lines will not reach Khomeini, since he is known to be quick to anger, I make so bold as to think that the Koran really is only a rehash of the Biblical events. Only in its version of Genesis is there a trace of a more original perception, namely in the idea that man was created from "a clinging drop" (Sura 96). That seed was therefore from God – how else – I deduce and therefore God is male. Man is therefore like God. How else? But that I sensed myself long ago. "There aren't enough men!" I heard a woman complain.

I rang the bell on the concrete gatepost and from round the corner of the house came the clack of slippers and then the painter emerged. It seemed to me that, in the course of those ten paces she was obliged to take with the key, she blushed with indignation from her face right down to the neckline of her blouse, but she made a laugh of sorts and with a black look quietly said: "Good morning." I came out of a sunny day into the gloom of her apartment, which looks like the home of a devout heretic: the holy images on glass are about something else entirely. We said almost nothing to each other. We drank tea. I related to her the previous night's dream about the snakes and she told me that in the night she had gone round on a chain merry-go-round and I was there too, from which she guessed I would probably come. "What did you do all summer?" I asked. She gestured dismissively – she had cooked for ten people, washed and tidied, weeded the garden and even flailed corn. And she had etched a number of her metal plates. She was unable to show me any: she would have to print from them first.

"But there is one picture I will show you," she said. She reached over to the wall and put a painting on the easel. It gave me a start. I had to turn my head away before returning my gaze once more. Against a red background, but one suffused with sulphur, there hung a disembodied head: dark hair and an unkempt moustache, pale forehead, cheeks smudged with shadow; deep-set but piercing eyes behind spectacles; a mouth that smirked and pouted proudly at one and the same time; the whole face – both its light and dark areas – were of the same colour as the background. The background was divided indistinctly by a horizon line on which a distant flame flared up, or maybe it was a kind of tree. There could be no doubt: the portrait was set on Jupiter. When I had collected my wits, I said: "I'm glad that you didn't do my jacket." The painting is not finished, however, and it is not entirely certain that this version will be the final one. It was clear to me that I would not be required for the subsequent work.

In the tram I read Einstein's article "Geometry and Experience" once again from the very beginning. Some of the sentences gave me the impression that I had read it before. At home I found a letter from Jan Trefulka. He is out of the hospital already, but even more dejected than ever. Tomorrow I shall go to Brno. I told three of my pals to go with me, but no one wants to. Jiří would certainly go, but he is not in Prague. I shall make the trip, but how shall I explain why the rest didn't come?

SATURDAY, 22ND SEPTEMBER 1979

I found my reserved seat in the train, shoved my haversack of books up on the rack, hung up my jacket and sat down. In came a dark-suited man wearing a tie in spite of the heat, and a pink shirt, and a he had a reservation for the same seat. It turned out that some of the seats in the compartment had actually been triple-booked. Those who came first got a seat, the later-arrivals stood and waited fuming for the conductor. And I proved how much I had matured over the past ten years by feeling no anger towards the personnel of Prague Central Station, and instead left my tired old imprecations against the state behind me, picked up my things and found myself another, better coach just behind the locomotive.

It was warm. The sunlight was reflected off the bare fields of stubble and freshly-ploughed soil. There was only one man in the compartment, sitting on the sunny side in a thick sweatshirt. He had a bedewed bulging forehead, very little hair, a genial expression, two score years and ten and he did nothing during the journey but stare. He didn't even read. He didn't leave his seat once, whereas I always had to be doing something. I could not make up my mind whether to look at the scenery, read Sylvie Richterová, or think. The "Hungaria" was running late. What's the point of fast trains on slow tracks!

I had lots of jobs to see to on the way. As soon as we left Prague, I had to check how they were getting on with the work of bulldozing mud from the pond at Kyje; it has been dragging on for ten years already. Just beyond Kolín, I had to catch a split-second glimpse of Mr. Beneš's Red Cottage as it flashed by amidst level greenwood. Malín comes right afterwards with its bizarre assemblage of heavy grey towers that resemble wooden planking and have a medieval look. Then Čáslav appears in the distance in the form of a tall, white, slender spire. During our expedition on horseback in 1965, Josef and I had made an overnight stop in some farmyard just by the level-crossing gates at Golčův Jeníkov, and since then I have tried in vain to catch sight of the place again from the train. Then it is Okrouhlice and the mill by the weir, where I photographed Zrzavý. In other words, I was running back and forth from one side of the train to the other. Then I am free until Žďár, so off I went for a coffee in the dining-car. It was full of Germans all speaking at once. I drank my coffee in ten minutes at a window screened by an orange curtain. Then I had to rush off again because after Žďár there is a place of narrow winding lanes that meander off in the direction of Polná and Rudolec. And then comes Křižanov, where, on a line running through Osová Bítýška to Tišnov, I check the sites and the state of forest and meadow ponds, now assisted by the "Brno and environs" walkers' map. The wind ecstatically fills my head and inner ear, lifts my spectacles, which I retrieve at the last moment just above the track bed, and refuses to let me tear myself away from the window and read or doze. Sylvie Richterová remains *intacta*. I took her on the trip with me because of one sentence I turned up at random: "When we are old we will love each other and nothing will get in our way, not even me."

A landscape is properly explored on foot so that its every intimate fold is revealed. But an express train is fine for a comprehensive review, underscoring the slow, dangerous processes which a landscape undergoes at the pace of human habituation. I have never been able to pass up that view from the express. In the space of several hours' watching I would always manage to discern the landscape's physical and mental state: what was going on between it and us, what lies in store for us, and why we are not better off. I always hated to see the disappearance of hedges, the levelling of roads, the drying of wet land, the building of factories and towns on level fields, the growth of pit-heaps. All that ostensible prosperity has always filled me with the sort of anguish described in Zahradníček's poem: "... landscapes covered in deletions were being relentlessly erased..." But I am also a victim of a baneful self-restraint and pointless respect for the community; I ought to have berated the people and its government far more for their lack of common sense and repudiated their right to affluence, abundance and comfort. Only I thought, or maybe I thought, that communal wisdom (no such thing!) would take that landscape and pencil in other interesting and generous features in place of the deletions. This never happened, however, because of the niggardliness of the people and its government! Just utility, utility! Getting something from everything!

I now looked out at the plains and the long rolling hills to right and left and was filled with an increasingly troubled amazement that they say nothing to me, or almost nothing. For so long people have treated fields, meadows, woods and rivers like a factory, so that looking at them now is like looking at a factory. The landscape answers the questions while its spiritless face only mirrors the faces of the local savages. If only the so-called natural mineral wealth were all swallowed up irrecoverably! And let those who are not good enough for poverty take themselves off to some more affluent land! And let the engineers of death delete us from their plans for mineral extraction.

SUNDAY, 23ʳᵈ SEPTEMBER 1979

After Tišnov the landscape abruptly changed. (I had to abandon writing yesterday because my irritation turned my thoughts fruitlessly in an anti-government direction.) The train ran along high embankments above deep valleys. The evening sun turned the gables of the houses on the hillsides to gold. In the old gardens the summer-houses were falling apart. In the dry grass on the loose banks, grasshoppers chirped along the entire length of the train. And we were moving at the time! Here and there a tree with leaves already yellow would appear glowing in the bend of a road, at the top of a steep meadow or above a disused quarry, like a deliberate signal. I waited for one to appear nearer to the track in order to identify it – it was a sycamore.

Tortuous steep-sided valleys are naturally more resistant to lackadaisical construction, and so they function as a kind of reservation for old cottages and villas, affording picturesque views. People sat on the steps of the houses, stood about under the corner trees, chatted over backyard walls, pushed prams between the gardens in which the apples were turning red and out of which dahlias hung their colourfully cheerful heads. Higher up the slope, above the backyards, smoke rose from bonfires of potato stalks. At Královo Pole, all the old cottages – comically enough – had newly whitened concrete ridges on their weather-beaten roofs. In Prague, the outskirts are either deserted or neglected and the terrain is all dug up for some building project, either begun or unfinished. The lanes between the cottages are constantly being trampled on by some grotesque organisation or other, and nothing is ever tidied up afterwards. People cannot be sure what else will be demolished. The only thing that any of them can be sure of is a hutch in a prefab housing block.

Every time I arrive in Brno like this, I try to guess where Mahen's magical story "The Best Adventure" was set: "When, one day, the young schoolmaster caught himself teaching without any enthusiasm a topic that was once interesting but had now lost all interest, he felt troubled. It suddenly seemed to him that he was laying bricks but building nothing. He started up again and again became aware of the bricks in his exposition and fell silent. He looked around the classroom. He realised that no one suspected anything." – He was only a little over forty but he took retirement and went off to Brno, where he found himself lodgings in just such a secluded house with a garden on a slope above the River Svratka. He started to read, study and go for walks between the fences, around the gardens, above the abandoned quarries and there, one day, he met the Black Lady. What sort of relationship he had with her, if any, I have forgotten. What seized my imagination most was that part of the adventure which I have just outlined: the moment he realised he was dead, he changed his life! And also the autumnal nostalgia of the outlying slopes above Brno.

At the station I looked around me, though by then it would have been too late. The tramcar slowly wended its way out of Brno back to the places I had been looking at half-an-hour before. The place was new to me. I got out at the foot-bridge over the river, and following precisely the directions once given me by a friend, I strayed uphill through streets of old working-class cottages and then across a slope of dry dusty grass to a wire-netting lane of wooden chalets and huts. Everywhere deserted, shutters closed, gates padlocked. It was sweltering. I was carrying my jacket. I had my swimming trunks in my haversack: I was counting on Milan Šimečka to take me for a dip. "Milan!" I began to call, and started scaling fences by climbing onto compost heaps. But everywhere there were only asters and African marigolds; heavily-laden stunted dwarf trees bearing six or even a dozen modern apples; squashes lying about in the middle of vegetable beds. Either I have got it completely wrong or Milan has succumbed to homesickness and left for Bratislava. I had imagined myself saying to them both: "I'll come to Brno and take you out to dinner!" An attempt to make it up with Milan's wife.

Dusk fell. I walked back downhill, intent on finding another path to another part of the hill. Instead I got stuck in a new housing estate. I crossed it and at the point where the estate had jettisoned its burst bags of cement, lengths of cable and broken pipes, I found myself once more at the wire fence of the chalet settlement I had just climbed out of. "Milan!" I called. I was starting to feel miserable. A new house stood close by, so utterly luxurious and extensive that I doubted whether it could be a private home and thought it might be some minor research institute. I rang the bell and through the glass I could make out a figure approaching from a distance. I asked: "Would you have any idea, where a fellow by the name of Šimečka might be staying?" The man was dressed like the boilerman of the institute but he turned out to be the owner of the house. To my surprise, he displayed neither fear nor suspicion. "I don't know any Šimečka," he said, "but I'll help you look for him. Wait a sec." He went to put on some shoes, though he might just as easily have gone to phone for the police, it struck me. He came out dangling his keys from one finger and then took me on a tour of his garden. Then we walked the whole length of the chalet settlement together, calling as we went. I: "Milan!"; the man: "Šimečka!" The only response was the dry chirping of grasshoppers and the faint sound of traffic from the main road beyond the river below. "Careful, don't tread on that squash," the man warned me, and fell to the ground, having tripped over the wire holding up the fence post. I said: "I expect he's not here. He probably got depressed and went home." The man said: "No, hang on a bit longer – we'll go right through to the back, seeing that you've come all the way from Prague." And he fumbled along ahead of me in the dark. Above our heads, the tops of the apple trees joined to form a tunnel...

(I am incapable of finishing this account: I used up all my energy describing the journey. – I went back into town and spent the night at the Trefulkas. Jan was calm but sad. We sat for a while together, in company with Milan Uhde, and drank a little wine. I had the impression that Milan Uhde was alarmed at Jan's illness. The following day, I went with Milan Uhde to a Josef Čapek exhibition: Čapek mastered cubism, not vice versa! Then he pointed out Professor Komarková's house to me, and I gave her the three volumes of her writings. Then I went off to that hill again in search of Šimečka's chalet. I found it! Milan was writing. He was very pleased I had come. We arranged my next trip, so that we would not have to risk communications about it. I promised to have some pals in tow next time. Then he saw me to the station. Along the path by the Svratka, I picked Madla a bunch of Nezval's speedwell, because. I spent the entire return train journey reading Sylvie Richterová. She is a Brnonian living in Rome. The book ought to be transcribed. Rain and fog awaited me as we reached the hills. – It looks as if I am getting fed up with writing.)

TUESDAY, 25TH SEPTEMBER 1979

It has been raining for four days now. Our boys look up at the newly-painted kitchen ceiling and are pleased at how well they repaired the roof. President Svoboda has died; in places there are black flags flying. On Sunday evening Madla switched on the television and they were showing a Russian film. She changed channels and this time they were showing a Russian film with English subtitles. She rushed in to fetch me: "Come and look at this – would you believe it?" My first thought was that we had been annexed by Russia. But I instantly realised it could not be true as I had not yet committed suicide.

This morning I got up, showered nonchalantly in cold water, made myself some tea and carried the typewriter through to the kitchen. But I did not write anything. It's raining. Tomorrow I have to go to Dobřichovice and pick some apples, rain or no rain, because I will not be here next week. And I have to deliver some books again too.

As I was cold I got dressed and went out. I picked my watch up from the repair shop, bought some green trousers from the hunting suppliers, had a coffee at the bistro on Železná Street – it was raining – had a Becherovka, for a change, all alone. It was still raining, but I did not mind it so much now. I walked to Charles Bridge via the Old Town Square and Karlova Street. Hradčany was scarcely visible through the drizzle. I climbed up the bridge-tower, climbed down, and went to the tram stop. I took the tram home. The typewriter was on the table where I had left it. I made a further attempt at evading it: I raised the lid of the piano, opened the Wallachian song-book, and came upon a song with the following words:

> King Solomon said when he was alive
> That as each man works so should he thrive
> Eat and drink and merry be
> And ever praise the Lord, said he.

I walked along Příkopy, wondering to myself how I would learn the news if things here were suddenly to change for the better. Ivan Klíma would come and tell me. "Get your clothes on, let's go! You're in the dark as usual, aren't you! Well we've got to revive *Literary News*, Zdeněk Prokop's taking over the Writer's Union publishers, Pavel's flying in from Vienna tomorrow and Kostroun is returning to the party leadership and saying we should have some proposals ready – otherwise things risk going the way Pavel dreams it up on the flight here. I've already sent Saša a telegram, Karol's trying to locate a printer and they've released Václav Havel from prison – he's sleeping it off at the moment, but we have to wake him up on our way. So get a move on!"

"Not on your life!" I said out loud; so loud, in fact, that people turned round to look. "Things have improved, you say? Fine, then at last it's none of my business." And I got down to the sweet task of planning my trip to Norway. Vindictively. To disappear.

My day-dream was spoiled by the even sweeter, sticky fragrance of sugary delights that always wafts from the ventilators of the House of Children department store. I held my breath in disgust, crossed over, cut across Wenceslas Square via the underground passageway, and made my way to Jungmann Street. I rang the bell at the door of a fourth-floor flat. It opened a chink, and a tousled head like a black sun looked out. The door opened wider, I entered the hall and, my hands almost in my pockets, I got down to business in a brusque fashion made possible by Ivan's news that things in publishing had suddenly got better: "You told me you'd have it finished by the middle of September. You've had it for two months already." She started to squirm lithely, pouted her lips, and with a charm that is starting to leave me cold she whined: "Yeah, I know, but it's such a thick thing and it's not much fun…" – "Save that for someone else," I interrupted her. "You'll get your two crowns fifty a page." At that moment I remembered the change in the situation and added: "If you deliver it in a week, I'll give you three crowns a page – but if you don't, you can forget it." She looked me up and down facetiously and said: "I just might at that. Are you sure you won't come in just for a moment? I'll make some tea and I've got some cakes from mother. The thing is you've been giving me such tomes – there was that Komárková with all its foreign words. Well at least it was informative. But this *Lord of the Tower*!"

I took hold of the door handle and said goodbye in friendly fashion. "Next time I'll bring you something thinner – some verses or a play." She arched upwards in the doorway in such a way that one of her breasts was a breast higher than the other and drawled: "That's all very well, but it's such slow going because the margins have to be perfectly straight and it means counting the key-strikes!" I flashed her the best smile I could manage in the present miserable circumstances and declared in winning tones: "But Marcela, my dear, I know you'll cope as always."

In front of the Academy of Sciences bookshop I bumped into Petr Chudožilov. "You really have stopped going to work?" I said in greeting. – "But I told you so, didn't I, Mr. Vaculík? Don't you believe me? In that case you don't even believe that I want to write nine books in my lifetime! I have five to my credit already, so I should be able to manage. I'm thirty-five. How old are you – fifty-three if I'm not mistaken. – I went to see Karol straight after you suggested it and I gave him several manuscripts. He was quite surprised, so he probably didn't believe me either. I just can't understand why everyone thinks I'm only bullshitting." – "I expect it's because you're always bullshitting, Mr. Chudožilov. And what was Karol's answer?" – "The answer he gave me is immaterial. The important thing is what he'll tell you. So go and see him." – I said: "Me? Why should I? I'll wait for him to come to me. And how are you supporting yourself?" He smiled again and in the same pleasant manner said: "But you know very well that I have enough to live on for two months. If nothing happens in the meantime I'll have to leave. It's up to you." – I said: "But emigration permits aren't given on the spot, Mr. Chudožilov!" And I smiled too.

MONDAY, 1ST OCTOBER 1979

At the border, clouds float above the mountains. In the cool atmosphere beneath them, every fallen tree on the steep forbidden slopes is reflected in detail. I am old.

TUESDAY, 2ND OCTOBER 1979

The forest path emerged abruptly above a steep-sided hollow full of golden trees and their scarlet berries. Then another shadowy walk through the forest. Until at last something glistened at the bottom of the icy black lake: a memory of a treasure from when the forest was free. Yes, as a memento of that memory, I'll buy her, if I find one, a golden chain.

WEDNESDAY, 3ʳᴰ OCTOBER 1979

Do I put these on, or these? What shall we drink? Would you like a dance? Or would you rather go upstairs?

The menu of the Hotel Javor: Udder Pie, Cock in its Juice, Stuffed Bun, Morning Sour, Puffed Rehash, Ennui au Vin...

THURSDAY, 4ᵀᴴ OCTOBER 1979

"No, no," he said to himself, "it'll come to nothing, it's totally pointless and out of the question." – Adalbert Stifter, *The Forest Path*

FRIDAY, 5ᵀᴴ OCTOBER 1979

Or would you sooner go back to Prague already? – Not at all, I'm happy to be here! – Well, I'll go out then, and leave you alone so you can think your thoughts and write. I'll be back in about three hours. – Fine. Only don't get lost! – So what did you do? – Thought my thoughts and slept. – Great! And what shall we do now? – Come here.

SATURDAY, 6ᵀᴴ OCTOBER 1979

I stood on St. Anne's Hill waiting for a group of people approaching from the south. It was going to be Pavel accompanied by about five persons, only two of whom I subsequently recognised. Here at last was my chance to show Pavel the village and house where I was born, but it took a tremendous effort on my part to keep the view below us in existence, because it had a tendency to dissolve into an unpleasant reality. That reality was a felled wood to one side of me, and below the hill, in place of everything, just a factory, its walls surrounded by a wasteland churned up by machinery. Even now the reality is not yet so bad: the wood still stands, as does the chapel in the middle of it, and the factory has not yet gobbled up the whole of Brumov. I could still show my valley to friends, and would like to.

Pavel turned to face the view, and placed one foot forward in a patient stance, then he removed his spectacles and let them dangle from his fingers as if waiting to hear a commentary. The other guests stood, as was appropriate, a few metres away, talking to Jelena about something. She's going to be intrusive, I thought regretfully. There was one other figure standing there, somewhat apart from them, probably in order not to disturb them and to hear me better. It was her. But in the end I said nothing. I just concentrated once more on the image of the landscape and the village, and willed into existence our old street with the row of barns beneath the lime trees, and our cottage as it used to be before my brother-in-law converted it. They could all see it clearly, and obviously did, as a glance in their direction assured me. Even Jelena was looking. But I was unable to turn towards them or even speak to them because the valley would immediately start to twist and contort into something else. I could not afford a single word or gesture to the woman or even attempt to communicate with her. I had to hold on to the home.

Then I gave up and turned to Pavel. He was wearing a brown suit that looked more like one of mine; his face had aged, and I thought I saw tears in his eyes. But he was in danger of seeing the same thing in my face, so we agreed in an exchange of glances that we would not let it happen and swapped rueful grins instead. Beyond Pavel I could see her, standing apart, in a blue skirt that moved in the wind, and an orange blouse, her arms folded on her chest, her gaze fixed on the scene below as if seeking to find out more about me there than the others saw. I could not understand why she did not come closer to me, or who was preventing her. I looked at Pavel and would have liked to walk past him towards her, but his face seemed to tell me that he was the one preventing it.

Now that our professional matters had been dealt with, I thought I would accompany them partway back and ask Pavel what she was doing and how she was. We had already set off; Pavel and I in front, the rest following. But the order came for us to take immediate leave of each other. Pavel spread his palms in a feeble gesture of futility; I merely nodded and took a sideways step so that I might see her beyond him: with a forward thrust of my chin I intimated a greeting, having in mind a kiss. That was how she took it, forming her lips into a little even mound – her upper lip is more pronounced – and dangling her arms emptily at her side, the palms slightly turned towards me: it was that unconsummated embrace.

I had this dream after hearing the news from abroad last night that Pavel and Jelena have been banned from returning home. It almost made me ill. But it's taken the dream to bring home to me what it all means. I cannot get over it. Zdena and I are scarcely speaking to each other. This event was the death of all other topics and I dread talking about it. Zdena just observes me in silence.

SUNDAY, 7ᵀᴴ OCTOBER 1979

It's a pity that it ended sadly because of the news. I expect you'll be needing to spend more time with friends. You can give me a bit of a rest; I'll manage to cope pretty well for a while. Thank you for everything. Whether you've anything to thank me for is another matter. Don't tell me!

MONDAY, 8ᵀᴴ OCTOBER 1979

Starting today, I ought to write every record in the awareness that it could be the conclusion of this – what? What is this novel about? I don't have much idea, really, as I have not read it. I had intended, as soon as I picked the last apples, to withdraw from society, read the manuscript from the beginning, catch its drift and strengthen it without contrivance by minimal revisions, so that the final entry would also conclude the job of editing and I could get it typed out straight away. Typed out? But by whom? Zdena? Such a volume of joy!

But since I do not know which will be the last entry, I am leaving it up to my friend Slavík, if worst comes to worst, to edit the manuscript at least slightly on my behalf and then arrange its publication – in Padlock Editions first.

I got under way again after my week's absence. I put a couple of books in my briefcase, along with Tatarka's manuscript. But Mlynárik was not home. I walked along Mostecká Street and under the bridge tower onto Charles Bridge – that cosy enclosure in the sun where a warm breeze wafted and little children were pulling toy cars, tourists were taking snapshots and painters painting. At its highest point I turned and gazed once more at Hradčany, that favourite motif of the old postage stamps. I walked along the peaceful and almost deserted embankment to Café Slávia, which was full of people and smokier than I've ever known it. At the table there was only Hiršal and some lady. I greeted them and left. On Národní Avenue I met Petr Pujman, the translator. I said hello in a manner that left it up to him whether he wanted to go beyond a greeting, and I was pleased to find he did. He earns his living as a conference interpreter from English. I asked at the jewellers when they would be getting something in, as Christmas is coming.

On Jungmann Square I met Karol Sidon. I invited him to the Alfa for a coffee and there we talked. Karol said: "Do you know, Petr Chudožilov greatly astonished me. He's got a number of finished manuscripts. It's true they each need to be worked on some more, but they're good. Do you want it in writing?" – That took me by surprise, but I said I did. "What I'm afraid of, Karol, is that Petr has entirely the wrong impression of us. He seems to think that someone is paying us and that it's dead easy for us to be dissidents with the funds we supposedly have." Karol said: "He certainly does, I feel. And I can tell you that plenty of people think the same way, unfortunately." We laughed. "He treated me," I said, "as if I belonged to some committee capable of sorting out a stipend for him." We laughed. Karol said: "Apart from that, he has no idea, people have no idea, that it takes years for a book to make its way in the world. That's judging from my experience, I mean..." – "I know, Karol, but there's nothing I can do about it. Perhaps Pavel will be able to help us now."

We sat for about ten minutes more and Karol voiced an interesting thought: "Do you know, it always amazes me that we are such clever people and yet we can't think up a way to get rid of them!" I turned that true and simple remark over in my mind as I walked on through Prague. If we were incapable of stinging, it struck me, then perhaps we could try stinking. And since at that moment I was making my way to the Chramostová's, I immediately imagined to myself the sort of objection Standa would voice: "But could you stink foul enough for snouts like that? I don't think it's humanly possible!" And we're back to square one. The Chramostovás were not in and I dropped the book in the mailbox. I went home. From a telephone booth on the way I sorted out a long-standing matter: *The Pink Lady*. She is coming for her manuscript on Wednesday. But will I still recall what I wanted to tell her?

I discovered a moment ago from Voice of America that they have stripped Pavel of his citizenship. But the talk was mostly about the Pope's visit to the USA. He put on quite a performance there! I am even getting a bit worried that he might be secularising his Holy See a bit too much. I like the way he parried the women's movement: they asked him why he was against women priests, seeing that he is in favour of human rights. He replied courteously that Scripture does not recognise women priests. If I had been in his place I would have had no qualms at all. I would have said: But I was specifically talking about *human* rights!

Those fabled American cows are actually capable of demanding entry into specifically male organisations on the ground of equal rights! We are warning you! Women have already wrecked every sort of work that men had managed to bring to some kind of perfection before they came along. Women would have the effect of turning the clock back – first in the parish, then in the diocese and finally throughout the Church – to the days of interdicts, exorcisms, burnings at the stake – chiefly witches – and religious wars. Nothing could be more terrifying than a woman licensed to mediate between Man and God, one who has access to the secrets of the confessional and a pulpit into the bargain! God's scourge in the Devil's hands!

As I type this out in its final version in March 1980 I am admittedly astonished at the last paragraph, but with the best will in the world, I can find no fault with it. For safety's sake, however, I had better dedicate it to our friend Jiří Gruša.

TUESDAY, 9TH OCTOBER 1979

Today I heard, from five different transmitters, expressions of annoyance at how our authorities have treated Kohout. And our ambassador in Vienna has actually managed to offend Austria; the Federal Chancellor is demanding an explanation. "Cocky Kohout Crows His Last!" clucks today's *Rudé právo*. And in my mind's eye I can see Pavel in his temporary home, as – in between mental activity, telephone calls and interviews – he unerringly switches on the radio news at just the right moment and asks everyone to be quiet so he won't miss the world's reaction and can reassure himself that the play is proceeding properly.

A handful of us also got very hot under the collar this afternoon: Jiří Gruša, Petr Kabeš, Eva Kantůrková, Jan Vladislav and I. We were doing an interview for West German television. The two guys recording it were pleasant and accommodating. We'll see if they manage to get the recordings out of the country. We also had fun doing it, because each of us thought of phrases that Pavel deserved to hear – although not via television. Maybe he had planned to return calmly to the republic, counting on the fact that the interior ministry people, whom he knows only too well, would take over from there? "Don't even suggest it," Jiří said, roaring with laughter. "I said the same thing somewhere yesterday evening, and I was severely reprimanded." I said: "To tell you the truth, I could never imagine what he might do here, but I have no difficulty imagining what he'll do there."

After the recording I went to join Madla at Dobřichovice – in trepidation at what I would hear on the topic of Kohout. The apple trees, I immediately noticed, had been pecked clean, precisely to Madla's height above sea-level. Herself I found over a cup of coffee in a book on Mahen. "Just listen," she said, "to the answer Mahen gave when he was asked what the Czech nation needed – ten thousand Don Quixotes!"

I changed my clothes, stood the ladder against the walnut, climbed up and shook the nuts off the tree. Down below, she gathered them into a basket. "The trouble is," I called down to her, "First Republic Don Quixotes and today's Don Quixotes are two different things entirely!" – A few moments later she asked: "Was Ivan at the recording session too?" – "No, he's ill," I said reluctantly. – "Or Saša?" – "He wasn't there either," I said very reluctantly. "No one knows Saša's whereabouts." A few moments later she called up: "Kosík agreed with me on Sunday that Pavel must have known this would happen and was probably counting on it." – I started to see red. "What are you saying, then? That he shouldn't have left, or he shouldn't have returned?" I shook some sprays and the walnuts drummed onto the tins under the tree. She replied: "Why? It makes no difference. The upshot is, though, that you're here and he's over there." I cautioned her: "Pavel consulted us last year before he left and we all agreed he should go. The attempt had to be made." – "Exactly. That's just what I'm saying. Perhaps it's for the best," she said. I thought to myself: Agreed, but what will I be left with here, or what will I be left for?

In a few moments it will be midnight. A few moments ago Madla gave a whine in her sleep from behind her screen. "What's wrong, what's wrong?" I said, to pull her out of it. In an altered, calmly narrative tone she said: "I dreamed someone was imprisoning me in a room, someone outside was calling what's wrong, what's wrong, and the one in the room twisted my arm and took my diary."

She went back to sleep and I went to look at what kinds of things she has in her diary. She has only been writing about Mahen and noting his precise number of Don Quixotes: 10,000 – i.e. at pre-war values. However, 1 pre-war Qčs is scarcely worth 0.10 of a present-day one!

The doorbell rang and I went to see who it was. "Hi there, it's nice to see you," Mirka said. "They're real so-and-so's, aren't they? Were you expecting this? I was!" – I invited her in and when she was obliged to step over the shoes of the visitor who had arrived just before her, I said in embarrassment: "I have someone here already..." She looked at the two little shoes, one of which was standing up in well-bred fashion while the other was frivolously lying on its side, and said *sotto voce*: "Oh! Such a dainty shoe? Good luck to you!" I shoved her into the kitchen with the words: "It's only Procházka's daughter with a manuscript." She expressed surprise: "The late lamented Procházka, you mean?" and with arms a yard apart she indicated the extensive oeuvre of the late lamented Jan Procházka. I nodded. "There you go!" she laughed. "They can't win, life is irrepressible." She reached for the pencil and paper on the table and wrote: "Re. P.K., I'm game for anything." I nodded.

She moved back into the front hall. There she brushed against the over-turned shoe with her flat grey foot, saying: "Otherwise, all the best." I opened the sitting room door with the words: "Take a look, she's in here." In the gloom, silhouetted against the window, the dark figure of the "Pink Lady" rose from the armchair.

She was as swarthy now as she had been in the summer: dark, not pink at all. And she looked skittish, like a boy, not a lady. "For goodness sake, is punctuation so hard to learn?" I said. "A subordinate clause must be separated from the rest of the sentence by commas on each end! How old are you?" She told me, but I have forgotten again. Not yet thirty, I fancy. "And there's one particular Prague-ism you repeat in several places." – Quietly she said: "But we're from Moravia." – "So why do you write it? Do you have any children?" – "One." – "And what does your husband do?" – "He emigrated beforehand. And I'm..." she went even darker, "an unmarried mother." – "Well there you are," I consoled her. "And does he help you out with the child?" – "No, but he sold his car before he left and the money was supposed to go to us, but it turned out to be forfeit to the state." – I said: "You write here that the cows were mooing on the pasture. When cows are out to pasture they either graze or they lie and chew the cud. They moo when they're in a trampled yard, in the cowshed, or in a fenced meadow when they want to come home. Whenever have you seen a cow mooing for the sake of it!" – "In Prysko." – "So take a fresh look." – "At those cows?" she asked. – "Either at those cows in Prysko or at that sentence. What do you do you for a living?" – "I work as a cleaning woman for a few hours a day." – "They were supposed to be putting on some play of yours in the theatre but they banned it before the premiere, didn't they?" – "That was my sister Iva." I opened the manuscript at the title page: Aha, this one's Lenka.

"Look here," I said resolutely, "take no notice of what I'm telling you and give the manuscript to someone else to read. I am no good at judging manuscripts and I do not even want to. I read yours quickly, all in one go, because I found it thrilling. I liked that it ended happily. One can tell... well," I waved dismissively and decided against saying what I thought it implied about her life. "Plot is clearly your strong point. But it has to be expressed in some sort of language. I prefer language that is original, personal, witty and poetic. You're quite entitled to hold a different view, like your father did – the farmer takes a pitchfork and starts loading. But even then the pitchfork handle doesn't have to be covered in bumps and knots that chafe your hands. And here you write, 'Mummy assented.' That's a dreadful sentence! But like I say, give it to someone else. Or tell me someone whose opinion you'd respect and I'll take it to them." She quickly reached for the manuscript. "No, no, I'll take a look first myself – at the language."

This afternoon I went over to Ivan's to examine his disease. He was lying in bed, all tousled, and the whole bed was crumpled with fevers. He showed me his tongue: it was violet on top, which he could have done himself, and underneath it was all ulcerated, his gums too. Foot-and-mouth all right. It is a shame, just at the moment when we need to talk properly. It's the others who deserve foot-and-mouth. He gestured me away from his bed with the words: "It's not supposed to be infectious – through the air – but personally I wouldn't be entirely sure." He had difficulty opening his mouth; his speech was lumpy. "So what are we going to do – about – our young Pavel?" he said. – "That's why I came," I replied. "I think it's the moment to implement what we agreed on at Hrádeček for this eventuality." – "Quite right – who'll write it? You, most likely – I've already thought of two comments – do you want to – jot them down?" He held his hand in front of his mouth.

As I was leaving, he added: "Don't forget Franta Pavlíček and Jiří Hanzelka, they're friends of his too!" I said: "I don't know why, but I can't help thinking that it's not final and that Pavel will still manage to get back here somehow. It just seems inconceivable to me that he should be so poorly insured, politically speaking." – "Unless," said Ivan, "he's actually pleased it turned out this way, even if he wasn't planning on it. I'm not entirely sure." I said: "Ivan, I remember you predicting last spring that things were bound to take a turn for the better this autumn." He waved his handkerchief, blew his nose, waved it again and said: "Quite."

That makes no sense to me. I have yet to be convinced that foot-and-mouth is that much better than hay fever.

THURSDAY, 11ᵀᴴ OCTOBER 1979

"Hi!"– Martin starts his letter. He announces his marriage to Mlle. Isabelle Faugeras, which took place three weeks ago. So it is a bit late for us to send a telegram with our congratulations.

"We walked there. It's just round the corner. This time it was Bernard and Irena who arrived late, rushing in with an enormous bouquet, and we entered a large hall with enormous windows and seating for five hundred, and We Were a Handful (Poláček used to be bed-time reading in our home. – L.V.) The deputy mayor makes a dignified entry. He's a jovial old chap with florid cheeks, a red nose and a tricolour ribbon across his chest who has been marking time for quite a while behind a curtain. He read out to us the rights and duties of married couples, and then asked us if we still intended to get married. It did cross my mind to say something silly but in the end I said '*oui*' like millions of others, and then Isabelle did, though her voice did give way. We signed two registers and then the old fellow stepped down from the dais and shook our hands, telling us how pleased he was for us. And we didn't live far? No. 13 – the house with the chestnut tree, *n'est-ce pas*? Ah, oui. And if we had any problems we were to seek help from the *commune*. It was a big, rich *commune*, with lots of facilities: schools, nurseries and a maternity hospital, for instance. He could also see we were young and so drew our attention to the opportunities for taking part in sports activities in the gymnasiums, the swimming-pool and the stadium. Bernard omitted to point out that we also have a railway station. He would like to have given us a medal, but he had run out of them, *hélas*. He also congratulated the lady in white – the official who acted as usher. He put a record of march music on the gramophone and we left. The sun shone aslant (! – L.V.). I caught up with Isabelle, who was striding off ahead without me, and I scarcely had time to give her a kiss on the temple when the old fellow was back again, beckoning us to return because we'd gone out a different door into the same corridor. The whole thing took ten minutes from start to finish, five times less than this letter, which I am only just writing out ten days later. But you'll like it, I liked it too. Yesterday was a nice day.

"That morning we still had no idea what we'd wear. In the end Isabelle chose a white summer costume, with trousers and a jacket. I wore those very-deep-green trousers and the brown shirt with a fine stripe from Prague, and I thought to myself, all I needed was a dark red bow-tie to be the man of the moment. So I went off to buy one.

"Back home we drank wine and ate ham and a potato salad that I'd made, successfully, that morning. On the table was an enormous flower pot with pink flowers that *mémé* Marie had had sent. We opened champagne, and then ring–ring: telegrams arrived at the door from Bob and Bernard's mother. Then Bernard and I drove Isabelle's witness to the station – she'd come specially from Strasbourg – and went for a beer. The *mesdames* and *mesdemoiselles* stared at my bow-tie and there were smiles in the air. (Martin writes excellently. – L.V.). Then we finished up the salad, and appraised the photos from St. Tropez, after which, however, Irena adopted the expression she does when she's about to make a scene, saying she feels ill and has to go home and that Bernard's eye has gone cloudy. And the smile was immediately wiped off Bernard's face. He's a dreadful hypochondriac, besides which he suffers from some chronic throat and nose infection that has now taken hold in his eye as well. He is in low spirits and lives in fear of blindness and death: depression, in other words. He made a will and burned his lesser-quality por-nography in the garden. His step-father, Bob, saw him at it from a distance and started saying that he was only making a lot of smoke, that the paper would never burn that way, that it needed shaking up. He picked the lot of it up on a garden fork. Garter belts and black-and-white breasts started to spill all over the place. "*Bon, dis donc, mon cochon, ce que tu brûles là, c'est de la pornographie!*" – So I drove them to the station. Isabelle and I hope he won't marry Irena (though he promised her he would when he was in hospital).

"Bernard would like to return to Czechoslovakia, to go fishing with uncle Bartoš and eat kolaches at Mrs. Hubáčková's, who, he says, has a backside as big as a barn. Irena declared that she would knock the Czech language out of him. And every summer she drags him down south for preventive reasons. She regards me as Bernard's wicked alter-ego, and she and I silently detest each other.

"Continued. I'll get this letter together, you'll see. Bernard's snoring here on the couch; he's got some check-up or other in Paris in the morning and he doesn't fancy going into work, or home either. He has a dreadful job. He works as a commercial traveller selling teaching aids along the Belgian frontier: ten schools a day, from village to village; hotels and cheap meals, and no income. When the leaders are in crisis and they're raising the prices (V&W – L.V.) the industrial North can't afford to pay for its schools. On Wednesdays and weekends he goes back to Orleans. Things are pretty tough for him. (*N.B.* L.V.: Bernard is a Frenchman who studied labour movement history, there and in Prague, and now can't make a living with it. But I told him as much several years ago! He found himself an exceedingly beautiful girl here, married her and took her off to France. There they separated and she now lives in Scotland.)

"Bebelle asks me every day (Bebelle, that's lovely! L.V.) whether I've written my letter to you and when I'm going to finish it. But I can't write at any old time, I have to be in the mood and on the right wavelength. Yesterday I forced myself and today I'm having to rewrite it because I don't like it. There are people who toss things off quickly and badly. Quick and brief. Quick and mediocre. We are entirely surrounded by quick mediocrity, a shallow stereotype. I'm talking rubbish again, I'll delete that in the next version." End of Martin's letter.

I ought to report here the conversations I've had with people about the Kohout case, my attempts to frame the text of a protest acceptable to all our friends, and particularly my subsequent efforts to get Kosík to sign it. Or I ought to describe how I hunted for beef today and finally tracked some down. But I am not in the mood, it's probably the wrong wavelength.

So why shouldn't I resort to a ready-made chapter in which two characters finally get happily married, in order to have a well-rounded novel?

On the radio the same thing pounds from every quarter. I am not interested anymore in yet another special broadcast from Voice of America about the Pope's visit there and I am irritated by their arguments about what Brezhnev's real intentions are. On my way to Vienna I stumbled on Budapest, from which such beautiful music could be heard that I had to stop and dance with them to the end. I always dance the czardas sitting calmly on my chair with one arm in the air and moving my fingers gently. I can imagine it all perfectly and I collapse. I told myself I would go out shortly and buy a bottle of *Tokay Szamorodni* in the local supermarket and drink the whole thing by myself. And I would imagine it all and write it all down. But I must not throw any reject pages in the wastepaper basket, because Madla always finds them there and uses them against me: "You asked her if she thinks you're a parasite on her? What kind of answer did you expect? She's a smart one!" Magyar music resembles Moravian Slovak music, or rather Moravian Slovak music is akin in one respect to Magyar music – and we are hardly going to claim that the Hungarians copied us, are we? Half an hour in Budapest and we start suspecting the music of monotony and get the feeling that if we were back in Uherské Hradiště, there would have been a change of rhythm, key and theme by now. Moravian Slovak music is more ramified and plays on more spiritual strings. It took everything there was to take from its surroundings. Moravia is the capital of music.

It was fine and warm today – mournfully torpid. The barometer fell five divisions during the afternoon and is now very low. Everywhere the smoke descends and the stench of crude oil hangs over the gardens. I did not feel like climbing trees again and picked up the scythe. But it is late for mowing; October actually resists it, and to prove it I was in a foul mood. It might also have been because Mrs. Rohlenová's two sons came and started scraping the rust off the frame of the disputed greenhouse. I went over to them, said hello and: "You make me feel quite criminal." – "Oh, there is no need for that," said one of them. But I took the other ladder and carefully placed it against the top of the tree, unfortunately breaking a small twig in the process. Then I clumsily knocked down about three apples with the ladder. At that point I started to shake the ladder and did not stop shaking it until all the apples had rained down. Then I walked away. "Go and pick them up before I stamp all over them," I advised Madla.

And I went on a walk over to the Vodsloňs'. There I learned that another of their sons – the second already – had stayed abroad with his wife and child. That leaves them with only one, and he will be worse off here as a result. I suspect that the more likely cause of the parents' distress is that what they expected has finally occurred, rather than that something unexpected has happened. Vodsloň Junior, the last one left, declared that the workers in his factory had poked fun at *Rudé právo*'s article "Cocky Kohout Crows His Last." Pavel's adventure had gone down well with ordinary people, while the elite was engaged in honing its professional doubts: Hadn't it all actually been according to Kohout's plan? Why hadn't he taken a plane? Why was he returning just before the trials? Why did he have journalists with him?

Take my friend K.K.: "Ludvík, you know that, for some time now, I have made it a principle not to sign anything. I'm sorry." There is no reason for him to apologise, because he is right too: there are people who know how to take freedom by force, the upshot of which is that people close to them are obliged either to do something or to put up with something. "There is just no way of knowing," said Karel K., "whether or not it is some kind of game, and I don't want to be manipulated by any side." – "OK," I said, "but if you assure the StB once again of your intention of staying silent, they'll start to count on it, so you are being manipulated anyway. By not wanting to speak out on Kohout's account you end up staying silent on theirs." – "You're right there, too," said K. Kosík, and since he never again intends to serve any but an indisputable truth, he has an even greater duty to remain silent. "You're right again," I said, "whereas when I find something too complicated for me to work out all its ramifications, I let myself be governed entirely by my feelings, sympathies, habits or... promises. Do you know about Saša?" – "Not a thing," he replied. – "I'll probably put him down as signing, because last year he also promised Pavel." Karel shrugged.

I went on: "Karel, how am I to believe, then, that you will stand by me when I'm the one they arrest?" – He replied: "That's a different matter." – "In what way?" – "Because you don't go in for speculation or manipulation, you just live it."

Terrific. Terrific. I found that really nice. I left discreetly ashamed. I live it, but unfortunately I also write it. Should I, or shouldn't I, friends? You're right, both you and you. So there's nothing for it – seeing it's so complicated and you're incapable of working out the truth on your own – if worst comes to worst, but for you and you to kiss my incarcerated backside.

SUNDAY, 14TH OCTOBER 1979

From which Monday will I finally start my new life? The point is, dear reader, I have not even finished writing the entry for 24th September about my visit to Brno. It was going quite well – the train journey and looking for Šimečka. And then that man, the one who helped me, tripped up and I lost the beat. Then a day goes by and then another and then it is impossible. If I do finish writing up that entry, then it will be the only deception in this book. Otherwise, I have just gone on writing.

When will I manage to see Professor Machovec, to ask his permission to write about him in connection with Ella Horáková? I would have to delete it otherwise. When will Karol finally decide to bring me his appraisal of Chudožilov's manuscripts, so that I can discuss a solution with him, if he is amenable? And when will I smooth things over with Mojmír Klánský, now that the ball is in my court? It was Mojmír who got me into newspapers in 1956. Why hasn't Saša contacted me? It is interesting how one can stroll through Malá Strana twice a week, say, and not meet any of the Pitharts. I need to talk to Petr, but I will not go to their place. Jan Mlynárik was subjected to an overnight interrogation – twenty-five hours non-stop, apparently. I must confirm that or I will have to delete it. My book is coming to its end. All the characters I have started – how am I going to draw them all to a conclusion?

Today I visited one of Pavel's friends to ask for his signature. I did not get it, for sensible reasons: first and foremost, one need not be involved in everything – which is something I also maintain; secondly, one has the right to decide what to devote one's nervous energy to at this particular juncture; thirdly, it is one's duty to keep control over oneself and abstain from contingent enterprises if one has a long-term project of one's own already under way that requires a greater input of energy. The friend in question has already initiated a correspondence with the government: six months ago he sent them a long letter, which he gave me to read. It is a commentary on the state of the republic in the political, moral and, above all, economic fields. Although he has received no reply, he was invited for a chat on two occasions by an official of the government presidium. "If it looks as if they're willing to adopt a different tone in their dealings with me because they need my suggestions, then I feel bound, for the time being, to maintain that tone."

It is interesting but quite simple. That good official is just another policeman, in my view, ensuring our friend's pacification by other means. Tomin gets dragged downstairs by his pyjamas, I get summoned every month to the local police station for intimidation, our friend gets invited to the government presidium building. He is in a higher service category: deluxe.

I am off to bed for a read of Zane Grey's *Stairs of Sand*. There's a writer for you! It's still so topical! And I ban all dreams, such as last night's about a girl I had completely forgotten, who at the time certainly did not interest me enough in that sense for her to take such liberties with me now. In the morning I was amazed: it was as if I had dreamed about feasting on tomatoes when I do not touch the things in daytime. Whatever next?! Can there really exist punishable dreams of passion requiring a vigorous denial the very next night?

MONDAY, 15ᵀᴴ OCTOBER 1979

I'm dog tired, but I still ought to write something, even though I've nothing to tell. For several hours I managed to resist the inclination to put some paper in the typewriter, but at last I have succumbed. And it is half past one and actually Tuesday. I seem to have become accustomed to this writing as a kind of daily self-conditioning. What will I do when I have finished this?

I am dwindling into health again; I have started telling lies once more. I again have the strength to deny my illness properly. I am more laid back, and wiser. When I am beset by a fit of shameful weeping, sometimes in the small hours, sometimes late at night, I let it cry itself out – silently, because of surveillance. I just swear and that distorts their report. I think I am better equipped against fate than I was last year, being more resigned to it. I am also bound to have made strides in my preparation for an eventual trial, when the time comes. I have an inkling what sort of future there will be on this territory, and a timely departure will be a privilege. Bliss. When I look around me on the street or at the faces of our so-called statesmen, there is nothing to presage a peaceful old age. I am amazed that people have children when they have no life for them. I now read everything, maniacally, as a forecast of things to come, and it does not look good. On television yesterday, they showed some small Lithuanian song-and-dance group. I saw the lovely, gentle and graceful gestures of the young dancers with their refined, masculine features. I heard the sound of words modulated by the aged lips of the singers. Each one was different – those people were as different one from another as the nations of Europe. It affected me as if I were looking at the very last singers and dancers of that nation: it is the most they will be capable of, being totally wedged between the Russians and Poles. All they can do now is to go on polishing their lives to make them even more graceful; but they have no reserve of expansionist passion, and above all they are totally unarmed. – That choreography cannot be fortuitous.

This afternoon I was at Karol Sidon's. His flat is a sort of human poultry-farm or urban village in Dušní Street, Prague 1. Children and a slender little woman pass over one another and move among the toys and clothes in an incomprehensible fashion. The effect is pleasantly archaic and protective and Karol occupies very much a back seat. To the left is Vlastimil Třešňák's abode – bizarre burrow might be a better description: dark-room, studio and dormitory in one; two lots of children swarm over the tape recorder, his own paintings and the floor. I have yet to work out what sort of society this is a cell of; I hate to think. Třešňák gave me one of his stories, which describes what I saw there.

Třešňák confirmed the rumour that Svatopluk Karásek wants to emigrate. I almost regard it as a matter of course by now. After all, he wrote these courageous lines:

> You in the faith intrepid
> And in Scripture abiding
> Now they're beating the shepherd
> Where are you hiding?

I made some sort of face and Vlastimil told me that things really were bad for Svatopluk at this moment. I felt a bit abashed at this, because things are fine with me. I was pondering on that yesterday while climbing the Blenheim apple tree: the shortcoming of those people is not that they emigrate, but that they started fighting as if intending to keep it up. Courage has to be rationed like water in the desert or bread during a siege: when I run out of it, I shall simply stop moving. And I do not appreciate the fact that the ones rescued by helicopter will poke fun at me later: Ha, he's not moving anymore! I prefer the way Marta Kubišová sings.

Some people want to be shepherds but are surprised when no one defends them. I expect they do not actually acknowledge any shepherd. It is logical that a shepherd should get beaten. But I agree with Jakub Trojan that he should kick back as well.

WEDNESDAY, 17ᵀᴴ OCTOBER 1979

As I was walking across Mánes Bridge yesterday from the Rudolfinum to Klárov, the sun shone and there was a soft mist. The result was such a beautiful world that I stopped in the middle of the bridge and gazed at it. Not only yellowing Petřín Hill, hanging dreamily in the background above the white water, and, a shade nearer, pinkish-grey Hradčany, but also St. Nicholas' Church and all the houses were covered in a veil of light and mist, even the nearest buildings just across the water, along with the rowing boats and the end of the bridge. The people walking across Charles Bridge were clearly visible, and pigeons whirled above the gallery of the bridge-tower. Some man approaching me across the bridge stopped and took a look to see what I was staring at. I said: "I'm just looking." He smiled and said: "I look forward to you unearthing something nice out of it again, for us." And he walked on. I did not recognise him. I felt embarrassed by his words. I retrieved my bag from the stone parapet of the bridge and strode off into the watercolour.

The picturesque mood was not sustained throughout the afternoon; the collection of signatures is not meeting with much success. It almost looks as if we shouldn't have started signing anything at all, because when people answer the question, their answer generally goes beyond what they were asked. No one, of course, condones Kohout's brutal treatment, but everyone says: 'If someone doesn't want to get locked out when conditions here are so vile, then they must either make sure they do not leave, or not be Kohout.' But I will finish my rounds all the same; I find it interesting. I received a message from Petr Chudožilov saying that he is ready to sign. But I cannot take it into account right now, since he wants something from me. Not because of his feelings, but because of mine. His behaviour is entirely normal.

In the evening we were at the Kosíks again listening to... come on... quickly... Mozart. It was a lovely evening. When we got home the boys told me that two gentlemen had been looking for me. At night I dreamed I was explaining to a bright little German boy how to make and fly a paper kite. I showed him some of Čapek's drawings and woke dissatisfied with the expression *loslassen* for releasing a kite. So this afternoon I was already expecting them and when they came we immediately went off where they wished. It was Major Fišer and Non-Christian. Non-Christian did the talking this time. He was fierce and to the point. By appearing on West German television, I had supposedly damaged our republic's interests abroad, and if others did not decide to prosecute me, then they, State Security, would intervene. They would use all legal means. I had violated our agreement, even after my son had been accepted at university. Major Fišer added that I could emigrate within a month, to wherever I liked, to save me having to send kisses via television.

I asked what "all legal means" were: surely, according to law, one can either be prosecuted or not. Did it mean I would be beaten up as I entered the building like Tominová, or I would have to take a driving test every month? There had been no agreement. A conciliatory atmosphere had developed between us because they had done nothing to me, but I take the action against Kohout personally, for obvious reasons. Whoever decided on that particular action must have calculated with some repercussions, and our protest fell into that category. Non-Christian tersely repeated the warning, and Major Fišer added that I would find out soon enough. And I left, dealt with quicker than at the barber's.

Their patience and nerves are official, of course. Mine are personal. And so far I have been endlessly indulgent. Have they really done so little to me? But I still want to avoid sharp conflicts. I am quite prepared to retreat.

The more things one loves, the weaker one is.

I no longer find the prospect so intolerable.

THURSDAY, 18TH OCTOBER 1979

Although I arrived five minutes before nine o'clock, the table was occupied. Some elderly lady is sitting there, having breakfast: rolls and something, and a coffee. And alongside she has a cigarette case and a lighter all nicely laid out, so she will not be leaving for some time. I had to sit at the table which has a seat to one side only. I am therefore staring at the wall, on which has been scratched the outline of a larger pig being approached from behind by the head of a smaller one, so it is not entirely clear to me which is the bigger pig.

The staff brought me a Becherovka; I think it is the same staff because I was served with a smile. And there must be further smiles at the sight of me writing a letter – because with the one Becherovka instead of two, the table with only one chair and the letter, it must all be crystal clear to them!

I am trying to write neatly, but without success; I would have to make a real effort to write slowly and buy a guide-sheet. Please write and tell me sometimes what you're wearing. I haven't received the hat yet and cannot guess whence it will come winging onto my head. I am curious.

I am still waiting for the day when we shall see each other again, but it's been two months now. It can't go on like this, so what's likely to happen? I'm so crushed that I'm almost totally nice to everyone around me. I'm a living apology, in fact. Thank God I still have the thing I am writing; it is one place I can assemble some courage and purpose. It won't be long now. I refer to the book, and I need your final and carefully considered consent to the name. I couldn't bear an Irena or a Květa; I'd be inclined to kick her off the page.

I am getting to talk to quite a few people who want to know my view on Pavel's case and what ought to be done about it. And I spend my whole day writing, reading or dealing with things and nobody realises that my acute case is you. My in-patient. I have Pavel as my out-patient, of course. The goats of my childhood wander about among these thoughts; outside, the leaves are falling, and I do not know what to tackle first; I haven't even finished the first volume of my "memoirs."

They must have done something against the pigeons, because there is not a single pigeon on Malostranské Square, would you believe? You have a regular job now and who knows what sort of people you'll encounter at work. Will you have a staff cafeteria too? And celebrate International Women's Day and get drunk? And will someone start walking you home?

You said you'd like my advice. That's a very grand word. You'd actually follow some advice (from me)? It's more likely you want to get some cares off your chest. But let's play at giving advice: it would not be a good idea if, even for a decent salary, you let yourself be walled up in some hopeless, routine job that you'd gain nothing from. As soon as you were used to it and knew the ropes, you'd be only too relieved to conform to a calmer stereotype at last, i.e. you'd become reconciled to your situation. That is something to be avoided. It would be much better for you to get a clear idea in your own mind of what you personally want and are actually capable of. I'm not telling you this for your edification, I couldn't give a damn about edification. I am telling you this so that it might be useful, in case it occurred to you to choose that option.

What a blow: the lady isn't leaving but instead has been joined by two cronies and they're just starting to chat. And she is just telling them about some gentleman who has been coming here almost every day since June to wait for some woman. When finally he gave up this week, she arrived, and so they missed each other. The second old lady is asking how many days' leave are given when people get married. And the third elderly lady has just started to sing. Behind the curtain the staff are discussing how much they make each day: "I made six and a half thousand on Friday." – "Thursday, five two, me." – "Over ten, Sunday." I would be more interested to know how many times they made something else. (I am beginning to feel that Becherovka!) For shame. Sorry. I myself am making so very little use of my time, almost none.

Yesterday I was at another intimidation session. They told me they could arrange the papers within a month and I could leave. I received your bulbs and they're in the ground already; there are thirteen of them. I'll let you know afterwards how many come up, if I am here to see. I expect I sound darkly menacing, but I mean nothing by it, except that I really don't know. I am gradually growing firm in the determination that nothing should bother me. My patience is going to run out too: it really is I who have been terribly lenient with them, not they with me, and I can make murderers of them if I feel so inclined. You're lucky to be over there. Of course it grieves me that people leave here, but it is part of the grief I feel at the nation's dreadful apathy. No, don't go thinking I'll do something stupid; it is just that I won't let fear stop me. I do not mind humiliation when I choose it myself or calculate it in advance.

I won't write to you about my women, now or ever, and certainly there's no question of sending anything. Please do not distress yourself any more, you have no reason to. You're probably on a better footing with me now than you were before, because you opened my eyes to something. I am freer and all I can do is thank you for it. It's as if you led me up the Hill of Enlightenment. You gave me back a part of myself.

I have moved over into the front room of the café, to a marble table-top with a chair on each side. So you can come now; lateness up to one hour does not even require an excuse. And I have ordered a second Becherovka. Through the window I can see people walking past. There's an old fellow sitting just near me. He's unshaven, has a light-brown checkered jacket and a red checkered shirt, grey trousers and black elastic-sided boots. His pyjama bottoms are sticking out of his trouser-legs! He has an electric cable stuck in his left ear and it runs over his collar and inside his shirt. I'll have the same, Helena, before long. You're lucky to be over there. That second Becherovka has possibly improved my wit, but it has ruined my handwriting.

I much prefer the man at the tram stop – I can see him through the glass. He's wearing a light-brown jacket, and the tram has taken him away from me; he had a light-brown jacket, greenish trousers, a fine old hat on his head, and he had equipped himself for the times with a crooked stick. I'll have something to eat, as I had no breakfast. All they have is Hungarian salami, Csaba sausage, frankfurters. Should I send you some Tokay? To the school? It's lovely outside today after yesterday's rain: bright sunlight diffused through the upper mist. The streets have a freshly-washed look. Pithartová has her corner window wide open this morning. The old fellow smokes BT cigarettes and drinks white wine. I let nobody touch the wine, but was that beautiful request of yours under the wooden shelter transferable? You shouldn't have left. You could have taken me away, but even you must have realised that. God be with you, Helena.

FRIDAY, 19TH OCTOBER 1979

As I read what I wrote yesterday, it strikes me there is something very familiar about it – yes, of course, what a horrible thought: it has the same rhythm and tone as the father's letters in *The Axe*. A kind of delirium between reason and reality. I flee that topic in superstitious trepidation.

I went to see Karel Pecka at his new flat in Nerudova Street and he cheered me up a bit. He has a large well-lit room with a vaulted ceiling, simply whitewashed, and, opposite the armchair in which he seats his visitors, an enormous mirror, so guests can observe with ease how well their visit is going and whether they have been sitting too long already. He signed the statement about Pavel, of course. He said that Jan Mlynárik was going around in a state of dejection and had lost weight. We know the reason, and we spent a few moments talking about it. Karel Pecka is another candidate for dejection; he is actually plotting it like a geometrician. But it is not much good talking to him about it.

I took a tram to the New Town, changed to another, and rang the doorbell of a flat in Žižkov or Karlín. The door was opened by a woman saturated with rejuvenating creams. She invited me to a coffee-table on which stood two glasses, evidence of a visitor who must have left just before I arrived. "I've had it ready for ages, but I didn't know how to get a message to you." – "And how did you like it?" I asked. – "It's dreadful!" she sighed with profound conviction. "There were parts I found disgusting." – I stared at her in amazement and also with mortification, as I had previously praised the book to her: it was Eda Kriseová's *Woman of Pompeii*. I was at a loss for words and allowed myself to be served a little white wine in the rinsed glass. The lady poured herself some too and sat down opposite me, taking out a cigarette. She rattled a box of matches but did not light up, because she has been giving up smoking for the past year. The whole time she rolled the cigarette nervously in her fingers above the table top.

She said: "The point is, the woman's supposed to be a painter, and so she ought to have some sort of aesthetic sense. Yet in several places the author writes about the mess she had in her flat and the little children in the middle of it. That kind of society is foreign to me, perhaps young people do live that way nowadays, but I wouldn't like to know anything about it." As we were saying goodbye in the passage she said: "Don't you have something cheerful there at all, something I'd get more enjoyment from typing out, so I wouldn't have to keep getting up from my chair and rushing around the room, wondering whether it's a good excuse for another cigarette?" – "I'll have a look for you," I promised.

I took the packet of transcriptions and made my way to the bookbinders, but I walked past the building and went home. Something perturbed me. I have an aversion to two fellows sitting silently in a parked car. I will ask Eda to see to the rest of it herself.

I made myself some Chinese green tea and read about the witty detective Nero Wolf and the murder of Caesar the champion bull. That's a book to cheer one up! It is worth transcribing.

I stopped the car at the beginning of the bridge, but I can't have put the brake on properly, because as I walked round the car it started to roll away slowly. Oddly enough, it rolled forwards, even though the old stone bridge sloped upwards and only turned downwards beyond the crest. I reached out to try to stop the car, but my hands slipped on the metal and my feet on the snow, which sleds had packed smooth. The car slowly drew clear of me; it was not dangerous at all. People moved calmly out of its way and just talked about it in amusement. It was completely empty; through both windscreens I could see a boy reaching out to stop it. The car disappeared over the crest of the bridge when I started to run after it, slipping as I went. I reached the crest and saw that things looked bad. With inexplicable force the car had struck the stone parapet of the bridge, and its bonnet, actually crushed flat, was now sticking out over the water. And an old-time policeman was already standing there writing everything down in his notebook. He was an older chap, and I was surprised how calmly – more out of concern than anything else – he started to ask me how it had happened. "It's completely wrecked," he said, "but I expect you're insured." – He did not even want my papers. I was already beginning to imagine the painful moment awaiting me at home, when I'd tell them what I had done. What excuse shall I give? What can I blame it on, seeing that I can't even recall why I got out of the car in the first place. I suddenly realised that the policeman was apparently unaware of this. I told him. "So at the time of the accident you weren't at the wheel?" he asked, and as if relieved he slammed shut his notebook. And I was relieved too and started to tell him jokingly how the car, which couldn't have been properly braked – my own fault, certainly – had rolled off uphill. This caused the policeman to lose all interest in the matter. He dismissed it with a wave of the hand and turned away, commenting: "There's the wagon – it's already coming for the corpse." – I asked: "You mean there's a corpse in the car?" – "Of course," he said. – "But who could possibly be in it?" I said, racking my brains to remember who had been my passenger, though this only served to strengthen my conviction that I had been alone in the car. What was interesting, though, was that my fear – unfounded, I was sure of that – homed in on some very definite person. The policeman said: "That girl, of course." I looked inside through a hole in the metal. On the passenger seat I could see a white upturned face: dark-brown hair, ruffled and sweaty as if in the heat of sleep, the mouth half-open in slumber. Between the lips I could make out two bright incisors with a gap between them. It looked erotic. I recognised her instantly, but it was not sleep, because she gazed at me unseeingly from beneath her distinctive dark eyebrows, with clear, calm blue eyes. No verdict of acquittal, none at all, will ever exonerate me, I thought with surprise! Surprise that anyone could possibly think I would want to go on living. I sensed very clearly that I was the son of death, that I was actually dead already. And that was all right. Only now does my nightmare commence. But how can a life that I do not want be returned to her? A frightfully cruel convulsion of the will condensed into the wish for it not to have happened, for a chance to undo it all, for it not to be true! And I sensed that the futility of such a wish was the proverbial hell, eternal and feared.

Interestingly enough, all my well-tried safety devices failed in that dream: not the faintest hint that it might be a dream! It was the sternest truth. I can't recall ever having had such a convincing dream. The nastier or more absurd a nightmare has been, the more sceptical I have tended to be of it, and I have always managed to crawl through the flaws in its logic towards anticipated rescue. Last night there was none of that: only damnation deeper than anything I could ever imagine. And then I remembered – merely remembered – that last hope of all those in the deepest despair: God. At that moment I awoke.

SUNDAY, 21ST OCTOBER 1979

"So now I'll get that tea and an aspirin," Madla said a moment ago on her way to bed, "and I'm glad I've lived to see fifty-four. I must not," she said and repeated it, "I must not forget what I wished for when the boys were small: if only I live to see their eighteenth birthdays, at least! Because all through my young years I used to say to myself – if I had a mother, things would immediately be better!" I handed her her tea and said: "And now at last you can die, mother?"

Strictly speaking, I am the invalid. So much so that on Friday I was obliged to seek medical assistance. After the fiasco with the heart complaint last spring, here I am in autumn with a leg condition. In spite of my scepticism, the condition worsened until finally, on Friday, I was unable to lift my right foot higher than the street kerb. I sacrificed one signature for Pavel, who is a hopeless case anyway, and instead of making for Franta Pavlíček's, I set course for the clinic. The doctor prescribed me two different medicines, and I have an appointment with the orthopaedist tomorrow. One of the medicines is called Benetazon, and within an hour of taking it I was able to lift my foot as high as the tram step, so I went out – I no longer recall where; I would have to check back a couple of pages.

So on account of my condition and also partly because we did not feel like it, we did not go to Dobřichovice yesterday, but today we had to, what with all the piles of apples under the trees! It was not too bad during the day but towards evening I was unable to lift my foot onto the doorstep to unlace my boots. But it's all right, I am going to the orthopaedist tomorrow – that is, unless I get picked up on the way by StB agents working on the assumption that I'm headed for the courthouse on the day that the trial of the ten VONS members opens. I wouldn't be going anyway, because I have made it a practice not to attend trials, ever since the first one with Mr. Václav. On that occasion, Jaroslav Hutka wrote ironically that the next trial Vaculík would be sure to attend would be his own. Quite right, young man. You do not run away from your own trial. This afternoon, we finished picking the Fořt apples – Madla had to be up on the step-ladder with me below – and I said: "Another thing I don't like about those emigrants is that they think they're worthier than the rest of us. As if they were especially worth saving. If there had been freedom here, they'd have certainly stayed. So freedom's OK, a mass grave no? Who do they think they are?" Madla said: "Yes, I find it a bit offensive too."

I was lying on the carpet, a moment ago, exercising my leg. Egyptian soil is made of Egyptians and Greek soil of Greeks, isn't it, I said to myself, testing the correctness of my opinion. Suddenly something went in my knee and the thought flashed through my brain: and of their enemies! That, please note, is a thought from my knee alone! What would I manage to think upon that topic with my head? We had better leave it at that, in case they send us to prison before they are ready.

But I mentioned Fořt apples. This name is unknown even to the experts. When we bought Topič's garden, we were given a guided tour by a former Topič family servant who told us what she knew about each of the trees. Some of the apple varieties were unfamiliar to her, and I later had them identified at the pomological advisory bureau. The old lady introduced one spreading apple tree to us thus: "That one gives fruit every year. The apples are beautiful and last till June. But they don't taste good at all. Not even Dr. Fořt wanted them." Dr. Fořt was private attorney to Mrs. Blekastad-Topičová from Norway and looked after her property matters here. At the pomological bureau, the beautiful yellow apple with the red cheek and waxen-sheened skin threw the experts into a quandary. They sniffed it and took slices of it, but their sense of smell let them down and they had probably eaten a surfeit of apples that day. In the end, they told me to bring some further samples. But I never got round to it, and by the following year the apple already bore the sonorous name of Fořt. It is not the practice in pomology, though it is commonly done in medicine: I don't think Dr. Bekhterev wanted that illness, either.

MONDAY, 22ND OCTOBER 1979

It is automatic in nightmares that when you fear something it actually happens. No sooner does it occur to you that a red cathedral might disintegrate than it quietly starts to do just that. A wise head has a good rule: dread nought.

I washed, shaved, gave the avian life clean water, drank some tea and swallowed my medicine, got dressed, put on my cap, opened the door to the passage, and there sat two young uniformed policemen on chairs. One had a moustache like mine. The other one stood up and said: "Mr. Vaculík, would you show me your identity card?" – "I see you know who I am, but I will show it to you," I said. – He examined it and then came the obligatory question: "Where do you work?" – "At home," I said.

I went to the orthopaedic clinic, where, in my boxer shorts, I was examined by the doctor and then, in slightly dropped boxer shorts, X-rayed by a nurse. Apart from that I did not notice anyone following me. I took my prescription to the pharmacy and picked up two medicines, one of which I will have to go and have injected three times a week. As was to be expected, I have had no pain anywhere since this morning. I stopped at the stationer's for two rolls of toilet paper and at the chemist's for two bars of household soap and some toothpaste. At the grocery shop I took a half-loaf of bread, a plastic bag of milk and two bottles of lemonade. I thought of things to do and places to go to give the nightmare in front of my door an opportunity to change for the better. I looked in the mailbox and took out the latest issue of *Aeronautics and Cosmonautics*, from whose front cover a fiendish portrait of Jupiter's moon Io leered at me. I took the lift up and discovered that the situation had greatly improved: there was only one man sitting there; the other seat was empty. "Any news?" I asked, in the tones of prime minister Štrougal. Moustache shook his head silently. "Nobody looking for me?" I asked, imitating the minister of the interior, and had in mind the Soviet advisors. The man shook his head again.

I have made myself a cup of coffee and will now sit down in the armchair and study the lengthy and interesting report from my Jupiter correspondents.

TUESDAY, 23ʳᴰ OCTOBER 1979

When I left the flat this morning, one of the guards stood up and said: "I've got a message for you." Something from Gruša, perhaps? I thought to myself. "You're not to go to the courthouse, because you won't get in anyway." I went to be injected and to do some shopping. I came home, wrapped up a packet of books and took them after lunch to the post office. The men in uniform took no further notice of me. I could not stay indoors, I had the feeling that the sentries could unlock our door at any moment and look at what I was writing. I was suddenly struck by the frightening thought that in visualising it – by virtue of the automatism of the nightmare – I brought it closer.

I dropped in at the Slávia, where I learnt that yesterday they had picked up about thirty people in the vicinity of the courthouse, releasing the majority of them straight away. The presiding judge is pushing the trial ahead at full tilt: no presentation of evidence apart from written material, and nothing on the part of the defense. The prosecutor is demanding the severest penalties for the main defendants – that means up to ten years. There is a great storm of protest about it round the world, but it will blow over in a couple of days. One of the younger generation of poets, Andrej Stankovič, eagerly signed the statement for Pavel in the Slávia. Who else to approach? There are people who would eagerly sign, but on principle we are only taking writers.

It was marvellously windy on the embankment; the trees are almost bare. The sun shone but it was cold. What does our need for courage command us to do? – That question, phrased differently, I subsequently put to Karel Kosík during the evening. We were at a concert – some Beethoven sonatas or other. I did not get much out of it, my mind was on goodness knows what.

Karel also declared that he was annoyed. "We ought to think up something completely new, something they're not expecting," he said. The status quo depresses him too, and he is ever more single-mindedly seeking a solution that takes him as far away as possible from it. Doctor Kriegel was absent from the concert, as he has had a heart attack. During the interval I met Eda and my lady painter and just said hello. My painter appeared very concerty; alongside her jolly, extrovert husband she seemed rather curled in on herself.

In the concert programme it states that when Napoleon entered Vienna he placed a guard of honour in front of Beethoven's door. The composer derived little enjoyment from it, though, as he was too embarrassed to go out. Well, I'm not so fussy. "We ought to think up something completely new," Karel says, and he is right. I will give it some thought.

After the concert, we accompanied the Kosíks across the bridge. We were intending to have a beer at Schnells' pub but they were unwilling to serve us, even though it was still thirty minutes to closing time. We went across to the Malá Strana Café for a glass of wine, and it was the same story. Karel said: "What time do you close?" – "Eleven o'clock," replied the waitress. –"And it's twenty-five past ten. Bring me the complaints book," he declared with a severity we are not accustomed to from him. "Bring him nothing of the kind," I said. Madla and Marie laughed. "Am I supposed to tolerate this?" said Karel. "Write and tell Sartre," I said. As soon as the waitress heard this, she jumped and immediately brought us two fruit juices and two glasses of wine.

> Where the lions prowled
> Two idiots howled
> They howled in the lion pit
> In the Bible it is writ

This dreadful poem was written not by me but by one of the younger generation of poets, Andrej Stankovič.

WEDNESDAY, 24TH OCTOBER 1979

To open the door of one's flat and come face to face with two guards – policemen – in the hallway is, you must admit, an original experience. It is like suddenly finding yourself in a demonstration or at the scene of a disaster.

There's been a murder! the thought strikes you. I just cannot get used to the idea of being a designated enemy of the state: nothing I know about myself would support that conclusion.

Our pair gave us no trouble. There was only the cigarette smoke that seeped from them under the door into the flat and the occasional growl or cough, or the shuffling of feet, when a solitary grain of sand would scrape beneath their boots, resounding, I expect, throughout the entire quiet building. We have no idea what they were doing there the whole time or what their brief was. They certainly let no visitors past, as no one came. In the space of two days, about three pairs took turns. Some of them plainly found it irksome – a strange assignment. When we were leaving for yesterday's concert, Madla said to them: "We're going to a concert." They replied: "Have a nice time." When we returned after eleven, they were gone and I thought they would not appear any more, since the trial ended yesterday. But this morning there they were again.

Yesterday I got the idea of photographing them. I told it to Jan in a quiet whisper, right in his ear, so it must have been even quieter than the sound of a grain of sand scraping beneath those boots of theirs. Then I said to myself that I wouldn't bother. But when I heard the severity of the sentences passed by the court, I said to myself that I would photograph them after all. Our place is ideal for it: both men are seated on chairs side by side facing the lift, backs to the wall behind which our flat is situated. Set in that wall is a tiny window from the bathroom. If you climb onto the bathtub and stick your head out the window, our front door is on the right and framed within it would be two sentinels in twin profile, like on coins minted to commemorate the victory of some socialism or other.

That bathroom window is of enormous strategic significance in our flat, and I hit on it when thinking up my short story "Defending the Apartment" a few years ago. The plot: burglars pretending to be policemen try to enter a certain apartment, but the *paterfamilias* recognises their voices and refuses to open up. Instead, he organises his family to defend the home. The story takes place in a five-storey apartment block in an American city. The burglars want to break the door down, but it is buttressed by a system of planks. The mother keeps a pot of water boiling on the stove. The children shout down to the street that there are burglars in the building; they signal the news from the window to their friends in the yard and it is broadcast over the radio the same day and appears in newspapers the next. An inquisitive throng starts to form in the street: the crossroads on Veletržní Street is impassable. Having achieved nothing by stealth or direct assault, the burglars cut off the family's electricity. But they are unable to cut off the gas or water because those are inside. There was no telephone, the family was too poor to have one. The burglars decide to starve the family and weaken them by a lengthy siege, but invective starts to rain down on them from the tiny bathroom window and later – on this the choleric father is unable to agree with the conciliatory mother – turds as well. The enraged burglars, still posing as policemen, have the neighbouring flats cleared so as to get in by battering down the walls. At the same time, they bore a hole into the ceiling from the attic, as we live on the top floor. When I had thought the story out this far, I could see we were in a sorry plight. At that moment, another gang of burglars arrives, posing as firemen, and they have a special ladder with them. It is not a rescue ladder, however, but a wrecker ladder. Two burglars are already climbing it, hauling up a thick hose, even though there is no fire! For that reason, the prescient father, before he started writing, had had piles of paving stones brought up to the flat and now we see the eldest of the three sons hurling down those heavy grey blocks. The firemen can be seen tumbling all over each other down below. At this point, the door from the passage splinters, but the planks still hold it in place and the middle son is able to splash boiling water through the holes out into the passage. The youngest son has the job of keeping an eye on the walls and ceiling and shouting down to the street for help. None is forthcoming, however, because you're all lily-livered sons-of-bitches. The father is counting on news of the affair eventually getting out, if the burglars fail to break into the apartment by a certain time; then it will be spread about all over the place until it becomes too much for the authorities of that American city to bear and they will call their burglars off. Meanwhile, what about those breaches in the walls and ceiling? In my anguish while I was thinking out the story, I asked my friend Josef Zeman if he could make me a halberd: after all, that has a point for poking, an axe for chopping, a hook for hooking or pushing things away, and its long haft would enable relatively remote combat – out of the window and through holes. And so the father distributed the axes to his sons to chop off the first insolent arms penetrating the flat, and he took hold of the halberd himself. It's to be bloodshed then! Mother prepares bandages and puts water on to boil. And everyone takes care not to stand directly in front of any opening: the burglars might open fire!

I came to no final decision about what the price of victory would be. But a victory it ought to be, because in my view, Czech literature is in need of a story with a victorious ending, if it is to survive. But I just could not fathom how to engineer one, now that the passive gawpers had been cleared from the street below, which lay silent and empty. Maybe that explains why I did not start to write the story at all, and why Major Martinovský, when he really did arrive, found the halberd blade behind the cupboard, and it had not even been fixed on its haft yet! At the time – it's a good few years ago – he asked: "What's that?" – "A halberd," I replied, abashed. And it did not even occur to him, it did not need to occur to him, to ask the next question: "What do you have it for?" He was already inside the flat.

So it's a useful little window, as you can see! I loaded a 27 DIN film in my camera, got up on the bathtub in my bare feet, very quietly opened the little window, stuck out my head and gazed straight into the face of one of the policemen, who must have been given the order, in force from this morning, to turn his chair to confront my barely whispered nightmare thought.

That happened at nine o'clock this morning, and at ten thirty the sentinels left of their own accord.

THURSDAY, 25ᵀᴴ OCTOBER 1979

This morning, I received my anti-leg injection and headed for the streets. No one said I was not allowed to walk. This evening, however, it occurs to me that they merely forgot to tell me. I went across Letná Park, through the avenue of plane trees, and the wind swept the dry leaves into my face. A comforting, conciliatory melancholy. The rain of the lapsed season, raining back on one. I hope it will be a hard winter.

I am trying to find a present for Martin and Isabelle. I bought something today: two identical Molniya pocket watches. I have something similar my-self, and it had taken Isabelle's fancy: it looks a trifle anachronistic, you see, as modern chronometers go. The ones I bought today have a relief on the rear cover – some heroic figure and the inscription "Skaz ob Urale." They are massive and reminiscent of heavy-engineering "eksport produkts"; they are rather touching in their way. Whenever I look at my watch or at any similar product that embodies Russia's striving after human ingenuity, it causes me to reflect on those people and their past, as well as on the future that inexorably awaits us in their company, and I wish them well. The world is awful.

For Zdena I am trying to get a little gold chain from which she could hang the nugget we found in the Black Lake. Well, I *call* it a nugget – I hope the chain I buy will have a higher gold content. I do not know what to get Madla, but something special. Apart from that I already have one present hidden behind the piano: the antique mirror. For Helena I am trying to find the first volume of *Bohemia's Cultural Monuments*, which is now sold out, and for Pavel, one more signature: Věra Jirousová has just come to my mind. Boxes of Christmas biscuits have appeared in shop windows. It all fills me with confusion, alarm, sadness and dread.

There is an argument brewing at home. The boys have been avidly following the trial and the response it has evoked. Madla has been keeping a tally of the people's comments about the event and has come to the conclusion that the people is not very interested. And I sense she is peeved with the people over it, but also blames the defendants for their lack of success – for failing to be the sort of people whom the people could, or might wish to support. They are nothing but odd-balls – journalists, writers, psychologists, reformers. Their exclusivity sets them apart from people. People feel they were convicted chiefly for their pigheadedness, not for defending the truth. Truth? That's not hard to find, it's staring you in the face! When, out of a million people who know the truth, six allow themselves to be imprisoned for it, it has to be exhibitionism, vanity or political speculation, surely? "What you'd like," I shall roar if the threatening row finally breaks, "is for random examples of run-of-the-mill, common-or-garden, uninteresting people to be convicted for their courage, the ones who have things in order at home, who perform uninteresting jobs, are not aroused by any ideas and have no interest in politics!" – But she says nothing.

I am as disgruntled as a lame dog.

Věra Jirousová from the poem "September, October":

>...are covered in dust
>a lowland dell strewn with thorns
>the light blue of flowers on the breeze

a rain-faded slope
laughter in the seashells
the stench of death

be quieter still
morning purple for the naked man
there still remains

a rounded hiding place of pain

FRIDAY, 26TH OCTOBER 1979

It is hard for me to turn over in bed because my leg, once bedded, gets cross when ordered to change position. Thank goodness it didn't catch me while I was picking the apples and nuts. Not to mention between March and the twenty-fourth of August! However, if I remember to use the correct foot when going up steps I scarcely feel there is anything wrong with the other one. And I dance the czardas as well as ever.

Věra Jirousová never unlocks the door until she has satisfied herself that there is no chance of a house-search. Her head was wrapped in a white cloth because of a chill, and as she led me through bric-a-brac deeper into the flat, she excused herself: "Please don't look at the mess – I fear I really am an intellectual after all." I reassured her that she probably was not: "An intellectual likes to have ordered thoughts, and orders material objects accordingly." She sat me down at the table, where her dreadfully clever five-year-old son Tobiáš was at that moment looking in the encyclopaedia to find out which creature has an enormous brown-and-white-striped conical shell and discovered that it must be an Indian Wheel sea snail. However, he mistakenly calls his mother Věra, which strikes me as biologically unfitting: I am convinced she is his mummy and in fifty years' time he will recognise the fact, along with the whole of the Czech underground.

On my way down to Charles Square I remembered Mojmír: he had not been at the concert! Either I offended him by buying my own tickets or he is ill. I telephoned him but he was not in. When I hung up, the telephone returned my coin. Taking advantage of this rare and lucky fault, I made three more calls. Who else could I phone? O.S.! O.S.– Odious Sod! He answered,

... and keeping silent like a reminiscence of himself ... (p. 419)

and I said as politely as possible: "Mr. O.S., I still haven't received my photos from Ella Horáková's wedding that took place last winter, when you were booked as the photographer." He replied: "Yes, it's my fault. When would you like them by, Mr. Vaculík?"

Kolář's table at the Slavia was thronged with dissidents like a hive with summer bees. I squeezed a chair in between Jiří Pechar and Petr Kabeš. Someone had brought the latest issue of *L'Humanité,* and Zdena Tominová and Pechar were translating what it said about the Prague trial. Professor Černý was sitting by the pillar that holds up the entire Café Slávia, smoking from mouth to nose and keeping silent like a reminiscence of himself; now and then he would throw in a more appropriate Czech expression, even though he could not see the French text. I ordered myself a coffee and a soda water. Olga, Havel's wife, was there too, calm and entirely unliterary. Doctor Danisz invited all present to his wedding tomorrow, when he is getting married to Jiří Gruša's first wife, and I gave him the wedding present I had been saving for him: Tatarka's *Jottings*. He had been wanting to buy a copy from me a while ago, but I had none left, so now I have had to give him my own. Gruša read us out the official notification that criminal proceedings against him over *The Questionnaire* had now been suspended. That particular piece of "harmful literature" presented only a minor social threat. We all laughed and he was proud. Eva Kantůrková said nary a word the whole time. Jaroslav Kořán, the translator, gave me his signature. Professor Černý explained to me why Pavel Kohout could do quite well without his. I had to agree with him. I paid up and left.

At the tram stop I shook uncontrollably with the cold. On Fridays, the streets are something terrible. When the tram finally arrived, I felt like giving it a good kick, but my right foot is out of action and I am not much of a kicker with my left.

In the mailbox I found a letter from Mrs. P., from which I shall quote the following excerpt:

Dear Ludvík,
It looks as if I really am a writer now, because the most I can manage is a letter! But you, you are not even a writer, because you can't manage anything at all, apart from a taciturn diffidence whose chilliness I can feel all the way from Holešovice, or wherever it is you live! We've

had a dog for several months already and it's a month since I finished my story: "Wait for Me," and I would like to give it to you to read...

I will give it some thought until Monday before writing: "My diffidence is illusory. On the contrary, I am cast down with a sweet sorrow, which is to be prized at my age and not eroded with fresh sorrows. And my leg hurts too. So send 'Wait for Me' to my Holešovice address, and I will read it sympathetically and – if you've made a good job of it – with an enjoyment that cannot be equalled by any reality, at my age, and after a year like this."

I took the lift up to our floor; from now on I shall always be looking through the frosted glass for two dark shadows to appear. I prefer being home. And when they are all there. But I only found Madla. She stood leaning with both hands on the table, looking out the window at the dim backyard of our block. "Would you believe what just happened to me? I came in, put the light on, leant on the table like this, and all of a sudden I heard a kind of rattling – and can you see it?" She pointed at the window. In the exterior pane, there was a perfectly circular hole one centimetre across, from which cracks radiated. "I immediately turned the lights off and have only just switched them back on again."

First I wanted to telephone one of my keepers, but Madla said: "Won't we look silly?" I shall see tomorrow. If it looks like an accident or a prank, I shall report it to the police. However, if it is something more serious, we shall launch an investigation of our own, the boys and I. And Madla will put the water on to boil.

SUNDAY, 28TH OCTOBER 1979

This morning I examined the window and found two air-gun pellets: one between the outer and inner window, the other out on the window ledge. An air-rifle is nothing very terrible; on the other hand, two shots are no accident. What it does mean is that our disfranchised status is known to people in our backyard. I went to see the building's superintendent. "I'd call in the cops," he said, "but I realise you don't want anything to do with them." – "How right you are," I agreed. "They could use it as a pretext for giving me a permanent guard 'in my own interest.' I should just like you to see it. I shall put a notice up in all the houses that someone shot at our window."

Yesterday I woke up with the suspicion that my leg did not hurt any more, and lo and behold, it was fit for anything. In the morning I had to tidy up and after lunch we rushed off to Dobřichovice. It was terribly cold. The thought of again spending the next four or more months in a cool wind, mostly from easterly directions, makes me less than confident about those four months. In the garden, I was fit as a fiddle when I started shoveling compost out of a pit to make room for raked-up leaves, and after an hour I could scarcely climb out of the pit. And once more I was unable even to take my boots off. I never thought my health would take this turn!

The tall white-tiled stove burns well. In the space of two hours the room-temperature rose from five degrees to ten, and then quickly soared to twenty-two. Madla did some ironing; I read Mlynář and then listened to Voice of America, where they had an interview with Vilém Prečan. I could visualise his childishly pouting lips, but I think that the sense of intimacy I felt, the feeling of an unbroken relationship with him, also stemmed from the fact that his carefully worded opinions could still have been coming from the free radio transmitter set up at Bílá Hora that time, and not from America. Some speakers astonish one by the alacrity with which they adopt foreign viewpoints – unintentionally and through no fault of their own. He talked about the Charter and the trials. I admire the work of those unknown people who dispatch news from here to the outside world, very speedily in most cases.

I read Mlynář's *Nightfrost in Prague* until long past midnight; it is a remarkable book *per se* and also in terms of its contribution to Czech literature. It is written in a style that has been extinct here for the past three decades, whereby a text informs about the subject and the writer at one and the same time. It discards any attempt at unattainable objectivity and convinces through its plausible subjectivity. The Mlynář thus revealed brings back to the Czech political scene a phenomenon of earlier and better days: a figure who is not a public personality but one who serves the public for private motives, which – and why not – can be acknowledged without shame. In spite of its subject-matter – the rise and fall of the 1968 Prague Spring – the book cheered me up.

During the night I had about ten dreams. All I can remember is a lecture hall where I was sitting among strangers, and when the lecture ended and everyone stood up, I discovered, as I had many times before, that my bottom half was bare and that my vest barely covered my navel. I elected to walk in a tight group of people so that only those nearest me could observe my shame. Another brilliant idea I hit on was to limp slightly, which excused my bedroom attire. Having come to terms with it psychologically in that way, I immediately started to worry about something else: whether, now that it was exposed, my sexual organ was not ludicrously small. However, I did not wish to examine myself, so I can't even tell you.

In the morning I noticed I was covered in a rash – on account of one of the medicines, I expect. Outside there was a slight frost. I briskly went out into it and started with renewed verve and stupidity to shovel compost out of the pit. The outcome was the same as yesterday, so I contented myself with pruning the gooseberries, at least. In the process I thought about last summer: about the Sázava River minus Pavel, about Milan Šimečka and whether our St. Martin's Day reunion will really take place. Madla predicts that I shall end up going to Brno alone again and my friends will make their excuses. "Ivan told you he'd go? I don't believe it. At most you'll go with Gruša, or on your own. And if you do go on your own then I don't believe for one minute that it's because of the Brnonians. You've got some other motive." That angered me. I told her to leave me in peace, but soon she came back again and with a cunning look on her face declared: "But it's a working Saturday! Don't tell me that Šimečka and Kusý will be taking the day off from work!" – "We didn't know it was going to be a working Saturday," I replied. It's a fact: if they were both to apply for leave, it would look suspicious. "Unless Milan manages to send me a message somehow, I shall have to go. You can see that, can't you?" I said loudly.

But I would much rather go into hibernation.

WEDNESDAY, 31ST OCTOBER 1979

It was at most three minutes after eleven when I arrived at the café in Karlova Street, and Mrs. P. was already on her way out. "Where have you been?" she said, in a tone that told me how unbearable she finds it to sit for more than a minute in a pub unprotected by at least one credibly compromising male person and at the mercy of many and various conjectures on the part of all the men. "My dear Drahomíra," I said, "whenever I have a date with you, it always means that I have somewhere else to go both before and after, and I arrange it in order to be on the same route and to fit in with my timetable. At this moment, I am on my way from the post-office, where I had the misfortune to be standing in a queue behind some old woman with a huge pile of official mail. After you comes Eda Kriseová, whom I shall merely guide to the gates of the bookbinders, where she will conduct an experiment by leaving them her novel about virginity preserved, so that we may find out whether it is true that they're beginning to keep tabs on the binderies and confiscate manuscripts. And half an hour later I am seeing Mrs. Havlová at the Slávia. And but for the fact I'd made all those arrangements, I'd never have left the house today – look at the way I am walking."

I let her choose a table; she chose the most secluded alcove. I have a bad reputation – Madla's always telling me so. Now I acknowledged the fact: "Quite right, make sure no one sees you with me!" – "What are you talking about?" the lady said woefully. "And why are you being so cruel to me? You're the one who put the message in our mailbox, telling me to come. Why?" – "Because I don't intend to come to your place." – "In other words, if I hadn't taken this step, you'd never have come again, ever?" – "Of course I would," I lied. "I'd come if the need arose, and otherwise I count on meeting you on the bridge from time to time." I wriggled into my seat with difficulty. – "Don't you think you're being a bit silly as far as Petr's concerned?" she said. "You're behaving like a little boy." – I ordered myself some white wine, she asked for mulled red. "Are you pregnant?" I asked. – "No way!" she said miserably, "I'm cold." – "And I think I've got a temperature. Look!" I boasted, proffering my forehead across the table. – "I don't intend to feel your forehead! You've got plenty of others for that." – I said: "Quite right. Now show me that story and you can leave if you like." She handed me a sheaf of papers; I glanced at the last one: forty pages.

"How's your writing going?" she asked. – "Ever onward," I said. "And I'll have to initiate permission proceedings with the people I'm writing about. With you as well." – "In God's name!" she exclaimed classically. "What have you written about me?" – "Everything, of course." – "But I don't want there to be anything sensitive in it!" – "And where would I find anything of the kind, for goodness sake. I always substitute three dots for sensitive things." – "You beast! It never got as far as three dots!" – "I know, but people believe nothing these days unless there are three dots. They'll say to themselves: Why did he visit her?" – She squirmed helplessly and said crossly: "Just don't write anything at all about me! Leave me out entirely." I said: "That's out of the question. The whole basis of the book is that it includes almost everything, and the rest is represented by samples. Anyway, you will have an opportunity to correct your part afterwards. But the fact will be indicated." – She said: "You're nothing but an exhibitionist and are dragging the rest of us into your ignominy with you." – I stuck her forty pages of exhibitionism into my briefcase. "OK then," I said. At the same time I came across the envelope with the photos from O.S. "Do you want to see the photos from Ella's wedding?"

So far, everyone's reaction to those photos had been the same: that it was the last thing I had needed. "Whether I needed it or not," I say, "I did it extra!" To my mind, those photographs speak chiefly of desolation. "You don't happen to know what happened afterwards?" I asked O.S. when he delivered me the pictures. – "Apparently he threw the wedding cake in her face, like in a slapstick comedy, and she hurled the passports into the forest."

Drahomíra turned the wedding photos over in amusement before pushing them haughtily aside. "I'm more interested in those," she said. They are extra photos that I ordered from O.S.: various groupings of guests at the Kohouts'. That memorable evening when a woman I did not know got up on a chance impulse from her place opposite, crossed the room, and sat on my knee, like a child coming to her favourite uncle. At the time, the photographer's professional preparedness failed him: his camera did not flash until she had slipped off my lap and squeezed into a corner of the couch by my side. She had her hands clasped in her bosom, her legs crossed within her long skirt, her face turned towards me, but also tilted back and smiling blissfully with her eyes closed. It was the sort of gesture that no one found anything wrong with, not even my wife – at the time. But when Drahomíra had finished looking through the photographs, she pushed them over to me, took a sip of her warm fragrant beverage, heaved her bosom in her grey-green blouse gathered with a cord at the neck, and said: "Did you sleep with her? Yes or no?" – I had a drink from my own glass and declared tantalisingly: "You'll read all about it."

When we parted ways at the corner, she said: "You're a hypocrite!"

It is as if nothing concerns me. I look straight ahead and keep going. And I happily start to shiver. That happened yesterday. This morning I finally recognise my illness *de jure*, and I don't want to go anywhere, hear anything or see anyone for a long, long time to come.

November already. Today is All Saints, a public holiday in Baden-Würtemberg, Bavaria, North Rhine-Westphalia, the Rhineland-Palatinate and the Saar, as well as in Austria and partly in Switzerland. Here it's simply the saint-day for Felix.

Our Jan came home from college at mid-day, helped himself to bread and milk, and ate while reading the script of a play he and Ondřej are acting in somewhere tonight. Then he went back to the faculty. He needs little encouragement to study, I must say! It is mostly technical drawing. He often works till after midnight and I have to chase him off to bed. When we ask him how he feels compared to the other students, he replies: "So far I've been unable to work out whether I'm fairly good or whether I am underestimating the course. I have the feeling they get too worked up over it. They make out that they have to study all the time, but I can't see what." When he has everything ready, he plays the drums to a tape recording, fiddles around with Švácha, and occasionally spends a Saturday or Sunday at Zeman's, helping him with something or other and going horse-riding, but chiefly seeing some fifteen-year-old Monika who also travels there from Prague to go riding. But most weekends he spends at the building site with Ondřej: they have already plastered the inside walls of the flat and are now laying concrete in the stairwells.

Ondřej came home from work, lay down, and will sleep for an hour. Then he will load up some props and go off somewhere with Jan to act in that play. It is his play, in fact. The one time I saw it, I did not know what to make of it: it is a kind of poetic dada. In the course of the play a log of wood is realistically chopped, and they have to bring a new one from Dobřichovice for each performance. And until I put a stop to it they were taking my dry logs, the ones I plant seedlings in. Now they have to cut themselves a fresh one each time from a green trunk. But it only now occurs to me that I do not know if they take the chopped wood back to Dobřichovice. When the company's administrator was asked by some unpleasant person whether he knew he had two Vaculíks in his troupe, he replied: "Are there any objections? If so, then in writing, please." But the authorities have been decent; only fate has been fickle – after two or three performances the administrator has had to seek another hall.

I've read Mrs. P.'s story and it is good. She is taking risks again, though. She gave her heroine a good old-fashioned name, but in a neo-snob form:

Anny. This Anny ferreted out (via whom? – the author, of course) what I am writing; in the story my book is finished and she is reading it with excitement. "He recounted his sins with disarming candour and was thus in fact asking his fellows' forgiveness, in such a natural and poignant way that in several places Anny was moved to tears. His habitual arrogance, however, did not permit him to consider for a moment that he might stop sinning. But he had such a desperate need for forgiveness that he himself forgave everyone everything, so that they should do the same for him... The places in the text where he indulged in this 'tolerance' were noticeably weak." – End of quotation.

As the wife of a prominent dissident, Anny is well placed to observe the way dissidents associate and how they cope. It is life in a ghetto. Any attempts at breaking out incur the risk of losing one's freedom – if they are at all significant, that is; and if they are not, they merit derision and Anny derides them. In their kitchens, living rooms and beds, all those fighters for human rights are probably no better than their persecutors. And Anny actually embodies unbounded amazement at this. Not even in the Chartist nest, where everyone hopes the eggs of a better future are to be hatched, do women manage to lie with the right men. Crushed by her disappointments, Anny no longer requires anything of men except that they should be human. When one of these rare moments of untrammelled human warmth and tenderness occurs, even this must be destroyed: "For the first time in a long while she felt safe in his arms and started to drift into sweet slumber. But then she felt his hard member rise, without compassion, against her limp body."

"Poor Anny! What shall we give her, or write for her, in exchange for that?" is a question I shall have to ask the author, in all sincerity, the next time I see her – if I see her.

I pinned up a notice in the houses on the block and have already received several tips from the citizenry: to the right, from the window above the bistro, some youngster "of Gypsy origin" reportedly fires at the pigeons; on the second floor of the house opposite someone has an air-rifle, but it is a long distance away. I relaxed. But as soon as I am fit, and have got over this feeling of having a high temperature that refuses to be registered on the thermometer, I shall wash the kitchen window and take a photo of that intriguing, precise hole in the glass. And if the fancy takes me, I shall send it to the agencies as evidence of how dissidents get shot at every day. They will all print it, and it will be a fabrication! As far as my leg is concerned, I have resorted to extreme measures: I am staying home. That enormous rash is moving down my back and belly and I am just thinking that when it runs off onto the carpet I shall vacuum it up and be done with it.

But it is November the First, Felix's day, and I have no idea whether I shall get another opportunity to incorporate a little poem that has been on my mind the whole of this autumn, for some unknown reason. I learnt it from a school reader, and I cannot even recall whom it is by. It is to be recited slowly without any expression at all, without punctuation and above all, without a full stop at the end:

> The yellow leaves fall from the trees
> Yonder the birds fly away
> And the flowers on your tomb Daddy
> Are shedding their blooms today
>
> They'll shed their blooms and disappear
> Borne off on the chilling blast
> And soon your darling grave Daddy
> Will be left alone at last

SUNDAY, 4ᵀᴴ NOVEMBER 1979

"Would you believe what people now want decided for them? And by the state!" I was raking the leaves together into a preliminary pile. "I was there on my own by then, yesterday evening, when in comes a woman, one of that self-assured variety, with her hair and her face done up, and something round her neck here that went straight down her cleavage. In a word: el-e-gant! She lit up a cigarette right away, of course." – I entreated her: "Get to the point, would you?" – "And from a distance and at great length she starts to tell me how she has a husband who's devoted to his children, what a good father he is and how the children adore him. I said to myself straight off, Aha, you've got a W." – I asked irritatedly: "What are you talking about? What's a W supposed to be?" Even though I know perfectly well that in Plzák's algebra M stands for husband, F for wife and W for the third party. But when I am raking wet leaves and they keep clogging the rake, obliging me to keep cleaning it all the time, I am short-tempered.

Madla continued: "And immediately she blurted it out, her husband was fine for the family, but her lover was unbeatable in bed." – "So what's her problem," I asked. – "He wants to divorce her, her husband. Mind you, I think he's just trying to put pressure on her, but she doesn't know that, and most of all, she doesn't want to give it up, He was the first one to make a woman out of me! The lover, that is. What a cow! She has two kids with the one, while the other one makes a woman out of her!"

Leaning on the rake, I asked her for a second time: "So what's the problem?" I employed my most academic tone. Madla always uses her professional cases as a means of re-educating me, to which I respond with a professorial expression. – "The problem is that if it came to a divorce she might lose the kids. And now she isn't sure – isn't sure! – what to go for: the children or the lover. And do you know what she wanted? It's the first time anyone has come up with this one, that we as an institution should give her statistics to indicate what gives women more happiness – children or sex with a guy?" I asked: "She said 'sex with a guy?'" – "They're my words, she said 'sexual harmony with another partner'" – "There you are. See how you spoil them?" I said. "If people didn't have your expert terminology to hand, they'd never dare talk out loud in some state institution about the people they're fucking. Have you been up to see to the stove?"

She went off to feed the stove and I started to get more and more incensed with that painted cow: using the power of the Union of Women, they really will set up a single State Semen Bank with donations from screened party cadres (What is your opinion about the intervention of the five Warsaw Pact armies in 1968?) and artificial insemination, which would have nothing to do with their orgasms, cultivated by means of courses at other state institutions.

I laid aside my rake and went upstairs. "What did you tell her?" I asked. – "I wasn't entitled to tell her anything. I was supposed to listen to her and book her for a consultation, but who with, a lawyer or a psychologist?" – "So what did you tell her then?" – "'Look here, Mrs. So-and-so,' I said – of course she has an engineering degree – 'what are you worrying about? What *you* need for happiness is your sexual harmony. So go and get it then. And leave your husband and children to seek their own happiness as they please without you.'" – "Just as well you're retiring," I said. – "Yes, it is just as well!" – "Otherwise they'd fire you. Was she pretty?" – "She would have been quite pretty, but for those cold, hard features that technicians have," indicating the corners of her mouth and the area around her eyes.

I went back to raking. When she followed me down a moment later, I asked: "Does the Phantom know about it?" – "I reported it to him, naturally, and do you know what he said? Our big high chief said that she was a reasonable woman and that was how we ought to operate. He immediately set our young things the task of thinking about how to find a key to establishing such indicators of happiness." – "And what did the young things say?" – "I'm sure you can guess – i.e. a possible topic for post-grad research. The horror of it doesn't occur to them. Their first thought is for the career opportunities it might hold." – "Who will she be seeing, that woman?" – "She didn't turn up. She was supposed to come in the next day, and she didn't turn up. She probably took the hint." – "She doesn't know that what you said was at variance with your institution's task of nationalising people's privacy." – "If she were to tell on me, I'd be out the door in a flash."

It is Madla's birthday at the end of the month and her workplace intends to take the opportunity to say its farewells to her in advance. They have a farewell party planned for her, where she is to make a speech, and she is already worrying what to talk about. "That's simple," I say. "You'll tell them what it was like to work with a bunch of informers." – "Don't be so silly. On the contrary, they're all nice to me. There are only two informers. Everyone knows about them, fears them and avoids them. One of them is now leaving for another institution." – "What institution?" – "Some magazine or other. And that's a sure-fire way of telling a cop, they are able to move on anywhere without any continuity. And the other one was betrayed by the Phantom himself. He is terribly dissatisfied with her and would love to throw her out. On other occasions he has had no trouble getting rid of people he doesn't want, but this one he isn't allowed to." – "Here you are retiring and we still have no answer to the question whether he wanted to get rid of you and wasn't allowed to, or whether he wanted to hang on to you and for that reason was required to vouch for you to someone." – "That would also help explain why he treats me the way he does. I prefer to believe the nicer alternative."

The past two days we have been making apple juice. We already have more than a hundred litres and are not properly equipped for it all. We dribble it all over the place; sometimes we sterilise it, sometimes we do not. I have drunk at least five litres of it. It must be terribly healthy, because my leg has almost stopped aching. Before going to bed I took two tablets of aspirin, had a good sweat, and this morning am a new man. I went out elated and stood beneath the bare trees, scanning the sky, and was overtaken by an immense suicidal melancholy, outwardly inexplicable.

A new man but an old fool.

MONDAY, 5ᵀᴴ NOVEMBER 1979

I am rewriting last night's naughty dream for the third time in an effort to find expressions at least slightly in keeping with these surroundings. But I'm still not sure I shall have the courage to admit to it.

On Friday, six more VONS members were arrested, including Otka Bednářová's two sons. (Most of them have been released by today.) An event like this always sets me fretting over the old question: how should one react to it, if one wants to keep control over one's own life at the same time? Consistent resistance to lawlessness transforms people into professional outlaws. The point is it leaves one with neither the energy nor the time for anything else. It is a cyclotron! Between bouts in prison, a fellow has his work cut out getting food and fuel. In the end, a life-style like that whirls a kindred companion into his arms: they have children who learn to divide people into plainclothes cops and uniformed ones. Friends, things and places have code names. Peace, order and discipline are suspect. What happens when these youngsters reach an active age? Will they still have any idea what the original, normal state of society is like – the one that the struggle is supposed to restore? I am fearful of the eventual bitterness these youngsters will feel when it turns out that the next renewal will not be the work of those who were denied education and employment, but rather of those who had the opportunity to study, get jobs and mature become coming to the right conclusions.

As I write this I have no one specifically in mind. It is a random reflection. There are other times when I know full well that these youngsters will bring forth people of deep intellect, introspection, fortitude, dauntlessness and foresight.

I wanted to go over to Kosík's to ask him, mischievously, what our courage required of us. But I had no time, and anyway I knew his answer: hadn't I set myself aside this year of restraint in order to complete my dreambook? And what about *Dear Classmates*? If I end up not finishing anything, how will I support myself? And how much time will I be granted for the things I still want to do? Clearly it will be my turn next. The only thing I can do is to steal a march on an alien fate by acting in accordance with my own code.

After a short sleep I woke to black images of my future. A child about an inch high was swarming up some scaffolding made of thin, red-leaded iron tubing. The child would slip but always managed to catch on with one arm like a monkey. When I could stand this no longer, I started to climb up the construction after it, but the frame started to warp beneath me and it tilted into a space that suddenly was infinitely deep. – A whole year without a single fair, decent, male dream?

And now that it has come I am ashamed to describe it. I am now confiscating it – 2nd April 1980.

TUESDAY, 6TH NOVEMBER 1979

At supper I asked: "Would anyone possibly like to read Mrs. Pithartová's latest short story?" Madla asked to, and a moment ago she was already here to scold me on account of it. What sort of perverted woman was it who had a shampoo and then objected to an erect male member? What was she after, who did she think she was – and poor Petr. "What Petr do you mean?" I said in earnest surprise, which took the wind out of her sails. She did a verbal U-turn, backed off from the author and set off in pursuit of poor old Anny. "The name's bad enough – Anny!" she spat.

I told her it was part of the author's intention to depict a frail woman unsuited to the circumstances which her husband has to grapple with, and that it was a good position from which to debunk dissidence, and it was only the author's temporary lack of literary experience, detachment and refinement that allowed her to be identified with the central character. In spite of certain similarities, she was a practical enough woman in her attitude to life, with well-brought-up children, a clean home, sufficient sanity to use writing to analyse her extreme states and sufficient brazen reliance on her husband to allow him to read her outrageous writings and for him to allow them to be made public. And I was sure that at the right moment she welcomed a male member, I did not add. "I really would like to talk to Petr some time," said Madla. – "Well so you could, if we didn't refuse their invitations all the time."

In the latest issue of *Czechoslovak Photography*, they reprint Robert Capa's famous photograph *The Falling Soldier* of 1938 and say that it was arranged. Negatives have been found after the Great Photographer's death showing the same hero posing for something else. And some daft dame writes there that it does not matter; after all, she says, Štursa's sculpture "The Wounded Soldier" is also artificial, like anti-war graphics... and anti-war films... What is important, she maintains, are the feelings and thoughts the photograph evokes, and the role it played in promoting an anti-fascist and anti-war climate. Can you believe it? The daft dame elevates the personal interests of Art above the interests of people. That partisan in Saigon, in the act of being shot with a pistol to the right temple, paid for his best snapshot with his life. And I hope that the kneeling woman with her child being shot point blank by a Nazi soldier did as well. And the next argument that the daft dame trots out as if it were self-evident, whereby she floors me for the second time, is that Hájek's photo of a fleeing hare – that heart-rending picture of the animal horror of a field creature – is also arranged, it seems: the hare is stuffed and the convincing effect of frenzied flight is created by camera movement. Would you believe it?

I talked to Jiří about it and he expressed surprise too. We agreed that if that were true, there was more human truth in pornography: there too several heroic deeds are arranged with a single erection, but we have the assurance that during the final one, the hero falls.

And before we go off to bed, here is Madla again, coming to say to us: "And the conceited way she writes about Kosík!" – "What? There's no Kosík in it." – "He's given a different name, of course, but it's him all right. How on the day after that party where that Anny talks to him she brings something to his flat and he doesn't recognise her! He dared not to recognise her!" After brief, but thorough reflection I said: "Don't be stupid. Kosík never goes to parties."

I can see I will be the best off: all ludicrous speculation about who's who will be avoided, and the most they will be able to find after I'm dead will be proof that it is all even truer.

I sent a card inviting Drahomíra to the Jadran wine cellar, which is unburdened with past associations. She arrived in an almost crimson costume from Germany that made her look just like a school-girl. Her hair was beautifully buoyant; I expect she had been washing it again: she just won't listen! She was calm the whole time and her speech and gesticulations were almost light-hearted. I was glad – it gave me a chance to take Anny to task.

"Unless you revise the story you can't include it with the rest. Madla has already drawn up an entire diagnosis on the basis of it. – She said calmly: "Is she biased against me already?" – "I mediate badly between the two of you. I realise that now. It would help if you could manage to talk together face to face. She would be able to see you're more normal and you would stop thinking she's being jealous. You'd realise that she's actually an awful sceptic most of the time. She has an aversion to artificiality and hates the sordid being made sensational."

She took a sip of her red wine and said, as if she had every right to do so: "You've ruined her and damaged her image of the world. Everyone who knew both of you before says so." – I said: "If you like." – "And you've ruined Zdena's life too, do you hear me?" – "Okay, okay, I'll make a supreme effort to take myself in hand." – She reached across the table to touch my sleeve. "And what will you do, Ludvík?" – "I'll enter my invisible cloister." – She recoiled with a jerk and said: "How come? You've pinched that from me! That's shameful. It's me who wanted a cloister! And now you'll be there with her? With that one?" – "Leave me alone! I've had enough of you all!" I said so loudly that some people looked round.

And actually I have no wish to write anything else about it.

At last they have filled in the pits in front of our house, and now they are covering them with a layer of asphalt: the house is full of fumes. Even our birds are irritated. Today I asked Karel Kosík what our courage now demanded of us. He replied that this morning he had met a certain journalist of the fifties and sixties and exchanged a couple of words with him, and ever since he has been seized with horror at the incorrigibility of that type of person. "Fine," I said, "but research, reflection and work on a *magnum opus* does not discharge one of the duty, the need, or the temptation even, to react to daily events."

Karel said that his work might turn out to be futile, but nonetheless he felt it to be his chief task: each of us had to do the thing to which we felt best suited. The events surrounding the VONS trial had shown that there were enough people, thank God, young ones especially, who were capable of reacting honourably to events. "And you," he grinned slightly, "are that balanced type of human being who goes on creating his *opus* while selecting, from the problems of the day, the ones he intends to react to." – "Oof!" I gasped, gratified by the bit about balance, but disconcerted as regards the *opus*.

Then I said: "But one has to dress according to the season. So far I've found a raincoat sufficient, now I'm looking around for a winter coat. I can't wait to read – that *opus* of yours!" – "But Ludvík, you'll never read it!" – "I'll make the effort and toil through," I said, making scout's honour with my right hand. – He shook his head: "You'll read the first page and say, Goodness, do I have to read all this nonsense?" – I asked: "When will you finish it?" He replied: "That's the very same question I was asked on Monday by the StB at Bartolomějská..."

He had received a postal summons. They led him into a room with a Stalin, and as if to break the ice asked him politely what he was writing, how far he had got with it, and where he planned to publish it. He heard them out and then said he did not think that was the purpose of the meeting. Of course not! they said, and immediately turned to the real question: some intellectuals were circulating some newsletter in Prague and the general opinion was that he was the author. Was this true? He replied that he knew nothing about such a newsletter. They noted his reply and let him go. "What was it they were after, do you think?" – "They wanted, Karel, answers to the real questions," I replied, "what you're writing, how far you've got with it, and where you intend to publish it." – "That's what I think too," Karel said. In the end I asked him if he would go to Brno with me, but he told me he was not feeling well.

I arrived home and on the very threshold I was overcome with such a foul mood that I turned tail and went out again. I walked the whole length of Belcredi (ex-"Peace Defenders") Avenue, looking in shop windows full of totally uninteresting things, and then stood for a moment in front of the local police headquarters. There were lights in only five or so windows of the building: what crime could they be working on? I went to the Belvedere for a bad dinner. There I observed the staff and clientele and then examined my

1980 engagement diary, noting that it was identical with this year's. On the way out I stuffed five one-crown pieces into the slot machine in front of the cloakroom. Some of them returned to me multiplied and I kept shoving them back in again until there were no coins left. I had the feeling I was acting like an unknown man who has nothing to do and nowhere to go, but is on the brink of an adventure he does not suspect.

The adventure was entitled *The Holy Year*. Commissaire Maigret was playing a bogus bishop who escaped from jail by using bed-bugs in his cell as an excuse, but the plane to Rome was taken over by hijackers. However, Maigret took the million dollars off them and used it to buy freedom from the Italian police to escape to a chapel which he did not find in its proper place, so his plan to live off money stolen some time earlier collapsed. But he took it like a man – an old man. That helped cheer me up a bit and encouraged me in my criminal activity, because I saw something that appeals to me: so long as I can, I shall go on evading them and doing what I want. When they catch me I shall glower at them and refuse to talk.

I had one weak moment right at the beginning of the film: there were several minutes of people rushing about some beautiful foreign city by car and on foot.

It is night again. Madla came and wordlessly placed a square of paper on my desk. On it was written in pencil:

> Daddy, are you actually
> running away
> from us? Even
> abroad maybe?

FRIDAY, 9ᵀᴴ NOVEMBER 1979

FRIDAY, 9TH NOVEMBER 1979

There was such a crush at Kolář's table that I was unable to squeeze another chair in. I sat nearby and waited for Jiří Gruša, in order to remind him about Brno. When he arrived he said he might not be going as they are expecting visitors. I observed how Professor Černý sat there, silent and motionless, just smoking; there is no way of telling how he perceives events; he rarely reacts to anything. I am amazed at his interest in this youthful bustle; by his age I'll be crabby already and find everything so loathsome that I won't even leave my burrow; that is obvious already. You will not find me asking for the latest news. His eyes are bad, and he never stops reading and writing. Everything that once formed his external spiritual world is gone, and he is left to himself. So he has emigrated inwards. No, that's where he was always at home. That is why he is not so pathologically dependent on the outside world. I would rather like to ask him what he sees, but I do not know how to talk to him; it could be that I'm frightened of him.

As I am going away and have no idea what might happen, I needed to find someone to help me sort something out. I chose one particular person for the purpose and hoped he would turn up there. When he arrived, I took him to one side and put my request to him. The answer I received was: you received a fee for it, so do it all yourself. These words sounded like the truth, but consider the context they were uttered in! For years I have performed work without reward. Other people have made use of it and it has never bothered me: maybe someone somewhere else was doing something for me, in turn; in life such accounts are always settled in some roundabout way. I felt I had never received such a slap in the face, ever. As I rose to leave, Jiří got up too. He asked me what was up. Then he mocked me for turning to that person in the first place. I took a walk and turned over in my mind what had happened. Why had I turned to that person in particular? A good question. Because I realised the critical state of our relationship and as a petitioner I was offering reconciliation and trust. The answer that came is perfectly correct. It is more natural than my request. It helps correct my inaccurate notions about the way things are here: remove the pressure that squeezes us round Kolář's table, and a harsh struggle would be unleashed – over money, status and glory. Having thus analysed what had happened to me, it started to bother me less.

So I set about sorting the matter out, tendered my apologies to Zdena, and thought to myself ruefully how late I would get home and what sort of things I would hear. It was already dark when I got to the Pitharts. Mrs. P. let me in. It was Petr I wanted; he was in the bathroom and shouted to me in an extremely rude fashion, but one, nevertheless, that accorded precisely with my own feelings and state of mind: "I've just come in. I'm in the bath and I shall be here for another three quarters of an hour!" I left the thing on the table and departed. Outside I could not help laughing: Serves me right for having a finger in every pie!

The train was half empty. In our compartment two men were sitting opposite each other speaking some Romance language or other, but most of the time they slept. Ivan, in the window seat opposite me, was reading *Svědectví*, Karol was quietly saying a Sabbath prayer from a Hebrew book, I was looking out the window. The sun shone weakly through heavy, humid clouds. The fields flying past were now only brown, the meadows rusty, the trees black. The cold streams cheered me with their meanderings and the shimmering surface of the flood water on the meadows whetted my appetite for sailing the seas in a yacht.

The express left Prague precisely on time, Japanese-style, but as we arrived at Havlíčkův Brod the timing was rather more Turkish. Ivan pointed this out sulkily from within his reading. In an attempt to take his mind off it I told him the complimentary things I had heard about his book of short stories *My Merry Mornings*. I was pleased when he took out a roll and started to break pieces off it. Two days before he had felt so bad that he almost pulled out of the trip. I said: "I'd like to thank you very much, Ivan, and you too," turning to Karol, "for coming with me. You have no idea how disappointed they'd have been if I'd arrived alone again." Ivan said: "Well, I'm missing the Dukla-Bohemians match on TV today!" We recalled the charming scene that Vladimír Blažek once made when someone forgot to give him a ticket for some match. He trembled with self-pity: "But everyone knows that it's study material for me as much as anything else, and that I'd do a piece for *Literary News* about it, and most of all – I just enjoy it so much!"

After Havlíčkův Brod I invited good old Karol for a coffee. The waiter in the cold and almost empty dining car welcomed us in three languages. Over coffee, Karol explained to me the pre-Christian origins and significance of the symbol of the Virgin Mary standing above a moon and stamping on a snake, but I have forgotten it again. In exchange I told him the latest news about conditions on Jupiter's moons. He was surprised. When we returned to the compartment, we got a reprimand from Ivan: "Must you be spending money all the time? I warn you that the Writers' Union won't be paying any expenses this time!" Karol said: "I wouldn't even turn to the union, seeing that they ignore us. But there must be someone we could send the tickets to – Radio Free Europe. They never miss a trick." Ivan said enthusiastically: "I think that's an excellent idea, let's send the tickets straight to Schulz."

Shortly afterwards, Ivan went to the lavatory and came back in a more cheerful mood, with the news that there was an interesting inscription there. Karol and I rushed to look. Written in black on the window were the words "Free the Chartists!" in Slovak. We were passing through a landscape of beautiful, deserted fishponds. In the corridor I related to Karol the plot of a Hungarian television film about Sinbad searching for his lost Sheila, and how he eventually found her, with the help of a faithful female slave, after surmounting terrible dangers. But when he embraces Sheila, he discovers that he does not want her any more and yearns instead for someone else. In his struggle to remember, the image of the faithful slave, who was there just a short while before, floats vaguely before his eyes, but she is already lost and gone. Karol was moved.

That (?) brought us round to Genesis, and Karol said that the dogmatic interpretation of the creation of the world out of nothing had only arisen from a translator's misapprehension. God – and in Hebrew they are actually gods – *gods created* the world from *what was*. We were passing through Osova Bítýška when I said that, for me, the most important question was no longer whether the universe was finite or not, nor whether it had sprung into existence and would eventually expire, nor even whether it was eternal. I was not interested in the debate about the relationship of matter and spirit, and I no longer anguished over whether God existed or not. No, for me the ultimate question was: How come anything exists at all? After all, it was equally possible for nothing to exist! And that had come home to me with a vengeance when I personally saw that the surface of Ganymede was curved into a ball shape like everything else, and that the ice on Europa, perhaps a hundred kilometres (or metres?) thick, was cracking and under it there was probably water. I was not expecting an answer either from philosophy or physics, or even from theology, because I could not conceive how they could ever reach one. It actually seemed to me that there was no compunction or need for us to look for an answer or dream one up, because one had always existed and all that was necessary was to recollect it. This made Karol laugh and we arrived in Brno.

The Moravian metropolis appeared half-busy and half-dead on that working Sabbath. Karol and I first went for lunch, while Ivan went looking round the shops for something dietetic. Seeing that the bill was on Mr. Schulz, we chose beef and lentils. This is a very luxurious dish, now that lentils can only be obtained from Tuzex at fifty cents (US) a kilo. Back on the pavement Ivan was already waiting for us, chewing a half-unwrapped square of processed cheese. Brno is not Prague: no ham or decent salami even. Karol wanted to look for a synagogue, but we no longer had the time. We set off for the hotel, from which we will not be allowed to emerge until tomorrow.

The plan for this visit was Milan Uhde's brain child. If Milan Šimečka and Miroslav Kusý could manage to evade surveillance in Bratislava, they would book into one of the older hotels on the outskirts of Brno, one that is usually occupied on weekdays by workmen who go home to their families on weekends. They would book two rooms, with at least two beds each, and next door to each other if possible. (There were supposed to be more of us coming: I had in mind Kosík, Gruša, Vladislav, and even, at the outset – Kohout!) We would enter via the hotel's café; from there you do not have to pass the reception desk, so we could just run upstairs and there we would be.

In the hotel café, Šimečka was already sitting at one table, Kusý at another. We split up and joined them. Then Uhde arrived too. Trefulka was away at a spa. Shortly afterwards we were all upstairs in one of the bedrooms, laughing. "Where's that Martinmas goose you promised?" I asked Milan Šimečka. He shrugged apologetically: after all, just three hours ago he was still being interrogated. They had come for him at work that morning and he thought the game was up. How he had rejoiced to find they knew nothing! All they asked him was what Jan Šimsa had wanted; they had arrested Šimsa the previous evening in the passageway in front of Šimečka's flat. "How should I know, seeing that you picked him up before he had a chance to tell me?" The answer seemed logical even to them, so they let him go.

Kusý now handed round glasses and poured us new wine from a demijohn standing by the table leg: it was still untamed and full of conflicting flavours. Ivan became slightly downcast – or rather he did not, that sort of thing does not bother him – and I pulled out a bottle of our excellent apple juice, which I had brought from home for him. We spent that evening (and part of the night) in the room. The other room was for resting. Karol went there first to say the evening prayer, and then Ivan went to air his lungs after all the smoke, and I went there for a half-hour nap. Around nine o'clock, Milan Šimečka said: "And now friends, I will present a futurological commentary on the situation, on which Mirek Kusý and myself agree..." And he expounded a thesis according to which, a year from now, we should be living in a changed situation, and so much better, apparently, that Kusý, on hearing this, could not help remarking: "Well, even I don't believe that." It electrified Ivan: here at last was someone with a different point of view who had reached the same conclusion. Karol maintained a sceptical silence and he strove – from memory, as he unhappily did not have the necessary tools with him – to ascertain what the stars had to say about it. For my part, I did not really care. But I enjoyed listening. The only thing I insisted on was that we should agree on a date to meet again like this – whatever the situation, for heaven's sake! And no more writing about it! We agreed on the 2nd of February, Candlemas, and made a mental note of it.

Another nice moment came when Milan Šimečka, leaning on the corner of a cupboard, glass in hand, started to congratulate each of us on the way we write. He even went so far as to praise Eva Kantůrková's *The Black Star*; I must tell her. Coffee was constantly being brewed with the help of a miniature immersion heater. Milan Uhde set out the plan for the next writers' congress, which we adopted, and then he went home. I mostly drank lemonade, for some unknown reason. The demijohn ended up slopping about between the two Bratislavans. Kusý spoke very little. He was pleased when we praised his intermittently ironic study of Charter 77, which had been published in *Svědectví*. For a while we discussed how it could have got there, and we vented our spleen. Nothing but trouble! The first to fall asleep, as early as ten-thirty, was Karol Sidon, on his stomach, fully-dressed. Milan Šimečka asked how sincere Karol was with his Hebrew prayers and Ivan said: Completely. They started to ask me how far I had got with what I was writing. "I'll have it finished as soon as it's done," I said. They told me I was as bad as Kosík.

At about one a.m. – Kusý was baffled why so early – Ivan and I got up, leaving Karol where he was lying, and went to the neighbouring room. Milan Šimečka accompanied us to our beds, wished us good night and said: "Boys, it's a pity. I thought about one thing, but I didn't know how you'd take it. I wanted to bring you a beautiful young student. This would have been the cue for her entry." Ivan, already lying straight on his back, turned on him: "That's what you promise me every time!" When Milan disappeared I asked Ivan: "Did he mean it?" He replied: "It would seem so, but in fact, he wouldn't dare." I asked him: "What would you do?" Covering his face with a scarf, he replied: "I wouldn't want her." That surprised me.

At last the first real sad November day, when to go out into the street is to convince oneself that the best thing is to stay indoors and let all the anxieties creep back where they came from. In the flat there is lots of heat and plenty of blank paper, or lots of books, at least. The telephone is determinedly silent, the years roll back, and all stupidities can be changed into wisdom. We shred the summer sun within the cabbage into the barrel of sorrow, and we shall tread it really well. Dear Ester!

When I got up this morning and discovered what sort of day it was and that my leg did not ache, I washed the kitchen window that looks onto the yard. In the process I noticed that tiny white scales of snow were flying about outside. Then I wiped the floor in the entrance hall and in the hallway in front of the door. After that I gave the birds a shelled nut and stuck a crescent of apple between the bars. Only then did I put on the water for my morning tea; it was ten o'clock. I stood by the window and gazed into the grey courtyard, at the roofs of the workshops and garages, at the ventilation ducts and pipes of the cheap cafeteria round the corner, and at the mighty chestnut tree that takes up almost a quarter of the yard – our enormous spring garland, the autumn lodgings for thousands of starlings, now a thick black scaffolding of branches.

After my tea I returned to my room, sat down at the typewriter, typed today's date, drew aside the curtains, the better to see what I wanted to write. But what I saw I didn't like. I was longing to write a dream about Ester, only I never dream about her. And everything else I might have written went off at such a completely differently tangent that I got dressed, packed my briefcase and went out into the street. I shall not be doing this much longer.

Jiří Pechar is engaged in a psychoanalysis of recent Czech literature. He would also like to include the latest works by the main authors. Some titles he is unable to obtain include: Pecka's *Notes from Prison*, Klíma's *There Stands a Gallows*, and Kriseová's early things. I promised to help him with it.

He made me a coffee and we talked. He lives alone in a three-room coop-erative flat that lacks nothing, not even various frivolous decorations, and yet it is an austere environment. It reminds me of my years in a dormitory. He let me read what he had written so far about Kohout's *The Hangwoman*: "Readers of *The Hangwoman* are obliged to change their view of the author three times in the course of the novel. First, Kohout seems to be writing black humour, then political satire, and, finally, student pranking. The author's 'cynical machismo,' which is exhibited here in the end, is ill received by those who recall the days when he exhibited his restraint. One can only look forward to the time when he will come to us with the ostentatious modesty of wise old age." – Here was I holding a critique written at my own friendly request: originally Pechar had intended to spare Kohout by leaving him out, but I told him that would seem like an even worse criticism. Now he was looking at me with a sheepish smile.

"It's possible to say all that about Kohout," I said, "but he also deserves a little justice." Pechar turned over *The White Book*, which I had just brought him as a further illustration of Kohout's method, and said: "But just take this photograph. What do you say about it?" It is a detail of Pavel's face, with a facetiously defiant smirk: Pavel playing a role. I said: "That's a momentary likeness that was superseded by a different one a moment later, but it's typical that publicity should invariably choose – or he should choose for publicity – a likeness that fits the received image of Pavel Kohout the playwright. Admittedly, I have never seen him utterly miserable, but there are occasions when he does look rather more crestfallen." Pechar said: "I met him just once, in Slávia. And I also had that contradictory feeling you mention. He struck me as unostentatious, and most of all resembled a good – though admittedly conceited – well-brought-up little boy."

This gives me a chance: if something like psychoanalysis really does exist, if an author's work really does provide sufficient material for analysing his psyche, and if this man really is a psychoanalyst, I ought to give it a try. "If I had the power to," I said, indicating the photo, "I would crack this hard protective shell of Kohout's. Life has drawn him to a penetrating perception of the system, but he observes the people in it like a menagerie, and, most important, nothing has yet drawn him to an equally rigorous perception of himself, as if that dreadful outwardly-directed power of his required him to be inwardly insensitive." And I told Pechar something he was unaware of, and which Pavel has not yet spoken of publicly: the mental terror he had to withstand before he left. "The way I see it," I said, "it would do Pavel good to collapse inwards. There were hopeful signs that things were going that way here. That hope is now gone, and nothing over there will induce it. The world will go on fostering his existing image, and he will live up to it. The fact that they did not let him come home was a more serious blow to him than he thinks. But even as things are, if someone were to remove his protective mask and gently puncture his soul with a finger that he could grasp, he would at last be free... not to fight, but to weep."

Pechar tidied his papers without a word and then said: "I'm glad you told me."

At home I had a postcard from London from Jiří Kolář and his wife Běla: "We're crawling from one museum to another and recalling, at every step, your vain wish to take a trip somewhere." I made myself a tea, took an aspirin, lay down and started to read a manuscript by Lumír Čivrný entitled *Little Indulgences*. I adjudicate others, but I myself don't feel like doing anything!

I'm even afraid to pick up this manuscript of mine and read it from the beginning.

WEDNESDAY, 14ᵀᴴ NOVEMBER 1979

Damn! By mistake I picked up the phone and heard in English: My name is so-and-so, I'm a correspondent for the *New York Times*, I have come from Warsaw and would like to talk to you; is it possible? – I said something that I intended to mean: "It would have been possible had you not called but come straight here." The man pondered on what he had just heard and then asked: "Well, can I come straight there, then?" I replied in my Oxphord English once more: "Had you not asked me in that way, I could have probably expected you. I'm afraid, however, that now that you have asked me, I can no longer expect you." The man at the other end had not quite come to terms with his astonishment, because after a moment he said: "Bye bye!" – I'll learn you! You just watch out! I declared cheerfully out loud. Where do you think you are! *Nevertheless!*

I wrote for a while, then got dressed, put the ninth ampoule in my pocket, and went to get my jab. Then I set off for Mojmír Klánský's, but he was out, so I left a book for him and went to see "Mr. Wheeper." "We're coming to the end of the year," I said, "and you'll be able to award your literary prize, should you so decide. And seeing that the fiction doesn't impress you, I have brought you something more interesting." I pulled out Samalík's *Introduction to the Philosophy of Czech History*, Trojan's *Studies in Christian Philosophy*, some of Pithart's articles, Šimečka's *Restoration of Order*, and the first volume of Dienstbier's *The Square*, which contains articles on foreign policy by a number of authors. He perused them languidly and then said: "I won't manage to read them by the end of the year, anyway." – "So award your prize at Easter." – He asked me if I would like a whisky, poured me one and said: "I've been in France. For heaven's sake, it's the same as here! So there's no point escaping to somewhere else. Have you never thought about it?" – "Yes, I have." – "And what conclusion did you come to." – "None. That I don't feel like it. Come to that, I don't even feel like buying a new coat for the winter."

Then I set out for Zdena's. I met her on the street. She was coming home from a walk with Bibisa and carrying her in her arms. Bibisa is unable to walk. Two days ago, she leaped up, yelped, collapsed, and crawled under the armchair. Now she was an invalid. She greeted me with only a wag of her tail and a lick instead of climbing up my legs and leaping up and down as she usually does. We decided to drive to the veterinary clinic at Říčany. But we sat for a few moments and Jiří arrived. We chatted and he said: "Do you recall that girl who was collecting signatures on a petition to let Hutka sing? He wrote a feuilleton about her at the time." We do recall her; they expelled her from university afterwards. "She's committed suicide." News like that I never want to believe. "She was interrogated several times and couldn't take it." – I said: "I wonder whether Hutka knows." – Jiří said: "He does, and has written another piece about it, in Holland. It was from the second feuilleton that I found out about it."

We drove with Bibisa to the vet's. She was given two injections, but they could not diagnose anything. She just has to take lime and phosphorus for her spine and nerves.

On the way back Zdena asked whether I would like to stay for supper, now that it was so late. I told her I could not stay. She asked whether I was unable or unwilling. "If I say I can't, it means I don't want to, either," I replied. So far, it had been a mini-dialogue we had rehearsed a hundred times before; now came something new: "Why do I bother to ask? Everyone in Prague knows you're scared of Madla." – "It's better for you to put that construction on it," I said.

Conditions outside were foul from early morning. Hradčany was not visible from the bridge. The Malá Strana Café was full. I sat and drank coffee with Jiří Gruša and told him about Brno. He regretted missing it. I dropped by to see Pecka but he was out. I set off for the Chramostovás', but when I entered their building, I remembered that this was the time of day when Vlasta studies new scripts for the coming season of "the living-room theatre," so I dropped her book in the mailbox. There is no meat to be had. There will be no gold before the beginning of next month.

In the cage, Catherine was shaking the hook we hang lettuce leaves on, but there is no lettuce to be had either. The phone rang. I picked it up, but there was silence at the other end. I placed the receiver on the table, went into my room, did some reading, and half-an-hour later went and hung up. I am at a loss about what to do because I am avoiding this manuscript: if I start reading it and it turns out not to be good enough to remain as is, it will take another year's work, and part of its *raison d'être* would be lost, as well as its entire "point."

I am reading Čivrný; I have had him here for ages and every day I go in fear of his turning up on my doorstep. It is not easy for poets when they start to write prose: the simple meaning of words can never satisfy them; their sentences are packed with meaning, their plots creep forward so slowly. That was the way he wrote his first prose work, *The Black Memory of a Tree*, some years ago. It all then depends on the mood the book catches the reader in. It took me a long time to get into the novel, and then I enjoyed it very much. The present *Indulgences* are already from this post-occupation period. It is impossible for a Chartist-reader to be fair to an author who personally behaves with restraint but involves his characters in political activity. I am determined to remain fair; I am able to. But I had to put the manuscript down when I came to the point where a nude photo of the hero – a poet called Jan Šimon – and his mistress is published in a sensationalist socialist magazine. That story sounds a bit too familiar to me, and I find it rather offensive.

It is evening. In the next room, Ondřej is typing out his latest play, under a pseudonym. Pecka was here and left a moment ago. And just now Madla came in from work, put down her bag, and doubled up with laughter. She had bumped into Pecka downstairs. When he met her, he kissed her hand, something to which she is definitely unaccustomed. After another fit of laughter she said: "When we were saying goodbye I discovered I was proffering my hand again!" – "Who's a Silly Billy, then?" I said, and she laid her head on my breast.

SATURDAY, 17ᵀᴴ NOVEMBER 1979

It is nearly noon and the day is gloomy. I have drawn back the curtain. The roofs opposite shine slimily. On the window sill I have a black earthenware vase (Ida Vaculková) and in it ragged yellow chrysanthemums. Madla brings bunches of them home from work. She is given them by people who have heard that she is retiring shortly. Next door Ondřej is thumping the type-writer at a tempo even faster than mine. Our Jan has gone off to the Horses or monika, we'll discover which before long. Work on the construction site has been suspended *sine die* on account of irregularities whose complexities I refused to have explained to me.

We were supposed to be going to the garden, but I do not feel like it, so I am glad it is raining. Our untreated apple juice is bound to be fermenting in the cellar. I shall try and persuade it to turn into wine. Zdena is good at fruit wines. The Čivrný is extremely contrived and needs cutting. The hero of the last story is a complicated would-be philosopher who thinks so much that he has no strength left to make the right decisions. So he vacillates between being a dissident and an informer and only fully realises what a paltry state he is in when a woman he yearns to speak to remains silent. So in one of his better moments he goes to a wood and hangs himself. The whole book is nostalgia for a fleeting love, as well as a document for the International Red Cross about something I have long maintained: that in our society, peo-ple never manage to keep a grip on any human relationship, whether with friends, relatives or lovers. A third power always intervenes: a monster which on principle opens a bottle by smashing it against a girder.

But here comes Madla again, who has been working diligently in the kitchen the whole time and is now calling me to lunch, but says: "You ought to dust this place." – "That's the third time you've said that since this morn-ing," I say. She goes to get a duster and starts to wipe off last week's dust. "I've finally got a diagnosis for you," she says. – "I don't want to hear it," I say. – "Reactive depression following departure of the W." I am proud of it.

I forget my dreams and can remember nothing in the morning. I expect they are just fragments, nothing consistent. I write, read through what I have written, hide it in two places, turn off the two table-lamps I work by, switch on a smaller one above the couch, lie down and pick up some lighter reading. Generally it's a magazine – *Our Language* or *Universe* – though most of all I would like a decent detective story, but I have nothing of the kind. Camus' *State of Siege* is no detective story. And I have already had a gutful of those symbolic dramas where the characters include The Plague or Mr. Ubiquitous. Please don't write any more of them.

But I have not been sleeping too well in the recent period. I quickly fall asleep, wake up and for a long time am unable to fall asleep again. There is nothing on my mind, no panic, and no physical pain, I am simply awake, in the dark; it does not bother me and I have no idea whether it lasts a quarter of an hour or two hours. I know it means something, but it has not become apparent yet. I have considered the possibility that I lack or want something, but there is nothing I want. I do not think about death, but it would not bother me – it would just be a pity not to put the finishing touches to *Dear Classmates*; I almost have a feeling it will be something quite new: a case of continuity of opinion from childhood up to "maturity," without stupid revisions, so that the end could easily be stuck onto the beginning. It will be new because it's a substantiated case; otherwise, such cases are not a rarity among normal people, those who do not dabble in politics or literature (e.g. Madla, Uncle Jožek, etc.).

It is odd – I can't make my mind up whether I ought to die before Madla or after her. I would like whatever would be better for her, and that – in view of future uncertainties – is not a simple issue. I wish her a long life, so that she trounces her family spectre, and when I see her preparing for retirement as if it were just the beginning, I feel troubled.

I am calmer than I appear to be in these pages, because the things that annoy me only annoy for as long as I speak about them. It makes no difference. Women are moving away from me and going out of me; this can be measured even over this past year. I am returning to my better state, to the way I was when I started out as a young man, to the masochistic joys of heartfelt correspondence: it is something fan-tas-tic! For the time being, for a start, I rave and sometimes weep. This will last, I am assuming, a year or thereabouts.

When I eventually fall asleep, I sleep well, wake up quickly, and have no problem getting up. If I do dream anything, it is invariably something I have known for ages already. Every day I am amazed that I have managed to shave myself, needlessly, every morning for the past thirty years. Then I tidy away my sleeping things, make some tea, hope that no one will come, then sit and ponder and even do some writing. When no one comes I feel a trifle neglected. I have too much to do and never manage to get it all done. I am astonished at the freedom I have and fear for it. I know no one as well off as I. Apart from Kosík – because he knows. Ivan has to do the cooking and has frail health. Jiří has to put up with two dogs, a little kid, and a greedy young wife; and he gets stomach pains. Jan Vladislav looks cheerful, but has too much to do, trying to make a living and... and other problems that are none of my business. Mr. Václav or Otka are in prison. And poor old Pavel is banished, a condition he enjoys only by mistake, out of stupidity. What is all the rush?

I wish a metre of snow would fall, so it would be silent and impossible to do anything.

TUESDAY, 20TH NOVEMBER 1979

I had my first headache in a long time. I had no wish to stir in the least, but on account of the Georgians and Madla I got up and went. I was afraid a lot of people would skip it today. Subscription concert-goers are awful riff-raff: for fear of missing out on something, they buy season tickets year in year out, but since they have no need to hear the same things again and again, they then stay at home.

As I expected, the hall of the Rudolfinum, though sold out, was a third empty. This was partly due to Dr. František Kriegel, who is lying in hospital connected to a heart-support machine. The Georgians were four in number, which is customary with quartets, and were very nice and pleasant-looking: they are decently different. I did not hold much store by their repertoire, however: it struck me as rather complaisant – Haydn, Shostakovich and Beethoven. I would be rather more curious about the composers they play back home: Taktakishvili or Tsintsadze. But those of us who already have an inkling about how series, programmes and publishing plans are produced know how to ask the right question: Who knows whether they had any say in what they were going to play? Going to a concert these days in Mozart's Prague – compared to Mozart's Vienna, for instance – gives you plenty to think about, ponder on, and observe that has nothing to do with the cello, enough for an entire evening!

There is a good view from the third row, and I immediately noticed that Vardanyan, Zhvaniya and Chubinishvili are wearing patent-leather shoes, whereas Batiashvili has ordinary ones and very unpolished to boot. They launched into Haydn's G minor String Quartet, "The Equestrian." The first violin did not play strictly according to the music, and I do not think it is a particularly attractive piece anyway, apart from the finale. I derived unusual pleasure from something else: the fact that they did not know what to do with this Haydn. They struggled with the Largo like a dog eating hay. I had to suppress an urge to laugh. Lacking any personal motive for a slow, contemplative tempo, they merely played slowly and ploughed through it as if through treacle. And lacking any sense of the piece's inward dynamic, they exaggerated its outward dynamic. They doubled the length of the sustained notes (a slight exaggeration). On the other hand, when the allegro finale arrived, they immediately started to belt it out *con brio*.

They then played Shostakovich's String Quartet No.7. I am unacquainted with it and cannot tell how much responsibility lies with the composer and how much with this evening's interpreters. The strings just rattled away and the musicians swayed about like Gypsies. The composition has just one movement, during which, however, the rhythm alters several times: explosive ideas and amazing variations of tone colour from each of the instruments. The Georgians entered the work with their whole bodies, and kicked their heels behind them. – On top of that – Beethoven again: unremitting tedium. What do people see in that Beethoven all the time, I asked myself, echoing the Georgians.

In the process, my headache gradually disappeared. I should love to read a knowledgeable review of tonight's concert in tomorrow's *Times*, but no one here will write one! And so I shall never know whether my judgement is even a teeny bit right or not. On the homeward journey the weather was marvellously foul – misty and rainy, ideal for concert-going. Like in London.

The grey silhouette of Hradčany upstaged by the blue big top of the Circus Humberto is such an extraordinary funny-poetic composition that no one with an ounce of conscience could resist it: I bought two tickets to the circus.

I then realised, however, that no one had promised me an extraordinary spectacle of any kind: neither the posters, nor the bored young woman in the booking office, nor the announcer in his barman's clothes. All those state-owned circus artistes seemed to be admitting publicly that they expect nothing special of themselves – they just can't – and that the rest of us must surely understand: isn't it like that everywhere nowadays? And we do understand, of course, and just look forward to the animals – isn't it time for the animals yet? – there won't be any – of course not, they'll be wintering somewhere. Yes, of course, every self-respecting Humberto stows itself away somewhere and self-respecting travelling artistes go their separate ways to their original homes and spend the winter caring for their children and their legends. We all read Bass's *Circus Humberto*, didn't we – and that makes it even worse for us now! The state confiscated the firm, gutted it and stuffed it full of things in its own image. And of course it doesn't suit the image of the State to have people living during rainy days from the money they earned when the sun was shining. They mustn't and they can't: their duties and pay are deliberately calculated so that they should always have plenty to do and no chance to stop. The state has learnt only one trick and it uses it for churches and circuses alike: the punishment for being a successful priest is transfer.

It was so excruciatingly boring that I was intrigued to see how it would develop after the intermission. So I asked Zdena's assent for us to stay till the end. We were already cold. When two acrobats up under the dome elbowed each other until one of them really did fall and only by luck managed to catch on to a bucket hanging from the other's foot, no collective *Aaaah*! went up, and not even the little children were surprised. They've seen it all before on television. Such a mournful spectacle of so much genuine hard work is only so clearly visible in the circus; elsewhere it is not so public.

As I left with the rest of the ungrateful public, I pondered on the root of all this self-abasement, but again I hit on nothing but dynamite. I'm no genius either. But what if all those magicians and illusionists, all those jugglers and tumblers, all those acrobats and tightrope walkers declared they'd never go on television again? Then one would only be able to see circus at the circus, in the same way that the only way to ride on a train is to take a train-ride. – Magic to amaze you! Death-defying deeds! The likes of it never seen before! Only in the circus! The circus is in town!

We went to U Sojků for supper. Inside the restaurant it was warm, though smoky. "How far have you got with that dreadful job?" I asked Zdena. That dreadful job is always the one she is supposed to be doing and no one will tell her how to do it, because it is always something new and Sylva said she was not going to do it and would sooner hand in her notice, so Sylva got more pay and one of the firm's flats, whereas Zdena was told when she started: "Your starting pay will be the same as your leaving pay!"

Zdena had been given her latest assignment two days earlier. It is something they've known about for the past two years, but nothing has been done about it and now it has to be resolved over the next week. And that's something they can't expect of Sylva, who's younger, and in the party, and much longer in the firm, can they! "Why did you take it?" I asked her on Monday. – "Because I really couldn't give a damn. And because I felt sorry for Mr. Matouš."

I always let her explain all those jobs but I understand very little apart from the fact that Zdena is coming into contact with some of the most sensitive issues of current industrial economics. At present she is supposed to be introducing some kind of "optical data scanning" for computer processing. This includes all data about production, costs, prices, wages and so on. The data are written in a special pencil on red pre-printed forms and the colour alone hurts the eyes; it entails extra work and neither the accountants nor the planners were prepared to do it. But in the end someone from management has to lend an ear to the resistance, transform it into discussion and come to some agreement with the personnel. "Whenever someone yells at her, Sylva bursts into tears and runs away." – "You don't burst into tears?" I asked. – "No one yells at me." – "Why, do you think?" – "Do you know, I've no idea. The whole factory already knows I'm an odd case. People don't treat me as if I were from management, and for my part I don't act as if I was. Yesterday I discussed with them how many operations they would actually have to do, and in some cases it amounts to as much as an hour a day more. In the process it emerged that they do something extra anyway, while there are other things they don't do at all. They have no idea of their job descriptions. They've never known them, even though they're supposed to sign them! I brought them copies and they looked at me with alarm, as if I had taken the liberty of divulging managerial secrets." – "How many people are involved?" – "About forty." – "That's too many, they'll fire you. And how did it turn out?" – "I wrote a report, gave it to them to read, and then delivered it to Matouš." – "What did you suggest?" – "That some people's work load should be eased, that staffing levels should be increased in certain places and that some people should be given a pay raise." – I expressed surprise: "So where is greater profitability to come from?" – "From elsewhere, in the longer term."

Then she burst out laughing and said: "I'm beginning to be amazed. I get the impression that the management is doing something without knowing where it's leading or how it might stir up the whole firm." – I said: "You're either going with the tide or they'll have to throw you out." – She said: "Will you finally realise that I don't give a damn." – You're just saying that. What do you think they'd let you do?" – "I think," she said coquettishly, "that you'd give me a job again!" – I said: "And they'd shut you away somewhere again. And anyway, will you finally realise, Zdena, that I really am giving it up." – "And who'll take care of it?" – "Let it take care of itself." – "But at least you'll let me type out the thing you're writing now." – "I'm not even sure I'll let you read it." – She said: "Reading a book is no longer enough for me. I've discovered that only when I'm typing it out do I penetrate its skin."

I said: "The trouble is, Zdena, that I'm very much afraid this book of mine will get under yours." – She nodded: "I guessed as much. Because you never talk to me about it."

SATURDAY, 24TH NOVEMBER 1979

Dear year, we're coming to the end. Of what, in fact?

I am sitting in D. with a fire going in the white-tiled stove, listening on the radio to a fleeting station broadcasting some baroque music played by some night-time string orchestra conducted by someone called Kuschelbau-er, and am unable to make up my mind what to do about today in terms of writing. Censor it?

Tomorrow is St. Catherine's Day. Tomorrow is Madla's birthday, on account of which she was supposed to have had that "farewell party" yesterday. But she dutifully got her regular autumn dose of bronchitis that proved even stronger than her sense of duty, so she has been home for the past two days.

Whenever Madla is off sick, the first two days are bad because she suffers. She is always dying of something horrible and I have to overcome my fear too. When she is a degree or so better, she starts tidying, washing, dusting, making and mending, and criticising my existence: telling me I don't do anything for the home, that I just lounge in the armchair and read and am clearly fed up that I can't go out on the prowl, that I spend my days prowling and don't do a thing, just chase women. And the fact is I know I can't stand women, and shortly I won't be able to stand anything and I can see the moment is coming when I'll lose myself in something, because I'm letting go of the thing that I've been holding on to so tightly that I couldn't go out anywhere and therefore didn't.

"Why don't you buzz off to Zdena's at last?" she said as loud as she could manage. "But I don't want to go anywhere!" I roared. Very quietly she said: "Pity your Helena can't hear you now." Yes, that's just how it ought to be. So I went.

She has her (note)book on the coffee table: "I bought this lovely big diary on 17.6.1979. Olda Unger visited us that day. He's leaving for Austria with his family. He made me a gift of two cassette recordings of bird-song that he once recorded for the radio... The idea of getting myself a notebook for my retirement came to me at Dobřichovice while reading. I am going to note down the things I want to remember..."

Well, when I really intend to remember something I deliberately don't write it down. Don't think that writing a diary is easy! What, how, style – such things take years to develop!

"Today I was sterilising the apple juice. We've got about 50 bottles altogether. The garden is looking miserable; we haven't raked up all the leaves yet. But I've washed the cellar windows and dug up the last of the dahlias. I am reading Mlynář; his frankness and readiness to admit his mistakes make him a likeable person."

It was always my wish that she should write notes about her work. She could edit them subsequently. I know no one with her perceptiveness or with her capacity to link her insights together into an interesting construction. She started a number of notebooks. All our kids have journals which she kept about them from infancy up to writing age. Every book in our bookshelf has something filed between its pages: a picture, a cut-out review of the book, a postcard from its author. Throughout the flat one comes across bits of paper slipped in different places with Madla's comments, notes, quotations. On occasions I have tried to file all those wandering slips of paper in a single envelope. But almost all her notebooks ended up with recipes, while the blank pages at the back of her cook books are littered with her philosophical ideas.

Now at last she is taking the matter properly in hand with her thick journal: "Dad is off somewhere. He says he's going to Brno to see Šimečka but I don't believe him. He never tells the truth, so even when he does, it isn't the truth for me anymore. It's odd how everyone thinks of him as a fighter for the truth."

It's not my fault they're all stupid. I don't need any fighter for the truth, so let them do without one too! I have never, I hope, proclaimed myself to be anybody but me. My lies are as much mine as my truth, and I don't know which will prove the more reprehensible.

SUNDAY, 25TH NOVEMBER 1979

I only needed to rake over the ashes and add a few wood chips to get the fire going again. I washed and shaved while the water heated for my tea. I checked the weather from two different windows, poured the tea, and there is nothing here to eat the whole day. At mid-day I'll make do with cheese and this evening I'll cook up some of those wood blewits that are pushing up the needles under the pine tree, and tomorrow I'll go shopping. I'll call the Pink Lady from the post office to say that Tuesday's out. I'll make my apologies to Zdena. I won't pick up the books from the binders, won't go to the doctor's, won't go anywhere. I've been telling myself the whole year that I will shut myself up here for at least a fortnight. I've forgotten what it is to be alone long enough to really feel it. I'll take out this manuscript that frightens me and start reading it from the beginning. But if they come for me, I imagine it will be worse from here than from the Prague flat. In Prague, they have to ring the doorbell. Here they can walk straight in. In Prague, I would discover straight away what it was about, whereas from here they would have to drive me half an hour first, and I would have to endure their fragrance.

When I came down the steps, Don had already dragged Mrs. Hermerková back from a walk. Mrs. Rohlenová, in front of her separate staircase, was hackering some branches brought from the woods, using a small saw and short jabbing strokes. The verb hacker does not exist, but there is no other one to suit the purpose. I greeted her and she said: "Did you take that pretty white rose that was still here yesterday evening?" This was a denunciation of Mrs. Kopecká. I had not noticed any rose yesterday. "Mrs. Kopecká took it to the cemetery," I explained fully. – "And where is your wife?" she wanted to know. – "She's come down with a dose of birthday," I said. – "Which one?" – "Her fifty-fourth," I said and it sounded so bad I shuddered. "She'll have got over it by tomorrow then," she chuckled. "It always takes me a week to get over mine these days."

I started raking the leaves from the farthest corner of the garden, so as not to get round to the leaves in front of the house at all this year. I'm damned if I'll be your odd-job man! In places the leaves were already rotted into the ground. I worked an incredible five hours in one go. It seems to me now like half an hour. For the life of me I cannot recall what I thought about the whole time. Nothing, I expect, but just stared at the leaves and the grey bark of the trees, and when a branch knocked my cap off, just cussed. I never thought I would ever cuss the way I cuss these days. What will I turn into now? A miserable old custodian.

And if I were to vow never to set foot in Prague ever again? Which of my friends would take the trouble to see me – not counting those nearest to me, whom I would advise of my decision? Whose face would first come into view over there beyond the box-hedge? By now it's obvious it wouldn't be Saša's, seeing that he hasn't come running in alarm at the news that Pavel has disappeared into thin air. Pavel has disappeared into thin air – how else are we to explain the fact that he does not feel impelled to write to one of us, or all of us together: "I was forced. Kiss my arse"? The rake I am holding bears a white enamel label on its handle. It is one of the tools left me seven years ago by the emigrating Luděk Pachman. That was how it started.

But it is obvious! There is no other way of looking at it: everyone who left tendered me their resignation. Whenever I find myself amidst wind-torn trees, enveloped in a scent of rotting leaves that takes me back to a goat shed beneath a low grey sky in which snow clouds are already beginning to rumble inaudibly from afar, there emerges from deep within my awareness a sense of profound disappointment that the reading of adventure stories is one thing and life is something else: mother would always end up yelling at me to go for wood, or take the goats to pasture, or rake up leaves for litter. How mother would have laughed to hear such words as "première" or "matinee." Uncle

Jošek would have asked: "What do you feed it?" So I find myself again back where I started. It only goes to show that I am fit for nothing but to stay here. They had to have someone to leave the rake to!

"There's always plenty to do, isn't there!" Mrs. Hemerková said in jovial greeting as she was sharply jerked off on a walk.

All of a sudden I had the feeling I had been here a fortnight already and no one had come. I could work up no appetite for writing. And as I walked past a bed of still-flowering pink snapdragons, wheeling a wheelbarrow full of leaves, a dream from last night came back to me at the speed of light – a treacherous dream.

I was rushing without briefcase, coat or cap from some office across the street to some factory gate or other. I was just thinking up an excuse. At the entrance, the porter called me into his lodge. With foreboding, I entered a sort of waiting-room at the rear. There sat Madla, exhausted from lengthy waiting, holding on her lap a bright bunch of summer garden-flowers. She stood up stiffly, handed me the bunch of flowers, and said something to the effect that she had been obliged to come, hadn't she, seeing it was my birthday. I started to explain that I had been in the office and was on my way back to the workshop, really, and she could go with me and see for herself that I had my briefcase, coat and cap there. So it's my birthday today, I said to myself in surprise.

TUESDAY, 27ᵀᴴ NOVEMBER 1979

I entered Café Belvedere, and the Pink Lady – in reality the dark Procházková – was already sitting there. She jutted above the table, thin and willowy, in a black blouse, with her hair tightly drawn back, and with the tense, gaunt face of some she-beast. Around her neck, which was paler than her face, was wound what might have been a nylon scarf, the colour of ordinary tights.

"Talking is out of the question at our place," I explained, "and here it's quite pleasant." I looked around, and attention from neighbouring tables made me realise that more frequent meetings here would be out of the question, too: there was no way I could show myself anywhere with such a young woman. And the unpleasant sensation immediately seeped into me that I am always falling into some sort of trap. I really ought not be reading someone's manuscript, which is bound to spark off an exchange about life, whereupon I shall be obliged to say something about the way things are between people, and so end up giving the author, in return for her intimacy – which I have never asked for – part of my own. I will keep my distance, do exactly what I was "engaged" for and no more. "What do you have that ugly thong round your neck for?" I asked, because it annoyed me. The Dark Lady blushed pink, reached under her chin, undid the scarf, crumpled it up and hid it somewhere beneath the table, maybe in her lap, whatever that's like, I thought. (Barren, as will soon be seen.) "There you are, that's much better," I said, as she revealed her prettily anchored neck, too soon and too rapidly concealed by the neck of her blouse.

Sadly, I cannot reassure the more sensitive reader by confessing that I made up the foregoing scene, that it is mere literary convention. My nerves are in no fit state. My coarseness was a means of extricating myself from an obsession that had lasted several minutes: I was incapable of speaking about anything as I sat transfixed by that rag of hers, which jarred so much with the keen discernment of things and words displayed in her writing. Moreover, in April 1980, I believe the older man was resisting the young woman – it struck him as monstrous on the part of life to ignore his mental state and serve him up once again with something like this, something worse than ever, which clearly lacked the least trace of sympathy or piety.

I said: "You say the short stories predate *The Pink Lady*. But they're better written, some of them. Why is that?" – "Probably because I took more time over them." – In her last story she describes her plunge into pub life at the side of her boyfriend and her disillusioned exit from pub life and from love. It's a virtuoso display of feminine frankness and humour. "But 'Hen in the Club'..." I didn't know how to get around my suspicion that it encompassed a painful and very recent experience. – "That one's new," she said dryly.

We talked for about an hour. "How much time do you have for writing?" I asked. –"Plenty. I go to the theatre at eight in the morning and I'm finished by ten." On one occasion she had discovered a fellow from the country asleep on the floor of one of the boxes, where he had lain since the previous evening. When she woke him up, he got a fright: "Is it over? Is it over?" – "So you do your cleaning in a theatre. I thought you cleaned houses. Tickets don't ever come your way, do they?" – "No, unfortunately. But if you like, I could get you some free tickets to the cinema." – "Yes, please," I said. By this time we were already walking along the pavement towards the tram stop. "Don't worry, I won't be shy," I said, meaning: "to accompany you if you invite me," since I had no regard for such foolish, unwarranted shyness. However, I had managed to say the opposite of what I intended. As I analyse why I did in fact say it, though, it strikes me that I realised she was just debating whether it was proper for her to invite me. But that is absurd; why should she want to? – I am writing about it here because it bothers me and because I am faced with the awkward alternative of either making excuses before tickets arrive or making a point of saying nothing, so that she will not even have the nerve to broach the matter.

I made my way home again with some poems that she lent me to read. They are few in number and I read them straight away to get it over and done with. One of them I definitely do not like: it is about Jan Palach. I fear it risks creating a legend repugnant to the next younger generation. That old brazenness! – But there is one of them that – I like? – that struck a chord with me. It has a bad title: IT STARTS WITH LOVE

It starts with love
one second's enough
to fetter you fast
while months and years pass
UNENDING

You don't scorn the chance
or lose countenance
in the primeval text
you find a pretext
A MESSIAH

Hope ever welling
From spring until year's end
And then it is yelling
Naked and innocent
A CHILD

It grows and it bawls
your senses are mauled

you're battered and uptight
it's hard to keep upright
ON THE GROUND

Pain and dismay
the stench of clay
your wrists iron-bound
next night you'll be found
ON THE PILL

Your eyelids darkened
your lap now barren
veiled all in velvet
you yearn with Hamlet
TO SLEEP

no declarations
no expectations
JUST LIKE THAT

It strikes me as rather harsh. Which is why I would entitle it ADVENT.
Our advent. The advent of today's young woman.

It makes me feel very odd. My nerves are in a bad way.

THURSDAY, 29ᵀᴴ NOVEMBER 1979

The café is semi-transparent, but the table is taken again. I would have to
make an agreement – for a consideration – with the staff, if I wanted to have
a seat here, "every last Thursday in the month," say. From my 60x60 cm.
square of marble I can see the bottom end of Malostranské Square. I ordered
my notorious Becherovka (one, one!) because my book is getting used to
alcohol. But the Becherovka has been declining in quality over the past three
months: I drink it up, leave, and there's nothing more.

It is a few minutes past nine. A beautiful grey day. Graphic. Yesterday
evening I walked through the Castle. Some old chap was just addressing one
of the castle sentries in Slovak: "Excuse me, how do I get to the Martinský

Palace?" The private kept his lips buttoned. The man said: "So what are you standing here for?" Aye me! How I'd love to have a decent monarch!

I went through a hole into the First Courtyard. I was utterly alone there, something that is almost impossible to achieve in the daytime, and I was immediately oppressed by the monumentality of the place. Illumined by yellow globes on the walls all around, the courtyard gave the impression of an enormous hall with its ceiling gradually disappearing in the heights. At the neighbouring table they're eating frankfurters; I'm hungry. The feeling is growing on me that, any day now, they are bound to come and take away my manuscript, so this morning I could not get out of bed soon enough to remove it from the house. I had brought it home yesterday, weighed it in my hands, and divided it into five sections in five separate envelopes. I will work on one at a time only. I have not yet started, though. I fear the disillusionment that Karel Kosík experienced when they returned a confiscated philosophical manuscript of his two years ago: "I thought it was better!" He started to rewrite it, and he is still at it. Searching yesterday for a temporary hiding-place, just for the night, I hit on a brilliant place. As I reached in I had a shock: it wasn't empty! With amazement I withdrew my own plastic bag with some manuscripts I was missing.

I walked through the Castle, came out through the Matyáš Gate, and set off down Nerudova Street. I was due to deliver a letter from Munich to one of the houses. Someone had written the letter to someone whose address was unknown to them and Ota Filip had apparently told them to send it to me, as I could be relied on to deliver it. I tugged an old-fashioned bell-pull and the door was opened by quite a young and pretty woman. I told her my name and said I was there to deliver a letter. I handed it to her in its original envelope. She glanced at my address and said excitedly: "You're...? We're all keeping our fingers crossed for you!" I said thank you and was already on my way back down the steps, while she continued to stare supportively after me, so it is possible she caught my parting shot: "And how will I know?" That was yesterday and I am still not sorry.

If only they would form a union, at least, all those finger-crossers! And circulate their right attitudes in mildly-worded missives. I'll have a couple of frankfurters too. A group of young Germans has arrived. They immediately started taking chairs from neighbouring tables and shoving them round one table in the centre of the room. It instantly puts paid to the intimacy of the

Malá Strana Café, where we all talk in hushed voices or remember each other unobtrusively. Almost everyone I talk to has their fingers crossed for the jailed VONS members, but few are ready to fingerprint an appeal for them to be released at Christmas. I was given signature sheet number sixteen from the petition and have collected only six fingerprints so far over the past week. One man said to me: "Of course I want their release, but it strikes me as absurd to make my own protest right alongside the protest of people who were the cause of their being in prison in the first place." – I asked: "Whom do you have in mind, for instance?" – "Slánský's widow, for instance." – Those are historico-analytical types who would sooner silence their Yes on account of their No. I replied briefly: "Because you don't like one of its branches, you'd sooner let the tree be chopped down?"

In addition to the tree theory, I sometimes use the hedgehog argument. "Do you think," Lumír asked, "that our protest will really help them?" – I said: "I shouldn't think so, but hedgehogs are supposed to prick." – "What's that supposed to mean?" – "When a car runs over a hedgehog, it ought to be obvious it ran over a hedgehog." – "And not a worm, say?" Lumír said slowly, and added his fingerprint. Interestingly enough, it is exactly seven years ago that Ivan, Pavel, Saša and I rushed around before Christmas with the first petition for the first political prisoners. In those days it was still possible for us to go and see the likes of Neff and Kaplický, who did not sign, and Jirotka, who did, and then my friend Milan Jariš, who signed it and then recanted his signature in *Rudé právo* – and attacked us in the bargain. I then showed it to another of my friends, Alexej Pludek, who did not sign and immediately reported us, so that the next day they caught us on the street, took away our petition and held us hungry and harassed until well into the night. In those days we were dealt with by a man with the build of a butcher and the face of a ruffian in a bad mood, who had the improbably mild-sounding name of Pokorný. Mind you, it is my belief he was not entirely devoid of a sense of humour – of sorts. When, that night, he eventually had to release us, he leaned over the desk in his fury and said, within an inch of my face: "When you go with your 'petition' to the President, tell him Tigrid sends his greetings!" I replied: "I'll do that, but I'll say that the message comes via Pokorný at Bartolomějská police station, and that I personally wouldn't touch it with a barge-pole." Since that time our sense of humour has waned somewhat, it is true, but on the other hand, think of all the things they have had to learn to stomach!

And now the waitress has arrived and told the Germans coldly in Czech: "I'm afraid you can't sit like that!" And they immediately started, without comment, to seat themselves by twos and threes at different tables. "And those coats," she said, pointing at the backs of the chairs, "to the cloakroom, please," gesturing over her shoulder with her thumb. One of the young men gathered up all the coats in his arms and disappeared with them.

If I were Good King Louis of Bohemia, this is how I'd rule: The local population, unlike today, would have every advantage and priority over the tourists, who, on the contrary, would be robbed on the highway, well and truly intimidated and relieved of their tobacco and cameras. They would return home with their tails between their legs, because their currency would pay for nothing here and their intellect would make no sense of anything on account of everything being so alien. It would merely be bruited abroad that animals and people prosper in our fields, birds in our sky, fish in our waters, that our simply-attired folk earn enough from a bare half-day's work in our factories and offices for modest board and lodging, and spend the rest of the time having fun with their friends, wives and children, that in the concert halls music is played incredibly beautifully, that the orchard is bright with the blooms of spring, and that in the forests of our borderlands marksmanship is flourishing among our young swains. And everyone would yearn to see such a land, but it would be proverbially arduous to worm one's way in. – The only thing we haven't yet worked out is how we'd deal with the cases of those who once left here for some unfathomable reason and now wish to return. They would have to beg us, Louis, ever so humbly!

The bell of St. Nicholas strikes eleven as I pay my bill and leave.

SATURDAY, 1ST DECEMBER 1979

She recognised a familiar face in the crowd of strangers. She elbowed her way over and found herself among a group of friends. They immediately asked after me, but she did not know where I was. Then someone came up behind her and slipped a scrap of paper into her hand. She glanced back surreptitiously, for fear of giving the game away – and saw that it was someone like František Vodsloň. To be on the safe side, she did not put the paper into her handbag but kept it in her closed palm. And with that she had the feeling that something had been sorted out. She left. But of course she immediately saw that she was being followed. She wondered where to put the paper for me. Meanwhile she had reached the bus in which she was due to return to Prague. Everyone from the institute was already on board and waiting for her. She climbed aboard and the driver shut the doors. Those who had been tailing her were left outside. The bus drove off. She took a discreet look round to see where she might secrete the paper. As she was looking toward the back of the bus, she noticed that she was separated from the rest of the passengers by two people in the seat behind her. One of them was that randy young so-and-so, that lay-about who burgled people's country cabins and whose trial was already coming up – but the Phantom had vouched for him and taken him on as a maintenance man. However, the fellow used to arrive at work at ten in the morning and never did anything but the occasional errand, and when his father managed to hush up the criminal affair, he left again. The other one was that tart who was scarcely ever at work because she was either having an abortion, preparing for a graduate degree, or drunk – there was no other possible explanation than that she was on their payroll too. The two of them were now sitting behind her. It occurred to her that she might jump out of the moving bus, somehow. She leaned forward in order to see the driver, and he looked back and said with a smile: "You've got nothing to fear, lady." So she stood up, turned towards the passengers, and over the heads of those two police spies she delivered a speech to them: "Can't you see they want to separate me from you? Don't you find all the surveillance and denunciation demeaning? I work to the best of my ability, and this filth, these bastards, these parasites are allowed to snoop on me? Who are you so afraid of, you pathetic spineless creeps? I've had as much as I'll take!" And she started to slap the two of them round the face, from above, with both hands, left and right. And she went on slapping them over and over again until she woke up.

Her left hand still hurt the next morning. That was on Wednesday, when she does not start work until mid-day, so she used the time to bake some savoury biscuits to go with the wine at her postponed farewell party. She also baked another strudel, as the first one had already disappeared at home. All of a sudden she told me she was feeling ill, and I made her lie down and place a tablet of nitro-glycerin under her tongue. A quarter of an hour later she was incredibly fit, apart from a disturbing pressure in her head. "I don't know why I've been so upset over the past two days." – "I'll tell you why. It's from bad reading-matter." She has been reading Kaplan's manuscript,

Paths to Power, which I will not read because I have no intention of letting it upset me. I am quite satisfied with the gems she serves me up from it. I've had enough of things like that to last me to the end of my days.

Yesterday's party went badly. When they were ready, the Phantom told them all to have fun, but he still had work to do and went into his office. They stood there dumbfounded. But the glasses were already filled and Doctor Hájek, one of the old school, proposed a formal toast. From what I understand, it was something along these lines: "Mrs. Vaculíková, so dear to all of us, you have reached the young age when you are actually, and unbelievably for all of us, going into a retirement that I with my three score and five years cannot yet permit myself. You are the most senior member of the staff here and you taught most of us the ropes. You were virtually in on the founding of our institute. Your unstinting quiet efforts..."

To cut a long story short: he presented her with a fairly decent-sized pine-tree in a pot, and she is apparently to plant it – as an ever-growing reminder of an undying memory – in the place where she is looking forward to spending, starting next year, that new and better part of her life that they all fervently wish her. – But that is only my surmise, because she did not tell me anything coherent about it: she had run away from the party and walked until dark through the streets, weeping over and over again, left and right.

"You ruined their party, of course," I said. "But on Monday, I'm going in to punch that Phantom on the nose. I'm not putting up with that."

At half past eight she dressed up again, put on make up, and went out. She did not want to tell me where she was going, and did not want me to go with her. Ten minutes later I pulled myself together and went out after her, but I could not see her anywhere in the neighbourhood. I did the round of the streets which I myself rush up and down when I have had a row with her, and then went home. She returned two hours later, carrying the remnants of her banquet in her bag. "I'm not leaving anything there!" she declared.

When she had arrived back at the institute, two of the male participants were still at the party. They were a bit tipsy, and maybe that was the only reason the younger of them had the temerity to say, within those high-tech-equipped walls, something to this effect: "You're making a mistake. It's not him you've punished, but us. But you're also making a more fundamental mistake – you're an authority, which means that you only recognise authority, you need it, you have to have it. The trouble is the world has changed! The

464

sort of authority that you're looking for doesn't exist any more. So why did you get so upset on his account? After all, you know what he is! A paper devil! And you get yourself into such a state over someone like him?"

She looks dreadful: her face swollen and dark bags under her eyes. She did some ironing and now she is sleeping. She occasionally turns over pages in the air as if she were reading.

TUESDAY, 4ᵀᴴ DECEMBER 1979

When I went for the ultra-sound this morning (I am getting ultra-sound treatments) a huge golden sun was hanging in the sky directly above Žižkov, and its glow spread across the Vltava Valley as far as Strossmayerovo Square in Holešovice. It was warm and clean, the way it is before Easter, not Christmas. Heartened by the pleasant weather and the ultra-sound, I set off about my business. Attentive readers no doubt have, at number one on their lists, the thumping I promised the Phantom and are already looking forward to it. So slow down, slow down! Let's not start resorting to blows yet, eh, friends?

In second place readers have no doubt noted gold. It is the beginning of December, so the pre-Christmas dole-out of gold has commenced. I did the rounds of three goldsmiths. They were all filled with fretful crowds, in which those at the back craned their necks between the shoulders of those in front. On Wenceslas Square, the queue spilled out onto the pavement. No way, my precious!

I first popped into a milk bar for a bun and a mug of cocoa, and then made for the main post office to telephone Pavel in Vienna. It strikes me as almost metaphysical the way I can just dial a number and at the other end of the line is a banned individual from Vienna. You can almost see each other. We kept it short and the telephonist even gave me change for my hundred crowns.

I finally received Pavel's letter a month late, the one in which he writes how he will be thinking of us if he is forced to stay there. He will not be taking part in any exile political activity, though; he will just work in a literary way and for literature. – Well, I don't know. It looks as if he's going about it the way I'd try to myself, i.e. to build up a sort of demilitarised cultural zone, in front of which neither side would necessarily have to put up warning signs. Constantly paving the way for understanding and an honourable return. We have thousands of people abroad by now, but how many of them have thought up some way of helping us here while also being a bit interesting for the rest of the world? (Škvorecký)

Pavel writes that he did not go to the protest march that followed Mr. Václav's conviction, but organised a reading of his writings instead. "We projected enormous photos of our Sázava days, and played Třešňák, Hutka and the Plastics as background music. When the fire curtain came down at the end, the audience remained motionless in their seats until Hutka's "Havlíček, Havel" finished. Attending: representatives of the government and opposition, personalities from the arts, and lots of young people. The next morning, I received a request from Munich to repeat the event at the Bavarian State Theatre. The turnout was objectively good, relatively excellent. (...) Unlike Vienna, almost no compatriots showed up. The compatriots – they're a laugh a minute (...). Some of them send denunciations to the exile newspapers that would be the envy of *Rudé právo*. One gives interviews saying I'm a well-known showman and that my youthful misdeeds are unpardonable; another maintains that in fact I never had any influence in the Charter, and anyway the Charter needed showmen too..."

I don't know. I almost don't know how it could be otherwise. It would be foolish if – when the opportunity arises – neither foe nor friend could choose between us. After all, at negotiations no one is going to be speaking to all of us at once.

But there is something else in the letter that troubles me: Pavel writes that he wants to hold a similar evening's entertainment about me. I found it gratifying but it also perturbed me. What does he want to use for it? He's bound to resurrect the celebrated Writers' Congress of 1967 when the two of us first met (that is to say, when His Honour first spoke to me) and show that photo of it. And he will recall my "Words," though for the life of me I cannot remember how many thousand of them there were, and *The Axe* and *The Guinea-Pigs*... No, thank you!

Moreover, I would not like to be included there mainly as one of the participants at "our Sázava days," just because he used to keep a photographer. And in all events it is not right to go pointing up our similarities and showing us to be identical – Kohout, Havel, Vaculík... – when it is not true. I am with them, but a bit apart too. Each of us ought to be. If we constantly harp on what we have in common, people will have little trouble convincing themselves that something like this was bound to befall such a coterie. By

466

no means, your worships! This sort of misfortune deliberately targets those who are most varied!

From the post office I took the metro to Letná. I like the metro. Waiting on the platform I overheard an elegant grey-haired gentleman telling a woman about someone: "He was one of my pupils. And now he's vice-rector!" I said: "That doesn't mean much nowadays – goodness knows why he got the job." And I moved away, because on principle I do not interfere in people's conversations more than is strictly necessary.

I hauled home this entire manuscript, and in search of material for a Viennese evening more to my liking, I started to leaf through it. Oh, but I am disappointed! I thought it was better!

The beginning reflects well my dejection at the time. But I drivel on at sixes and sevens about friends, the family, and things I have read. It was my intention, at the time, not to falsify or embellish it afterwards. But what is to be done with it now? The writer oscillates between the need for sincerity on the one hand and shyness on the other; his words vary between a document that is not always interesting, and a stylisation that is clearly intended to rectify that. As the then-author, I am terrified at the work that still awaits me if this is to turn into a book. As the present-day reader, I feel a gloating satisfaction and my advice to the author is: Flush the whole thing down the toilet!

FRIDAY, 7ᵀᴴ DECEMBER 1979

I have read and corrected many manuscripts by other people in my time. And there are plenty of my own that I have re-written, over and over again, to their greater perfection and success! But I have never heard tell of a job like this. I pore over this manuscript almost every day and am at a loss which direction to urge it in. Which way would it sooner go itself? Towards a smoother shape, which would create a more definite impression, or instead back towards doubts, allusions, nothing but feelings, and a more fragmented style? In the first case, I would certainly find more truth, which I could tower above and lord it over. In the contrary case, let me be wrong, wilfully so, let the truth be elsewhere – but let it be at my side, at least. How great it will be, I cannot say.

I remind myself of my original intention: that my work should speak as much through what it is as what it says, and in the end I leave it in its original form. The next day the process is repeated: I fume over its blind alleys, meandering adventures, shamefully uneven style, its blemished finish, and I sit and read the same five pages over and over again... until in the end I say: So what! What is more congenial to me: my future reader or my own past? This past year of mine is a corpse: do I embalm it to make it smell nice, or let it fall into dust? – It's obvious, isn't it!

And besides that, there are the unexpected and painful moments of realisation that I have wasted my life writing, that was life and now it's gone. And the enormous losses all round! Human suffering! The interest of my book conflicts with the interests of the people that it is about!

What sort of idea was that – the puzzle! That six-branched wooden joke that I banged into the typewriter just to see whether something might come of it, something to write about, just for the sake of it. What's it doing now, the puzzle? What does it look like? Do I still have it? I interrupt my writing. And what about that sulphur-yellow flower, which must have dried ages ago? I want to see it!

I go over to the bookshelf, open the bottom cupboard and take out the cubic box. I open it with bated breath: I'll have some proof! Real proof! Proof that it wasn't a figment of my typewriter, but a headstrong amatory adventure. Should I, may I, say amatory? When the last piece is inserted, the shape is completed and makes sense; when it is removed, the shape immediately falls apart. There's ingenuity for you...! I open the box and stare at the thing in my hands: the puzzle, and to its top face is stuck a little flower, its stalk now scale-dry and transparent, its head grey and shrivelled beyond recognition. But in the gap between the pieces, a tiny slip of paper has been inserted! It wasn't there when I accepted the puzzle, examined it and put it away with a smile. I withdraw the slip of paper between finger and thumb: it is a descriptive label, of scholarly strict morals. I raise my glasses like a scholar and read the description, written in a well-known scholarly hand: ADONIS?? – I carry the strange exhibit over to my desk and stare at it for goodness knows how long. At last, in my mind's eye, I can see the unknown bank of clay whence this flower came. And louder than my recollection of the joke with the puzzle, crueller than my writing assignment today, the thought screams in my mind that my extremely ingenious and truthful amatory adventure took place entirely without me!

With a relish that will be understood by anyone who knows which spring flowers come first, I write the requested answer: NO! COLTSFOOT!! I replace the paper into a chink in the puzzle, very carefully, so as not to scatter the desiccated specimen, close the box and put it back in its place for a further period of silence.

TUESDAY, 11ᵀᴴ DECEMBER 1979

I feel that it is "running away from me." – That is an expression from the Baťa factory: the workman removes one shoe after another from a wire cage, known as a "warrior." He does his bit on it and then replaces it in the "warrior." Meanwhile the line of warriors moves slowly forwards. Every hold-up, because of mechanical failure, faulty material or the state of the workman, means that the workman must stretch to reach the departing warrior, delaying himself even more, and this leads to nervousness, panic... and finally, a red light: stop! I went through terrors enough on account of that. There was a time when the lining would always tear on me; until they started using stronger fabric, even the red light over the exit in the cinema gave me a twinge of alarm in my stomach. – Interestingly enough, I have never had dreams about it, either then or since. And what better material for a nightmare!

"Last night I spent half the night dreaming about a house I'm designing, and the other half was identical, but about you. It was about how I was looking into the house and trying to find the simplest solution, which has to be there, and I look and for a long time there's nothing, and then it leaps out and I know there can't be any other way, so that the moment I stopped dreaming about the house, suddenly there you were, Ludvík, and the simplest solution came to me and I just went to find you somewhere, where you were standing as large as life and completely free. Yet as I was waking up I forgot which route I'd taken, and then it misted over completely as consciousness returned. So I still don't know where or how! And yet, when I woke up during the night, I knew that I would not forget *this* by morning, that there just can't be any other way."

They led me into a more elegant office, in which an unknown man sat at the head of a table. Major Fišer, who had escorted me, drew himself ridiculously to pre-retirement attention and called: "Comrade Superintendent, Mr. Vaculík has presented himself per summons." – "Sit down," said the superintendent and continued, "I summoned you in order to issue you a caution in accordance with the law and paragraph so-and-so. Stand up."

469

We all stood up: myself, Major Fišer and another man – a driver, I expect. The superintendent picked up a paper and started to read: "In accordance with law so-and-so and paragraph so-and-so, I formally caution you that you are organising anti-social, coercive activities and furnishing distorted information to the foreign media, thereby damaging the republic's interests abroad. Sit down. Is there anything you wish to say?" I sat down, thought it over carefully and said: "I take note of the caution, I have no other option. I cannot agree with your characterisation of my activities. But I doubt you'll be ready to discuss that with me." – "No," the superintendent confirmed. – "Then I don't have a clue what we're talking about or what the caution relates to," I said. – Major Fišer said: "But you wrote a letter to the speaker of the Federal Assembly, didn't you? Do you really think that Kohout is such an important writer?" – I turned to the superintendent: "You see? The speaker of the Federal Assembly has yet to confirm that he even received the letter, and here you are giving me a caution on account of it! It's typical. What do you mean by distorted information? In the case against VONS, you didn't even investigate whether the information they were making public was truthful or not, and they were convicted simply because they made it public." – Major Fišer said: "Were you in court? You weren't!" – I turned to the superinten- dent: "You see? How could I attend the court when they forbade me to and kept me under surveillance? And that is really typical." – The superintendent stood up, walked up to me and offered me his hand with the words: "Mr. Vaculík, I personally regret having to issue a caution to you, of all people."

I escaped onto the street, into a warm breeze that was scented with the pure water of the dark clouds over Prague, and I cursed: Hell! Cautioned! Yet again!

Because I can't go thinking it means nothing, can I? Though I suppose a hero might. Up to now each of my actions gave them some scope for politico-psychologico-tactical speculation about what to do with me, but henceforth they have no freedom to take decisions about me. They've tied their own hands. It has been decided, and it is up to me to make the move that closes the cage on me. And I have so many jobs in hand at the moment! For heaven's sake!

At the corner of the street I halted for a moment and considered the wisdom of going straight from a police caution to the bookbinders for the bound 1978/1979 collection of feuilletons. In the end, with the sort of innate

And there sat Kolář! (p. 472)

sense of guilt I feel as a child of respectable parents – in this case guilt no doubt worthy of some better misdeed – I scuttled off home first. There I made myself some tea and sat down. I fell asleep.

As I roused myself and managed to push aside the chain-mail curtain in my head, it was time to go to Slávia, where I was to meet Eva Kantůrková. I entered the café, made my way to the corner, and in passing just glanced in the direction of Kolář's table. And there sat Kolář! I quickly backtracked and took a seat nearer the entrance so that I could not see him. Such moments with unexpected reactions are new for me, and I find them enjoyable. It is like a weary astronaut switching the controls of his spaceship over to automatic: one's weary intellect entrusts itself – with relief, after fifty years of resistance – to one's cerebral matter grown wise after fifty years of resistance. I can't take it all in at once, and I do not intend to.

From my spacious – though half-empty – briefcase, I took out the chapters of this manuscript that I propose to send to Vienna. I started to read and correct them; first in terms of style, then to see how intelligible it was for readers abroad, and lastly in the light of the caution I had just received. Time passed but Eva did not arrive. I must have got it wrong. She came an hour later. One of us must have been mistaken, but she had no wish to probe it further. "I wanted to talk to you about something you ought to know. They also called me in about that statement for Pavel, and I get the impression they're trying to pin it on you. I naturally responded in the proper way. I refused to answer questions about who drafted it and who collected signatures. The others did likewise, as far as I know. Nonetheless I got the strong impression that they're trying to pin it on you." – I said: "It's kind of you, Eva, but it's already pinned, and I went there this morning to have it formally attached. And they didn't even need to get any information from third persons, they made a simple and correct deduction. I sent the statement with a cover letter signed by me alone." – "But you shouldn't do that, Ludvík, or at least you could have told us so afterwards, so that we knew better how to deal with the interrogation." – "Hmm, it doesn't matter now." I said.

"You're not looking well and you're not getting out at all. Are you worried about something? she asked. – "There's nothing I'm worried about," I said, at which moment it occurred to me to test her concern, "except, maybe, for one minor matter at this particular moment." And I told her about my misgivings over the feuilletons, and she offered to pick them up from the binders, deliver them, collect the money, and hand it over to me in a week's time at the same place. It surprised me. When she left, I had, for the first time, the feeling that someone had given me a helping hand just when I needed it.

I got up and went over to Kolář's table. "It's marvellous here," Kolář declared, shaking my hand without getting up, thereby inviting me to join him. "No people, no cars," he said nasally. "Nothing's changed here! Well, do you have the impression I've been away for a year?" – "Not in the least," I said. "Looking at you now, I don't know whether you are here and now, or here and last year. It seems like no time at all."

WEDNESDAY, 12TH DECEMBER 1979

The ground beneath my feet wobbled, water-logged. The trees stood motionless and bare, but I had definitely heard a dark booming from somewhere and was looking for it. The clouds hung low over the oak trees, and their outlines were meticulously clear-cut, so that they looked like – heavy clouds, admired from incredibly close quarters. Crows wandered mutely above the desolate furrows. And that dark booming in the totally dead landscape was the water in the overflowing stream: its fused bubbling carried through the damp air, as in an enormous hollow balloon.

Řehonůřka – real name Arizona. A brown meadow undulating upwards to a small wood wedged into the marly hillside. I was never able to understand, and never will, through what play, and of what, it was created, and what gives rise to its spiritual personality. And I am not satisfied by the simple explanation – that the source is me. Its contours are as distinct as a letter A. That, too, is not the work of water, wind or time. Here's the throne hill, from which the entire prairie can be surveyed and controlled. It's the base. Suddenly I ran off light-footedly downhill, flying down into the valley and up the hillside opposite. I looked back in amazement, in my light black raincoat, to discover that I had taken the base with me; now it's here where I am. The prairie can be entirely surveyed and controlled from here! There are two spaces superimposed on each other. Is that the answer?

The only problem now is to make sure that no one ever transforms it! It is not possible to reach the one height from the other with a spear, but you can shoot an arrow the whole distance. From neither eminence, however, can one see into all the gulleys that criss-cross the prairie, making it an incredible

Its contours are as distinct as a letter A. (p. 473)

hiding-place for Indians, crawling strictly on their bellies, of course. It is a game that cannot be played with screaming and brute force; it is one that calls for intelligence, patience, and staying silent at the appropriate moment.

But beware of the forest at your rear when you're standing on either hill! I turned round and entered the ridiculous little wood. It is remarkable because of its composition: about a hundred trees of every kind, all of mighty growth, submerged in a hazel thicket. If I filled a vessel with the living air here, would I manage to carry it to Prague? My feet slip on the mouldering leaves. I do not know how to describe it and my quandary must have been obvious from the very beginning of this chapter. From each of the hills a footpath runs into the wood; inside, both paths meet in a clearing, ever open to the burning sun, an atmosphere entirely jungle-like. Weighed down by a summer downpour, the branches of the trees and bushes would join to form a vault beneath which reigned the darkness, the spiders and the ants.

And that was where the pit was! It measured about two metres by three – no, that's wrong, one metre by one-and-a-half. Everyone was bound to fall in it once, so well was it concealed by vegetation! There was nothing to indicate its original purpose, when it had been made, or where they had put the earth dug out of the hole. The damp, crumbling walls are still not overgrown with anything. I now stood above the pit and looked down into it, as I had forty years before. It's unchanged! I feel how warm and expectant it is.

I returned to the hill and made several attempts to reach the other hill with a spear, but in vain. I was unable to clear the linden trees in the valley. As I swung my arm back in my light black raincoat, I fell over on the damp prairie grass and got all muddy. I made my way to my sister's, cleaned myself up, had a wash, and then took a back street to the schoolmistress's house. The schoolmistress was cooking the Sunday lunch, Madla was sitting up in bed and coughing with a chill. They were both in excellent spirits, however, from one another's company. After lunch I looked for something really good to read and came up with *The Counterfeiters* by André Gide. When we were leaving I begged the schoolmistress to let me borrow the book, and she told me to keep it. Since then I have had it as bed-time reading; it is an excellent novel.

On Tuesday – yesterday, in other words – we went to a concert. It was given by the Smetana Quartet, one of whose members is Antonín Kohout (cello), who celebrated his sixtieth birthday with a *tour de force*: Pauer's twelve cello duets. He played the lot, with six cellists taking it in turns to play the second part. They included his daughter Marie (why, otherwise, would she have given him a kiss afterwards?), who played very well, I think. But whereas a man comes in, sits down, adjusts the position of the music-stand or his seat, leans the instrument on the ground or against his face, and starts to play, a woman arranges her skirt, then tidies her hair over her shoulder, then sweeps aside obtruding hair from her forehead – though she could have easily trimmed it off at home – then looks to see if we can see her properly, then twists her arms so that the fastenings of her sleeves should not get in the way later, then stretches her neck out of her collar, fluffing out her hair at the back again – which requires her to take the bow in her left hand so as to readjust her hair-do with the right – then she takes back the bow from its place of safekeeping, and then at last the men can start playing. "Get on and play, you ninny!" I always shout.

The second item was Martinů's piano concerto, and finally Smetana's E minor quartet No. 1, "From my Life." The hall was packed, only Kosík and Kriegel were missing. Kosík because there is no relying on him to attend anything at all, and František Kriegel has died. On account of the degenerate authorities, he could not have a decent funeral and was therefore merely cremated technically. A ceremony will be held after the revolution.

FRIDAY, 14TH DECEMBER 1979
There has been a snowfall, but it is now thawing. The streets are running with filth. I had three dreams.

I was wading in the brook at Brumov. It was murky, because sewage pipes discharged into it from either side. I walked with revulsion on the slippery stones, against the current; eventually I must come to the highest of the sewers, above which the water will be clean. I reached it: the brook beyond was clean.

I was walking along the bank of a shallow pond. I was intending to bathe. There was no one there, just a lonely fisherman in the distance. I entered the water in a t-shirt that came down to just above my knees. I only swam a few strokes and when I came back to the shallows, the tee-shirt barely reached my waist. The bank was full of people, I had to disentangle myself from fishing lines and carefully remove the hooks from my body.

The crocodiles did not bother the people at all, so it occurred to me that the brewery workers kept them as pets. (p. 478)

I wanted to show my friends the Brumov brewery and the cottage behind it, where I was born. You have to cross that brook to reach the brewery. As we neared the bridge I was afraid the water in the brook might be nasty. But when I reached it, I saw that it was clean; there simply wasn't much of it, which is usual in summer – a little water trickling through a wide expanse of gravel. Close by the bridge was an artificially scooped-out pool, "the splash" – like we used to make. People were swimming in it: they were all men in boxer-shorts, brewery workers. I was pleased my visitors could see it. A few yards lower down there was another pool. I leaned on the railing over the stream and saw, in the pool, a beautifully positioned dark-brown crocodile, curved into an S-shape so it would fit. I wondered whether it was the celebrated "Brno Dragon." Along with it there were two smaller light-green crocodiles, moving about in lively fashion. The crocodiles did not bother the people at all, so it occurred to me that the brewery workers kept them as pets. It made me proud.

Today I related those three dreams from one night to Karel Pecka. "They're not what you could call sweet dreams, are they?" he said. – "What's a sweet dream supposed to be? What's meant by it?" I asked him. That question took both of us aback. Was it when you dreamed you were eating something nice, or when you saw something splendid or were sleeping with a beautiful woman? I do not think I have ever dreamt about food in my life. About women I dream precisely as many times a year as is recorded here, and so far I have never had anything particularly first-rate. To see one's long-dead parents in a dream always has an element of sepulchral horror, as well as a dull sense of guilt in their regard. "I can't help it, Karel. Brewery workers and crocodiles swimming alongside each other in a clean brook in my native village, that has to be a sweet dream for me." Karel said: "True enough."

I feel sleepy all the time these days. I would be able to sleep anywhere. I fall asleep in the tramcar before I get from the National Theatre to the Rudolfinum. *Aeronautics and Cosmonautics* slips from my hands. The trams run badly, and when it is wet above and below, as it is now, there is always something burning out in the motor, and we end up standing at a tram stop as the cars spray us with muck. With both hands full of heavy packages, I decided it would be better to walk from the embankment if I was to make my date with Lenka Procházková. I left all my wet things, including the packages, in the cloakroom, chose a table, and started to drowse nicely at it. But after a cou-

I decided to get it over with as quickly as possible: I would return the texts, say what I had to say and that would be that. (p. 480)

ple of seconds I gave a start and became very angry at myself – why aren't I snoring at home instead? I decided to get it over with as quickly as possible: I would return the texts, say what I had to say and that would be that.

She arrived wearing a white blouse, cut like a man's shirt from coarse, but soft, material that came down over her hips. Jeans. She sat down and said: "I left my scarf in the cloakroom today." As planned, I returned her manuscripts, some of which immediately found themselves back in my care, so that I might give them to someone cleverer to appraise. I realised that I was in fact incapable of justifying my feelings to her. Ivan would be better. She agreed.

Then she told me she had cinema tickets for the revival of *Closely Watched Trains*. I told her I had seen the film when it first came out and had not liked it especially. (I had even found it unpleasantly coy at times.) Then I said: "And anyway there's no possible way I could go to the cinema with you. It was stupid what I said last time. I don't even feel comfortable with such a young woman, even here, I must tell you." She looked at me with amused surprise. "And there's yet another reason, which I have to tell you. What I'm currently writing is a sort of snapshot of the year. I describe everything that happens to me or that I dream – all my encounters with people and my feelings about them. You're in it too, now. Along with everything I think about you and your writing. On the other hand, there's no need to get too alarmed, because it's also a bit of a joke. I wouldn't have told you this, but now I have to, to give you a chance to keep away from me if you like. It'll continue for about another month, and it's unlikely you'll write another book in that time," I laughed.

This time, her gaze, which she had fixed on me without replying, was one of pure amazement.

MONDAY, 17ᵀᴴ DECEMBER 1979

Chance directed my steps to the street where the Wheeper lives. I entered the house and rang his doorbell with nothing particular in mind. He opened the door – and stared at me as if I was a ghost. When he gathered his wits, he said: "Well, that's decided it then. Come in." I took off my shoes, entered his study and sat down in the heavy leather armchair opposite his desk. Without asking, he poured me a glass of whisky. In silence he sat down in the chair where he works, looked at me, and, shaking his head, chuckled quietly to himself. Then he pulled open a drawer and tossed two 10-thousand-crown bundles of hundred-crown notes in front of me. "You must have caught a whiff of this money," he said.

Some aunt of his had died the previous year. It turned out that he stood to inherit, and at first it looked like there was a pile of rags and little else. Her furniture was neither usable nor antique. With annoyance he let the neighbours get rid of it. But the aunt had also owned a cottage in the Or-lické Mountains; never having been there, he made a trip to see it and lost any interest he might have had in it. He mentioned at the local town hall that he would consider selling and a buyer came forward. Contrary to current practice he sold him the cottage for the price at which it was officially valued, stipulating only that he intended to keep the tiled stove, which the buyer would dismantle and transport to the Wheeper's cottage in Southern Bohemia at his own expense. The money arrived today. The Wheeper was just wondering what to do with it when my name wandered into his thoughts.

"What do you want to call your prize, then?" I asked. – He raised his hands in protest: "No prize! Please! I've no wish, I'd hate to..." – "You don't want to commit yourself for the future, is that it?" I laughed. "Quite right. Here's the money, give it to anyone you like, and in fact I'd sooner you kept it yourself." – "That's foolish. It's a shame," I regretted, "because I could use it. But it would look to all the world that I had wangled twenty thousand out of you on the pretext of Czech literature's needs! Well, I just happen to know someone who needs it if he is going to finish his book..." – "I don't want to know who it is," he raised his hands again. "What if he finished it, you gave it to me to read, and I was pissed off at having given money for such nonsense?" We laughed. It only remained for me to ask about the final particular: "What about your wife?" He rose agitatedly from his desk, crossed the room and declared: "She'd just better keep really quiet, that's all. She couldn't abide her and actually went so far as to say that even on her death-bed she wouldn't accept a sip of water from an old bat like that. So..." – "She couldn't have put it better," I agreed, took the money, thanked him and left.

"Karol, old chap, something incredible has happened," I told him an hour later. "I might at last have some money for our colleague, but how can I give it to him without his getting the impression that it's just like the *Litfond*, and that stipendia are there for the asking." – "How much?" Karol asked. – "Twenty thousand." – Karol chuckled. "That's unfortunate. It's quite a sum. That would be enough for half a year, without a doubt. The trouble is he'll never believe us that it was sheer chance," he said, shaking his head and laughing at the unbelievable event. – "You'll just have to fix it up somehow, Karol," I said. In high spirits we went our separate ways, and at the last moment I remembered to say: "This is important, Karol! Tell him he should have a good story ready for the cops!"

WEDNESDAY, 19TH DECEMBER 1979

"Only five more days at work! How about that?" With those words Madla left the house. On the table she left a chopping board with some sliced orange peel. In the unlit oven, some meringue cake or other with raisins in the middle is drying out. And I have no Christmas tree. "It was your one and only Christmas task and you're incapable of fulfilling it! While *I* have to keep going like clockwork all the time! You don't do a thing for the family!"

For the past fortnight I have been compiling from this book a "sample cross-section for Austrians old and new." I have also written an introduction, which I have to record in German, plus a three-minute autobiography, sufficient for an understanding of the text. I have tried to make it a separate composition. If I succeed in my purpose, the emigrants will weep buckets and the foreigners will be enchanted. The only trouble is that I do nothing for the family, and that's the main thing. But I don't know what I would not do.

I was obliged to ask Zdena to type it out. When she started, she was happy and inquisitive; by the end she was taciturn. Yet again she is covered in injections and sticking plaster. There is a bandage round her wrist and one round her foot above the instep. A fortnight ago she arrived at work in the morning, sat down on her chair, and she was done for: she was unable to rise again. In pain and with her colleagues' help, she got herself to the doctor and from there to hospital, where they injected her and sent her home. The day before yesterday she went back to the factory for the first time in a fortnight. She returned triumphant: "I got a bonus: a hundred crowns! Do you realise what that means? That the boss must have defied instructions and decided to let me know I'm working well. I expect it'll be my last bonus too." – "What about your organisational suggestions?" I asked. – "I didn't want to ask too many questions, but my guess is that they are being implemented cautiously." – "And what do you say about my book?" I asked. – She remained silent and then said: "For weeks on end no one passes through that door, but over the past two days I've had Jirka, Sergej and Ivan here. They all wanted to know what I'm typing. 'Ludvík,' I told them. They were really curious to know what it was like. I gave each of them the standard reply you told me: 'I don't know yet, but apparently it's going to make us all shed a lot of tears.'" – "You put it perfectly," I said. – She fingered her bandaged wrist. "I look a real mess," she sighed, "but my typewriter still likes me."

Meat is suddenly in adequate supply again. I bought a turkey and we received a rabbit from Marie Kosíková's parents. It has been Jan's job and custom since he was small to buy the carp. Formerly he made a principle of bringing it home live and then talking to it, kneeling at the side of the bathtub. This year there is no frankincense on sale: they have banned its production because it smells of churches.

In the afternoon, Dark Procházková came and gave me an envelope. It contained a detailed typewritten questionnaire. I took it over to the desk to study it. In a preamble it states that in view of the fact that any sort of agreement with me is difficult to achieve, and particularly in our flat, the following procedure has been selected: I am to mark only one answer to each question. The questions were along the following lines: I am willing to accept an invitation on... (several dates). I'm not willing, because: I don't feel like it; I've other commitments; I don't want to be seen with "a woman so young"; I regard her invitation as impudent. In case of a favourable response I would prefer: the Lobkowitz Wine-Cellar; the Maecenas Tavern...

I lent it a moment's thorough consideration and then marked the appropriate answers: I don't want to be seen with a woman so young; I've other commitments; she's impudent; 29th December at 6:30 p.m.; Lobkowitz Wine-Cellar. I handed it to her and she said: "But it contradicts itself!" I shrugged to say: that wasn't my fault. She left.

Of course I know what would be better for me. But I am only small fry. My Book demands something else!

THURSDAY, 20TH DECEMBER 1979

It will soon be midnight. Outside it is snowing. We are just back from the Klímas. Saša Kliment has finished his book and Ivan held a dinner in his honour. On the table was the menu of the Hotel Eremurus: Main Course – Pork "Kung Mao." Saša's book is set in the fictitious Hotel Eremurus.

For half the evening I was half-dead, and even had to go to lie down in the other room for a few minutes, while in the main room the women were having a good time, I expect, but everything they said got on my nerves. In a quiet corner Ivan was discussing Saša's manuscript with him; he apparently has some comments. Ivan did not tell them to me and Saša has not yet offered me his manuscript to read.

Saša welcomed me warmly, saying he had already planned to come over to our place, which I would like to believe. I asked him if he knew I had signed the statement for Pavel on his behalf. He said he had already heard about it, though he did not know what it contained; however, he would not show me up. "Mind you, Ludvík, I didn't make any commitment to Pavel at Hrádeček that time. I think I was the only one who voiced serious misgivings. I thought he was taking a risk going there and regarded the eventual outcome as ninety percent certain. The other thing I said at the time was that my reaction would be governed by developments..." He extended his hand towards me when he saw I was unnerved, "but there's no harm done – there's nothing to worry about."

The only thing that worried me was Saša's wife, Jiřina, and I was glad she could not hear us at that moment. Last week – I did not even record it here – Major Fišer called me in again over Pavel. And I have another summons for tomorrow for some unknown reason, and I do not intend to write about that either. Jiřina talked to me normally today. The Klímas did their best to raise my spirits and offered me everything possible; I had to put a stop to their attentions, because Madla was looking as if she might turn savage. I was dreadfully angry with myself and for the first time in my life started to feel as if I myself were a stranger, someone who had nothing to do with me and for some unfathomable reason always gets me in trouble and still has it in him to cause me terrible, still undreamt of, misfortune. Then Helena Klímová asked with a facetious smile whether I wanted to lie down, and led me to their bed, leaving me there and switching off the light. I fell asleep and when I re-emerged into the company half an hour later, everyone pretended they had not noticed anything and I was right as rain again.

At noon today I had a brief meeting with Mrs. P. for the purpose of receiving from her, together with her comments, the pages of this work where I describe our meeting on 1st August. She approached me with an irate step. Silently we entered the Alfa (mulled wine – grog) and then I got the full force of her rage. She forbade me to write about our meeting because my account of our conversation is inaccurate. For one thing, I distort her views and statements, and from some frivolous literary vanity I added something that wasn't said, which provides readers with ample scope to deduce all sorts of things. I can treat my women however I like, but she never imagined that everything would form part of a record, in which, what's more, the only person I am shamelessly cheering for is myself. No, she has no objection to any harsh descriptions of her stories, but she does not want any personal remarks about her, none at all!

I replied that that was precisely why I had lent her that particular entry: so she could raise objections. Surely the reader of the book as a whole will recognise a game for what it is, and will realise that no friendship between a man and woman can exist without the conscious or unconscious possibility of its transcendence, a possibility that, in the case of lifelong friendships, is lifelong and provides them with a stimulating overtone. I would have expected her to be more receptive to such an idea. She replied that she would be, in real-life terms, if only I didn't write about it or at least were more skilful and capable of portraying it. But all I was capable of portraying was myself and no one else. My overriding tone was one of self-pity, while towards others I was pitiless.

By now I just remained silent and fiddled with a button that, in my agitation, I had pulled off my shirt cuff. She also fell silent, and when the button fell from my fingers and rolled across the table-top, she seized it, beating me by half a second, and then swallowed it. That made me angry. "What are you up to!" I said. – "There you are," she said didactically, "if you had any flair at all for sublimating reality, you'd say, for instance, in place of your stupid outrages, that I'd eaten a button. I'd allow you to do that." – "You must be crazy!" I said. "You call eating my button some kind of sublimation of reality, but that would be far worse in everyone else's eyes!"

We soon parted company, curtly. I told her I would delete all mention of her. But, I now realise, that is out of the question and have no wish to. So for the time being I am just deleting the conversation from 1st August, and I'll take another look at the rest. And write about a button, as she suggests? Not on your life!

Yes, the moments I expected are now arriving. I spent the whole afternoon sitting numb and amazed, like a good pupil who has just failed an exam. I am not going to haggle for a better mark. I know a lot of people will share her view of me. But there is no way I can delete everything. All I can do is try to rewrite it, more and more, against myself. And then I'll stop having anything to do with people.

SATURDAY, 22ND DECEMBER 1979

To bash away at the typewriter to the sound of Schubert's B minor, with rough gusto, almost in time with those rustling semi-quavers that are so refined and mysterious, is a way of suppressing shameful sorrow. Thirty-eight years ago, when I myself played this piece as fiftieth violin or whatever, in Zlín, I had no idea what I was playing, of course. Now I have to face the music!

Christmas began for me today. I drove to Josef's for a tree. I had not planned to at all, but when I turned up at his place, he acted as if we had always agreed on ten-thirty sharp. He locked the stable and took a different coat, and we drove to the sawmill at Kosova Hora, where we arranged for them to cut four two-metre trunks into planks for me. On the way back we stopped at a pine thicket and cut down the tree. There are white shadows of snow lying in the black fields: summer in negative.

It is past midnight again, and I am drinking white wine from Uherské Hradiště. It will soon be Christmas and the end of the year. I have almost no presents and almost no money. Just piles of books for delivery again. Eva Kantůrková said to me: "They say you're writing against everyone." – "No one has been authorised by me to announce that." The petition for the prisoners to be released for Christmas was signed by over seven hundred people, which is very good. The trouble is it's the same ones again.

Josef's yard is a swamp, churned up by tractor wheels and trampled down by horse's hooves. In it, two girls, still kids, were moving to and fro, grooming horses and carrying manure. One of them was the Monika from Prague. Josef's wife invited me to lunch, Monika carried the food to the table. Whoever comes to help with the horses on weekends is naturally Josef's guest. Monika is small, frail and slightly pale, and has a modest though resolute demeanour. As I was leaving, she boldly sent her best wishes to Jan. I liked that. I told her what I knew – that Jan was intending to come there for St. Stephen's Day.

When I was driving to Prague, the weather was grey with moderate visibility, temperature about three degrees above zero, and a steady cold breeze.

Once again I saw, jutting up out of the horizon, that same mysterious lonely church that has lured me for the past fifteen years. I set off for it. It is smaller than it appears from a distance. It stands on the foundations of a Romanesque church from the twelfth century or thereabouts. It is newly repaired and painted, and in fact the scaffolding had only just been removed. There is no village nearby, but there is a cemetery, whose old stone wall is crumbling in places. The church is surrounded by mighty, spreading trees. The hillside below the church is covered by a dense old cherry-orchard. The view of the grounds creates a sense of mystery: as if, beneath them, there was buried a palisade with moats, drawbridges and gateways, covered now with a further layer of decaying leaves. I walked through them cautiously, hesitantly, looking around and measuring distances. There was a faint but constant hiss of air everywhere, as if summer had withdrawn, leaving in its wake a vortex to be filled with cold air from the north, and now it was necessary to wait for summer to return once more from its circuit of the globe.

MONDAY, 24TH DECEMBER 1979

It is nearly six o'clock and the carp has almost finished frying. There is an enormous pile of presents under the pine tree. Most of them were added by Ondřej and Jan. I have never had so few presents ready as this year. The pine tree that Josef and I selected was quite crooked, so it was no easy job to fix it upright in the stand. I spent the afternoon decorating it and have just finished. Every year I get the feeling that I have only just packed the glass balls away, a year has gone by, and there has been none and I am still there holding the decorations. It is the feeling I have each time I climb the cherry tree. About twenty years ago I wrote a story about decorating the Christmas tree; it was the first things I ever published in *Literary News*. Each time I try to think up a new arrangement of colours and I plan to buy decorations of a single colour for next year: either blue or green.

I had been wanting to hand this job over to the boys, but they refused. They walk past with eyes closed lest they see the tree before the end of dinner. When they were small, they would blindfold themselves of their own accord. I would stand here mumbling and pretending I was talking to Krakonoš – that Old Man of the Mountains – who assisted me and then left the presents. Old Krakonoš has been coming to us for the past thirty years, at least. When in those days the state authorities started suppressing the Baby Jesus and imposing in his stead a certain Grandfather Frost – an old devil from goodness knows where, who purported to be one of the people, whereas he was in fact a product of party bureaucrats' mental masturbation – we enlisted the help of Krakonoš. For one thing he did not need to pretend like an idiot that he had arrived on a Russian sleigh, when outside there was nothing but mud. Moreover, there was copious background material about him written in Czech and he had the reputation of being a fair and fun-loving being. Krakonoš became established in our family and never caused any problems for us – or for the Baby Jesus. Krakonoš can happily join us in the singing of "Christ the Lord is Born."

We are in excellent spirits; peace and harmony always triumph in the end. The boys think up humorous wrapping for their presents; Madla makes a potato salad, guts the fish, bakes a plaited Christmas loaf, and grumbles, now notoriously, every Christmas, that she could use another day to prepare. I leave the presents in the shop's wrapping, and just tie them with different string. Madla buys herself decorative Christmas paper. Each of us openly hides his or her presents in some corner or other, and secrecy is never violated. Madla alone rewraps each of her gifts twenty times, examining it and seeking the advice of everyone except the person it is for. This is something the boys and I object to. In the end, all the wrapped presents are entrusted to me.

We have already burnt the only cone of frankincense saved from last year. They are not allowed to make frankincense anymore, because it smells like church incense, and public carol-singing is also banned. A fortnight ago we were at the annual concert of the Chorea Bohemica folk group: it was forbidden to put books in the basket for charity donations, and after the performance, which traditionally used to end with community carol singing, we were allowed to sing just one before being shooed out the door. For the whole of Christmas Eve the radio broadcast scarcely more than a half-hour dose of carols, measured out like a burst from a machine-gun and sincerely intended by the state to convey just such a message. In place of carols they broadcast songs about Christmas: Christmas, dear children, is a sort of festival about nothing, when we rejoice over clothes and piles of food. So in our family we mostly put on records for music.

Jan helps out in the kitchen, preparing dishes of fruit and sweetmeats. We change for dinner, and when we are seated I am asked to make a speech.

Ever since Martin made fun of me during the first words of my speech, saying "here comes the speech," my speech goes as follows: "There was a time when I would deliver a fine speech. Ever since your foolish brother Martin made fun of me, saying 'here comes the speech,' I no longer make speeches." The boys give satisfied nods that tradition is upheld, but Madla is dissatisfied and must wish us all good health, including Martin, now with his Isabelle. First of all we eat a sliver of wafer with honey. Then comes fish soup, fried carp, various preserved fruits and ice cream. The boys always used to get hold of some bottles of fruit juice; this year we have our own apple juice. Wine is also poured, but the glasses are rarely drained.

Dinner is over. We were still at the table when the telephone rang. Jan grabbed it: we were expecting Martin. But it was Zdeněk Mlynář. Exceptionally, I was prevailed upon to use the phone, and I spoke with him. He sent us his best wishes and I am to convey his greetings to friends. When I replaced the receiver, we all thought about it for a moment and I started to be cross with myself for having been terse with him. Madla and the boys said: "You didn't speak to him very nicely." It grieved me so much that I decided to come and make a note of it here. Then the boys washed up, and I went to light the candles and sparklers on the tree. Then I opened the door and the children called out, Ooooh! We sat for about half an hour singing carols. We start with "Christ the Lord is Born" and wind up with "Bethlehem is where it happened, now's no time to sleep." Then our Jan delivers the pile of presents, because he is the smallest and enjoys doing it. It also gives him a chance to practise his reading. No one ever wants to open their presents and waits for someone else to start. Ondřej received a camera bag and gadgets to make it easier for him to photograph locomotives out in the field, plus a few little items for the darkroom in the new flat. Jan got a set of drawing pens, a shoulder-bag, and *Czechoslovak feuilleton 1978/1979*. Madla, gold earrings. In addition, we all got lots of things to wear and read. Madla and I got a slide-projector from the boys.

The worst thing is having to clear up the bits of paper and string. The paper has to be piled up and Madla saves the nice pieces for future use. The string I take because I play Krakonoš the whole year round for the benefit of Šimečka, Uhde and Trefulka. Then I go back into the kitchen, where we drink coffee or tea and Madla gives a detailed account of how she searched for it until she found it, bought it and exchanged it for a larger size. At this point some of the gifts are immediately tried on, shown off and poked fun at. We call Martin's number in Paris but no one answers.

Then we go to bed and each of us takes along a book to read. I took a children's book that Ondřej gave me. It is called *The Story of the Sad Tiger*, and it is all about how the tiger was sitting sadly in his cage when in flew a little bird who told him that if he ate seeds like a bird he would eventually be able to creep out through the bars. The tiger says he would like to try and at the cost of terrible hunger (about which the book remains silent) he dwindles into a little bird and flies out. The story ends with a sentence that Ondřej pasted over – in case, he says, it upset me. He does, however, quote it in the dedication, for the sake of information: "But such things only happen in fairy tales, don't they!" I expect he did not want anything to discourage me.

It cheered me up instantly.

SUNDAY, 30TH DECEMBER 1979

I am coming downstairs; it is becoming lighter. On the last landing, by the window, two women are prattling, prolonging their stupid encounter just to get a look at me. I enter their field of vision feet first. The old bags stop talking and squint hatefully at the bloody smears on my thighs. I don't care. I've just come from a screaming woman; it wasn't supposed to be me. Her head is screaming but she frenziedly takes me with her loins. I am hurting her, but she can put up with it for a moment, can't she, for God's sake? She thrusts her head backwards so that all I can see is the rim of her mouth and nostrils. I grow suspicious. This isn't Ester! The words are spoken of their own accord, and straight away regret starts to collect there, and collect and collect. I churn the regret into an unspoken reproach, like a burning cord. I shake the woman's shoulders, trying to jerk the head up towards me for a second at least. Instead she stiffens in my hands and thrusts herself away in disgust. I inject my regret into her and smite her in anger. After this vengeance she is exhausted, but not in any sweet sense. I can now raise her head by the hair. A total stranger! But she's a woman made for compassion; I collapse onto the recess between her nape and shoulder. I caress her hair. I don't know her. What now? Am I to blame? I was, but now she has my blame inside her. It's hers now! I'm now blameless – an amazing revelation! I'm finished. There's something terribly wrong, but I'm not going to wash myself, I'll go blood-stained as I am. I want to. At last I am in the passage, making for the door of the building, and opening it onto the street. Where is she? Ester? The street is empty, snow-covered as in the early morning of some holiday, but I am a year late. A little dog is attached by a leash to an old-style street lamp. The dog has slender, fleet legs and a narrow fox-like head with short spiky ears. I recognise him and go to speak to him. I can see him shuffling on the spot and stretching out inquisitively to sniff the bottom of my coat. I make a step towards him, but he recoils in panic, and finding himself held by the leash, he twists his head out of the collar in practised fashion and runs off, zig-zagging freely up the white, empty street.

TUESDAY, 1ST JANUARY 1980

It is the fourth hour of the new year. New Year's Eve was a success –wait and see.

I spent the day printing photos to accompany the text I am sending to Vienna. Madla was already dressed up and in party mood while I was still flattening curled-up photos across the table edge. In that light, and with a nocturnal dusting of snow, the walk up the Old Castle Steps and through other parts of the Castle was right out of a story of Old Prague. Pale stars were shining. At the Castle gate I greeted the sentry. He responded. Madla kept stopping, turning round and scanning the towers, windows and gables. She spends half her time in the past, and histories are her favourite reading: her current choice being Vavřinec's *Hussite Chronicle*, which I put under the Christmas tree for her.

At the Kosíks', there was music and the fear that some Italians might turn up. "Mrs. Vaculíková," Karel declared ceremoniously, "the thought of entering the new year in such dependable company gives me the greatest joy. I would immediately express the hope that this year will be at least as good as last." The recipient of those wishes beamed appreciatively and Karel, with festive gestures, showed us to our places in his black-timbered penthouse. He was wearing an elegant, unprecedented brown suit with long narrow lapels. Marie was gentle, modest and charming in her Sunday best: a crocheted see-through white costume. Music was playing powerfully; it was Mahler. Then there arrived two different ladies by the name of Marta. And Kosík's cellist son popped in for a moment to say hello. Karel proposed we take a nip of

*He was wearing an elegant, unprecedented brown suit
with long narrow lapels.* (p. 491)

slivovitz. We did. I brought Karel my "cross-section" for Vienna, because he is impatient to see my Book, and I am even more impatient to know his opinion. I am actually a bit apprehensive. After all, it is full of references to him.

In addition to Kosík's slivovitz, which came courtesy of Kléma Lukeš, two others were also featured: one I had obtained from my driver brother in Uherské Hradiště, the other from Miroslav Zikmund, in Zlín, who distils it himself and sticks his *ex libris* on the bottle. We decided to make a careful comparison of them. Meanwhile Marie offered round things to eat. Madla admired Karel's suit and he told us, with renewed exasperation, that a German had brought it – second-hand, of course, and that he had felt ashamed but had not wanted to give offence; from this he realized that foreigners were unable to see, and would never understand, what we really need. "So why are you wearing it?" I said. Karel, smiling with taut lips, replied: "Isn't it a beautiful suit?" It's a case of the unfortunate "true enough." The phone rang. Karel was frightened that it might be the Italians and sent me to deal with it. "Police station," I announced into the phone. That definitely put them off, and suddenly it was our Switzers: Bruno, Jürgen, Líza, and Pavel with Jelena. Jürgen wanted to know when I would be delivering the manuscript. I told him to come to Vienna in January and I'd explain matters to him. He asked excitedly whether I'd be there and I replied that I would, to a certain extent. I thanked Pavel for his help and Jelena whispered in my ear that we'd probably see each other soon. Then Karel Kosík, with an immense smile (a pity they could not see it), conveyed greetings and best wishes full of confidence in the future. However, his confidence was based more on slivovitz than on an assessment of the situation. Then I tried to call Zikmund in Zlín to tell him how much we were enjoying his *ex libris*, but no one answered the phone.

Someone rang the bell below the iron staircase. Karel was frightened that it might be the Italians, but it was only Karel Pecka. He had come to invite us all to his place on Nerudova Street. There was a short argument about this; we did not feel like going into the unknown, now that we were so nicely settled, but Pecka coerced us with charm, and midnight was approaching. He promised me there was a letter waiting for me there. I was curious. Eventually Karel Kosík decided that we should go, as he would be safe from the Italians there.

Pecka's flat was full of people. Some of them, particularly the womenfolk, I had never seen before. I was afraid the unfamiliarity would bother Madla. But she formed a women's corner at the table in the front room and took no notice of anything else. There was lots of food; Kostroun had spent two days cooking. Pecka declared that he and Kostroun had decided to live together, so these were the banns. Pecka's "old girl," Majka, is leaving for Germany in January or February, I do not understand why, although Pecka denies they are breaking up. She is of German origin.

Kostroun squeezed his way toweringly through the crowd, choosing those who had not yet eaten this or that, selecting teams of diners and sitting them at the table with polite coercion. I ate next to Marta Slánská. I am surprised I have never met her before. She is a fine, tall woman, who was named after her godmother, President Gottwald's wife. Those children must have had a hard adolescence. It strikes me that Marta puts up quite philosophically with her dual-clan Slánský stigma and is very level-headed. Speaking about her mother, she declared with affectionate frivolity that she "is embarrassing, the way she plays the nation's widow." Whenever I talk to Rudolf Slánský Jr., I am never quite sure what to feel: at first I used to feel a need to say something out of the ordinary; then I realised it was not necessary – by now there has grown up between us a steady relationship of unstated trust, respect, and, for my part, a certain degree of pity. It is my belief that these cautionary offspring of a deed committed by the nation and the state function as an extremely useful moral institution. Marta spoke to Madla about her mother; with me she only spoke about the Germans: "The German threat means nothing any more to me or my generation." – I said: "It would only need a slight relaxation of the dreadful Russian grip and you'd all feel it again, though in a different way, of course, than during the last war or in the last century. Gruša is planning to write a book about it, an anti-German one, in fact." (This paragraph contains some reckless statements, but I wrote it on New Year's Night. – April 1980.)

After eating, what I wanted most of all was cold water, and this was something else Kostroun had, in a jug in his cellar, and he took me to get some. Kléma Lukeš spent his time walking from one room to the other and although it was only his second visit, he managed to break only one glass. I cannot recall what people talked about. An unshaven Jan Mlynárik, annoyingly neither drunk nor sober, assailed me and told me that I had to see about publishing Tatarka's political articles, and once more I told him that someone should edit them first and supply a Slovak typist, damn it! At this, Karel Kosík took issue with me, saying that it was a document, so why should it need editing, and clearly I had a low opinion of Tatarka. That finally got to me, because I think I do appreciate him, which is precisely why articles of his from twelve years ago ought to be edited by someone, with care. And if people do not agree with me, let them do what they like – but on their own! Jan wandered around the flat aimlessly with a glass in his hand and everyone knew what had happened to him over Christmas.

Then Kléma and I got up and went to stand in the doorway, where we started to sing. We sang for about half an hour and everyone enjoyed it, apart from Bartošek, who started to lobby for some songs from Bohemia, but he only knew those inane things that are done to death at school. I was the only one able to sing an unknown Bohemian song: "Look up at the sky, how clear it is, at the sparkling stars..." It has a lovely, stately melody, chorale-like almost.

I declared that the songs of Bohemia reflect a feeble mind that is incapable of celebrating anything properly; they are just childishly descriptive: "Oh, my lily of the valley, Oh, my scented garden rose, never I'll forget you, and ne'er shall find repose." By comparison, the most ordinary of Moravian Slovak songs fills one with a feeling of wonder:

> "Oh, lassie from Ždánice,
> Why do you nothing give?"
> "What can I give to you at all
> For I am yet too small
> And nothing yet to give."

That's it, the whole song! Perfect, definitely ambiguous, and now gradually acquiring another, third meaning. (Unless it is a return to the primary meaning that comes with the wisdom of experience.)

All of a sudden, what do I see – Zdena! Somewhere by the door they had taken her coat and now she was bobbing and turning in a cluster along with the Kantůreks. She was wearing her long mauve dress with the black flowers, which I will not go out with her wearing because it is so strikingly solemn. Everyone looked at her. "Who's that?" some dolts asked, and Madla explained: "That's my husband's mistress." And the black waves of Bibisa were already coming to me between people's legs, and now she was leaping up at me, her head high, rolling her dragon's eyes and wagging her tail. So far Zdena had taken no notice of me but went on greeting and introducing herself to people. I would have sooner had the Italians, but the justice of the entire event was obvious to me. My Book will be overjoyed; it had to happen one day, even though it did not happen of its own accord but was the work of the dreadful Kantůrková, who knew I was going to be here – the letter Pecka had mentioned was from her, and it told me how to care for her book of feuilletons. An ashen Karel Pecka came over to me and said: "What's all this about?" – "I've no idea. What am I supposed to do?" I replied. – He spluttered: "Don't ask me, buddy! You should have sorted things out before!" That made me angry. Sorted things out. What's that supposed to mean? Zdena can visit whomever she likes. After all, she has typed out books for all of them. She is not my dependency.

Kléma turned to me. "They say Zdena is here! Where? Lead me to Madla, men!" he bellowed intimately into the unknown around him. "Surround Zdena, we have to keep them apart!" And I just looked on in astonishment as an audacious old dream of mine finally came true. By audacious, I mean the dream was audacious in its treatment of me.

I went over to Zdena and said: "Hi! Well, seeing you're here, all the best..." and I kissed her on the cheek. She picked up Bibisa and said into her predatory face: "Look, Bibiska! It's our master!"

WEDNESDAY, 2ND JANUARY 1980

I have not yet made up my mind whether the New Year's Eve adventure was the last item of last year or the first of this. I feel good. Every morning, I expect a pasty-faced man with a hoarse breathless voice to appear at our door, wearing a short fur coat and fur hat. As I shave myself in the bathroom at nine o'clock, I listen through the strategic window to the banging of the lift door and the direction the steps then take. I need to finish writing this. The beginning of the manuscript displeases me – it is unreadable, and what irks me, I think, is not so much my inability to improve it, but my lack of courage to leave it as it is. I really did think it was better. There is an impending risk that I shall flush it down the john, but there exists a copy, so why the melodrama? People are already asking when it will be ready. I cannot help wondering why Slavík did not warn me when he was reading the instalments of the manuscript. I am not going to change or rewrite anything, just delete things. Then there is the unfinished entry for 24th September: what shall I do about that now? It was to stop the letters from trickling out of a hole that I shoved in a couple of sentences and brought the trip to Brno to some sort of close. I would like to simplify my life in the coming year.

Last night I had a beautiful dream at last: we had moved into an enormous peaceful flat in an old two-storeyed house, where we were able to hang up our pictures. We had also acquired a neglected garden that sloped up from the back of the house. I saw a number of aged, tall-trunked fruit-trees that looked as if they needed felling, and suddenly I saw how I could restore them to rampant growth. It was late August (!) in the garden, the grass dry, the soil grey and crumbly. The garden was surrounded by a wall with cracks in the mortar. I felt as if I was finally where I had always wanted to be. Madla and I had bedrooms at opposite ends of the house. When I went to see her, it was almost as if I would have to take a train there, and I actually looked forward to it.

If they intend to go on interrogating me on a monthly basis this year, I shall initiate a new manner of negotiating, one that I have already devised. Last year, before they arrested him, the astrologer Michal Kobal predicted that this year my personal freedom would be restricted, and that two years later I would have "a major spiritual success." I would like to test – cautiously, with one finger – whether the two things are necessarily linked. Michal Kobal is already out of prison and wants to emigrate. I predicted for him by guesswork that he would not be happy there either, and I feel sorry for him. It has started to freeze, there is a cold wind blowing, and I am pondering how to proceed.

I intend to continue writing this only a few days more, depending on when I manage to conclude it with some good idea or an important event. I would like to find space to record Milan Šimečka's visit, planned for the 12th, as well as a metre of snow, were it to fall, and some concluding dream about Ester.

THURSDAY, 3ʳᵈ JANUARY 1980

I spent the morning writing. In the afternoon I took a bag and went to pick up Pecka's bound stories. I wanted him to sign them for me, but he has gone off again to the place he measures water levels somewhere out of Prague. Outside, the snow has been flying about all day and Kolář has gone off to see the world again.

It is a year since he said to me in the Slávia: "Look here, if you're unable to write, write about why you're unable to write, for goodness sake! Keep a record of what you see, what you hear and what comes into your head. You've already developed your own style for it in your feuilletons, which are excellent, after all!" If I kept it up for a year, he said, I'd have a book. Maybe I'd even create some "new novel," because what was a novel these days, and where were they to be found? He also said that if I wrote regularly, he would give me something. I started to think it over, and what tempted me most of all was that he would give me something!

Ella Horáková sent me a New Year's card, which I don't think I'll be able to show to any women. ("See what use she makes of you, you stupid fool of a Czech?") It's a photograph: she and the bridegroom are standing listening to the official's words (whom the state hath joined let no man put asunder); I am standing behind them but am turned completely away from them. The two of us look very good on the photo. In front of the newly-weds a picture of a babe in a crib has been pasted, and if, heading into 1980, this really means what it ought to mean, we could send congratulations. Yet another woman ruined by her brain has been given an opportunity to help herself onto a better path by means of her breasts! I shall have to go and see Professor Machovec some time.

"Oooh, that's nice. You're coming to wish me a Happy New Year?" she said, unlatching the door and letting me in. – "You take me for a chimney-sweep?" I said. – "Not a chimney-sweep, sort of a St. Nicholas or Infant Jesus. You've got something?" – "Naturally. And I was hoping to give it you before the holidays. Where were you?" – "I've been... well..." – I gestured my indifference, what concern was it of mine! I paid her for the previous job and explained the new one: "Just this one, Marcela, and that's the last we see of each other. That's the end." – She took the book over to the lamp and leaned so far over the table that an amber pendant slipped out of her well-rounded bosom. "Not that Kantůrková again?" she said miserably. – "But Marcela, I'm sure you're going to like this one," I said. "But, careful, these two articles are to follow it, and it ends with this letter." She made marks on the papers.

The letter had been written to Eva by Ota Filip. "...this morning I read your feuilletons and my cosmopolitan soul quivered – a rare occurrence indeed. It was as if you had tickled my roots with a living stream and shaken my trunk. I trembled like an aspen, not with fear, but from the gusts of warm sorrow…"

Right. And now, while my hastier readers are thinking how noble I am – maybe even an idiot – I would ask them to be so kind as to find the entry for 23rd May, where I write: "she was in a long red dress that reached the pavement and was open to reveal one leg. It suited her, but nice she was not." The words "it suited her" are to be deleted and between "one" and "leg," the word "hind" to be inserted.

FRIDAY, 4TH JANUARY 1980

Two facts confront each other within me: that Madla has gained enormous freedom, which I do not begrudge her, and that my own freedom has diminished. I used to wake up each morning in the condition I had been in last thing at night. I could sit down at the typewriter and continue. I could look out the north window into the street and check if the roofs were wet and the traffic poisonous, then out the south window to see whether I ought to write or go out. I could calmly devote myself to my feeling of illness or health. Put some paper in the typewriter or tickle the ivories… that is all in the past now. My first thoughts each morning now confront the thoughts of another person. And straight away the mood I am in is no longer my own, but is induced. If I do not start working after breakfast, I am asked whether I'm planning to go out. Were I to tickle the ivories, it would be: Who am I pining for?

My friends share my view of what a marvellous being she is, but they do not know what an aggressive power she can be as well. (Naturally, otherwise she wouldn't tolerate living with you. – Helena Klímová.)

A cry went up over my Viennese phone calls: Senile folly! Unprincipled weakness! I say: But I'm old enough to be foolish, and as for my principles, they are mine to decide on. Nero Wolfe leaned back in the armchair: "One of the hallmarks of intelligence," he said slowly and patiently, "is the capacity to do something extraordinary or unique when the vital need arises…" I envy that fat detective for staying so cool. I always regret it afterwards when I shout.

I have never known anyone as well equipped as Madla for enjoying ordinary happiness. She does precisely what she was looking forward to: she has a proper sleep, then she tidies the clothes, does some washing, some ironing, some sewing, reads Vavřinec's thick *Chronicle*, falls asleep, wakes up, gets dressed, goes out. She comes back and she has been at the Kotva department store, visiting someone, or at the gallery in St. George's Basilica. In the evening she cooks something for Ondřej to take to the building site, while at the same time listening to the television. Then she switches it off, reads, chats with the boys – while darning clothes – goes to bed, and reads until she falls asleep. She is already asleep: I can see her light is off.

TUESDAY, 8TH JANUARY 1980

I am not even sure what I do all day. I do not feel like doing anything. It is always as if I were waiting for a more favourable moment to write. I am never alone. I am at a loss what to do about it. I have nowhere to go, either near or far. We were not at Dobřichovice even once during the entire Christmas holidays, and I do not feel like going there, do not want to know which of the old ladies have frozen pipes and no water, and am not curious to know which way the hare got in again.

Over the weekend, when equipment was out of action and nobody put salt on the streets, Prague looked like a human city. We went for a walk in Stromovka, where I like going and Madla does not. I looked at the way they treat the massive, spreading beeches. They always prune them at the "branch ring," with a saucer-shaped recess so that it should close as soon as possible, and paint them with varnish. I began to suspect I had too gloomy an attitude to the world. Stromovka was full of people, sledding and skiing. Holiday in White! There was skating on the pond. Mothers are getting younger all the time. There was gaiety everywhere. Young couples walked arm in arm or threw snowballs at each other, and all the youngsters are now wearing long colourful scarves down to their knees. Then I had a row with a young fellow who was letting his brat drive his sled through a clipped hedge, causing the twigs to fly in all directions. "Just go and have a look at what they're destroying over there," he said, pointing in the direction of the Russian embassy compound, where they were felling yet more trees. I refused to echo his familiarity and said: "Well, go and protest, then." He shouted in annoyance: "Why don't you go yourself, you old windbag!" I said: "I've already been, but I didn't see you there." I did not move from the fence until he had departed, taking his little twit and the sled with him. I did not lose my temper, though. I did it out of curiosity. Today, all that remains of the snow in the streets is a nasty slush.

WEDNESDAY, 9ᵀᴴ JANUARY 1980

There was a fine frost on the windowpanes today. Standa answered the door and there came a holler from the bedroom. "You're to go in and see her," he said, and led me in. In a wide dramatic bed Vlasta was sitting up, sewing lampshades. "Shall I leave you alone for a moment?" Standa asked anxiously, albeit willingly, or maybe vice versa. I had come to make sure that the Saturday performance, to which I had invited Milan Šimečka, was going to take place. Vlasta's motor is humming at high rpm and she looks five years younger. For the past few weeks she has been immersed in her play with Božena Němcová, and now news is coming in of the success enjoyed by her Lady Macbeth when it was shown on Austrian TV. Standa is overjoyed, but is tense whenever he answers the doorbell.

Jiří Lederer is being released from prison on Sunday. I wonder how they will treat him and what he will do. I am glad that *Czech Conversations*, one of the reasons they locked him up, has come out after all. I saw a copy of the book at someone's place, and it looks nice. It's not nice, though, that they have omitted yet again to send me a copy, although I think I did quite a bit towards its counter-publication.

I took Bibisa for a walk – ten minutes are enough for her in the frost – and then read for a while until Zdena arrived. "There's something I need," I said. – "Can you think of anything I wouldn't do for you?" she answered. I can think of at least two things, naturally, that she ought not do, but I would not dare name them, lest she do them. She was wearing a blouse she had made herself. It suited her, and because she filled it out properly, there's no need to delete that. I made coffee and she started to make something to eat. I wasn't hungry, but she maintains that I help her eat when I at least sit opposite her. First she drank her coffee and smoked a cigarette and then nibbled her food. I asked her if, by Friday, she would manage to type a seventy-page play by František Pavlíček, which Vlasta was going to perform on Saturday. "Will you take me along?" she asked. – "But you're invited there on your own account, anyway," I said. – "I'll look forward to it," she said. – I asked her: "Have you had any interesting dreams for me, by any chance?" – "If you stayed the night, we might come up with one, mightn't we?"

THURSDAY, 10ᵀᴴ JANUARY 1980

I was walking along the crest of a remarkable mountain, whose existence so near Prague surprised me. On one side, whence I had come, there stretched the familiar basin of the Vltava meander, with the National Theatre, the Museum, Hradčany and Žižkov Heights, while on the other was revealed to me a totally unfamiliar view: a drawn-out range of uninhabited mountain ridges and sun-drenched valleys with glittering streams. I was so thrilled that I immediately made my way downhill to tell someone about it, and didn't even have time to scrutinise it properly. I arrived home, which was just close by. Josef Zeman was waiting for me there. "Quick, come on, there's something you have to see!" I said, and led him back towards the mountain. I was carrying my grey winter coat over my arm. As we reached the foothills, I was bewildered to discover that things had changed, somehow, but we were going in the right direction and the mountain towered before us. Where I had previously taken a field path, there was now an asphalt footpath, ending at a cliff that we had to climb by means of a wooden ladder. If I was to hold on, I would have to wear my coat. When I stopped to put it on, Josef overtook me by two paces and started to climb the ladder ahead of me. He was wearing a nice grey overcoat, and under it a dark-blue suit and white shirt; he had come to see a play. He was bare-headed. He was therefore the first to reach the entrance of the mine shaft in the cliff – which had also not been there before. Two guides sat by the opening to the shaft, one at each side, showing visitors what to do: it was necessary to grasp a wide strap hanging from the ceiling, slide down it about a metre, kick away from the wall and swing across a deep, dark well into an opening that was a continuation of the lighted shaft, and after a few metres one would emerge onto a plain, along which the path continued without further obstacles to the top of the mountain. Even though none of this had been here before, I remembered it. When Josef reached the entrance, the two guides immediately handed him the strap, explaining to him that he had to slide down a bit, kick away and swing across to the other end of the shaft. I knew very well that I ought to go first, because I was already familiar with it, but Josef, ever the sportsman, was already hanging from the strap, at which it occurred to me whether the hook was well attached, I looked up at the hook... and everyone knows what happened next: the hook started to open. I wanted to shout out, I wanted to reach for the strap, but at that moment Josef said: "Hey, Ludvík, isn't something wrong here?" and disappeared down into the darkness, still holding the strap above his head. Then, much later, came the sound of an enormous splash.

Horror glued me to the spot and my first thought was to jump in, but the splash of water was grounds for hope, if something was done straight away. I sped back down the rock-face – though "fell" might be a better word – as the rungs of the ladder gave way under me, and then I dashed to the maintenance workshop. I did not even have to tell the whole story, the maintenance man already knew. He found a sort of hempen rope, working it in his hands without any haste, and handed it to me as if there were no danger in delay. I went out and once more hoisted myself up to the shaft, where the two guides were still squatting; I rushed up to them with the rope – they stepped aside from the hole and I saw the shaft was full of water. I left the rope there and walked slowly homewards. I just could not understand how a moment before I had been with Josef and now he was gone. There was still a slim chance that I would arrive home and find him sitting there, wearing the blue suit for the theatre, but I knew it was out of the question. Why had I brought him here, why had I ruined my life?

FRIDAY, 11TH JANUARY 1980

I am pleased. The frost is increasing and that is something that will take care of the greenfly, pear suckers and spider mites. Mojmír came here early this morning for the first time in ages. It turned out he was not offended, just ill and writing. He has written a book, a historical study of agrarian policy from 1945 to 1968. He brought me several copies. We talked for a while and then I left him sitting with Madla while I went off to write. I am writing, and have now delivered, a contribution to an anthology in honour of Václav Havel and Co.

Every day I rewrite the previous day's entry. *Some entries I don't even rewrite much. By doing so I break my resolution, though was it really a resolution?* When is something actually created? *Maybe there is no such thing as creation.* Maybe we only discover what is, what endures, in which case we must not limit this process of discovery, lest we should discover nothing, confirm nothing and the thing should remain as if it never even existed. *Maybe it never even existed.* When I said I was rewriting today's entry, *it does not mean I shall actually rewrite it. In the end most of it will remain unchanged. Everything in fact. Or almost everything. Or I am not really sure.*

I am reading Šikula's *Vilma* and that is the way he writes. Sometimes I split my sides laughing. It is village life, related by a grown man through the eyes of the little boy inside him. Inevitably the detailed description of the environment, the local characters, and his feelings must, if only for reasons of accuracy, be accompanied by reservations and doubts about the reliability of observation and memory. It gives rise to a magical chain of certainties or uncertainties, the unwinding of the magician's formula of "now you see it, now you don't," and above all it is something with an original style, at last. The man almost announces that the boy in him loved the woman Vilma, or maybe he didn't. "She has her faults! If one wanted to, it would be possible to find them and perhaps even exaggerate them. Sometimes she even seeks them herself, and occasionally finds them, though she doesn't know whether she's found the right ones. Was there any need to look for them at all?"

I got dressed and went round to see Bibisa, who was alone at home dozing in the armchair, took the tied-up packet of Pavlíček's manuscript for Vlasta, and drove to the bookbinders. An hour later, I was walking down a clean and freeze-dried Wenceslas Square with nicely guillotined booklets ("put a pile of books on top of them when you get home"). There were few people about, the easier to be captured on an old etching. They were walking along contentedly in their fur coats and jackets. But maybe they weren't walking along contentedly.

MONDAY, 14TH JANUARY 1980

Milan Šimečka did not come on Saturday, for some unknown reason. People were disappointed, such as Petr Pithart. It was a good evening. Vlasta acted even better than at the premiere. Or I appreciated it more. But this time, too, I was obliged to keep my eyes shut for the first quarter of an hour, and when I peeped at Sergej he was also frowning terribly. Pithartová wriggled nervously.

"It's raining," says Vlasta-Božena, because that is all she knows for the moment. The play is only just beginning and she dashes with an umbrella from the suitcase to the bed. This is a trifle drastic for my stodgy nerves. If I were to write a play for a solo actress, she would have to stand or sit calmly, and say her lines without any grimaces, and only when the words had started to evoke an emotional response in the onlookers would she be permitted to move her eyes and hands, and only then take a step. The thread between her and the audience would first have to be tightened imperceptibly before she could pull on it – with care. Krejča's theatre, on the other hand, thrusts us into the mood of his denouement like so much straw into a sack. Once upon a time I felt like going and kicking his Lorenzaccio off the stage, until I eventually got used to his ways.

Pavlíček's *Report on Burial in Bohemia* is a new treatment of an old patriotic melodrama about a woman writer-martyr. We all see through the trick and are pissed off, but when the lights go up we are all wiping our emotional noses. Vlasta plays solo for two hours. Her capacity to transform herself is enormous. After the performance I went to congratulate her. It is only now, from a need to reflect on it, that I have determined the cause of my initial dissatisfaction.

I pondered yesterday on how I would write a play for her with two or three female characters: in what way each of them would differ, what it would be about – and I even started to get an inkling of how badly it would turn out... if I felt like doing it and found I was capable. I told Madla what I was thinking. She was actually convinced that I would be good at it. Most important, she said she already knew which women I'd give preference to. So with relief I decided to take offence and give it no more thought.

This afternoon I said to Zdena: "I was thinking about how I might write for the theatre." She said: "You'd be good at it." I went on: "I imagine two female characters. Each of them would be different but they would both say exactly the same things. And their interplay, like when you put two halves of an empty mould together, would give rise indirectly to a third character – a despicable male." – She was silent for a moment, going on with what she was doing, and then said: "I happened to pick up that feuilleton of yours from last year, about courage, and I've only just now realised what made you write it. But I'd only offend you." I said nothing, and shortly afterwards, after she had come to terms with my anticipated umbrage, she said: "It wasn't just an expression of your political maturity and weariness with civic life, but your total collapse as a man, because you didn't do anything when they interned me in the VD clinic the previous August. And you even went off on holiday with your wife."

I made a reply, but it made no difference. Nor will it.

TUESDAY, 15TH JANUARY 1980

The waiting room was full. An old man in a black winter coat suddenly stood up. He had a hat, strong glasses, and a red face from which there issued a loud roar: "This is preposterous! Who do they think we are? They've already forgotten they're accountable to the people!" That's my kind of talk, and I hoped to hear more. Walking stiffly, the man started to pace the area in front of people's legs and went on speaking in a series of explosions: "Would this – ever happen – anywhere else – in the world? What have we – these past thirty years – though it started much earlier – accustomed ourselves to!" From one of the white doors a nurse appeared and said: "Excuse me, sir, what is it you want? And could you possibly calm down?" He turned towards her and, standing near her, gave such a shout that she took a step backwards: "How dare you ask me to calm down. How can I be calm? Calm is absolutely the last thing I can be!" he bellowed, with one hundred percent justification. "The trouble is that the lot of you," he gestured over our heads, "are now so sunk in your putrefaction that you're oblivious to everything," he correctly declared. "I had an appointment for nine thirty! And now it's ten o'clock!" roared the man, now – regrettably – veering away from the main point. The nurse said: "But it's not always possible to estimate exactly. That's unavoidable, surely…" – "Silence! I am going to report you!" the man said, and squeezing his briefcase, which was also full of goodness knows what, he left.

I knew what would happen next. Two minutes later he was back. Quietly and intelligently he went from one door to another looking for the nameplate with the name of the head dentist, Dr. Kubcová. When he found her door, he studied it for several seconds, took a step back, and then ran up to it and belted it three times with his briefcase. "Would you believe it?" he yelled rightfully, in desperation. "They send me here but they know she doesn't have any consulting hours!"

After those blows, all the nine doors to the surgeries, laboratories, and even the X-ray room opened and someone came out of each of them. And Dr. Kurka addressed the man, smiling: "Sir, you are in a health facility here. We require peace and quiet. If there's something you don't agree with, go and complain." The man went up to him, gripped him by his white lapels, and said firmly: "Show me your identification!" I got up, and two young men with me. I didn't want this critic of the state's basic principles to take it out unjustly on Dr. Kurka, of all people. I said: "Sir, I agree with you on all counts, and have done so for thirty years already" – this impressed him – "but you'll only bring down greater misfortune on yourself. There's nothing else for you but to do the same as us, sit and wait for the dentist to call you." The man uttered with bewilderment, more calmly now, almost crushed: "Dentist! What dentist, for heaven's sake? It's a woman!"

"My dear sir, I entirely sympathise with you," I said, taking him by the elbow and directing him to the nearest seat. The white coats all disappeared. The man sat down, folded his briefcase on his lap, and stared at the floor. I returned to my place at the other end of the waiting room. In the silence, the man started to say in a plaintive voice: "I expect you're all laughing at me. But you've got it wrong, because in reality you're the ones who are weeping and I'm the one who's laughing. What spiritual degradation. What a decline in taste and manners! Nothing like this went on in the past. Not at all. But it's been going on for a thousand years. And no one sees it. Nobody notices we're in the hands of mobsters. It's quite simply the underworld, what the Germans call the *Unterwelt*!" We all remained silent. "I'm going home," the man declared, utterly dispirited, "I won't accomplish anything here, but it's dreadful, dreadful, quite dreadful..." the words tailed off as he made his way out.

It was a few minutes later when two burly men in white coats arrived. "Where's the agitated gentleman?" they asked. "He went home," someone said. The men went into one of the surgeries. Someone said: "What's it coming to? You come to have your teeth done and the next thing you know you find yourself in the loony-bin." The men came out and took another look around the waiting room, but they didn't recognise me and left.

(...)

I now live in a sort of anticipation of the evil and the good. For some un-known reason I want the year to get a move on, so that something should happen at last, though I don't know what. We have snow here, so I'm glad there's a sharp frost. I don't feel like going to the garden, that's another place I fear bad tidings. On Sunday we were intending to go there, for some apples, at least, but I couldn't get the car started. Are you getting started? It's been such a long time! It's like talking across water; in other words, I hear my own words come mumbling back into my head, but it is impossi-ble to tell how far they're carrying. Jiří Lederer is home now. Our Jan took his first exams and got a decent grade in both. Most of his fellow-students failed. I went with Madla on Sunday to the Wallenstein Riding-School to see an exhibition of ancient artefacts from local collections: shards, statues, vessels, jewellery, shreds of fabric, sarcophagi, fragments of mouldings, in-scriptions... It's pathetically skimpy and touchingly unique, owing to our lack of any proper source, not even a sea. But apart from that, the exhibition as such failed to stimulate me; it's always the same thing, after all: a jug can't do without a handle, so it always ends up looking like the one my sister-in-law brought us from Georgia – and that one comes from a modern state work-shop. Aphrodite rising from the foam – an authentic Roman replica of the original, that is – is a fairly corpulent woman: her lap has a charming little ripple of marble flesh. They shouldn't have done it to her! – All the while a tamed minus-twelve frost breathed in through the high windows from the Vojanov Gardens. I was thoroughly cold in that hall, with the instruments down near the floor ticking away and scratching their records. One no longer enters the exhibition space from the lane, but from the handsome space by the metro entrance, with its hedges of heather – now all covered in snow, of course. The metro pumps air back and forth along the tunnels, now hot, now cold. The trains are full of people and each journey takes only a couple of minutes and you can't get anywhere. People are totally uninteresting, apart from the ones who are exceptionally ugly. I never see an attractive woman. Mind you, though, at that exhibition there was a strikingishly graceful figure moving among the glass cabinets – we had winter coats, she had left hers in the cloakroom – a pleated grey skirt, and over it, coming down to her hips, a round-necked jumper with horizontal blue-grey stripes, the sleeves rolled up. Her long hair was combed back and clasped together at the nape of her neck in such a way that it formed a perfect jug handle. It was almost comical the way she moved here and there like an echo of the exhibits. But how is it possible that even someone like that fails to realise that she ought not wear the bottom of her jumper so low on her hips? It gave her a long trunk and short legs. What's the point of all these exhibitions if even after thousands of years... Ah, that just reminds me. You know how those Greek jugs always have drawings on them and the men are shown with tiny tools; well all of a sudden I espy a decent-sized prick at last. Naturally, I immediately start to scan the accompanying notes and there I see: *148. Goblin.* – Any idea why? Just recently I got a toothache again, and I had to get it drilled and filled, and so it goes on. Before long, it'll be obvious that one is beyond repair and then one would be justifiably inclined – albeit without gestures or pathological symptoms, just freely and level-headedly – to make use of the remedy that you once had in your possession but relinquished. I've just read quite a good book – *Vilma* by Šikula (a Slovak), and by "quite" I mean that it would be a very good book had the author not descended into the usual sort of drivel in the end. So much of the book was precise, witty and evocative. A sense of proportion! That's something that worries me, too, as you are aware. I'm now reading reminiscences of Hemingway by some fellow called Hotchner, and whereas it is interesting because of the Hemingway, it gets on my nerves because of the Hotchner. He's a youngster who happened to find himself in close proximity to Hem., who took some kind of fancy to him and dragged him round all over the place, and the young man seems to have dragged round a tape-recorder, and that's where it started. When I read about all that grandiose loafing about in bars, on the ocean, around Africa, and all that money for work with distant deadlines – and which, following a kiss from a certain being, is suddenly completed – that charming claptrap about animals, women, etc. and in the space of a single word the action shifts from New York to Paris or Venice, I discover I have a petty little envious soul which I mock and spit at inwardly. JesusJesusJesusJesus...

The day before yesterday I entered a maze–like house up some green steps, but no one was home and I just put that bottle of French wine on the cupboard opposite the door and went away. Then I took the stone steps up to the Castle, where the ramp was quiet and freezingly draughty and I was numbly indifferent. Our Philip has started his spring song and Catherine will start laying her eggs all over the place. Then all the rest – snowdrops, winter aconite, daphne, erica, and the third degree of torture: anemones, daffodils and cherry blossom.

THURSDAY, 17ᵀᴴ JANUARY 1980

They summoned me to the Ministry of Finance to show them documents about my foreign earnings. As I left the house I opened the mailbox and found a letter from Karel Kosík: "Dear Ludvík, I found your manuscript so evocative that I have decided to adopt its main slogan: You can all get lost! – Karel."

So from the ministry I made my way to Karel's. Since I had phoned beforehand to announce my arrival, he opened up, otherwise goodness knows. Three times last week I stood outside his door in vain. There was somewhere we were supposed to go together; I had made a preliminary arrangement and suddenly he was unavailable. I left him a note in his mailbox that was a trifle sharp, which probably explains the answer: "I found your manuscript so evocative..." There are only three entries where he appears in the Vienna-bound "cross-section" that I sent him: 2ⁿᵈ June, 13ᵗʰ October and 18ᵗʰ November. I cannot think what could have offended him.

I said: "Are you angry with me?" – He answered: "No, I'm not, but I've decided to isolate myself totally from everything that turns me into a cog in anything." – "Does that mean," I said, "that you won't even be holding any Mozart sessions?" – "Probably not." – "You won't go to concerts?" – "I don't know." – "Does it mean you won't be reading my manuscript in its entirety?" – "I think it's unlikely." – "But to a great extent I wrote it for you. It's also a book about tolerance, written under your influence. You've only read a tenth of it." Karel shrugged. "Does this mean," I said, "that you won't be giving me your book to read?" – He replied: "Probably not, Ludvík. When it comes out it'll be available for everyone." – I said: "When it comes out... we might be dead by then." He shrugged. I said: "Are you writing it for some actually functioning life, or for the truth that moves upon the face of the waters?" – "We shall see," he said and shrugged again. – I still wanted to ask how it would affect Marie, but it was not the right moment. "And how about Marie," I asked. – He replied: "Ludvík, haven't you enough troubles of your own?" – "Certainly. And whom will I be able to talk to about them, if things go on this way? I was able to talk to you." He smiled. He had said everything with his wide close-lipped smile. I could not think of any other question of interest. All I could do was get up, give him a hug and go. Which I did.

I walked across Hradčany Square to a telephone box to call Lederer. But his phone just goes too-too-too-too. The square is covered in snow smoothed by people and cars. I lost my footing and fell over, and my trouser legs ripped open from the crotch to below the knee. I walked down Nerudova Street feeling sorrow-free, joy-free, fear-free, depression-free – free, in a word. I said to myself: One could call it a winter harvest. I am starting to reap.

FRIDAY, 18TH JANUARY 1980

I rang Professor Machovec's doorbell. "You've come at just the right time. Do you want to see something?" he said and opened the living room door slightly. I caught sight of an enormous pile of books shaped like a low cone about a metre high: a bookcase covering an entire wall had fallen over. "What are you doing with it?" I asked. "What do you think, I'm putting them all back," he said in a conciliatory tone. If something like that happened to me, I would toss them back on the bookshelf with a pitchfork and the ones that failed to stay put would get chucked out of the window. I'm no philosopher.

He sat me down in a smaller room – his study. We talked for about an hour and a half and drank schnapps from tiny goblets with tall stems. I didn't even need to explain the reason for my call, he broached it himself: "If you hadn't come, I shouldn't think we'd have ever met each other again, because I'd have never sought you out, although during Advent, every day at around seven in the morning, I was going into the self-service diner round the corner from you for a bowl of soup. You've come about Ella, of course." We clinked glasses. I said: "Are you really so angry?" – "Of course. The thing is I've thought again about that single sentence of yours – and it was a profound one, Maestro – that it was a mere formality to accommodate her, whereas to refuse her would have been a deed. You were duty bound to do that deed!" – "But why," I asked, "why do you ask me to have stood in judgement over her life? That was a role I refused when everyone else chose to judge her!" – "So you became an assistant to a police wedding. Twenty cops and you – it must be unique and it ought to be documented." – "What twenty cops...?" – "That's what Ella herself told me, that there was nothing but cops and it was even a

511

cop who performed the ceremony." – "That's nonsense! If she told you that, it was self-pitying self-deprecation. She was married by the local official and there was absolutely no one else there apart from the four of us. Did she send you a New Year's card?" He pointed behind him at a desk covered in papers: "You mean that insolence, that vulgarity, that tastelessness? A decent person either does not write at all or sends each of his friends a separate handwritten greeting! She wrote to me twice. I didn't reply, nor will I. As far as I'm concerned it's all over – the greatest disappointment of my life, the death of a woman philosopher. Her brain and talent were those of a De Beauvoir, but her vagina, unfortunately, was... for which I had an understanding, of course, and did not begrudge her anything, but not like you, handing her over to a fellow who'll destroy everything – but everything – there is within her."

I said: "How do you interpret the picture? Are they going to have a child?" – "Ella? A child? You're not serious. But I forget, you'd like her to have one, because you're a peasant. Woman – child – procreation, procreation! You exploit nature and lord it over the woman. She nurses the children and you conquer the universe and destroy the planet. Don't you realise, Maestro, that you're just a male waving a stick on the edge of a biotope..." – "Stop calling me maestro!" I said crossly, but he went on: "How long do you think this male civilisation is going to last? Another fifty years and it'll be finished! The only ones capable of changing the fate of humanity at the last minute – and that's right now! – are gifted women with a larger dose of humanity. Women like Ella, something you didn't realise! The StB noticed it, though, which is why they conspired with that worthless fellow who – with your, *your*, assistance carried her off abroad. Trinkewitz hit the nail on the head when he called it the Rape of our little Sabine. Sabine – Sabina, get it? She was no Karel Sabina, naturally, but they must have had something on her and she didn't have the strength to deny it, so she thought it better to leave." – "But she'll be back, won't she?" I said. – "Maybe she thinks she'll come back. But she'll never return. Never." – "Were she to return, how would you speak to her?" – He replied: "How would I speak to her? How would I speak to her? It would depend on how she came... Whatever do you mean, for heaven's sake?" – I said nothing, and then plucked up the courage to ask: "May I write, Professor, that you love her?" He stared at me, breathing agitatedly, before saying resignedly: "The whole of Prague knows I do, you wouldn't be saying anything new... but... for heaven's sake, you do write about other things, don't you?"

We left his house together. On the stairs he declared sorrowfully: "She could have become a human being. She remained a woman."

SUNDAY, 20TH JANUARY 1980

I have done nothing for the past two days except read and rewrite the last entry over and over again. Rewriting and shortening, until now it is down to a half and I am incredibly fed up: I wanted to achieve directness with frugality of expression, and I am not sure. I did not put a foot outside the door for two whole days and now it is Sunday evening and I am fed up. And I have no one to blame but myself, and I have no idea how to step back. I stretch out on the floor and have a yen for something, or to smash something to pieces.

A film about Kuks Castle and Count Špork ended on the television a few moments ago. The camera traced the church paintings, angel faces, and the statues, and the commentary said: "The count wanted the children to enjoy going to church, and the joys of paradise after death were intended to make them forget the misery in which they lived." – Ondřej said: "They have to decry him or they wouldn't be allowed to mention him. Yet without him they wouldn't have anything to show." – "That's right. He ought to have established a cholera pit instead," I said. This was immediately followed by Part 758 of the serial *Virtue in Uniform*. It's all about how truth, honour, courage and pride are the monopoly of the police and the state, where in the end they are more profitable. It has been running for at least ten years already.

I got hold of a copy of the *Frankfurter Rundschau* in which Milan Kundera answers questions from some German about Czech culture. "In the nineteenth century," the German mocks, "the Czechs resisted German influence and turned towards their Slav neighbours. So you are simply where you wanted to be." – Kundera replies that the Czech nation asserted its identity in those days just like the Austrians or Hungarians. That does not mean they renounced their adherence to Central Europe. The latter was destroyed, however, after 1945 as the first step in the destruction of that great multinational cultural tradition without which Europe is inconceivable. Kundera refuses to be counted as an East European writer. He says: "I belong to the last generation of a dying Central European culture." – Well then, the German continues to taunt, if the Czech national identity is now mortally threatened, shouldn't Czech art start engaging in political struggle? Kundera replies that culture defends a nation not through some struggle or other, but by creating irreplaceable values. – "What constitutes these irreplaceable values of Czech culture?" the German asks pointedly. In reply, Kundera uses the ploy of the likeable grammar-school pupil who is not so familiar with this particular detail of the topic, and goes back to the Gothic and the Reformation, and then how Bohemia was brutally Germanized, and then how, in the nineteenth century when the revivalists tried to resuscitate a virtually forgotten tongue, they became aware of the question: Is it worth it? It was a gamble (in the Pascalian sense) and there are bound to be many who will say it wasn't worth it, because its consequences paved the way for Hitler and Stalin. In Kundera's view, the Czech nation has yet to give a final answer; however, the wager still stands! Only it now encompasses every nation in a world that is becoming ever more centralised, collectivised and uniform, so that "sooner or later, both France and Germany will find themselves counted among the small, superfluous nations."

I like that very much.

But I was disheartened by Kundera's parting shot, because it tallies so closely with my worst nights, when I don't have a single dream: "The tragedy of a Czech nation swallowed up by Russian civilisation will soon turn out to have been just one episode in a sea of far more bloody and more dangerous tragedies. In that respect the Czechs' fate mirrors the fate of humanity as a whole, in which the greatest injustice is not violence but oblivion."

Our Jan has come back from Bezejovice redolent of horses and satisfaction. On Friday, he passed another exam with top marks. Madla has spent the entire two days reading, typing out excerpts, taking naps, listening to music, and writing letters. The nation's fate, it seems, is something that only I here and Kundera there worry our heads about.

I sense with my whole skin that world events are bad; I don't even have to know what they are. My current bad state is beginning to make me suspect that I might be wrong and that the cause is elsewhere. And I say to myself: Is it possible that that one thing should continue to play such havoc with me? I am such a fool – how can I make these my closing sentences, with me half out of my wits? That is no way to finish my Book, is it?

Outside there is a blizzard. The illusive grey light lies evenly both outside and here indoors, so in a way it is snowing right onto my desk and I enjoy being in my room and nothing tempts me out. When a person whose headache has just started to ease remains perfectly still, the pain shifts and disappears. The same applies to me in my entirety, not just my head: when I stop wanting anything, keep away from all memories, am oblivious to all the threats surrounding me, am not the slightest bit jealous of anything; when, carefully, even in my mind I stop resisting wrongs and renounce my legitimate rights; when I recall how nothing matters any more to my dead parents – and indeed nothing does matter! – then I start to be happy. Just keep perfectly still!

I look at the Vlastimil Beneš paintings, and have everything here I need. If only I could play my thoughts on the piano. I dream confused dreams and I immediately forget them. Last night it was something about our Jan and Karol. Jan was still a little boy and Karol Sidon was paying us a visit, and I was so pleased about it in the dream that now I cannot understand why. Jan has gone off to another exam today, not worried at all, and he was already on the phone arranging to go and do something straight afterwards: he takes it entirely for granted that he will be in good shape afterwards. And that dream reminds me I have to go and see Karol: it will soon be Candlemas. A card arrived from Šimečka on a skiing trip in the Tatras; that is why he didn't come.

No feeding the birds, no washing up, watering the plants, wiping the doorstep. I have no work to do. I do not even go shopping, or roast chickens. And when I consider the further curbs and restrictions (and emigrations), I have no idea what my Book would be about if I were starting it now!

I have just been in the kitchen for a drink. Madla is in there kneeling on the couch, resting on her elbows, reading. When I came in she just raised her head and grinned like a Cheshire Cat. She has got it all done in advance: her chores, her housework and her cooking. I had a peep at what she has been typing out from her reading. "For goodness sake, what do you copy out the whole paragraph for when you've got the book at home!" It's Vavřinec's *Hussite Chronicle*. And she's copying out the course of events of 1419! "I know it's silly," she replied, "but by spending time over the description I become involved in the events, and anyway I'm retired, aren't I?"

When a person whose headache has just started to ease remains perfectly still,
the pain shifts and disappears. (p. 515)

She wants me, too, to try and imagine what would have happened if King Wenceslas IV had ignored the advisors who were recommending that he make peace with the Taborites, after they had defenestrated the town councillors, and punished them instead. And what if he had actually managed to wipe them out! – A lovely thought. It didn't happen though, and those vandals are still with us, only they are a bit lazier and podgier by now. They are the ones who put on the never-ending serial *Virtue in Uniform*.

WEDNESDAY, 23ᴿᴰ JANUARY 1980

"Any idea why you're here?" Major Fišer asked and brandished *Svědectví* No.59 – "The Prague Issue." "Haven't a clue," I answered properly.

It is known as "The Prague Issue" because its introduction says it was edited in Prague. The articles carry on a debate, direct and indirect, with the emigré community, and whoever put it together is a pretty good fellow. But it looks as if he had neither the time nor the peace of mind for it – that is if one can believe it really was someone from here. I find it unlikely that I should have failed even to overhear something about it. Or have I really become so isolated? They included an old piece of mine in which I reply to a question about whether I would stay or leave.

Major Fišer wanted to know how and why I had sent my contribution, whether I had received a fee for it, and whether I was aware that I was contributing to a journal engaged in hostile propaganda against our state. I replied that I had the right to write for any journal whatsoever in the world and bore no responsibility for what anyone thought about it, only for what I actually wrote. Unless he could tell me what was objectionable in my contribution, there was nothing for us to discuss. To that Major Fišer made no reply, merely warning me in the vaguest terms that I might make things difficult for my student son. I told him that was already ample grounds for a complaint, but for the sake of goodwill I would not take it further.

On my way home I realised that I have referred from time to time in this book to assignment "D," which looks rather ill-considered in this context. With the assent of friends A., D., and G(ruša), since I can no longer jeopardise assignment "D(ictionary)" and most of all because there is nothing illegal about it, I hasten to explain that it concerns *The Dictionary of Czech Writers*

1978, which will soon be published, we hope. Unless, that is, friend B. causes any further confusion.

On this occasion Major Fišer was brief, calm and to the point. He was wearing a new chocolate-brown suit cut from high-quality cloth, a brown-patterned tie and nice brown shoes. I got the impression he was smoking less. As he saw me to the door I said that if he managed to stay the course and would still be inviting me for these chats every month, I was intending, like him, to keep a "record of statement," and supply him with a copy and include any comments or objections in the subsequent "record" and... "And in three years' time you could turn it into a book, eh?" he declared perceptively. – "That's right," I agreed. "And there'd be quite a demand for it. And I'd name you as co-author, naturally." We laughed.

"I need your advice on something," I said. Zdena adopted an alert pose with two grey-green eyes and one cigarette, and I said: "I have the chance of engaging a geisha. What do you think?" – She replied effortlessly: "Is she Japanese? Because if she isn't she is a category lower from the outset." – "Well, she's not exactly Japanese..." I said shamefacedly. – "And have you spoken to her or her manager? If she doesn't have a manager, she's an additional category lower." – "My first contact was with her, but if I am interested I am supposed to speak to her manager, she says," I lied. – She gave it some thought, had a smoke, and then said: "What can she do? Can she do anything we can't? She must know how to sing, dance, discuss with you at a high level about literature, music and other things. Can she?" – "I don't know yet," I said. – "How does she look?" she asked. But that was something I was not telling. "A geisha, eh? Well, of course that's something I'd recommend! Except that to be a geisha for you," she said through half-closed eyes, "would be damned hard! Send her to see me first of all and I'll give her a couple of tips. Such as when she ought to sing and when she is to leave the singing up to you. And something about black holes and the Milky Way!"

FRIDAY, 25ᵀᴴ JANUARY 1980

I typed the date and realised what day it was. I look out the window into the street, where the sun is shining on the snow. The snow is thawing and water is dripping past the window. The sky above the roofs is blue, only lightly overlaid with disintegrating clouds. What intense radiance, all of a sudden!

And at that a brutal urge almost lifts me from the earth and drags me straight out, somewhere, where? I'm already there, in my mind, futilely, and I pull myself together standing by the window with my hands behind me.

A five-month-old foetus would already swell the belly. A five-month-old child, as I vaguely remember, already purses its little lips and lets out long velvety coos: Coooh! goooh…! Then it coils up convulsively, kicks its arms and legs and shrieks with joy.

The five-month-old manuscript of a good author numbers one hundred and fifty finished pages. In that amount of time I've written two hundred and forty, and now I'm tinkering and messing around with them; it is getting on my nerves, I hate it and just want to run away.

It turns out, for instance, that one character who is so prominent at a moment when she is virtually disappearing from the plot was not conceived with the prescience we would expect of the author. She ought to have been introduced by means of an unprovable and discreet hint, or – better still – an emphasised (suspicious) inconspicuousness, which would, however, correspond to her role in the second third of the book. As it is, the reader will gape uncomprehendingly at how such a drastic complication could have arisen: either the author lied to us and concealed it before, or he has just dreamed it up. The author did not lie, however; nor did he conceal it. He merely failed to realise immediately – when he was living it – what effect it would have on his, er, writing activity. The book, as it nears its conclusion, draws his attention to the fact and demands the undeniable truth, which the author – naturally enough – could otherwise have concealed, had he been content merely to live it and not had the intention to write about it as well! For as we know, a deed can be kept secret, but the offspring of the deed will shout to us in the street.

Attention has been aroused and the author can no longer keep the cat in the bag: the entry of 30th January 1979 (the one you happily read without any sense of discontinuity so long ago now) was written today, 25th January 1980!

Who would have the heart to reproach the author for artistic license, when you surely must see how much genuine sorrow it ushers in?

519

SATURDAY, 26TH JANUARY 1980

Today I pruned the trees; it is two degrees above zero; the snow has an icy crust in which tracks of cats and squirrels have hardened, along with the heavy prints of dopey dog Don. And the characteristic sets of two round and two long prints betrayed a visit from the Hare, who again neatly nibbled the lower branches of the cordon. I made a tour of the fence and discovered two loosened stakes: they had been pulled away from the Hare's side of the fence!

I walked round the garden like a stranger. It is small. Arizona also used to seem small to me each winter. So I walked around inspecting the trees and noting with disappointment that I would have to mow under them again in the summer, as well as count the bees, water the roses, chase the butterflies, listen to the thrush in the late afternoon, drink coffee at the white table, read in the shade, pick currants, then apples... and what for? I thought that when it had been written, as it now has, it would be over and done with and we would move onwards, where to? Yes, I have succumbed to a curious effect. Previously, whenever I wrote, described or related something, I would part with it forever. Now it feels like returning from a funeral in which I took a full and proper part and with a sense of well-performed mourning – only to find the deceased waiting for me at home! Oh, God, life really does continue like this? Until final unconsciousness! But where is the grass of yesteryear? Yesteryear!

I left the hare a couple of prunings by the cordon and took the rest to the chopping block. I picked up the chopper and at that moment out of a bush leapt... Škvorecký. I started to offer him my Book and, with each of his objections, I was getting angrier and angrier: What do you mean it is not a novel! It's long – so what? No, I'm not going to cut it. Take it as it is or leave it. A dithering start and no obvious genre? – But that's deliberate (That is always a good excuse: that it was deliberate, or there was a precedent.) Until I realised with relief that he is not the one I ought to deal with; it is not he who is the publisher, but Mrs. Santner. No problem there, with such a long lovely piece of gossip as this...! Until I realised that the whole time, as an undertone to my thoughts, my words to myself, and my sentimental axe strokes, could be heard: Niagara so sadly roars... The song, as if it were only waiting for me to push aside the floodgates for it, at once burst into my gardens with a roar, and overwhelmed me with its melancholy foam, bawling in true fashion: alas that bea-u-tiful vision I cannot embrace!

I took the first section of the retyped and edited Book – about a quarter of it – to the typist. Once I had the opening sections behind me, I noticed that the manuscript started to improve and arrange itself. It was as if the author had gradually found a style in which to write about himself, to all appearances sincerely, but without doing himself any harm. In some of the chapters we encounter those well-known Vaculíkian leaps from the willow-tree to the parsnip, with some masterly vaulting from the opening sentence to the punch-line; we recognize the author of outstanding feuilletons, and already we have an inkling – may he, too, realise it in time – that this could at last be a work about our present day as a whole.

Such a positive assessment is not as yet shared by Pavel Kohout in Vienna. He wrote to me that he did not think he could stage what I had sent him so far in the Burgtheater. For one thing it was too long for a single evening, and for another, the montage in question, while admittedly it gives some idea of one of the strands of my book, fails to do so for the book as a whole – which in this case is a more serious error than it might appear to me: such evening entertainments being also conceived as publicity for a book. But not only is this one not yet in the bookshops, it is not even at the publishers! Thirdly, I seemingly fail to appreciate that because of my years of literary sloth I have faded as a writer from the consciousness of the enlightened public there, being known solely as a fomenter of political scandals (I am translating freely from Czech into Czech), which is why he would consider the first task to assemble a selection of my earlier pieces and put me back where I belong. Fourthly –

Fourthly, he is in a quandary over the way I write about friends, which is uncustomary – it does not worry him personally, of course, because he knows me, but someone listening to this part and unaware of what else I no doubt say about those people might get a false idea of them, as well as about the way I treat my friends. Fifthly –

Fifthly: "I can well imagine that the party and government would like to see me in my states of greater dejection – but that YOU should? What business of yours, or of any of you, are they, my dejected states. Thank your lucky bloody stars that there's someone, at least, who doesn't feel obliged to air his fear and his defeats in polite company. For heaven's sake, I've known Cyrano de Bergerac by heart since I was nine. If you want to confide your mistress problems to your wives and tell your friends how much your haemorrhoids hurt, good luck to you, but don't expect me to follow suit! I can't wait to hear – because I don't intend to censor you, naturally – some famous actor here declaiming those golden words of yours: 'The way I see it, I said, it would do Pavel good to collapse inwards. There were hopeful signs that things were moving in that direction while he was here. That hope is now gone, and there is nothing over there that will induce it.' – Oh dear, my good old friend, is that what you really think? Do you realise how much inward collapse I've already gone through or what sort of stakes were driven carelessly into my soul from the mid-fifties to the end of the sixties? After all, I'm the only one, out of all of you, whose membership of the Communist Party was always being harped on, and still is. Over here, for the first year, they were quite unhappy that it wasn't appropriate to mention it. Now that those restraints have gone, do you have any idea how I'm treated here, particularly by my fellow-countrymen? Tell me what further opportunities for total collapse were left for me in Prague, if they hadn't been enough to bring about my collapse in the previous ten years? Anyway it's almost foolish what you say. In Prague we're no more than national martyrs and it would take some skill to undo that fact; whereas here – here! – everything's at stake: my honour, my art and maybe my life, even… That's a bigger misfortune than you think, Ludovico, and what I actually miss about Prague – of all the absurd things! – is comfort. But if you don't mind, even now I don't intend to show anyone either tears or tantrums. The most I'll show you – you, Karel, and Mr. Pecka – if you continue to treat me this way, is my backside. – Love, Pavel."

TUESDAY, 29TH JANUARY 1980

This is the end – all I need is some handy dream. Looking back through my notes and the discarded documents I wanted to incorporate somehow in this manuscript, I come across a forgotten pre-Christmas letter from Ivan Kadlečík:

"You haven't written anything, but I received probably all the books and send you one as a Christmas gift (Šikula: *Vilma* – L.V.) Another one out recently is Laco Ťažký's *The Gospel According to Sergeant Matthew* – pretty good; better, I suspect, than what he's written before; he's grown up a bit. I haven't published anything, probably for the good reason that I haven't written anything; I don't have the time. At the moment I'm smoking sausages; the rosehip wine is almost fermented, and there's been a snowfall. What are you up to? Drop me a line, for solitude is like good wine, but one shouldn't drink three litres at once. I wish you and your family a peaceful holiday and New Year too, however it turns out; I hope I'll be reading your new book in it."

And come to think of it, when my Book is finished and I shall be obliged, willingly, to make myself scarce, Pukanec in Central Slovakia is also a possibility.

This evening we were at a concert. It was the Kreuzburg Quartet playing Schubert, Bartók and Schumann. The first violin was Friedegund Riehm; she had straight shoulder-length hair and she sat down any old way, in a black dress with a faint, vaguely purple pattern. The gown spread out in several folds on the floor, which was all the more charming in that she sat side-saddle on her chair. I was particularly taken by a mistake that she made several times, and one I had never previously encountered at the Rudolfinum: I mastered it perfectly when I was working from Book Three of *Malát's Violin Method* and have never managed to unlearn it since. If the right and left hands are not perfectly synchronised, each time you move the bow, you catch a bit of the previous note, and when it happens in a cascade of semi-quavers you end up with a cascade of slurred notes, which, once it starts, has to continue to the very end and all you can do is be more careful next time. It was the reason, in fact, why I gave up any hopes of playing at the Rudolfinum. Surely not, Friedegund? I said to myself, and felt satisfied. She is thirty-seven. At home, later, I was unable to find any Kreuzberg on the map. Karel Kosík did not come to the concert.

WEDNESDAY, 30ᵀᴴ JANUARY 1980

Nothing yet. I go to bed late, feeling like a conscientious workman. I have no idea what goes on in my dreams at night.

I dropped over to Ivan's and to Jiří's to remind them about Candlemas. Ivan scratched behind his ear. I looked in at the Slávia and saw Jan Vladislav for the first time in ages. He told me they were constantly dragging him in for interrogations these days, after seeming to be oblivious to him for years. It is a refined process: his children are in Canada, his wife is visiting them at the moment. In other words, he looks all set, ready to fall, so they start chopping. "It looks as if they want to chase me out as well," he said dejectedly, which is a mistake, because they might hear it!

From the Slávia I went somewhere and then somewhere else, which I am now deleting on 10th April 1980 to make room for some fresh and far more interesting news that Madla has just brought from Dr. Kurka. In the park above the Letná Tunnel, two scoundrels mugged a young American woman. She returned to her hotel black and blue and with her clothes all torn, and it did not occur to any of the staff to send her to the doctor and the police. It was not until the following morning that the interpreter who had come to pick her up found her all swollen and took her to the police station and the polyclinic. There they discovered that two of her teeth had been knocked out, which she had not even realised, being unable to open her mouth. She ended up in Dr. Kurka's chair and just as he was wondering what to do with her, two policemen arrived, having found the two teeth at the site of the assault. Dr. Kurka cleaned them up, inspected them, and having ascertained that they were unharmed and healthy, suggested to the girl that he might be able to replace them in her jawbone if she was able to endure it without anaesthetic. Such cases are described in the specialist literature and he also had an opportunity to try it six years earlier on some man, and the tooth was still in place. The American woman agreed and subsequently left his surgery tortured but whole. The following day she was due to fly to Rome. Dr. Kurka asked her to seek out a dentist as soon as she arrived and afterwards to write to let him know how she got on. "You're lucky," he said, "that it happened to you here and not in Rome. There it would probably cost you a pretty penny, here you had it done free."

Sometime in mid-February – to continue interrupting the chronological order – I was once again a guest of the Klímas. The Kliments and Grušas were there too. On that occasion I got drunk, surprisingly. We all sang; in addition, I sang some folk songs and other things, and we were completely knocked out by Havlíček's parody of the Czech national anthem. I got really drunk; afterwards I could not recall anything I had said. I only know that they wheedled out of me some advance information about my Book, and that I told them nothing, except that they would soon read something about themselves. At that, Jirka started to slump into his armchair, because he knows full well what. Ivan expressed relief that, luckily, we had seen little of each other during the year of my Book-keeping, and Saša learnt from me that his absence is a constant throughout the manuscript. I told Jiřina that I spoke approvingly of her, on several occasions, with the words: "Jiřina spoke to me normally," and she laughed. Then the Kliments drove me home. Saša took excellent care of me, even letting me vomit somewhere. In front of our building he borrowed my keys, opened up and led me up to our floor, opened the door again and delivered me to Madla and the boys with the best references and recommendations. At the time I decided that this event – in which I finally come off worse than Saša – had to be inserted organically into my manuscript, and now it is.

The next day, Helena Klímová sent me a letter: "Dear Ludvík, last night I composed a letter to you. I can't recall ever enjoying an evening as much as yesterday's… I think Saša was right in saying that you were pleased with your book and I'm beginning to get an inkling, an idea what it's probably going to be like. I'm coming to see it more and more as a kind of complement to *The Axe*… When you'd all gone we kept talking for a while at home and said how terrible you are, the way you torment women and yourself… The way you grieved over Saša's absence, the fact that Pavel is gone and you saw so little of Ivan, what with young Jiří having a girlish side to him, it suddenly struck me with great sorrow that in fact you have an enormous capacity for friendship… And that those two tendencies in you are mutually antagonistic. Therein lies your uniqueness, your strength, and your danger, in my view… I don't like people getting drunk, but I've just now realised that I understand for the first time why people drink, that it can achieve (though not necessarily) an uncanny transformation… During the evening I had an almost cathartic feeling, a sense of closeness with others… Ivan was angry with me for objecting when he tried to stop you drinking. He said you'd drunk a lethal dose and you'd suffer alcohol poisoning at the very least…"

But the next day I felt absolutely fine after Ivan's whisky. I do not understand how it was, either way.

On Saturday 1ˢᵗ March, Major Fišer wanted to talk to me urgently. After the preliminary mandatory mystification about something entirely different, he came to the point: "Mr. Vaculík, you keep complaining about not being allowed to travel. Apply for a passport. Go and do a bit of foreign travel. It'll do you good. I am authorised to guarantee you that you'll return safe and sound. It needn't be for long, about a fortnight – to Vienna, say."

It was an odd moment – I had been expecting it. We stood looking at each other, smiling, with total mutual understanding.

It's a very beautiful dream, but by now I am too much of an expert on dreams!

THURSDAY, 31ST JANUARY 1980

Sometime this spring the number of Padlock titles will reach two hundred. It crossed my mind to take the jubilee number for myself, seeing as I already had the first. But then I had a better idea: I called in on Karel Šiktanc, who has published three books in Padlock but has been unwilling to let me have the fourth, *Dance of Death*, for the past two years, and I made him a fabulous offer: I would award him the jubilee title No. 200! He asked for time to think it over and then refused. It is seven years now since Ivan and I asked Zdena – who had just been fired from her job – to type out our manuscripts. We paid her for the work, and since something like that is very costly for an author, we let interested parties have the surplus copies in return for a contribution to defray the costs. It was a spontaneous idea, not planned at all. Other friends picked it up from us. It did not receive its name until a year later, when, shortly before Christmas, I was in a tram, looking at a poster advertising some publishing house: "Key Books," it said, "open the treasury of Czech literature." "Bullshit!" I thought to myself.

I sat at home this morning on my own, thinking about my Book and what it lacks, what I have forgotten to put in and how I shall deck it out for the public. I would like to include photos of the main characters, but there is a snag: I would be definitively identifying each of them with what I write about them. Unless, for instance, I wrote under the picture of Jiří Gruša: Any resemblance between this photo and Jiří Gruša is entirely coincidental. I am simply no longer capable of assessing whether the way I write about people is acceptable. I sometimes wake up in the middle of the night and as I stare into the darkness in my eyes, I find myself staring into the question of whether the way I write about myself might also be damaging.

I have decided to have the manuscript read by a number of people whom I trust to be capable of judging both the literary and factual aspects, from the point of view of both the present moment and the more distant future, and I will be guided by their suggestions.

When our boys see me constantly straightening typed sheets, taking them away and bringing them back, they smile and make silly faces. "I expect you're looking forward to reading something nice and instructive very soon," I said. "Forget it! It's not for children." – "No, no, no," they replied, "we want to read it when we're grown up!" As for Madla, she declared ages ago that she had no desire to read it. "You ought to have second thoughts," she told me in the garden. "You're about to lift your siege of those people. I'm not even particularly worried about myself anymore."

This evening, our Jan said at table: "Apparently they've already arrested ten people from the management of the housing cooperative. The story goes that they made four million from bribes and fraud." I asked: "What does it mean as far as you two are concerned?" Ondřej said: "I wouldn't be surprised if the investigation concludes that a co-op so rotten must be disbanded, and then all the flats would be forfeited to the state." Madla said: "But you should have had them approved by now!" – "Exactly," said Ondřej. "It looks to everyone as if instead of trying to complete the construction as fast as possible, they're deliberately holding it up." I said: "Elect some new officers straight away. Don't wait for someone to make a stupid decision; put forward your own proposals for solving it." Jan said: "Yes, that idea's already been put forward at the building site, but others said it would be better if we didn't make too much fuss, otherwise it might start looking like Sixty-Eight all over again." Madla said: "But they can't go taking away finished flats from you, after you built them yourselves!" – "They can," I said. – "Mind you," she admitted, "since 1945 it's been nothing but a story of confiscations. They've already taken something from everyone, even the things they gave. Now there's no one left to take anything from, except for the co-operative farms and these building co-ops."

At mid-day the doorbell rang: it was Josef. He was wearing a grey raincoat over a dark suit with a white shirt and a tie. I recalled a mine shaft full of water and asked: "Are you going to the theatre?" – "No way! A horse ripped the sleeve off my everyday clothes." – "Really! How did it happen?" – "Just like that. I was doing something next to his stall and because I wasn't taking any notice of him or talking to him, he wanted to attract my attention. But the sensitivity of the animal! He didn't bite me, just ripped my sleeve off."

We walked down Celetná Street to the Old Town Square, popped in at Rotts' hardware store, where Josef asked about some electrodes for welding cast iron, from there along Melantrich Street to the surplus store where he wanted to buy something fantastic, really cheap, no matter what, and to the Two Cats for goulash, then through the ravine of Perlová Street to Jungmann Square, where we visited an exhibition of grandiosely banal photos about work, past the violin shop where we looked at the violins and trombones in the window, through the Shoe Store arcade onto Wenceslas Square, then turning right past the confectioners' and the shop with gentlemen's clothes for us, and into the Alfa Arcade where the Semafor Theatre and the Světozor Cinema are. There we just took a look at the programmes, then walked through the subway to the corner where the Academy of Sciences bookshop is and where I asked about the latest astronomy year-book, but it is not out yet, so a quarter of the ephemerides can get lost. We checked out the programme of the Lucerna and Hvězda cinemas, looked at the Slovak books in the window at Slovak Books, and from there across the tram tracks to the agricultural publishers, where we did not need anything either, then along Opletalova Street to the corner of Růžová, where, at the metallurgical suppliers, Josef asked whether they had electrodes for welding cast iron, and we ended up at the Jindříšská Tower, where there is a shop that sells expired photographic paper, which on principle we never buy, then through the arcade by the Slavonic House, out onto Příkopy, where we did a left turn and reached the Savarín Café, at which I treated Josef to a coffee.

We sat by a window, outside which people were walking past but could not see us through the net curtains, and Josef said: "Yesterday evening, as usual, I went to shut the chickens in. But they were nowhere to be found, the little devils! I rushed here, there, and everywhere trying to find the wretched creatures, but not a sign of them. Would you believe it, I'd forgotten to let them out yesterday morning! They'd spent the whole day sitting in the hen-house – and were they miserable!"

FRIDAY, 1ST FEBRUARY 1980

I was surrounded by the towering stone walls of grey palaces. Am I on the square I have been seeking so frantically? I vaguely remembered the heavy figurative relief carved into the oaken gates. The sun divided the area into light and dark halves. I gazed attentively from the light into the shadow and caught sight of a diminutive white figure by the gloomy portal of a palace.

I walked over uncertainly, and it was her. I had to take her by the hand before she noticed me. She did not recognise me, she had been waiting too long and was in a bad way. I said: "Remember!"

As if it were a magic word, she came to life. Her motionless eyes focused on me. Her face was traversed by a sequence of stills: first her features sagged into the despair they were moving towards before they froze so long ago; having reached bottom they stopped and her face started to brighten up and regain an expression of interest and lively expectation. I allowed this heart-rending process to run its course – how else? – waiting until she herself recognised me. Then her mouth twisted as if she were about to weep, but immediately she smiled painfully. Her head fell back exhaustedly, and she stayed leaning against the grey stone, her eyes closed and her mouth in a smile. I took her by the shoulders and said: "Can you walk?" She was silent. I squatted down and felt her legs from the heel to above the knee; they were as cold as granite and rough as sandstone. I ought to carry her out into the sunshine, but I was shy to, as there was no one about. I looked around and just then a throng of people swarmed out of a narrow lane. So I bent over, and raised her in my arms, and carried her calmly and proudly over to the other side of the empty square.

I stood her up in the blazing sun against a mighty pillar that formed part of a colonnade. She immediately laughed as if at a joke in company, and with brisk movements started to smooth down her skirt, readjusting her belt that I had moved while carrying her. She shook out her hair, looked behind her at the back of her legs and her high-heeled shoes, turned round several more times, and then took me by the hand and made as if to go.

But I could not go anywhere! She gazed at me with joyful urgency, playfully imploring me with grimaces; she came closer, and taking hold of my fingers kissed me lightly. I said clearly: "Wait here for me, I'll be right back. Don't go away." I led her to the corner pillar, at whose foot a stone post, rough, warm and ancient, stuck out of the pavement. I placed Ester on it in the full (golden) sunshine. She sat there happily, gazing skywards.

I walked away, looking back at almost every step. I'll be back soon, before that pillar sinks back into the shade, I said to myself. When I turned for the last time, another group of people was trooping in from the narrow street opposite; some of them started to talk to Ester and, unbelievably, she got up and started to leave with them, hesitated a moment, and left. And then a whole stream of cars flooded into the empty square. I stood on tiptoe in order to catch sight of that small white figure amidst the crowd.

Suddenly the question bellowed in my head: why am I courting such disaster again, and on account of yet another trivial matter somewhere? I stood my bulging bag against a wall, abandoned it there and ran back. From far off I could already see that the stone post was empty. I could not bring myself to believe it. How could I make the selfsame mistake twice in succession? At the same time it struck me that if I could not hold on, then she at least could – and should! – have. And there she was, sitting two pillars further away on the same kind of post. She was wearing a one-piece creamy-white dress, with a wide skirt, furbelows in place of sleeves, the neckline high but slit and unfastened. On her lap an open handbag, in her hand a mirror: she was putting make-up on. I had the oddest feeling, like the thought "we belong together."

I grabbed her by the hand. She scarcely had time to throw her tools back in her handbag than I had her white figure in tow. Nothing but the sound of little hooves behind me. And we flew through the colonnades, a strip of sunshine, a strip of shade, then another square paved with light and dark slabs, the pigeons flew up from beneath our feet. Then through streets full of shop-windows, their lights and colours reflected in the damp heat of the asphalt, then a market with fruit and flowers, then the coolness from open church doorways. I turned back to look at her; she was gasping open-mouthed, trying to keep together the posy on her breast – she already had a red posy! A more relaxed pace now beneath the overhanging branches of linden trees, then some timeworn fountains and stone steps up to moss-grown statues. Then a yellowish early-evening glow reflected in the flat windows of the houses in the narrow lane, at whose end there stands a gloomy house, with – suddenly – a night lamp already shining in front of it, and I awoke with the humiliating awareness of a fundamental physical law: if you do not wish to lose something, you must cling to it tightly. It is unforgiveable.

The happy details of how I had found her again were still coming back to me while I was shaving – I left the door open so I could hear the telephone! – and from my discovery there was gradually formulated the second paragraph of that same law: or else one must book it in one's own name. And that came as a minor – very minor – relief. And then the phone rang.

Since that conversation I have been shaking the whole day – Tuesday, 15th April 1980. I could distinctly hear a desperate dilemma, unhappily controlled disappointment and reluctantly acknowledged regret over the way I had put my tenure and title (at that point it was up to 11th September 1979) in my book. I did not entirely understand, but even after my urging on Wednesday, I did not receive anything more by way of an answer than astonished pained amazement, which I took to be a question whether what I had written and the way I wrote it could possibly express a relationship and feelings which I declare to be good and positive. – After that, what can I hope from other, worse afflicted characters in my book? So I don't want to wait for the reproach I have no trouble imagining: that the way I dragged certain persons into my Book is a breach of their agreement – more extorted than voluntary – with the way I had already drawn them into my life.

On Thursday my Book is awakening to the long-feared realisation that its interests are at variance with the interests of the people and things it deals with. Exploiting the last shred of my better nature, I have made up my mind (making a virtue of necessity – L.V.) to lay it aside, to let other wills decide. Let the living dream take precedence over the paper dreambook.

You have no idea, all of you, how much this decision of 18th April 1980 relieves an anxiety that has afflicted me for over a year.

SATURDAY, 2ND FEBRUARY 1980

The train was again half-empty. Ivan sat down by the window facing the engine, I threw my bag down opposite and Karol Sidon sat next to me. I got out again, went back into the station concourse, and found an out-of-the-way corner to observe events. I saw Jiří Gruša arriving and Karol waving to him from a window of our carriage. It did not look to me as if Jiří was being tailed, so after scanning all the people waiting round I returned to our compartment. "How many pages have you written?" I greeted Jiří. – "Only ninety. But there's already a pile of corpses," he replied.

Ivan said he'd look for a better compartment and set off to inspect the train. Jiří bellowed: "I don't believe this! Kosík's here!" – "The beginning of our journey is marked by unnatural phenomena," said Karol, shaking his head. Kosík entered, smiling his broad tight-lipped smile, and said: "Hello, friends! Pretty good, eh?" – "Not bad," said Karol. Kosík hung up his coat, sat down in the corner by the door and said: "Well, gentlemen, would it have been conceivable, back in the so-called good old days, for us to set off on a trip for the hell of it like this, and in such excellent company?" He embraced us all with a ceremonial flourish.

Ivan came in and said: "Gentlemen, I propose we move up two carriages. It's the only one in the train with running water." Karol said sulkily: "Do we have to?" – "It's got cleaner windows too," Ivan added. Kosík showed displeasure, at which Ivan implored, with a touch of pique: "We'll be further from the dining car, so we won't have the whole train walking past us all the time." I intervened in the silence of contention: "Let's go then," picking up my own knapsack and reaching for Kosík's. "At least, Karel, you'll be in Brno two carriages sooner." That was a cogent argument in his case, as he hates travelling. We squeezed our way along the corridor, with Jiří behind me complaining: "Catch me going anywhere with Klíma again! Why didn't we go by car? Just because Klíma doesn't want to burn the oil of some stupid Saudis!" – "It's mainly because it's less conspicuous this way," shouted Ivan from in front, "and also cheaper. Particularly as an express goes there anyway!" – "Pipe down!" I reproved Jiří, and he started to mumble to himself as he went.

We were already sitting down again when Saša Kliment arrived. "Good morning, gentlemen. It truly is a rare pleasure to see you altogether like this." You should talk, I thought to myself, but aloud I said: "Now that you're here, Saša, this train is transformed into the Prague-Brno Pleasure Express." – "You make me out to be far too much of a rarity, Ludvík, one might even say, an attraction." – "No, no!" Ivan objected sharply. "The attraction is Karel Kosík." Kosík smiled graciously.

The train wasn't due to leave for another ten minutes. I stepped down onto the platform. Jan Vladislav was approaching with small rapid steps. Smiling like a good-humoured Buddha, he declared of his own accord: "Don't worry, Ludvík, old chap, if I thought they were following me I certainly wouldn't bring them here." I led him to our compartment, where he declared: "Friends, I don't understand why we didn't take an earlier train." – "There isn't anything earlier," I said. – "I was thinking about one last year, Ludvík, or the year before." Saša turned to Jiří : "How many pages have you written?" – "Ninety, and I'm stuck. One character I forgot about when she went into a coma two months ago has suddenly come to life and is starting to interfere."

A whistle blew, doors slammed, and we started to move. Ivan asked to borrow my train timetable and I gave it to him. "You've got black on your fingers," I pointed out, and he spat on them and cleaned them with his handkerchief, and Jiří said: "Well, at least we're sitting in the only carriage with running water!" We were passing by the enormous grey ball of the gas holder in Libeň, when along the corridor, turned slightly sideways in order to get through, came Karel Pecka. He slid the door open and declared with annoyance: "Well, friends, who was in charge of this? I could have easily missed out!" – "You were never home," I apologised, "and I didn't want to leave a note." – "So how did you find out?" Kosík asked in amazement. – "How? How do you think? They announced it on Radio Free Europe, of course!" Ivan exploded: "What a bloody fool that Milan Schulz is!"

We were nicely settled now. Karol picked up my cap, put it on, opened his Hebrew book and started to recite. That plunged us into embarrassed silence and Jiří said: "Has anyone got anything interesting to read?" One of us got up, reached for his bag, and handed out envelopes with our names. We opened them: in each of them were several photocopied cuttings from Austrian and German newspapers and in each of those someone was writing about Pavel Kohout, everyone favourably, except for Jan Beneš and some Morava or other. "Pavel sends these to you." Ivan shook his head. Kosík smiled, almost out loud, and Jiří, chuckling, declared: "It's perfect, I like it! He's sticking to his role!" Each of us also received a reproduction of a poster announcing the premiere of Pavel's latest play: *The Labyrinth of the World and the Paradise of the Heart*. We waved them at each other, laughing gaily, and J.G. exclaimed: "I've got an idea! Let's hang them up in the train." – "That's an excellently crazy idea," said Ivan; he opened his knapsack, took out his pyjamas, tipped out about five kilos of sausages, found his travelling first-aid kit, removed sticking plaster and scissors from it, and we all went, except for Kosík and Karol, from carriage to carriage. Jiří wanted to stick the posters up in the toilets, but in each of them the slogan "Free the Chartists!" was written in black letters. It was inexplicable (I looked at Ivan's freshly spittle-cleaned fingers) and Pecka said we shouldn't turn the toilets into a political education centre, so we stuck the posters up in the washrooms.

We came back in and Kosík declared with concern: "Do you think that was reasonable? Wouldn't it be more appropriate to write and tell him? Are any of us writing to him from time to time?" We exchanged glances and were all ashamed of ourselves apart from Pecka. He took his heavy haversack down gingerly from the rack and took out a demijohn of wine. "Friends," he said, "let's drink his health. He doesn't have it easy, poor chap. Tell me,

It was inexplicable... (p. 533)

frankly, which of you would like to be in his place?" No one volunteered. Everyone said that here one was better protected against those emigrants who felt obliged to use their new-found freedom in order to publicize their old antagonisms, jealousies, envies and umbrages. It was shameful, we all said. And we drank to Pavel's health.

Jiří expressed surprise: "You're taking wine to Moravia?" – "What sort of stupid question is that?" Pecka replied. "I am, of course, going to Moravia for wine, but I'm hardly going to carry an empty demijohn, am I?" He poured us all some more, but Ivan said that without sausage the wine was making him nauseous, so he opened his haversack, took out the first-aid kit, pyjamas and finally a string of sausages, and started to pull them off and hand them round. Only Karol Sidon refused one, so I offered him a piece of the strudel that Madla had given me for the journey, with the words: "Off you go, boys, have some fun. It's time you did. After all, you deserve it." Kosík's glasses glinted and he said: "Ludvík, were you serious when you said you thought there'd be music there?" – "I don't think so, Karel, I know so. Because Trefulka said so, so it's a certainty." – "And will Šimečka and Kusý be there, Ludvík?" Karel asked next. "I've been looking forward to meeting them for so long!" I shrugged: "I can't say. If they do things according to the plan Milan Uhde worked out, they could make it. In fact, Tatarka might even come." – "Dominik, Dominik!" several voices clamoured. "Dominik. It must be ten years since I last saw him," said Pavel Kohout. "So let's drink to his health too," said Pecka and poured Pavel a glass. "Why didn't you invite me on this excursion before," said Pavel. "After all, I used to invite you over so often!"

We were pulling into Havlíčkův Brod – ten minutes late by Ivan's reckoning – when Jan Vladislav said in elation: "And I didn't have a clue you organised outings like this. You're real friends!" – "Well, there you are," said Ivan, who comes to everyone. – "You've got everything so well arranged," Jan continued. "Some girls, too?" The compartment went silent, and Ivan and I exchanged glances and exclaimed together: "That student! But of course!" Pecka got hot under the collar: "Whoah! Steady on! Let's get things straight. I was informed this would be a gentlemen's outing." – "It is! It is!" Ivan blurted, almost losing the bread and sausage from his mouth in his haste to explain: "But Šimečka always brings along some beautiful student, and Ludvík and I always refuse her." Vladislav found this surprising. Pecka said the student would get the cold shoulder once more. Mr. Václav remarked that we shouldn't be rash but should deal with the situation as it arose, and Jiří called out: "A triplet is best!" Kabeš gave him a withering look and said, not to him but to me: "Did you hear him? A reverse triplet – that's a comedown for you!" Pavel said: "I agree with our friend Pecka that we shouldn't let women spoil it, apart from the fact, Ludvík, that even a sturdily constructed book such as yours could hardly sustain another female character." And no one knew what he was talking about, just Pavel and I.

Beyond the train window the dark fields had a light toning of frost. The duckponds weakly reflected the grey calm of the sky as we rolled into Brno. I went out into the corridor, followed shortly by Karol. We looked out the window and I recalled that old piece of weather lore: At Candlemas the lark must sing, even if she do freeze, poor thing.

(Prague, 23rd April 1980)

A Czech Dreambook invites readers to share a year in the life of the writer Ludvík Vaculík. It details his experiences from 22nd January 1979 to 2nd February 1980, blending together many different levels: everyday conversations with neighbors, family, and friends; shopping trips and visits to the dentist; detailed accounts of gardening, weeding, grafting, and hewing; arguments about literature and politics with other writers; meditations on world events; intimate details of two extramarital affairs; reports on police surveillance and interrogations; and descriptions of the inner workings of one of the most impressive underground publishing operations in the Soviet bloc under communism. It is an eminently political book, about defending one's integrity in the face of state repression, negotiating the boundaries between public and private, and talking to the police; it offers a compelling portrait of Prague's dissident community just a couple years after the appearance of the human rights declaration Charter 77. But it is also a book about everything that politics *isn't*, a book that shows how any human life overflows its political bounds and reaches out in other directions. It is a book about a remarkable marriage sorely tested by infidelity, about the infidelities themselves, about parenthood and the release of children into the world. It is also a book about love (both romantic and familial). And it is, preeminently, a meditation on friendships, portrayed in all their density and contradictions – a reminder that true friendship contains equal parts exasperation and devotion, and summons up deep conflicts that would remain invisible to mere acquaintances (as well as to mere enemies). Controversial and edgy, it is a book that does not shy away from provocations; sometimes obnoxious, often wise, it bares its own imperfections even as it strives for immortality, and then begins to record its readers' objections even as it is being written. It is the greatest work of one of the greatest Czech writers of the twentieth century.

None of this was clear when Ludvík Vaculík sat down on the evening of 22nd January 1979, rolled a sheet of paper into his typewriter, and began describing why he couldn't sleep the night before – and why, nevertheless, he didn't get up to start writing in the middle of the night. "So shall I really start keeping a diary like this? After resisting it for all these years?" At the time, Vaculík was undergoing something of a writer's crisis. For political reasons, he was banned from official publishing. He was devoting much of his time to running Padlock Editions (*Edice Petlice*)[1], an underground publishing house for banned Czech authors, and to dealing with the attendant police attention (surveillance, harassment, the constant

---

1) Pronounced "EH-dit-se PET-lit-se." Vaculík's own name is pronounced "VAH-tsoo-leek."

threat of house searches, and regular monthly interrogations). At the age of fifty-two, he had three novels under his belt, and numerous newspaper articles and radio pieces from his earlier career as a journalist, but his recent writing was almost exclusively limited to short essays. "Everyone knows my genre," he writes on 25th January 1979, and indeed, Vaculík was well-known for the three-to-four-page essays that in Czech are called *fejetony* ("feuilletons"). His latest project, an annotated edition of his teenage diaries called *Dear Classmates!* – he continued working on it throughout the year of the *Dreambook* – was also hard to classify, a return to older writings rather than something new.

About this time, as Vaculík reveals toward the end of the book (in the entry for 3rd January 1980), he had complained of his lack of productivity to the poet Jiří Kolář. Kolář (whose own intensely rigorous poetics had once led him to advise spending "a day and a night" on each line of verse) replied: "Look here, if you're unable to write, write about why you're unable to write, for goodness sake! Keep a record of what you see, what you hear and what comes into your head. You've already developed your own style for it in your feuilletons, which are excellent, after all!" This advice provides us with one more paradoxical designation for *A Czech Dreambook*: it is a beautifully written book about why Vaculík was unable to write.

What does the title mean? A "dreambook" describes dreams and offers interpretations of them – along the lines of "if you dream you are flying, you will soon inherit money." It is, by its nature, a compendium of folk wisdom and superstitions, as well as a catalogue of human fears and desires; it encodes a faith in the interpretability of the world, as well as a sense of its depths and mysteries. Vaculík's text shares these qualities, although, strictly speaking, it is not a dreambook at all. He does relate many of his dreams, but rather than offering stock interpretations of them, he lets them reach out ambiguously to other passages, mingling with memories and speaking to his angers and fears. In one sense, the designation "dreambook" was a canny way to avoid specifying just what Vaculík thought he was writing, and in particular whether the book is real or fictional. Is it a novel, a diary, a *roman à clef*, a memoir, or something in between? Or is it simply a collage of myriad smaller parts – portraits, anecdotes, short stories, songs and poems, political essays, reportage, found documents, book reviews, and of course dreams – that come together in an unclassifiable whole?

The first readers of the *Dreambook* were Vaculík's friends and acquaintances. As with all clandestine literature circulated during the Communist period, the book was not printed normally; rather, typewritten carbon copies were distributed to a relatively small group of people. When Vaculík wrote this text and gave it to friends and family, he could expect readers with a good deal of inside knowledge about his life as well as the fortunes and attitudes of particular characters.

Even so, much would have remained to decipher in a text that plays frequently with themes of the unconscious and its manifestations, private and public, censored and uncensored, secret and shared. In 2012, Vaculík published some of the correspondence surrounding the 1986 translation of the *Dreambook* into Swedish, in which his translator Karin Mossdal posed questions about particular passages. Reading Vaculík's answers today, it is clear that parts of the book must have been mysterious even to its contemporary Czech readers. At one point, when Mossdal asks about the mention of a key in the entry for 30th August, he reproaches her: "You ask, dear Karin, what kind of key this was, which is none of your business as a translator, because it is meant to remain hidden from the reader." To another question, he says: "Once again you are more curious than required."[2] And even in its home context, the book is emerging into a world of much different readers who no longer have personal memories of life under communism, or even textbook knowledge about the political and philosophical stands of various dissident figures, not to mention forgotten films, vanished landscapes, and the obsolete technology of underground publishing.

The *Dreambook* has been translated into French, German, Hungarian, Bulgarian, and Swedish; now it appears in Gerald Turner's superb English translation, which is both meticulously accurate and wonderfully expressive. How should today's English-language reader approach the *Dreambook*? It would be tempting to provide extensive footnotes in the text, explaining every historical reference and political allusion, with capsule biographies of all the book's many characters. This approach would have both strengths and weaknesses. Footnotes would elucidate many references, but would also bog the text down in a critical apparatus of dozens of pages, constantly interrupting the fictional dream with information that will, to some readers, seem extraneous. Vaculík does not write for a foreign audience, but he does create a rich, detailed, self-sustaining world for patient and attentive readers. Many quirks of style, "information deficits," and surprising formulations are meant to give *all* readers pause; many strange puzzles are resolved within a paragraph or two. This consistent readerly disorientation, pursued by a narrative voice that seems self-assured and omniscient, is one of the basic stylistic devices that give the text its unity. Vaculík wants his readers to ask what they know and how they know it, and to cross-check various accounts – in other words, he wants to model the kind of reader who is skeptical about rumors and opinions, and seeks to filter them through his or her own judgments.

---

2) František Janouch and Ludvík Vaculík, *Korespondence Janouch/Vaculík* (Praha: Mladá fronta, 2012), p. 107–108.

Since Vaculík gives us fictionalized portrayals of many real people, there is a related editorial temptation to give mini-biographies of all the writers and politicians he mentions in the work. Any editor would be tempted to provide entries such as: "p. 15: Karel Kosík (1926–2003), Czech philosopher, member of anti-Nazi resistance (imprisoned 1944–1945), reform Communist and leading theorist of humanist Marxism in the 1960s, author of *Dialectic of the Concrete* (1963), dismissed from university teaching in 1970, later dissident and signatory of Charter 77; author of open letter to Jean-Paul Sartre after secret police confiscated over a thousand pages of his philosophical manuscripts in 1975." But such glosses would pose problems of their own. Not only would they still end up swamping the text with hard-to-digest information, but they would also bring in extraneous information that may not be relevant to Vaculík-the-narrator, who is drawing his own portraits of friends and acquaintances. Rather than treat the book as a storehouse of trivial gossip about real people, it is advisable to let the book's "characters" emerge as Vaculík creates them, without constantly indexing them against some condensed versions of their biographies – biographies that would, in turn, only index our own obsessions as foreign readers, as historians, and so on, overlaying a strange and confusing set of coordinates onto a text that strives for its own authenticity and precision. In the end, Vaculík does not write "Karel Kosík, Czech philosopher"; he just writes "Karel," leaving it up to the reader whether to fill in any background information or not. Does it matter that Kosík is Czech, a philosopher, a former member of the anti-Nazi resistance, a dissident, and so on? As readers, we will only get more and more confused if we constantly struggle to draw lines from these characters to our own preconceptions about their "real-life" equivalents. Understanding the text means letting it build its characters on its own terms; only then can we step back and think about Vaculík's own blind spots, motives, and insights.

At the same time, it seems helpful to give foreign readers some basic information about Vaculík's life, writings, and political history, as well as explaining references to moments in Czech culture that may be unfamiliar to an English-language audience. This afterword seeks to give enough background information to orient readers in the basic coordinates of Vaculík's world; many readers may want to consult it before proceeding to the book proper. *A Czech Dreambook* moves in several large thematic circles. A brief introduction to some of them may orient the reader better than a series of extensive and intrusive footnotes in the text itself.[3]

---

3) One other place where a foreign reader might be at a disadvantage is simply in registering the repetition of unfamiliar Czech names and nicknames as they recur from entry to entry. In this respect, a quick guide matching first and last names may be useful: in most cases where another meaning is not clear from context, "Ivan" refers to Ivan Klíma, "Jiří" or "Jirka" to

Vaculík was born on 23rd July 1926 in the Moravian town of Brumov – at the south-eastern edge of the current Czech Republic, on its border with Slovakia. Brumov is in a region known as Moravian Wallachia (*Valašsko*), and Vaculík occasionally makes references to the dialect and folk songs of his Wallachian homeland, as well as to his larger sense of his Moravian identity. Although Brumov was near a railroad line, Vaculík grew up surrounded by farm people, close to the land. His rural childhood would become a touchstone of his own upbringing, as well as of his personal mythology as a man of the countryside who has been transplanted into the urban Czech capital of Prague. Vaculík's childhood games playing "cowboys and Indians," frequently mentioned in the *Dreambook*, reflect his own idyllic fantasies and reading of Westerns and adventure tales for boys. But they also embody his sense of a set of moral coordinates rooted in a local environment and local practices.[4] Looking back on these games, he still appreciates these moral coordinates – even as he understands that such certainties belong to a children's world, where the good guys and the bad guys are easily identified.

As a teenager, Vaculík took an apprenticeship with the large Baťa shoe company, owned and run by Tomáš Baťa, the foremost Czech entrepreneur of the interwar years. Baťa had created a commercial empire around his shoe business and had built an entire micro-society in the city of Zlín about twenty-five miles away – not just a factory, but a whole company town that provided standardized housing for adult workers as well as dormitories for student apprentices, who applied for jobs from all over the country. The company also ran schools, cinemas, musical societies, athletic and social clubs, and other forms of education and entertainment for its workers. Although Baťa was a capitalist par excellence, his vision of collective discipline and cultivation of the individual through productive labor was actually not all that far from many Communist tenets. Vaculík would retain a lifelong respect for Baťa and the lessons he learned as an adolescent worker in Zlín. It was here, during the war, that he met his future wife Marie (Madla) Komárková, who

Jiří Gruša, "Pavel" to Pavel Kohout, "Karel" either to Karel Kosík or Karel Pecka, "Saša" to Alexandr Kliment, "Otka" to Otka Bednářová, "Mirka" to Miroslava Rektorisová, "Zdena" to Zdena Erteltová, "Eva" to Eva Kantůrková, "Eda" to Eda Kriseová, "Vlasta" to Vlasta Chramostová and "Standa" to her husband Stanislav Milota. "Mr. Václav" is Václav Havel, who spent much of the *Dreambook* year first under house arrest and then in prison, and never makes a personal appearance. "Mrs. P." is Drahomíra Pithartová, "Petr" is often her husband Petr Pithart. Vaculík's wife, Marie Vaculíková, is called by her lifelong nickname "Madla," and their three sons are Jan (the youngest), Ondřej, and Martin (the oldest, who lives in France). 4) See "Nechci se dohodnout" ("I don't want to come to an agreement"), Pavel Kosatík's essay on Vaculík in *Česká inteligence* (Praha: Mladá fronta, 2011), p. 329–333.

had also come to work for Baťa. She was much less content there, but eventually found her niche as an outstanding *vychovatelka* – something like a combination tutor, governess, and dorm advisor for the young women who had come from all over the country to work in Zlín.

As a young man, Vaculík was attracted to Communist ideas, and after the war he joined the Communist party. He would remain loyal to this decision, if not strictly to the party itself, for the next twenty years. In February 1948, the Communists took control of the Czechoslovak state and rapidly began to institute one-party rule, including massive surveillance by State Security (the secret police were known by the acronym StB, for Státní bezpečnost) and the systematic, violent repression of political opponents, religious orders, and "class enemies" – not just wealthy bourgeoisie but also independent tradespeople and better-off peasants. Like many young Communists in their early twenties, Vaculík seems to have made his peace with this state-sponsored violence; he believed that sacrifices were necessary to build a new society, and he felt that the sins of Communist rule could be blamed on bad actors rather than on the system itself. In his 1967 speech to the Writers' Congress, he talked about the role played by "altruistic but ill-informed enthusiasts like myself" in consolidating Communist power. Despite the mounting evidence of corruption and violence inside the new regime, he held out hopes that its problems and errors were temporary and had to be accepted on the way to a new social order. Nevertheless, he always retained some critical distance from the party. Madla – who, herself, never trusted the party and never joined it – later noted that "Vaculík wasn't a fanatic. For him, an injustice was an injustice even if it was committed by the Communists. This is why he didn't write at all in the 1950s – when it was only possible to do so dishonestly. On the other hand, at that time he thought things would get better if different people took over important posts."[5] This comment accurately reflects Vaculík's long-standing focus on character rather than ideology as a determinant of social and political systems.

Vaculík began studying at Baťa's business academy in Zlín just after the war, but soon relocated to Prague to study politics and sociology. At the same time, Madla had been transferred to help run a dormitory for young girls in northern Bohemia, in the borderlands that had formerly been heavily populated by German-speaking citizens of Czechoslovakia, many of whom were expelled after the war. Vaculík moved to the borderlands to be with her, also taking on work as a *vychovatel* (advisor) in the dormitories for young workers. The couple married in

5) Madla Vaculíková, *Já jsem oves: Rozhovor s Pavlem Kosatíkem* (Praha: Dokořán/Jaroslava Jiskrová-Máj, 2002), p. 30. See also the interview with Vaculík in Antonín Liehm, *The Politics of Culture,* translated by Peter Kussi (New York: Grove Press, 1973), p. 183–201.

June 1949, but Vaculík was far less successful at his work than Madla, and eventually was forced to resign from the job. He relocated to Prague in December 1949 – Madla went with him. After another stint as an advisor for young Prague factory workers, Vaculík served his two years in the army and then, with Madla's help and at her urging, he began to work for a state publishing house. Meanwhile, they had started a family: their eldest son Martin was born in 1950, then Ondřej in 1954 and Jan in 1958.

In 1959, he began his journalistic career as a reporter for Czechoslovak Radio, where he first specialized in youth programming. He would remain there for seven years; even in the restrictive world of state-controlled broadcasting, he steadily acquired a reputation as an original, bold reporter who avoided ideological clichés and did not hesitate to improvise. In September 1965, he became an editor at *Literary News* [*Literární noviny*], the weekly organ of the official Czechoslovak Writers' Union, which had been evolving over the course of the 1960s from a relatively reliable regime organ into one of the most provocative, innovative, reform-oriented journals on the Czechoslovak political scene. During the 1960s, Vaculík would find himself combining his professional identities as radio and print journalist, novelist, and *homo politicus* into his own unique blend.

JOURNALISM, LITERATURE, AND POLITICS

After the repression and show trials of the late 1940s and 1950s, the 1960s saw a gradual opening up of Czechoslovak culture as reform currents began to take hold even at the highest levels of the Communist Party, spurred on by the need to reform a stumbling economy. Vaculík played an important role in the long process whereby intellectuals, journalists, and writers helped to push against censorship and cultural repression, and to expand the boundaries of what it was possible to say in print and on the air. The process culminated in 1968, when the reform wing took firm control of the party under the Slovak Communist Alexander Dubček, inaugurating the short-lived but far-reaching process known as the Prague Spring. For eight months, from January through August, reform-oriented Communists dominated the party and the state; they sketched out economic and political reforms, some of which began to be implemented. One of the most important shifts was the virtual lifting of censorship in the spring of 1968, opening up a new public sphere. But even before censorship was lifted, Vaculík and writers like him had been pushing the envelope of what could be talked about in public. The second half of the 1960s would become the first culminating point in his career. The tension between collective responsibility and individual reasoning is a constant in Vaculík's writing, and this tension was pushing him further and further away from orthodox communism.

The split is already fully evident in his semi-autobiographical first novel, *Rušný dům* (The unquiet house, 1963), about a dormitory advisor; much of the text is taken up with the narrator's efforts to cultivate both party discipline and independent thinking in the teenaged workers under his care, although in the end orthodoxy seems to win out over individualism. This novel's literary qualities go well beyond the standards for official prose in the late 1950s and early 1960s, and it is still quite readable today: the dialogue is witty, and the structure, blending different time layers, is sophisticated. Nevertheless, it is beholden to the ideological clichés of the day. There is no mention of the show trials or massive repressions carried out by the Communist Party in the early 1950s, and there are plenty of moments where the narrator reinforces the reigning ideology, with its official badges and work campaigns, stereotyped jokes about American capitalists, and reading of inspirational books by the first Communist president, Klement Gottwald. Yet, even despite this relative orthodoxy, party officials asked Vaculík to rewrite the novel before it could be published – and he obliged.[6] Although he would continue to negotiate with the censors throughout the 1960s, this would be one of the last such sacrifices to party orthodoxy that he would make.

The 1960s saw a series of spectacular public statements in which Vaculík definitively broke with the party and began to speak for himself. His complex and nuanced novel *The Axe* (*Sekyra*, 1966) portrays a middle-aged journalist coming to terms with the failures of socialism in Czechoslovakia and, in particular, with his own father's role in the forced collectivization campaigns of the 1950s, when farmers were driven to surrender their land and livestock to state-run cooperative farms. Like Milan Kundera's *The Joke*, with which it was often compared, *The Axe* would become one of the main cultural events preceding the Prague Spring of 1968 – an aesthetically complex but undeniably critical account of the sins of Communist orthodoxy. In terms of Vaculík's political development, however, this novel turned out to be a mere prelude to his most striking and public act of coming to terms with Communist power, his speech at the June 1967 congress of the Czechoslovak Writers' Union. A number of writers at this congress (including some who are represented in the *Dreambook*, like Karel Kosík, Pavel Kohout, and Ivan Klíma) spoke vociferously against censorship and ideological conformity. But Vaculík went even further, stunning everyone by giving a provocative speech in which he analyzed the shortcomings of Communist power and stated matter-of-factly that "in the past twenty years not a single basic human problem in our country has been solved, from primary needs like housing, schools and economic well-being to those more subtle requirements which the world's undemocratic systems cannot

6) Vaculíková, *Já jsem oves,* p. 49.

fulfill – the feeling of playing a full role in society, for example, or the subordination of political decisions to ethical criteria, the belief in the importance even of humble work, the need for trust between individuals, or elevating the educational standards of the entire public."[7]

The speech was clearly a moment of catharsis for Vaculík. In his lively account of the Writers' Congress, Dušan Hamšík, one of the editors of *Literary News*, wrote:

> His delivery was calm and factual; he neither gestured nor raised his voice for emphasis. Even the most dogged and rebellious passages [...] sounded in his delivery bitter and nostalgic. Vaculík spoke with utter and surprising candour. He made no use of subtle formulations or prudent innuendoes. Listening to him, I realised how far we had accustomed ourselves to wrap up all our criticisms and misgivings in a thick disguise so that they should not only pass the censorship but also conform to those standard patterns of public opinion which – we had come to believe – must be accepted if there were to be any dialogue without scandal and disgrace. Vaculík discarded these assumptions.

Hamšík gives a good sense of how Vaculík was coming to terms, not just with the demands of ideology itself, but also with the rules of convention and propriety that always underlie ideological correctness. According to Hamšík, when Vaculík then had to defend himself to party authorities, he said: "I spoke because I wanted for once to have things straightened out in myself. I challenged myself to say the plain truth about everything, because the plain truth is something I hardly ever find myself telling these days."[8]

The speech at the writers' congress marked Vaculík's "stepping out" as one of the most outspoken intellectuals among the reform Communists. He was effectively burning his bridges to the party. The evening after the speech, Hamšík and his other colleagues were sure he would be arrested on one pretext or another; in the event, he was expelled from the party and, if the hard-liners had stayed in charge, he would surely have suffered further consequences. When the reform wing came to power in January 1968, he received a temporary reprieve. Throughout 1967 and 1968, he would write frequent feuilletons and investigative articles on the political situation in the country. His June 1968 article "The Revival Process in Semily," examining the progress of the Prague Spring in a small town, is a classic of reportage that observes, with great acuity and irony, how national politics filter down

---

7) The speech is reprinted in Dušan Hamšík, *Writers against Rulers*, translated by D. Orpington (New York: Random House, 1971), p. 181–198.
8) Hamšík, *Writers against Rulers*, p. 59 and 67.

to the local level. He also began writing a regular column for *Film and Television News,* where – under the pseudonym √l, "the square root of L" or also "VL" – he captured many of the promises and paradoxes of the Prague Spring. With his typical flair for contradiction, he would even use these essays to argue with other texts that he had written under his own name.

It was in the early summer of 1968 that Vaculík would write his most dramatic and influential short text, one that would ensure his place in Czech history even if he had written nothing else. In the spring of 1968, a number of scientists came to Vaculík asking him to draft a statement of support for the reformers. Vaculík responded by authoring a manifesto that he called "Two Thousand Words," in which he said that the socialist program had fallen "into the hands of the wrong people"; he criticized the "leaders' mistaken policies" after 1948 for creating a party in which power mattered more than intelligence or integrity. The party had been built on ideas, but it had become "highly attractive to power-hungry individuals eager to wield authority, to cowards who took the safe and easy route, and to people with bad conscience." Under the rule of such a party, society itself had deteriorated: "Personal and collective honor decayed. Honor was a useless virtue, assessment by merit unheard of. Most people accordingly lost interest in public affairs." The manifesto warned that many people within the power apparatus were still resistant to change, and it appealed "to those who so far have waited on the sidelines" to help push change forward. In its appeal to character and independent thought, it bore the hallmarks of Vaculík's thinking: "Let us forget the impossible demand that someone from on high should always provide us with a single explanation and a single, simple moral imperative. Everyone will have to draw their own conclusions. Common, agreed conclusions can only be reached in discussion that requires freedom of speech." In this spirit, Vaculík appealed to "the everyday quality of our future democracy," calling for local action among factory workers and at the district and community level of government. If local officials abused their power, "ways must be found to compel them to resign. To mention a few: public criticism, resolutions, demonstrations, demonstrative work brigades, collections to buy presents for them on their retirement, strikes, and picketing at their front doors… For questions that no one else will look into, let us set up our own civic committees and commissions. There is nothing difficult about it; a few people gather together, elect a chairman, keep proper records, publish their findings, demand solutions, and refuse to be shouted down."[9] "Two Thousand

9) For the text of "Two Thousand Words," see Jaromír Navrátil, ed., *The Prague Spring 1968: A National Security Archive Documents Reader,* translated by Mark Kramer, Joy Moss, and Ruth Tosek (Budapest: Central European University Press, 1998), p. 177–181.

Words" was one of the fullest expressions of the grass-roots political sociology Vaculík had developed over the past ten years, identifying the personal virtues that help collectives function, and ultimately cutting free from ideology in favor of fine-grained accounts of local and individual behavior.

This text was published simultaneously in several different newspapers on 27th June 1968, and it immediately struck a chord with readers – hundreds of thousands of people sent in letters asking to sign on to this statement. The popularity of "Two Thousand Words" infuriated the reform Communists, who were struggling to maintain control of popular opinion, and further sharpened tensions with the Soviet Union. Vaculík had become, de facto, one of the public spokesmen of the reform movement, even as he maintained his stubborn individuality and unpredictability, as well as his own quirky writing style that relied on surprising formulations. An interesting perspective on this period appears in the *Dreambook* entry for 24th April 1979. While acknowledging the outpouring of support – including dozens of letters from people who felt he was speaking for them – Vaculík here frames 1967 and 1968 as a period when he was learning "to act publicly in a purely private capacity." He reflects that "my speech at the Writers' Congress had merely been intended to show how I thought everyone should be talking." In other words, he wanted to model a kind of civic virtue rather than rally people around a particular platform or ideology. An important concomitant of this is that he could continue to explore all the contradictions underlying his own beliefs – such as when (in a 7th August 1968 feuilleton published in the voice of "the square root of L") he attacked Ludvík Vaculík for "coming down from the mountains every six months to raise a ruckus in the pub and then disappearing again."[10]

When the Soviet invasion came in August 1968, it was clear that Vaculík could only stand in opposition to the new regime. There were rumors that he had been shot by the Russians. His son Martin, at that time eighteen years old and on a trip to a kibbutz in Israel, decided not to come home; he ultimately emigrated to France.[11] In the event, Vaculík was not arrested, but he did settle into a life of uncompromising opposition to the government.

"NORMALIZATION"

In the months following the Soviet invasion, the reform government, despite its massive popular support, was gradually sidelined and then completely forced from power. In April 1969, Dubček was deposed as first secretary of the party and his place was taken by another Slovak Communist, Gustáv Husák, who would preside

---

10) Ludvík Vaculík, *Stará dáma se baví* (Praha: Lidové noviny, 1990), p. 96.
11) Vaculíková, *Já jsem oves,* p. 136.

over an ever-tightening repression. This process came to be called "normalization," and the term eventually took hold as a label for the twenty years of Communist rule following the invasion. While a number of the government's most vocal opponents were put on trial and imprisoned, the new regime relied much more on a slow demobilization of the social energies unleashed by the Prague Spring and by the invasion itself. A gradual tightening of the screws was combined with targeted repression against outspoken regime opponents. A pall settled over cultural life as harsh censorship was reinstituted. Reform Communists were forced from power at all levels, expelled from the party and often from their jobs as professors, researchers, writers, and journalists; in order to remain gainfully employed (and avoid prosecution under the law against "parasitism," which required adults to have a stamp confirming their employment in their identity booklets), many intellectuals had to take on blue-collar jobs: driving taxis, stoking boilers, guarding parking lots, washing windows. A fascinating and politically savvy view of this period comes from Vaculík's diary entries from 1969 to 1972, published in 1998 as *Nepaměti* (Non-memoirs or Anti-memoirs), and not yet translated into English.

Vaculík himself slowly but surely lost all his publishing possibilities. His pessimistic situation and limited possibilities were reflected in a grotesque, semi-fantastic short novel called *The Guinea Pigs* (*Morčata*, 1973), which he published in his own underground publishing house. But conditions in the 1970s were not ideal for writing. As a prominent regime critic and active organizer of underground publishing, Vaculík was subject to heavy police surveillance. He was never imprisoned, but was regularly called in for interrogations, and he knew his house could be searched at any time. Under these circumstances, the journalistic genre of the feuilleton took on new meaning for him as a way of commenting on the ongoing crackdown without attempting a larger synthesis.

Vaculík's first feuilletons had appeared in the 1960s, when he wrote for *Literary News, Film and Television News,* and other venues. Usually three to four pages in length, his essays generally moved from some everyday event (a visit to the movies, a story in the newspaper) to an unorthodox meditation on morality or politics; Vaculík's favorite technique was to plunge his reader directly into the description of some unfamiliar situation that would only gradually become clear as he teased out its deeper meaning. He continued this technique – turning an unfamiliar lens on the everyday – into the 1970s, but this was *not* a kind of allegorical writing to avoid censorship; Vaculík knew full well that his texts were unpublishable in any form. Rather, it continued to reflect his own vision of political sociology, in which there was no clear hierarchy between politics and everyday life, as well as his general desire to cultivate a skeptical reader who would ask questions about even the minor details of daily life. Over the years, Vaculík had written dozens of these feuilletons and had become one of the recognized Czech masters of the genre, but he had not managed any longer, more ambitious work. Hence that sigh, early in the *Dreambook*, that "everyone knows my genre."

PADLOCK EDITIONS AND CHARTER 77

One reason Vaculík felt that he was writing less in the 1970s was that he had thrown himself so energetically into organizing oppositional culture. In the Czech sphere, he was instrumental in developing and solidifying a new form of underground publishing, known as *samizdat* – the term is the Czech version of a Russian neologism that means something like "self-publish."[12] One of Vaculík's many enormous contributions to oppositional culture in the Czech lands was the underground publishing house, Padlock Editions (*Edice Petlice*), that he founded in 1973. Padlock was one of the first underground publishers to get going in the 1970s, and it would become one of the most consistent, stable, and ambitious of samizdat publishers, ultimately releasing over 350 titles throughout the 1970s and 1980s – novels, poems, plays, philosophy, and essays that could not appear officially because of the massive censorship (aimed both at specific authors, who were outright banned, and at sensitive topics) re-instituted under the Husák regime.

When we speak of underground writers, "publishing" is something of a euphemism. Censored writers had no access to printing presses and official distribution networks. Samizdat generally involved typing multiple copies of works on mechanical typewriters; the most common technique was to interleave 8, 10, or 12 pieces of thin onionskin paper with pieces of carbon paper and to roll the stack into a typewriter, so that the keystrokes would impress the carbon ink on each successive piece of paper. This technique allowed typists to make multiple copies at one time, although the overall process was still painstakingly slow. Many samizdat "editions" appeared only in a few dozen copies. Once typed, copies were often proofread by groups of editors – as in the scene from 7th March, where Vaculík joins the Slovak-speaking Ján Mlynárik, his wife Edita, and an unnamed woman (likely someone whose name Vaculík withheld so as not to create difficulties for her) to go through thirty typed copies of *Písačky* (Jottings) by the Slovak writer Dominik Tatarka. (*Jottings* was Tatarka's own first-person, erotic account of life as a regime opponent in Slovakia: an interesting counterpart to Vaculík's *Dreambook*.)

Vaculík avoided the term samizdat as a Russian import – in fact, the word does not appear in the entire *Czech Dreambook* – and yet he must be counted as one of the most important actors in European samizdat culture under communism. And the

12) On samizdat, see, for example, Tomáš Glanc, ed., *Samizdat Past & Present* (Prague: Karolinum, 2018).

Dreambook offers one of the best accounts of the mechanics of running an underground publishing operation. Vaculík illustrates the whole range of his activities, from meeting with unpublished authors and editing their work to delivering the finished typed copies to readers (and struggling to get them to pay for their copies so as to cover the costs of production). We see him trying to arrange a stipend for banned authors, dropping off typescripts at various bookbinders, and hiding manuscripts in unnamed places to protect against police searches. Appropriately, he emphasizes the extent to which samizdat publishing rested on a whole network of volunteers; foremost among them were the so-called "copyists," predominantly women, who typed multiple copies of innumerable texts. Many of these copyists appear in the *Dreambook*, including figures who were already well-known to the secret police and who are mentioned here by name – like Miroslava (Mirka) Rektorisová, Otka Bednářová, and Zdena Erteltová – as well as others who appear under pseudonyms, or anonymously, to protect their identities. Although Padlock was one of the largest and, in underground circles, best-known publishers, it was just one of many. A number of other samizdat "editions" were founded and became long-term, sustained operations. Two that are mentioned in the *Dreambook* are Edice Expedice ("Dispatch Editions"), founded by Václav Havel, his brother Ivan Havel, and his wife Olga Havlová, and Edice Kvart ("Quarto Editions," named after the distinctive square-shaped books it published), run by Jan Vladislav.

As intellectuals gradually adapted to the new conditions under the repressive Husák regime, more coherent oppositional networks began to coalesce. Samizdat played a large role in this, providing a set of unofficial cultural coordinates and a way to create a self-consciously alternative culture that could grow, comment on itself, and orchestrate larger debates. Another important development was the rise of the music "underground," the groupings of mostly young people that centered around banned rock groups like the Plastic People of the Universe. (Vaculík gives an outsider's somewhat bemused view of this alternative youth culture in his comments on the underground poet Věra Jirousová, in the entries from the end of October.) But the key event in the self-constitution and self-awareness of the Czech opposition was Charter 77, a proclamation issued in January 1977 that drew together a wide spectrum of intellectuals, artists, and former politicians who had been sidelined after 1968, along with members of the music underground and others who had hardly ever participated in "official culture" to begin with. Vaculík attended the meetings at which the Charter was drafted, and was among the first group of signatories. The Charter's original proclamation detailed human rights abuses in the country and called on the Czechoslovak government to honor its commitments to human rights treaties, including the recently signed Helsinki Accords. Emphasizing solidarity rather than ideology, the Charter called itself an "informal organization." It operated under a system of three rotating spokespersons, and would eventually evolve into a loose but unbreakable dissident grouping that provided support and solidarity for its members and issued periodic communiqués about regime repression and the state of life in Czechoslovakia.[13]

LIFE IN OPPOSITION: CHARTER 77 AND REGIME REPRESSION
The government did not sit by quietly while its opponents began to organize alternative forms of cultural life. Vaculík's fate was typical of many opposition intellectuals in this regard. Slowly but surely, publishing bans extended over his work, until his only income came from publications abroad. Vaculík and his family had long been under surveillance, and police attention only increased in the 1970s. He was regularly called in for interrogations; in 1975, he was one of many writers subjected to a wave of alarmingly thorough apartment searches. In the first half of the 1970s, the Vaculíks' case was the special purview of a secret policeman who identified himself to them as Major Martinovský; he is mentioned several times in the *Dreambook*. Such repressive measures continued and intensified after the publication of Charter 77 in January 1977. In the regime's initial, apoplectic response to the Charter, dozens of signatories were repeatedly interrogated, harassed, and subjected to a nationwide slander campaign that saturated newspapers, radio, and television for weeks.

Vaculík, of course, was just one of many people who were targeted in this way, but he came in for special treatment – in part because, as the author of "Two Thousand Words," he remained one of the living symbols of the Prague Spring, in part because of his samizdat publishing activity. He had also authored a manifesto called "Ten Points" on the one-year anniversary of the invasion; signed by Vaculík, Václav Havel and others, it had little broad impact, but resulted in a formal indictment and singled out the signatories for closer attention from the police. When Havel asked Vaculík: "You can't have forgotten, surely, that you – like myself, incidentally – are still formally indicted on a charge dating back to 1969?" (in the entry for 26th January 1979), he is referring to the charges related to "Ten Points."

In particular, Vaculík was the target of one of the more bizarre episodes of regime repression in the 1970s, an episode that also casts a long shadow over the *Dreambook*. Since the early 1970s, Vaculík had been carrying on an extramarital

---

13) For an overview of the music underground as well as the formation and operation of Charter 77, see Jonathan Bolton, *Worlds of Dissent: Charter 77, The Plastic People of the Universe, and Czech Culture under Communism* (Cambridge: Harvard University Press, 2012). There I also give further details about samizdat publishing, as well as the political debates surrounding *A Czech Dreambook*.

affair with Zdena Erteltová, herself a courageous regime opponent and one of the most active copyists for Padlock Editions. At one point, she and Vaculík had taken photographs of each other lying naked on tombs at a cemetery. These photographs had been confiscated during the 1975 house search, and the secret police had repeatedly tried to blackmail Vaculík, threatening to publish the photographs unless he agreed to shut down Padlock Editions, or even to emigrate. He had always refused. On 21st January 1977 – in the midst of the massive slander campaign against the recently proclaimed Charter 77 – the official magazine *Ahoj* published the photographs (with a black square virtuously covering the sensitive parts) along with an attack on Vaculík, claiming he had "put a series of pornographic pictures into circulation." Although the regime's indignation was feigned and manipulative, the photographs are indeed puzzling, and it's still something of a mystery as to what Vaculík and Erteltová were thinking. Jan Vladislav, in his diary, posited that they were modeling the poses of medieval *ginants*, the statues lying recumbent on medieval tombs; in Vaculík's manuscript prose *The Old Bed*, the narrator describes an intense and moving encounter, half-game, half-quarrel, in which two lovers court death by lying on tombs.[14] Of course, the photos were never meant to be circulated, and of course, none of this was very transparent to readers of *Ahoj*, or to Vaculík's family and friends.

This episode would have been well-known to every early reader of the *Dreambook*, and it would become a key moment in Vaculík's life. In the entry for 25th January 1979, he mentions that other dissidents thought he had been "demoralized by Martinovský" – in other words, that he had lost his oppositional fervor after the affair of the photographs. But in fact, the public shaming failed to break either him or his wife (at whom it was equally directed): Madla would stand by Ludvík despite his repeated wanderings. (The long-running affair with Erteltová, as readers of the *Dreambook* will see, was not Vaculík's last.) When Vaculík looked at his own secret-police files after the fall of communism, he surmised that this failed operation was the reason Martinovský had been removed from his case and replaced by the "ashenly menacing Major (?) Fišer," who would become one of the main representatives of the secret police in the *Dreambook*.

More broadly, as Vaculík would later write, he had braved the worst the regime could throw at him, and emerged with strengthened self-confidence and perspective. The question for him would no longer be how to *protect* his private life from public harassment, but rather how to *present* his private life – on his own terms. In a 1997 retrospective, Vaculík wrote: "This event had an instructive and encouraging effect on me that lasted the rest of my life. Once I had taken the decision to preserve

14) On the photographs, see Ludvík Vaculík, *Tisíce slov* (Brno: Atlantis, 2008), esp. p. 298–304.

my honor in its entirety, even with my sins – that is, to defend my soul, warts and all – everything else was much easier for me. I had given the enemy evidence that not even the worst would affect me, and it really seemed to me that they took my impregnability into account. [...] The lifelong instruction and encouragement was this: life is life, and you shouldn't surrender it – not for glory, not for money, not because of promises, not under threat. Of course, I don't know if I could have acted this way had my family not been able to hold out, had they cracked."[15]

INTELLECTUAL AND POLITICAL DEBATES OF 1979

After his short novel *The Guinea Pigs*, Vaculík had focused ever more on running Padlock Editions. This is what he means when he says, in the entry for 26th January 1979, that in "Year seven" – that is, entering the seventh year of his work for Padlock – "my real trade is falling into decay. Madla told me the other day what our boys say about me behind my back, i.e. that it's shameful really – all the things he could be writing, instead of traipsing around Prague with other people's nonsense!" In the entry from 28th January 1980, Vaculík paraphrases a comment from his friend Pavel Kohout, at that time in Vienna: "because of my years of literary sloth I have faded as a writer from the consciousness of the enlightened public there, being known solely as a fomenter of political scandals."

The beginning of 1979, as Vaculík began work on the *Dreambook*, was a time of intense intellectual discussions among the Charter community – discussions in which, as usual, Vaculík played a key part. Police harassment of oppositional activities was continuing as strong as ever, with many acts of brutality resonating among the Charter community – on 5th June 1979, for example, Charter spokesperson Zdena Tominová was severely beaten by a masked assailant as she entered her apartment building. The government had instituted a coordinated secret-police campaign code-named "Decontamination" (*Asanace*) to harass and terrorize many Charter signatories, forcing hundreds into emigration. But the regime had ceased its front-page attacks on the Charter, which was falling out of public memory and risked becoming yet another obscure petition. Many dissidents worried that they had lost touch with their fellow citizens, the vast majority of whom were not in open dissent against the regime, and some spoke of a dissident "ghetto," as if the dissidents were a sealed-off community. One of Vaculík's great projects in the *Dreambook* is to explode this myth of the "ghetto," by showing all the many contacts between his own "dissident" world and people around him.

---

15) Blanka Císařovská, Milan Drápala, Vilém Prečan, and Jiří Vančura, eds., *Charta 77 očima současníků: Po dvaceti letech* (Praha and Brno: Ústav pro soudobé dějiny and Doplněk, 1997), p. 190.

Under these conditions, many dissidents were looking for a new way forward. Some were struggling to find a more tenable form of existence under close police surveillance and harassment; others were trying to intensify their activity and fight back more forcefully against the government. One of the major initiatives seeking a higher-profile form of opposition was called the Committee for the Defense of the Unjustly Prosecuted, or (by its Czech acronym) VONS. It was organized in February 1978, and sought to publicize the arrests and trials of political prisoners, while providing material aid and moral support to prisoners and their families. This was an extremely risky activity. Indeed, in May and June 1979 – during the year of the *Dreambook* – fifteen of the seventeen members of VONS were arrested, and six of them were put on trial in October; these included a number of people mentioned in the *Dreambook*, such as Otka Bednářová, who had been a prominent radio journalist in the 1960s (and later became a copyist for Padlock), and Václav Havel. Vaculík, however, held back from VONS. In his entry for 5th November, in response to a further wave of arrests, Vaculík makes a characteristic observation: "An event like this always sets me fretting over the old question: how should one react to it, if one wants to keep control over one's own life at the same time? Consistent resistance to lawlessness transforms people into professional outlaws. The point is it leaves one with neither the energy nor the time for anything else. It is a cyclotron!"

Given the ongoing pressures of opposition and government repression, many chose simply to emigrate. Vaculík's friend Pavel Kohout, a playwright who had gone through many different metamorphoses – as loyal party member in the 1950s, prominent reform Communist in the 1960s, and then regime opponent and founding member of the Charter in the 1970s – accepted an invitation to travel to Vienna in 1978. He knew full well that he might not be allowed back into Czechoslovakia, and indeed he was turned back at the border when he tried to return in October 1979. Kohout's name in Czech means "rooster" – hence the headline in the official newspaper *Rudé právo*, "Cocky Kohout Crows His Last," mentioned in the entry from 9th October. Kohout was one of the most active dissidents, and characteristically he began promoting Czech literature and culture abroad. From Vienna, he continued to communicate with Vaculík and even proposed to arrange an evening at the Burgtheater of readings from Vaculík's work. The entry from 28th January 1980, conveying some of Kohout's reservations about the *Dreambook* excerpts Vaculík had sent him, is an interesting early meditation on how the book might appear to a foreign audience – as well as how one of its "characters" might react to his own portrayal.

Emigration is one of the ongoing themes of the *Dreambook*, as Vaculík reflects on those who have left (like the folk singer Jaroslav Hutka) and speaks with people who are preparing to emigrate (such as the writer and artist Karel Trinkewitz). Both Hutka and Trinkewitz were targets of Operation Decontamination and had been placed under extreme pressure before they left the country, but Vaculík still does not hesitate to record his opposition to emigration, in judgments that might seem harsh to many: "the shortcoming of those people is not that they emigrate, but that they started fighting as if intending to keep it up. Courage has to be rationed like water in the desert or bread during a siege" (15th October 1979). Or, as Vaculík says with characteristic forthrightness: "I can't help feeling that every departure weakens me" (26th March 1979). Vaculík would explore another route, asking how to stay in Czechoslovakia and oppose the government without turning his entire life into a political demonstration or a dissident "cyclotron."

Thus, as the *Dreambook* gets going, he has just ignited a fierce debate among the Charter community with a short essay called "Remarks on Courage." This was a piece written for the fiftieth birthday of Vaculík's friend Karel Pecka, who had been arrested in 1949 – at the age of twenty – because of an amateurish oppositional flyer he had copied and distributed with a couple friends. Pecka did ten years of hard labor in a uranium mine. Consciously breaking many taboos, Vaculík asked if the crime was worth the punishment. He suggested that Pecka's true courage was visible, not in the initial act of futile resistance, but rather in his ability to resume his life after this catastrophe. He went on to ask, implicitly, what *kinds* of oppositional activity the Charter should be cultivating, and suggested that hardcore activism was setting the bar too high for most Czech citizens.

This is a line of thought that Vaculík would explore in other writings as well. His feuilleton "Attempt at another Genre," which is mentioned in the entries for 8th and 26th February, as well as 20th April 1979, was dedicated to the Protestant minister Jan Šimsa, who had manhandled a secret-police officer during a search of his home, and gone to jail as a result. In this essay, Vaculík wondered if the heroic view of dissident life ends up isolating all evil outside of us, suggesting that we ourselves are the embodiment of good while the regime is the source of all evil. Instead, Vaculík asks whether we can imagine a life in the presence of evil, accepting evil as a necessity rather than pretending we are immune. In a strange way, this question runs through Vaculík's life like a leitmotif; back in his first novel *The Unquiet House*, the narrator argues with his wife, who is not a party member: "She would like to have the fire without the ashes – she would like to have this system without its mistakes. Who wouldn't? I argue with her: she can either have this system with its mistakes, or another system. There is no third path."[16] Over the next twenty years, Vaculík would explore many third paths, but he would

16) Ludvík Vaculík, *Rušný dům* (Praha: Československý spisovatel, 1963), p. 222.

often refuse simply to identify with the forces of good against the forces of evil. The *Dreambook* is full of meditations that would have seemed heretical to fellow dissidents – attempts to understand what the regime is thinking, an abiding effort to ascribe reasonable motives to his opponents rather than simply scorning them, and an openness about the flaws (internal squabbling, pettiness, resentment) of dissidents themselves. Life is complicated and people cannot choose perfect allies (or perfectly evil enemies). Here is another reason why, almost as a point of principle, Vaculík reveals his own imperfections to friend and foe alike. His intriguing discussion with Šimsa, home from jail, is described in the entry for 26th February 1979. And even though the feuilleton "Attempt at a Different Genre" seemed to push against the heroic view of dissidents, he nevertheless had to answer for it in his interrogation described on 20th April 1979.

Readers of the *Dreambook* will see how upset many dissidents were by "Remarks on Courage." A major discussion ensued, several dozen replies were written and circulated, and the first month or so of the diary devotes a great deal of time to the ensuing debates. Vaculík clearly wanted to work out a better response to regime harassment than the ongoing call-and-response where regime repression provoked protests, which provoked more repression, which provoked more protests, and so on. Vaculík's real reply to this vicious circle was the *Dreambook* itself, a meditation on how to maintain an oppositional stance without responding endlessly to the regime's provocations. Schooled by his own brushes with the police, he sought to bare his doubts and internal debates, his fears as well as his convictions – his "soul," "warts and all."

Here we might productively compare Vaculík with the most prominent Czech dissident, Václav Havel. Over the course of the 1970s, Havel had worked out his own conception of political opposition in essays such as "The Power of the Powerless." He allowed for fear and ambivalence, but he wanted each person to articulate his or her own truth and then take a stand for it, often with a sense of higher responsibility to a mystical, transcendent "absolute horizon" – a sense that our actions have moral consequences even if we can't discern them.[17] Vaculík represented a different strand of dissent, woven more around sincerity than truth: through his own behavior, he implicitly encouraged people to investigate their (often contradictory) emotions and beliefs, and then to think carefully about how to express themselves as openly and completely as possible. The moral universe for him was not transcendent but concrete, rooted in the natural world and in specific relationships with specific people. To recall his admonition from "Two Thousand Words": "Let us forget the impossible demand that someone from

17) See Kieran Williams, *Václav Havel* (London: Reaktion Books, 2016), esp. chapters 4 and 5.

on high should always provide us with a single explanation and a single, simple moral imperative." His hopes for democracy were founded on this vision of sincere citizens, unencumbered by ideology or inherited preconceptions; this kind of free self-expression was the ultimate political virtue for him, whether or not one took part in each act of protest or opposition. Here we see yet another of the great paradoxes of the *Dreambook*: Vaculík attempts to articulate a political stance that rejects the paramount importance of political stances. And indeed, no matter how important the book's political coordinates are, it would be a grave mistake to read it merely as a portrait of oppositional life under a repressive regime. Part of Vaculík's very project was to show how much of his life *wasn't* subsumed under, or consumed by, politics.

CZECHS IN THE WORLD

During the Cold War, travel abroad was closely monitored and restricted, and we often have a vision of the Communist countries as sealed behind an Iron Curtain that prevented the movement of both people and information. While there is much truth to this view, the *Dreambook* is striking in its portrayal of Vaculík's many international contacts. Far from being ushered into a hermetic, sealed "ghetto," we see all the ways in which Czechs were interconnected with the outside world, through what historians have only recently begun to label "transnational ties." In the very first entry, Vaculík has spent the day with a visitor from Hamburg; he talks to Jiri Gruša about the German translation of Gruša's novel *The Questionnaire*; he refers to their connection with a Swiss publishing house, run by Jürgen Braunschweiger, who published German translations of a number of banned Czech authors. These "international" moments contrast with the title (it's a *Czech* Dreambook, after all), and remind us that the Czech dissidents, even in the closely guarded confines of communism – where the border was carefully monitored and most people did not ordinarily speak with Westerners – still kept in touch with the rest of the world. Vaculík implicitly argues against the idea of a "dissident ghetto" by tracking these contacts – he listens to Voice of America, fends off a *New York Times* reporter, comments on major news stories of the day, reads foreign authors, and entertains foreign visitors: from his brother's Georgian wife Lina and his son's French fiancée Isabelle to the Norwegian human-rights activist Thorolf Rafto.

Yet, even as the book undermines our sense of a society hermetically sealed behind the Iron Curtain, *A Czech Dreambook* remains true to its title: it is a sustained meditation on a *national* community, its fate under communism, and what it means to be (and speak, and write) Czech. For this reason, it is helpful to consider the underlying regional identities in Vaculík's composite world. Vaculík is very much a Prague writer: he lived in Prague much of his life and was fully involved in its cultural life. But he does not speak or reproduce dialogue in so-called *obecná čeština* or "common Czech," the vernacular form of Czech commonly spoken in Prague. His written and spoken language is often inflected by Moravian word choice and word endings. And within Moravia, he often hearkens to the folk culture – songs and stories – of his native region of Wallachia.

More broadly, Vaculík negotiates between his own urban and rural affinities. He grew up on a small farmstead in the village of Brumov, in a house his father-carpenter had designed and built. In his games of "cowboys and Indians," he had crawled and crept through every inch of the surrounding countryside – the landscape he named "Arizona." His love of nature is clear in his attention to the changes of seasons, his knowledge of plants, trees, and flowers, and in his wonderful descriptions of landscapes. It may also tie in to a patriarchal streak that runs through much of his thinking, as well as to his frequent laments about the environmental devastation wrought by industrial and urban life – sometimes this is associated with Communist neglect of the environment, and sometimes it is simply recognized as a symptom of modernity. "It is marvelously possible," he wrote as the square root of L in a 1967 feuilleton, "that what we have grown used to seeing as the history of our civilization's technological development is really, much more, the history of nature's extinction."[18] Thus, if Vaculík is a sharp observer of urban life – the streets and cafes, concerts and theaters of Prague – he seems most at peace when he is tending to his garden at the family's villa in Dobřichovice, outside of Prague, where he and Madla spend many weekends as well as longer stretches during the summer months. The villa is, characteristically, no idyll – it is divided up, as many suburban villas were under communism, among a number of different tenants, and so it bears as much witness to political conditions as anything else. But it does represent a kind of way-station between the urban world of Prague and the rural traditions Vaculík grew up with.

Even as folk culture pulls Vaculík to the eastern parts of the country, he is also fully immersed in the high culture of Czech literature, although he often takes a subversive view of it. As a master of the feuilleton, Vaculík is frequently compared to two nineteenth-century Czech journalists, Jan Neruda and Karel Havlíček Borovský, who also specialized in political-cultural commentary about Czech life. But the characters in the *Dreambook* refer back more often to the cultural world of the "First Republic," the interwar Czechoslovak state founded in 1918 and presided over for almost twenty years by its president Tomáš G. Masaryk. During the year of the *Dreambook*, Vaculík, Madla, and their friends read and talk about many of the touchstones of Czech interwar literature, often figures who, to some

18) Vaculík, "K výročí bitvy, která se nekonala," in *Stará dáma se baví*, p. 31–33.

extent, represent the country's liberal, democratic, or Catholic traditions rather than its Socialist ones. The great interwar literary critic F. X. Šalda (1867–1937) had a villa near the Vaculíks' house in Dobřichovice, and they often walk past it on what they call "the Šalda Trail" even as Madla is immersed in reading Šalda's correspondence. (The subversive view of Šalda offered by Madla and Karel Kosík, focusing on the romances of this authoritative literary presence, can be seen as a kind of counterpart to Vaculík's own "self-demystification" in the *Dreambook*.) Vaculík reads the correspondence between the left-wing poet Stanislav Kostka Neumann and the brothers Josef Čapek and Karel Čapek, all leading figures of interwar culture. Madla reads to Vaculík about the Catholic poet Jan Zahradníček (1905–1960), who was imprisoned by the Communists in 1951 and died soon after he was released from prison in 1960; Vaculík later quotes his 1951 jeremiad "The Sign of Power" ("landscapes covered in deletions were being relentlessly erased"), an apocalyptic vision of the Communist takeover.

Vaculík also treats us to portraits of some of the central figures of Czech literary culture of his own day. As a samizdat editor, he spoke frequently with both established (albeit banned) and beginning authors; many dissidents were banned writers, and so we see portraits of figures who may be familiar to English-language readers, such as Vaculík's friends Ivan Klíma, Pavel Kohout, and Jiří Gruša. And we also see vivid portraits of older writers – for example, the commanding literary critic Václav Černý, and the poet Jaroslav Seifert, both of whom came of age during the First Republic but played a great role in Czech literature throughout the century. (Seifert would win the Nobel Prize for Literature in 1984, a few years after the *Dreambook* was finished.) Vaculík even tries to arrange a film of Černý interviewing Seifert, a project that, alas, never seems to have been realized. Vaculík occasionally stops in at Café Slavia, just across from the National Theater in Prague, which was a favorite hang-out for banned writers – it was here that Jiří Kolář, the poet who would tell Vaculík to write about why he couldn't write, presided over his own table, "thronged with dissidents like a hive with summer bees," as Vaculík writes on 26th October.

In the entry from 18th March, Vaculík discusses the novel *The Engineer of Human Souls*, by Josef Škvorecký. Škvorecký had emigrated after 1968 to Toronto, and there he and his wife Zdena Salivarová opened Sixty-Eight Publishers, one of the most important émigré publishing houses for Czech literature. Many of these volumes were smuggled back into Czechoslovakia and read widely there. Vaculík admired *The Engineer of Human Souls* and imagined that it was Škvorecký's attempt to write something like the great Czech novel, "uniting the Czechs' sundered destiny. There is a new story on every page." But it's clear that Vaculík had aspirations to do the same thing, painting his own mosaic of Czech history through hundreds of daily observations and micro-stories that would draw together Bohemia and Moravia, city and countryside, oral and written (and typewritten and printed) culture, folk song and classical music, art, photography, and theater, into a panorama of Czech history and life in the twentieth century.

FAMILY, FRIENDS AND LOVE AFFAIRS

A Czech Dreambook is an acute evocation of a marriage – one that is both sorely tested and yet remarkably resilient. Vaculík's wife Madla emerges as a finely drawn character with a strong and distinctive voice. In a way, this is a shame, since she can speak for herself, and has done so.[19] But the *Dreambook* is Vaculík's book, and in it, Madla often represents a foil to his own views and vices. Always distrustful of communism, she had lived through the same history as Vaculík, but had a different view of it. She hated the collective discipline of Baťa's factory in Zlín. She never thought that communism was a promising ideology ruined by careerists and power-seeking cynics, and she never bought into the idea, so dear to Czech Communist intellectuals in the late 1940s and 1950s, that the party should force (other) people to make sacrifices now in the name of their future happiness. Where Vaculík had meant his first novel *The Unquiet House* as an internal critique of mindless discipline, bureaucratic in-fighting, and the bad actors who were sabotaging the work of the party, Madla thought the book deficient because it made no mention of the show trials or police repression that were taking place at the time. All this is clear from her own writings and pronouncements. But one thing she shared with Vaculík was a fascination with the politics of daily life; like Vaculík, she was less interested in ideologies and systems than in the micro-politics of everyday behavior. In the 1970s, she was working as a marriage counselor in a state-run institute, and her conversations with Vaculík about her workplace and her boss (whom they have nicknamed "the Phantom") are a fascinating commentary on workplace ethics under normalization. When the cultural historian Pavel Kosatík asked whether she and her husband talked about politics, she said: "Of course, all the time. And we fought. We hardly had any arguments about raising our children, about money, none of the things that married couples usually argue about. We were always quarreling about politics – terribly!"[20]

---

19) After 1989, Vaculíková began to correspond regularly with Jiří Kolář (who thus served as a muse for her, as well as for her husband); she published her letters in two volumes called *Drahý pane Kolář...* (Dear Mr. Kolář...), in 1994 and 1999. In 2002, she published a book-length interview with Pavel Kosatík called *Já jsem oves* ("I am oats" – a reference to the *Dreambook* entry from 14th February).
20) Vaculíková, *Já jsem oves*, p. 43.

The marriage was honored as much in the breach as in the observance. Among so many other things, the *Dreambook* is the story of Vaculík's love affairs, and the interplay between loyalty and infidelity is one of the book's most fascinating, occasionally troubling themes. Without giving away too many of the year's events, we can return to Vaculík's affair with Zdena Erteltová, which we have already mentioned – and which the Communist régime had already publicized. Erteltová is another of the *Dreambook*'s strong female characters, and someone who would deserve a book of her own. As one of the most dedicated copyists for Padlock Editions, she played a key role in Czech samizdat literature, a role that demanded both literary acumen and political courage; she was under police surveillance and suffered harrowing persecution, at one point being forcibly hospitalized, as Vaculík describes in the entry for 14th February. Of course, it is the nature of the *Dreambook* that other people emerge only in fragments of conversation and everyday interactions; Vaculík does not let other characters steal the spotlight. Given this caveat, it is worth noting that he paints many arresting portraits of women. It is unfortunate that more writing by women from dissident circles, including Eda Kriseová, Lenka Procházková, and Eva Kantůrková, has not been translated into English; among other things, this reflects particular conceptions of dissent that have been embedded in both Western journalism and historiography going back to the 1970s. And like most of his contemporaries, Vaculík was no feminist, nor was he the only dissident of outstanding political credentials who cheated on his wife or partner, or even the only one who maintained long-term relationships while still remaining in a marriage that held up under the unique strains of dissent and infidelity.[21] But it is nevertheless worth noting that he sketched some of the most effective and enduring portraits of women in Czech dissident writing. He gives voice to many compelling female characters, many of whom castigate him sharply and persuasively.

A revealing moment comes in the entry for 24th November, when Vaculík looks into Madla's diary. This entry is not only a confrontation of two different writing styles, two different ways of recording a life, but also a kind of *apologia* for Vaculík's wanderings. Madla writes: "He says he's going to Brno to see Šimečka but I don't believe him. He never tells the truth, so even when he does, it isn't the truth for me anymore. It's odd how everyone thinks of him as a fighter for the truth." This is a stark and effective confrontation of Vaculík's political reputation, both at home and abroad, with his marital infidelities; it also comes in a passage where Vaculík is snooping about in his wife's personal writings, in a way that uncomfortably mirrors the police surveillance they were all subject to, and publicizing her intimate

21) Another was Václav Havel. On this point see also Williams, *Václav Havel*, p. 129.

thoughts in a way that highlights the controversial nature of the *Dreambook* itself. We see Vaculík in a negative light – and then, of course, understand that he has carefully arranged this scene to prove a larger point. "Fighting for the truth" is not just a political pose; it also means staying true to one's opinions and desires, in a way that will prove unpopular to many people. As he portrays himself to us in the *Dreambook*, Vaculík was seeking no one's approval; indeed, the very project of baring his soul, warts and all, was also meant to teach his readers to stop looking for heroes. Instead, he wanted them to start thinking for themselves, rather than outsourcing their virtue to someone else. It's a finely balanced moment, in which we see Vaculík both manipulating his wife's voice and letting it ring out loud and clear – the kind of moment, as in all great literature, that will evoke different, deep responses from different readers. Vaculík's skill at balancing these responses over the course of an entire year is one of the things that make the *Dreambook* so compelling.

THE AUTHENTICITY EFFECT

The *Dreambook* falls into a clearly identifiable tradition in Czech literature, the publication of diaries, letters, and first-person texts as a form of "public intima-cy." Vaculík's own literary tastes in the book often foreground this tradition: as we mentioned earlier, he reads the correspondence of the interwar writers Josef and Karel Čapek, while Madla reads that of critic F. X. Šalda. Vaculík discusses reactions to the Padlock edition of the first-person (and sexually explicit) writings of the Slovak writer Dominik Tatarka, and he makes a pilgrimage to the home of the writer Jakub Deml (1878–1961) – a renegade Catholic priest who also wrote extensive first-person diaries and essays, including accounts of his romances. He meets several times with Drahomíra Pithartová, the wife of the active dissident Petr Pithart, to discuss drafts of her story "A Short Exercise in Ruthlessness," in which the first-person narrator offers a withering view of her husband, a promi-nent dissident. (Vaculík's discussion of this story with Madla, in the 6th November entry, is a surrogate discussion about the *Dreambook* itself.) And one of his literary discoveries of the year is *Nightfrost in Prague* by Zdeněk Mlynář, an architect of political reforms in 1968, who had signed Charter 77 and then emigrated under heavy political persecution. In his praise for Mlynář's memoir, Vaculík certainly expresses some of his own literary ideals: "It is written in a style that has been extinct here for the past three decades, whereby a text informs about the subject and the writer at one and the same time. It discards any attempt at unattainable objectivity and convinces through its plausible subjectivity" (28th October 1979).

To this day, Czech writers frequently publish diaries, *romans à clef*, and other texts that deal with real people, settle scores with their rivals or enemies, and paint a nuanced portrait of Czech cultural life through the portrayal of an individual's experience. Lenka Procházková's *Smolná kniha* (Black book, 1991 – the title refers to medieval court protocols of witness testimonies often extracted under torture) was a *roman à clef* based on her own relationship with Vaculík, which began during the year of the *Dreambook*. A recent memoir by another former dissident, Tereza Boučková's *Život je nádherný* (Life is wonderful, 2016), pays tribute to Vaculík as a proponent of this genre, while settling scores with him at the same time. Book-length interviews, ranging widely over a famous person's life and experiences, are another common genre – for our purposes, a notable one is Pavel Kosatík's interview with Madla Vaculíková, *Já jsem oves...* (I am oats...), in which we get Madla's view of the events of *Dreambook* and much else besides.

These works are an accepted part of the Czech literary landscape, valued for the insight they give into the lives and creative struggles of well-known personalities. Periodically, they also ignite discussions about how far a writer can and should go in talking about other people. Vaculík was well aware of the potential for controversy, and as he was finishing the *Dreambook*, he began distributing copies of the manuscript to many of his friends and asking them for their responses. Reactions varied from embittered disgust to unbounded, even ecstatic enthusiasm. On one side were readers who felt that "fictionalizing" real people was a form of manipulation, a violation of confidence and abuse of friendship; on the other were those, more numerous, who allowed that Vaculík was presenting his own subjective view of the world, and granted him considerable leeway in how to render it. Many of them felt that he had given a unique and inimitable expression to the world they were all living in, and had thereby helped them to understand and withstand the pressures of normalization in a way that no other literary or essayistic account had been able to do.

Vaculík eventually collated the reactions, positive and negative, and published them all in a separate volume. But he had already begun to incorporate people's reactions into the *Dreambook* itself, and one of the most dramatic and fascinating threads of the last third or so of the book traces his own doubts as he begins to assimilate the reactions of his readers. These interact with his own editing of the manuscript as he reads through it in 1980, a year after writing it, registering his own reactions to what he said and wrote a year earlier. Various passages imply that different characters requested particular edits, while also suggesting that he didn't honor all of these requests; at other times, he makes a point of saying that he is adding information that was not in the original entry, or that he is leaving something out. If we read the reactions of his critics and characters, it becomes clear that not every detail in the text is reliable. In his otherwise enthusiastic response to the text, written in June 1980, Milan Šimečka felt compelled to add a postscript responding to the entry for 11th November 1979, in which he is portrayed as saying he wanted to bring "a beautiful young student" on a weekend trip to Brno: "The literary character who appears in the book sometimes as Milan, other times as Šimečka and sometimes as Milan Šimečka seems to me to be portrayed in a favorable and friendly light. It is a shame that, against the background of somewhat loose relationships between male and female characters, the author neglected to highlight his moral constancy and irreproachability, because even that student was made up."[22]

The *Dreambook* has earned a lasting place in Czech literature. It is now widely recognized as one of the canonical books of Czech literature of the second half of the twentieth century, and many Czech critics simply treat it as a novel. In addition to being a work of literature, it is also a valuable historical document, painting an insider's portrait of dissident life; it would be difficult to get a full picture of Charter 77 and samizdat publishing without knowing Vaculík's text. Its publication in English translation should now make it required reading for any historian working on dissidents and dissent under communism. For just this reason, it is all the more necessary to ask how reliable the "facts" of the text are. Is it all real? It must be acknowledged that Vaculík creates an overwhelming "authenticity effect." By revealing intimate details, and publishing frank and open criticism of his friends and political allies, he creates the impression that he is holding nothing back. As readers, we feel we are reading a remarkably sincere, raw, no-holds-barred act of witnessing. For all his artfulness, Vaculík's style seems frequently to cut to the quick of a question or debate, revealing painful contradictions and sparing neither himself nor others. Indeed, we may be fooled into reading the book as a simple historical document. Nothing would be less wise, and more against Vaculík's intention.

For a sense of all that has changed in the telling, we might consider a case where we *can* verify the text's accuracy. In the entry for 20th April, Vaculík describes an underground lecture given by a professor visiting from Oxford.[23] "She began with a quotation from Hobbes: If we swapped the brains of a prince and a cobbler who would then be the prince and who the cobbler?" When, in 1991, Gerald Turner wrote to Professor Kathy Wilkes of Oxford about this lecture, she replied that she remembered it quite well, and vividly remembered Vaculík's presence. And she

22) Ludvík Vaculík, ed., *Hlasy nad rukopisem Vaculíkova Českého snáře* (Prague: Torst, 1991), p. 70.

23) On this lecture, and philosopher Kathy Wilkes' visit to Prague, see Barbara Day, *The Velvet Philosophers* (London: Claridge Press, 1999), esp. p. 33–39. I am grateful to Gerald Turner for showing me his correspondence with Kathy Wilkes.

did give a lecture called "The Identity of the Person." But she spoke of Locke, not Hobbes, who proposed a scenario of trading souls, not brains: "For should the soul of a prince, carrying with it the consciousness of the prince's past life, enter and inform the body of a cobbler...," wrote Locke in *An Essay Concerning Human Understanding*. Why did Vaculík change Locke to Hobbes? Did he realize he had made an error, or not? Did he misunderstand (he was, after all, listening to the lecture in a foreign language, with interpretation into Czech by Julius Tomin)? Or did he intentionally sow this error, perhaps as part of a general policy of lightly "shifting" the text away from reality? (Some of the *Dreambook's* first readers would also have been at the lecture, and could have readily recognized any errors in Vaculík's transcription.) Did he intentionally change "soul" to "brain," perhaps for thematic reasons, or perhaps because the idea of swapping brains was simply more congenial to him? (With his intense devotion to personal individualism, Vaculík as a rule thought souls were *not* interchangeable...) Or was he thinking of the discussion of brain-swaps that *did* take place later in the lecture? Did he want to say something more generally about cultural miscommunication between Czechs and visiting foreigners (a recurrent theme in the *Dreambook*)? Who knows? The discrepancy opens space for interpretation (including for the question of just what kind of discrepancy Vaculík thinks it was, provided he noticed it in the first place), and gives a sense of how this book reaches out to the "real world" and yet maintains its own fictional nature at the same time.

Another moment of misdirection concerns Vaculík's affair with the dissident writer Lenka Procházková. It is not difficult to discern the beginnings of their romantic relationship in the *Dreambook*. Vaculík would have a daughter with Procházková in August 1981; he would go on to found a second family with her, while never definitively leaving Madla, and both Vaculík and Procházková would give fictionalized renderings of their relationship in later novels. In the first two editions of *Dreambook* (the 1980 samizdat edition in Padlock and a 1983 exile edition with Sixty-Eight Publishers), Vaculík even included photos of himself with their newborn daughter, but he took these out in later editions.[24] Here is another clue that the *Dreambook* is not a faithful, blow-by-blow rendering of Vaculík's emotional life, but rather a literary creation, shaped and pruned to achieve its own thematic unity. Meanwhile, at least if we are to believe Vaculík's comments on ed-

---

24) On this question, as well as the role of photographs and photography more generally in different editions of the *Dreambook*, see the insightful discussion in Barbora Chybová, "Český snář objektivem vypravěčova fotoaparátu. O Vaculíkových fotografiích v textu i mimo text," *Slovo a smysl* VII: 14 (2010).

iting within the text, the book's main romantic line did not appear spontaneously in the original diary entries but was filled in at a later date.

In other words, it would be foolish to rely on the text for exact details about historical reality, or to ignore the fact that the book's narrator emphasizes and conceals different facts to create his own literary structure. *The Czech Dreambook* is not a *documentary* image of anything, and its narrator Ludvík Vaculík is as much a literary creation as anything else. Above all, this book demands readers who understand that "an authentic picture" of any age will never be an exact copy. This may lead us to ask what kinds of truth claims are made in a book like the *Dreambook*. In her 2002 interview with Pavel Kosatík, Madla Vaculíková described her reactions when she first read the book: "I was shocked. Above all I thought that everything he wrote about me had happened differently. That's the reaction of every participant. Anyone who is written about there will say: But I didn't say it like that! So first I was overcome with horror at how Vaculík had revealed all of us. He uses a lot of direct speech – but he could not have remembered all of it, he doesn't have a tape recorder... He objected to me that he wrote down everything immediately, the same day. And that it's nonsense to try to disprove it a year later."[25] One can hear her skepticism, as well as a certain resignation: her reaction was inevitable, perhaps predictable. Readers might themselves try the experiment of writing down a few lines from a conversation they had the day before – they will probably come away with the same ambivalence. We certainly remember some lines clearly, even as we might hesitate to stake much on the reliability of our memories. At the same time, it's worth remembering that Vaculík was a trained reporter who worked in radio for many years, and was used to interviewing people and pulling quotations from their speech.

In a passage on 22ⁿᵈ March 1979, Vaculík himself writes a caveat:

People might well be amazed at the liberties I take. When I describe my own actions here, I have either carefully considered them or disguised them anyway. As far as Padlock is concerned, it is all common knowledge. When this work comes to be published I will not be doing it anymore and other people can tackle it the way they like. If someone protests that I have failed to give a true or faithful rendering of their words, it is my wish that his or her version be given preference and greater credence. For reasons of courtesy, if nothing else. I don't care. I cannot see any other way of producing an authentic picture of the present day, and a more favourable situation might never occur again.

25) Vaculíková, *Já jsem oves,* p. 109.

There's a certain bravado here: if you prefer life to literature, feel free to take life! But there is also the sincere desperation of a writer who senses that he has begun work on something great, but has also realized that it will demand some sacrifices. What does it mean when Vaculík says that a more favorable situation might never occur again? We can imagine that he has discovered the harmony between his *capabilities* – his talent for fresh and careful observation, his stylistic precision, his political acumen – and his *situation* – the strange world of normalization, where everyday life continued in the midst of police repression, and thus where those careful observations would resonate outward with unusual force, both politically and personally. He has realized that, in writing this public diary, he can both come to terms with himself and create "an authentic picture of the present day" – but also that this will have a price.

Vaculík was criticized for his exhibitionism, but it would make more sense to see him as a writer who is probing the social limits of self-expression. In his speech to the Writers' Congress, in "Two Thousand Words," in his reporting and feuilletons, he had perfected the idea of self-expression as a political ideal: a functioning polity needs citizens who communicate their beliefs clearly and sincerely. It needs people who trust their instincts, don't drown in abstractions, aren't baffled by theories, and aren't overwhelmed by the demands and interests of others. These are the ideas of a radical democrat, someone who believes in the worth of every individual – if only they can be roused to speak their minds! – and is a little bit worried that *any* political institutions tend to muffle and standardize our originality. ("Only now does it strike me: I did not want to control politics, I wanted to destroy them." 24th April 1979.) For Vaculík, the imperative of self-expression tells us first to observe the world with care and compassion, and then to take stock of our own emotions, thoughts, and reactions; we must know our own minds, and learn how to formulate our ideas for others. But how do these same ideals play out in our personal lives, in marriage and in families, and between lovers and friends? When does an effort to be true to our emotions become a self-serving pursuit of our own desires? ("Authors have the right to deal with anything; what counts is whether they do so successfully: success justifies everything." 29th January 1979.) It is one thing to speak truth to power, and quite another to tell a painful truth to a friend. ("Oh, the anxiety it arouses, the simple threat of losing friends!" 25th January 1979.) In exploring this conflict, *A Czech Dreambook* transcends its political situation to become something more, a book that navigates a path for self-expression through the thickets of love, family, and friendship – and speaks to readers in any country, under any regime.

Jonathan Bolton
Harvard University

I first met Ludvík Vaculík in 1977, when I was still working as a translator from French at the World Federation of Trade Unions in Prague. I received a phone call one Sunday morning from a friend asking if I could interpret for "a visiting English writer." On learning that the writer in question was Tom Stoppard, already well-known for his activity on behalf of banned writers, I realised it would be an undercover assignment. I was driven down to the square in front of the Castle, where Stoppard was already waiting in the back of a car and we drove to Dobřicho-vice to meet Vaculík, about whom I knew little at the time, apart from having seen the naked photos of him and his lover in the magazine *Ahoj*.

By the time I came to read the *Dreambook* I was already familiar with those "well-known Vaculíkian leaps from the willow-tree to the parsnip, with some mas-terly vaulting from the opening sentence to the punch-line" (28th January 1980), having already translated a number of his feuilletons.

I was also familiar with the setting of the novel and many of its characters. During the seventies I had come to know personally Svatopluk Karásek, Nikolaj Stankovič, Jan Lopatka and Zbyněk Hejda (who was a close friend of my wife Alice), as well as other Charter 77 activists. I was living in Prague throughout the period of the narrative and left the country to return to England with my wife and her two daughters shortly before the novel was completed in 1980.

In 1985 I was engaged by Vilém Prečan, the director of the Centre for the Promotion of Independent Czech and Slovak Literature, which was then located in Hanover, but soon after re-located to Castle Scheinfeld in Bavaria, to translate the Centre's periodical ACTA and other texts. As a result of this, I translated a number of Vaculík's feuilletons and his own history of Padlock Editions. We were therefore eager to read the *Dreambook* and obtained a copy of the edition published by Josef Škvorecký in Toronto.

When I embarked on the translation in earnest in 1990, we were already living in a country cottage in County Wexford, Ireland. Living in the countryside was a new experience for me, and it helped me relate more profoundly to the narrative. Indeed, I was soon engaged in activities that feature largely in the book, including cutting the grass with a scythe – possibly inspired by what I was translating. I was also becoming familiar with the Hiberno-English that surrounded us, and we would listen with enjoyment to Sunday Miscellany, Radio 1's selection of prose and poetry. My growing awareness of the peculiarities of Irish speech, particularly in terms of word order, would come to my aid when facing the challenge of rendering Vaculík's turns of phrase typical of his native Wallachia.

Background research for the translation was a more cumbersome business pre-internet and entailed periodical day trips to the library of University College Dublin, to which I gained access thanks to Věra Čapková of the Department of Linguistics and the philosopher Richard Kearney, who was deeply interested in Václav Havel. In my efforts to discover common English names of some of the wild flowers and insects mentioned, I enlisted the help of my father in England, who contacted Kew Gardens and the Natural History Museum on my behalf, and received approving comments from Vaculík for my thoroughness. Some of my researches proved fruitless, however – such as my attempt to clarify the content of the talk given by the Oxford academic, which the author records. I managed to identify the speaker as Sally Wilkes and wrote to her, but as Jonathan Bolton notes in his afterword, Vaculík's account proved to differ fundamentally from the lecture she gave.

Readers may be puzzled why the present translation has taken almost thirty years to appear.

In September 1990 the Peter Pont agency informed me that they had negotiated a contract with Random House, who then controlled a large part of publishing both sides of the Atlantic. However, when it eventually arrived the following April, I was astounded to find that a single contract had been issued to author and translator jointly, from which it transpired that my translation fee would have to be paid from the author's advance. I immediately wrote to the publisher asking for a separate translation contract. The publisher unfortunately refused to comply with my request. Thus, long after the translation was completed there was a constant to and fro of correspondence with Random House, who insisted on sticking to the joint contract before passing the matter to one of its English subsidiaries to resolve. Eventually, in 1993, the author, with my agreement, proposed that the advance be increased in order to cover the cost of translation; the publisher's rejection of this led to both parties withdrawing from the contract.

Yet there continued to be lively interest in the novel, particularly from the United States, and some sections of my translation were printed in a number of literary periodicals and anthologies.

When I moved to Prague in 1998, I would regularly sing with Ludvík at the weekly sessions of the *Wlastenci* glee club that he founded with the writer Alexandra Berková as part of the Czech centre of PEN International, and he would often ask me about the fate of our "joint project." My hopes received a boost in the early years of the new century when several publishers expressed an interest, but it was only in 2015 that Jantar Publishing of London came with a concrete proposal to bring it out as an e-book, news which Ludvík was overjoyed to receive, and he readily gave his consent. Sadly, he died just a few months later when the publisher was finalising the matter of rights, so he did not live to hear the good news that Karolinum, in agreement with Jantar, had decided to take over publication of the translation.

The challenges of translating *Dreambook* were enormous, both in terms of language and factual detail. I derived great satisfaction, for instance, in finally deducing the identity of the mushroom Vaculík refers to in his entry for 25th November 1979 by a name that did not appear in any of the various Czech mushroom guides available to me. (Identification would be instant nowadays thanks to search engines.) I don't recall how I discovered it was simply a wood blewit, but I certainly started collecting and enjoying them from then on.

The translation would not have been possible without that close collaboration with my then-wife, Alice. It's an ill wind, etc., and the failure to find a publisher after the first contract fell through meant that I was able to return to the text again and again in subsequent decades and "tweak" it here and there.

I am deeply grateful to Jonathan Bolton for painstakingly reviewing the entire translation with me for the present edition, even if it meant the sacrifice of some of my carefully crafted Anglicisms, which would unfortunately have been misleading or meant nothing to the American reader. I also wish to thank Mike Baugh of Karolinum Press for his useful comments and suggestions, and of course Martin Janeček of Karolinum, who seized the opportunity.

Last but not least, I am grateful to Paul Wilson and Tom Stoppard for their invaluable moral support over the past decades.

Gerald Turner, Prague

Ludvík Vaculík (1926–2015) was born in eastern Moravia in 1926. After an apprenticeship at the well-known Bat'a shoe factory during World War II, he moved to Prague, where he became a journalist, making his name in the early 1960s as an investigative reporter. He joined the subsequently banned literary journal *Literární noviny* in the mid-sixties and stepped up his critical involvement in social and political issues. His speech to the 4th Czechoslovak Writers' Congress in 1967 was an open challenge to the regime. During the Prague Spring of 1968, he sought to bring pressure on the reformist Communist leadership to make genuine moves towards democracy by publishing the now legendary "Two Thousand Words" manifesto, which Czechs signed in droves. Vaculík made his début as a prose writer in 1963 with the novel *The Unquiet House*. While his next novel, *The Axe*, was highly acclaimed during the Prague Spring, the one that followed– *The Guinea Pigs* (1970) – was never officially published in Communist Czechoslovakia, although it was translated into many foreign languages and, like *The Axe*, was published in Britain and the USA. As a prominent opponent of the regime and publisher of samizdat literature, Vaculík's writing was banned throughout the seventies and eighties. His short commentaries on topical issues published in samizdat were circulated secretly among the Czech public and won him great respect and a wide audience. In 1977, he was one of the founders of the Charter 77 human rights campaign. Starting with the novel *A Czech Dreambook* (1981), Vaculík perfected his technique of merging the personal and the political, combining meditations on his country's fate with the intimate details of his own life. Vaculík maintained his critical engagement after November 1989 and he particularly supported various environmental campaigns, speaking out against what he saw as the mistaken thrust of Western civilisation. In 1997, he received the Erich Maria Remarque Peace Prize, awarded by the German city of Osnabrück for outstanding literary works on the theme of peace and human rights. In 2008, he won the Czech Republic's National Literary Award in recognition for his life's work.

Gerald Turner (b. England, 1947) is a widely-published translator of Czech and French. During the 1980s he translated banned Czech authors, including Václav Havel, Ludvík Vaculík, Milan Šimečka, and Ivan Klíma under the pen-name of A. G. Brain. From 1985 to 1990 he was sole translator for the Documentation Centre for the Promotion of Independent Czech and Slovak Literature (Schein-feld, Bavaria). His published translations include novels, short stories, and plays. His translation of Ivan Klíma's novel *No Saints or Angels* was shortlisted for the Weidenfeld Translation Prize of the British Translators' Association in 2002, and his translation of Patrik Ouředník's *Europeana* received the US PEN Translation Award in 2004. In recent years, his translations of works on theology have been highly commended, particularly in the United States, where his translation of Tomáš Halík's *Patience with God* was awarded the best theological book prize for 2009–10. He was private translator to President Václav Havel (2004–2011).

MODERN CZECH CLASSICS

The modern history of Central Europe is notable for its political and cultural discontinuities and often violent changes, as well as its attempts to preserve and (re)invent traditional cultural identities. This series cultivates contemporary translations of influential literary works that have been unavailable to a global readership due to censorship, the effects of the Cold War and the frequent political disruptions in Czech publishing and its international ties. Readers of English, in today's cosmopolitan Prague and anywhere in the physical and electronic world, can now become acquainted with works that capture the Central European historical experience – works that have helped express and form Czech and Central European identity, humour and imagination. Believing that any literary canon can be defined only in dialogue with other cultures, the series publishes classics, often used in Western university courses, as well as (re)discoveries aiming to provide new perspectives in the study of literature, history and culture. All titles are accompanied by an afterword. Translations are reviewed and circulated in the global scholarly community before publication – this is reflected by our nominations for literary awards.

Published Titles
Zdeněk Jirotka: *Saturnin* (2003, 2005, 2009, 2013; pb 2016)
Vladislav Vančura: *Summer of Caprice* (2006; pb 2016)
Karel Poláček: *We Were a Handful* (2007; pb 2016)
Bohumil Hrabal: *Pirouettes on a Postage Stamp* (2008)
Karel Michal: *Everyday Spooks* (2008)
Eduard Bass: *The Chattertooth Eleven* (2009)
Jaroslav Hašek: *Behind the Lines: Bugulma and Other Stories* (2012; pb 2016)
Bohumil Hrabal: *Rambling On* (2014; pb 2016)
Ladislav Fuks: *Of Mice and Mooshaber* (2014)
Josef Jedlička: *Midway upon the Journey of Our Life* (2016)
Jaroslav Durych: *God's Rainbow* (2016)
Ladislav Fuks: *The Cremator* (2016)
Bohuslav Reynek: *The Well at Morning* (2017)
Viktor Dyk: *The Pied Piper* (2017)
Jiří R. Pick: *Society for the Prevention of Cruelty to Animals* (2018)
Views from the Inside: Czech Underground Literature and Culture
(1948–1989), ed. M. Machovec (2018)
Ladislav Grosman: *The Shop on Main Street* (2019)
Bohumil Hrabal: *Why I Write? The Early Prose from 1945 to 1952* (2019)

Forthcoming
Jiří Pelán: *Bohumil Hrabal: A Full-length Portrait*
Jaroslav Kvapil: *Rusalka*
Jan Procházka: *The Ear*
Ivan Jirous: *Collected Works*
Jan Čep: *Common Rue*
Jiří Weil: *Lamentation for 77,297 Victims*